PENGUIN CLASSICS

COUNT BELISARIUS

ROBERT GRAVES was born in 1895 in Wimbledon, son of Alfred Perceval Graves, the Irish writer, and Amalia Von Ranke. He went from school to the First World War, where he became a captain in the Royal Welch Fusiliers. Apart from a year as Professor of English Literature at Cairo University in 1926 he earned his living by writing, mostly historical novels which include: *I, Claudius*; *Claudius the God*; *Sergeant Lamb of the Ninth*; *Count Belisarius*; *Wife to Mr Milton*; *Proceed*; *Sergeant Lamb*; *The Golden Fleece*; *They Hanged My Saintly Billy*; and *The Isles of Unwisdom*. He wrote his autobiography, *Goodbye to All That*, in 1929 and it rapidly established itself as a modern classic. *The Times Literary Supplement* acclaimed it as 'one of the most candid self-portraits of a poet, warts and all, ever painted', as well as being of exceptional value as a war document. His two most discussed non-fiction books are *The White Goddess*, which presents a new view of the poetic impulse, and *The Nazarine Gospel Restored* (with Joshua Podro), a re-examination of primitive Christianity. He translated Apuleius, Lucan, and Suetonius for the Penguin Classics series, and compiled the first modern dictionary of Greek Mythology, *The Greek Myths*. His translation of *The Rubáiyát of Omar Khayyám* (with Omar Ali-Shah) is also published in Penguin. He was elected Professor of Poetry at Oxford in 1961, and made an Honorary Fellow of St John's College, Oxford, in 1971. Robert Graves died on 7 December 1985 in Majorca, his home since 1929. On his death *The Times* wrote of him, 'He will be remembered for his achievements as a prose stylist, historical novelist and memorist, but above all as the great paradigm of the dedicated poet, "the greatest love poet in English since Donne".'

JOHN JULIUS, second Viscount Norwich, was born in 1929. He was educated at Upper Canada College, Toronto, at Eton, at the University of Strasbourg and on the lower deck of the Royal Navy before taking a degree in French and Russian at New College, Oxford. He then spent twelve years in H. M. Foreign Service, with posts at the Embassies in Belgrade and Beirut and at the Disarmament Conference in Geneva. In 1964 he resigned to become a writer. Among his many publications are *The Kingdom in the Sun*, *A History of Venice*, *The Architecture of Southern England*, *Fifty Years of Glyndebourne*, a three-part series – *Byzantium: The Early Centuries*, *The Apogee* and *The Decline and Fall* and *Venice: A Traveller's Companion*.

ROBERT GRAVES

Count Belisarius

with an Introduction by

JOHN JULIUS NORWICH

PENGUIN BOOKS

PENGUIN BOOKS

Published by the Penguin Group
Penguin Books Ltd, 80 Strand, London WC2R 0RL, England
Penguin Group (USA) Inc., 375 Hudson Street, New York, New York 10014, USA
Penguin Group (Canada), 90 Eglinton Avenue East, Suite 700, Toronto, Ontario, Canada M4P 2Y3
(a division of Pearson Penguin Canada Inc.)
Penguin Ireland, 25 St Stephen's Green, Dublin 2, Ireland
(a division of Penguin Books Ltd)
Penguin Group (Australia), 250 Camberwell Road,
Camberwell, Victoria 3124, Australia (a division of Pearson Australia Group Pty Ltd)
Penguin Books India Pvt Ltd, 11 Community Centre,
Panchsheel Park, New Delhi – 110 017, India
Penguin Group (NZ), cnr Airborne and Rosedale Roads, Albany,
Auckland 1310, New Zealand (a division of Pearson New Zealand Ltd)
Penguin Books (South Africa) (Pty) Ltd, 24 Sturdee Avenue,
Rosebank, Johannesburg 2196, South Africa

Penguin Books Ltd, Registered Offices: 80 Strand, London WC2R 0RL, England

www.penguin.com

First published by Cassells 1938
Published in Penguin Books 1954
Published in Penguin Classics with an Introdction 2006
008

Printed in England by Clays Ltd, St Ives plc

ISBN-13 978-0-141-18813-3

www.greenpenguin.co.uk

CONTENTS

LIST OF MAPS AT END OF BOOK

INTRODUCTION

All forms of literature are dangerous; but in none is the danger more acute than in historical fiction. The writing of straight history is essentially a matter of reportage, with attempts to explain and interpret where necessary; pure fiction is an exercise of constructive imagination. But the moment an author attempts to combine the two, he finds his way beset with perils and pitfalls. Certainly he can now fill out his historical narrative, giving it a dash of liveliness and colour which it could never otherwise have hoped to attain; but he will need all the novelist's skill and all the professional historian's knowledge of the period of which he is writing if he is to persuade the reader how it would have felt to be living in distant days. Conversations will become a particular problem for him. He will have to steer a careful path between modern colloquialism on the one hand – slang, it need hardly be said, is to be avoided at all costs – and any suggestion of gramercies or gadzookeries on the other. Most important of all, he must decide precisely where the line between these two opposing disciplines is to be drawn. How historical is he going to be, or how fictitious? And how is the reader to know where history ends, and fiction begins?

In most historical novels, this last question at least does not arise. They are, for the most part, costume dramas – modern stories set in the past, with a few stage-coaches and crinolines thrown in. But in an age when every station or airport bookstall is bursting with bodice-rippers, there are perhaps half-a-dozen genuine historical novelists that stand out from the crowd. They do so for two reasons. First, they are superb writers on their own account. Second, it is their characters as well as their settings that are historical. Of the twentieth century, the names that spring immediately to my mind are Marguerite Yourcenar (*Memoirs of Hadrian*), Maurice Druon – whose dazzling series *Les Rois Maudits* has been translated under the title of *The Poisoned Crown* – and of course Mary Renault (*The King must Die, The Persian Boy*). To many of us, however, one author will always stand out in a class by himself: that man is Robert Graves.

Graves's two novels set in the early Roman Empire, *I, Claudius* and *Claudius the God*, are deservedly famous: the more so in this country thanks to their admirable presentation some years ago on BBC television. *Count Belisarius*, on the other hand, has remained comparatively unknown – not because it is in any way inferior (which to my mind it is not) but for the same reason, I suspect, that it has not been dramatized. The average western European reader may have a fairly clear (if not always entirely accurate) picture in his mind of Ancient Rome; but where Byzantium is concerned – about which, in this country at least, there seems always to have been a conspiracy of silence – he has always remained a little vague.

Why this should be remains a mystery. Byzantium was after all only the same old Roman Empire, continuing more or less as it always had after Constantine the Great had transferred its capital to his new city of Constantinople (the old Greek colony of Byzantium) in 330 AD. True, because it was now centred in the Greek-speaking world it gradually over the centuries abandoned Latin and became more and more Greek, both in language and in spirit. To its citizens, however, it remained the Roman Empire – and they remained Romans – until the eventual capture of Constantinople by the Ottoman Turks in 1453. Here then is a great nation, which even after the change of scene endured for over eleven centuries – a period of time comfortably longer than that which separates us from the Norman Conquest – for several of which it was the richest, most powerful and certainly the most colourful on earth; why, in our schools, is it so unaccountably ignored?

Count Belisarius is set in one of the most astonishing periods of all Byzantine history: the age of the Emperor Justinian in the sixth century AD. Justinian, for all his many and grievous faults, was the first truly great Emperor since Constantine himself. Thanks largely to his general, Belisarius, he regained Italy and parts of Spain from the Goths; he achieved the complete recodification of Roman law; and he left behind him a number of superb buildings, two of which still survive. The earlier of these, the little church of St Sergius and St Bacchus, is the most exquisite in Constantinople; the later, the Great Church of St Sophia less than a mile away, ranks among the supreme architectural monuments of the world. Justinian also happens to be the only Byzantine Emperor of whom a true portrait has come down to us: the two great mosaics in his church of S. Vitale in Ravenna, featuring himself and his Empress Theodora with their respective retinues, were created in their lifetimes and are probably reasonable likenesses. They are certainly not idealized.

A further word or two must be said about Theodora – and not just for the important role she plays in Graves's novel. Her father had been a bear-keeper in the Hippodrome, her mother some kind of circus performer – probably an acrobat. She herself by her early adulthood had become Constantinople's most notorious courtesan and theatrical performer – though we may doubt whether, even in her most abandoned moments, she altogether deserved her description by the contemporary historian Procopius:

> ... The wench had not an ounce of modesty, nor did any man see her embarrassed; on the contrary, she unhesitatingly complied with the most shameless demands . . . and she would throw off her clothes and expose to all comers those parts, both in front and behind, which should rightly remain hidden from men's eyes.

He continues at some length in the same vein; readers wishing to pursue this line of study need only turn to his gloriously scurrilous *Secret History*.

Such stories may be true or false; in any case, Justinian recognized quality when he saw it. Surmounting all obstacles, he married Theodora on 4 April 527, and four months later the pair found themselves sole and supreme rulers of the Byzantine Empire. The plural is important: Theodora was no Empress Consort. At her husband's insistence she was to reign at his side, taking major decisions and acting on them in his name. Her future appearances on the public stage, in short, were to be very different from those of the past.

So much for Justinian and Theodora; what do we know of the hero of this story, Belisarius himself? Edward Gibbon, normally all too ready with his darts, is for once disarmed:

> His lofty stature and majestic countenance fulfilled their expectations of a hero . . . The sick and wounded were relieved with medicines and money, and still more efficaciously by the healing visits and smiles of their commander . . . In the licence of a military life, none could boast that they had seen him intoxicated with wine; the most beautiful captives of Gothic or Vandal race were offered to his embraces, but he turned aside from their

charms, and the husband of Antonina was never suspected of violating the laws of conjugal fidelity . . . The spectator and historian of his exploits has observed that amidst the perils of war he was daring without rashness, prudent without fear, slow or rapid according to the exigencies of the moment; that in deepest distress he was animated by real or apparent hope, but that he was modest and humble in the most prosperous fortune.

A Romanized Thracian like his master, this paragon was while still in his twenties one of the Empire's leading generals at the time of the riots of January 532 (so brilliantly described in Chapter IX). His military gifts were unquestioned: his personal courage had been proved again and again, and he was a natural leader of men. He had but one liability: his wife, whom he had married soon after his return from Mesopotamia in 531. Antonina's background was not unlike that of the Empress, whose closest friend she became. The relationship was valuable to them both: Theodora knew that she could always control Belisarius through his wife, while Antonina could rely on the Empress to protect her from the consequences of her endless adulteries. At least twelve years older than her husband – Procopius says twenty-two – she already had several children, in or out of wedlock. Unlike Theodora, she had made no attempt to reform her character after her prestigious marriage, and in the years to follow was to cause her husband much embarrassment and not a little anguish; but he continued to love her and – perhaps as much to keep an eye on her as for any other reason – took her with him on nearly all his campaigns.

All this is clear enough – even if we occasionally have to read between the lines – in the pages that follow; and indeed as we turn those pages we are struck again and again by how closely the author sticks to the facts as we know them. The Carthaginian expedition in 533, Belisarius's Triumph in the following year, the campaign in Sicily, the double-crossing of King Vitiges to win Ravenna – all these in fact occurred; so too, did his accusation and disgrace at the hands of Theodora, and his pardon by – and partial reconciliation with – the Emperor. We also recognize all too well the constant *leitmotif* of Justinian's jealous hatred of the man who showed himself, again and again, the most loyal of all his subjects.

But adherence to historical fact as far as we know it – for early medieval sources are always inadequate, while even those that we have are seldom if ever entirely reliable – is only the beginning of Graves's achievement, and indeed the easiest part of it. Where he truly excels is in his recreation of the atmosphere of sixth-century Byzantium, and even – to a most remarkable degree – in his ability to enter the minds of its people. For a perfect example, we have to look no further than the first three paragraphs. There, first of all, is the all-pervading Christian faith – of which no true Byzantine, however serious his transgressions, was ever for a moment unmindful. There are also references to the nature and importance of oaths, the education of children, the emptiness of fashion and 'the world of men, women and clerics' – these last being men of such huge power and prestige in the Empire that they might indeed have been considered a third sex. Equally telling is the scene which immediately follows of the drunken Cappadocians in the inn, discussing – as was the way in Byzantium – not politics or women but the nature of the Second Person of the Trinity. This passion for theological speculation was one of the characteristics of the Byzantines by which visitors to Constantinople were immediately struck. Already at the end of the fourth century St Gregory of Nyssa had wonderingly written:

> If you ask a man for change, he will give you a piece of philosophy concerning the Begotten and the Unbegotten; if you enquire the price of a loaf, he replies: 'The Father is greater and the Son inferior'; or if you ask whether the bath is ready, the answer that you receive is that the Son was made out of nothing.

By Justinian's day the habit had spread even to the charioteers in the Hippodrome. Of the two leading teams, the Blues – favoured by the Emperor and Empress – maintained that Christ had two Natures, the Human and the Divine; a view hotly disputed by the Greens, who allowed him only one.

The second chapter of *Count Belisarius* in particular – begun on the author's forty-second birthday – always strikes me as a *tour de force*. Here we have a description of a banquet given by a rich and somewhat pompous nobleman – during which, incidentally, Belisarius and Antonina fall in love. We are given every detail of the decoration, the clothes, the conversation, the food and drink, and the entertainment – this last provided by Antonina, at that time still a dancing girl from the theatre at Constantinople, who sings ravishingly to her lute and performs several extremely lascivious dances. The narrative is a perfect blend of scholarship and imagination, its effect rather like that produced by a brilliant portrait of an unknown sitter; the face is unfamiliar, but the individuality so strong that one instinctively recognizes a perfect likeness.

And what of the eunuch Eugenius, that devoted slave of Antonina, by whom the entire story is told? He is the only major figure in the book for whom there is no historical authority; but he is none the less real for that. He was first introduced – only when the work was well under way – at the suggestion of Graves's mistress (and for the previous eleven years his inspiration) Laura Riding, and he must have proved a godsend. He lends distance to the view, allowing us to stand – with him – aside from the action and to enjoy his commentary. More important still, he adds enormously to the verisimilitude. Imagine if we had only a straightforward, third-person narrative – it would have read like history – or if Graves had permitted himself direct speech, like a novel. Thanks to Eugenius, we feel we are reading neither: here instead is a chronicle, related by an eye-witness of the events described.

And so *Count Belisarius* continues, with one dazzling set-piece after another, effortlessly carrying us back over fifteen hundred years, bringing back to life a whole company of men and women before our eyes. Justinian lives again – though we may frequently wish to throttle him – and Theodora, and the odious John the Cappadocian, and Narses, the octogenarian Armenian eunuch whose generalship proves second only to that of Belisarius himself. The battles – and the strategies that dictated their course – are wonderfully described; and there is a memorable account of Belisarius's defence of Rome against the Ostrogoths in 537, with his wife at his right hand. But this is a domestic drama as much as a military one: among other pages that stick in the memory are those describing Antonina's passion for their adopted son Theodosius and its extraordinary consequences. Thus, chapter by chapter, Graves – in the words of the novel's huge admirer Winston Churchill – 'rolls back the time-curtain' and recreates the Byzantine world as no author has ever done before.

The book was published in early April 1938, in a first edition of twenty thousand copies. It sold well and was for the most part enthusiastically reviewed, the principal criticism being that the author had made Belisarius himself a little too perfect. Graves responded indignantly to the *Sunday Times*, denying that he had falsified history; It was, he wrote, 'a shocking comment on twentieth-century literary taste that when . . . a really good man is shown . . . it must be said that he does not really come to life.' In fact, the critics had a point. Belisarius must have had his occasional outburst of cruelty – if not, he was the only Byzantine general in history who could make such a claim. Similarly, he must sometimes have answered back when Justinian was at his most offensive. (We must certainly hope he did.) In giving us instances of such moments, Graves would have been doing his hero no disservice: the *chevalier sans peur* may be all very well, if somewhat lacking in imagination; the *chevalier sans reproche*, one suspects, must all too often have been a very boring man indeed.

However that may be, in *Count Belisarius* you will not find a boring sentence. Winston Churchill told Graves that he could not put it down; nor, I am delighted to confess, could I. And so, dear reader, the time has come for you to turn the page and begin: 'When he was seven years old, Belisarius . . .'

John Julius Norwich

FOREWORD

MOST people find it difficult to make a logical connexion in their minds between the characters of the straightforward Classical age and those of the romantic age of medieval legend. King Arthur, for example, seems to belong to a far more antique epoch than Julius Caesar; yet his Christianity dates him some centuries later.

How these two ages overlapped will be seen in this story of Count Belisarius. Here is a Roman general whose victories are not less Roman, nor his strategical principles less classical, than Julius Caesar's. Yet the army has by now changed almost beyond recognition, the old infantry legion having at last disappeared, and Belisarius (one of the last Romans to be awarded the dignity of the Consulship and the last to be awarded a triumph) is a Christian commander of mail-clad Household knights, nearly all of barbarian birth, whose individual feats rival those of King Arthur's heroes. In his time occur characteristically Romantic situations. For example, caitiff rogues lead away captive maidens to dolorous castles in the hills (during the Moorish raids on Roman Africa), and his knights chivalrously prick out to the rescue with banners and lances.

The miraculous element in the story of King Arthur is partly primitive saga and folk-tale, partly monkish mysticism of a far later date. But in Belisarius's case the chief authority for his private life and campaigns was not any Hunnish or Gothic member of his Household – who would doubtless have made a rambling epic of it, for the monks to embroider in succeeding centuries – but his educated Syrian-Greek secretary, Procopius of Caesarea. Procopius was on the whole a Classically well-informed, judicious writer, as was also Agathias, who supplies the final military chapter; so there has been no romantic distortion here, as in King Arthur's case. The historical King Arthur seems to have been a petty British King, a commander of allied cavalry, whom the Romans left to his fate when their regular infantry were withdrawn from the garrison towns of Britain at the beginning of the fifth century. If a Procopius had been his chronicler, the ogres and fairy ships and magicians and questing beasts would not have figured in the story except perhaps as a digressive account of contemporary British legend. Instead we should have a lucid chapter or two of late

Roman military history – Arthur's gallant attempt to preserve a remnant of Christian civilization in the West country against the pressure of heathen invasion. And Arthur's horse would have been a big-boned cavalry charger, not a fairy steed flying him wildly off towards the Christian millennium.

Belisarius was born in the last year of the disastrous fifth century (King Arthur's century), in which the Anglo-Saxons had over-run Southern Britain; the Visigoths, Spain; the Vandals, Africa; the Franks, Gaul; the Ostrogoths, Italy. He died in 565, five years before the birth of the Prophet Mohammed.

Wherever surviving records are meagre I have been obliged to fill in the gaps of the story with fiction, but have usually had an historical equivalent in mind; so that if exactly this or that did not happen, something similar probably did. The Belisarius-Antonina-Theodosius love-triangle, however fictional it may seem, has been adopted with very little editing from the *Secret History*. Nor is the account here given of sixth-century ecclesiastical and Hippodrome politics exaggerated. The only invented character is Belisarius's uncle Modestus, a familiar type of the tinsel-age Roman man of letters. The two Italo-Gothic documents quoted in the text are genuine.

The distances are given in Roman miles, practically equivalent to English miles. Place-names are modernized wherever this tends to make them more recognizable.

The maps are by Richard Cribb. I have to thank Laura Riding for the great help she has given me in problems of language and narrative.

1938 R. G.

CHAPTER I

THE BOYHOOD OF BELISARIUS

WHEN he was seven years old, Belisarius was told by his widowed mother that it was now time for him to leave her for a while, and her retainers of the household and estate at Thracian Tchermen, and go to school at Adrianople, a city some miles away, where he would be under the guardianship of her brother, the Distinguished Modestus. She bound him by an oath on the Holy Scriptures – she was a Christian of the Orthodox faith – that he would fulfil the baptismal oath sworn on his behalf by his god-parents, both of whom were recently dead. Belisarius took this oath, renouncing the world, the flesh, and the devil.

I, the author of this Greek work, am a person of little importance, a mere domestic; but I spent nearly my whole life in the service of Antonina, wife to this same Belisarius, and what I write you must credit. Let me then first quote an opinion of my mistress Antonina on the subject of this oath sworn at Tchermen: she held that it was most injudicious to bind little children by spiritual oaths of such a sort, particularly before they have even attended school or had the least experience of the world of men and women and clerics. It was no less against Nature, she said, than if one subjected a child to some bodily handicap: for example, that he should always carry about with him, wherever he went, a small log of wood; or that he should never turn his head in the socket of his shoulders, but either bend the whole body around or move his eyes, perhaps, independently of the head. These would be great inconveniences, admittedly, but not nearly so great as those attendant on a solemn oath, to renounce the world, the flesh, and the devil, taken by a young nobleman destined for the service of His Sacred Majesty the Emperor of the Eastern Romans, who rules at Constantinople. For either, on the boy's reaching adolescence, temptations come on him and the oath is broken, and his heart is filled with remorse – in which case he loses confidence in his own moral fortitude; or else the oath is broken in the same way but no remorse is felt, because world, flesh, and devil appear delightful things – in which case he loses all sense of the solemn nature of an oath.

Yet Belisarius was so exceptional a child and grew to be so exceptional a man that no difficulties whatsoever put in his way could have greatly troubled him. To take the absurd instance that my mistress used: he would easily have accommodated his body to the rule of never turning his head on his shoulders and would have made this habit seem nobility, not stiffness. Or he would have carried about his perpetual log of wood and made this seem the most convenient and necessary object in the world – a weapon, a stool, a pillow – so that he even might have set a City fashion in handsomely carved and inlaid logs of wood. And certainly this fashion would be no sillier or more superstitious than many current today among the young dandies of the rival factions at the Hippodrome, and many more that have come in and gone out again in this wearisome century: fashions in beards, cloaks, oaths, toys, scents, games of chance, carnal postures, terms of endearment, aphrodisiacs, religious argument and opinion, reliquaries, daggers, comfits.

Belisarius, at all events, took this dangerous oath with the same innocence of purpose as when once young Theseus of Athens swore before his widowed mother to avenge his father's death on the monstrous Minotaur of the Cretan Labyrinth, who ate human flesh.

Whether or not he was true to the oath you shall judge after reading this story. But let me assure you, if you are perhaps Christians of the monkish sort who read this, that Belisarius was not at all of your habit of mind, and cared little for dogma; and that when he became master of a large household he forbade all ecclesiastical disputation within the walls of his house, as being unprofitable to the soul and destroying the family peace. This was my mistress Antonina's decision first of all, but he agreed with her after a time and made it his, and subjected even bishops and abbots, if they happened to be his guests, to the same discipline.

So this was the first of the three oaths he swore; and the second was to his Emperor – to the old Emperor Anastasius, in whose reign he was born, and subsequently to the two successors of Anastasius; and the third oath was to my mistress Antonina as his wife. These remarks will serve as preface to the work which follows, which I am writing in extreme old age at Constantinople in the year of our Lord 571; which is the thirteen hundred and sixth year from the foundation of the City of Rome.

Belisarius was born in the year of our Lord 500, and his mother regarded this as ominous. For the Devil was, she believed, allowed dominion on this earth for a thousand years, and at the close of this time mankind would finally be redeemed: therefore the year of her only son's birth came, as she said, in the very centre of the long black night dividing the first day of glory from the second. But I, Eugenius the Eunuch, confess that I regard such opinions as superstitious and altogether unworthy of sensible persons; nor did my dear mistress Antonina think otherwise in these matters.

This young Belisarius dutifully said good-bye to his mother and the household retainers, who (taking the slaves with the free and counting in children and old people) numbered some two hundred souls; and mounting his fine white pony rode towards Adrianople. There accompanied him John, the bailiff's son, an Armenian boy of his own age who had played the part of Belisarius's lieutenant in the small private army he enrolled from children living on the estate; and Palaeologus, a Greek tutor who had already taught him the rudiments of reading and writing and ciphering; and two Thracian slaves. Palaeologus was unarmed, but the slaves carried swords, and Belisarius and Armenian John had light bows suitable to their strength with a few good arrows. These boys were already very handy with their bows, both on foot and when mounted; as might be expected. For the Armenians are a sturdy race and Belisarius was of Slavonic stock – as his name Beli Tsar, meaning the White Prince, indicates; the heathen Slavs, who live beyond the River Danube, are notable archers and horsemen. His father's family had been settled at Tchermen for a hundred years, and was wholly Romanized and had been raised to the second of the three ranks of nobility.

This journey from Tchermen was by the fields, not by the main road from Constantinople to Adrianople, which passes near this village. Several times Belisarius and John, with their tutor's permission, rode off the track in pursuit of game; and Belisarius was fortunate enough to shoot a hare, which provided a meal for them that night at the inn where they proposed to lodge. It was only a small inn, not much frequented, and the old landlady was in deep distress: her husband had recently been killed by the fall of an elm-branch while tending his vines, and their man-slave had thereupon run off, stealing the only horse in the stables, and might be anywhere by now. She had only a young girl slave left, who inexpertly tended the animals and vines while she herself worked in the house. The travellers perceived that at this inn they must provide their own food and do their own cooking. Of their two slaves, one was a porter, a strong, brave man without knowledge or adaptability, and the other was a youngster, Andreas, who had been trained as a bath-attendant; neither of them could dress a hare. Palaeologus sent the porter off to gather firewood and draw water, and set Andreas at scouring the greasy inn-table with sand. He himself skinned and jointed the hare, which presently was simmering in a pot with bay-leaves and cabbage and barley and a little salt. Armenian John stirred the pot with a horn spoon.

Belisarius said: 'I have a packet of black peppercorns from Ceylon, which my mother is sending by me as a present for my Uncle Modestus. I like this Indian pepper. It stings the mouth. It will not detract much from the gift if I grind a few peppercorns in the little hand-mill that goes with it, to flavour our hare-soup.'

He opened his saddle-bag and took out the packet of peppercorns and the hand-mill and began grinding. Being only a child, he ground too much for a meal for five persons; until Palaeologus, observing him, exclaimed: 'Child, that is enough pepper for a Cyclops!' Then, while the hare was stewing, Palaeologus told them the tale, which they had not heard previously, of Ulysses in the Cyclops' cave and how he charred a stake in the fire and, making the Cyclops drunk, thrust out his one eye with the flaming point. The boys and the slaves listened laughing; for Palaeologus, quoting the play of Euripides, was very droll in his imitation of the stricken Cyclops. Then they set the table for three – the slaves would eat apart afterwards – and poured wine into the cups from a smoky earthenware wine-jar that they found in a cupboard. The slave Andreas cut slices of bread for them with his hunting-knife.

At last the meal was practically ready, the hare only wanting a few more minutes to be cooked. Palaeologus had added to the pot two or three spoonfuls of wine and a pinch or two of pepper and a small sprig of rosemary and a little sour sorrel which the old woman fetched from the back-garden. Every now and then they tasted the soup with the horn spoon. Four tallow candles had just been lighted, which it was Andreas's duty to snuff when the wick grew cauliflowered. But at this happy moment a great noise was heard at the door and in burst six truculent armed men, Asiatic Greeks by their speech, and disturbed everything.

With them they had a decently dressed, mild-featured young man, bound hand and foot so that he could not walk. He seemed a well-to-do artisan or tradesman. The leader, a very burly fellow, carried this prisoner on one shoulder like a sack of grain and flung him into the corner by the fire – I suppose because this was the place farthest from the door, if he should try to escape. The man was plainly desperate and in full expectation of being murdered. His name, it proved later, was Simeon, a burgess of that district. It had fallen to him by lot to go on behalf of his fellow-burgesses to a great land-owner named John of Cappadocia, begging him to pay the land tax due from him, or at least a part of it – an obligation which this rich young man had long evaded. Now, the district was called upon to pay so many pounds of gold annually to the Imperial Treasury, and the lands of John of Cappadocia were assessed at a rate which was less than their value indeed, but which amounted to one-third of the total tax of the whole district. The burgesses, because of bad harvests and a recent plundering raid by the Bulgarian Huns and being assessed greatly above the value of their holdings – they had been presented by the Government with worthless strips of country, all marsh and stone, yet valued as good farm-land – were so deeply in debt as to be nearly ruined unless John of Cappadocia consented to pay his share. But he always refused. He had a retinue of armed men, mostly his own Cappadocians, as these six fellows all were, who insulted and beat the representatives of the burgesses when they came to his castle to sue for payment.

In my story there are likely to be many Johns besides these Armenian and Cappadocian Johns, John being the name that foreigners commonly take when baptized into the Christian faith (calling themselves either after John the Baptist or John the Evangelist), or that Christian masters give their slaves. It is also frequent among the Jews, with whom it originated. So we shall distinguish these Johns either by their country of origin or, if that happens to be insufficient, by their customary nick-names: John the Bastard, John the Epicure, and Bloody John among the rest. But there is only one Belisarius in my story, and he as unusual as his name.

It appeared, then, from the boasts of the Cappadocians and the complaints of this wretched Simeon, that he had gone boldly with an armed body of constabulary to the castle of Cappadocian John, intending to overawe him into paying at least a reasonable part of his debt, but had been set upon with swords and clubs by the armed guard at the gate-house. The constabulary had deserted Simeon at once, so that he was captured. Then Cappodocian John himself, who was spending the autumn on his estate for the hunting and fowling, had come swaggering out and asked the sergeant of the guard who this fellow might be. They made a low obeisance to John, who exacted from them the sort of respect a patriarch or the governor of a Diocese is usually given, and answered: 'A sort of strange tax-gatherer, if it please your worship.' Cappadocian John cried: 'Give him a sort of strange end, so that no tax-gatherer may trouble me again on my Thracian estates.' Then six of them, led by the Sergeant, bound Simeon hand and foot and put him across a horse and rode off with him at once, hoping to please their master by their alacrity.

As they rode, they discussed the fate which their captive should suffer. The Sergeant invited his men to make suggestions. One said: 'Let us tie a stone to his neck and throw him into a pond.' But Simeon objected loudly: 'It is a crime before God to poison water. My corpse would spread a pestilence. Besides, what you propose is not a strange death: it is the common death that slave girls give to puppies. Think again!' The Sergeant agreed that Simeon was right, and they rode on farther.

Then another of the Cappadocians proposed that they should lash him to a tree and shoot him full of arrows. Simeon again interrupted: 'Would you blaspheme by inflicting on a mere tax-gatherer the very death suffered by the holy martyr Sebastian of Milan?' This also seemed an objection to be respected, so they rode on farther yet. A third man suggested impaling, and a fourth flaying, and the fifth was for burying Simeon alive. But each time Simeon poured scorn on these suggestions, and told them that they would certainly be punished by their master if they were to return and report that they had put him to death by so commonplace or trifling a means. The Sergeant took his part and said at last: 'If you can tell us a sort of death that is strange enough, I shall be grateful to you and carry it out just as you wish.'

Simeon replied: 'Let your master pay his debt voluntarily. Then, be sure, I will die of astonishment, and no stranger death will ever have been recorded in the Diocese of Thrace.'

The Sergeant struck him on the mouth for his impudence, but was still undecided as to the manner of his death. It came on to rain, and the Cappadocians saw a light burning in the inn, so they tied up their horses in the stable and came inside for a drink of wine and further consultation.

Palaeologus now heard them mention their master's name, and knew him by reputation for a rancorous and quarrelsome man, so was anxious to do nothing to affront these servants. He asked them whether they would do him the honour of drinking wine at his expense.

The unmannerly Sergeant made no reply, but, finding himself near the cooking-pot, which was giving off a very savoury smell, turned to his companions and cried: 'We are in luck, bullies! This old bearded fellow has foreseen our coming and cooked a hare for us.'

Palaeologus pretended to take this in joke. He said to the Sergeant: 'Best of Greeks, this hare is not sufficient for ten grown men and two boys, one of whom, moreover, is a nobleman. But if you yourself, and perhaps one other, care to join us...'

The Sergeant replied: 'Impudent old beard, you are well aware that this is not your hare. It is a stolen one, doubtless the property of my master John, and you shall have no share in it at all. What is more, when our meal is over you shall pay me, on my master's account, a fine for your theft. You shall hand over ten gold pieces or as much more as I find in your pockets. As for your nobleman, he shall wait on us. Bullies, guard the door! Now disarm the two slaves!'

Palaeologus saw that it was useless to resist. He told Andreas and the porter to give up their arms peaceably, and they did so. But Armenian John and especially Belisarius who had shot the hare and was eager for a taste of it, were greatly enraged. But they said nothing. Then Belisarius remembered the cave of the Cyclops and decided to make these ruffians as drunk as possible, so as to have the advantage of them if it came to a struggle.

Very politely he began acting as cup-bearer, pouring out the wine without any admixture of water, and saying: 'Drink, gentlemen, it is good wine, and you have nothing to pay.' Because the pepper made the soup very hot for the Cappadocians, they drank more wine perhaps than they otherwise would have done. They toasted him as their Ganymede, and would have kissed him, but he eluded them. Then one of them went into the kitchen to catch the slave girl and began pulling off her smock, but she ran out of the house and hid among the bushes, where he could not find her; so he returned.

The Cappadocians began in their cups to discuss religious dogma.

This is the disease of the age. One would expect farmers, for instance, when they come together, to talk about animals and crops, and soldiers about battles and military duties, and prostitutes perhaps about clothes and beauty and their success with men. But no, wherever two or three are gathered together, in tavern, barracks, brothel, or anywhere else, they immediately begin discussing with every assumption of learning some difficult point of Christian doctrine. Then, as the main disputes of the various Christian churches have always been concerned with the nature of the Deity, that most tempting point of philosophical debate, so naturally these drunken Cappadocians began, not without blasphemy, to lay down the law on the nature of the Holy Trinity and especially of the Second Person, the Son. They were all Orthodox Christians, and seemed to hope that Palaeologus would raise his voice in dispute. But he did not, for he held the same opinions as they.

However, Simeon soon revealed himself as one of the Monophysites. The Monophysites were a sect powerful in Egypt and Antioch, and during the last generation or two had brought the Empire into much danger. For the Emperors at Constantinople were obliged to choose between offending the Pope of Rome, who was the recognized successor of the Apostle Peter and had condemned the sect as heretical, and offending the people of Egypt on whose goodwill Constantinople depended for its corn. Some Emperors had inclined to the one view and some to the other; some had tried to find grounds for a compromise. There had been destructive riots, and wars, and scandals in the Churches because of this dispute; and at the time of which I write there was a clear schism between the Church of the East and the Church of the West. The reigning Emperor, old Anastasius, tended to favour the Monophysites; therefore the burgess Simeon, to annoy these Cappadocians, made his loyalty to the Emperor equivalent to his Monophysitism.

Simeon proved too eloquent for them, though all shouted at once; so they called on Palaeologus as a scholar to defend the Orthodox point of view on their behalf, which he gladly did. Armenian John, nudged by Belisarius, plied them with more drink as they listened to the disputation.

Palaeologus quoted the words of Pope Leo, which I forget myself, if I ever heard them, but which I gather were to this effect: that the Son is not God only, which is the view of the insane Acuanites; or man only, which is the view of the impious Plotinians; nor man in the sense of lacking something or other of the divine, as the foolish Apollinarians hold; but that He has two united natures, human and divine, according to the texts 'I and My Father are one' and also 'My Father is greater than I'; and that the human nature, by which the Son is inferior to the Father, does not diminish from the divine nature, by which the Son is the equal of the Father.

The Cappadocians cheered Palaeologus when he recited this decision, rattling their cups on the table or banging with their beechwood bowls. They did not notice that Belisarius, under the table, was tying their feet together with a length of tough twine – not so tightly that none of them could stir his feet for comfort, but tightly enough to incommode them greatly if they all tried to rise together; for he had tied them in a narrow circle.

Then Simeon ridiculed Palaeologus, and said that to brush aside false doctrine of Acuanite or Apollinarian or Plotinian was not by any means the same as stating true doctrine; and that for a priest to be elected Pope of Rome did not give him a right to lay down the Christian law finally; and that a Pope might say and do things for political reasons that were injurious both to his God and to his Emperor. Simeon also said that the Son's nature could not be split into two as a man splits faggots with an axe. The Son's doings and sufferings were neither wholly divine nor wholly human, but all of a piece – Godmanlike. Thus: the Son walked on the waters of Galilee, which was an act performed through the flesh but transcending the laws of the nature of flesh.

So far, both my accounts agree as to the order of events, but at this point there comes a difference. First let me give the story as I heard it from a man of Adrianople a great many years later; who had heard it, he said, from Simeon's elder son.

According to this Adrianopolitan, Simeon closed his exposition with the following words: 'But Pope Leo also remarked on this head – I can quote his very words: "*Ardescat in foco ferrum. Sunt vincula mea solvenda. Mox etiam pugionibus et pipere pugnandum est. Tace!*" How can you be obedient to such gross folly, men of Cappadocia?'

The Sergeant of the Cappadocians, pretending to understand Latin, cried out recklessly: 'The Blessed Pope Leo spoke very good sense. He was right in every word. Out of your own mouth you are confuted.' For they were all unaware that Simeon had conveyed a secret message to Belisarius to heat the spit in the embers, to cut his bonds, and to be prepared to do battle with daggers and pepper.

But, according to the version that I heard from Andreas not many years ago, it was Belisarius who spoke the Latin words, pretending to confute Simeon, and crying out: '*Ardescit in foco ferrum manibus tuis propinquum. Vincula solvam. Mox etiam pugionibus et pipere pugnabitur*' – at which (Andreas said) the ignorant Cappadocians cheered the boy as a stout champion of the true faith. These words of Belisarius, if spoken, conveyed a message to Simeon that the spit was already heating in the fire close to his hands, that he would cut his bonds, and that a battle would soon be fought with daggers and pepper.

Against the acceptance of Andreas's account is the well-known tendency in old people to exaggerate or distort the experiences of their youth, especially when telling of a person afterwards famous. Thus, St Matthew learned from certain old gossips that the infant Jesus once restored a dead sparrow to life for them when they were playmates together; and has recorded this in his second Gospel with such other extravagances as that He spoke from His Mother's womb and reproved His stepfather Joseph. But in favour of this version I can say that it came to me not at third but at first hand, and that I knew Andreas as a man of confidence. Nor must it be objected that so young a child as Belisarius then was could not have spoken good Latin, the Latin of Rome: for good Latin was his mother's native tongue. Her own father had been a Roman Senator who left Italy with his family, fifty years before this time, when the barbarian Vandal, King Geiserich, plundered the temples and noble houses of Rome; he came to the Eastern part of the Roman Empire for security, and his family remained true to good Latin. So it was that Belisarius spoke three languages already: the Thracian vernacular of his family estate, and Latin, in which his mother and her chaplain always conversed with him, and Greek, the common language of the Eastern Empire – but Greek not fluently as yet.

Well, whoever it was who acted as general on this occasion, I can tell you at least how the battle went. First, Belisarius secretly cut Simeon's cords with his dagger. He was unperceived by the Cappadocians, who had finished their meat by now but were still seated drinking at the table. Then, nudging Armenian John to preparedness, he took a great fistful of ground pepper and came up to the table and whirled it in their faces, blinding all six of them. Up jumped Simeon with a roar, brandishing the red-hot spit which Belisarius had put to heat in the hearth; and the Thracians, Andreas and the porter ran to catch up their weapons, which had been stacked not far from them.

The Cappadocians roared like bulls with pain and helpless anger. They were fuddled with wine, entangled with the cord at their feet, blinded with pepper, and paralysed by sneezes. Simeon at the first onset struck two of them terrible blows on the head with the red-hot spit; so that even though Palaeologus took no part whatsoever in the fight, the Cappadocians were now outnumbered, four by five. Their stools were pulled from under them, and they fell sprawling to the ground. The boys and the slaves stood over them with drawn swords and daggers raised.

Simeon hurriedly fetched some pieces of harness from the stable and bound them one by one – he was a saddler by trade, and handy with knots. He, as it were, knotted each bond with a Monophysite argument, saying: 'Escape this logical predicament, Sir, if you can' or 'That text draws tight on your conscience, does it not?'

They answered piteously: 'For Christ's sake, best of men, bring sponge and water, or we shall go blind with this fire-dust.'

But he began in a powerful voice to sing the Hymn of the Seraphim with those interpolations in the Monophysite style which had caused scandals, riots, and bloodshed in many Christian churches. When they were all secure, Simeon informed them that Christ had enjoined him to forgive his enemies; and sponged their inflamed eyes tenderly, saying, 'In the name of single-natured Christ.' So they thanked him.

When Simeon learned from Belisarius how he had planned the battle he turned to Palaeologus and said: 'I had thought it a simple miracle, and was not therefore greatly astonished, just as I think the prophet Balaam was not greatly astonished when his ass suddenly spoke in God's name. For all things are possible with God, and one should no more be surprised at such obvious irrationalities as speaking asses or food sufficient for twelve men being stretched to feed 5,000 (and even leaving a superfluity), than at the natural braying of asses or at citizens starving naturally because no food is left in their city. For in the one case you have God, whose function it is to transcend the impossible, and in the other you have nature, whose function it is to obey the ways that God has indicated for beasts and men. But where justifiable astonishment arises is in a case like the present, where nature excels herself by neither divine nor demonic aid. If this child is spared until manhood he will make a general of the first rank: for he has the six chief gifts of generalship – patience, courage, invention, the control of his forces, the combination of different arms in attack, and the timing of the decisive blow. I was with the remounts in the Persian wars and came across both good generals and bad; and I know.'

Palaeologus answered: 'Yet if he does not add to these the gift of modesty, he will be nothing.' Which was a wise remark in its way, and a fitting seventh virtue to cap the rest.

The hare had been eaten, and most of the fresh bread, but there was biscuit left in their saddle-bags and some sausages, so they did not go hungry. They thought it unsafe to stay at the inn for the night, fearing lest someone should give the alarm at John's castle: so they tied the Cappadocians on their horses, and Simeon and the slaves were each to conduct two of them, tying the horses' heads together. The old woman had run out of the house when the fighting began; when she returned, to find these desperate fellows tamed, she was all gratitude, as if it had been done wholly on her behalf. Nevertheless, they paid her well.

Belisarius rode ahead with Palaeologus, and Armenian John acted as rear-guard. At dawn they rested in a wood, where one of the Cappadocians died of the injuries to his head. The others cursed and swore continually, but made no attempt to break free. Later in the day they reached Adrianople, without further adventures, where Simeon handed the Cappadocians over to the judge. Simeon's fellow-burgesses greeted him with joy and astonishment, because the constabulary had reported him captured.

The men were confined to the prison and held there until John should ransom them. They could not be charged with murder, nor indeed with anything worse than stealing a cooked hare, for it was not clear whether they had intended to obey John's murderous orders. John sent a message saying that he was justified in binding and removing Simeon, who had insolently trespassed on his estate.

The judge could not allow John to be charged with any crime, for fear of antagonizing other powerful land-owners. He also knew that, as a point of honour, John could not acquiesce in the punishment of his servants and fellow-countrymen. Nevertheless, there was a strong case against master and men. So an amicable arrangement was made, by which the men were openly released, but John secretly paid over one-half of his debt, amounting to 200 pounds of gold by weight – more than 14,000 gold pieces – by which means John's honour was saved and the burgesses also were saved from ruin. This Cappadocian John, whose avarice, unneighbourliness, and frequent devotions in church were all remarkable in so young a man, later became Commander of the Imperial Guards and Quartermaster-General, and as such did Belisarius many injuries in later life.

Belisarius and Armenian John and Palaeologus and the slaves now went to the villa of Belisarius's uncle, Modestus, guided by Simeon, who knew him. It lay outside the City, near a trout-stream, in well-wooded grounds. There Belisarius greeted his uncle, who was a tall, thin, unwarlike man of literary tastes, and gave him what was left of the pepper. The boy was made welcome, and Armenian John and Palaeologus with him. They talked together in Latin, and Modestus heard the story of the battle. His comment was: 'Well done, nephew, well done! It was contrived in the thorough Roman way – the way of Marius, Metellus, and Mummius. But your Latin contains many barbaric words and phrases, which sound as if uttered through the snorting snout of an African rhinoceros, and grate against my ear. We must eradicate them, cultivating in their place the elegant language of Cicero and Caesar. My friend Malthus, to whose school you will go, is fortunately a man of considerable taste and learning. He will explain to you the difference between the good Latin of the noble pagans and the base Latin of the ignoble monks.'

Or this, rather, was what his comment amounted to when translated into plain terms. But Modestus could never permit himself to make the least remark without wrapping it in an approved literary allusion, a paradox, or a pun, or all three together; so that Belisarius had great difficulty in understanding him. I myself shrink from reproducing the affectations that crackled from his lips, because no nonsense would read absurdly enough to do them justice – if indeed justice is what they deserved. The fact is that whereas Greek is a pliable language, good for the turns and twists of metaphor and for the humours of comedy, Latin is stiff and does not readily lend itself to these uses. It has been said of Latin rhetoric: 'The falsetto of a female impersonator.'

*

Malthus's school was in the centre of the town of Adrianople, and was not one of those monkish schools where education is miserably limited to the bread and water of the Holy Scriptures. Bread is good and water is good, but the bodily malnutrition that may be observed in prisoners or poor peasants who are reduced to this diet has its counterpart in the spiritual malnutrition of certain clerics. These can recite the genealogy of King David of the Jews as far back as Deucalion's Flood, and behind the Flood to Adam, without a mistake, or can repeat whole chapters of the Epistles of Saint Paul as fluently as if they were poems written in metre; but in all other respects are as ignorant as fish or birds. Once, when I was with my mistress Antonina at Ravenna in Italy, I came upon a bishop who failed to grasp a conversational reference that she made to the pious Aeneas, the Trojan hero, and his betrayal of Queen Dido of Carthage. Now, Heaven forbid that I should claim to be learned, for I am a mere domestic, whose only education has been listening to the conversation of intelligent people. Nevertheless, I should be ashamed to confess to the ignorance of this bishop. He did not know in the least what my mistress was talking about. 'Aeneas?' he echoed, 'Aeneas? I know the text in the Acts of the Apostles well; but, I assure you, my sister in Christ, that you will find no statement there, nor even a gloss by any well-informed commentator, that the pious Aeneas of Lydda whom the Apostle Peter healed of a palsy (though he had kept his bed for eight years), afterwards visited any Queen Dido at Carthage, much less betrayed her.'

In Malthus's school, which was under Imperial control, some instruction in the Scriptures was given as a matter of course; as bread and water appear on the table even at banquets. But the main fare was Latin and Greek literature of good authorship. Such books encourage children to accurate expression, and thus to clear thought; and at the same time supply them with an extensive knowledge of history and geography and foreign customs. I have heard it argued that soldiers should not be educated, on the ground that among the most vigorous barbarian nations, such as the Goths and Franks, whose principal men are all soldiers by trade, book-learning is despised. But the proverb 'a scholar made is a soldier spoiled' applies, in my opinion, only to private soldiers, not to any sort of officer. At any rate, there has never, to my knowledge, been a general of repute in any nation of the world who was not either to some degree educated or, if only poorly educated, did not regret this.

Belisarius in after life told his friends that the account of the long war between Athens and Sparta given by Thucydides, and Xenophon's account of fighting in Persia (both of which books were read and commented upon at Malthus's school at Adrianople) taught him more about the principles of war than he ever learnt in the military academy at Constantinople. At a military academy the instruction is in drill and simple tactics, and the use of siege-engines, and the duties of staff-officers, and military punctilio – the lesser rather than the greater arts of war. The greater arts are strategy, and the use of civil power and politics to assist military aims, and especially the art in which Belisarius learned to excel – the art of inspiring the love and confidence and obedience of his troops and so making good soldiers out of rabble. Belisarius held strategy to be a sort of applied geography, and in later years spent a deal of money on supplying himself with accurate maps: he had a professional map-maker, an Egyptian, always attached to his staff.

Belisarius used to say also that the training that he had been given at Malthus's school in accountancy and rhetoric and law had been of the utmost use to him: for Government officials, who excel in these civilian arts and are always very clannish, enjoy making fools of barbarian military commanders, whose chief qualities are courage, horsemanship, and skill with the lance or bow. He let them see that he was no barbarian, in spite of his name and in spite of his feats in hand-to-hand fighting, to which the smallness or cowardice of the forces at his disposal sometimes unwillingly reduced him. He would often call for the account-books of men under his command and, if there was a discrepancy anywhere, would point it out gravely, like a schoolmaster. In ordinary matters of law, too, such as the rules of procedure in a civil court and the rights of various classes of citizens and allies, he was not easily deceived by professional lawyers. Again, he knew enough rhetoric to be able to present a case simply and cogently, and not to be misled by ingenious arguments. For this he acknowledged a heavy debt to Malthus, who cared little for far-fetched allusions and fanciful tropes and Athenian traps and predicaments of logic. And it was a saying of Malthus's that a few well-armed words in disciplined formation would always prevail against words crowding along in enthusiastic disorganized mass.

On the first day of his attendance at school, Belisarius did not arrive in the early morning at seven o'clock, which was the usual hour, but shortly after noon, during the hour of intermission, when the boys were eating their luncheons in the schoolyard – such of them at least as did not live near by, so that they could go home quickly and eat and return. Now, it happened that in Adrianople it was not the custom, as at Constantinople and Rome and Athens and the great cities of Asia Minor, for a boy to come to school accompanied by a tutor as well as by a slave carrying his satchel of books for him. Even satchel-slaves were rare at this school. Thus the boys mistakenly thought that Belisarius must be the coddled sort of rich boy, since he came into the schoolyard with Palaeologus at his side, and Armenian John half a pace behind, and Andreas in attendance with the satchel.

One biggish lad, whose name was Uliaris, pointing at the venerable Palaeologus, called out: 'Tell me, bullies, is this grandfather bringing his grandchildren to our school to learn his *hic, haec, hoc* – or is it contrariwise?'

As they crowded round, munching their bread and fruit and hard-boiled eggs, a boy who had remained behind happened to throw a fig at Uliaris, to tease him. The fig was soft and sour with the heat, and seemed fatally destined for use as a missile. It narrowly missed Uliaris, but burst on the shoulder of Palaeologus's gown, which was fresh from the fuller's and of particularly fine woollen cloth. Then a louder laughter still arose; but immediately Belisarius ran angrily through the crowd of boys, and stooped to pick up a large, round stone which some of them had been trundling backwards and forwards on the smooth flags of the yard; and, before the boy who had thrown the fig realized what was happening, Belisarius had rushed towards the bench and struck him on the head with this stone, so that he fell forward stunned. Belisarius, without saying a word and still carrying the stone, returned to his tutor's side.

Palaeologus trembled, expecting the other boys to avenge their playmate, and indeed some of them now advanced with threatening cries and gestures.

Belisarius did not retreat or apologize. He said: 'If any others of you dare to insult this old man, my tutor, I will do again what I did.'

Because he showed courage, a party of boys led by Uliaris rallied to him. Uliaris asked: 'What is your Colour, boy? We are Blues. The boy you struck, Rufinus, is leader of the Greens.' They expected him to proclaim himself a Blue too, in self-protection, and to be of service to their faction at some later time.

But, strange as it may seem, Belisarius had been brought up at

Tchermen in so unworldly a way that he had never even heard of the rivalry of the Blue and Green chariot-racing factions; which was almost as strange as if he had never heard tell of the Apostles Peter and Paul. For in both halves of the Roman Empire the factions are everywhere constantly spoken of, and they are no new invention either; but date from at least the reign of the Emperor Tiberius, who was a contemporary of Jesus Christ.

Belisarius answered Uliaris: 'I belong to the Whites, and this is my lieutenant.' He pointed to Armenian John. Belisarius in his troop of boys on the estate had employed a white standard, to match his name, so the troop was called 'The White Troop'.

They explained, surprised at his words, that every boy must be either Blue or Green, or a turn-coat, or a trimmer. It was true that there were originally Red and White factions at the Hippodrome, representing the colours of summer and winter, just as the Green represented spring, and the Blue autumn. But chariot-races are now run two chariots against two, and not all four chariots each against the others; so White and Red no longer exist as independent factions, having long ago become affiliated, respectively, to Blue and Green, and disappeared.

Belisarius realized that he had said what sounded foolish, but none the less decided to abide by his words. He answered: 'If there are not yet any Whites at this school, Armenian John and I must make a beginning.'

They grew angry then, Blues as well as Greens, and told him that it was a strict rule of the schoolyard that knives or stones or other dangerous weapons should not be used in their tussles, but hands and feet only, and soft missiles like mud or snow.

Belisarius mocked at them for this and said: 'And it was you who called me a girl-boy!'

This provoked a noisy rush against him and Armenian John. But Andreas dropped the satchel and ran to their rescue. Meanwhile Palaeologus had gone to fetch aid; the undermaster soon appeared and prevented further mischief, for he induced Rufinus to make his peace with Belisarius.

Rufinus had recovered from the blow and, being a noble-minded boy, said that he admired Belisarius for avenging what seemed to be an insult to his tutor. He told Belisarius: 'If you and your comrade care to join the Green faction as members, you will be welcome.'

Uliaris shouted: 'No, let them come to us. We were the first to ask.'

It was unheard of that two faction leaders, such as Uliaris and Rufinus, should be competing for the support of a new boy. Usually it was only with difficulty and bribes that such a one obtained full membership in a faction: he had to wait for many months as a mere hanger-on to the faction that he favoured.

Belisarius thanked Rufinus for his invitation, but excused himself, as being a White; and Armenian John did the same. So Rufinus laughed. He did not appear insulted, but said: 'If your huge White army needs help against the Blues, you know what allies to summon to your aid.' The affair ended more quietly than it had begun, and when the boys heard that it was Belisarius and Armenian John who had fought the pepper-battle against the Cappadocians, grown men, they treated them with respect. With both Uliaris and Rufinus separately Belisarius became friendly; and even succeeded in making them work together when he was leader in some adventure. They played an important part in a famous snowball battle fought under Belisarius's generalship against the boys of a monastic school near by.

The story, though a boyish one, may be of interest. The monastery pupils were oblates – that is to say children dedicated by their parents to the monastic life. There was a breach in the monastery wall from which the oblates, armed with clubs like the Egyptian monks of the Sinai desert, used to descend and waylay boys of the Imperial school returning to their midday dinners, and beat them viciously. One snowy day Belisarius, with Armenian John and Uliaris as decoys, drew a large number of these oblates into an ambush – a timber-yard belonging to the father of Rufinus. There the Blue and Green factions, at peace for the occasion, nearly smothered them with snow and made prisoners of twenty boys, locking them in the wrestling-shed in the Imperial schoolyard. But unfortunately Uliaris had been captured, close to the breach in the wall.

Among those who fought along with Belisarius on this day was a small body of 'allies', namely four or five satchel-bearers, Andreas among them, and half a dozen poor boys known as 'servitors'. These were not regular scholars, but were allowed to sit apart at the back of the schoolroom and receive free instruction. In return they performed certain menial services: such as cleaning the school privies, and scrubbing out the classroom when the lessons were over, and distributing ink when it was needed, and smoothing out the wax on the used wax-tablets of the other scholars, and minding the furnace which in winter heated the rooms with pipes under the floor. These servitors were looked down upon by the ordinary scholars and treated as interlopers. But Belisarius had promised them privately that if they fought well and obeyed orders he would see that their condition was improved.

He now put himself at the head of these allies and led them at a run towards the monastery, to the postern-gate behind the kitchen. It was here that at this time of day a few poor persons of all ages were admitted to gratuitous meals of soup and stale bread and broken meats. Belisarius and his band entered quietly, pretending to be beggar-boys, but then skirted round the kitchens and passed through the monks' cabbage-garden, meeting nobody, and reached the schoolhouse beyond. There they came upon Uliaris in a shed, bound hand and foot, and with a bloody head. He was not guarded; for the enemy were now all anxiously gathered at the breach of the wall, wondering about their friends. Uliaris urged an immediate attack on the oblates from the rear. But Belisarius considered the suggestion dangerous, because of the difficulty of escape should the oblates call for help to the monks and lay-brothers. He was for retiring quickly again by the way that they had come.

So they escaped, taking with them, as legitimate plunder, apples and nuts and honey-cakes and spiced buns from a line of satchels hanging in a row in the shed. (This was Shrove-tide, when the oblates were given a dole of dainties to reconcile them to the coming rigours of Lent.) Singing the paean of victory, they returned to their own school and there made a fair division of their plunder among the scholars. But Belisarius allowed nothing to be given to those few boys who had held back from the fighting; and one of these, by name little Apion, Malthus's most industrious pupil, treasured a lasting grudge against Belisarius. As for the twenty captured oblates, they were released by Malthus's orders, but excommunicated by their Abbot for a full month.

*

Belisarius (whose mother died about this time) grew to be a tall, strong lad, with great breadth of shoulder. His features were noble and regular, his hair black, thick, and curly, and he had a frank smile and a clear laugh. Only from his cheek-bones, which were somewhat high, would his barbarian descent have been guessed. At school he satisfied his masters with the lively attention he gave his studies, and his schoolfellows with his courage and skill in wrestling and football. He was also a strong swimmer. He formed a small troop of young cavalrymen from the elder boys of the school, supplying them with cobs from his estate if they could not afford to mount themselves, and trained them in his uncle's park. They exercised chiefly in archery and lance-work upon stuffed sacks hung from the boughs of an oak. But they did not omit to engage in tourneys and skirmishes with one another, using blunt weapons; and even in miniature sea-battles from boats on the River Hebrus that runs past the city of Adrianople. Thus they became proficient soldiers before they went to train at the cadet-school at Constantinople, as they all did in a body – disdaining to enter the Civil Service. Some of them, the sons of tradesmen and debarred by decree from leaving their hereditary occupations, had first to buy exemption with bribes at the Palace.

CHAPTER 2
THE BANQUET OF MODESTUS

I HAVE already written something about Belisarius's uncle, Modestus, with his Roman ways and his strained rhetorical talk full of puns and recondite allusions. I met him once only, nearly sixty years ago, but my memory of that occasion was often afterwards refreshed by Belisarius, one of whose favourite diversions in private was to mimic Modestus and make my mistress Antonina laugh. I have also inherited a volume of Modestus's poems and another of his painfully composed letters, in the style of Pliny, both of which are inscribed with a dedication to Belisarius. Moreover, when I was in Rome during the siege I met many noble Romans who spoke and behaved in very much the same manner as he, so I know the type well.

The scene is the dining-room of Modestus's villa. There are present: Modestus himself, the burgess Simeon, Malthus the schoolmaster, three other local dignitaries, Bessas (a big, tough Gothic cavalry officer quartered in the town), Symmachus (an Athenian professor of philosophy), Belisarius, now fourteen years of age, with Rufinus and Armenian John and Uliaris and Palaeologus the tutor. Everything is arranged exactly in the old Roman style, for Modestus is an antiquarian and makes no mistakes: he can justify everything by quotation from some Latin author or other of the Golden Age. His guests feel a trifle self-conscious, especially Simeon, who is a convinced Christian and somewhat scandalized by the lasciviousness of the painted frieze that runs between windows and ceiling – the subject being Bacchus, God of Wine, on his drunken return from India. In deference to the wishes that Modestus has expressed in his letter of invitation, most of his guests are dressed, Roman-fashion, in long, white, short-sleeved woollen tunics. But the burgess Simeon is true to the smoky woollen blouse and loose pantaloons that every ordinary inhabitant of Thrace wears, who is not a cleric; and Bessas wears a linen tunic with broad vertical stripes of yellow, green, and red, and breeches of sewn skins, because he is a Goth. Bessas also wears a brownish-yellow military cloak fastened with a large amethyst brooch that sparkles magnificently when it catches the light.

They recline on couches at a round table of ancient sumach-wood; which Bessas finds awkward, being accustomed to sit up to the military board on a hard bench. He envies the boys, who, since they are not yet of age, are provided with chairs, not couches; they sit at a side-table. It is four o'clock now, by Modestus's water-clock, of which he is so proud and which keeps such poor time, and Greek servants bring in the appetizers – dishes of olives, chopped leeks, young onions, tunny-fish in vinegar, prawns, sliced sausage, lettuce, shell-fish. Malthus has been appointed wine-master, but Bessas's high military rank entitles him to the consular seat at the tip of the crescent in which they recline. Symmachus the philosopher resents that the principal honours should go to the brownish-yellow cloak of Bessas, a barbarian, rather than to his own grey professorial cloak; but does not dare to show his feelings openly.

Malthus's duty is to see that every man's cup is filled and to regulate the proportion of wine to water: it is a duty that he has often performed for Modestus. He can be trusted to whisper to the man with the wine-jar and water-pot 'More wine', when conversation is formal and frigid, and 'More water' when the conversation is becoming too free or quarrelsome and spirits need cooling. A hired dancing-girl supplied by the Theatre at Constantinople, with a wreath of roses on her head, bare legs, and a very short tunic, hands the cups around, making pretty jokes as she does so.

Now Simeon the burgess says something in a low tone to Palaeologus (who is reclining on his left), indicating the frieze with a critical inclination of his head. Palaeologus replies with a warning frown, and Modestus calls out: 'Hey, Sirs, is this proper banquet comradeship? Did not Petronius the Arbiter lay down hundreds of years ago in his famous satirical novel that at a courteous table all offensive comments should be made aloud? Come, let us have it! What do you find amiss with my frieze? It is a reproduction by a gifted contemporary copyist of a major work of Gorgasus the mural painter. The original was at Corinth, but is now destroyed, which makes this doubly precious to me and to all connoisseurs.'

Then he goes on, in a chanting voice: 'Observe how Bacchus, having ravaged India, the land where the sages, called fakirs, nude but for a loin-cloth, sleep (praying to their gods) supported by nothingness three feet above the parched serpent-haunted ground – how great Bacchus, ever youthful, is harnessing the tigers to his triumphal chariot, wreathed with vine-clusters, with vines for bridles! From his curly head sprout golden horns, symbol of valour, which themselves sprout lightning – that very lightning in which Jove begat him on astonished Semele. His smooth temples, you will notice, are adorned with poppies ...'

'If I may be pardoned such a rude interruption of your charming and eloquent speech,' Malthus puts in – he sees that the guests, having drunk little so far, are growing restless at the prospect of a long, dismal, classical recital, and he knows the only way to silence Modestus – 'those are not poppies, they are intended for asphodel. Poppies are proper to Morpheus and to Ceres and to Persephone; but asphodel to Bacchus. Gorgasus was too well-informed an artist to make such an error in floral attributes.' Then, hastily to the servant: 'Boy, pour again, and let it be all wine!'

Modestus apologizes: he meant asphodel, of course – 'A slip of the tongue, ha, ha!' But his confidence is shaken; he hesitates to resume his recital.

Simeon considers that the half-clothed women of the frieze, in attendance on Bacchus, are not proper ornaments for a Christian dining-room. Looking up at them, one might imagine oneself inside a brothel at Tyre or Sidon or one of those heathen places, he complains.

'I was never a customer at any such haunt,' says Modestus sharply, 'but perhaps you know best. At the same time let me tell you that I regard the attitude to nudity as one of the tests of civilization. The barbarians hate the sight of their own unclothed bodies: just as the singing, illiterate, savage fraternities of monks do.'

Nobody takes up the challenge on behalf of the monks, not even Simeon, but Bessas answers stiffly: 'We Goths regard the sight of a person unclothed as ridiculous – just as you, Modestus, laugh at a person who cannot sign his own name – as many a noble Goth cannot do, I among them.'

Modestus, in spite of his crotchets, is a good-humoured man and does not want to pick a quarrel with a guest. He assures Bessas that he is surprised that a man with so noble a name cannot record it on paper or parchment.

'For what were Greek secretaries created?' laughs Bessas, ready to be appeased.

Next, Modestus tells his Thracian guests how proud he is, though a Roman of exalted rank, to be resident in Thrace, once the home of great Orpheus, the musician, and the cradle of the noble cult of Bacchus. 'Those naked women, Simeon, are your own ancestresses, the Thracian women who piously tore King Pentheus in pieces because he spurned the God's gift of wine.'

'My ancestresses all wore long, thick, decent gowns!' Simeon exclaims; and his indignation raises a general laugh.

While the appetizers are being cleared away, the dancing-girl gives a clever performance of acrobatic dancing. As a climax to her hops and skips, she walks about on her hands and then, curving her body into a bow and arching her legs right over her head, picks up an apple from the floor with her feet. Continuing to walk on her hands, and even slapping the floor with them in time to the apple-song she is singing, she pretends to debate with herself as to who shall be awarded the fruit. But her mind has long been made up: she lays the apple on the table beside young Belisarius, who blushes and hides it away in the bosom of his tunic.

Simeon quotes a text from Genesis, how Adam says: 'The woman gave me the apple and I did eat'; and Modestus a text from the poet Horace: 'Galatea, wanton girl, Aim an apple at me,' and everyone is surprised at the unanimity of sacred and profane literature. But the dancing-girl (who was my mistress Antonina) surprises herself by the sudden liking she feels for this tall, handsome youth, who looks at her with such fresh admiration as Adam is credited with having felt at the first sight of Eve.

Now, this liking came, I think, very close to love, an emotion of which my mistress's mother had always warned her to beware, as a hindrance to her profession. Antonina was nearly fifteen years old then, a year older than Belisarius, and had already lived a promiscuous life for three years, as public entertainers cannot avoid doing. Being a healthy, vivacious girl, she had thoroughly enjoyed herself and suffered no ill-effects. But amusement with men is an altogether different thing from love for a man, and the result of the look that Belisarius gave her was to make her feel not exactly penitent for the life she had been living – penitence is a declaration of having been in the wrong, and that was never Antonina's way – but suddenly modest, as if to match Belisarius's modesty, and at the same time proud of herself.

I was squatting on the floor in the background all this time, in attendance on my mistress; providing her, when she clapped her hands, with garments or objects from her property-bag.

Modestus resumed his painfully fanciful description of the meaning of the frieze... 'There, you will observe, captive to the jolly Deity of Wine, goes the river-god Ganges with green watery looks and cheeks bedewed with tears that mightily swell his heat-shrunk stream, and behind him a company of inky prisoners carrying trays loaded with varied treasure of ivory and ebony and gold and glittering gems (sapphire, beryl, sardonyx) snatched from jet-black bosoms....' So my mistress Antonina earned the gratitude of all present by calling for her lute.

She sang a love-song, the work of the Syrian poet Meleager, to a slow, solemn-ringing accompaniment. At the close, not having turned once in Belisarius's direction, she looked sharply towards him and quickly away; and he blushed again, face and neck, and when the blush had gone he turned pale. Never in her life did she ever sing better, I believe, and there was a great rattling of cups in her praise – even Simeon contributed a 'bravo', though he did not greatly care for pagan music and had tried to look indifferent while she was dancing. Symmachus the philosopher congratulated Modestus, exclaiming: 'Now really you have provided us with a rare phenomenon: a singing girl who keeps both her instrument and her voice in key, accentuates her words correctly, prefers Meleager to the nonsensical ballads of the streets, is beautiful. I have not heard or seen better at Athens itself. Here, girl, let a grateful old man embrace you!'

If the invitation had come from Belisarius, my mistress would have been on his lap with a single bound, twining her arms about his neck. But on lean, snuffling, pedantic old Symmachus she had no favours to bestow: she cast her eyes down. For the rest of the meal, though she sang and danced and joked beyond her usual best, she allowed nobody to take any liberties with her – not even Bessas, though he was a man of the world and good-looking and strong, in fact just the sort whom she would otherwise have marked down as a worthy lover to spend the night with. She behaved modestly; and this was not altogether an affectation, for she did not feel her usual bold self.

When the principal meats are brought in, served on dishes of massive ancient silver – a roast lamb, a goose, a ham, fish-cakes – Modestus glows with satisfaction. He begins a long, involved speech, recommending his nephew Belisarius to Bessas as a young man who intends to take up the profession of arms, and who will, he hopes, restore the old lustre to the Roman military name. 'It is long years since a soldier with true Roman blood in his veins led any of the armies of the Emperor. Nowadays all the higher commands have somehow fallen into the hands of hired barbarians – Goths, Vandals, Gepids, Huns, Arabians – and the result is that the old Roman military system, which once built up the greatest empire that the world has ever known, has lately degenerated beyond all recognition.'

Palaeologus, who is reclining next to Bessas, feels obliged to pluck at the striped tunic and whisper: 'Most generous of men, please take no notice whatsoever of what our host is saying. He is drunk and confused and so old-fashioned in his ways of thinking as to be almost demented. He is not purposely insulting you.'

Bessas chuckles: 'Have no fear, old beard. He is my host, and the wine is good, and this is excellent lamb. We barbarians can afford to let the Romans complain a little of our successes. I do not understand one-quarter of his jargon; but that he is complaining, that much at least I understand.'

Modestus goes on, inconsequently, to point the close resemblance – has Malthus noted it? – between this villa and the favourite villa of the celebrated author, Pliny. 'The entrance hall, plain but not mean, leading to a D-shaped portico with the same glazed windows and overhanging eaves as Pliny's, thence to the inner hall and the dining-room with windows and folding doors on three sides. The same view of wooded hills to the south-east; but south-west, instead of the view to the sea which Pliny had – in rough weather the breakers used to drive up to the very dining-room, which must have been both alarming and inconvenient – the river valley of Hebrus, and the fertile Thracian plain beloved of the drunken devotees of the Wine-God, who ran with their breasts uncovered, their loose hair speed-tossed, and carrying in their passionate hands wands ivy-wreathed and tipped with pine-cones – why, observe, there they are so in the frieze just above the window; beloved also of Orpheus, pictured with his lute, who made rocks dance that should have stood still, and waters stand still that should have danced – the waters of the very River Hebrus that rolls yonder. Such stilling of waters was a feat that no other man has ever performed before or since. . . .'

'Who divided the Red Sea?' Simeon breaks in, indignantly. 'Or who in later times passed dry-shod over Jordan? As for dancing rocks, does not David the psalmist write: "Why hop ye so, ye high hills?" surprised at the power of his own sacred melody?'

'The Thracian plain,' resumes Modestus with a grimace of contempt, 'first bloodlessly annexed to Rome by that scholarly Emperor who conquered foggy Britain and added Morocco to the Empire – Claudius, his name – ah, you Greek-speaking inhabitants of the Eastern half of our Empire, you mixed multitude, do not forget that it was we Romans, not half-breed Greeks, who first won for you the dominions in which you now boast yourselves – it was our native-born Mummius, Paullus, Pompey, Agrippa, Titus, Trajan . . .'

'A most unselfish set of gentlemen, I am sure,' puts in the burgess Milo, a Thracian, drily; and he, too, feels it his duty to propitiate Bessas, muttering something behind his hand.

'Drink up, Sir!' orders Malthus. 'A new round of wine is about to begin. Let us all pledge the name of Rome, our common mother!'

Simeon agrees recklessly: 'I am ready, Schoolmaster. That wine which was poured during the marriage-feast at Cana of Galilee would not yield in quantity and quality to this; and as for these fish-cakes, why, the miraculous draught of fishes itself could never . . .'

So unpleasantness is once more avoided, but Modestus cannot resist continuing on the topic of the unconquerable Roman soldiery. 'Now tell me, my learned friends at that end of the table, and my gallant friends at this – what was the secret of the Roman soldiers' unexampled success? Tell me that! Why did they win battle after battle in Southern sands, in Northern snows, or against the painted Briton and the gilded Persian? Why was it that Rome, the capital of the world, had no need of walls and that almost the only fortresses in the whole Empire were block-houses on the remote frontiers? Why? Let me tell you, my gallant and learned friends. There were three reasons. The first: these Romans trusted to their own visible tutelary gods, the golden Eagles of their legions, who guarded them and whom they themselves guarded, and to no hypothetic divinity in Heaven above the clouds. The second: they trusted to their own powerful right arms for hurling missiles – sharp javelins – not to the adventitious bowstring; and in these right arms wielded the short, stabbing sword, the weapon of the courageous, civilized man, not the cowardly lance or the hurtling, barbaric battle-axe. The third: they trusted to their own steadfast legs, not to the timorous legs of horses.'

'Ho, ho, ho,' laughs Bessas. 'My worthy host, Distinguished Lord Modestus, will you forgive my frankness if I tell you that you are talking a great deal of nonsense? I shall leave the more religious-minded of the company to dispute your account of the power of the Eagles as gods, which I certainly think, though I am not an expert in such matters, is not only blasphemous but an exaggeration of fact; but I will take you up most strongly on the other points. In the first place, I understand you to despise the bow as a weapon of no account . . .'

'Have I not the authority of Homer for doing so, who presents his noblest heroes as fighting at Troy (dismounted from their chariots) hand to hand, with javelin and sword? The bow at Troy was the weapon of the effeminate and treacherous Paris, and of Salaminian Teucer, who skulked behind his brother Ajax's shield, and who later was refused permission to return honourably home to his violet-scented island city, because he had not avenged his brother Ajax's death as any decent shield-and-sword fighter would have done. In the only passage indeed where the word "archer" occurs in all the divine works of blind Homer, it is used as a term of ridicule. Diomede named Paris, in the Eleventh Book, "An archer, a jokester, a dandy with a lovelock, who gapes after girls"; and "archer" was the hardest name of all. The archer in Homer's poems skulks behind a comrade's shield, I repeat, or behind a mound, or a pillar, or a gravestone, and the shield-and-sword man resents his existence, as stealing from the battle (which he never enters) something which is not his. Is this not the truth, you scholars? Malthus, Symmachus, Palaeologus, I appeal to you.'

They acknowledge that Modestus has neither misquoted nor misinterpreted Homer.

But Bessas snorts and asks to hear more. 'Tell us about the Roman warriors of your golden age. They trusted to their legs, did they? Was it perhaps because they were such unskilful horsemen?'

Modestus's eye kindles. 'The infantryman is the acknowledged king of the battle-field. Horses are useful for mounting scouts upon, and for conveying generals and their staff quickly from one point of the battle to another, and for pulling wagons and siege-engines, and – yes, I grant you this – we may allow a small proportion of cavalry to every large body of infantry, in order to disperse the skirmishers of the enemy who, from a flank, may annoy the steadily advancing ranks of our foot-sure legions. But the Romans of old so disdained cavalry-service that, as soon as their conquests permitted them, they compelled subject nations to undertake that menial task for them – as they also ceased to drive the plough themselves or to plant cabbages, entrusting such employment to slaves and men of inferior race. Is that not so, Malthus, Symmachus, Palaeologus?'

They agree that the Romans early came to depend on allied cavalry. But Malthus, in historical honesty and fairness to Bessas, adds: 'Yet I think that no nation disdains what it excels in. The Roman cavalry were never very skilful. In Spain, on the last occasion that they were employed as a field-force they made a sorry exhibition of themselves; or so we read. Similarly, neither the Greeks nor the Trojans of Homer's day seem to have been capable archers, according to modern standards. They drew the bowstring back only to their breasts (not to the ear, as the Huns do, or the Persians), and the penetrative effect of their arrows seems only to have been slight. Ulysses was more successful, I grant you; but his archery against the suitors was at close range, and against unarmoured, unsuspecting men.'

Then Bessas has his say. He speaks slowly and judiciously, being the sort of man whom wine makes cautious, not rash. 'Modestus, my generous host, you live in a world long dead, shut in that book-cupboard yonder. You have no conception of the nature of modern fighting. In every age there are improvements. In this age we Goths have hit upon a perfected mode of fighting. Now I do not wish to denigrate the successes of the Romans, your ancestors, in olden times – they are undeniable. It is clear that they made a virtue of their deficiency as horsemen by perfecting the discipline of their foot. But clearly their battles were won in spite of their mistrust of horses, not because of it. Had they been natural horsemen and applied their courage and good sense to the evolution of the cavalry arm, they might well have conquered not merely the whole Western world, but India, I believe, and Bactria, and even China, which lies, by land, a year's travel away. But instead they relied on their infantry, and at last their armies were matched against a brave nation that was also a nation of horsemen – a nation, moreover, that obeyed its chiefs – the Gothic nation – my nation. That was the end of the Roman legions. These Thracian plains, Distinguished Modestus, have seen sterner sights than drunken women and dancing rocks. Simeon, Milo, Theudas' (this was the other Thracian, a land-owner) 'and you boys too, as soldiers to be, am I telling the truth, or am I not?'

They acknowledge that he is telling the truth, and Theudas adds: 'Indeed, Bessas, you are right, it must have been a terrible slaughter. Forty thousand Roman infantry butchered, with all their officers, and the Emperor Valens himself at their head. It was on fields now owned by me about eight miles to the northward of this city that the battle was fought. The thirty-acre plough-land is still full of bones, skulls, and fragments of armour, and arrow and javelin heads, and shield bosses, and gold and silver coins: every spring we turn them up.'

At this Modestus's assurance suddenly deserts him. The great battle of Adrianople is an historical calamity that he has from time to time succeeded in forgetting, but never for long; and here it starts up again at his very table. He quavers, with an appealing glance at his supporters, and speaking for once in straight language: 'We were betrayed. It was our Thracian light cavalry, on the left flank, that first gave way. We had almost won the battle. Our legionaries were cutting their way through the barricade of enemy wagons and in another half-hour we would have driven their main body off the field – but unexpectedly the Gothic heavy-cavalry squadrons returned from a foraging expedition and thundered upon these Thracians, who were driven off in all directions. So the Goths easily rode down our allied infantry, and pressed the survivors of these against our brave legionaries, who were busy enough already with the fight at the wagons. Next, the cavalry that was supposed to cover our right wing (Low Country horse, I believe) galloped off in disgraceful flight; and finally, out swarmed the whole barbarian mass from behind the wagons. Assailed in front, rear, and flank, we were hugged tight, as in the sudden embrace of an angry mountain she-bear . . .'

Bessas agrees: 'Most of the legionaries could not raise their arms to strike a blow, being pressed shoulder to shoulder, like a Hippodrome crowd, and some were lifted entirely off their feet. Spears snapped right and left, because the spearmen could not extricate them from the packed, swaying crowd, and many a man was accidentally impaled upon the sword-point of his rear-rank comrade. All day long until nightfall my ancestors, horsemen born, brave men, handy with the lance and the sword, killed and killed and killed. Our infantry poured in arrows. The dusty field was slippery with blood.'

Modestus mutters again, a great tear splashing down his cheek into his cup: 'Our allied cavalry betrayed us. That was all. The legions fought to the death.'

Malthus asks: 'But my dear Modestus, had not the same thing happened once before, in the war with Carthage? Did not Hannibal's heavy cavalry at Cannae break the Roman light cavalry to pieces, so that our allied cavalry on the other wing fled too? Were not the legions then also pressed together into a mass and slaughtered? The Romans should have profited by that lesson. For though they were not born horsemen, as it seems agreed, neither were they born seamen, as the Carthaginians were; yet finding a stranded Carthaginian war-vessel they built others like it, and practised sea-fighting in the safety of their own harbours, and finally sought out the enemy fleet off Sicily, and destroyed it. They should have bred big-boned draught-horses to replace their smart Gallic ponies, and climbed on their broad backs and disciplined themselves into heavy cavalry – within the safety of the walls of Rome if necessary.'

Bessas takes pity on Modestus, who is weeping again: 'Courage, Distinguished Lord Modestus! It was you Romans who first instructed us barbarians in the warfare by which we defeated you here at Adrianople. It was you who taught us to co-ordinate our military movements, and showed us the importance of defensive armour, and of fighting in regular formation. We merely applied your teaching to cavalry fighting. And though we were lucky enough to defeat your main army we did not destroy your Empire; far from it. We admired too much your civilized ways, your firm roads and lofty buildings, your good food, your useful manufactures and extensive trade; thus it was you who conquered us in the end. Our nobles became the sworn henchmen of your Emperor, the successor to the Emperor we had slain, and a few years later marched with him to rescue Italy from the rebellious Gauls; whom we defeated in pitched battles, cavalry against infantry again. That was in the time of my great-grandfather. We have remained within the Roman Empire ever since, to protect it against the new nations of barbarians that press against the frontiers, and against the ancient Persians, your neighbours.'

But Modestus remains sunk in gloom. He recalls other incidents of the battle. The legions fought on empty stomachs, because of some foolish Christian fast . . .

Then Belisarius asks permission from Bessas to speak; because being only a boy he must in general refrain from doing so until addressed. Bessas nods consent, and Belisarius speaks, stammering a little from embarrassment, what is in his mind.

'"Roman" is a name borne by hundreds of thousands who have never seen the City of Rome, and never will; and so it was, I believe, in the greatest days of the Empire. To be Roman is to belong not to

Rome, a city in Italy, but to the world. The Roman legionaries who perished with Valens were Gauls and Spaniards and Britons and Dalmatians and many other sorts; of true-born Romans among them there cannot have been many hundreds. Then, I do not think that perfection in equipment and military tactics has been attained by the Gothic lancer. The Gothic lancer is a brave man, and his charge is terrible because of the weight of his horse, and because of the heavy armour he wears – cuirass, shield, helmet, greaves. But the Hun horseman is a brave man too, and he can let loose a rain of arrows while riding at full gallop; only his horse is too light to carry a fully armoured man. Thus the Hun has not attained perfection either. Yet, noble Bessas, was it not fear of the Huns that first drove you Goths over the Danube into our Thrace? For your foot-archers could not overtake them, nor could your lancers withstand their volleys of arrows. Now, suppose that one could combine Hun archer and Gothic lancer into a single fighting man and civilize him as a Roman, and put him under proper camp discipline – that, I think, would be to breed a soldier as near perfection as possible. And he would be a Roman both in name and spirit. I intend to command such troops one day.'

Belisarius spoke with such quiet sincerity and such good sense that everyone applauded loudly, and the heart of my mistress Antonina went suddenly out to him in unmistakable love.

When dessert was brought in, Antonina gave an exhibition of sword-dancing in the old Spartan style. By now the dispute had ended, for it was realized that Belisarius had said the last word that needed saying; and that the future of warfare lay with him and his boy-companions. Modestus called his nephew to him, and embraced him drunkenly. 'When I die this villa of mine is yours – tables, plate, frieze, and all. I could not leave it to better hands.' Indeed, the poor fellow died soon after, and was as good as his word. The property was a very valuable one.

There is little more to be recorded of the rest of the banquet, which lasted until a late hour. Everyone but my mistress and Belisarius was very drunk – even Malthus – and young Uliaris grew boisterous and seized up a carving-knife and had to be disarmed. Modestus began, once more, his rambling disquisitions, and tied himself into such knots that he won almost as much applause as my mistress did with her last dance, when she so contorted herself that her legs seemed arms, and her belly, buttock. Being drenched in wine, he utterly forgot that he was a Christian and indulged in the most scandalous abuse and blasphemy of the Son (whether single, double, or many-natured) – though not of the Father, whom he generously identified with Jupiter, the supreme Deity of his own race. He went on to tell how the ruin of Rome had been her forsaking of the Old Gods and her taking up of this Galilean impostor – whose meek, unwarlike philosophy had rotted the Empire through and through; so that unlettered barbarians must be hired to undertake the defence of the Empire not merely in the lower ranks of the Army, but also in the capacity of colonels and generals and even commanders of armies.

Now, while I am on this subject, let me copy out from Modestus's book of poems an example of his Latin hendecasyllabics – the metre that he favoured most. It will show both the weakness and the occasional strength of his verse. Its weakness, in the continual puns and word-play – *cuneus*, a military column, or phalanx, and *cuniculus*, a rabbit; *rupibus*, rocks, and *ruptis*, broken; *late*, widely, and *latet*, lurks. Its strength when, for once, an antithetic contrast (the triumph of the rabbits, that is to say the Christians, by means of their unwarrior-like meekness) is felt with a noble and sincere disgust. Chorazin, I believe, is a village in Galilee which Jesus cursed, but is used instead of 'Galilee', the part for the whole, according to poetical convention.

DE CUNICULOPOLITANIS

Ruptis rupibus in Chorazinanis
Servili cuneo cuniculorum
Late qui latet, allocutus isto
*Adridens BASILEUS, inermis ipse ...**

ON THE INHABITANTS OF RABBITOPOLIS

In Galilean rocks the rabbits breed,
A feeble folk, to whom their frail LORD said,
Smiling: 'Be bold to cowardice, yea with speed
Dart from your Foe – unless he too has fled.'

To our Eternal City these short-lived
Prolific coneys came, and burrows found
In catacombs, where they in darkness wived
And numerous grew and pitted all the ground.

* [Literally:
To that servile phalanx of rabbits that lurks in the broken cargo of Chorazin over a wide extent of country, the KING, Himself defenceless, spoke smiling...
R. G.]

Thistles of controversy, coney-burrows,
Injured the farming of our frontier lands:
No more the Roman sword with straight plough-furrows
Securely drove through all marauding bands.

Soon rabbits everywhere swarmed over-ground –
Constantine took to him a rabbit bride,
A white scut to his purple back he bound
And two long ears exchanged for laurel pride.

Rabbitopolitans, long sunk in shame,
You bribe the fox, the ferrets and the stoats
To constable your warren in Rome's name:
So blood spurts frequent from your furry throats.

The next morning my mistress was thoughtful and silent, and I asked her at last what was on her mind.

She replied: 'Did you notice that boy Belisarius? Last night after the banquet he declared his love for me.'

'There was surely no harm in that, was there, Mistress?' I asked.

'Such a strange declaration! Eugenius, imagine, he spoke of marrying me if I would have the patience to wait for him, and meanwhile he would look at no other woman. A boy of fourteen, indeed! Yet somehow I could not laugh.'

'How did you answer him?'

'I asked him whether he realized who I was – a public entertainer, a charioteer's daughter, a Megaraean Sphinx – and his answer was: "Yes, a pearl from the muddy mussel." He was evidently unaware that marriage between a man of his rank and a woman of my profession is forbidden by law. I did not know what to answer the poor fellow. I could not even kiss him. It was a foolish situation.'

'And now you are weeping, Mistress. That is more foolish still.'

'Oh, Eugenius, sometimes I wish I were dead!' she cried.

However, the melancholy fit soon passed when we were back again in Constantinople.

*

The story of how I had come to be in attendance on the dancing-girl Antonina, my mistress.

There was a Syrian merchant from Acre, by name Barak, and his trade was in Christian relics. If any of these relics happened to be genuine, it was accidental, since I cannot remember that he ever handled any object for which he had to pay a fancy price. His chief talent lay in investing a worthless object with a spurious sanctity. For example, on a voyage to Ireland he carried with him a relic which he confidently ascribed to St Sebastian, martyred under Diocletian. It was a worn-out old military boot (appropriate because Sebastian had been an Army captain) picked up from the roadside in a suburb of Alexandria. Barak had been to the trouble of drawing out the rusty nails from the boot-heel and replacing them with golden ones, and lacing the uppers with purple silk cords, and finding a crimson-lined cedar-wood casket to hold this fine relic. He also brought with him the harsh, heavy loin-cloth of St John the Baptist, enclosed in a casket of silver and crystal. It was made not from linen but from asbestos, a substance which can be shredded and woven into a rough, fire-proof cloth. To the ignorant Irish it was an undeniable miracle that this loin-cloth could be passed through a fierce fire without either changing colour or crumbling away. He also had with him the jewel-encrusted shin-bone of the martyred St Stephen; and the backbone of a shark, its vertebrae bound together with gold wire, which he said was the backbone of the giant Goliath whom David killed; and a rounded piece of rock-salt, mounted in silver, which was supposedly the fore-arm of Lot's wife; and many other such wonders. The richness of the settings seemed to prove the objects themselves authentic, and he had with him parchment letters of testimony from Eastern bishops, recounting at length the miracles of healing which these relics had already effected. All the letters were forged. The Irish petty kings paid enormous sums to secure these treasures, and genuine miracles were soon reported from the churches where they were stored.

Barak returned by way of Cornwall, the extreme western cape of Britain, and touched at the Channel Islands, where he bought me, a six-year-old boy, from a captain of Saxon pirates. My name was Goronwy, the son of Geraint, who was a British nobleman. The Saxons had carried me off, together with my young nurse, in a sudden landing in the Severn estuary. I remember the grey, yellow-lichened keep of my father's castle, and my father himself as a grave, black-bearded man dressed in a speckled cloak and saffron-dyed trews and wearing a chain of gold and amber about his neck; and I remember the harpers in the rush-strewn hall, and even some fragments of the ballads that they sang.

My master Barak starved me and treated me very cruelly, and

brought me with him to Palestine, where he changed my name to 'Eugenius' and castrated me. Then with the money that he had earned in Ireland he bribed the Bishops who ruled in the Holy Places to appoint him general overseer of monuments and chief guide to pilgrims. By their leave he greatly enhanced the wonder of the shrines, and grew very rich. It was he who put the two stone water-pots in the marriage-chamber at Cana of Galilee. They were so constructed that if one poured water in at the mouth they discharged wine in return. For there was a partition to each bottle, just below the neck, and water poured through a funnel into one part of the bottle did not mix with the wine already stored in the other. Barak also supplied the Potter's Field, called Aceldama, with the original iron chain from which the Apostle Judas hanged himself; and, because pilgrims in the Church of Constantine at the mount of Golgotha often inquired after the sponge of hyssop from which Jesus was given sour wine to drink during His Crucifixion, Barak rediscovered this sponge – pilgrims could drink water through it if they fee'd the attendant well. In the synagogue at Nazareth he also deposited the identical horn-book from which the infant Jesus had been set to learn His alphabet, and the bench on which He sat with other children. My master Barak used to tell the pilgrims: 'This bench may be easily moved or lifted by Christians, but no Jew can stir it.' He had a Jew or two always within call to prove the truth of one-half of this assertion; the pilgrims themselves could prove the other half, if they paid for the privilege.

To the Church of the Holy Sepulchre my master Barak had no need to make any pious additions, for the brazen lamp which had once been placed at Jesus's head was already there, burning day and night; and the stone by which the tomb was closed lay there, too, at the entrance. It was as large as a millstone, and encrusted with gold and precious stones. From iron rods on the walls of the shrine hung armlets, bracelets, chains, necklaces, coronets, waist-bands, sword-belts, crowns bequeathed by Emperors, of pure gold and Indian jewels, and a great number of rich head-ornaments bequeathed by Empresses. The whole tomb (which recalled the winning-post at the Hippodrome on New Year's Day hung with prizes for the Inaugural Stakes) was plated with solid silver – walls, floor and roof. An altar stood in front of the tomb, under hanging golden lamps in the form of suns.

Barak visited Constantinople one summer (the pilgrim-seasons being spring and autumn) to sell relics to the monks there. He had forged a document purporting to be a testimonial from the Patriarch of Alexandria that a certain couch was the identical one on which Jesus had reclined at the Last Supper. He was asking ten thousand gold pieces for it. It happened that the private secretary to the Patriarch had just arrived in the City; hearing of the matter, he denounced the testimonial as a forgery. But my master Barak, not wishing to be scourged and mutilated as the law required, fled away at once, and took ship, and was not seen again in our Eastern part of the Empire for a great many years. Then a warrant was sworn against him by the landlord from whom he had rented a furnished house. This landlord was a Hippodrome charioteer, the father of the girl Antonina. He was owed a considerable sum of money; and the judge allowed him to distrain upon any goods that Barak had left behind. But Barak had succeeded in carrying away all his possessions except myself; for I had been sent by him on a shopping errand and had lost myself in the City streets. When I came home at last, very late, expecting a severe beating, I found my master Barak gone. Thus it was that I passed into the ownership of the charioteer, who handed me over to his wife to help in the kitchen, who later bequeathed me to her daughter Antonina, whom I served faithfully for more than fifty years.

CHAPTER 3

MEGARAEAN SPHINXES

You may perhaps have been puzzled by the term 'Megaraean Sphinx': that was the name given by some epigrammatist or other to the prostitute of Constantinople. The Sphinx was a devouring monster that kept its secrets to itself, and it was from the Greek city of Megara that Constantinople was first colonized. The story is that the prospective colonists were instructed by an oracle to sail to the north-east until they came to the land opposite to 'the city of the blind men'; they were to found their own city there, which would become the finest in the world. So they sailed north-east across the Aegean, and up the Hellespont until they reached the Bosphorus, and there they founded their city on the European bank – opposite Hieron, which was already colonized. This was clearly the place intended, for the men of Hieron had built their city on the more unfavourable bank, where currents were troublesome, fish scarce, and the ground unfertile, when they could readily have chosen the other bank with its fine natural harbour, the Golden Horn – so blind they were. Now after all these centuries Hieron is still a small place, but the Megaraean foundation has become a place of a million inhabitants, with magnificent buildings enclosed by a triple wall. It is the city of many names – to the Greeks officially 'Constantinople', familiarly 'Byzantium', to literary Italians 'New Rome', to the Goths and other German barbarians 'Micklegarth', to the Bulgars 'Kesarorda', to the Slavs 'Tsarigrad' – the wonder of the world, which I regard as my home.

My master, the father of the girl Antonina, was as I have said a charioteer of the Green faction at Constantinople. His name was Damocles, and he treated me kindly. He won many races for his Colour before he died, as quite a young man, in circumstances which require that I should tell the story in detail. He was a Thracian from Salonica, the son of a charioteer at the Hippodrome there, where the racing standard is a very high one – though not, I admit, as high as at Constantinople. He was noticed one day by a wealthy supporter of the Greens who had come to Salonica in search of talent; and, in return for a large sum of money paid to the local faction funds, his services were transferred to the Capital. There he drove the second chariot in important races, his task usually being to make the pace and jostle the two Blue chariots off their course, in order to give the first Green chariot, which had the faster horses, an opportunity for a clean run through. He was very skilful at this business, and sometimes at the last moment won the race with his own chariot by a feint at jostling that allowed him to slip in and thrust ahead himself. He had a great talent for getting the best out of difficult or lazy horses. He was also the cleverest manager of the whip in the whole profession: with it he could unerringly kill a bee in a flower or a wasp on the wall at five yards' range.

This Damocles had a friend, Acacius of Cyprus, to whom he was greatly devoted, and one of his conditions for coming to Constantinople was that Acacius should be given an appointment of sorts at the Hippodrome: enough for a decent living, because he was married and had three little children, all girls. The condition was faithfully observed, Acacius being appointed Assistant Bear Master to the Greens. Later he was given the Chief Bear Mastership, a responsible and lucrative post. Here I must go back in history, to make everything plain.

Now, the year of our Lord 404, exactly a hundred years before the story that I have to tell, was marked by two very inept innovations. In the first place the Sibylline prophetic books, which were consulted by the Senate in all cases of national perplexity and danger and had been kept carefully stored in the Palatine Library at Rome ever since the reign of the Emperor Augustus – these precious and irreplaceable treasures were wantonly burned on religious grounds by an illiterate Christian, a German general in the service of Honorius, Emperor of the West. This stupidity was foretold in the books themselves; for it is said the final set of hexameter verses ran:

> When two young fools between them do divide
> Our world, the elder (on the younger side)
> By banning bloodshed in his Hippodrome
> Bloodshed redoubles, while in elder Rome
> The younger, yielding to barbarian folk,
> Sees his most trusty Council rise in smoke.

Arcadius, the Emperor of the East Romans ('the younger side'), fulfilled his part of the prophecy in the same year. One day, in the

Hippodrome at Constantinople, à mad monk darted between two armed gladiators just as they had reached the most exciting phase of their combat. He called on them in a loud voice to refrain from murder, in Christ's most holy name. The gladiators were chary of killing the monk, which would have brought them bad luck – gladiators are naturally superstitious. They broke away, and by signs asked the Emperor, who was acting as President, what they were expected to do next. The spectators were affronted by the monk's tasteless interference with their amusement; swarming over the barrier, with lumps of concrete in their hands and bricks torn from the seats, they stoned the monk to death. Arcadius was equally affronted at this usurpation by the audience of his authority as President. He took the very severe step of forbidding all gladiatorial displays for an indefinite period. This decree provoked riotous protests, in punishment of which he dissolved the gladiators' guild altogether and allowed the monk, whose name was Telemachus, to be proclaimed a martyr and honourably enrolled on the diptychs. The consequences were not happy.

In the first place, as the Sibyl seems to have foreseen, the populace, denied its customary pleasure of seeing men kill one another publicly and professionally, sought satisfaction in unofficial sword-fights in the streets and squares between the young coxcombs of the Blue and Green factions. In the second place, the disappearance of the gladiatorial part of the Hippodrome games raised bear-baiting from an inferior position to a very high one. The mastiffs which fought the bears were, I may mention, not jointly owned by the faction, as the bears themselves were, and the horses, but privately trained by wealthy sportsmen. Occasional fights were also staged between lion and tiger (the tiger always won) or wolves and bull (the wolves always won, if in health, by attacking the bull's genitals) or bull and lion (the odds were even, if it was a strong bull) or wild-boar and wild-boar. But bear-baiting provided the most consistently good sport, and was more popular even than the spectacles, still permitted at some hippodromes, in which armed criminals attempted, more or less ineptly, to protect themselves from the attacks of these various wild beasts.

The more devout Christians either left their seats or shut their eyes during such set fights; and by some encyclical letter or other bear-keepers and lion-keepers and chariot-drivers and other Hippodrome entertainers were not allowed to profess Christianity. Or rather, they were forbidden to take part in the Eucharist, since their professions were supposed to be wicked ones that excited men's minds and drew them away from calm contemplation of the Heavenly City. For this reason the entertainers were naturally hostile to the Christian religion as one that despised their traditional callings, of which they were by no means ashamed. They took pleasure in circulating stories to the discredit of Christianity, especially about the hypocritical behaviour of devout Christians. There was more than one high officer of the Church who used secretly to send a present of money to the Green or Blue Dancing Master, asking him to select a clever woman to enliven a dinner-party; and yet, in the streets, these same men would draw their garments away in horror if they met an actress, as though afraid of pollution.

I was at one with the entertainers in this: my experiences while in the employment of my former master Barak had given me profound suspicions of the Church, suspicions which I still retain. It is something ingrained in me and not to be washed away; just as the colour Green was ingrained in my master Damocles' soul. But I have met some honourable men among the Christians, and therefore cannot in justice write anything against Christianity itself – only against those who have used it to their own ends and made a parade of holiness as a means of self-advancement. At any rate, there was this hostility to the Church among the Hippodrome people (I include in this term the entertainers from the Theatre, which was closely connected with the Hippodrome); and their rooms and offices were a sanctuary for the few priests of the Old Gods who survived, and for Egyptian and Syrian sorcerers and fortune-tellers and Persian mages, who were adepts in the interpretation of dreams. Only the Dancing Masters, who acted as our intermediaries with the faction management and thus with the Court and the Church, were, by custom, Christians; and a sly, unlovable set of men they were, to be sure.

Damocles' friend, the Bear Master Acacius, was killed in the exercise of his duty. The he-bears were excited by the presence of a she-bear in a neighbouring stall. They became refractory. One of them managed to break his chain and then beat in the door of his stall, furious to get at the she-bear. Acacius offered him honeycomb on a stick, and tried to persuade him to return peaceably to his stall. But the bear seemed insulted to be offered one sort of sweetness when he had set his heart on another, and struck petulantly at Acacius, though with no intent to hurt him seriously, and tore his arm. The wound became poisoned, and Acacius died that same evening, to the great grief of his associates of the Green faction, and especially of my master Damocles; and to the grief, I am told, of the bear, who mourned for him like a human being.

The Assistant Bear Master, Peter, was a sort of cousin to Damocles – most of the Hippodrome people were related by marriage – and it was decided that he should marry Acacius's widow and apply to the faction management to be appointed Bear Master in his place. This was done; and, though the marriage might seem a little lacking in good taste, celebrated so soon after the Bear Master's death, it was necessitated by circumstances. None of the Greens thought any the worse of either of the contracting parties.

But the dead Bear Master's term of office had been so successful – he had improved the defensive powers of the bears by giving them regular exercise and a careful diet, instead of keeping them always locked up in the dark, as the custom had been – that the management had recently voted for his salary to be doubled. It now amounted to 500 gold pieces a year, apart from perquisites. This bounty was justified by the huge increase in the ringside betting on the bear-baiting shows, for three per cent of the winnings went to the faction funds. Five hundred a year was a tempting sum, and the Dancing Master, who was typical of his class, did not wish to give it away for nothing. When Cappadocian John, who happened to be a prominent Green, offered a thousand for it on behalf of a retainer of his, the Dancing Master was not deaf. The matter was easily arranged, Cappadocian John being chairman of the Committee for Appointments. The Dancing Master stated at the meeting that the only other candidate was Peter, the Assistant Bear Master, who not only should be refused the rise in position but did not deserve to keep his present post. He insinuated to the Committee that Peter might have had something to do with the escape of the bear that killed Acacius; and made Peter's haste in marrying his dead master's widow seem indecent.

The Committee not only dismissed Peter's application, but also Peter himself. When Damocles heard of the decision he was rightly disgusted. He went to his fellow-charioteers to complain. He asked them to sign a petition to the Governors of the Hippodrome, who were a higher authority than the Green-faction management, complaining of the double injustice done to the Bear Master's widow and three children, and to the Assistant Bear Master.

The charioteers were not eager to do anything in the matter, however, though the new Cappadocian Bear Master had openly boasted that the post had been bought for him, and though he was an outsider with no previous connexion with the Hippodrome. Their reasons were that they were not interested in bear-baiting themselves, being charioteers; that Cappadocian John was a powerful man at Court and in the faction; and that they held it as unreasonable to carry a matter which touched the honour of the Greens before the Governors, among whom there were Blues as well.

Damocles refused to let the matter rest. He interviewed other prominent Greens, trying to persuade them to take an interest in the case, but none of them would listen to him.

The Blues soon came to hear the whole story and sent two of their charioteers to sound Damocles secretly. They asked him whether they could assist him in any way to get justice done. Damocles was so distracted that he answered bitterly: 'Yes, indeed! I would accept assistance from anyone, even from the Blues, nay even from the accursed Christian monks, if they could bring about the disgrace of this Dancing Master and this Cappadocian.'

The charioteers said: 'Suggest to the woman and her children that they put garlands on their heads and take posies in their hands and go out as suppliants, escorted by Peter, to the lower race-post just before the bear-baiting is to begin. The better-minded of the Greens will intervene on their behalf; and we can promise that the Blues will support the appeal vociferously.'

He agreed to this plan, which was only, of course, intended by the Blues to discredit the Green management; they had no genuine desire to help the woman and her children. But strange things now began to happen. In the first place, by a remarkable coincidence, the Bear Master of the Blues dropped dead that same afternoon as he was walking across the Square of Augustus. In the second place, Thomas, the Treasurer of the Blues, had a dream that night in which a big black bear, wearing a Green favour and ridden by a little girl with a garland on her head, came shambling into the Blue committee-room, tore off the favour, trampled on it, and began distributing crowns and palms of victory and pawfuls of newly-minted money.

The next day, as soon as the suppliants had presented themselves at the race-post, as the Blue charioteers had suggested, Cappadocian John sent a party of Greens to remove them. The Blues raised a fearful outcry, and most of the Greens among the audience did not understand the rights and wrongs of the case: so far from showing sympathy, they hissed the poor creatures as they were being bustled out through the Green benches. Damocles grew more angry than ever.

The last race that afternoon was a most important one. It was the anniversary of the Emperor's accession and he had promised to award a work of art, a chariot team in full career (the horses executed in silver, the chariot and driver in gold) to the management of the winning faction. It would be a close race, to judge by the betting. Damocles determined to gain popular applause by driving as he had never driven before. He knew that when he was conducted by the faction-leaders, garlanded and with a cross of flowers in his hand, to prostrate himself in homage and accept the prize from the Emperor's hands (as would happen if he helped to win the race), he would have an opportunity to make an appeal. The Emperor Anastasius was an affable man, and ready to do justice in cases of this sort.

It would be out of place to give a full account of the race; but let me at least describe the seventh and last lap of it. First one Colour had led, then the other, then the first again. By the end of the fifth lap, when the competitors had already covered a full mile, the position was that the first Green chariot was in the inside berth, hugging the central barrier; the second Blue chariot, which had been making the pace magnificently, lay just a little behind, in the next. Next came Damocles' chariot, the second Green, in the outside berth, closely challenged by the first Blue in the berth next to him on the inside. Victory seemed assured for the Greens now, and the Blue benches were looking glum when the final turn of the course was reached. But then Damocles suddenly knew that his horses were exhausted: no amount of skill with the whip or exhortations with the voice would draw another spurt of speed out of them. The distance between the two inside chariots, the first Green and the second Blue, and the two outside ones, the first Blue and the second Green, had lessened greatly, though the same relative positions were maintained. The first Blue was going strongly now and was capable of snatching a victory not only from Damocles, in the second Green, but from the two leaders. So Damocles took a swift decision at the turn: he slightly infringed on the first Blue's course and then reined in suddenly. His intention, of course, was to foul the off-wheel of the enemy chariot, and so put it out of the running – leaving his partner in the inside berth to make sure of victory. This trick is a legitimate one, but seldom played, because of the danger to the life of the man who plays it: the chances are that the chariot will overturn and that he will break a limb, or be kicked to death, or strangled in the reins, which are tightly tied around his middle, before he can cut himself free with his hook. Damocles, however, risked the danger, and was so intent on not missing his aim, and there was so much dust and shouting, that he did not notice what was happening in the two inner berths. His partner, the first Green, had been jostled by the second Blue and had fouled the race-post and come to grief; but the near trace-horse of the second Blue had strained a tendon in the course of the manoeuvre, which obliged the team to pull up. As a result, the first Blue was able to avoid the danger from Damocles' wheel, as he could not have done if his partner had still been running just ahead of him: he made a wonderful inward swerve and scraped past, to win comfortably from Damocles, who was left standing.

It was a clear case of bad luck, as all discriminating judges would have agreed; yet the Greens were so disappointed that they felt obliged to find a scapegoat. The scapegoat was not the first Green charioteer, who was lying stunned on the ground in the ruins of his chariot, but my master Damocles. For Damocles, after his partner had crashed, had been left in the leading position with only a hundred yards more to go for victory, and had unaccountably reined in. It can be imagined that Cappadocian John put the worst possible construction on his behaviour, and accused him of selling the race to the Blues. The evidence that he offered for the accusation was that two Blue charioteers had been seen speaking to Damocles on the previous morning in a City wine-shop, and that Damocles had a grudge against the faction management in the matter of the Bear Mastership. So at a committee-meeting held immediately after the race he was suspended from driving for a year; and that night he killed himself, after an assault on the Green Dancing Master, one of whose eyes he struck out with a flick of his whip, aiming across the full length of the charioteers' dressing-room.

Our fortunes now seemed at a very low ebb, because my master Damocles had been generous with his earnings and saved practically nothing; and now his wife and Antonina his daughter were cast off by the faction as the relicts of a charioteer who had disgraced his Colour. As for myself, I was in danger of being sold again to another master.

But all ended well, because at a meeting of the Blue management two days later Thomas the Treasurer related his dream about the bear. He assured the committee that the little girl who had ridden on the bear's back in his dream was one of the daughters of the deceased Green Bear Master, who had sat garlanded as suppliants at the race-post. He urged them to offer the vacant post of Blue Bear Master to Peter, who was now stepfather to these little girls: for it was clear that good luck would come to the Blues if they did so.

There was some opposition to the suggestion, but Thomas pointed out that Peter was well trained in the Green bear-stables, and that they would be doing themselves a service as well as putting the Greens to shame, if they chose him. Peter was appointed the Blue Bear Master and made a success of his term of office, and the whole family changed their colour from Green to Blue; which is a very rare occurrence among Hippodrome families. To show his gratitude to the family of Damocles, he gave us board and lodging in his own house; and his wife and daughters as well as himself swore by the God Poseidon (the most respectable oath among Hippodrome people), that they would do everything in their power to assist us. So we were comforted, and Damocles' widow did not need to sell me. But in order not to be a burden to Peter, she persuaded the Dancing Master of the Blues to employ her as an actress at the Theatre – not as a dramatic actress on the stage, because she had not sufficient training for this, but as a variety actress in the orchestra-area. She could dance a little and strum a little on the lute and manage a tambourine quite well, so he used her. She trained her daughter Antonina from her earliest years as musician, juggler, dancer, and acrobat, and Antonina grew up as Blue in her feelings as her father Damocles had been Green. Antonina was soon greatly in request at supper-parties like Modestus's at Adrianople, and at community-dinners among the young coxcombs of the Blue faction, to which each member made some contribution either of food or drink.

Antonina remained on terms of intimate friendship with the three daughters of Acacius. Their names were Comito, Theodora, and Anastasia. But of these I wish chiefly to write about Theodora, the middle one in age, who was Antonina's senior by some two years and became her particular friend. As the three girls grew up they were each in turn put on the stage. Comito was a sleek, superbly made creature, and made a great success with the men, in spite of being a poor actress. She began to treat Theodora and Anastasia with disdain, because neither of them had her good looks, but she died pretty soon of the disease of her profession. Anastasia became contaminated too, and lost most of her teeth in a brawl at a community dinner. But Theodora was undamageable. It was generally agreed that she had a devil in her – a devil of implacability and insatiability. How often in after-life did Antonina have occasion to thank the gods that Theodora was her ally, not her enemy!

I remember Theodora first as a six-year-old child, dressed in a little sleeveless frock of the sort that slave children wear, carrying her mother's folding-stool for her to the orchestra-area before a performance. She scowled or snapped at any other children she met; her mother used to say that one ought to hang a notice around her neck like those seen in the bear-stables warning visitors: 'This animal is malevolent.' Theodora had become embittered by being jeered at by her former little friends among the Greens for that unlucky history of her father's death and her mother's remarriage.

Antonina, too, had insults thrown at her, as the daughter of a charioteer who had sold a race to the Blues. But she was not a physical fighter like Theodora, who went for her tormentors with nails and teeth. She took her revenge in other ways: chiefly – as she grew a little older – by frightening her enemies into imagining themselves the victims of her magical powers. She gradually came herself to believe in the magic. Certainly she had one or two remarkable successes with it. One day she was rudely kicked from behind by Asterius, the Dancing Master of the Greens, whose machinations had been the original cause of all the trouble. She made an image of him in tallow – paunchy, big-nosed, one-eyed – and uttered certain prayers to Hecate, who is the Old Goddess who manages these things, and then drove out his remaining eye with a pin. Before the moon had reached her third quarter, this villain was blinded: a spindle thrown by an angry woman at her husband somehow struck him instead, as he was passing by their street door. Theodora much admired Antonina for this action, and together they tried to destroy Cappadocian John too. But I suppose that his many prayers in Church hindered Hecate's action; for he continued to thrive. Then they swore by the Sacred Rattle – a most terrible oath – that they would never rest until one or other of them had reduced John to the nakedness and beggary which were his due. The sequel will be told before this book is over.

An old Syro-Phoenician sorcerer from whom my mistress Antonina learned her magic – my master Damocles had befriended him – cast the two girls' horoscopes one day, which amazed and terrified him by their brilliance. He told Theodora that she was fated to marry the King of the Demons and to reign more gloriously than any woman since Queen Semiramis and never to lack for gold. As for Antonina, she should marry a patrician, the one good man in a wholly bad world; and, whereas Theodora's share of misfortune would occur in the earlier part of her life, Antonina should be spared misfortune until extreme old age, when it would be soon done.

Theodora bent her brows at him and said: 'Old man, are you trying your usual flattering tricks on us? Are you unaware, for a start, that men of birth are forbidden by ancient law to marry women of our profession? Confess that you lie!'

He trembled, but would not retract a word, inviting her to show the figures of these horoscopes to any reputable astrologer. So she did so, and the second astrologer, an Alexandrian Greek, made much the same deductions as the first.

Then she said to my mistress Antonina, laughing: 'Dearest girl, what your husband will not be able to accomplish for us by goodness, I shall make my husband accomplish by demonry.'

Another memory that I have is of Theodora going into the Theatre wearing nothing except the obligatory loin-cloth and a large hat. That was when she was almost fully mature in body. Her game was that her loin-cloth was always coming untied: she used to go with it in her hand to the busy faction-official who attended people to their seats and complain that 'certain men of Belial' had rudely pulled it off her. She desired him to escort her to some private place and assist her to put it on again. Meanwhile she modestly covered her thighs with her hat. Her gravity, her mock-distress, her persistence, used to exasperate the official, to the delight of the benches.

Theodora was small and sallow complexioned. She was not a particularly good dancer or instrumentalist or acrobat; in fact, she was rather below the average of excellence at all these things. But she possessed an extraordinarily quick wit and a complete freedom from sexual shame: she seems, indeed, to have shown a singular inventiveness in her carnality, so that 'I learned this from Theodora' was a current joke under the statue of Venus, the chief trysting-place of the brothel district. And all the time that she was apparently engaged merely in money-making and pleasure Theodora was busily studying Man; and there is no better way to study this subject than as a Megaraean sphinx, to whom young men and old reveal their true selves more openly than to their chaster mothers, sisters, or wives. My mistress Antonina was a student of Man, too, and she and Theodora soon learned to despise even the gravest of their clients for their unquenchable conceit and credulousness and ignorance and selfishness, and to turn these traits to their own advantage. By charms and remedies they both managed to avoid pregnancy, except Theodora, who had to procure an abortion on a couple of occasions, but without ill-effects.

They had only two intimate friends, Indaro and Chrysomallo, girls of their set; with whom, some six months after Antonina's visit to Adrianople, they planned to leave the stage, if they could get permission, and set up independently. Permission was extremely difficult to obtain, but Chrysomallo and Theodora had the good luck to gain the favour of the Democrat of the Blues, who controlled the political side of the faction, while Indaro and Antonina laid successful siege to the Demarch, who controlled the military side. The usual ruling was that the husband of any actress who left the stage for the sake of marriage must pay a heavy contribution to the Fund. No other excuses were accepted except penitence, but no penitent might return to her old employment under a penalty of being shut in a house of correction for the rest of her days. Nevertheless, these four girls won permission to leave, on the understanding that they remained good Blues. With their savings, and money borrowed from their backers, they clubbed together to take a well-furnished suite of rooms in an elegant house close to the Statue of Venus, and opened it as a place of entertainment: being officially backed by the faction, it soon became the most fashionable resort of Constantinople. By this time my mistress Antonina's mother was dead; Antonina had inherited me from her. The club catering was entrusted to my charge. As independent entertainers the ladies were no longer forced to pay a high proportion of their private earnings to the Dancing Master; instead, they became full members of the faction, paying their subscriptions regularly to the Fund. Indaro and Chrysomallo were both highly trained, the first as an acrobatic dancer and juggler, the second as a singer and instrumentalist; and my mistress Antonina was equal to either of them in those accomplishments. Theodora was their manager and their clown. The four of them had some very happy, amusing, altogether shameless times together, and I am glad to record that they remained good friends both then and throughout their subsequent lives; and I, who have survived them all, regret them all.

One day Theodora told us – for I was treated more as a friend than a slave, and they all confided in me – that she had been invited to accompany a patrician named Hecebolus to Pentapolis, of which he had been appointed Governor, and that this opportunity of seeing the world at her ease was too good to be missed. We all begged Theodora not to leave us, and Chrysomallo warned her that Hecebolus was not a man to be trusted – was he not a Tyrian by birth and so a born trickster? Theodora replied that she knew how to take care of herself and that her only anxiety was about leaving us to manage without her. Off she went; after a couple of amusing notes from cities on the route to Pentapolis, we heard nothing more either from her or about her for a very long time. Then a staff-officer came on leave from Pentapolis and told us that one evening Theodora had lost her temper with Hecebolus, who had tried to keep her in a sort of cage all to himself: she had emptied a pail of slops over him, brocaded tunic and all, as he was dressing for dinner. He had thrown her out of his residence immediately, and refused even to let her remove her few clothes and jewels. The staff-officer believed that she had then persuaded the captain of a vessel to take her to Alexandria in Egypt; but he could tell us nothing further.

It was a very different Theodora who limped back to Constantinople many months later. The misfortunes prophesied for her by the Syro-Phoenician had been concentrated into a single year, and they had been very bitter ones. Our gay, self-reliant Theodora, who had never failed to tell us her most ludicrous and painful adventures, kept pretty silent on the subject of her experiences in Egypt and her humiliating return journey by way of Caesarea and Antioch and the interior of Asia Minor. We nursed her slowly back to health, but even when she was strong enough, to all physical appearances, she did not feel equal to resuming her work at the club-house. 'I would rather spin wool all day than begin that life again,' she cried. Much to our surprise, she actually borrowed a spinning-wheel and began learning to use this melancholy if serviceable instrument in the solitude of her room. The other ladies did not laugh at her, because she was their friend and had evidently suffered almost beyond human endurance. So the steady sound of the spinning-wheel was now heard in the club-house at all hours of the day and night; and when clients asked, 'Will that damned whining noise never stop?' the ladies would answer, 'That is only poor Theodora earning an honest living.' But they took it for a joke. They never caught sight of her.

One of our clients was a strange, round-faced, smiling, lecherous fellow named Justinian, a nephew of the illiterate old barbarian commander of the Imperial Guards, Justin. Justin had sent for Justinian when a youth, from the mountain village in Illyria where he had himself once been a shepherd-boy, and had given him the education that he regretted himself not having had. Justinian – whose baptismal name was Upraudа, 'the upright' – still talked Greek with a strong foreign accent and far preferred Latin, the official language of his native province. None of the ladies knew what to make of Justinian, and though he was courteous and amusing and seemed destined to become a person of importance, he made them feel uncomfortable, in some obscure way, as if he were not quite human. None of them enjoyed taking him to her private room. My mistress Antonina, for one, successfully avoided doing so on every occasion, and without incurring his hostility. Indaro told a queer story: how one evening she had fallen asleep while Justinian was in bed with her and, suddenly waking up and finding herself alone, had seen a large rat scuttle from under the coverlet and out through the window. With my own eyes I saw a still queerer sight. Justinian said one night, as he and the ladies were talking together, 'I heard noises at the front door.' But all were too lazy to investigate, and I was busy at some task behind the wine-bar. Then I noticed an emanation float out from Justinian's shoulders, a phantom head which swooped out of the door and presently returned. Justinian said: 'The noise was nothing: let us continue our talk.' The ladies had not seen what I saw; but it was a characteristic of these phenomena that not more than one person ever saw them at a time, so that each one doubted his senses, and no argument was possible as to the authenticity of any particular vision.

He was a Christian and revelled in theological discussions, as much as, or more than, in faction gossip and salacious jokes and stories; and he used to fast regularly. He always came to the club-house at the close of his fast-days and would eat and drink enormously. Sometimes he had fasted, he said, for three days, and his appetite would have supported his boast if he had called it three weeks. But he never lost that rosy complexion of his, not to the day of his death in extreme old age.

My mistress Antonina used to call him Phagon, after the famous old trencherman who once, giving a display before the Emperor Aurelian, devoured at a sitting: a pig, a sheep, a wild-boar, and 100 loaves of full weight.

Justinian, too, complained of the spinning-wheel whine and derided our explanation of it. But one morning, when he happened to be there on a visit, Theodora came into the club-room to warm her hands at the fire, not expecting to encounter any guests at that hour. When she noticed Justinian on a couch behind the door, she was going away again; but he pulled at her dress and begged her to stay. So she stayed and warmed her hands. Justinian began a religious discussion with Chrysomallo, who liked that sort of thing, and was getting the better of her as usual when Theodora suddenly interposed with a quiet comment which showed her to be extremely well-informed on the doctrine of the Incarnation of Christ, which was the subject under dispute. Justinian exclaimed admiringly: 'That is most ingenious, but also most unorthodox,' and turned his attack on her.

They continued to dispute endlessly, even missing the hour of their midday meal, until Justinian rose and left us in a hurry at the sound of the dull booming of mallet against board, which is the customary summons to public prayer in the City. Justinian's Orthodoxy was also due to foreign travel: he had lived for some years at the centre of Orthodoxy, Rome, as a hostage to King Theodorich of the Goths. Theodora routed him in a way that surprised us; but it seems that she had profited by her stay at Alexandria to learn these fine points of doctrine from the schoolmen there. Thus intimacy between these two started, and he was fascinated by her as by a repentant Magdalene – for had not St Mary Magdalene also been a prostitute? Whenever he came to the club-house Justinian now regularly went straight up to Theodora's room. What passed between them besides discussion of the nature of the Trinity, and of the fate of the souls of unbaptized infants and such topics, I do not know; at all events, her wheel was quite silent during those interviews. The other ladies were glad to be relieved of his company and of the sound of the wheel.

CHAPTER 4

AN IMPROVED CAVALRY

THESE opening years of the sixth century of the Christian era were evil ones for the Empire. Belisarius's mother may be pardoned for her superstitious belief that the Devil was then at the height of his power. The reigning Emperor was old Anastasius, known as 'Anastasius Odd-Eyes' because one of his eyes was brown and the other blue (a peculiarity occasionally noted in domestic cats but never before, to my knowledge, in human beings); or as 'Anastasius the Usher' because he had once been an officer of the Gentlemen Ushers at the Court of his predecessor. He was an energetic and able ruler, despite his age, and no blame could be attached to him personally for most of the misfortunes of his reign: such as earthquakes, which greatly damaged some of the richest cities in his dominions, and the first appearance in the Bosphorus of Porphyry the whale, and the plague that spread from Asia, and a wide failure of crops, and an embitterment of the rivalry between Blues and Greens which led to mutiny and sedition. All these things occurred in or about the year of Belisarius's birth, together with vexatious wars with the Saracens in the country inland from Palestine and with savage Bulgarian Huns raiding across the Danube. Orthodox Christians ascribed all these misfortunes to a religious portent, namely the simultaneous appearance of two rival Popes; holding that it was blasphemy for two Vicars of Christ to exist simultaneously. The election of one Pope, at Constantinople, took place on the same day exactly as that of the other at Rome, the slowness of communication between the two capital cities causing the inadvertent confusion. But, once entrusted with the Keys of Heaven, neither of the rivals wished to yield his bunch to the other: the Roman Pope standing for rigid Orthodoxy in the (to me) highly fanciful dispute as to the single or double nature of the Son, while the other, Anastasius's nominee, stood for graceful compromise. Each anathematized the other as Anti-Pope, and we Hippodrome heathen were much amused at the spectacle and exacerbated the conflict by taking sides, Greens for one Pope, Blues for the other.

As if all this trouble were not sufficient, Anastasius became involved in a war with Kobad, King of the Persians, who utterly destroyed one of our armies and ravaged Roman Mesopotamia in a dreadful manner. Anastasius was forced to buy peace at the price of 800,000 gold pieces, and at a time when gold was scarcer than it ever had been, owing to the exhaustion of the principal European and Asiatic mines. In the year that Belisarius went to school at Adrianople, the Bulgarian Huns were ravaging Eastern Thrace again, and actually pasturing their horses in the kitchen-gardens and parks of suburban Constantinople. Anastasius set to work and built a great defensive wall at thirty-two miles' distance from the City, straight across the isthmus. This has been a comfort to us ever since, though it has been allowed to fall into disrepair and is not difficult to turn at either end.

As for the religious disputes: Anastasius, though inclined to the theory of the single nature, had, as I have explained, found it politic to nominate a Pope who favoured a compromise between this and the Orthodox, or double-nature, view. The Blues were Orthodox for political reasons; the Greens were either for compromise with Monophysitism or for plain Monophysitism. One day such rioting broke out in the Hippodrome over these religious differences that the old Emperor had to stand as a suppliant by the race-post (as Theodora and her family had done some nine years previously), and offer to resign his throne. The Blues pelted him with stones, but the Greens stood by him, since to them, as the stronger faction, he had allotted the best seats in the Hippodrome. In gratitude, he gave the Monophysite cause every possible support. But not long afterwards the Blues massacred a party of arrogant Monophysite monks; and because Anastasius did not venture to avenge their deaths, the power of the Blues became dominant in the City and Senate. But Vitalian, a Green of patrician rank, raised an army of 40,000 Thracian Monophysites and led them against the Blues, laying siege to the City. In fear of his life Anastasius then announced that he would assemble a General Church Council to resolve the whole religious difficulty; at which Vitalian disbanded his army before any fighting had taken place. But Anastasius did not keep his promise.

Such matters concern my story more closely than appears at first sight, because this queer fellow Justinian played a leading part in the negotiations between the Emperor, the Blues, and Vitalian on behalf of the Greens. Justinian represented the Blue faction, and assured Vitalian that matters could be arranged honourably to the satisfaction of both Colours and both Dogmas and of the Emperor himself. He even took the Eucharist at Vitalian's side as an additional proof of the Blue faction's good intentions towards him, and swore an oath of brotherhood on the Bread and Wine. Justinian was offered patrician rank for his services, but did not wish to accept this honour until he had first married our Theodora, with whom he was still infatuated. His aunt, Justin's wife, however, a virtuous old country woman who could talk no Greek, or very little, opposed the marriage – horrified that her nephew should consort with a woman who had once been a prostitute. Justinian was thus in a predicament: once he had accepted patrician rank he could not marry Theodora, and yet to refuse the honour would seem disloyal; and he was afraid of his aunt. He consulted with Theodora, who smiled and said: 'Accept the rank, for I cannot stand in the way of your advancement.' Theodora also went to the aunt, to tell her the same thing: which so pleased the old dame that she withdrew her opposition to Justinian's friendship with Theodora, if only she would leave her quarters at the club-house – as a decently repentant Mary Magdalene should already have done. So Theodora left us for a fine mansion, well-staffed and furnished, that Justinian gave her, and drove about in a carriage drawn by a pair of white mules. Justinian himself used a chariot with silver wheels and frame, and a team of four black horses harnessed abreast.

It was not long after this time that Belisarius came to Constantinople to study at the cadet-school, but my mistress Antonina saw nothing of him. She and the other ladies had given up the club-house, which had proved very profitable. Chrysomallo had married a rich wine-merchant, and Indaro had gone to live with Theodora, as her companion. My mistress thought that she might as well marry too. She found a solid, middle-aged Syrian merchant whom she could rely upon to treat her indulgently, not to live too long, and to leave her comfortably off when he died. She met him by accident: he was on a business visit to Constantinople and had taken a furnished house near the docks, of the sort that the owner lets, wife and all complete, while he lives uproariously by himself at a wine-shop. In this case the rented wife had died suddenly and the merchant was left without either a bedfellow or a house-keeper. My mistress consented to manage for him temporarily; and pleased him so well that they were legally married within a few days. He is not of great importance to this story, because (to be frank) he was not even the father of the two children of my mistress who survived – her son Photius and her daughter Martha – and of only one of the two who died. But he did just what was expected of him in life and death, and it seems that my mistress satisfied him as the best of wives, since he described her so in his will.

Their home was at Antioch, where he was Treasurer of the Blues at the local Hippodrome, and president of the silk-merchants' guild. He proved to be a much richer man than we had suspected. Peace to his memory. It was to please him that my mistress was baptized a Christian, along with three other women. That was a memorable ceremony in the hearty Syrian manner, with a young priest and a young deacon officiating. The women were immersed naked; but for decency's sake no man beside the priests was permitted to be present. I was not excluded, being a eunuch. Well, the proceedings at that baptistry included many jokes, drinks, kisses, and a little Christian ceremony. All seven of us ended in the water.

In the second year of our life at Antioch, which is a city of which I was extremely fond (especially when one can escape the heat in summer, as we did, by retiring to a country estate in the Lebanon among flowers and cedars), we heard news of the death of the old Emperor Anastasius. Soon afterwards came the surprising report that his successor was not one of his three worthless nephews, Green factional rubbish: he was Justin, the veteran commander of the Imperial Guards. Justin had been given a great deal of money by Anastasius's Court Chamberlain with which to bribe the Guards to support his own candidate for the throne. Justin gave the Guards this money honestly enough, but he tricked the Chamberlain: he himself put on the purple robes panelled with cloth of gold, and the purple stockings, and the scarlet jewelled slippers, and the white silk tunic, and the crimson scarf, and the pearl diadem with the four great pearls dangling behind. The Guards cheered him enthusiastically. Justin's baptismal name had been Istok and he had no surname, but he had arranged to be adopted into the ancient and noble family of Anicians. His old wife, however, said that all this pomp was ridiculous for a woman like herself: she refused to wear her own Imperial finery, or to move into the Sacred Imperial suite, until Justin had given her a new name instead of her old one. So from Lupchin (which signifies 'sweetheart') she became Euphemia, and caused a great deal of merriment in the City by her country ways. It was a sight to watch her distributing Sunday alms to the poor in the Cathedral Church of St Sophia, with her elegant train of women and eunuchs behind her. Lupchin had an excellent sense of the purchasing power of money, but could not accustom herself to the notion that gold coins by the hundred thousand were now hers for the asking. So she would solemnly deal out single pieces of silver to the long line of approved beggars, and if one old woman perhaps, having received her coin, took her place again at the end of the line, Lupchin would not fail to recognize her and would box her ears soundly; as she still used to box Justinian's ears if he spoke out of turn or otherwise displeased her.

Justin was Orthodox and inclined to the Blues. He found it necessary to rid himself of one or two dangerous Greens; among these was Vitalian. Justinian had Vitalian murdered at a banquet at which both he and his Imperial uncle were present. He justified his breach of the oath sworn on the Eucharist by some theological quibble to the effect that an oath sworn to a heretic was not binding. Justinian proved invaluable as a minister to Justin, who could not read or write – having to sign all documents with the assistance of a golden stencil which forged the letters LEGI, meaning 'I have read and approved'. Justin adopted him as his son, awarding him the dignity of the Consulship and appointing him Commander of the Armies in the East; but he was not a soldier, and preferred to remain at Constantinople with Theodora. The Greens took up arms to avenge Vitalian's death, but Justinian was kept informed of their secrets by Cappadocian John and suppressed the rising ruthlessly; and you may be sure that Theodora encouraged him in this. Cappadocian John, though a Green, happened to be Orthodox in his views and made this an excuse for his treachery; for he saw which way the wind was now blowing Justinian rewarded him with large presents of money and an important position at Court. Theodora could afford to wait for her revenge on him.

Meanwhile the breach with the Pope had been healed, because Justin was more Orthodox than the Pope himself, as he used to boast rather childishly; and all Monophysite bishops and priests were removed from their appointments. A curious circumstance was that, although Theodora was so loyal a Blue, or rather so vengeful an enemy of the Greens, she was intellectually a Monophysite, just as Cappadocian John, though a Green, was intellectually Orthodox. She took the view, which seems a sensible one to me, that if anything so singular as a double nature had characterized the Son, someone at least of the Evangelists or Apostolic Fathers would have mentioned it, if not the

Son Himself; but none had. Justinian's counterview was that a double nature was common enough; though in ordinary men it was, more usually, part human and part demonic. (This was true enough of himself.) Theodora replied to this: 'Demons are numerous, and as many as seven at a time can occupy a man's body, I admit. But God is eternally One, by a theological axiom, and therefore if Jesus was indeed God He was One also.'

Belisarius – who was Orthodox, though not fanatically so – graduated from the cadet-school with honour and proved an excellent officer of the Guards. His uniform was now the green tunic faced with red, golden collar, red shield bordered with blue and starred in black. He did not mix in faction politics or spend his time in idleness, so Justin noted him as due for quick promotion and encouraged him to work out a new system of cavalry training with the men under his command. He elaborated the plan that he had clearly hinted at, during that banquet at Adrianople, for arming heavy cavalry with bow as well as lance and thus making them proficient both as skirmishers and shock troops. Justin was a seasoned soldier, and Belisarius's views pleased him; he also admired the unanimity that he found between Belisarius and his brother-officers – Rufinus and Armenian John and Uliaris. When he became Emperor he permitted them to train a company of recruits in this new style and take them raiding across the Danube.

Belisarius, then, armed all his men with the lance, and a stiff bow that had a slow shooting-rate but could drive an arrow through any corselet. He also gave them each a small handy shield, strapped to the arm, which acted as a receptacle for half a dozen sharp darts. These darts were useful at close quarters. They were seized by the feathered end, held upright like a torch, and flung with a forward and downward motion; the heads were heavily weighted and the feathering kept them steady on the mark. As a final arm for use when even the lance failed they carried a heavy broadsword in a sheath on the left thigh. To control all these weapons, and the horse at the same time, needed many months of practice. A bow, for example, is a weapon that needs both hands; so Belisarius trained his men to manage their horses without the bridle, by pressure of the knee and heel. But he also introduced the novel device of steel stirrups, which were suspended by straps from the saddle as an aid in mounting and riding the very large horses that he favoured. Stirrups are now in general use throughout the army, though at first despised as womanish. Lastly, he supplied his men with wide, well-stuffed saddles, in front of which were strapped, when not in use, their woollen cloaks for cold or rainy weather. They wore sleeveless mailshirts of thigh length, and tall rawhide boots. When not in use, the bow was slung behind the back; the arrows were contained in a quiver next to the broadsword; the lance was carried in a leather bucket on the right side.

The recruit was trained to do everything methodically, so that each action became habitual: for example, the action of stringing the bow was undertaken first with the horse walking, then at a trot, then at a gallop. The right hand reaches behind for the bow, pulls it forward, rests the strung end on the right foot, and bends the bow by pressing it downwards. The left hand, which has meanwhile snatched an arrow from the quiver, unties the loop of the bowstring and slips it up over the catch; then down comes the left hand to the centre of the bow, transferring the arrow to the right hand – and in a moment the bow is in action. Belisarius learned this method from the Huns. From the Goths he learned the proper management of the lance and shield and taught his men to tilt against one another with light, untipped spears. The final exercise for the trained cuirassier was to gallop across a field from the end of which the Hanged Man approached. This was a stuffed figure suspended from a gallows on a low, wheeled trolley; the trolley came rolling forward down a gentle slope. The rider must string his bow as he rode, aim three arrows at the swaying figure, and then be ready to follow with the lance, or with darts. Rank, pay, and rations were awarded according to proficiency in these and other exercises. Belisarius required from his officers exceptional faculties: skilful use of country in manoeuvre, promptness and accuracy in reporting to headquarters, a quick appreciation of a tactical difficulty or advantage, but, above everything, the power to control their men both when in a body and when dispersed. This power comes more naturally to some men than to others; and none have it who failed to earn the respect of their men by bodily prowess. Therefore Belisarius insisted that every officer must be at least as proficient with bow, lance, darts, sword, and as good a horseman as the best men under his command.

Justin had asked Belisarius: 'What sort of recruits do you want? Have you a preference for any particular class or tribe or race?'

Belisarius's answer: 'Give me men who can drink foul water and eat carrion. Let them be a mixed force of mountaineers, sailors, men from the wide plains. Give me no estate-levies, except with the privilege of choice, and no factionists, and no men who have served as soldiers in any other corps.'

Justin approved the answer. Disease carried off more men on some campaigns than wounds, and its victims were for the most part those who were unused to bad food and water. Mountaineers were in general bold, hardy, independent men with well-developed sight and hearing; they were invaluable as scouts and guides in broken country. Men from the wide plains understood the management of horses and the art of open warfare. Sailors were ingenious with their hands and knew how to make themselves at home in strange places and how to establish understanding with foreigners. Each of these classes of men could learn from one another; the more diverse the ingredients of the mixture, the better would be the discipline in any squadron, and the better the terms on which one squadron met with another. For close racial and religious ties uniting men under a single standard often make for mutiny, discontent, and quarrelling with other corps. To enlist in the army should be like becoming the citizen of an entirely new world, not like moving from the centre to the suburbs of one's native town. These were Justin's views as well as those of Belisarius. Belisarius had wanted no estate-levies – that is to say no serfs contributed by landowners to the army in lieu of a tax – because the landowners would in general send their weakest and most useless men; but he had added 'except with the privilege of choice', knowing that in these levies a man was sometimes included merely because he was too active and independent-minded to please his landowner – and, properly handled, might turn into a fine soldier. Finally, he had wanted no factionists, because they were a disturbing element wherever they went, and no men with previous military service in other corps, because these always considered that they knew better than the officers and sergeants of their present squadron or company, and taught the recruits traditional tricks for evading duty, and for stealing, and for bettering themselves at other people's expense.

Justin allowed Belisarius his pick of the recruits who came forward that year from Thrace, Illyria, Asia Minor; he chose according to the specifications he had made.

With a well-trained squadron Belisarius raided across the Upper Danube in the summer of the year of our Lord 520. He engaged with the Gepids, a troublesome Germanic race that had been settled in this region for about a hundred years. The Gepids fought from horseback with long battle-axes and talked in loud voices and greased their yellow hair with rancid butter. They were organized, like most German tribes, into *gaus*, communities of 5,000 or more souls, each under a nobleman, and providing a thousand or so armed warriors for the national army. The *gau* thousands were subdivided into 'hundreds', troops of mounted freemen who had taken an oath of personal loyalty to a lesser nobleman and who were members of a single clan, or group of families among which there was a regular exchange of women in marriage.

Belisarius's commission was to engage small forces of the Gepids, to take prisoners, to lose no men himself, to teach this nation a new respect for the Imperial name. All these tasks he accomplished. Even the noblest Gepids wore little armour, relying on leather jerkins and helmets and hide-covered wicker shields; and only their infantry, who were serfs or slaves, used the bow. Belisarius's tactics were to draw the Gepid cavalry away from their infantry, and to keep them just within bowshot; not letting them come to closer quarters with their battle-axes and short javelins until they were demoralized by their losses; first dismounting as many of them as possible by the shooting of their horses. Then he would charge, yet would not press the pursuit, merely capturing the dismounted men and as many others as held their ground. In this summer's campaign, of which I can give no geographical details, because there are no settled towns or other well-known features in that district to indicate its extent, he raided over a distance of 400 miles. The food his men carried with them was barley-meal and dried goat's flesh, always a ration for ten days. He kept a supply-boat on the river, with stores of arrows and a repair-shop in it: this was his base. By the end of the campaigning season three of his men had been wounded, and one drowned in a marsh; but he had captured not less than forty Gepids, all of whom, rather than be sold as slaves for menial work, applied for permission to enlist under his personal command as cavalrymen. They were the first barbarian recruits to the Household Regiment of Belisarius, for so Justin gratefully renamed the force, allowing the men to swear personal allegiance to their commander.

These Gepids have a shortage of metal, iron as well as gold, and their jewels are of trifling value.

Many of the officers who later distinguished themselves under his leadership in his four principal wars were trained in this campaign; or in the punitive expedition that he made in the following summer against the Bulgarian Huns of the Lower Danube, who had lately been active again on our side of the river. He had 600 heavy cavalry with him on this occasion, not 200. With the Bulgarians, who are horse-archers, the problem was how to come to close quarters with them, not how to hold them off. His method was to use live bait, a small body of men on fast horses, and draw the greedy Bulgarians into an unfavourable position, from which their retreat could be cut off. The Bulgarians, like the Gepids, protected their communities, when halted during the march, by barricades of wagons. Belisarius would ride to the windward of these and set them alight by means of fire-arrows. He caused the Bulgarians heavy losses and took numerous prisoners, but the plunder that the captured camps yielded was small.

For his feats Belisarius was promoted in title from 'Distinguished Patrician' to 'Illustrious Patrician'. Justinian was now Commander of the Imperial Guards under his adoptive father the Emperor Justin. He was, however, no soldier, and in practice army matters were still controlled by Justin. On the other hand, Justin had no understanding of statecraft or civil business, and let the officers of State do more or less what they pleased, under the supervision of Justinian.

Belisarius was now employed as general supervisor of military training, and spent the next four years going from one garrison town to the other throughout the Eastern half of the Empire, writing detailed reports on the condition of the troops he inspected and on the capacity of their officers, and making recommendations for improvements in training and equipment. He gained many friends among steady old officers whose work he praised, and active young officers whom he recommended for promotion; but more enemies. He always refused to turn a blind eye to incompetence or to deficiencies in equipment, and was known to be unbribable.

He remained in high favour at Court, yet when he was pressed to marry this high-born woman or that, he always excused himself as at present too much of a traveller. When he could settle down he would marry, he said. But he had no love-affairs with women, married or unmarried, and abstained from visits to the grand brothel which Constantine had built and which was the general meeting-place of all the wit and fashion of Constantinople. His enemies hinted that he was no lover of women merely because he preferred his own sex; but that was a foolish lie. If he did not marry, that was, in my naturally prejudiced view, because the memory of my mistress Antonina had remained with him; and he abstained from the brothel because to attend it was against the Christian law which he had sworn to observe. Besides, his work was enough to occupy his mind, and should he want amusement he would go hunting with his staff. If there was a shortage of deer or hare or other game, this would not trouble him much: he would shoot as readily at hawk in the sky or snake in the hedge as at nobler game, and not less accurately. He encouraged his officers at the same practice; for hunting, he said, was a sort of drill. Boar-hunting with the lance he especially recommended.

He came to Antioch twice in the course of his duties, but on the first occasion my mistress and her husband happened to be staying at their villa in the Lebanon; and on the second she did not meet him either, though she longed to do so. Her husband invited him to a dinner at the house, but he refused, pleading his official duties. However, he wrote a letter in his own hand as a particular compliment to my mistress's husband. My naturally prejudiced view was that he would have felt embarrassed at meeting my mistress again as the wife of another man.

This may seem an extravagant story, but I later met its parallel in Italy: a young patrician had fallen in love with a married woman when he was only thirteen. Not only did he abstain from love of any other woman, but he went out into the wilderness and lived in a cave, and later formed a society of hermit monks whom they now call Benedictines after this desperate Benedict. They were a decent fraternity, whose employments were three only – namely, worship of God, reading, manual labour; they abstained from butcher's meat, politics, and vice. But they came to hold with Benedict that man and woman should not merely be strangers to each other but natural, irreconcilable foes; which, to me, is nonsensical. I visited their high-walled hermitage on Mount Cassino once, above the Latin Way between Rome and Naples, and found everything under the strictest and exactest discipline. I reported what I had seen to my mistress, who by the rules of the monastery was not permitted to enter, and said to her of Benedict: 'A good soldier is lost in him.' Belisarius, who was present, answered me in the Christian sense: 'No, Eugenius, a good soldier found.'

This Benedict was nearly defeated once, for the woman with whom he was in love took pity on him at last, and engaged a party of theatre-women to come with her one evening to the monastery, one woman for each monk. They knocked at the great door; and when the porter – a gigantic Goth – opened to them he was assaulted by fondling arms and smothered in scented kisses, and led away prisoner. The attack was carried out most vigorously, and all the monks succumbed except two or three, who locked themselves in their cells and threw the keys out of the window to be rid of the temptation: as Ulysses in the story immobilized himself against the temptations of the Sirens by ordering his sailors to lash him hand and foot to the mast. Only Benedict stood his ground. He took the leader of the enemy by the hand and spoke to her with loving frankness, and made her bitterly ashamed of her action. If this story be true, Benedict was as staunch a character as Belisarius. Or perhaps the woman had lost her looks in the meantime; for she was certainly a good deal older than he, and patrician women at Rome are gluttonous and lazy and soon grow as fat as the captive carp in their fish-pools.

At all events, Belisarius lived an upright and regular life, and in these years only failed on one expedition: that was against Porphyry, the famous whale, who now for twenty-five years had harassed the shipping of the Bosphorus and Black Sea, and could not by any means be killed or trapped. This Porphyry was the only whale that was ever known to enter the Mediterranean Sea. Much larger whales, called sperm whales, are frequently met in the Atlantic, and one of great size was once stranded at Cadiz. Larger still are met with in the Indian Ocean by Red Sea traders, who sail to Ceylon every year with the monsoon-wind – these are the whales that yield whalebone, and are often 400 feet in length. Porphyry was no more than one-eighth of that size; but unlike the Indian whales, who are shy creatures and avoid shipping, he carried on a destructive war with the Empire. Whales do not, as one might suppose, eat large fish and dolphins and seals and sharks, but only the smallest fry: they rush through the water with their mouths open and engulf millions at a time. Porphyry would cruise about in the Black Sea, feeding on the sea-bottom in the breeding grounds of fish, and sometimes would disappear for months on end. But always he would return and station himself in the narrows of the Bosphorus, or the Hellespont, and let swarms of fish be swept into his mouth by the current. It happened at Porphyry's first appearance that a bold fisherman, annoyed at having his nets broken, managed as he shot by in a small boat to throw a heavy fish-spear into Porphyry's flank. This was a formal declaration of war, and Porphyry, whose intentions had hitherto been peaceable enough, charging after the boat, broke it with a swing of his tail. Then it was realized that Porphyry was not a young whale of the usual unwarlike sort but a full-grown killer-whale, as they are called, such as have been observed by sailors on the Indian voyage in the act of making war on the great whales and flogging them to pieces with repeated blows.

Porphyry would lurk in the depths of the sea and suddenly appear, spouting water from a hole in his head, and dash at any boat or small ship he saw, and strike at it with his tail, and destroy it. He also sank two ships of considerable tonnage, at different times, by rising suddenly from beneath them and starting their timbers with the impact of his head against them. This was perhaps an accident, however.

All sorts of explanations were given for Porphyry's ravages. The Orthodox held that he was sent as a punishment for the heretical sin of Monophysitism, but the Monophysites said that this could not be so, for Porphyry struck at Orthodox and Monophysites alike. (And by the time of which I speak the breach with Rome had been repaired.) Others said that he was looking for a Jonah – and many an unpopular sailor, Orthodox or Monophysite as the case might be, had been thrown out to him as a sacrifice. Bishops of both opinions had been sent to preach to him from the shore, and texts floated down the current to him, written on strips of paper, conjuring him in the name of the Trinity to return to the Ocean whence he came. But Porphyry was unlettered and unbaptized, and paid no attention.

Belisarius volunteered to hunt Porphyry. He stationed himself at the entrance of the Black Sea about the time that the whale was expected to return to its usual fishing grounds. He was in a ship of a size greater than Porphyry was accustomed to attack, and it was armed with a siege-catapult of the sort that throws not the usual short bolt with wooden feathers, but a heavy, long spear. Justinian provided, for the management of the catapult, a detachment of City militia of the Blue faction – the responsibility for the defence of the walls of Constantinople was divided between the Demarch of the Blues and the Demarch of the Greens – who were animated by a desire to earn glory for their Colour by the extinction of Porphyry. The ship's crew were also Blues. They painted the catapult spears with blue paint, and painted the cheeks of the vessel blue too, and the blades of the oars.

Reports arrived at last that Porphyry had been sighted farther along the north coast, moving slowly down towards the City, and that he was in a mischievous mood. Belisarius ordered a keen look-out to be kept; and tested the catapult, giving the militia-men a drill in its management to make them perfect. He instructed them to aim at a cask which he had thrown overboard until they could calculate to a nicety the propulsive force of the ropes when tightened with a crank. Presently the look-out sighted the spouting Porphyry at half a mile's distance. Porphyry came closer, swimming on the surface, and made straight for the vessel, as if he intended to ram it. He was an animal of intelligence and wit, and knew how terrible his reputation had become: at a sight of him ships used to put on all sail and flee before the wind, sometimes going fifty miles or more out of their course. But this ship held its ground.

Nearer and nearer came the beast, and now Belisarius gave the order to shoot. The spear hurtled through the air – and went clean through the cask at which the prudent militia-men, terrified of Porphyry's anger, preferred still to aim. Porphyry contented himself with a flourish of his tail – which snapped two dozen oar-blades – and then dived and disappeared. But before he went Belisarius had driven a heavy arrow into him, from a stiff steel bow of the sort used in siege-warfare against enemy who try to force city-gates under the cover of shields of extreme thickness. He aimed where he reckoned the brain would be; but the anatomy of the whale is peculiar, and the arrow sank out of sight in protective blubber.

That was the last that the hunters saw of Porphyry; after cruising about for a few days they returned. The crew had talked matters over among themselves, and agreed on a story that satisfied their pride. According to them, Belisarius had shot with his bow but missed, and they had then shot with the catapult. The spear had gone straight into Porphyry's open jaws, but Porphyry had bitten the shaft off and gone away bellowing, with the head of the spear deeply embedded in his throat. 'Soon he will die of his wounds,' they boasted, 'and you will recognize our spear-head by its colour.' The Greens refused to accept these claims, particularly as Belisarius had not supported them. All that he would say was: 'The militia-men fought their catapult energetically and showed themselves accurate marksmen. I have handed in an official report to his Serenity the Emperor. Doubtless he will publish it, in due course.' But, for the honour of the Blues, Justin withheld the report.

Porphyry continued to destroy nets and shipping for many years after this. The Greens, though convinced that the Blues had been cowards, were not anxious to make fools of themselves by volunteering to put an end to Porphyry.

CHAPTER 5

WAR WITH PERSIA

THE Emperor of the Romans and the Great King of the Persians are ancient enemies; yet they think of themselves, together, as the twin eyes of the world and as the joint light-houses of civilization. Each finds the existence of the other a comfort to him in the loneliness of his sacred office, and there is a note of comradeship which constantly recurs in the royal letters that they exchange – in time of war no less than in time of peace. They greet each other like two veteran back-gammon players who play together in the wine-shop every day for the price of the day's drinks. One eye, or one light-house, shines over a great part of Europe, and over Asia Minor, and part of Africa; the other, over immense territories in Greater Asia. It is true that in both cases the sovereignty exercised over many regions is only titular. The Persian cannot control such distant satrapies as Bactria and Sogdiana and Arachosia; and the Roman, at the time of which I am writing, had in all but title lost Britain to the Picts and Saxons, Gaul to the Franks and Burgundians, North Africa to the Vandals and Moors, Spain to one nation of Goths, and Italy, with Rome itself, to the other. Nevertheless, the true control of a large part of the world remained, and remains, in the power of one or the other, and so also does the nominal control of another large part.

Fortunately for world peace, there are deserts of sand and great rocky uplands intervening between the two realms for practically the entire length of their common frontier – which runs from the eastern end of the Black Sea through Armenia and behind Syria and Palestine to the northern end of the Red Sea. Seldom in the history of the world have Western armies succeeded in conquering parts of Asia beyond these boundaries, or Eastern armies overflowed into Europe or Africa. Even when this has happened the invasion has not been lasting. Xerxes the Persian failed to conquer Greece, despite the immense armies he brought over into Europe by his bridge of boats across the Hellespont; Alexander the Greek conquered Persia, but his swollen Empire did not survive his death. More usually the invaders from either side have been defeated close to the frontier; or, if successful, have not attempted to retain the territories occupied, but have retired home after exacting tribute in some form or other. Such conflicts have almost all taken place in Mesopotamia, in the region between the upper waters of Euphrates and Tigris. This is the most convenient campaigning ground – which, however, favours the Persians in the matter of ready access to food depots and garrison towns.

For several centuries after the time of Alexander, the Persian Empire was known as the Parthian because the Arsacids, the ruling dynasty, were of Parthian origin; but, about a hundred years before Constantine turned Christian and transferred the capital of the Empire from Rome to Constantinople, a descendant of the old Persian Kings, by name Artaxerxes, had revolted and overthrown the Arsacids. His new dynasty, the Sassanids, restored the Persian name and tradition to the Empire and has maintained itself in power ever since. (At the time of which I write, Kobad, the nineteenth of the line, wore the regal diadem.) The Sassanids had purified and strengthened the ancient religion of the Persians, which is the worship of fire according to the revelation of the Prophet and Mage Zoroaster. This religion had been much corrupted by Greek philosophy – as the ancient Roman and Jewish religions had also been, and the Christian religion too. (Compare the fine, simple story contained in the four Gospels, obviously born among illiterate peasants and fishermen who had never studied either grammar or rhetoric, with the wearisome philosophic Christianity of our time!) But King Artaxerxes banished all the philosophers from his realm. They returned to us with Persian notions and inflicted on Christianity a new heresy, the Manichean. These Manichees have hit upon a totally original theory of the nature of Christ. They hold that it was dual, and not only dual but contradictory: Jesus, the historical man, being imperfect and a sinner, and Christ, his spiritual counterpart, being a Divine Deliverer. Manichees are hated both in Persia and Christendom, and I have not a word to say in their defence. The Persians encourage them only in Persian Armenia, in order to weaken the bonds of religious sympathy between that country, which is Christian, and Roman Armenia, which is Christian too and rigidly Orthodox.

By forbidding talk of an unnecessary sort – this is all that philosophy appears to be to a practical person like me – and ordering a return to a primitive directness of action, speech, and thought, Artaxerxes restored the native power of the Persians alike in the civil and military sides of government. Great wars were waged between his descendants and successive Roman Emperors, in which, on the whole, the Persians had the advantage. But the fourteenth of the line was Bahram the Hunter, so called because he had a passion for hunting the wild ass of the desert. He became involved in a war with us because he persecuted Christians as fanatically almost as we persecute our fellow-Christians; and was conquered in battle and forced to pledge his royal honour to keep the peace for a hundred years. His sons and grandsons, for fear of provoking the anger of his ghost, kept the peace strictly, and the hundred years did not expire until modern times. Then, as I have already mentioned, war broke out again, and Anastasius's army, disgracefully led, was disgracefully defeated. This was the campaign which the burgess Simeon had witnessed.

The quarrel had several causes, but the chief of these was the wholesale price of silk. Silk is a material for clothes that is far superior in coolness, lightness, and handsome appearance to any other known. It was invented by a primitive Chinese queen, and for centuries it has been imported from China by sea and land for the use of rich and well-bred people and for dancing girls and prostitutes and such; and from a rare luxury it has become a common vanity. Silk takes dye readily, especially the purple dye of the shell-fish. Cotton is another useful importation from the East, principally from India; it is the fibrous flower of a marshy shrub, and can be woven into a light, tough cloth, cooler than woollens and easy to wash. However, cotton has not the glossiness or fineness of silk. There was never any mystery about cotton; but what the nature and origin of silk was nobody but the Chinese themselves knew, and they would not reveal the secret, because they wished to preserve their most valuable monopoly. Raw silk came to us in yellowish skeins wound on grass-stalks, each skein containing a certain weight of thread. Natural historians guessed that it was the thread of a gigantic Chinese spider, but others believed that it was fibre drawn from the bark of a certain palm-tree, and still others that it was made from the scrapings of the furry undersides of mulberry leaves. However, nobody could prove his own view to be the correct one, because our relations with China have always been maintained through middlemen – except for a short period 400 years ago when our ships sailed directly into the ports of Southern China. We have dealt either with the Persian merchant colony in Ceylon, by the sea-route, or with Persia itself, by the land-route. The silk caravans from

China take 150 days to reach the Persian frontier by way of Bokhara and Samarkand, and another eighty to reach our frontier by way of Nisibis on the upper Euphrates; from thence a journey of twenty days brings the silk to Constantinople. The sea-voyage is perhaps less hazardous, but the silk must go through the hands of the Abyssinian traders of the Red Sea, and thus pay a double toll.

As the demand increased, the Chinese merchants raised the price of raw silk; and the Persians, unwilling that the Chinese should be the only ones to profit, increased the re-sale price more than was equable. Then our merchants, unable to make any profit by buying at this rate, decided to deal direct with the Chinese, if possible, by reopening an old trade-route passing to the north of the Persian territories, beyond the Caspian Sea: this long but practical route entered our territory through a narrow pass of the Caucasus mountains, to the east of the Black Sea and at the boundary of Colchis, a rich land friendly to us. It was to Colchis that Jason of old went in company with the Argonauts to fetch back the Golden Fleece; which was, I think, a parable of Eastern riches brought by this northern route. In deciding to reopen it, our merchants were aware that they must pay toll to the savage Huns through whose territory it passed, but hoped that they would be satisfied with less money than the Persians. The nearest and most powerful of these tribes were the White Huns, so called because they were European in appearance, unlike the other Huns, who seem to us a sort of evil yellow animal. They lived between the Caspian and the Black Seas and were inveterate enemies of the Persians. A timely gift to these White Huns to persuade them to attack Persia from the north had more than once saved our frontiers from serious invasion.

But the merchants' plan failed. The Persians heard of it and persuaded the Chinese to deal only with themselves. Then King Kobad wrote sarcastically to the Emperor Anastasius that the White Huns had now made him responsible for the toll that the Romans had promised to pay them for the use of the northern route. If Anastasius still wished to buy silk, he must therefore first lend the Persian Government money with which to appease the disappointed Huns. Anastasius, of course, refused this demand with indignation, so Kobad invaded Roman Armenia with a small but well-trained army, besieging the important city of Amida on the Upper Tigris. Anastasius despatched an army of 52,000 men to its relief, entrusting its command, however, not to a single worthless general, as was customary, but to several worthless generals of equal rank – who constantly opposed one another's plans and could not agree on any single point. This huge force was therefore beaten, division by division, in several pitched engagements; and some parts of it fled without daring to come to grips at all. Our name thus won such discredit in the East that had Kobad not been distracted by a Hunnish invasion from the north – Anastasius had bought the services of the White Huns by paying the promised toll twice over – he would doubtless have attempted to overrun all Syria and Asia Minor, and doubtless would have succeeded. He had already taken Amida after a long siege, owing to the negligence of certain Armenian monks, supposed to be on sentry duty at one of the towers, who had eaten and drunk too generously after a long fast and fallen asleep: the Persians crept into this tower by an old underground passage that they had discovered and slaughtered the monks, every one. At the assault Kobad himself showed great energy for a man of sixty years. Mounting a scaling-ladder, sword in hand, he threatened to run any Persian through who turned back. It is said that the Persian Mages had dissuaded him from raising the siege, as he had intended to do when it grew wearisome, because of a sign: a group of prostitutes on the walls had taunted the Persians by lifting up their skirts at them, exclaiming, 'Come in and enjoy yourselves.' The Mages interpreted this as a sign that the city would soon reveal her secrets to them; and the discovery of the hidden passage proved them right. Kobad, returning to give battle to the White Huns, left a garrison of a thousand men behind at Amida, who succeeded in holding the city against the Roman relief-force and only consented to evacuate it, two years after its capture, on payment of 70,000 gold pieces.

Peace was concluded for seven years between Anastasius and Kobad, but continued much longer, because Anastasius was too weak and Kobad too preoccupied to continue the struggle. But two hostile acts were committed, one by each side. Kobad seized the Caspian Gates, the pass through the Caucasus through which our caravans were to have gone in search of silk; and Anastasius fortified the open city of Daras, close to the Persian frontier and commanding the main road joining the two countries.

To give an explanation of what these acts signified. The Caspian Gates are of great strategical importance. They are the only practical pass through the lofty and terrible Caucasus range, which acts as a barrier for many hundreds of miles between the broad Asiatic steppes, where the nomad Huns roam, and our civilized world. Alexander the Great had been the first to appreciate fully the importance of this pass, which is seven miles long and begins, at the end nearest to us, with a natural door, set in precipitous cliffs, that can be defended by a small garrison. He built a castle there, and it has been held by many different princes in the last eight or nine hundred years. The present constable was a Christianized Hun, whose grazing-lands on this side of the mountain the castle protected against the heathen Huns on the other.

This constable felt death approaching and, being able to place little reliance on the good sense or courage of his sons, wrote to Anastasius, who had shown him many marks of favour, and offered to sell him the castle and the pass for a few thousand gold pieces. Anastasius called his principal Senators together and asked them for their opinion on the matter, which they gave as follows: 'The Caspian Gates would have been of great commercial importance to Your Sacred Majesty, had you been able to use the northern caravan-route for direct trade with China; but as this has been denied you by Persian intrigue there is no profit to be derived from them. Your Majesty will realize that the present constable, or his sons, will continue to hold the fortress without any inducement from you, merely to restrain raiders from the steppes from overrunning their own country. Moreover, to post a Roman garrison there would be both dangerous and expensive: for the Caspian Gates are situated two hundred miles beyond the eastern end of the Black Sea, and more than that distance from the Diocese of Pontus, which is the nearest of Your Clemency's personal dominions on the southern shores of that Sea: the Persian satrapy of Iberia lies between. We therefore advise Your Greatness to thank this Hun most courteously and to send him a worthy gift, but not to throw good money after bad; the Eastern frontier has already cost the Empire too dear.'

Anastasius unwisely took their advice. The constable died shortly afterwards, and the sons quarrelled over his will. Then the youngest of them, who was robbed of his inheritance, wrote to Kobad suggesting that a strong Persian force should seize the Gates, and that he himself should be appointed constable with a large yearly salary. Kobad sent the force, seized the Gates, killed all the sons, including the youngest one, and congratulated himself that his extreme Western dominions were now secure from attack by the Huns. If Anastasius had only had the courage to garrison the Gates, he could, whenever he pleased, have let loose swarms of raiders on the Persian part of Armenia, as easily as a gardener removes a stop from a garden reservoir and floods the irrigation channels.

So much for the Caspian Gates. As for Anastasius's fortification of Daras: it was forbidden by ancient treaty for either side to build any new fortifications on the frontier. The Persians greatly resented his action, but Anastasius further fortified the village of Erzeroum in Roman Armenia, and made a strong city of it. This, too, the Persians took very ill, and also his intriguing with the Manichean monks in Persian Armenia, pretending to be a secret convert to their sect.

When Anastasius died, and Justin succeeded, Kobad grew anxious about the future. He knew Justin for a capable soldier and he felt his own death approaching. Like so many Eastern Kings, he hated his natural heir, whose name was Khaous. He doted on his youngest son Khosrou, the child of his second wife who by her self-sacrifice had once enabled him to escape from the so-called Castle of Oblivion, where he had been confined for two years by a usurper. She had changed clothes and places with him, and when the deception was discovered had been put to death by very cruel tortures. Kobad had sworn to her before he escaped that if ever he recovered his throne her son should be his successor. Besides Khaous, there was another son, Jamaspes, who was the most capable soldier in all Persia and had the confidence of the entire nobility; but he was not eligible for the throne because he had lost an eye in a battle with the Huns. No man with any deformity or mutilation is permitted to rule in Persia, and it is a peculiarity of Persian laws that they may never be cancelled or amended. Kobad pondered for years as to how he could set aside Khaous, who was loyally supported by his brother Jamaspes; but could hit on no answer to the problem. It was only when Anastasius died and Justin became Emperor that he decided on a course of action. He wrote Justin a strange letter, accompanying it with some very handsome presents of jewels and works of art. I quote it here with a few immaterial omissions.

*

'Kobad of the Sassanids, Brother of the Sun, Great King of the Persians, Acknowledged Emperor of Media, Iraq, Transjordania, Hither Arabia, Persarmenia, Kirman, Khorasan, Mekran, Oman, Sind, Sogdiana, and other lands too numerous conveniently to name in the course of this short letter, to Justin the Christian Emperor of the Romans, resident at Constantinople, sends greeting.

'Royal cousin, at the hand of your father Anastasius we have suffered great injustices, as you in your well-known nobility of soul will be among the first to acknowledge. Nevertheless, we have seen fit to abandon all the grave charges that we could bring against the Romans, confident that in your Royal Father's lifetime you deplored as much as ourself his unreasonable actions, though in filial piety you refrained from mitigating their effects. And we are assured that true victory lies with him who, though knowing himself to have been abused, is yet ready to be overcome by his enemies when they plead for friendship with him. Such is the proposed magnanimity of Kobad, and he is willing to bind himself to Justin with the closest possible ties of friendship.

'Our royal cousin cannot be unaware of a notable transaction that took effect between his ancestor the Emperor Arcadius, and mine, the great Yesdijerd, self-surnamed (in his great humility before the Sun God whom we worship) "The Sinner". This Arcadius, being grievously sick, and having no grown son, but only a child, Theodosius by name, was afraid lest this child should be cast aside from the line of succession by some powerful general or by one of his own ambitious kinsmen. He was equally afraid that his subjects would take advantage of the political uncertainty that so often marks the reign of an Emperor of tender years. He therefore boldly wrote to our ancestor Yesdijerd and begged him to act as guardian to his child until he came of age, and to preserve the throne for him against all rivals. Our noble ancestor, Sinner in name but virtuous in deed, accepted the charge and wrote to the Senate at Constantinople a letter threatening war on any usurper of the throne of Theodosius. He then preserved a policy of profound peace towards Rome until his death.

'In commemoration of this noble history, which honours Arcadius no less than our ancestor, and in hopes of another century of peace such as the Emperor Theodosius subsequently swore with our ancestor Bahram the Hunter, and which terminated only lately, we have the following proposal to make: that you, Justin, make our beloved son Khosrou, who is our chosen successor to the Throne, your adopted son. Do this and we shall love you, and our subjects shall love yours, and the Great King and Emperor of the Romans shall no longer be cousins, but brothers. Farewell.'

*

You would imagine that Justin, and Justinian as his prospective successor, would have been delighted with this letter as portending a happy solution to all their difficulties, including even the old dispute about the price of silk; and you would not be wrong. None the less, they thought it advisable to call the principal Senators together to ask their advice, as Anastasius had done in the matter of the Caspian Gates. It is well known what happens on such occasions. The simplest and most obvious conclusion is rejected as unworthy of such experts in wisdom as these ingenious hoary old men, and an obscure alternative is warmly debated and then rejected; finally, a most far-fetched and marvellously improper conclusion is found and unanimously accepted. There is a popular story which has aptness in this context. Once two clever Athenian policemen were pursuing a Theban thief towards the city boundaries when they came upon a sign: 'The Sign of the Grape. Thebans made welcome.' One said: 'He will have taken refuge here.' 'No,' cried the other, 'this is just the place where he will expect us to look for him.' 'Exactly,' rejoined the first, 'so he will have decided to outwit us by entering.' They therefore searched the place thoroughly. Meanwhile the Theban thief, who could not read, had run on to safety across the boundary. Thus now the clever Senate argued about Kobad. Was he being simple, or cunning, or mischievous? Or what besides?

All sorts of views were examined, and finally the Lord Chancellor, as an expert on law, gave it as his mature opinion that Kobad was hiding extreme cunning under the guise of extreme simplicity: he intended to have Khosrou adopted as Justin's son so that he could legally claim the Empire when Justin died! Any ordinary person – but no ordinary person was present – would have realized at once the absurdity of this argument. In the first place, the Persians are a truthful people, and the Great King would not be capable of lowering his royal dignity by such a pettifogging trick; in the second, no Persian had the least prospect of being accepted by us as a candidate for the Roman Throne, not even if he allowed himself to be baptized a Christian, which would, of course, cut him off from communion with his fellow fire-worshippers. The fact was, that Kobad was making a sincere and neighbourly offer (light-house signalling to light-house), just as Arcadius had once done. But the Lord Chancellor's view frightened Justinian, who wished to have no rivals to the succession; and even Theodora, who judged the letter to be what it purported to be, could not persuade him to return to a sensible view of the matter. So Justin was obliged to return an inept answer to Kobad, in which he offered to adopt Khosrou by the ceremony of arms, but not by Imperial charter. The former method of adoption is used chiefly among the Goths. The prospective father presents a horse and a complete suit of armour to the prospective son and utters the simple formula: 'You are my excellent Son. This day, after the custom of the Nations and in manly fashion, I have begotten you. Let my foes be your foes; my friends, your friends; my kin, your kin.' The difference between this formula and civil adoption, by charter, is that it is not recognized by Roman Law as conferring on the son any title to the patrimony, but only as a contract of legal protection on the one hand and filial obedience on the other.

Before calling the Council, Justinian had privately assured the Persian ambassador that the Emperor would, he thought, accept the charge with alacrity; and the ambassador had thereupon sent a message to Khosrou to be ready at the frontier, whence he would shortly be escorted to Constantinople for the adoption ceremony. But now, of course, things were altered. Khosrou felt bitterly insulted at the shabby reply which a Roman ambassador brought to his representative at Nisibis on the frontier. A simple 'no' would have been far less galling than a 'no' masquerading as a 'yes'. Did Justin really expect that the ruler of the oldest and greatest kingdom in the civilized world would allow his favourite son, his chosen successor, a prince with the blood of Artaxerxes and Cyrus in his veins, to be treated like a barbarian German man-at-arms? War broke out soon afterwards; and in it Belisarius was given his first important command.

Before giving an account of his exploits, I must tell you a little more about my mistress and myself at Antioch. One day at noon – it was the twenty-ninth day of May – in the year that this new Persian war broke out, we were sitting in the garden porch of the house, waiting for luncheon to be announced. It was a cool place, beautifully tiled in blue, with a perpetually playing fountain and a white marble pool, full of vari-coloured fish, surrounded by pots of flowers, some of them very rare ones imported from the Far East. My mistress sleepily held a piece of needlework in her hand, unable to sew because of the oppressiveness of the day; I, too, was painfully slack-limbed and slack-minded. Suddenly I began to feel sick. The whole earth seemed to heave and rock about me. I was terrified: was it the cholera? Would I die within a few hours? Cholera was raging in the poorer quarters of the city, killing 5,000 a day. Not far off stood a magnificent temple in the Corinthian style that had once been dedicated to the Goddess Diana (who is also the Syrian Goddess Astarte), but had now been used for a hundred years or more as the official headquarters of the Blue faction. Looking out through the porch, I tried to steady my gaze on the broad peristyle of this substantial building and its columns of yellow Numidian marble ranked in tall rows. But these, too, were swaying about in a drunken manner, and at a particularly violent lurch they all seemed to topple sideways – and down came the peristyle with a rumble and a resounding crash! I realized suddenly that it was not myself who was sick, but our mother the Earth! What I was experiencing was an earthquake of immense and horrible violence. I snatched up my mistress's boy Photius and her little Martha, who had been playing on the floor near me, and ran out into the garden, my mistress stumbling after me. We were only just in time: a still more violent heaving of the earth flung us all to the ground, and with a roar our beautiful, costly, comfortable house collapsed into a confused mass of rubble and broken timber. Some flying object struck my head and I found myself automatically making swimming motions with my arms, as if I had been flung into the sea from a wrecked ship and was being overwhelmed by hugely swelling waves. Indeed, at that very moment, though I did not know it, many thousands of my fellow-citizens were swimming too, and in desperate earnest. For the great River Orontes, swollen with its spring flood, had been driven out of its course by the convulsions of the earth; and now swept through the lower city to a height of twenty feet, carrying all before it.

When my head cleared a little, I caught at my mistress's hand and we ran back to where the house had been, frantically calling the names of the two elder children, and the names of their tutor and of the other domestics. But all were buried under the dusty ruins, except for two gardeners, and a footman who had rushed out of the back door when the first shock was felt, and one badly injured maid. We tried to free someone who was groaning close to us in the ruins – I think that it was my mistress's sister-in-law – but a sudden wind blew up, and a fire spread through the shattered mass, making rescue-work impossible. Once I thought I heard my mistress's elder boy screaming; but when I went to the spot I could hear nothing. After this the shocks gradually diminished in violence. A few hours later we were able to reckon up the day's horrors.

Antioch, the second city of the Eastern Empire (though Alexandria and Corinth and Jerusalem boldly disputed the title), lay in ruins. Of those who survived of its three-quarters of a million inhabitants, all but a few thousand were homeless; for a raging fire had destroyed the wooden houses that the earthquake had spared. Not a church or a public building was left undamaged. Immensely deep, long chasms had appeared in the earth, engulfing whole streets of houses. The most fantastic damage was in the Ostracine and Nymphaean quarters, but the greatest loss of life was at the Public Baths (named after Hadrian and Trajan) which were crowded at the time of the first shock.

The usual evils that accompany an earthquake of such magnitude were not lacking: pillage, rioting, contamination of the water supply, the spread of infectious diseases among the inhabitants (the cholera with increased force), and bitter religious argument as to the cause of the disaster. Fortunately we had an able governor who kept the confidence of the better elements among the survivors. He organized parties for releasing victims trapped in the ruins, for fighting the fires, for burying the dead, for building temporary shelters, and for the collection and distribution of food. If it had not been for him our situation would have been desperate indeed.

My mistress's husband had been caught in the collapse of the Temple of Diana, and his body was never identified; but we were able to recover a large sum in gold from the cellars of the house, and his will was safe in the crypt of a church at Seleucia, under the charge of priests, and the store-building in which he kept his bales of silk had neither collapsed nor been burned. The villa in the Lebanon would be unaffected by the disaster. It might all have been much worse, we decided. Of my mistress's four children she still had two. She suffered the usual mother's pangs for the two that she had lost, telling herself that they were her favourites and the most beautiful and gifted of the four; but whether this was really the case I do not know. It is true that Photius did not prove a good son to her, but I preferred him to his brother who died.

When Justin was informed of the disaster, which had involved not only Antioch but the great city of Edessa on the road to Persia, and Anazarba, and Pompeiopolis, and, in the West, Durazzo and Corinth, all principal cities, he was overcome with grief. He took off the diadem from his head and put on a grey mourning cloak, and offered sacrifices at a shrine outside the City walls, and refrained from washing or shaving for a whole month. He also closed the theatres and the Hippodrome by decree for the same length of time. He contributed 2,000,000 gold pieces to the rebuilding of Antioch and proportionately to the other cities; he also remitted their taxes for a number of years. The loss in Imperial revenue was staggering.

As for my mistress, Antonina: she waited for two years at Antioch until conditions there had improved sufficiently to restore land values to a reasonable level. Then she sold all the property that she had inherited from her husband, and returned to Constantinople, with her two children, accompanied by myself. She bought a small house in the suburb of Blachernae, overlooking the waters of the Golden Horn, and did not announce her presence in the City to Theodora or any other of her former associates, preferring to live in seclusion.

Shortly after our arrival, Justinian became Emperor in succession to Justin. Theodora was already his wife, for his old aunt had died and he had persuaded Justin to repeal the law forbidding patricians to marry women who had been stage-actresses.

So my mistress's former club-mate now wore the Empress's crown of gold heightened with sprays of jewels, and strings of pearls over her shoulders, and a purple silk mantle, and a red gold-brocaded skirt, and golden slippers, and green stockings. My mistress thought it better to let Theodora seek her out, if she wished, than wait upon Theodora herself. For all we knew, she might wish to forget or destroy all evidence of her former life.

My mistress eagerly followed the news of the Persian War, and came to take a secret pride in Belisarius's achievements. He and another young commander named Sittas had raided Persian Armenia and carried away a number of prisoners. This was the only success that the Romans could show in the war, which so far had gone badly for us. The Iberian subjects of the Persians, who were Christians, had revolted from Kobad because he had tried to force Persian burial customs on them. The Christians dig graves and the pagans practise cremation, but the Persians expose their dead, in towers, for the carrion-birds to feed upon: they regard fire and earth as elements too sacred to contaminate with corpse-flesh. Help had been sent to the Iberians from Constantinople in the form of a distinguished general, money, and a small force of friendly Huns from the borders of Colchis; but this was not enough to prevent the Persians from reconquering the Iberians.

In the mountain-range between Iberia and Colchis there are two passes, dominated by ancient forts. The men of Colchis who manned these forts made the war an excuse for sending an ambassador to Constantinople, asking to be paid for maintaining their difficult and disagreeable service; but saying that if the Emperor preferred to hold the fortresses with his own men, he was at liberty to do so. This was while Justin was still alive, though in his dotage. Justinian, who now took all the important decisions himself, was determined not to repeat the mistake that Anastasius had made over the Caspian Gates. Without calling a meeting of the Senate, he informed the ambassador that Justin would accept the second alternative. The Colchians therefore withdrew their garrisons, and Imperial troops were sent to take their place. But unlike the castle at the Caspian Gates, which was easy of access and situated in a fairly fertile region, these fortresses were in wild and barren country, and the provisions that they needed could not be brought to them even by mules – only human carriers could scale the rocks. Nothing edible grew for miles around, except for a kind of millet on which the Colchians could subsist but which our men regarded as food fit only for birds. The Colchian carriers now charged so highly for the conveyance of bread and oil and wine to the Imperial garrisons that the two commanders soon exceeded their subsistence allowance and, their soldiers refusing to touch millet-bread, were forced to withdraw to the plains. When the Persians in Iberia heard of the withdrawal, they seized the fortresses themselves and thought it worth while to feed their garrisons on the best food procurable. Justinian should have left the garrisons in the hands of the Colchians, paying them well for their services.

Another mistake on our side was a raid into enemy territory near Nisibis, undertaken by a Thracian general commanding the troops at Daras. The object of a raid, so Belisarius used to say, is to thrust as far inside enemy territory as is possible without endangering one's retreat and, while there, to do as much military damage as is possible; but one should avoid committing acts of unnecessary cruelty. A successful raid alarms the Government of the land raided and discredits it with the inhabitants: the alarm and the discredit are the measures of its success. Thus the cavalry raiders of Belisarius and Sittas, in the previous campaigning season, had swept for a hundred miles up the valley of the Arsanias, crossed the river by a bridge, which they then destroyed, and retreated slowly by the other bank – plundering systematically as they went – before the advance of a large Persian column.

There were only a few hundred of them, all trained men. But this Thracian conducted his raid with a large, ill-assorted force of cavalry and infantry and made the pace of the horses conform with that of the marching men. He reached no place of importance, committed several acts of senseless cruelty, and, on the unconfirmed and inaccurate report that Persian reinforcements were marching along the road to Nisibis, turned about and hurried empty-handed back to Daras, from where he had started.

Such cowardice and foolishness cancelled the wholesome effect of the previous raid. Belisarius and Sittas were therefore ordered to ravage the Arsanias valley again; and did so. The Persians were on the alert this time, however, and soon surprised a squadron of Sittas's men, who were not only encumbered with heavy plunder but intoxicated as well. Belisarius was forced to fight a difficult rearguard action to cover their retreat, and was lucky to get the greater part of his force away intact after causing the Persians heavy losses. But he left a large herd of captured horses and a number of captured Persian notables in the hands of the enemy. It was after this raid, in which his former schoolmates distinguished themselves greatly, that Belisarius first announced his stern rule against drunkenness while on active service: death without appeal was the penalty, and death according to whatever was the most shameful method established in the drunken man's own nation – the sentence to be carried out by his fellows.

One of the first acts of Justinian on his accession was to dismiss the Thracian from his command and appoint Belisarius Governor of Daras in his stead. We heard a rumour, which troubled my mistress greatly, that Belisarius had advanced his position by becoming betrothed to Anastasia, Theodora's sister, in spite of her lost teeth and unhealthy condition; but it was untrue. It was Sittas who was the fortunate man.

One day, while the war was still in progress, the course of my mistress's fortune was again changed by the arrival at our house of two haggard and wayworn monks, the elder carrying a little basket. They had traced her whereabouts with great difficulty, having walked all the way from Antioch, where they had expected to find her. Only after many fruitless inquiries from one end of the City to the other, and much prayer, had they come upon her house. When we first looked into the basket it seemed to contain only a few freshly plucked mulberry leaves. Yet in those leaves was stored a fortune of colossal size. My mistress immediately took them to the Palace and asked for an audience with Her Resplendency, the Empress Theodora. She had put on dull-looking clothes and described herself as the pious relict of Such-and-Such, late Treasurer of the Blues at Antioch; not as Antonina of the club-house. She refused to particularize her business, but said that it was an important matter of State, and that if she announced it she would not be believed. She knew Theodora well enough to be sure that this statement would be irresistible.

CHAPTER 6
THE SECRET OF SILK

THE part of the Palace to which my mistress Antonina went was the vestibule, called the Brazen House. Its roof is of brass tiles, and there is an image of Christ over the Gate. Here the four battalions of the Imperial Guards are quartered; here also are to be found the Throne-rooms and State banqueting halls, and the State prison for men and women accused of treason. The other principal buildings of the Palace are the Daphne, where most of the Imperial business is transacted, and the Sigma, where the Emperor and Empress have their sleeping-quarters, and the Residence of the Eunuchs. There is also a little square palace with a pyramidal roof, built of purple-speckled marble – the others are of white, yellow, red, or green marble – where all Empresses must, by an ancient rule, be brought to bed of their children, who are then said to be 'born in the purple'. Theodora bore Justinian a child here, a girl; but she died in infancy. The Palace and its annexes and grounds cover one-tenth of the total area of the City, and occupy a triangle of land between the Bosphorus and the waters of the Sea of Marmora.

My mistress was kept waiting for hours in the reception lobby of the Brazen House, a small, stuffy apartment, and questioned by a number of important and unimportant people, mostly eunuchs, each in turn trying to break her persistent silence. The Empress, she was continually assured, refused to see claimants unless they expressly stated their business in detail. My mistress answered that if the Empress knew that they were keeping away so important a petitioner, she would punish them for their interference. Surely they could judge from the seriousness of her person that she was not one to petition the Empress idly?

She was at length successful. They admitted her to Theodora's silk-hung audience chamber at the second audience, which began at two o'clock. She had with her, besides the basket, the children Photius and Martha; and they were cross and tearful because they had missed their dinner, having been kept standing about in the reception lobby since before eight o'clock. My mistress recognized one or two of the officials and Guards officers from her club-house days, but took care that no one should recognize her. The handsome gold cross on her breast and her widow's weeds were a sufficient disguise; and she had grown a good deal plumper since her acrobatic dancing days. She had been ten years away from this part of the world.

My mistress watched the preliminaries of the audience, which Theodora conducted at a different hour from Justinian's, so that the chief Officers of State should be free to assist her. A priest opened proceedings with a short prayer, and a few responses were sung, during which Theodora trimmed her nails with a tiny knife and looked contemptuous. Next, retired officials and women of note came up one by one to her throne very reverently, to kiss the hem of her robe or the instep of her feet. She greeted them coldly. Then the first petitioners were announced. Theodora listened to some attentively and to some impatiently with bent brows. Her decisions were short and pointed. 'A present of gold to this woman', 'This plea must be referred to His Clemency, the Emperor', 'Take the impudent fellow out and whip him.' Everyone seemed to stand in awe of Theodora.

Yet she had not changed at all, my mistress thought. At last Narses, the eunuch Chamberlain, announced her apologetically to Theodora: 'Antonina, widow of Such-and-Such, silk-merchant, late Treasurer of the Blue faction at Antioch: with a personal plea. Obstinately refuses to state her business; insists, however, that it is of importance to the State and to your Resplendency.'

My mistress advanced and made a deep obeisance.

Theodora listened quizzically, her head tilted a little in a familiar attitude. My mistress almost forgot herself, almost sprang forward to embrace her old friend; tears started to her eyes. She was very fond of Theodora, and felt a deep pride in her as she sat there on a golden throne with such grace and assurance.

Theodora addressed my mistress. 'That is a pretty little girl. Is she your own?'

'Yes, Resplendency.'

'Name?'

'Martha, Resplendency.'

'Why Martha?'

'A Christian name, Majesty. The child is baptized.'

'But why not Mary? Or Elizabeth? Or Dorcas? Or Ann? Or Zoe?'

My mistress grew bolder: 'I named her Martha after the sister of that Lazarus who was raised from the dead. Martha, I am told, preferred the practical routine of household life to taking part in perhaps heretical religious discussion.'

The priests were scandalized, but Theodora laughed softly and said to the Major-Domo: 'Clear the room, and be quick about it. I wish to have private conversation with this intelligent and pious widow.'

Before the last of the petitioners and Guards were well out of the room the Empress had descended from the throne, run towards Antonina, and was embracing her tenderly, weeping for pleasure. 'O my Antonina, I thought you were dead. They told me that you were killed in the earthquake at Antioch! I did not recognize you until you spoke. Why did you not seek me out before? You were the best friend I ever had, dearest Antonina.'

My mistress asked for forgiveness, explaining that she had not been sure whether Theodora wished to see old associates, now that her position had become so exalted.

'That was unjust of you,' Theodora said, embracing her again. She fingered the cross at my mistress's breast. 'So you have turned Christian too? I should never have thought it of you – you pagan, you witch!'

My mistress's confidence had returned completely. 'I learned it from Theodora,' she joked.

Theodora slapped her lightly, and assumed a mock-scowl. My mistress, with no least feeling of anxiety or embarrassment left now, remarked that the children had had nothing to eat since breakfast. Theodora summoned the Major-Domo again and told him to punish the person responsible for starving her guests. She also said that the audience would not be resumed that afternoon, and that the remaining petitioners must return on the next day. Then she took my mistress and her children to her private room, off the banqueting hall, where a wonderful meal was served from gold plate encrusted with amethysts. There followed easy, placid talk of old times. My mistress learned that Indaro had made a good marriage and gone to live at Smyrna, but that Chrysomallo was still here – she would be summoned presently. And what did my mistress say to becoming a Lady of the Bedchamber, with patrician rank, like Chrysomallo, and living at the Palace?

My mistress did not dare to ask Theodora about her relations with

Justinian, but Theodora told her a good deal of her own accord. 'He is a clever fellow, cowardly, vacillating, manageable. The one difficulty I have with him is that he is religious, guiltily religious, and anxious, above all things, to keep his soul clear of any taint of heresy. He and I have a compact to be known to disagree on theological questions but not to pull in opposite directions. This keeps the general peace and brings intriguers to us from both sides, the Orthodox and the heretic; we pool our information.'

'And Cappadocian John?' my mistress asked.

'Our oath still holds.'

'To reduce him to utter beggary?'

'Presently, presently. Antonina, my dear friend, you will marry again, of course?'

'Why not?'

'I have a husband in mind for you.'

'O Theodora, a suitable one, I hope?'

'A man who is altogether too pious and upright, a man who avoids marriage by all manner of excuses – afraid, it seems, of falling into sin by making the wrong choice. I wish to do both him and you a service.'

'A patrician?'

'A patrician. Young, handsome, a fine soldier – the finest cavalry-leader we possess.'

My mistress began to laugh. 'O Theodora, you and I have evidently hit on the same choice for me. But what if Belisarius refuses?'

'He will not refuse. It will come as an order from me, in the Emperor's name.'

In her joy my mistress remembered her basket. She said: 'Theodora, this is the luckiest day in my life. Yet I have it in my power to make a present to the Emperor and yourself which, I believe, will repay your kindness to me a hundred times over.'

She took out a spray of mulberry and showed Theodora three caterpillars feeding on it. 'The secret of silk,' she said.

The Empress looked incredulous. But then my mistress showed her the silk-cocoons in which the caterpillars, when wishing to become moths, are accustomed to wrap themselves; and told the story of how she came by this precious merchandise, as follows.

'My late husband happened to be a Nestorian in his religious opinions, because he was born at Antioch, where the heresy originated.' – She did not need to explain to Theodora what Nestorianism was, but to my readers let me explain that it was merely another of those various opinions concerning the nature of the Son, and a logical rather than a mystical creed. The Nestorians hold that the Son had two complete natures, human and divine, and that each was complete, and each therefore personal, personality being an essential part of a complete nature; and that in consequence one could not think of these two natures as united (which was the Orthodox view) but only as conjoined. As for the divine nature of the Son, this was an indwelling of the Father in Him, comparable with the indwelling of the Father in the Saints; though the Saints had it to a far lesser degree. This view was anathematized as lessening the dignity of the Son, and as approaching dangerously near the Plotinian heresy, which brutally denies to the Son any divinity whatsoever.

'One day two Nestorian monks came secretly to my husband and complained that their monastery in the Lebanon had been closed by order of the Patriarch of Antioch and that they were now cast adrift on the world. They proposed to go to some far-off country – India or Abyssinia or China – and preach the word of God there. But they had no money, and their sandals were already worn out and their robes in rags, and alms scarce. So my husband comforted them and arranged that they should join one of his caravans going to Persia, and gave them money to proceed, if they wished, as far as China, where the mission-field was wide and where a Nestorian community had already settled. So they praised God and thanked him and inquired whether they could do anything for him in return. He replied, half in jest: "Pray for me every morning and evening and, when you return, bring back the secret of silk; for that will earn you religious freedom for the rest of your lives."

'These simple men went to China, suffering much by the way, and stayed there for a year, preaching the gospel. They trusted that the gift of tongues would descend upon them as upon the primitive Apostles, so that they could make themselves understood by the natives. But it was not granted; and the Chinese language is most difficult to learn by human means, consisting, as it does, of very few words, which change sense continually according to the accent with which they are spoken. These monks, therefore, could only sigh and frown and point to the sky and speak earnestly in their own Syrian dialect, as they went from village to village. Of the inhabitants some laughed, some pitied, some took them for holy men and gave them alms.

'One day they passed through an unguarded mulberry plantation and saw women in a shed near by unwinding silk from cocoons and winding it up again in skeins. They stole a cocoon, unravelled it, and found a caterpillar inside, resembling the caterpillars that they had noticed as swarming on the mulberry leaves, and guessed that the cycle must be: grub, caterpillar, cocoon, moth, egg, and grub again. They waited in the neighbourhood until it was the season of moths; then they returned to the plantation and collected what they deduced to be silkworm eggs and hid them in a hollow stalk of bamboo – as the legend is that Prometheus once hid the fire stolen from heaven in a hollow stalk of fennel. Having sealed the stalk tightly with wax, they set out on the long journey homewards, returning by way of Persia. They arrived at Antioch one year and two months after the sealing up of the eggs, but these hatched out after being laid in a warm midden; the grubs fed on mulberry leaves which the monks had ready for them. Some cocoons, see, have already been formed.'

You may imagine with what delight Theodora greeted my mistress's story. The monks had attentively observed the routine of the silk-farming industry, and it was clear that with these small beginnings a silk industry could be started which would eventually make us independent not only of Persia but of China. Factories for weaving and dyeing the raw silks were already established in many of our cities. Theodora promoted the monks to be abbots of Orthodox monasteries, and wrote a letter to the Patriarch of Antioch informing him that they were under her protection. These two monasteries became silk-farms, with forests of young mulberry trees, and the abbots, though not recanting their Nestorian views, were too busily employed to argue fine points of dogma with the monks. The scandals of heresy are the product of idleness.

Soon Justinian made King Kobad a present of a costly silk cloak dyed in Tyrian purple which, he pretended in the accompanying letter, was made by Syrian silkworms; and sent cocoons of silkworms in proof. This was a great vexation to Kobad, who had also recently come to know the secret of silk: it had been communicated to him by one of his vassals who married a Chinese princess – she had concealed a batch of eggs in her turban upon leaving her own country. But he had made no attempt to exploit his knowledge. It was safer to let things continue as before, making his middleman's profits on the sale of silk to the West cover the expense of his own large consumption, rather than inaugurate a new industry and risk its being observed and copied by ourselves. Now the worst had happened: his monopoly was broken and the higher the price he now asked for silk, the greater would be the encouragement to our Syrian silk-farmers. He therefore informed the Chinese that both Persia and Constantinople knew the secret of silk, and did not wish to pay such high prices abroad for what they could raise cheaply at home. The price fell somewhat, but even now our silk-farms cannot clothe us without help from China and Persia; for the rearing of silkworms is by no means a simple matter. Justinian made the sale and manufacture of silk a State monopoly.

Within two days of her arrival at Court my mistress Antonina was created a patrician, the Illustrious Lady Antonina of the Bedchamber; and was presented to Justinian, who was condescending to her, but pretended not to know her. Meanwhile she had been involved in an alarming adventure. On the evening of the day that she had this audience with Theodora, she left the Palace and went on foot to the nearest point of the Bosphorus where she could hire a boat to row her home past the docks of the Golden Horn. But a burly-looking, black-bearded fellow in a merchant's cap stopped her in the street. He drew her aside and asked whether her name was Antonina; for if so he must have a word with her. 'I am an official from the Palace,' he said.

My mistress refused to go with him into a nearby house, as he suggested, because the man might be an impostor who intended in reality to carry her and her children off, after stupefying them, and sell them as slaves to some chieftain of Colchis or the Crimea or some other wild region. There was considerable traffic in kidnapped women and children to remote parts of the Black Sea coast. She replied: 'No, come into this church with me. We can talk privately there.'

He agreed, and they went in. My mistress said: 'Now show me your warrant. How can I be sure that you are from the Palace?'

He drew out a commission written in purple ink, which is only used by the Emperor. It was to the effect that the loyal and beloved patrician, the Distinguished So-and-So (but he held his finger over the name) was commissioned as a superintendent of secret police in the City of Constantinople by the grace of His Most Sacred Clemency the Emperor Justinian. My mistress read it only in the flickering light of the long, scented candles burning in a draught before the shrine of some martyred monk or other; but it appeared genuine.

'Well, what do you want of me?' she asked.

'An account of everything that passed between yourself and the Empress this afternoon.'

She laughed, resolved not to display the least fear. 'It would surely be better to ask the Empress. I have a wretched memory for royal interviews.'

'Prison and a little torture would improve it,' he threatened. 'And there is another more important matter which His Clemency is anxious to learn about, and which you as a former associate of the Empress . . .'

My mistress interrupted: 'If the Empress has been gracious enough to recall certain trivial services of mine to her in the years before she was raised to the purple, that is her affair. I have no recollection of them myself.'

He lowered his voice and said: 'No hedging, I beg of you. Is it a fact that the Empress had an illegitimate son in her theatrical days by a Red Sea merchant who visited frequently at your club-house?'

My mistress raised a cry, and two monks who were hovering in the shadows darted forward. 'This man is blaspheming the Christ,' she said. 'He is an idolator, a Manichee, a vile sodomite, and I do not know what else. Protect me from him, you pious monks!'

The Superintendent flourished his commission in their faces. 'The woman lies,' he said. 'I am questioning her in the Emperor's name. See, I am a superintendent of police. Go away, holy brothers, and leave me to conduct this inquiry in private. I have soldiers waiting outside.'

My mistress asked the monks: 'On whom does this church of St Mary Magdalene depend for its endowments? On His Sacred Clemency the Emperor, or on Her Sacred Resplendency the Empress?'

They made a reverence as they acknowledged their indebtedness to Theodora. 'I am in the service of the Empress,' she warned them. Then she asked the Superintendent, stretching out her forefinger: 'Do you recognize this ring?' It was a small gold ring with a blue human eye pictured on the enamel, and in the iris of the eye was a tiny golden initial, a capital *Theta*. Theodora had just given it to my mistress, as a token that she was now one of her trusted people.

He attempted to pull it from her finger. My mistress struggled with him and kicked him in the groin and escaped. She ran with her children for sanctuary to the high altar, where he did not dare pursue her. Then she said to the younger of the two monks: 'Run to the Palace, brother in Christ, and let the Empress know at once that the woman of the mulberry leaves is in danger here in your church.'

The terrified monk excused himself: 'I am not permitted to leave this church without the orders of my Superior, and he is attending mass in the Cathedral.'

My mistress asked: 'Are you more afraid of the Empress or of your Superior? Off now, and the sooner you start, the sooner you will be back.'

He hitched up his gown and ran. Then the Superintendent sullenly left the church, and said: 'You will fall under His Clemency's grave displeasure.'

My mistress replied: 'Or perhaps under the pleasure of Her Resplendency.'

Soon a full company of Guards came to escort my mistress back in safety to the Palace, where she told Theodora something of what had happened, but not all: she discreetly made no mention of the question as to the illegitimate son. Nevertheless, Theodora looked grave. She asked for a description of the man, but his burliness and a black beard and a slight provincial accent were his only distinguishable features.

'He is none of the Emperor's usual agents,' she said. 'Either he is someone with a secret commission, unknown to me, or else he is an impostor. I will find out soon enough.'

But she could not trace him, though she examined the monks and obtained from them a description of him. One monk suggested that his accent was Cilician, but my mistress did not agree with him on this point.

My mistress had no further encounter with this supposed superintendent of police, but became aware that her movements were constantly watched. Her house in Blachernae, before she gave it up, was broken into and her box of private papers rifled; fortunately none of these was in the least compromising, either morally or politically. My mistress had not, I admit, been living a particularly chaste life of late; and having been in conflict with the law in the matter of some property of her husband's, she had been obliged to buy justice in a lower court from an official of the Green faction who controlled it. Otherwise, her conscience was clear, and no record of any of her lapses existed in writing. She was a woman who never wrote or preserved love-letters, never asked or gave receipts for money where the transaction was questionable. But she soon realized that she must behave with even greater circumspection than usual if she would avoid being harmed by secret enemies who were apparently trying to strike through her at Theodora.

My mistress felt the full force of their assault one Holy Day. After attending Theodora's morning audience she followed close behind her in the usual Royal procession to the Cathedral Church of St Sophia. (This was the old church, which was a splendid building, though not to be compared with the present church on the same site, which is acknowledged to be the finest sacred edifice in the whole world.) She was dressed in her best flowered silks, with all the scarlet and purple additions to which her rank as the Illustrious Antonina now entitled her, and wore her heaviest and most exquisite jewellery – part of it a present from Theodora, who was, in a literal sense, 'as generous as her mouth was wide'. Naturally she also wore an exquisitely curled and coiled auburn wig, with a number of ringlets bobbing pleasantly on her neck, to supplement her own good but not profuse auburn hair. My mistress always enjoyed these processions – unless of course it was raining; even those to distant churches on the name-days of the saint to which they are dedicated. For on such occasions the Superintendent of City Streets has the roadways and pavements swept; and the whole population wears festival clothes and appears with clean faces and hands and feet and casts itself down in adoration as the Emperor and Empress pass; and embroidered cloths hang from the windows, and there are ingenious decorations everywhere of myrtle, ivy, rosemary, box, and meadow-flowers, forming letters that couple the Imperial honour with that of the Saint. Gay marching hymns are chanted by the monks in the procession, and throughout the City is heard a rhythmic drum of mallets on sounding-boards, summoning the faithful to prayer; each church has its different characteristic rhythm.

On this occasion my mistress was in her customary good humour as she reached St Sophia's. Passing through the line of penitents in the vestibule, who are cut off from the Eucharist and may approach no nearer, she climbed the stairs and sat down next to the Lady Chrysomallo, in the front row of the gallery-seats, which were reserved for women. She leaned over the carved sill and began signalling merrily to her male friends in the nave below; for a great deal of intimate information can be exchanged thus with the aid of hand and kerchief. At St Sophia's, as at most fashionable churches, the sacred nature of the service is not taken over-seriously: clothes and gossip provide the greatest interest in the gallery, and a buzz of political or religious argument from the nave invariably drowns the reading of the Scriptures. However, the singing of the eunuch choirmen is usually listened to with some respect, and nearly everyone joins in the chanting of the General Confession and other prayers; and if the sermon is being preached by an energetic preacher it is often greeted with appreciative clapping and laughter or with earnest hissing. The Eucharist is dispensed at the conclusion, and then the blessing spoken, and out we go again. 'Against such civilized and sociable Christian functions it would be foolish to bear any grudge,' my mistress used to say – 'they are merely a quiet variety of the Theatre performances.'

The preacher on that day was a bishop whom we had not heard before, but who was known to be greatly admired as a theologian by Justinian. He held some Italian see or other, and was good-looking in rather a foppish way. He took for his text the verses in the first epistle of the Apostle Paul to the Corinthians, which lay down that men should wear their hair short and not pray with their heads covered; but that women should wear their hair long and not pray with their heads uncovered. He dwelt most gravely on the verse: 'For if a woman be not covered, let her also be shorn'; which was to say that if a woman attended service in a church without a head-covering she should be punished by having her hair clipped close to her head. The audience settled down to an entertaining homily, though not without nervous looks on many faces, male and female. For there was many a woman there whose head-covering consisted of no more than a spray of jewels, and many a man whose hair was cut in the Hunnish mode then fashionable – clipping the front part off as far back as the temples and leaving the back hair to grow down the shoulders. What if the Emperor or Empress should be persuaded by this bishop to take severe steps against the law-breakers? Nevertheless, it was not these people whom the Bishop intended to denounce: for the sermon, most illogically, was directed against women who wore wigs. As though a wig were not a head-covering of the most complicated and effective sort!

He started gently in a musical voice with general thoughts on the subject of women's hair, appreciatively quoting the pagan poets of both languages – to make it quite clear to us that he was a man of polite education, not an ignorant, narrow-minded, monastery-bred preacher. He cited Ovid as having said this, and Meleager that, in praise of a fine head of hair. Nor were these praises anti-scriptural, he pointed out: for the Apostle Paul himself, in the very passage from which the text was derived, had written: 'If a woman have long hair it is a glory to her.' And in praising length the Apostle no doubt meant to praise strength and glossiness, for no hair that is not strong or glossy can grow to commendable length. '*But*,' he said, putting tremendous emphasis on the word, '*But*, during any religious ceremony and on any but the most intimate private occasions, this long, strong, glossy, beautiful hair must be decently covered, *out of respect for the angels*.'

For the Christian angels – he proceeded to explain, as if he had had a long and troublesome acquaintance with them – are all eunuchs; they look down from Heaven on human worshippers, and from that vertical angle see little but heads and shoulders. 'Any honest person who has had any experience of eunuchs,' he went on – with a sly glance at the choir and at the long aisle reserved for eunuchs of the Civil Service and for personal eunuchs attached to prominent courtiers, such as myself – 'Any such honest person will support me when I assert that the lack of the customary male organs of generation does not, as might be supposed, free the heart from carnal affections. Not by any means! I have indeed seldom known a eunuch who could confess truly to having no tender feelings for women's hands and eyes and feet and hair – oh, but especially for their hair! I know many a rich and learned eunuch who spends his leisure time, wantonly and shamefully, in the slow combing of the hair of some frivolous woman of his household! You may laugh, my sisters, but you know it is so, and it is a great sin that you are committing if you pander thus to the ineffectual lusts of the castrated. Angels are no less subject to temptation than eunuchs: the Arch-Fiend himself was an angel who fell from Grace – was it perhaps partly from delight in the hair of some daughter of Earth? Out of respect therefore for these blessed but beauty-loving angels, who must not be distracted from their religious duty of perpetual hosannas and hallelujahs, it is the first duty of all Christian women with fine hair to keep it securely covered. It is surely evil enough to wean human worshippers from their devotions by an ill-timed display of the crowning glory of women, without seeking to drag angels down to earth and thus add to the race of demons – already numerous enough, God knows!'

But the pagan poets, even – he quoted Martial, Propertius, and Juvenal – had written with the utmost horror of women who wore hair that was not their own. Wigs were thus proved to be an offence not only against the Laws of the Church, but against secular canons of beauty and good taste. 'As for the Orthodox view of the Holy Fathers, it could not be clearer, and may be summarized as follows. Male wigs are in general designed to cover baldness: they are therefore in the nature of a skull-cap and constitute a covering, and are therefore anathema. Women's wigs, however (for a bald woman is a rarity), are designed to add to the hair already in existence on their heads, to heighten and improve its effect: they therefore do not constitute a covering, and are anathema. The righteous thunders of the Church, Council after Council, have always been directed at wigs of both sexes: both the cowardly male wig and the immodest female wig. Tertullian has said – but what has Tertullian not said against these stitched and coiled monstrosities of wigs? He has said, amongst other things, that all personal disguise is adultery before God. All wigs, paint, powder, masks, false bosoms are disguises and inventions of the devil.

'Moreover, my erring sisters,' the Bishop proceeded, suddenly pointing very rudely at Chrysomallo and my mistress, whose wigs, after Theodora's, were the two most elegant monstrosities in all St Sophia's that day, 'Tertullian makes a powerful appeal to your common sense as well as to your religious scruples. He writes: "If you will not fling away your impious false hair, as hateful to Heaven, cannot I make it hateful to yourselves as women of worldly discernment, by reminding you that those lascivious, bought ringlets of yours may have had a detestable origin? They may well have been cut from the corpse of some woman dead of the plague, and still retain the seeds of plague alive in them; or, worse, they may have adorned the head of a blasphemer irretrievably damned by Heaven and carry in them God's heavy curse, ineluctable."

'What does wise St Ambrose say of wigs? "Do not talk to me of curled wigs: they are the pimps of passion, not the instructors of virtue." What does downright St Cyprian say? "Give heed to me, O ye women. Adultery is a grievous sin; but she who wears false hair is guilty of a greater." What does the famous St Jerome say? He tells an instructive story, on the truth of which he stakes his reputation as a Christian teacher – yes, if this story is a fabrication, the great name of

Jerome must be erased from the diptychs as though he were a heretic or forger! He tells of a respectable matron of his acquaintance, by name Praetexta, who had the misfortune to be married to a pagan. Now it is well known that a wife should obey her husband in all things, and indeed this very text in Corinthians makes it plain, when it says "the head of every man is the Son, but the head of the woman is the man". But there is a reservation implicit in this first phrase, namely that if the husband be no Christian, the Son, not he, becomes her Head in spiritual matters; as, with widows, the Son becomes their sole Head, unless they marry again in discourtesy to the Son.

'This husband, therefore, whose name was Hymetius, said one day to Praetexta: "Our orphan niece, Eustochia, whom we have tenderly nurtured in our home, is not an uncomely girl. She might easily find a rich husband, and thus relieve us of the expense of a dowry, but for one fault in her looks – her thin and ragged hair. Do you therefore, my good wife, repair this defect of nature, by going secretly to the hairdresser's and ordering a fine curly toupee for her." This Praetexta did, hoping the expenditure of five gold pieces to save a thousand or more, and forgot entirely both her duty to God and her respect for the angels. That very night, as she lay beside her husband, dwelling with satisfaction upon Eustochia's remarkable transformation, to that sinful bedside descended a tall angel, piping in wrathful falsetto. "Praetexta," cried this angel, "you have obeyed your husband, an unbeliever, rather than your crucified Lord. You have decked the hair of a virgin with superfluous ringlets and given her the appearance of a harlot. For this do I now wither up your hands, and command them to recognize the enormity of your crime by the measure of their suffering. Only five months more shall you live, and then Hell shall be your portion; and if you are bold enough to touch the head of Eustochia again, your husband and children shall die even before you do." O my erring sisters, what a sin that was, and how fully deserved that anguish of corporal punishment!'

It was only natural that my mistress Antonina should giggle a little at this story. It was no great interest of hers that the name of this St Jerome should remain on the diptychs; and he certainly deserved to have it removed, she considered, for so outrageous a story. If Praetexta's hands had really been withered, how was there any possibility of her using them again on her niece's head? She remarked on this to the Lady Chrysomallo, who giggled too and, signalling to her husband in the nave below, flapped her hands about dramatically, as if they, too, were withered. Such levity angered the Bishop. He began to rail at my mistress and the Lady Chrysomallo, mentioning them by name, though he was a stranger in the City: which made it clear enough to us that the instigation to preach against them had come from some enemy of theirs at Court. He threatened them with exclusion from the Eucharist, and branded my mistress as a shameless, ill-living widow who painted her face and lived as merrily as the Great Whore of Babylon instead of wearing sad raiment and weeping for her sins and ministering to the poor, as widows should. He said that my mistress brought dishonour upon the Pious and Superbly Beautiful Sovereign who employed her, and upon the whole city of Constantinople; and that if a sudden pestilence broke out, spreading from my mistress's abominable wig and from the filthy red ringlets pendant therefrom, the faithful in the City would know whom to thank.

This indelicacy was too much for Theodora, who was sitting enthroned at Justinian's side. She rose, excused herself with a respectful obeisance to Justinian, and began to walk away down the nave, her pages behind her, without waiting either for Eucharist or blessing. Etiquette demanded that the ladies in the gallery should rise to accompany her. The Bishop was now demanding that my mistress's head and the Lady Chrysomallo's be shorn until as bald as ostrich eggs. Theodora answered him indirectly; for to have answered him directly would have been an insult to Justinian, who remained silent. She paused in her progress, to call to Cappadocian John, across the benches: 'Pray tell your eloquent, smooth-chinned friend that it is not becoming for the Razor to preach anathema against the Comb – or wise.'

The ladies clattered noisily down from the gallery to her, and only men and eunuchs were left in the Church to hear the sermon out. But in the buzz of indignant or excited talk that we raised the Bishop soon found it expedient to wind up his argument, with an abject apology to His Clemency if he had perhaps spoken with too great frankness and to the personal offence of his most Chaste, Gracious, and Lovely Empress whose glories it was beyond the skill of poets, Christian and pagan alike, to match in their most melodious verses. The Bishop was indeed in a dangerous position, and would never have dared to preach such a sermon if he had not been privately assured by someone or other that the Lady Chrysomallo and my mistress were in disfavour at Court. As for the Razor and the Comb: Theodora's point was that this Bishop was himself offending against Church Law by appearing with a shaven chin. Only scissors were allowed to pass over a priest's face. His hair had been irreligiously pomaded too, for he was a typical Ravenna dandy. Before the day was out he had been re-embarked in a small trading vessel and was on his way back to Italy. Theodora made it plain enough to Justinian that she stood by her old associates, so long as they remained loyal to the Throne, as firmly as she stood by her convictions about the single nature of the Son.

These events made a great impression in Constantinople, and my mistress's name became the subject of many untrue but not altogether discreditable tales in the Bazaar. By now her history was well known, and that Theodora had acknowledged her as a friend by the public reproof of a bishop greatly strengthened her position. Nevertheless, to protect her against personal violence a permanent guard of two Ushers was thenceforth attached to her when she went out for walks or drives; and a whole detachment of Guards when presently she was sent out to the Persian frontier as Theodora's emissary to Belisarius, in circumstances which the next chapter will explain.

CHAPTER 7

THE BATTLE OF DARAS

I MUST at this point give a short account of events in Persia since Belisarius had been appointed to the command of the troops at Daras. The impregnable city of Nisibis, fifteen miles to the eastward, had once been the principal Roman frontier station. It had successfully withstood three long sieges against Sapor, the eleventh Sassanid, when it was peacefully handed over to him by the disgraceful treaty which the Emperor Jovian signed, yielding to Persia five frontier districts. To supply the place of Nisibis, Anastasius had fortified Daras, which remained in Roman territory; but an outpost was needed to secure it against a surprise attack. Justinian therefore permitted Belisarius, at his own request, to build a castle at Mygdon, which was three miles away and only a few hundred yards from the frontier.

Belisarius had made a study of the art of fortification. He sited the castle in a strong position, and began building at a great pace, intending to make it ready for occupation by a garrison before the Persians could interrupt the work. The masons, who were very numerous, built hurriedly, sword at thigh, just as the Jews under Nehemiah are said to have rebuilt the walls of Jerusalem under the jealous eyes of their Samaritan neighbours. Before he began the work Belisarius had gathered together at Daras a great quantity of timber and dressed stones and lime; and the castle walls, which enclosed two acres of land, were soon two men high and rapidly rising higher.

The Persian commander at Nisibis handed an immediate protest to Belisarius, a copy of which he also sent to the Commander of the Roman Armies in the East, with a covering letter to the effect that the Persians took a serious view of this further breach of the treaty clauses relating to frontier fortifications. If building operations did not cease forthwith he would be obliged to resort to compulsion.

This protest was referred at once to Justinian, who replied that it was to be disregarded, and that Belisarius must be reinforced at once. The reinforcements sent were a mixed division of cavalry and infantry under two young Thracian noblemen, brothers, named Coutzes and Boutzes, who jointly commanded the troops stationed in the Lebanon.

By the greatest ill-luck the clash with the Persians in front of Mygdon Castle took place on a day when Belisarius was lying sick, in the worst stage of malarial fever, and fit for nothing. Not more than 8,000 troops were engaged on either side in this battle; in the course of which Boutzes, with half the cavalry, allowed himself to be drawn away in pursuit of a small body of the enemy, and left exposed the flank of the main body, which was composed of infantry. The Persians made a concentrated attack on Coutzes's cavalry on the other flank and routed it, capturing a number of prisoners, including Coutzes himself. The infantry, protected in their flight by Belisarius's Household cavalry under the command of Armenian John, streamed back to the castle. At nightfall Boutzes, returning with his forces intact and proudly exhibiting his plunder, learned of the fate of his brother and grew very angry. He ordered the castle to be evacuated, as a place of evil omen; and the whole Roman force, infantry and cavalry, retired on Daras, carrying the sick Belisarius with them on a litter. Two days later Belisarius, recovered from the delirium of fever, but still so weak that he could hardly sit his horse, made a counter-attack on the Persians, who had occupied the castle and were already dismantling it. At the head of his Household Cavalry, who numbered a thousand men, he drove them from the walls; but Boutzes, who should then have led the infantry back again with supplies for a siege, could not persuade them to follow him; so Mygdon Castle was abandoned once more for lack of a garrison. The Persians razed it to the ground and retired victoriously to Nisibis.

Justinian, on reading the reports that came to him, decided that the Commander of the Armies in the East had made an error of judgement in sending Belisarius inadequate and ill-led forces, and that Belisarius was the only soldier who had not tarnished his reputation. He therefore dismissed this Commander of the Armies and appointed in his place Belisarius, whose age at that time was only twenty-eight. Justinian also sent out to the frontier the Master of the Offices, one of his chief ministers, whose duties included the supervision of posts, communications, and arsenals throughout the Eastern Empire, and foreign embassies abroad. This Master of Offices was charged with resuming peace-negotiations with the Persians but protracting them as long as possible, thus giving Belisarius time to put Daras and the frontier generally into a posture of defence. Belisarius took advantage of this truce to make a tour of inspection of the frontier, strengthening fortifications, raising and drilling troops, collecting military stores. It was hoped that a renewal of hostilities might be avoided, because Kobad at the age of seventy-five seemed likely to prefer a tranquil old age to the anxieties of a major war. But this was not to be.

Belisarius, who had succeeded in getting together an army of 25,000 men (of whom, however, he could not count on more than 3,000 to show hardihood, either in attack or defence) soon heard that a well-trained army of 40,000 men under the command of the Persian generalissimo Firouz was marching against him. Then came a Persian messenger with an arrogant message for Belisarius: 'Firouz of the Golden Fillet spends tomorrow night in the City of Daras. Let a bath be prepared for him.'

To which Belisarius replied with the amiable wit which became his handsome person: 'Belisarius of the Steel Casque assures the Persian Generalissimo that the sweating chamber and the cold douche will both be ready for him.'

The person who felt most insulted by Firouz's message, strangely enough, was not Belisarius but a bath-attendant. He was that same Andreas who had been Belisarius's satchel-slave. Andreas had been given his freedom some years before at Constantinople, and had been employed as instructor at a wrestling-school near the University until he came East to rejoin Belisarius at Daras.

Belisarius's tactical problem now was the familiar table-problem of the poor country inn-keeper who is forced to provide a banquet at short notice for a number of hungry guests: namely, how to make a little go a long way. Like the inn-keeper, he knew that his little was of inferior quality, and like the inn-keeper, too, he solved his problem by a carefully laid table and a brave smile and by putting the best food and wine foremost, keeping the coarser food and the worse wine in reserve. The coarser food and the worse wine were his infantry, half of whom were recent recruits. He had decided, because of the short time at his disposal, not to attempt to train these recruits in more than one art: he therefore chose to make archers of them. He provided them with long, stiff bows and regulated their pay according to their gradually increasing skill with these weapons; but it was only what he called 'random shooting'. He demanded no more than that each man should be able to send his whole quiverful of forty arrows a distance of at least a hundred yards, keeping them within an angle of not more than ten degrees. Against a massed enemy this would be sufficient aim. He had already manufactured an enormous quantity of arrows, and continued to keep his artificers busy at forging more arrow-heads and trimming and feathering more shafts. The trained infantry he also perfected in a single art, namely the defence of a narrow bridge against cavalry or infantry charges; he found them all chain-armour and spears of varying lengths, drilling them in the phalanx-formation used by Alexander, the front of which bristled with spears like an Indian porcupine. The half-trained infantry he practised in javelin-throwing.

The better food and wine, in this metaphor of the poor inn-keeper, were his cavalry. He had temporarily broken up his Household cuirassiers into six parties, which he sent as model troops to the six regular squadrons of heavy cavalry, to set them a standard of training for emulation: he did not represent them as instructors, only as challengers in the arts of shooting and tilting and rapid manoeuvre – but instructors they became. He also had with him two light-cavalry squadrons, of Massagetic Huns from beyond Bokhara and Samarkand, old enemies of Persia. And half a squadron of Herulian Huns whose summer quarters were in the Crimea; they were archers, with a quick rate of fire, and for fighting at close quarters they carried lances and broadswords. They wore buff-coats, with light metal plates sewn on them, but no other body armour. (Light cavalry is essential for outpost work on the frontier, Belisarius held, but must be supported by a strong striking force of heavy cavalry garrisoned not far away. The Empire was poor in light cavalry; as might be deduced from the fact that both the Herulian and Massagetic Huns live many hundreds of miles from the Roman border.)

Belisarius went out in front of Daras, just beyond the parade-ground which borders the fosse. He staked out a crooked system of trenches to be dug, six feet deep and twelve feet wide, with a narrow bridge at every hundred paces. The system, viewed from the battlements of the fortress, was like a drawing of a square-crowned, wide-brimmed hat, with the top of the crown resting on the farther edge of the parade-ground. Since this was to be a battle of the Persians' own choosing, and since their object was the capture and dismantling of Daras, Belisarius could afford to remain on the defensive; and indeed to have taken the offensive with troops like his would have been most unwise.

Around the three sides of the open central square, or re-entrant, of the trench-system, Belisarius stationed his infantry, with phalanxes of spearmen guarding the bridges, supported by the javelin men, and with the archers lining the length of trench between. The trench was set with pointed stakes along its whole extent and was too broad to be leaped by cavalry. Forward on the wings, behind the advanced trenches (the brim of the hat), he stationed heavy cavalry. The bridges across the trenches were somewhat wider here, to allow for more rapid movement. As a connecting link between centre and wings, 600 Massagetic Huns were stationed inside each corner of the re-entrant, ready to bring a cross-fire of arrows against the enemy should they advance against the infantry, or to go to the help of either cavalry wing that might be involved in difficulties. In reserve he kept his own Household Cavalry, now reunited, and the Herulian Huns.

These were his dispositions. Everyone approved them at the council of war at which they were explained. The men were in excellent health in spite of the very hot July weather: the expected outbreak of dysentery and other hot-weather sicknesses, almost inevitable at Daras at this time of year, had not taken place. The fact was that Belisarius had issued most strict regulations about the mixing of all drinking-water with sour wine to purify it; and about the cleanliness of latrines and field kitchens; and especially about allowing no harbourage for flies – for he said that Beelzebub, the Lord of Flies, was the chief devil of destruction and that where there were flies, there was sickness. Moreover, all military exercises had been carried out in the early mornings before the sun was strong; after which the men slept until noon. In the evenings he had sent them out on night-marches to keep them in good physical condition, or employed them in digging. Belisarius never allowed his men to stand idle. They were now in proper fighting spirit, and had the greatest confidence in their young commander.

At sunrise on the day after Firouz's messenger had come, the look-out on the battlements reported clouds of dust rising along the road from Harmodius, a village near Mygdon in the direction of Nisibis. Soon the Persian columns came in sight, forming up in close order out of range of the Roman bows; with infantry, concealed behind enormous oval shields, in the centre, and cavalry on either flank. It was estimated that their army numbered 40,000 men. But Belisarius's comment was: 'There are few generals capable of controlling forty thousand men in battle. Firouz no doubt would feel easier in mind if the armies were more equal in numbers.'

The Persians tried to provoke the Romans to attack by challenging and derisive shouts, but they held their ground and kept silence; and for a long time nothing happened. The Romans did not even retire for their midday meal as their custom was, but cold food – salt pork and wheaten cakes and wine – was distributed to them at their stations. Firouz had been convinced that the sight of his enormous forces would frighten our men out of their wits, and that the luncheon-hour would be a good enough excuse for the more cowardly commanders to withdraw their forces. He still anticipated no serious fighting. 'Wait,' he said. 'They are only Romans. Soon they will think better of it.' But nothing happened.

Late in the afternoon the household troops of a Persian named Pituazes, who commanded on their right flank, came riding out against Boutzes's Thracian cavalry, who were opposite him. Boutzes had sworn to Belisarius to fight that day in loyal co-operation with the rest of the forces, and be drawn into no private adventures. As had been agreed, therefore, he withdrew slightly from the trench as soon as Pituazes's men, all mounted on greys, came at him. His object was to decoy the Persians across and then to turn and charge them while they were still bunched at the bridges, not yet properly deployed. The Persians, however, did not venture to cross the trench after all, so Boutzes and his men returned to their station, shooting from the saddle as they went. The Persians retired. These Persian horsemen have highly ornamented weapons and shields and especially beautiful quivers, and wear gloves (for which our men ridicule them) but no helmets. They also carry riding-whips; for whips our men have no use in battle.

Seven Persians fell in this skirmish, and Boutzes sent a party out beyond the trench, who brought the bodies back. Then the two armies stood watching each other for a few minutes more in silence. Firouz is said to have remarked to his staff that the Romans kept remarkably good order, but that he would send for the garrison of Nisibis, 10,000 more men, and doubtless their arrival on the following day would have the effect of breaking the enemy's obstinate mood. Then a young Persian, whose name I do not know, an aristocrat by his dress and weapons, galloped out on a beautiful chestnut horse, towards the Roman centre. He knew some words of Greek and, as he reined in suddenly, he uttered a loud challenge to single combat, undertaking to cut into small pieces any Roman knight who dared oppose him.

Nobody accepted the challenge, because there was a general order that ranks should not be broken on any pretext whatsoever. The young man continued shouting and brandishing his spear and laughing contemptuously. Suddenly there was a murmur from the side-trench on the Roman left. A horseman, bending low over his horse's neck, came dashing over a bridge, past the Massagetic Huns in the angle, and went straight for the Persian. The Persian saw the charge too late. He tried to avoid it by suddenly whipping his horse forward, but the lance struck him full on the right breast and toppled him over. He lay stunned. The Roman, hastily dismounting, cut his throat – as if he had been a sacrificial animal. A mighty shout went up from the Roman army, and from the walls of Daras, which were crowded with townspeople. At first it was thought that the hero was Boutzes, avenging the capture of his brother Coutzes. But when the victor rode back at leisure across the trench, leading off the Persian's horse, with the dead Persian thrown over the saddle, it was seen who he was – bold Andreas the bath-attendant!

For Andreas, whose duties were light and whose character was energetic, had for some time, unknown to Belisarius, been taking part in the early morning cavalry exercises under Boutzes, who was now Belisarius's Master of Horse; and his training as a wrestler had made him a formidable fighter. Belisarius sent a staff officer to him, congratulating him, with a present of a white-tufted steel cap and a white-pennoned lance and a gold neck-chain as a sign that he wished to give him sergeant's rank in his Household cuirassiers. But the Master of Offices, who was acting as marshal to Belisarius, deplored the breach of discipline – though delighted with Andreas's success. He sent a message to all commanders of squadrons that nobody else must answer another challenge to single combat, under penalty of a severe whipping. Belisarius took the Master of Offices to task over this, because it was a threat that could not be carried out. A man who rode out to accept a challenge would either be victorious, in which case there would be a popular outcry against his punishment; or else defeated, in which case the Persian would carry off his dead body out of range of Roman whips.

A second challenge soon came. It was from another Persian, who had been vexed that the first challenger had ridden out against the rules of courtesy. For there is a strict punctilio in these matters in the Persian army: the challenger must always be of the noblest family represented in the battle. The second such challenger therefore came riding out rather to reassert his family's pride than because he was thirsting for combat. He was no youth, but a man in the prime of life; he managed his horse and weapons with an air of experienced decision. Nor did he shout excitedly like the youth whom Andreas had killed, but only cracked his whip with a stern 'ho! ho!' at intervals in his slow ride down the Roman lines. At one point he reined in and called out something in Persian which was thought to be an invitation to Belisarius himself to come out against him. But when this was reported to Belisarius by some of his staff, who urged him to accept the challenge for the heartening effect that victory would have upon the army, he replied with contempt: 'If he wishes for death, why does he not put his head in a halter, privately, instead of trying to implicate me as an accessory?'

So for a long time nobody went out against the second challenger. He was returning to the Persian lines, perhaps relieved at having performed an honourable obligation to his family without serious consequences to himself, when, as before, a sudden murmur rose: again a horseman, this time wearing a white-tufted cap and carrying a white-pennoned lance, came charging across the bridge. The Persian turned, grasped his lance, spurred his horse, and met the challenger in full career. Each lance glanced off the polished corselet against which it was driven; but somehow the horses, instead of passing each other, as usually happens in such a tilting match, crashed together head on with a clang of frontlet and poitrail and were thrown back on their haunches. The riders were projected forward and collided in mid-air, falling to the ground in a tumble together. This was the moment when every spectator held his breath. The Roman made the quicker recovery. As the Persian rose to his knee he struck him in the face with his fist, then seized his foot and threw him head over heels, in the well-known wrestling-school style; and dispatched him with a single blow of his dagger. Then a roar went up from the Romans behind the trenches and on the walls, even louder than before, and it was seen that it was again Andreas, in a sergeant's uniform of Belisarius's Household, who had taken it upon himself to maintain the honour of Rome. The Persians withdrew to their camp, judging the day ill-omened; and the Romans raised the victory song and marched back behind the walls of Daras.

But Andreas resigned his sergeant's rank in the Household Regiment.

He had done a great feat that day in sight of 70,000 men, and had then proved that it had been due to skill, not chance, by repeating it: however long he lived he would never surpass these twin glories, which would always be remembered by the camp-fires and in the wine-shops and in the written histories of war. He therefore returned to his towels and sponges and furnaces, a simple bath-attendant once more, and was never seen in armour again – except on a single, most urgent occasion, to which I shall refer in due course.

Early on the next morning the garrison of Nisibis arrived, increasing the strength of the Persians to 50,000 men of all arms, which was twice the strength of Belisarius's forces. He commented, when he heard the news: 'Few as are the generals capable of controlling in battle an army of forty thousand men, there are still fewer who can control fifty thousand.' His conjecture that Firouz was somewhat embarrassed by the unwieldy size of his forces appeared to be justified. For they were now reorganized into two equal lines of battle, one supporting the other. Belisarius commented: 'A drill-sergeant's solution. He could have used the front formations to mask Daras, and with the remainder struck at my communications!' Meanwhile he and the Master of Offices sent a joint letter to Firouz, suggesting that he withdraw the Persian army to Nisibis instead of forcing a desperate and unnecessary battle. The wording of this letter was for the most part Belisarius's, and one characteristic sentence has been recorded: 'Nobody with the smallest claim to common sense enjoys fighting, even when fighting is necessary; and the general who begins hostilities has a grave responsibility not only to the men under his command but to his whole nation for the distresses and horrors that are inseparable from war.' The Master of Offices contributed a passage to the effect that negotiations for peace were about to be resumed by Justinian, whose ambassador was now on the way from Antioch, but that a clash at Daras would put an immediate end to all hopes of a peaceful settlement.

Firouz replied that Persia had been so often deceived by the peaceful protests of Roman ambassadors that her patience was exhausted: war was now the only remedy for wrongs. No peace treaty could any longer be taken seriously, especially if concluded by Roman oaths.

Belisarius and the Master of Offices replied that they had said as much as could honourably be said, and that the present correspondence would be fixed upon the Imperial standard next day – true copies of their own letters and the Persian reply – as a witness to the God of the Christians that the Romans had made every effort to avoid a needless battle.

Firouz replied: 'The Persians have a God too, more ancient than yours, and more powerful, and he will bring us safely into Daras to-morrow.'

Belisarius now addressed his forces, which were drawn up in mass behind the trench in the centre. He pitched his voice high and spoke slowly and enunciated clearly, so that every man heard as plainly as if it had been a conversation in a private room; and he spoke familiarly, first in Camp Latin and then in Greek, so that all might understand. He explained that the reason why Roman armies had not in the past invariably beaten the Persians, who were inferior to them alike in courage, arms and physique, was merely that their discipline had been faulty; and this was an easily remedied matter. If every man obeyed his officers, during both advance and retirement, defeat would be impossible. A battle should be fought by the common soldier as if it were a drill; and in drill it was surely easier to obey than to break ranks or act on a private impulse? The tactical control of the battle must remain in the responsible hand of the commanding general, namely himself, and he had given clear alternative instructions to his subordinate officers as to how to behave in this possible development of the battle and that. The common soldier should be so occupied with his own weapons, and with keeping formation, as to have no time to speculate irrelevantly on the general progress of the fighting. Full reliance must be placed on the tried intelligence and loyalty of the officers. He also made a laughing reference to the enemy infantry, only half of which consisted of trained soldiers. 'You Roman recruits have in a short time learned to do one thing well, which is to shoot strong and straight; their recruits have also learned a single military art, and that is to protect themselves behind those enormous shields of theirs. They are merely crowds of rustics brought up for effect, like stage armies, and will prove a great embarrassment to their generalissimo before the day is over. They have spears in their hands, it is true, but this no more makes spearmen of them than if one were to arm them with flutes and call them snake-charmers!'

The warning was then given from the look-out tower that the Persians were beginning to marshal their forces; so, with loud cheers for Belisarius, the parade moved off. The heavy cavalry rode to their stations on the flanks, the light cavalry posted themselves in the two angles of the re-entrant, the archers once more lined the nearer trenches, the phalanxes of spearmen posted themselves at the bridges with the javelin men behind and beside them. Then Pharas, the little bow-legged leader of the Herulian Huns, trotted up to Belisarius and said to him in the almost unintelligible trade-Greek that these Crimean savages use: 'I not harm the Persians, not much, here under tall walls: send I behind that hill on the left, away. I hide behind that hill. When Persians come, I hurry to their behind; I charge, shoot, shoot.'

Belisarius eyed Pharas steadily, who dropped his gaze. Pharas evidently doubted the issue of the day and wished to be in a neutral position; his final charge would be against whichever side seemed to be winning the battle. Belisarius noticed that Pharas's finger was bleeding from a slight scratch: he therefore quickly seized it, for they were knee to knee, and thrusting it into his mouth sucked it. Then he said: 'I have eaten your blood, Pharas: you shall be my *anda*, my blood-brother. Go now, dear Pharas, my *anda*, and do as you say. Hide behind that hill and charge the Persians neither too soon nor too late.' Pharas complained whimpering: 'You eat my blood, now give me yours, *anda*!' For by this one-sided action he had come (according to Hunnish superstition) under Belisarius's magical power. But Belisarius replied: 'After the charge has been made you may eat your fill. I have no blood to spare now, *anda*.' Thus Pharas was securely bound to loyalty.

The Persians held their positions all the morning, until they heard the bugles blowing from the fortifications as a signal for the ration men to fetch the midday meal up to the trenches. As soon as Firouz calculated that the distribution of food was about to start, he launched the attack. Persian soldiers are accustomed to eat in the late afternoon, and consequently do not feel hungry until the sun is low in the sky, whereas the call of the Roman appetite comes when the bugle sounds at midday. However, Belisarius had anticipated a midday attack, and advised the troops to fill their bellies well at breakfast; so they fought none the worse. The Persian cavalry advanced to within bowshot of the Roman cavalry on the wings and began to shoot; and a mass of foot-archers also pressed forward into the re-entrant and began firing clouds of arrows at the Roman infantry and at the light cavalry in the trench-angles. These foot-archers moved forward in parallel single files, with a single pace's interval between files. As soon as the man at the head of each file had fired one arrow he retired to the rear and then gradually came again to the head of the file; and by this means a steady stream of arrows was maintained. They greatly outnumbered our own archers, but they suffered from three great disadvantages. First, the stiff bows that Belisarius's recruits were using had a greater range than their own lighter ones; next, the wind was blowing from the west, so that their arrows lost speed and fell short; lastly, they were being fired at from the front and both flanks and were tightly enough packed to make the most random Roman shooting effective. The pressure of fresh troops from behind urged them farther forward than they wished, and though this brought them into closer range, they lost the more heavily. A half-hearted attempt on the part of their spearmen to capture two of the bridges simultaneously failed; the javelin men drove them off. But, an hour or two later, both sides having exhausted their missile weapons, there were desperate battles at the bridges all along the line with lance and spear, and attempts to cross the trenches with planks. Belisarius broke one dangerous thrust with dismounted cavalry – the right-hand squadron of Massagetic Huns, now recalled this side of the trench.

At last the attackers gained a slight advantage against Boutzes's Thracians on the left. They forced one of the bridges and managed to deploy on the other side. The enemy troops engaged were Saracen auxiliaries, well mounted and savage. Boutzes fought vigorously, but the issue was in doubt until the left-hand squadron of Massagetic Huns, who, like the right-hand squadron, had now been recalled across the trench, galloped to their aid. They had just been provided with a supply of Persian arrows that a crowd of boys from the town had been hurriedly collecting from all sides and tying up in bundles of forty. The Saracens were driven back across the trench with great slaughter, and had no time to reform before Pharas and his half-squadron of Herulians unexpectedly charged them in the rear from the hill. It is said that Pharas's men did more damage, proportionately to their numbers, than any other force on the field that day. They were using their broadswords now, and between them and Boutzes's Thracians and the Massagetic Huns, the Persian cavalry of that wing lost 3,000 men. The survivors broke back to the main body; but Boutzes had no instructions as to pursuit and returned dutifully to his trench.

Belisarius immediately recalled the Massagetic Huns and Pharas's men. He embraced Pharas and completed the blood-brotherhood ceremony by allowing Pharas to suck an arrow-graze on the back of his hand. These fine fighters were now urgently needed on the other flank, where Firouz had just sent 'The Immortals' – the Royal Heavy-cavalry Corps, 10,000 strong – to break the defences at all costs. The Immortals succeeded in forcing two bridges. Our cavalry there, Armenians for the most part, then retreated slowly, but, according to instructions, diagonally away to the right. This left a clear field for a strong Roman counter-charge from the centre. The right-hand squadron of Massagetic Huns, now remounted and joined by their compatriots fresh from their victory on the left wing, and by Pharas's Herulians, and by Belisarius's own incomparable Household Regiment, broke into a canter, and then into a gallop. Such was the weight of this charge, which caught the Persians in the flank, that it drove right through the column, breaking it into two unequal halves.

The Persian General commanding on this wing was one-eyed Baresmanas, a cousin of King Kobad's. He was riding comfortably along with his staff in the rear of what he thought was a victorious pursuit of the crumpled Roman right; when suddenly, from his blind side, he heard wild shouts and cries, and the Massagetic Huns were upon him with their short, tough lances and whirling broadswords. These Huns had good reason to hate Baresmanas, for he was the general who had dispossessed them of their grazing lands in the far east. In revenge they had made a journey of many hundreds of miles and taken service in the Roman army. Their leader Sunicas drove with his lance at the Grand Standard-bearer, who was some strides ahead of Baresmanas, and caught him under the spole of his raised arm, so that the crimson standard embroidered with the Lion and Sun dipped suddenly and fell. A yell of rage and alarm from the rear halted the leading Immortals when they saw that their Grand Standard was down; they rushed back to the rescue. But it was too late. Sunicas, drunk with glory, had sought out Baresmanas himself and killed him with a lance-thrust in the side, and at that sight the Persians in his rear turned to flight. The main body of Immortals was now surrounded, for the Armenians had recovered and were fighting fiercely again; and 5,000 of these noble Persians fell before the day was ended.

Soon the unprotected Persian centre broke and streamed back towards Nisibis; and the Persian infantry recruits confirmed Belisarius's poor opinion of them by throwing away their great shields and their spears as the Roman main body rushed after them. The Roman recruits, though only trained in random archery, picked up the fallen spears and played at being spearmen; the Persian ranks were in such disorder that even this awkward spear-pushing turned their retreat into a rout.

But Belisarius did not allow the pursuit to be pressed beyond a mile or so, because it was always a principle with him not to pursue a beaten enemy to the point of despair; which had been a maxim also of Julius Caesar's. He thus preserved the victory unmarred. It was the first time for more than a hundred years that the Romans had decisively defeated a Persian army; and he had fought with a great numerical disadvantage. The Great Standard of Baresmanas, spotted with blood, was picked up from the battlefield, and Belisarius sent it to Justinian together with his laurelled dispatches announcing the victory.

The Persian Army did not recover from its surprise and shame for a long time. Only skirmishes took place for the rest of the year on this part of the frontier, since Belisarius could not risk an attack on Nisibis or even another attempt to rebuild Mygdon castle. As for Firouz, Kobad accused him of cowardice and deprived him of the golden fillet that he wore in his hair as a sign of exalted rank.

*

To tell more particularly of the Huns. There are many nations of them, and they occupy all the wild land to the northward of the Roman and Persian Empires from the Carpathian mountains as far as China. There are White Huns and Massagetic Huns and Herulian Huns and Bulgarian Huns and Tartars and many more. All have the same general customs, except that the Herulians have lately professed Christianity. Huns are wheat-coloured, with crooked, sunken eyes (always red with wind and dust), insignificant noses, fat cheeks, lank black hair which they wear shorn in front, plaited at the ears, and hanging long behind, shrunken calves, powerful arms, small feet turned inwards. They navigate the desert, like sailors the sea, in long caravans of black-hooded wagons. Their horses can gallop twenty miles without a halt, and cover 100 miles in a single day. Upon some wagons they tie great wicker-baskets covered with black felt, in which they store the whole of their household treasure; and upon others they tie bell-shaped tents of the same construction, which are their only homes. They drive from pasture to pasture as the seasons change; going in a year, it may be, a distance equivalent to that from Constantinople to Babylon and back. Each tribe and every clan of each tribe has its own hereditary pastures. Most of their wars are due to disputes about grazing rights. In the summer they set their faces to the North, following the snow-bird; in the winter they return to the South. They do not till the ground, but obtain corn either as barter or as tribute from their settled neighbours. Their chief refreshment is mares' milk, which they call *kosmos* and drink either fresh, or as buttermilk, or as whey, or as the intoxicating *kavasse*. Plain water they abhor. They eat all meats, but only game and horse-flesh is of their own supplying, for swine or oxen would die in the cruel winds of the steppes where they travel. They cure meat by drying it in the sun and wind, without salt. That they eat horse-flesh makes them detestable to civilized people.

The Huns wear fox-skin caps and for warmth in winter two long fur coats, the one with the hair turned outwards, the other with the hair turned inwards. A man's rank is shown by the sort of fur that he wears: the common person wears dog's or wolf's skin, but the nobleman sable. Their breeches are of goatskin. They carry gerfalcons on their fists for hawking, by which means they obtain a great quantity of wild geese and other game. Their other chief sport is wrestling from horse-back. They are very quarrelsome; yet, when two men fight, no third man dares intervene to part them, not even a brother or father of either man. Murder is punished by death (unless the murderer was intoxicated at the time), and so are fornication, and adultery, and theft, and the making of water upon a camp-fire, and even lesser offences, unless these are committed outside the clan or tribe or confederation of tribes, in which case all is permissible. Their personal habits are most filthy, and they do not wash, but smear their faces with horse-tallow. They worship the blue sky and employ magicians and, for fear of evil spirits, no sick man of them may be visited by any but his servants. They are terrified of thunder and lightning, and hide in their tents during storms. Marriage with them is by capture or pretence of capture, and a son inherits and marries all his father's wives except his own mother. Their weapons, as I have told, are light bows and arrows, and tough lances and curved broadswords. In battle the nobler men wear leather coats armoured in front with overlapping plates; but not behind, because they consider this cowardly. They talk an almost unintelligible language, piping like birds.

For the most part they live in disharmony, tribe with tribe and clan with clan, but occasionally a single nobleman rises to be a prince having many clans subservient to him, and is called a Cham. It is when a Cham arises that the two Empires must beware of raids over the frontier.

So much for the Huns.

CHAPTER 8

THE UNNECESSARY BATTLE

THIS victory was the occasion of my mistress Antonina's journey to Daras: the Empress Theodora sent her there to Belisarius with a letter of personal congratulation and presents. As was natural, the Emperor Justinian also sent a letter and presents, but he was unaware that Theodora was doing the same, for she had not taken him into her confidence. The two missions sailed independently. Justinian's presents were a ceremonial robe exquisitely brocaded in heavy thread of gold and pearls; and an illuminated missal bound in carved ivory; and a valuable relic – the authentic begging-bowl of the blind St Bartimaeus, whom, according to the Evangelist Mark, the Saviour restored to sight. This bowl, which had come to Justinian from the treasures of a monastery lately dissolved on account of its immorality, was of olive wood, silver-grey with age. It was not adorned, as these relics usually are, with precious metals and jewels, but was a simple begging-bowl of the sort that beggars still commonly use on our church-porches and in our Squares. Around the rim had been carved at some time or other the Greek words 'Poverty and Patience'. In the letter, written in Justinian's own hand, there was great praise for Belisarius's skill in battle and his loyalty to the Imperial cause, and an encouragement to repeat his glorious deeds, blessed by God, if ever the heathen Persian dared again to violate our frontier. But at the same time Justinian counselled the utmost economy in fighting men: while the present poverty in soldiers continued, the injunction to patience carved on the holy relic must be observed religiously.

Justinian's envoy on this occasion was Narses, the Court Chamberlain. Off Lesbos, the ship in which he sailed overtook the one in which my mistress and I were, and he courteously invited her to join forces with him. Narses was a dwarfish and repulsively ugly figure; a native of Persian Armenia, he was reputedly the cleverest man in Constantinople and, of course, a eunuch. My playful mistress, to relieve the tedium of the journey, which occupied three weeks, began teasing Narses as 'a traitor to his sex'. For, as I overheard her one night whispering to her tiring-maid, Macedonia: 'He shows none of the usual traits of a eunuch – luxury, sentimentality, timorousness, and argumentative religiosity. He betrays not the least inclination to comb my fine auburn hair or fondle my pretty feet, and even seems to have no envy of my good looks; which is the most outstanding trait of all in a eunuch.' (I have omitted to mention that, not merely by virtue of expensive embellishments at the hands of hairdresser, chiropodist, manicurist, and the rest, but in her own natural right, my mistress was now known as one of the three most beautiful women in Constantinople; and the first place was, of course, unattainable, being reserved for the Empress.) Narses talked very practically on the problem of frontier defence, and recruiting, and the commissariat problem; and when he addressed the escort of Guards he gave clear, abrupt orders in a very good imitation of a military voice, which made my mistress smile a little. Her smile offended him, and he said so frankly.

Now, we eunuchs are a prominent feature of Eastern Roman civilization, and perform a very useful part in it. My own history was exceptional – most eunuchs are imported when young from the Black Sea shores, about Colchis, and educated at a special Palace School in the routine of the Imperial Civil Service, which is almost entirely controlled by eunuchs. It is a principle first learned by our Emperors from the Persian Court that eunuchs, since they are ineligible for sovereignty and incapable of founding dangerously powerful families, can safely be honoured with the royal confidence and used as a bulwark against the possible usurpation of the Throne by a conspiracy of powerful nobles. Eunuchs on the whole make milder and more loyal and more industrious officials than their unstoned colleagues, and their pettiness in routine matters – I do not deny the pettiness – is a strong conservative force. It has therefore long been the practice of rich middle-class families who have enough male children to carry on the line, deliberately to castrate one of the younger ones and dedicate him to a profitable career in the Civil Service. The bastard sons of Emperors too, or of their sons and daughters, are regularly castrated, in order to make useful citizens of them and prevent them from aspiring to the Throne. Nor are eunuchs debarred from the priesthood, as they were in pagan times from all priestly orders but that of the Attis priests of Mother Cybele. The City Patriarch himself is now frequently one of our number.

Thus, to be a eunuch is, in the worldly sense at least, more of an advantage than a disadvantage, as may also be seen by a comparison of slave-market prices. A eunuch house-slave fetches three times the price of an unstoned one; he is worth only a little less than a trained house-physician or a skilled artisan. But a eunuch is seldom a happy man, because the operation has almost always been performed on him before the age of puberty, and he secretly imagines that to be a whole man is something very fine; if only because whole men are apt to jeer at eunuchs and to swear that they would rather be blind or dumb or deaf, or even all three of these things together, than debarred from the sweet and wholesome act of love. Naturally, the eunuch has a ready answer to such boasting: that sex is a madness and never brought anyone much luck. But secretly, as I confess, he is apt to envy the man who can take a woman to bed with him and do more than embrace her as a sister and chastely kiss her eyes.

My mistress Antonina said to me once: 'For my part, my dear Eugenius, if I were not a woman I would much rather be a eunuch than a man; because men find it most difficult to find a mean, in sex, between debauchery and asceticism. That we women are regarded with such suspicion by the Church and so scurrilously preached against from the pulpits as tempters and destroyers, I have always understood as a roundabout confession that men envy the evenness of women. And this evenness the eunuch enjoys to a certain degree, and would enjoy it nearly to the full but for the jeers of the happy-unhappy unstoned. In this context, Eugenius, you should consider the fable of Aesop: of the fox who lost his tail in a trap and tried to persuade the other foxes how convenient such mutilation was. They jeered at him, saying that he only took this view because he was mutilated himself. Aesop is said to have been a eunuch domestic as you are. The moral implied in the fable is therefore not what it is usually taken to be, namely that misery loves company – as, for instance, monks, who have lost their liberty by taking strict vows, try to persuade their old friends to do the same. No, the moral is rather the impossibility of arriving at a logical decision in the question of whether men are happier with or without full sexual powers. For my part, I am happy to be a woman and not to be personally involved in the argument.'

My mistress said much the same to Narses. He had replied soberly to her chaff and told her his life-story, which explained why he was not contented with his sexual estate. He had been captured in battle when he was eleven years old, and had already at that tender age killed a man with his little sword – for he came of a well-known military family in Armenia. He detested office-work, he said, and hoped one day to persuade the Emperor to give him a military command; he had studied strategy and tactics intently all his life, and if he were only allowed the opportunity he believed that such royal gifts as he was now bearing to Belisarius would one day be brought in gratitude to him, or even perhaps greater!

It is well known that almost everyone in the world is discontented with his trade or profession. The farmer would like to be an emperor, the Emperor would like to plant cabbages; the lean captain of a trading-vessel envies the big-paunched wine-shop proprietor – who returns the envy, dissatisfied with his stay-at-home life. But it is wise not to laugh at such men when they pour out their dissatisfaction as a confidence: my mistress first learned this rule of tactful behaviour when working at the club-house in the old days. So she affected to realize that she had been mistaken in talking to Narses as to an ordinary unwarlike eunuch from Colchis, and to sympathize with his discontent. If ever he were rewarded for his great services to the State by a high military appointment she would be the first to congratulate him, she declared, and to wish him success. For the rest of that journey they were at peace; and he became a good friend of hers. A quarrel, an apology, and a reconciliation are as favourable an introduction to friendship as any. But you may imagine that my mistress could not take his military ambitions very seriously, even when he proved by his conversation with the two Guards captains who commanded his escort and hers to know a great deal more about the theoretical side of soldiering than they did. For though he had perhaps killed a man with his little sword at the age of eleven, that was forty-nine years ago, and since then he had hardly set foot outside the Palace; where for a long time, until his education was complete, he had worked at a loom in the company of the Palace women.

We went by sea, for the first part of our journey, in a warship with three banks of oars. It was a pleasant but not eventful voyage past the usual green hills and white cities. When at last we disembarked at Seleucia and came by road to Antioch I was delighted to see how quickly the ravages of the earthquake were being repaired: it was our dear, bustling, luxurious, old Antioch once more. Narses and my mistress were entertained by the local Senate and by the Blue-faction officials, who were very obliging to my mistress – and she to them. Then we took the paved road to Zeugma, famous for its pontoon-bridge, 120 miles away; from which it is another 200 miles, through mainly fertile country watered by four principal tributaries of the Euphrates, to Daras and the frontier. We travelled in post-gigs and found the heat very trying, in spite of awnings and briskly trotting ponies. From Edessa, where we halted for two days, we sent fast riders ahead to announce our approach.

When we arrived at Daras, etiquette demanded that the letters should be delivered not directly to Belisarius (and to the Master of Offices, who was also honoured with a letter from the Emperor) but to his domestics. My mistress greatly regretted that this should be so, because she knew the contents of Theodora's letter, which had been written in her presence. She would have given much to watch Belisarius's face as he read it. It went as follows:

'Theodora Augusta, spouse of Justinian, Vice-regent of God and Emperor of the Romans, to the Illustrious Patrician Belisarius, Commander of the Victorious Armies in the East: greeting!

'Tidings have come to my royal husband, the Emperor, and to myself, of your well-deserved success over the Persians. You are enrolled now with the heroes of the past, and we praise you, because you have greatly benefited us, and we wish you well. Two of the Emperor's presents, the bowl and the missal, do honour to your religious nature, and the third, the cloak, is a foretaste of the appreciation in which you will be held at our Court on your return from duty and victories. It becomes me therefore – for a lady's presents to a retainer should be complementary to those given by her lord – to send you three other gifts by the hand of my trusted Lady of the Bedchamber, from which you may derive an altogether different sort of pleasure. The first of these gifts I have chosen for you because he wears your household badge and is, moreover, the most excellent of his race in our dominions; the second I send you because your plunder will have put you in need of it; and as for the third it is a present above rubies, and you will greatly incur my displeasure if you presumptuously refuse it. For it is a characteristic of Theodora that in gratitude she always gives of her best. Farewell.'

Belisarius sent word that the representatives of their Majesties were welcome, and presently received Narses and my mistress in the cool, arched tribunal-hall where he dispensed discipline and gave daily audiences to his subordinates and allies. Narses was admitted first, as emissary of the Emperor. Belisarius, it seems, greeted him affably, inquiring first after the health of his royal Master and Mistress and of the principal Senators and then for news of affairs in the City and Empire. They drank a cup of wine together on the tribunal, and Narses asked searching questions about the details of the battle. Belisarius answered, not in an off-hand manner as to a mere Palace eunuch, but considerately and in detail, weighing every word. Narses wished to know why Belisarius had temporarily dismounted the Massagetic Huns to defend the central trench. Belisarius replied: because the attack was a formidable one, and because nothing so greatly encourages hard-pressed foot-soldiers ('the latrine-men' as they are sometimes contemptuously called because of the many thankless tasks that they are called upon to perform) as when mounted comrades nobly renounce their opportunity for flight, by sending their horses back a little way under charge of grooms, and fight for once, cut and thrust, on their own legs.

Then the Emperor's presents were delivered, admired, and given thanks for; and soon Narses bowed and withdrew.

Meanwhile my mistress Antonina was sitting in the ante-room at the end of the hall, and Rufinus, who was now Belisarius's standard-bearer, was most attentive to her. But she answered his polite remarks in a confused, random manner, because, for once in her life, she was feeling altogether ill at ease. The matter had seemed simple and certain when Theodora and she discussed it at the Palace; but now, as she rose at the summons from the tribunal-hall, her knees were trembling and her tongue dry.

She stood half-way down the hall and signalled to her guards to lead forward the first of Theodora's three presents, which was a tall, fiery three-year-old bay stallion with a white blaze on its forehead and four white socks. It was to these marks that Theodora had referred when she wrote that her first present wore his household badge. A murmur of applause went up from the cuirassiers of the Household, who were standing at attention along the walls of the hall with their lances held upright at their sides, and from all the cavalry officers ranked around the tribunal. My mistress overheard Rufinus, who stood near her, muttering to himself: 'This one gift of the Empress's outweighs by itself the Emperor's three.' For it was indeed a superlative animal, of the famous Thracian breed of which the poet Virgil makes mention in the fifth book of his *Aeneid*.

The stallion was led off to the stable, and my mistress Antonina beckoned for the second present to be brought forward. My mistress had been anxious lest this might perhaps not arrive in time, though we had sent it ahead from Antioch as soon as we had disembarked and overtaken it a day out from Edessa; but here it was – a consignment of 500 complete suits of cavalry mail-armour from the arms factory at Adrianople. Theodora knew that Belisarius's plunder included a large number of Persian horses, and inferred rightly that he would enrol in his own forces the sturdiest of the 3,000 prisoners that he had captured and make cuirassiers of them. But the Persian cavalry-armour which had fallen into his hands was not suitable, being both too thin and too complicated for use in the field; so these 500 suits were a most welcome gift. Again a murmur of applause arose, for it was seen that the steel helmets all carried white plumes. The Empress clearly understood the art of giving appropriate presents.

Then at last my mistress found her voice and spoke: 'The third gift, Illustrious Belisarius, is, by the order of Her Resplendency, my royal Mistress, to be delivered to you in private.'

Belisarius had not recognized her, she felt sure, because his voice was cool and natural as he replied: 'As my Benefactress wishes. But you, my lords and gentlemen, pray do not retire! The Illustrious Lady of the Imperial Bedchamber will perhaps be gracious enough to meet me in the ante-room from which she has just emerged, and deliver the third present to me there in the privacy that her Glorious Mistress requires of us.'

My mistress Antonina bowed and retired to the ante-room, and presently he entered and closed the door.

They stood facing each other without speaking, until at last she said in a low voice: 'It is myself, Antonina. Do you remember me – the dancing-girl at the banquet that your Uncle Modestus gave at Adrianople?'

Either he had never forgotten or else the memory now leaped suddenly back to his mind. He answered: 'And this is still myself, Belisarius.' He clasped her hands in his, and the third gift was taken.

Then Belisarius said: 'Tell your royal Mistress that never, I believe, in the whole course of history have such welcome gifts been given to a subject by his Imperial Mistress; and that I accept them in loving wonder at her marvellous divination of my needs and desires. But, O sweet Antonina, tell her that enjoyment of the third gift, immeasurably the best of the three, must be postponed until my recall from the wars; for I have a vow to keep.'

'What vow can that be, my dear Belisarius?' she asked him.

He replied: 'My officers and men have taken a vow upon the Gospels, in which I have joined them, that they will neither shave their chins, nor fall into the sin of drunkenness, nor either marry a wife or take a concubine, so long as they remain here on active service against the Persians.'

'Could you not appeal to the Patriarch for a dispensation from this vow?' she asked.

'I could do so, but I would not, because of the others, who must remain still bound by it. My beloved Antonina, whose image has lingered in my heart these fifteen years, be patient and wait! To know that when I return to the City the greatest reward in the world will be awaiting me, this surely will hasten the victorious return that the Emperor has wished for me.'

Though my mistress Antonina could not press him in a matter which touched his honour, neither could she conceal her disappointment. She asked: 'Oh, Belisarius, are you sure that you are not making excuses to gain time?' But this was pure rhetoric, for never was delight written so plainly on any man's face as on his.

Belisarius and my mistress returned to the tribunal-hall, and both resumed their official looks and accents. Belisarius recalled Narses, and invited both him and my mistress, and the officers of their escort, to a banquet with himself and his staff that night. My mistress had no further opportunity to speak to Belisarius in private, and both of them were careful not to reveal by word or look the great love that each felt for the other. The banquet was a sober affair, because of the vow against drunkenness which nearly everyone present had taken, and because table-delicacies are not easily procured at Daras. On the next morning Narses and she returned home, armed with letters of humble gratitude to their royal Master and Mistress. But Narses had guessed my mistress's secret, and whispered to her as soon as they were seated privately together in a gig: 'May he be as fortunate in your love, most Illustrious Lady, as you in his!'

My mistress replied in words that pleased him as much as his had pleased her: 'And may you, Distinguished Chamberlain, be as successful when the general's purple cloak flaps from your shoulders as you have been these many years while dressed in the stiff crimson silks of your Palace appointment.'

When we were back again at Constantinople my mistress found

two letters from Belisarius waiting for her that had come by a quicker route. They were written in such simple, elegant language and indicative of such honest ardour that, since this love was not only sanctioned but positively enjoined upon the two of them by Imperial orders, she broke a life-long rule, and committed her own amorous feelings to writing. Many scores of long letters passed between them until his return to her some eighteen months later.

The next phase of the war was a Persian invasion of Roman Armenia; but it was energetically checked by Sittas, Belisarius's former comrade, who was brother-in-law to Theodora. The Roman name being now held in greater respect than formerly, a number of Christian Armenians from the Persian side presently deserted to the Imperial armies. Kobad also lost the revenues of the gold-mine at Pharangium, a town situated in a fruitful but almost inaccessible canyon on the border between the two Armenias; for the chief engineer there elected to put the city and mines under Roman protection. Kobad, with the obstinacy of old age, refused to withdraw his troops from the neighbourhood of Daras, though Justinian sent an embassy to re-open peace negotiations. Each side tried to fix the moral responsibility for the conflict on the other. Kobad told the Roman ambassador that the Persians had done meritoriously in seizing and garrisoning the Caspian Gates, which the Emperor Anastasius had refused to buy from the owner even at a nominal price; since, by doing so, he had protected both the Roman and Persian Empires from barbarian invasion. The garrison was costly to maintain, and Justinian should, in justice, either pay a half-share of the expenses or, if he preferred, send a detachment of Roman troops there sufficient to permit half the Persian garrison to withdraw in their favour.

Then King and Ambassador discussed the breach of an ancient treaty regarding frontier fortifications. The Roman fortification of Daras, Kobad pointed out, had made it strategically necessary for the Persians to keep a strong frontier force at Nisibis; and this again was an unfair tax on his country's resources, and was one injustice too many for him to accept. He now offered Justinian three alternatives to choose from: contributing to the defence of the Caspian Gates, dismantling the fortifications of Daras, renewing war. The ambassador understood the King to mean that a money tribute, speciously disguised as a contribution to common defence against the barbarian menace, would end the conflict.

Justinian could not yet decide whether or not to offer a money tribute. While he deliberated, Kobad was visited by the King of the Saracens, his ally, with a plan for a severe blow at the Romans. The Saracen was a tall, lean, vigorous old man, whose Court was at Hira in the desert, and who for fifty years had been raiding Roman territory between the Egyptian and Mesopotamian borders. He would appear suddenly from the wilderness with a force of a few hundred horsemen, plunder, burn, massacre, take prisoners – by the thousand sometimes – and then disappear again as suddenly as he came. Several punitive expeditions had been made against him, but all had been unsuccessful; for the art of desert warfare is only understood by those born to the desert. He had cut off and captured two strong Roman columns operating against him and held their officers to ransom.

This old king, then, suggested to Kobad that instead of campaigning as usual among the head-waters of Euphrates and Tigris, where the Romans had a number of walled cities to fall back upon if attacked, he should take a southerly route, which no Persian Army had ever taken before, following the Euphrates. At the point where the river-course turns from west to north he should strike across the Syrian desert. For here, beyond the desert, the Romans, trusting to the natural defences of waterless sand and rock, had built only few fortifications, and these were manned by no troops worth the name. If vigorously attacked, Antioch would fall into their hands without a struggle, because – he was justified in this comment – Antioch is the most unserious city in the entire East, the inhabitants having only four interests, namely wine, sex, Hippodrome politics, and religious argument. (Trade is not an interest, but a disagreeable necessity to which they submit in order to keep themselves in funds for the active prosecution of these four exciting interests.) What a magnificent city to plunder! And the raiders could return safely with their spoils long before any rescue could arrive from Roman Mesopotamia.

Kobad was interested but sceptical. If no Persian Army in the past had found this approach feasible, in what way had conditions altered to make it so? How would an army, unaccustomed to temporary starvation and thirst, maintain itself in the parched, pastureless desert?

The King of the Saracens replied to the first question that hitherto the Great King had never called upon an experienced Saracen for advice. As for the second question: the Persian force should consist entirely of light cavalry – infantry and heavy cavalry were ruled out – and they should make their expedition in the spring, when there would be ample pasture, even in the wildest desert, for those who knew where to look for it; and they should travel light; and the Saracens would be waiting for them, at a point on the river well within the Roman territories, with sufficient food and water for the last and most difficult stage of the journey.

Kobad was persuaded by the King of the Saracens, though Saracens are a notoriously faithless race; because he could surely have no motive in making these suggestions but to obtain Persian help in a profitable raid which was on too large a scale for himself to undertake alone. All that Kobad needed to guard against was treachery during the return journey, and he would therefore insist on the King of the Saracens leaving his two sons and two grandsons as hostages at the Persian Court at Susa until the campaign was over. The Saracen agreed to do so, and by March of the next year – the year following the battle of Daras – all preparations had been made. The expedition assembled at Ctesiphon in Assyria, 15,000 strong, under the command of an able Persian named Azareth.

They passed the Euphrates just above the city of Babylon and continued along the southern bank through uninhabited country until they reached the Roman frontier station at Circesium, where there were only a few Customs police. From there they pushed on rapidly astride the Roman road, which, after following the river for a hundred miles, curves south to Palmyra and Damascus. They were now joined by a large body of Saracens under their King; who told Azareth that the route lay straight across the desert to Chalcis, a walled town, which was almost the only obstacle to be encountered between them and Antioch, and this was no obstacle either, because it had a garrison of only 200 men. Azareth did not altogether trust the Saracens, though they had brought the stipulated amount of provisions. He therefore waited until scouts, sent ahead under Saracen escort, should report back that the desert pasture was plentiful, and that no ambush had been laid for them on the other side.

But to allow himself this delay was to underrate the energy of Belisarius, who had recently introduced a system of linked look-outs, with agreed smoke-signals, as a protection against frontier-raids. Within an hour of the Persians' arrival at Circesium, 200 miles across the Southern desert, Belisarius at Daras had learned the numbers and composition of their forces and had taken his decision. Leaving only slight garrisons behind in Daras and the other frontier cities, he hurried by forced marches to the relief of Antioch at the head of all the trained troops that he could assemble – which, at such short notice, amounted to only 8,000 men; but he picked up reinforcements on the line of march to the number of 8,000 more. He took the southern road, by way of Carrhae (famous for the crushing defeat by the Persians of Crassus, colleague to Julius Caesar) and managed with his main cavalry forces to reach Chalcis, 300 miles way, in seven days, just in time to man the fortifications. But it was a close race, for by now Azareth was across the desert and only half a day's march away from Chalcis – among the very rocks where St Jerome and his mad fellow-ascetics once lived like angry scorpions, worshipping God indeed, but ungratefully rejecting God's creation of all pleasant and beautiful things. On the same morning Belisarius was joined by 5,000 Arab horsemen from the Northern Syrian desert, where they had been pasturing their horses. They were the subjects of King Harith ibn Gabala of Bostra in Transjordania, to whom Justinian paid a yearly sum in gold on condition that he checked Saracen raids on Syria. These Arabs were not reliable soldiers, however, and King Harith was suspected of having an understanding with the Saracens, because whenever there had been a Saracen raid his men had always arrived two or three days too late; but Belisarius was glad to have them with him, because in the absence of his infantry, who were still on the way, they increased his numbers to 21,000 men.

Azareth was disgusted with himself when his vanguard, pressing on to Chalcis, was suddenly thrown back on the main body by a Roman cavalry charge. He had let his opportunity slip, and could not now reach Antioch without risking a battle against the same general and the same troops that had fought so well at Daras. If he were defeated at such a distance from the frontier, and on the wrong side of the Syrian desert, it was unlikely that a single Persian would survive the return journey – the Saracens would save their own skins, melting into the desert which they knew so well. Even if he were victorious, he would not be able, probably, to prevent Belisarius taking refuge with the surviving remnant of his forces behind the walls of Chalcis. It would be dangerous to continue the raid on Antioch, with Chalcis lying uncaptured in his rear and Roman reinforcements on the way. So he took the wise decision to retrace his steps, with no gains and no losses, while he still had provisions and while the weather remained temperate. He consoled himself with the reflection that even if he had reached Chalcis before Belisarius, and pushed on to Antioch, and plundered it, then his forces – especially the Saracens – would have been disorganized by victory, and Belisarius would have intercepted him on his return and again had the advantage of choosing the battle-ground and standing on the defensive, as at Daras. The King of the Saracens agreed that retirement was now the only course; he did not dare to break his own forces up into small raiding parties and go off plundering to the southward, for fear that Azareth would report to Kobad that he had been deserted, and that Kobad would put his Saracen hostages to death. So the Persians and Saracens faced about and marched homeward, and Belisarius followed close behind them to make sure that they did not turn and come back again into Syria by some other route. Neither army hurried or attempted any hostilities against the other. Belisarius remained at a day's distance behind Azareth and encamped each night at the place which Azareth had abandoned that morning. He kept a sharp look-out on his own flanks and rear, in case of sudden surprise by the Saracens.

It was the seventeenth day of April, and Holy Friday, the anniversary of the crucifixion of Jesus. The feast of Easter, which is the day on which He is said to have risen again from the dead, was due to take place two days later. The Persians had now regained the bank of the Euphrates and marched fifty miles along it to the point where the road from Damascus and Palmyra curves round to the river. It was clear that they meditated no alternative plan but would continue on their homeward march along the river. Now, Belisarius had, at Chalcis, severely reprimanded his vanguard commander for engaging the enemy without orders, and thus spoiling a tactical scheme by which the whole Persian Army was to have been trapped; and would have relieved him of his command but for the intercession of the Master of Offices. That Belisarius seemed to discourage the offensive spirit in his men and did not attempt to harry the retreating enemy, made the loud-mouthed talkers of his army accuse him of cowardice; but only behind his back as yet.

Then the Christian fanaticism of Easter, which is always celebrated by a great feast after forty days of frugal living and one or two complete fasts, overcame them. They clamoured to be led against the Persians so that they might win a resounding victory for celebration on Easter Sunday, the luckiest day in all the year. Belisarius that night entered the small town of Sura; but the Persians had been making so slow a pace, because they did not wish to seem in any hurry to return home, that part of his infantry had now come up with the cavalry. These battalions had not marched all the way to Chalcis, but had taken a short cut down the Euphrates, turning southward from the Carrhae road. Their arrival was the signal for renewed battle excitement: it was said that with 20,000 men Belisarius had no right to avoid engaging a dispirited and weary enemy.

On the following morning a number of officers came to Belisarius and informed him that his courage and loyalty were being called in question by their men, who could no longer be restrained from challenging the enemy. If he still attempted to hold them back there was likely to be a mutiny.

Belisarius was astonished. He explained that he must obey Justinian's explicit orders to avoid all unnecessary wastage of troops. The Master of Offices supported him in his view; but they were both argued down.

Then Belisarius ordered the bugles to be blown for a general assembly, and addressed the troops as follows: 'Men of the Imperial and allied forces! What dog has bitten you that you have sent your officers to me with so mad a request? Do you not know when you are well off? Here are the Persians, who came into our territory with no less an intention than that of sacking the great city of Antioch, now forced by our prompt action to retreat, empty-handed and chagrined, back to Persia. "Do not spur a willing horse" is a proverb of proved merit, as you horsemen know, and it has appositeness here, especially when linked with the proverb "Leave well alone". So much for worldly wisdom; but let me further remind you in your Christian enthusiasm that the Scriptures strictly enjoin us "Thou shalt not kill!" This is interpreted, I hasten to say, as an injunction only against wanton slaughter, since otherwise we should be forbidden to serve as soldiers, even in defence of our country. But I must ask you to decide whether the battle which you wish to fight does not come under this very heading of wanton slaughter; for I can see no good reason for it myself. The most complete and happy victory is this: to confound one's enemy's plans while suffering no material or moral loss oneself. And such a victory is already ours. If we force a fight on the Persians we shall not hasten their departure by a day, even if we are victorious; whereas if we are defeated ... Here I must ask you to remember that

Providence is kinder to those who fall into dangers not of their own choosing than to those who deliberately seek them out. We cannot afford to be defeated, remember! One last word: you know how even a rat will fight fiercely when cornered, and these Persians are by no means to be despised as rats. Moreover, this is Easter Saturday and all of you but those of the Arabians, who worship demons, and those of the Massagetic Huns, who worship the Blue Sky, have fasted since early last night and must keep your fast for twenty-four hours. Fasting men do not fight at their best, especially on foot. I refrain from reminding you infantrymen that you have marched three hundred miles in twenty days – a magnificent but exhausting feat – and that a number of the slower battalions are still on their way.'

But they would not listen to him and howled 'Coward' and 'Traitor' at him – cries in which even some of his officers joined.

He changed his tone and told them that he was delighted at their confidence and courage, and that if some good angel was perhaps prompting them to offer battle, it would be impious for him to check them; and that they could count on him to lead them vigorously against their hereditary foes.

He hurried out from Sura and caught up with the Persians at midday; and by harassing their rear-guard with constant arrows forced Azareth to turn about and fight. The river was on the Roman left; and on the opposite shore, a little down-stream, was the Roman trading city of Callinicum. Between the shrunken river and the great sloping banks which restrain it in the season of floods was a space of a few hundred yards; here the battle was fought.

It was a very bloody battle, and began with the usual exchange of arrows. Belisarius had put his infantry on the left, with the river providing a defensive flank, and King Harith of the Arabs, on the extreme right, on the rising bank. He took the centre himself with his cavalry. Azareth opposed the Saracens to King Harith's Arabs, who are of the same stock, and engaged the centre and right himself. The Persians fired two arrows to every one of the Romans; but, the Roman bows being much the stiffer and the more tightly strung, and the Persian armour being more for display than for defence, twice as many Persians fell as Romans in these exchanges.

The afternoon was drawing on, and neither side had the advantage, when Azareth suddenly led two squadrons of his best cavalry up the bank against King Harith. The Arabs turned to flight, which is the usual tactics of these desert fighters when charged, and thus left the Roman centre exposed. Azareth, instead of pursuing the Arabs, swerved round against the rear of the Roman centre – and broke it. A few cavalry squadrons, notably the Massagetic Huns and Belisarius's Household cuirassiers, held their ground and inflicted heavy losses on the enemy; but the rest dashed for the river and swam out to a group of sandy islands near the shore, where they were safe from pursuit. The Arabs made no attempt to retrieve the battle, but rode hurriedly back to their tents in the desert.

The Roman infantry consisted partly of those raw recruits from the south of Asia Minor whom Belisarius had trained in archery, and partly of trustworthy spearmen. The former were cut to pieces without making any attempt to use the swords which they carried; and they could not swim. These were the men who at Sura had been the loudest in their clamour for a battle. But Belisarius rallied the spearmen and formed them up in a semicircle with their backs to the river; and, with the survivors of his own squadron, dismounted, he warded off the Persian attacks until nightfall. They were only 3,000 men against the whole Persian army, and faint for want of food; but the front rank, kneeling on one knee, formed a rigid, unyielding barricade with their shields, from behind which their comrades fought with spears and javelins. Again and again the Persian cavalry charged, but Belisarius made his men clash their shields together and shout in unison, so that the horses reared up and threw everything in confusion.

When night fell the Persians withdrew to their camp, and a freight-boat from Callinicum ferried Belisarius and his comrades in batches across to the islands, where they spent the night. On the next day more boats appeared, and what remained of the Roman Army was transported to Callinicum, the horses swimming. The Easter Feast was celebrated there, but with little jubilation: the more ignorant and foolish Christians accounting for their defeat by saying that God died each Crucifixion Day and remained dead on the next day, until His Resurrection at Easter; and that therefore the battle should have been postponed for a day – for God, being dead, could not help them. This Belisarius wrote to my mistress in a letter, mocking at the would-be theologians.

The Persians stripped the Roman dead and their own, who were no less numerous. The detachment that had suffered most on our side was the Massagetic Huns: only 400 of their 1,200 survived, and most of these were wounded. Belisarius had lost one-half of his Household Regiment, which had consisted of 3,000 men. He waited for the rest of his infantry to arrive and then returned with them to Daras; his total losses were some 6,000 men.

Azareth returned to Persia and claimed a victory, but Kobad, before praising him, instructed him to 'resume the arrows'. It is a Persian custom that, when any military expedition sets out, each soldier deposits an arrow in a heap. These arrows are then bound together in bundles and kept under seal in the Treasury. When the campaign is over the survivors 'resume arrows'; and by seeing how many of these remain may calculate their losses. Seven thousand arrows remained unclaimed, so Kobad dismissed Azareth from his command with disgrace. The King of the Saracens also was blamed for his foolish advice, and the annual subsidy that he had long been drawing was discontinued.

Belisarius wrote a dispatch to Justinian, excusing himself for his losses, and the Master of Offices sent a confirmatory dispatch, explaining exactly what had happened and praising Belisarius's courage; so Justinian continued to place confidence in him. But my mistress wished that this senseless war were over, which could easily have been settled by the payment of a few thousand gold pieces and a few courteous phrases from the rulers of the opposing Empires. She must have shown her anxiety on Belisarius's behalf more plainly than she intended; for Theodora now persuaded Justinian to recall Belisarius, on the ground that a capable soldier was needed in the City as a protection against the increasing mob-violence of the Blue and Green factions. Sittas was appointed to deputize for him on the frontier.

So Belisarius returned, bringing his Household Cavalry with him; and married my mistress on the feast of St John the Baptist at St John's Church. It was an occasion of great pomp and joy, Justinian himself acting at the altar the part of my mistress's parent; for she had no male relatives surviving. Theodora settled upon her an extensive city property, with a huge annual rent-roll: she held that a woman who is beholden to her husband for every copper she spends is little better than a slave. My mistress warned Belisarius that in future she would accompany him on his campaigns, as Antonia the Elder had once accompanied the famous Germanicus in his campaigns across the Rhine, to their mutual comfort and the great advantage of Rome. To remain tamely at Constantinople in ignorance of what might be happening to him on some distant frontier and to be exposed to wild rumours of his defeat and death – this was a torture that she refused to bear again.

They occupied a great suite at the Palace, where there is room for everyone.

CHAPTER 9

THE VICTORY RIOTS

IT was ten years before Belisarius returned to the Persian frontier. Of what happened in the East during his absence, especially the further misfortunes that overtook our dear Antioch, I promise you a round account when my story reaches that point. Meanwhile a few words will suffice. King Kobad died, shortly after Belisarius's recall, at the age of eighty-three, but not before ordering a further invasion of our territories. His forces were so strong that in Roman Armenia our soldiers were obliged to retire into their walled cities while the Persians laid the country waste. The succession to Kobad's throne was then disputed by three claimants. These were Khaous, the legitimate heir; one-eyed Jamaspes, the second in age, as regent on behalf of his infant son (himself debarred because of his deformity); and Khosrou, the youngest, whom Kobad had nominated in his will. Khosrou was acclaimed by a vote of the Grand Council and duly crowned. He soon destroyed his brothers, who revolted against him, and all their male heirs. But he did not feel himself secure upon the throne, even after this massacre, and decided to come to terms with Justinian.

These twin eyes of the world therefore synoptically signed a peace, named 'The Eternal', under which all territory whatsoever conquered by either side during the late wars should be restored, and Justinian should pay Khosrou a large sum for the perpetual maintenance of the Persian garrison at the Caspian Gates – some 800,000 gold pieces – and, without dismantling the fortifications of Daras, agree to withdraw his advanced headquarters to Constantina, which was less dangerously close to the frontier. There was also a curious condition: that the pagan philosophers who had fled to the Persian Court from Athens when Justinian closed the University there, four years previously – poor Symmachus was among their number – should be allowed to return temporarily to the Roman Empire, without fear of persecution, for the purpose of setting their affairs in order and of collecting a library of the pagan Classics for Khosrou's own edification. Justinian agreed to this, content that he had dealt the Old Gods their death-blow not only at Athens but throughout his dominions: he had everywhere converted their venerable temples into Christian churches and sequestrated their treasures.

So much for Persia. But Theodora was right in anticipating trouble from the factions, and Justinian in consenting to the recall of Belisarius – but for whom, as I shall show, he would certainly have lost his throne and almost certainly his life.

Must I repeat what I have already said about the virulence of the hatred between the Blues and Greens? Preoccupied now by increasingly bitter disputes as to the nature of the Son, they were engaged in justifying a Gospel prophecy. For, according to the Evangelist Matthew, Jesus told His twelve Apostles, when He first sent them out preaching Christianity: 'Do not think that I am come to send peace on earth. I came not to send peace, but a sword. For I am come to set a man at variance with his father, and the daughter against her mother, and the daughter-in-law against her mother-in-law. A man's foes shall be the members of his own household.' So it was in many a Christian household in the City. Son and daughter perhaps wore the Blue favour, and were Orthodox two-nature people, while father and mother and daughter-in-law wore the Green and maintained the single nature. They threw kettles of boiling water at one another as they sat at meals, or poisoned the wine; and blasphemed most learnedly. If the Greens set up a statue of a victorious charioteer and inscribed it: 'To the glory of Such-and-Such, winner of the Foundation Stakes, and the greater glory of Christ single-natured', the Blues would gather together at night and deface the inscription, then behead the statue and paint it blue; however, the Greens would perhaps retaliate by attempting to set fire to some wine-shop or other which the Blues used as their headquarters. It was not safe to be out in the streets after dark, not for physicians hurrying to attend the sick, nor for priests going at a more leisurely pace to administer the last Sacrament to the dying, nor for midnight adulterers, nor even for the poorest sort of outcasts. Gangs of young coxcombs ranged the streets at night, murdering and robbing indiscriminately; and the police were either bribed or terrorized into inertness. The war was even waged against the dead. Holes were bored at night in the tombs of departed factionists, and through them were dropped lead tablets of execration: 'Sleep unsoundly, vile Blue [or Green] until Judgement Day, dreaming of Green [or Blue] victories, and awake only to be damned to everlasting perdition!'

The Greens had been easily the stronger faction in the days of Anastasius, and had enjoyed his royal favour, and been awarded the best seats in the Hippodrome. But Theodora insisted on Justinian's reversing these conditions. The Blues were given the best seats now, and favoured in every possible way – by political and Court appointments and grants of money, and especially by legal protection, the Greens' monopoly of justice in the lower courts having at last been broken. It may be imagined that the Greens did not yield to the Blues without a struggle, and a very fierce one. While they had been the bullies they had made the Blues sing very small; and the Blues were now having their revenge, behaving, I admit, in a rather more violent and arbitrary way than the Greens had ever done. Robberies with violence became frequent in broad daylight, and if a Green happened to be killed and the murderer arrested by the police it was enough for a Blue official to swear in court that the Green had been the aggressor: the accused was at once dismissed with a caution. The carrying of arms by any private citizen was unlawful, but the enactment had become obsolete. The contemporary fashion was to wear short cutlasses by day concealed under the tunic, strapped along the thigh; while at night everyone carried arms openly. One result of these street disorders was that false jewellery came into fashion: substantial citizens no longer appeared in jewel-studded golden belts and valuable rings, but wore brass and glass instead.

Justinian intended his persecution of the Greens only as a temporary measure. When he had chastened them thoroughly he would allow them equality with the Blues, and try to preserve a balance of power between the two Colours. But meanwhile he made it a very unpleasant thing to be a Green. There were mass desertions to the Blue cause and much assistance to the Blues from criminals, who trusted that the wearing of a Blue favour would afford them immunity. Extraordinary scenes were now witnessed. Young women joined faction murder-gangs and killed and were killed along with the men. (It must be noted that women can have only an indirect interest in the factions: for they have not been admitted since pagan times to watch the chariot-races in the Hippodrome, unless they have happened, as in the case of Theodora and my mistress Antonina, to be the performers' own women-folk.) Then there were cases of needy or greedy sons levying blackmail on their prosperous fathers: 'If you do not give me a hundred gold pieces I will come tonight with my gang and burn your warehouse down.' As a matter of course anybody with a grudge against a neighbour who was not known to be a Blue denounced him as a Green. The murder-hour had now receded from dusk to the early afternoon; the young roughs prided themselves on being able to kill casual passers-by with a single sword-stroke, like professional executioners. It was a particularly bad year for money-lenders: the gangs used to visit them in their offices, on behalf of debtors of the faction, and compel them at dagger-point to hand back the loan-contracts. Also, women and boys, even of the upper classes, were forced to submit to the amorous wishes of the gang-leaders, and there were actually cases of public rape committed in the streets by groups of factionists, as in a captured barbarian city. To crown all, Justinian instituted a heresy-hunt against the Greens; so that priests and monks began wearing the Blue favour and taking part in faction politics. These heresy-hunts were used as an excuse for dissolving rich monasteries and sequestrating their treasures.

A great many prominent Greens fled away from the City to distant parts of the Empire, out of Justinian's immediate reach, and even across the frontier to Persian or barbarian territory. I could feel no pity for them, because my former master Damocles' miserable death was due to the hard hearts of the Greens; and I sympathized with the Empress, too, for avenging the injustice with which the Greens had treated her family when she was only little Theodora, the Bear Master's daughter. But Cappadocian John, who had long deserted the Greens and was now a leading Blue, was Justinian's chief instrument in the religious persecutions. Though no soldier, he had been appointed Commander of the Guards. He filled the Treasury with the monastery spoils, grew richer than ever by retaining part of his takings, and delighted in watching the torture of miserable heretics. John made a great show of respect for Theodora, but she treated him with polite contempt, and my mistress Antonina needed no encouragement to follow her example. Theodora was aware, of course, that Cappadocian John slandered her to Justinian. 'I shall wait patiently for twenty years, if need be,' she confided to my mistress, 'like the elephant of Severus.'

The elephant of Severus is commemorated by a statue close to the Royal Porch, nearly opposite the main entrance to the Hippodrome. It had waited twenty years to catch a certain money-changer on whose evidence its master had been committed to a debtor's prison, where he had died. At last, while taking part in a procession, it had recognized the money-changer in the crowd lining the street and had seized him with its trunk and trampled him to death. Investigations proved clearly that the money-changer had been a thief and a perjurer, so the elephant was honoured with this statue, which represents it with its master seated upon its neck. The motto is: 'It will be avenged at last.' Many who labour under private and public injustice comfort themselves with the elephant's message.

You may wish to hear more of Justinian as Emperor, how he behaved. The man was a mass of contradictions: most of which, however, were to be explained as the result of great ambitions struggling with cowardice and meanness. Justinian wished, it seems, to make himself remembered as 'Justinian the Great'. His talents would indeed have been equal to the task if he had only been less of a beast in spirit. For he was incredibly well-informed and industrious and agile-minded and accessible, and no drunkard or debauchee. On the other hand, he was as irresolute as any man I ever met, and as superstitious as an old church-widow. There was something about him, inexpressible, that made one's flesh creep – whatever it was, it certainly was not greatness, rather a sort of devilishness. He had decided, after studying the history-books, that sovereigns are honoured as 'Great' for four main reasons: for successful home defence and foreign conquest, for the imposing of legal and religious conformity on their subjects, for the building of great public works, for personal piety and stern moral reform. He set to work on these lines.

He began on the legal side with a recodification of the laws, and I own that this was greatly needed. No single code existed, but a variety of codes side by side, all contradictory, obsolescent, and obscure, so that a judge could not give a fair decision in any but the simplest cases, even if he so wished. Justinian's industrious legal officers eventually ordered the great confused mass into a single fairly intelligible and not wholly contradictory system – but it took no less than 3,000,000 lines of writing to do this. If only he and his judges and lawyers and the general population had been the moral equals of this formidable task! Religious conformity he tried to attain by the smelling out of heresies; but he was not consistent in this, because, for fear of Theodora, he chiefly persecuted Jews and Samaritans and pagans and the minor sects of Manichees and Sabellians and such-like, while allowing the Monophysite and Nestorian heresies, wherever there was no proved connexion with Green faction politics, to continue unchecked. Not only were they rife in the provinces, but he allowed them to be exported by foreign missions to Ethiopia and Arabia. His great public works consisted chiefly of the building and restoring of monasteries and churches. These were, of course, profitless to the Empire (except in a vague spiritual sense) and not to be compared with the building and restoring of aqueducts and roads and harbours and granaries, to which he did not pay nearly so much attention. His plans for foreign conquest, of which he made Belisarius his chief instrument, I shall soon have occasion to mention more fully.

His moral reforms were for the most part inspired by Theodora, and were extremely severe. Now, it had been a very long time since a really capable woman had been in so powerful a position as Theodora was. That was the fault of the Church, which – having originated in the East, where women are little better than playthings or slaves or beasts of burden – tended to seclude women from public life and give them no education worth the name. In pagan times the Empress had often been the second ruler of the state and had acted as a powerful check on the caprices of the Emperor; and this was made possible because she had been brought up in a free and educated atmosphere, not severely confined to the women's quarters until called upon to marry some man whom she had never seen – as is the rule now with women of the upper classes. Theodora was no fool of the priests. She had seen the world, and she understood men and politics, both lay and ecclesiastical. She ruled Justinian as absolutely as it is said that the great Livia once ruled Augustus, the first Emperor of the Romans.

Theodora determined gradually to restore wives to the powerful position that they had lost. This bias of hers explains Justinian's legislation, which she sponsored, against prostitutes and sodomites. While husbands were free to take their pleasure in the public brothels or with state catamites, their wives could not easily manage them. The Association of Procurers, formerly under Imperial protection, was broken up; and procuring made a criminal offence. Sodomy was now punishable by castration, and there was also a great rounding up of common prostitutes of the sort who charge a few pence only and are known as 'the infantry'. Theodora called these unfortunates 'a standing offence to the dignity of women'. She allowed them three months to make themselves respectable by marriage; then, if still obstinately unmarried, they were arrested again and shut up in the so-called Castle of

Repentance on the Asiatic shore of the Bosphorus. (A considerable number of the 500 women confined there jumped to death from the castle walls in their vexation and boredom.) But to those who chose marriage Theodora offered a dowry, and a great many benefited by her generosity. Nevertheless, she did not touch 'the cavalry', as the more accomplished prostitutes were called, who were their own managers, possessed valuable jewellery, and were organized as a guild. She employed them as her secret agents, and provided good physicians for them when they fell sick.

It was a bad time for husbands. Theodora made it quite plain that wives no longer needed to live chaster lives than they. If a husband had been companying with prostitutes – as practically every husband did at some time or other – the wife was at perfect liberty to amuse herself with lovers. If he then grew angry with her, she could make an immediate appeal to Theodora and bring a counter-charge against him, of cruelty, or failure to support his family, or something of the sort; and Theodora never failed to bring the charge home, accepting the wife's account of the matter without question. Often a jealous husband had to pay a fine amounting to double the wife's dowry; which was then handed over to her in Court, after a small deducation had been made for costs. He was also likely to be scourged and usually given a few days in prison. Husbands after a time grew very careful how they behaved themselves, and also very careless how their wives behaved. The scourge was a five-strapped leather whip with an iron tag at the end of each strap; and the public slaves laid on extremely hard.

As a good example of Theodora's way with husbands, let me describe how the son of the Master of Offices fared. He wished to marry a second cousin of his; but Theodora, who had decided to match him with the Lady Chrysomallo's daughter, told him that this was quite out of the question: she disapproved of marriages between cousins. He was obliged to yield, of course, because Theodora was to the Court what an old grandmother is to the members of a large country family. He was lucky enough to be marrying the Lady Chrysomallo's daughter, who was young and pretty and intelligent; but after the wedding he grumbled to a friend of his that the girl had been 'tampered with'. The fact was that the Lady Chrysomallo, though nominally a Christian, kept to the customs of her family – which, because of its connexions with the Hippodrome, was a pagan one. Thus the girl, instead of presenting her husband with an intact maidenhead, had undergone the traditional pagan ceremony of defloresœnce – namely, equitation of the stone phallus of a Priapic image, to induce fertility. The bridegroom's complaint came to Theodora's ears, and she was very angry. 'What airs these young gentlemen give themselves to be sure!' she cried. 'I suppose he has never in all his life tampered with a girl himself! "Tampered" indeed!' Then she gave orders that he should be tossed in a blanket by her servants, just as vain and unpopular schoolboys are tossed on the way to school by their schoolfellows. And, after the tossing, they thrashed him.

Theodora, as the story of Severus's elephant reminds me, never lost a chance of paying off an old score. The patrician Hicebolus was among the first to pay for his former ill-treatment of Theodora: he was brought back from Pentapolis on a charge of sodomy, Theodora herself judging the case, was convicted (not without justice) and sentenced to castration. He died of blood-poisoning after the operation.

Here, too (because of the sequel), I should tell the comic story of Hippobates, the old Senator who came to Theodora's audience one morning to appeal to her for justice against Chrysomallo's husband, one of her gentlemen-in-waiting, who owed him money. This Hippobates had once in the old days been brought by a friend – none other than the Demarch of the Blues – to spend an evening at the clubhouse. He was expected to choose one of the ladies to pair off with, while the Demarch chose another, but for some reason or other he did not feel equal to female company. Then instead of plainly confessing – as a man of honour would have done – that he was a Christian, or impotent, or that he preferred the other sex, or whatever else ailed him, he began to find fault with the physical charms offered him. Indaro was too tall and too square-shouldered, he said; and Theodora too skinny, and her mouth was too large; and my mistress had red hair, which he could not abide, and 'a mattock-shaped face'. I forget what was wrong with Chrysomallo – perhaps her hooked nose. Since he was a detestable old satyr, all felt relieved to be excused from entertaining him. Still, he had no right at all to criticize the ladies in this way, and his remarks were strongly resented. It was unfortunate that the Demarch had introduced him, for the ladies must keep on the very best terms with the Demarch. Otherwise, they would have punished him in the humiliating ways in which they were adept.

Theodora knew in advance that Hippobates was coming to appeal for the money, so she had everything carefully prepared for his reception. He entered with a very unhappy countenance, and grovelled most abjectly as he kissed her insteps, and pretended to weep. I do not think that he realized that Theodora the Empress was Theodora of the club-house, whom he had once insulted. She asked him kindly what his trouble was. He began in a most unbecoming beggar's whine: 'Oh, Resplendency, it is a grievous matter for a patrician to be penniless. My creditors dog my steps, duns rap perpetually at my door, I have hardly a crust of bread in my house. I entreat you, most gracious and lovely Empress, to persuade your servant to pay me the money that he owes me.'

Theodora began: 'Oh, most excellent and Illustrious Hippobates...' From behind the curtains a concealed choir of eunuchs, formed into two semi-choruses, broke into a mysterious, soft chant:

First Semi-chorus: Excellent Hippobates,
You have a bald pate!
Second Semi-chorus: Excellent Hippobates,
You have a bad breath!
Full Chorus: You have a big belly,
Excellent Hippobates –
Bald pate, bad breath,
Big belly too!

She turned to my mistress: 'My dear Lady Antonina, did you hear a queer noise then?'

'No, Resplendency.'

'And you, Lady Chrysomallo?'

'Nothing at all, Majesty.'

'It must have been a singing in my head. Proceed, Hippobates!'

Hippobates, not daring to notice what he had heard, nervously recommenced his petition: 'If a patrician like myself runs short of money, through no fault of his own, he is ashamed to mention the incongruous fact to his creditors. They would not at first wish to believe it. When they did finally realize that he was a beggar, he would have to suffer social disgrace as well as bankruptcy; and social disgrace, as you know, Your Loveliness...'

Theodora began again: 'Oh, most excellent and Illustrious Hippobates...' And again the concealed choir struck up, a little louder this time:

First Semi-chorus: Excellent Hippobates,
You have a humped back!
Second Semi-chorus: Excellent Hippobates,
You have a hernia!
Full Chorus: You have haemorrhoids,
Excellent Hippobates –
Hernia, humped back,
Haemorrhoids too!

'Lady Chrysomallo, did you hear anything then?'

'No, Resplendency.'

'And you, Lady Antonina?'

'Not a murmur, Majesty.'

'I could have sworn I heard a sort of noise. But proceed, Hippobates!'

And still he had to pretend to have heard nothing himself. Each time he began his petition the choir broke in upon it, and each time the verses were increasingly scurrilous. In the end, he had to give it up, retiring in frantic discomfiture, but with the obligatory serene obeisance.

The sequel was that his creditors, who had originally prompted his appeal to Theodora, became more insistent than ever, until he was forced to apply to his old friend, the Demarch of the Blues, who sent a group of factionists to protect Hippobates' house. There ensued a riot, in which two of the creditors, who were Greens, were killed and a number of Blues wounded. News of the disturbance reached the Palace; and Cappadocian John, aware that Hippobates was out of favour with Theodora but not realizing that some of the men engaged had been sent from Blue military headquarters, thought that he would please Justinian by intervening in the name of public order. He sent a strong force of Guards to the scene of disturbance, who arrested Blues and Greens indiscriminately, several of each Colour. A hurried trial was held, four of them were sentenced to decapitation for being found in possession of weapons, and three to the gallows for conspiracy to kill; and all were marched off to execution.

It happened that the gallows rope was not stout enough. It broke twice – under the weight of a Green and of a Blue. These miserable men fell to the ground and were left lying for dead, it being assumed that their necks had been broken. That evening, however, some monks sought out the bodies and found life still in them; and conveyed them to St Lawrence's Hospital, where they recovered. This Hospital was a sanctuary. But Cappadocian John arrested them again, violating the sanctuary, and put them into the State Prison (which, with the police-barracks, comprised a whole wing of the Brazen House on the side nearest to the Hippodrome).

The Demarch of the Blues then took a remarkable resolution. He went at once under a flag of truce to Green headquarters, and in an interview with the Demarch of the Greens suggested joint action against the police who had dared to interfere in the traditional feud between the two Colours. The Demarch of the Greens was most eager to declare a temporary truce. The thirteenth day of January was near, the date of the New Year's Races. They agreed that, after their usual loyal greeting to Justinian as he entered the Hippodrome, they should all, Blue and Green alike, appeal for the release of the prisoners, whose lives God had spared by a miracle, and for the dismissal of Cappadocian John – whom the Blues loathed as a turncoat and envied for his wealth, and whom the Greens hated as a traitor and oppressor. So this was done, and I think that Theodora had a hand in the plot. But Justinian took the matter very coolly and made no reply to the appeals for release, which continued throughout the day, after each of the twenty-two races that were run.

The two Demarchs then agreed on more vigorous action and on a common watchword, which was 'Victory!', for the two factions. That evening after the races they surrounded the State Prison and demanded the persons of the two men who had been removed from sanctuary. No answer was given them, so they set fire to the porch with torches. The flames spread and destroyed the whole wing, police-barracks and all. Most of the prisoners were rescued, but a number of warders and police were burned to death. The Guards, who sympathized with the rioters, did not intervene. Their own quarters in the centre of the Brazen House had not been attacked, and the fire was now under control.

The next morning Justinian decided to continue the Races as usual without taking any notice of the outrages committed; but the factionists surrounded the Palace, demanding the dismissal of Cappadocian John and of Tribonian the Lord Chief Justice, and of the City Governor. When there was still no reply, and no Guards or police arrived to disperse them, the factionists knew that they were at liberty to riot to their hearts' content. First, they heaped wooden benches, dragged from the Hippodrome, against a number of public buildings and sct fire to them. Then under the cover of the smoke and confusion they began joyfully murdering, robbing, raping, and plundering. Convinced Blues showed a preference for damaging Green property, and convinced Greens for damaging Blue property; but most of the rioters were not particular in their choice of victims, because of the truce. The watchword was, as I have said, 'Victory!' and the combined Colours won a great victory indeed over the City. Soon the central district was alight in several places; the fire-brigades did not attempt to extinguish the outbreaks – most of the firemen themselves were busy looting. The flames spread unchecked. Fortunately it was a windless day, or the whole City would have burned down. There was a general rush to the docks, where people offered the boatmen enormous fees to ferry them across to safety on the Asiatic shore.

I was at our suite in the Palace as usual, in attendance on my mistress Antonina, and I must confess that the whole household was terrified, in spite of Belisarius's calm, not to say scornful, demeanour. Imperial orders came that none of us should leave the Palace grounds under any pretext. Vigorous action of some sort should clearly have been taken long ago, but Theodora could do nothing with Justinian, who was praying in his private chapel. Cappadocian John had disappeared, and the Guards, in the unburned part of the Brazen House, were consequently without orders. However, the rabble would certainly have slaughtered them if they had attempted to intervene. Belisarius was still nominally Commander of the Armies in the East, but had no authority in the City. When my mistress urged him to offer Justinian his services and those of his Household cuirassiers – they were quartered not far away – he refused: as a servant of the Emperor he must not speak out of turn, but wait for orders. No orders came. Justinian was as obstinate as a mule; praying fervently and assuring Theodora that Heaven would provide.

At last, on the fifteenth day of January, Justinian moved to end the disorders. His method was to appeal to the Christian scruples of his subjects. He sent out a deputation of bishops and priests with banners and a parcel of sacred relics – a small portion of the True Cross, and the authentic horn of the Patriarch Abraham's ram, which will be sounded upon Judgement Day, and the serpent-shaped rod of Moses with which miracles were once done in Egypt and Sinai – and, besides these, the bones of Zoe the virgin martyr and of some other martyrs of lesser importance. But no miracle resulted, and the clergy were forced to retreat to the Daphne Palace, pursued by a smart shower of stones and bricks. Justinian was watching from a balcony and called out: 'Oh, protect them, quickly! Let someone go out at once and protect them!' Belisarius went out, glad of an opportunity for action, with a party of forty Thracian-Gothic soldiers who were on permanent duty in the Daphne colonnades; and drove the rioters back, killing a number of them, so that the clergy returned with the relics undamaged.

This action of Belisarius's enraged the factions, which were now altogether out of control. On the next day Justinian sent out a herald to the Square of Augustus to announce that Cappadocian John had resigned his command and that the City Governor and Tribonian, the Lord Chief Justice, had also retired from office. (Tribonian had been so busy with his work of re-codifying the laws that he had not had sufficient time to supervise the administration of justice.) But this concession was no longer enough to restore peace, especially as the truce between the factionists had been broken in quarrels over the division of plunder, and the Green cause had revived with unexpected strength. By the seventeenth of January there had been sacked and burned: the churches of St Sophia and St Irene, and the Royal Porch, which was a famous library containing among other curiosities the complete works of Homer written upon the intestines of a serpent forty yards in length, and the Baths of Zeuxippus lying between the Brazen House and the Hippodrome, and the silversmiths' colonnades, and the High Street as far as the Square of Constantine. A vast amount of treasure was thus destroyed. We domestics watched the fires from an upper window and did not dare to go to bed at night for fear of being burned to death if we did.

It was not until the fifth day of the riots, which was the eighteenth of January, that Theodora managed to persuade Justinian to enter the Hippodrome and make a public appeal for peace. The Hippodrome runs parallel with the Palace, on the slope leading down to the Sea of Marmora. At the northern end are two towers, and stables, chariot-sheds, and offices for the entertainers, and, high up to one side, at the point commanding the best view of the start, the Royal Box surmounted by the gilded horses from Chios. This Box was reached by a private colonnade from the Daphne Palace, skirting St Stephen's Church, so Justinian did not need to risk driving through the public streets. Holding a copy of the Gospels, he appeared in the Royal Box before the packed Hippodrome and began one of those vague paternal exhortations to peace and harmony, combined with vague promises, which are usually effective, after a riot, when popular heat is beginning to cool somewhat and the graver sort of people have begun to reckon up the damages. But it proved perfectly useless, because not backed up by any show of force. Half-hearted cheers came from the Blue benches, interspersed with hisses – but yells of execration from the Greens, who were now in the ascendant again, many deserters having returned to their old allegiance. Stones and other missiles were thrown at the Royal Box, as once in Anastasius's time, and Justinian retired precipitately, the mob streaming out of the Hippodrome in pursuit of him. Thereupon the Thracian-Gothic Guards withdrew from the Palace and joined their fellows in the Brazen House. The mob plundered and burned down the extensive block of Palace buildings, adjacent to St Stephen's Church, which was the residence of the eunuchs of the Civil Service.

Now, the least worthless perhaps of Anastasius's worthless nephews, of whom one or other had been expected to succeed to the Throne before Justin seized it, was Hypatius. He had served under Belisarius at Daras, somewhat ingloriously indeed – it was his squadron that had been forced from the trenches on the right wing when the Immortals charged; but it could at least be held of him that his ambitions did not exceed his capacities. As soon as the riots broke out he came modestly to Justinian, with his brother Pompey, and said that the Greens had made approaches to him, offering him the Throne; that he had indignantly refused to countenance any movement on his behalf, and that to show his loyalty he now put himself at Justinian's disposal. Justinian praised and thanked Hypatius, though unable to understand his frankness in admitting that he had been offered the Throne – unless possibly as an attempt to disarm suspicion and seize the supreme power as soon as a favourable opportunity offered. But after this attack on the Palace, Justinian sent word to him and Pompey that they must leave at once if they did not wish to be executed as traitors. As soon as dark came, they slipped away, very unwillingly, and managed to enter their houses unnoticed. Unfortunately the news somehow reached the Greens that Hypatius was at large. They surrounded his house, forced it open, and carried him off in triumph to the Square of Constantine. There, at the centre of a tightly packed, screaming crowd, he was duly proclaimed Emperor, and crowned with a golden collar for want of a diadem, though the remainder of the insignia was available, having been plundered from the Palace. Hypatius was genuinely unwilling to accept the Throne; and his wife Mary, a pious Christian, wrung her hands and wailed that he was being taken from her along the road to death. But the Greens were not to be gainsaid.

Green representatives went to the Senate House and demanded that an oath of allegiance be sworn to Hypatius. The Senators (as always happens in cases of this sort) did not wish to commit themselves. Their loyalties were fairly evenly divided; though most of them were professedly Blues, many were secret Greens who regretted the 'good times of Anastasius', as they called them, and despised the upstart Justinian. They took refuge in rhetorical talk, coming to no decision. At the Palace, too, there was a certain number of Senators assembled, all Blues and all very frightened. Justinian himself was trembling with fear and asking everybody he met – man, woman, or eunuch; patrician, commoner, or slave – what he ought to do next. A regular Council was hurriedly called together. Most of those wretched cowards advised instant flight, on the ground that the Palace Guards were clearly not to be depended upon and that the Greens now dominated the City. Only Belisàrius, with Mundus, favoured a vigorous stand against the rebels – Mundus was Commander of the Armies in Illyria, and happened to have arrived in the City two days previously to see about remounts for his cavalry.

Theodora entered the Council Chamber uninvited. She was so terrible in her scorn and rage that not only Justinian himself but everyone else present would sooner have died a hundred times than oppose those blazing eyes. She said: 'This is all talk, talk, talk, and as a woman of sense I protest against it, and demand that strong action be taken at once. This is already the sixth day of the disturbances, and each day I have been assured that "the matter is well in hand", and that "God will provide", and that "all possible steps are being taken", and so on and so forth. But nothing has been done yet – only talk, talk, talk. Bishops sent out with frivolous relics. The Gospels flourished in the faces of a great rabble of impious pigs – and then we run away when they grunt and squeal! You seem almost to have decided on flight, Justinian the Great. Very well, then, go! But at once, while you still possess a private harbour and boats and sailors and money! If, however, you do go, remember: you will never be able to return to this

Palace, and they will hunt you down in the end and put you to a miserable and deserved death. No secure place of escape is left to you. You could not even take refuge at the Persian Court: because once, greatly against my advice, you mortally insulted Khosrou, who is now King, by refusing to adopt him as your son. But go, I say, go, take your chance in Spain or Britain or Ethiopia, and my scorn follow with you! As for myself, may I never be separated from this purple, or survive the day when my subjects fail to address me by my just and full titles. I approve the old saying: "Royalty is a fair burial-shroud." What are you waiting for? A miracle from Heaven? No, gird up your robes and run, for Heaven hates you! I shall remain here and face whatever doom my dignities enjoin upon me.'

Then Mundus and Belisarius put themselves under Theodora's orders – for nobody else seemed inclined to give them any. Justinian was wearing a monk's habit, as if for humility, but rather for a disguise should the Palace be attacked again. He was hard at prayer in the Royal Chapel, his face covered with the coarse brown cowl. At this juncture an unexpected message came from Hypatius to Theodora: 'Noblest of women, since the Emperor suspects me and will do nothing for me, I beg you to trust my loyalty and send soldiers to release me from this predicament.' Theodora thereupon told Belisarius to place himself at the head of the Guards, rescue Hypatius, and bring him back to the Palace. Belisarius summoned the men of his Household who were encamped in the Palace grounds, and Mundus summoned his escort of Herulian Huns. The two forces together did not amount to more than 400 men, for the greater part of Belisarius's people had been lent to the Imperial Forces and were away in Thrace, under the command of Armenian John, enforcing the collection of taxes. Belisarius desired Mundus to take his Huns round by the winding alley called 'The Snail' to the Gate of Death, at the south-east of the Hippodrome, through which the dead bodies of gladiators had formerly been dragged. He was to wait there for orders. Then Belisarius himself rode with his people through the Palace grounds to the end of the High Street, where the Senate House is, and turned left to the gates of the Brazen House. Finding no sentry outside and the gates still shut, he rapped with the pommel of his sword and shouted: 'I am Belisarius, Commander of the Armies in the East. Open in the name of his Sacred Majesty, the Emperor Justinian!' But no answer came. The soldiers preferred, like the Senate, to wait on events. The gates were of massive brass and not easily forced, so after a second summons he went back to the Palace and reported to Theodora that the Guards were not available. She told him that he must do what he could with the few men at his disposal.

He decided to go past St Stephen's Church, now also burned, and straight up to the Royal Box. To do so he must pass through the ruins of the Eunuchs' Residence, which were still smouldering. Every now and then a wall would collapse or a sudden fire blaze up again. The horses were terrified by the smoke, and would not face it, so he gave the order to dismount and sent them back. Wetting their cloaks and wrapping them about their faces, his people rushed across in twos and threes and reached the Blue Colonnade of the Hippodrome (it is ornamented with sheer lapis-lazuli) which mounts gradually to the Royal Box. But they found the door at the end barred and guarded. It was dangerous to force it: that would mean fighting a way in darkness up a narrow staircase, while perhaps a crowd of Greens was sent round to attack them in the rear. Belisarius gave the order to turn about. This time he led his people along to the main entrance of the Hippodrome, on the northern side, between the towers.

I cannot say what the Greens were doing in the Hippodrome all this time, but I know that the Demarch and Democrat of the Greens both made boastful speeches, while the Blues present sat in glum silence. It was now plain that the Greens had succeeded in appointing an Emperor of their own colour; and the Blue Demarch bitterly repented having made that truce with them. Then suddenly a cry arose and Belisarius was seen marching into the Hippodrome, with his sword drawn, at the head of his mail-clad soldiers. He turned and called out to Hypatius as he sat in the Box above him: 'Illustrious Hypatius, it is the Emperor's seat that you have taken; and you have no right to occupy it. His orders are that you return at once to the Palace and place yourself at his disposal.'

To the general surprise (for only the leading factionists were aware how unwilling a monarch he was), Hypatius rose obediently and moved towards the door of the Box; but the Demarch of the Greens, who was seated near him, roughly forced him back into his chair. Then a crowd of Greens began to threaten Belisarius's men. He charged along the benches at them. They yelled and scrambled back in disorder. They were only a mob of City loafers, and their weapons were adapted for murder, not for fighting; moreover, they wore no armour. So Belisarius's 200 men, fully armoured, were fully a match for their thousands. Meanwhile Mundus, waiting outside the Gate of Death, heard the roar of alarm from within, and realized that Belisarius's people were engaged. He charged in with his Huns against the Greens, who were leaping over the barriers into the arena, and slaughtered them in droves. Some of them tried to take refuge on the pedestals of the statues ranged along the central barrier – that of the Emperor Theodosius with the napkin in his hand, and the three great twisted serpents, brought from Delphi, which once supported the priestess's tripod there, and the statues of famous charioteers, including one of my former master Damocles which Theodora had recently erected there – but these fugitives were soon pulled down and killed. Then the Blues, who were all seated together as usual, joined in the fight. Led by two of Justinian's own nephews, they made a rush for the Royal Box and, after a severe struggle, killed the Green Demarch and his men, secured Hypatius and Pompey and handed them over to Rufinus, who was assisting Belisarius. Rufinus conducted them to the Palace by way of the narrow staircase and the Blue Colonnade.

The Greens had now recovered from their surprise and began to fight desperately. Belisarius and Mundus were forced to go on killing methodically until once more the silk-clad simpletons with their billowing sleeves and their long, pomaded hair retreated in panic. At last Belisarius was able to withdraw some of his men peaceably to the North Gate and send others to guard the remaining gates; and Mundus also called off his Huns. But there was no holding back the Blues, who would now be satisfied only with a total extermination of the Greens. Belisarius and Mundus did not think it wise to interfere: they stood and grimly watched the fratricidal slaughter, as one might watch a battle between cranes and pygmies – with sympathies somewhat perhaps inclined to the side of the pygmies, who were almost as inhuman as the cranes, though not less grotesque in appearance. When it was clear that the Blues had won a handsome victory (in the names of the double-natured Son of his Vice-regent, the double-dealing Emperor), Belisarius returned to the Palace for further orders, and Mundus with him. Soon my mistress was embracing her dear husband, all bespattered with blood as he was. But a whole horde of Blues from the suburbs, where the Colour was very strong, now came running up with all sorts of weapons and burst into the Hippodrome to assist in the massacre. They had been armed at the Arsenal by Narses, who had bribed the Democrat of the Blues to call for volunteers against the usurping Hypatius. They were followed by the Guards from the Brazen House, equally eager now to show their loyalty to Justinian by a butchery of the Greens.

Thirty-five thousand Greens and a few hundred Blues were killed outright before the day ended, and a great many more were severely wounded. The crowd had also attacked the Green stables – killing grooms, and hamstringing the horses and burning chariots. Then began a furious hunt for unrepentant Greens throughout the City, and by the next morning there was not a man or woman left who was still wearing the hated favour.

When Hypatius and Pompey were brought before Justinian he said to Belisarius: 'Excellent, but you should have caught these traitors sooner, before half our City was burned down.' Then he sentenced them to death – the action of a scoundrel, as Theodora told him to his face. But his answer was, as usual, a soft one. What a fellow he was, even in those days!

Thus ended the so-called Victory Riots, and with them, for a time at least, the feud between Greens and Blues. The Greens were utterly broken, and Justinian stabilized this happy state of affairs by putting an end by edict to all chariot-racing in the City. However, it was revived again a few years later; so the Green faction was bound to be revived too. The Blues could not, after all, compete against themselves. In a few years' time the Greens had become as rowdy as ever, gathering together under the protection of their Colour all elements in the City hostile to the Emperor and to the Orthodox Faith; and once more there were murder-gangs abroad at dusk.

Belisarius was always neutral – a White, as in his schooldays; but my mistress Antonina was a Blue, because of the wrong done to her father, and because of the club-house, and because of Theodora, who was her sworn friend.

CHAPTER 10

THE EXPEDITION AGAINST CARTHAGE

JUSTINIAN now planned a great expedition against the Vandals, a much-travelled people whose capital city was Carthage in North Africa; and, at Theodora's insistence, he entrusted the sole command to Belisarius.

Who the Vandals were and what they were doing in Africa can be told shortly. They were Germans of sorts, and first reported as residing on the frozen shores of the Baltic Sea at about the time that Jesus was alive on earth among the Jews. They migrated southward by slow stages to the rich plains enclosed by the Carpathian mountains, where they increased their numbers by alliance and intermarriage with the Hunnish tribes who already occupied this territory. By the time that the Emperor Constantine adopted Christianity as the State religion they had outgrown their new kingdom: because of a scarcity of provisions and the fertility of their women, a large number of them were obliged to cross over into the Roman Empire on this side of the Upper Danube, where they were given lands and the status of allies, and learned Roman methods of warfare. Two generations later they crossed the Danube again and invaded Germany, plundering and burning as they went, and then marched northward. They debated an invasion of the island of Britain, which had just been denuded of its Roman garrison. There were transports enough in the French ports, but the Vandals were not experienced sailors, and the English Channel seemed too rough a sea-passage. So, leaving Britain to the mercy of Saxon pirates, they invaded France instead, crossing the River Rhine on New Year's Eve when it was frozen over. For two years they raided and plundered in France, and then marched into Spain, where they established themselves in the southernmost part, and called their kingdom Andalusia. But a few years later they were invited to Carthage by Count Boniface, the Roman Governor of North Africa. Count Boniface had been wrongfully accused of plotting against his Emperor and needed allies to save him from a shameful death: he offered the Vandals one-third part of the lands about Carthage for their own if they came to his help.

The Vandals had made sailors of themselves while in Spain, though there was a law among the Romans decreeing death to anyone who should teach any German barbarians the art of building or managing a ship. So they crossed over by sea from one of the two rocky Pillars of Hercules, namely Gibraltar in Spain, to the other, which is Ceuta in Morocco, and then marched eastward along the coast. There were 200,000 of them in all, but only 50,000 fighting men, the rest being women and children and the aged; for they came all together and only a very few elected to remain behind. These Vandals were Christians, but like most other German tribes, they were Arian heretics. Alas, here is one more theory of the nature of the Son to expound.

At the time that the Germans were converted to Christianity by one Ulfilas, a contemporary of the Emperor Constantine, who translated the Scriptures into the Gothic tongue – all but the Books of Kings, which he feared might inflame their military passions – this Arian heresy was a widely-held one and had nearly become the orthodox view of the whole Church. The Germans welcomed it because it seemed a simple, barbarian creed, substantiating their own conception of the Deity. The Arians hold that the Father is immeasurably superior to man, and that there is no real mediation between the Father and man: not even the Son, who never perfectly knew the Father and while He lived here on earth was subject to all the affections of man, such as anger, grief, despair, humiliation – as is indeed described by the Evangelists. Nevertheless, the Son (according to these Arians) is a sort of demigod: not God, but a middle being, of a different substance from, and perfectly unlike, the Father, who existed before the world and was created out of nothing and became man. Since the Germans already believed in a God of immeasurable power and freakish temper, whom they called Odin, and also in a demigod and racial ancestor called Mann (which is the German for 'man'), who originated out of practically nothing, their change of faith was one of names rather than of beliefs. They now agreed to abstain from human sacrifices, because these (according to their new faith) had been forbidden by God since the time of the Patriarch Abraham; but continued to engage in bloody wars and massacres. For, though the good Ulfilas had omitted the Books of Kings from his translation, he had included the Book of Joshua, which tells of the merciless massacre by the Jews of such pagan tribes as they met in their 'promised land'.

To the Vandals, Roman Africa was a promised land too, and resembled Canaan of old in its vineyards and corn-fields and fig-plantations and walled cities. But when the moving multitude was already close to Carthage they were coolly informed by Count Boniface that he had made a mistake: the Emperor, or rather the Empress Regent, now trusted him again, and there was no need for Vandal allies – would they, please, return to Andalusia, and he would pay them for their trouble. Naturally they felt grossly insulted and refused to go. From allies they became enemies and defeated Boniface in battle; after which they occupied not only one-third of the lands about Carthage, but the whole Diocese of Africa, enslaving the inhabitants.

Carthage itself, which next to Rome was the greatest city of the Western Empire, held out for some years. But this was because it was supplied with food from the sea and had very strong fortifications, which the Vandals were not experienced enough as engineers to reduce; not because of any heroism among the defenders. The Roman Africans had become unwarlike, owing to centuries of peace, the richness of the soil, and the enervating heat. Further, they were divided among themselves by the Donatist schism. This, for once, was not a heretical view about the nature of the Son, but a quarrel about Church discipline: the Donatists held that to be blessed by a priest who lived an evil life or who had committed some such impious act as burning a religious book when ordered to do so by the civil authorities, was no blessing, and that no sacerdotal act whatsoever performed by such a person was valid. But the Orthodox theory was that the water of life could flow through the jaws of a dead dog (as it was expressed) and still heal the soul. The Donatists formed a separate communion, separating themselves from the Orthodox in order to avoid contamination by them. The Vandals made an alliance with these Donatists, as a temporary convenience: they were Donatistical, too, in their Arian way, they said.

The Vandal King, lame Geiserich, who had somehow been born an Orthodox Christian, was now an Arian; and soon began persecuting all the non-Arians of Africa, whether Donatists or Orthodox or heretics of whatever sort, with all the violence of a convert. At last the whole Diocese of Africa was under his power, and as a precaution against revolt he dismantled the fortifications of all its towns but Hippo Regius and Carthage, both of which he garrisoned strongly. Then he increased his fleet and began capturing islands, among them Sardinia and the Balearic islands, and raiding the coasts of Spain and

Italy and even Greece. His principal feat was the sack of Rome, from which, after a fortnight's stay, he carried away immense booty, public and private – including the golden treasures of Solomon's temple that Titus had brought to Rome centuries before, and one-half of the roof of the Temple of Capitoline Jove, which was of fine bronze, plated with gold. As I have mentioned, it was because of Geiserich's depredations that Belisarius's maternal grandfather had abandoned Rome for Constantinople.

The Emperor of the West – for the Eastern Emperors at Constantinople still had colleagues at Rome in those days – was unable to resist these many acts of piracy; but a punitive expedition was sent to Carthage from Constantinople. It consisted of 100,000 men carried by the most formidable fleet of ships ever embarked on the Mediterranean Sea; and they should have had no difficulty at all in overwhelming the Vandals. Geiserich pretended the utmost deference to their commander, and obtained from him an allowance of five days in which to 'prepare the city for surrender', as he put it. Then he secretly collected his forces and on the fourth night sent fire-ships sailing into the Imperial fleet, following up with armed galleys. Between blazing fire and savage Vandals the surprised Romans were utterly destroyed. Only a few battered ships and a few hundred soldiers returned to Constantinople. This disaster took place two generations before the reign of Justinian.

Since then there had been several successors to Geiserich, who had decreed that among his descendants the regal power should always pass entire to the eldest surviving male. This was to prevent the partition of the kingdom, with a consequent weakening of central authority, and also the troubles that so often occur when a regency is proclaimed on behalf of a child ruler. Thus, the eldest son of the king would not inherit at his father's death, while he had an uncle or granduncle living, but must yield the succession to him. Geiserich did not perhaps sufficiently consider that this law of succession tended to favour princes who were more remarkable for their longevity than for the soundness of their wits.

At the time of Justinian's accession the Vandal king was Hilderich. He had signed a defensive alliance with the King of the Goths who ruled in Italy. (By this time, the whole Western part of the Empire – though nominally under the sovereignty of the Eastern Emperor at Constantinople, there being no longer an Emperor at Rome – was dominated by various German allies, who acted as its garrison. They had chosen its most fertile regions to settle in, and were all Arian heretics.) Hilderich was also on good terms with the Eastern Emperor and continued to send to Constantinople the annual tribute-money agreed upon by Geiserich in the peace treaty which ratified his conquests. He was an old man, unfit for public business, and almost as suspicious in temperament as Justinian himself. The widow of his predecessor was still alive, a sister of Theoderich the famous Gothic king. She had brought with her as dowry a guard of 6,000 Gothic cavalry and the sovereignty of Lilybaeum, which is a promontory in Sicily only 100 miles distant from the coast of Carthage; and somebody assured Hilderich that this former queen intended to murder him and seize Carthage for the Goths. He had her confined to prison and subsequently strangled, and massacred the 6,000 Goths. This greatly offended Theoderich; he broke off his alliance with the Vandals, but would not risk a military expedition against them.

Justinian was a personal friend of Hilderich's, and there was a frequent exchange of letters and presents between them. Hilderich had befriended Justinian at Rome at the time when he was an unimportant hostage at Theoderich's Court; and Justinian also valued Hilderich for his indulgence to the Orthodox Catholics – previous Vandal kings had persecuted them savagely. When news came to Constantinople that Hilderich had been deposed and imprisoned by his nephew Geilimer, Justinian was affronted. He felt that Geilimer should be taught a lesson; for he himself had once been in the same sort of position as Geilimer, when his Uncle Justin grew decrepit and for the last two years was Emperor only in name. He considered that he had chosen the virtuous course in having been content with the title of Regent instead of anticipating sovereignty, and that this gave him a special right to protest to Geilimer. It was a mild letter, according to diplomatic usage: to the effect that, if the old man were released and restored to his royal dignities, God would be favourable to Geilimer and Justinian would be his friend.

Geilimer's excuse for imprisoning Hilderich had been a slanderous accusation that he had become a secret convert to Orthodoxy and wished to bequeath his throne to Justinian; so he made no reply to the letter when the ambassadors brought it, except an unseemly noise with his mouth. Hilderich was put into a darker and more disagreeable dungeon than before.

Justinian wrote again, more firmly this time, to the effect that Geilimer had seized the royal power by violence and must expect the divine retribution which usurpation always invites. He demanded that Hilderich be at least sent to Constantinople to end his life in comfortable exile, and threatened to declare war on the Vandals if this were not done.

Geilimer replied that Justinian had no right to meddle in the internal politics of the African kingdom; that Hilderich had been deposed as a traitor – an action approved by the Vandal Royal Council at Carthage; and that, before making war, Justinian should recall what had happened to the last fleet that visited Carthage from the East.

Justinian would not have granted King Khosrou such easy treaty-terms if he had not already considered the possibility of withdrawing some of his forces from the Persian frontier for an expedition against the Vandals. But when he mentioned the project to his chief ministers they all advised him against it as extremely dangerous. They were right enough in their view, of which Cappadocian John, as Commander of the Guards and now also Quartermaster-General of the Imperial forces, was the spokesman. Carthage lay at least 140 days' journey away from Constantinople by land. To transport an adequate force there by sea would mean the requisitioning of a vast quantity of ships; and this would greatly hamper the Empire's trade. It was difficult enough to raise troops for frontier defence in the North and East, without wasting them in unnecessary wars at the other end of the world. Even if it were possible to defeat the Vandals, it was strategically unwise to occupy North Africa unless one also controlled Sicily and Italy – which Justinian could not hope to do. Besides, the expense of such an expedition would run into millions. Cappadocian John was also afraid, though he did not say so, that Justinian, in his efforts to raise the necessary money, would go carefully into the accounts of the Quartermaster-General's office at the War Ministry and find evidence there of frauds on a large scale.

His arguments, however, decided Justinian against the project. Everyone was relieved, especially the Treasury officials, who would have been responsible for raising vast sums of money in new taxes. The generals, too, felt easier: each of them had feared that his own merits would single him out as commander of the expedition against the Vandals.

Then a bishop came from Egypt, asking for an immediate audience at the Palace; for he had dreamed a dream of some importance. Justinian received him with his customary affability and the Bishop explained that God Himself had appeared in this dream and ordered him to go and rebuke the Emperor for his irresolution: 'For if he will only undertake this war in defence of the honour of My Son, whom these Arian heretics impiously deny to be My equal, I will march before his armies in battle and make him master of Africa.' This message is less likely to have emanated from the Deity than from a group of African Orthodox clerics, friends of Hilderich's who had fled from Carthage on Geilimer's accession. But Justinian gave it perfect credit, and assured the Bishop that he would obey the divine order at once. These, then, were the circumstances in which he called for Belisarius, whose loyalty and courage had been proved beyond all doubt in the Victory riots. He told him in Theodora's presence: 'Fortunate patrician, it is to you that we are entrusting the capture of Carthage!'

Belisarius, who had been warned by my mistress what Justinian really had in mind, replied: 'Do you mean me alone, Your Serenity, or a dozen commanders each of equal authority with me? For if you mean the former, I can offer you loyal gratitude; but if the latter, only loyal obedience.'

Justinian was about to prevaricate when Theodora broke in: 'Do not trouble the Emperor with unnecessary questions. Certainly he means you as sole commander, do you not, my dear Justinian? You, Narses, see that the commission is drafted at once and brought to the Emperor for signature: the Illustrious Belisarius is to be described there as vice-regent to the Emperor. The great distance between Carthage and the City will unfortunately make it impossible for the Emperor to give his advice in urgent matters, or to ratify high political appointments and treaties with the necessary dispatch. Write, therefore, good Narses: "The orders of the Illustrious Belisarius, Commander of Our Armies in the East, shall, during the conduct of this expedition, be deemed to be Ours."'

Justinian blinked and swallowed a little when the matter was arranged for him in this style. But he did not venture to return to his original plan of multiple command. It was politically plausible in that no one general could hope to gain all the glory and so become a possible rival to himself; but would have been disastrous from the military point of view – as had already been proved in Persia in Anastasius' day. He signed the commission.

This was in the autumn of the year of our Lord 532, a few months after the riots, and the winter was spent in making all necessary preparations. My mistress was glad that the expedition was not sailing until the spring, for about New Year she was expecting a child by Belisarius, and she had determined not to be left behind when he went to the wars. She intended to find a foster-mother for the child and give it into Theodora's charge. This she did, and the child proved to be a daughter whom they named Joannina. The Emperor and Empress stood sponsors for it at the font. This was the only child that my mistress bore to Belisarius, and she proved a disappointment to them in the end.

There were dismal feelings of foreboding in Constantinople when the details of the expedition were announced. The City Governor is reported to have said to Cappadocian John one evening at the Palace: 'I fear that this disaster may prove as great as the one that our grandfathers suffered at the hands of Geiserich.'

And Cappadocian John to have replied cheerfully: 'That cannot be. For in that campaign we lost one hundred thousand men, no less; but now I have persuaded the Emperor to send only fifteen thousand, and most of these are infantry.'

The City Governor again: 'At what fighting strength do you reckon the Vandal army?'

Cappadocian John's reply: 'At more than a hundred thousand, counting their Moorish allies.'

The City Governor, astonished: 'Best of men, what possible hope of success can Belisarius have in that case?'

But Cappadocian John, shrugging: 'A bishop has a right to his dreams.' The phrase became proverbial.

The infantry were of good quality, mostly Isaurian mountaineers; Belisarius had been training them in marching and digging, as well as in the use of weapons. The cavalry numbered only 5,000, because of the difficulty of transporting horses a distance of some 1,500 miles. But among them were the remnants of the Massagetic Huns who had fought so well at Daras and by the Euphrates, 600 of them (for many of the seriously wounded had recovered); and Pharas's 400 Herulians; and Belisarius's well-trained Household Regiment of 1,500 cuirassiers. The remainder were Thracians who had served under Boutzes; but Boutzes himself had remained on the Persian frontier. Belisarius had entrusted the command of these Thracians to Rufinus and to a Massagetic Hun called Aigan, the son of Sunicas, whom Sunicas had commended to Belisarius as he lay dying on the battle-field. Belisarius's chief of staff was an Armenian eunuch named Solomon; he was a eunuch not by deliberate castration but by an accident which had happened to him when a baby in swaddling clothes, and had lived with soldiers all his life.

It needed a fleet of 500 transports to convey this army to Carthage. They were as mixed a collection of vessels as were ever brought together, their burden varying from 30 to 500 tons. They were manned by 30,000 sailors, for the most part Egyptians and Greeks from Asia Minor, and commanded by an Alexandrian admiral. Besides these transports there was a flotilla of ninety-two fast single-banked galleys, all decked in as a protection to the oarsmen in case of a sea-battle. There were twenty oarsmen to each galley, men of Constantinople of the sort called 'marines', who are paid above the usual rate because they can be used as infantry in an emergency. Cappadocian John was made responsible for victualling this fleet, and two officers were sent to the royal pastures in Thrace to round up 3,000 horses and have them ready at Heraclea, on the northern coast of the Sea of Marmora, when the fleet touched there.

We started at last, at the time of the spring equinox. Belisarius and my mistress had an impressive godspeed from Justinian and Theodora, and a blessing from the Patriarch of Constantinople. We embarked at the Imperial harbour, which is close to the Palace, at the point where the Sea of Marmora narrows into the Bosphorus. Here there are broad white marble steps, and gilded state barges, and ornamental trees from the East; and a graceful chapel in which are shown the authentic swaddling clothes of Jesus, and a portrait of him in later life attributed to the Evangelist Luke. Above the harbour stands a sculptural group of a bull in a death-struggle with a lion. We eyed it with superstitious interest, for the Bull is a symbol of the Roman armies, as the Lion is of North Africa. My mistress Antonina said, grinning, to the City Governor who stood by: 'I will wager you five thousand to two thousand that the Bull brings it off. The Lion is under-muscled, and the Bull, though small, is of the fighting breed.'

For good luck Justinian put aboard our vessel, the flag-ship of the fleet, a young Thracian who had just been baptized into the Orthodox Church. He was one of a dwindling sect, the Eunomians, whose peculiarity is that they deny that the Son can be God and eternal, on the grounds that He was once begotten: for eternal generation is, they say, a nonsensical idea. That which is begotten cannot possibly be of one substance with the unbegotten; and contrariwise. The unbegotten remains eternally unbegotten, and the begotten cannot deny the act of begetting. Therefore ... But, at all events, this young man was converted from his heresies and became godson to Belisarius and my mistress Antonina, and took the new name of Theodosius.

He was the handsomest man I ever saw, and I have seen many. He was not so tall and magnificently muscled as Belisarius, but he was strongly and gracefully built and had an extremely mobile face. (The only defect that I could find in him was that the nape of his neck was a trifle narrow and had a deep cleft in it.) But besides all this he was the only man that my mistress had ever met who could talk her own particular sort of happy nonsense with her. Belisarius was witty and eloquent and affectionate and had all the qualities which are admirable in a man, and there was never a woman who was so lucky in her husband as my mistress. He was like the Sun that runs around the heavens – warming creatures and buildings; but, like the Sun, his circle was not complete – he could not shine from the North. It was an incapacity connected with his loyalties: faith and ignorance occupied that quarter of his orbit. But Theodosius shone from the North, as it were, with a laughing light, the quality of which is very difficult for me to express. I can only say that, whatever Belisarius lacked, with this Theodosius seemed to supply my mistress. It was little enough by comparison with what Belisarius had, yet extremely precious to her, even for its littleness.

It is almost impossible, I believe, for one man to love two women at the same time, without a secret reservation in his mind, 'this one I prize the most'. But a woman may very well be in such a situation, as my mistress soon discovered – at once the most happy and the most miserable one possible. She can reconcile the two in her heart, but in their relations with her each ignores her love of the other. The better man (and my mistress would never at any moment have failed to acknowledge Belisarius to be such) is tempted to behave rather unkindly towards her – from an inability to understand the phenomenon of radiance from the North, and from a desire to make a complete orbit of love around her. The other one is so free of jealous or intense feelings that he regards her loving someone else with as little seriousness as her loving himself. His equable humour makes any strong emotions seem absurd.

It was Theodosius's serene airiness in contrast with Belisarius's deep moral gravity that first made my mistress Antonina pair them together in her mind. There was the occasion of the drunken Massagetic Huns at Abydos; and then that matter of the water-bottles, as we neared Sicily. Both must be told about in detail.

After taking the Thracian horses aboard at Perinthus we continued down the Sea of Marmora until we came to the Hellespont, and anchored off Abydos one evening, intending to set sail early the next morning. The currents are very difficult here, and one needs a good north-easterly breeze to assist one in navigating them; but the next morning there was no breeze at all, so we were obliged to wait four days until one sprang up. The men, having been given shore-leave, found themselves at a loose end: there is not much to be done or seen in this part unless one has a taste for antiquities – then one may ride along the coast to the site of Troy and, dismounting, run around the Tomb of Achilles for good luck.

The Massagetic Huns carried with them what is called a 'bee', a sort of yeast that they put into mare's milk to make it ferment after they have beaten it in a bladder with a hollow club to thin it of its fatty parts. At Perinthus they had bought a quantity of mare's milk and treated it in this way, so that by now it was a very potent drink – they call it *kavasse* or *kumys*. In politeness to Aigan I tasted it once and found it far too pungent for my liking, though the after-taste was not unlike the taste of almond-milk; and there seemed something disgusting in its being drawn from a mare. But, as we say when the habits of others are not ours, 'Every fish to his own tipple', and 'Thistles are lettuce to the ass's lips'.

Belisarius did not know about the bee, and had taken what he thought were sufficient precautions against the soldiers supplying themselves with any intoxicating drink beyond the day's ration of sour wine, which they mix with their water to purify it. The Huns, then, had a drunken party ashore, in the course of which one of their number ridiculed two other Huns for losing their way in a ballad – and was immediately killed by them. Belisarius ordered a court-martial on the murderers, who seemed to take a very light view of the crime and pleaded drunkenness as an excuse: they were prepared, they said, to pay the customary blood-money to the dead man's kinsmen. But Belisarius held that to kill a fellow-soldier on the way to the war was a most infamous act. He asked Aigan what was the most infamous death that could be inflicted on a Hun, and Aigan replied 'death by impaling'.

The two Huns were duly impaled on the hill by Abydos, to the great indignation of their comrades, who declared that they were allies of Rome, not Romans, and that their own laws did not make death the penalty for manslaughter committed under the influence of drink. Belisarius paraded them for a personal address, and, so far from making an apology, told them that it was high time that their barbarous code was revised: drunkenness was, in his view, an aggravation of crime, not a mitigation, and while they served under him they must obey his laws. He warned them that he would not overlook any acts of private violence whatsoever committed against fellow-soldiers or prisoners or civilians, unless great provocation could be proved. 'This army must go to battle with clean hands.' Then he took possession of the bee, until such time as the Huns should be safely garrisoned in captured Carthage.

At supper that evening his table-companions sat silent. Belisarius, knowing what was on their minds, nodded in the direction of the hill and asked: 'And what is your frank opinion? And yours?' Armenian John replied: 'It was well deserved.' Rufinus said the same, and Uliaris grunted out: 'A man should not handle a weapon when he is drunk.' Finally, Theodosius, called upon for a comment, remarked carelessly: 'There should have been a third, surely?'

My mistress was the only person present who understood the mocking reference. Belisarius replied seriously: 'No, the other men at the camp-fire were not implicated, according to the evidence.' But my mistress looked at Theodosius and said: 'And if there had been a third, your godfather would not have rewarded him with a drink of wine.' At which Theodosius smiled gratefully to her, and no more was said; but it is a great bond between two strangers when they can carry on a private joke together without anyone, even their intimates, suspecting that their words hold more than they seem to do. For Theodosius meant something of this sort: that the hill suggested Golgotha, the place of the Crucifixion, but that there was missing from this impressive execution a third victim more glaringly innocent even than the other two. My mistress's remark about the sour wine was a reference to the merciful Roman soldier who gave Jesus to drink from the hyssop-sponge raised at the point of a spear.

Theodosius was not a religious-minded person. His baptism into the

Orthodox faith had been a matter of convenience, as my mistress's had been, and he never lost the practical, faintly mocking way of looking at things that I have always found characteristic of the Thracians. He could detect inconsistency and pretentiousness even in the most admirable characters, though not setting himself up as a moral paragon. His emotions and thoughts were at least his own, not borrowed; he conformed outwardly to current conventions, yet in private he acknowledged no authority but his own sense of what was fitting.

As for the incident of the water-bottles: that occurred some weeks later on our way to Sicily. The voyage had been a much longer one than anyone had expected: because, though from Abydos we had a strong following wind which carried us out into the Aegean Sea as far as Lesbos, it dropped to almost nothing at this point, and we were three weeks in rounding the southern coast of Greece. Moreover, the speed of the whole fleet was that of the slowest ship, since Belisarius was anxious that no unit should become detached and arrive at Carthage before the rest of the fleet, thus preventing a surprise. He painted the mainsails of the three leading vessels, ours and two others, with broad vermilion stripes as a guide by day; at night he used stern-lanterns. No ship was allowed to steer more than a cable's length away from its neighbour. At times there was a good deal of bumping and cursing and use of boat-hooks, but no ship lost touch or was stove in.

Then the wind failed completely, and Belisarius ordered a general disembarkation at Methone, a town on the south-western promontory of Greece. This was done as a drill practised in full armour, and the inhabitants were most alarmed. The men were in a listless enough condition by now, and the horses too, so marches and sham-fights were the order until the wind rose again. It was extremely hot at Methone. The soldiers' biscuit-bread which had been brought in sacks from Constantinople began to turn mouldy and stink. Belisarius immediately used his Imperial warrant to requisition fresh bread from the neighbourhood, but did not obtain it before 500 men had died from colic.

He investigated the matter of the biscuits and reported to Justinian. His findings were that the biscuits had been supplied by Cappadocian John in his capacity as Quartermaster-General to the Forces; that, on account of the loss that fresh bread suffers in weight on being hardened to biscuit, the Quartermaster-General had been paid the customary one-fourth more for his contract than for an equal weight of fresh bread, in addition to a fuel allowance for the baking; that he had only slightly baked the bread, and thus not reduced its weight by the necessary one-quarter, while accepting payment as if for proper biscuit; and that he had also pocketed the fuel allowance, though his partial baking had been done for nothing at the furnaces that warm the Public Baths. Justinian later complimented Belisarius on his report, while exonerating Cappadocian John (who had found a scapegoat among his subordinates) from the suspicion of deliberate fraud.

But nobody, not even Cappadocian John, could be blamed for the tainting effect of the heat on the casks of fresh water that we shipped from our next port of call, the island of Zante. Our voyage from Zante across the Adriatic Sea to Sicily was lengthened by sudden calms to sixteen days; and a miserable time it was, because this was now mid-June and cruelly hot weather. My mistress had taken the precaution at Methone of sending me to buy in the open market a number of glass jars of the sort used for pickling olives, to be filled with fresh water and stored in the bottom of the ship up to their necks in sand; it was my task to keep them moist with sea-water. The result was that ours was the only ship's company that had untainted water to drink; and this greatly embarrassed Belisarius, who made a pride of eating the same food as the men under his command, and drinking the same water. What made matters worse was that the supply of sour wine had given out, because of the unexpected length of the voyage.

Belisarius explained the position to his Household officers and asked their advice. He pointed out that there was not enough clean water to be worth the sharing with all the other ships' companies in the fleet; nor could he share with two or three only, for fear of jealousy. Perhaps the noblest course would be to follow the example of the great Cato, who once, on a sultry march in Africa, reproved a soldier for bringing him a helmetful of water when the rest of the army was thirsty, and dashed it to the ground; and of King David of the Jews, who had once done much the same thing with water brought to him from the well at Bethlehem. Now, these lieutenants of Belisarius were all cast in the same mould: they were heroes to a man and honourable to what seemed to me at times an extravagant degree. They were all convinced that they ought not to benefit by my mistress's prudence, but empty the water-bottles overboard! Naturally she grew very angry. At first nobody supported her in her view that it would be not only foolish but an insult to her to drink tainted water when she had been to the trouble of providing fresh – as anybody else with sense had been at liberty to do. Then Theodosius came forward smiling and said to her: 'Godmother Antonina, if nobody else wishes to be the first to forfeit empty honour by drinking your excellent water, I offer myself as a glad victim. Here is my cup. May I help myself? I shall not venture to accuse my godfather of disloyalty to his Emperor in risking the infection of dysentery when the safety of the expedition depends so largely upon his keeping in good health. But I shall at least remind the company that the five wise virgins in the Gospel parable would not have been praised if, on learning that the five foolish virgins had forgotten to fill their lamps, they had poured their own oil away and disabled themselves from attendance on the midnight Bridegroom.'

In a dead silence he filled his cup and drank, throwing his head right back, then filled again and offered the cup to Belisarius. Belisarius held it for a moment in his hand, considering, and finally said: 'Theodosius, you are right: duty takes precedence of honour.' He sipped and handed the cup to Armenian John and Aigan, who sipped too. So here was another bond between Theodosius and my mistress, whose honour he had protected at the risk of losing his own.

We anchored in a desert place near the volcano Etna. There was water there, and grazing for the horses, and we still had enough sacks of biscuit from Methone to last us for some weeks. But Belisarius needed fresh supplies, especially of wine and oil and vegetables. He sent his secretary, Procopius of Caesarea, in a fast galley to procure these things at Syracuse, the capital city, and bring them to us at the port of Catania, where there was safer anchorage. Belisarius knew that a compact had lately been made between Justinian and the Gothic Regent of Italy, Queen Amalasontha (Theoderich's daughter, whose young son, Athalrich, was now king), according to which she should grant him an open market in Sicily for his armies if they happened to pass that way. Amalasontha had been glad to sign this, because her political position was precarious, and Justinian's friendship counted for much.

The Governor of Syracuse accordingly sent a number of vessels along the coast to us filled with the required provisions, and also a few boat-loads of horses to take the place of those that had died on the voyage. That we had not lost more was due to Belisarius's ingenious way of exercising them on ship-board: he had them hoisted in their stalls with a rope under their forelegs until they were standing balanced on their hindlegs. In this position they pawed and staggered about angrily in an attempt to regain their natural posture, and sweated out the bad humours. Procopius brought back extremely good news from Syracuse. A boyhood friend of his, a merchant from Caesarea in Palestine, had just received a cargo from Carthage; and his agent reported that not only did the Vandals not suspect that an expedition was approaching, but they had recently sent away their best forces under the command of Zazo, the brother of King Geilimer, to put down a revolt in Sardinia, which was a Vandal possession. That, further, there had been a successful revolt against the Vandals by the natives of Tripoli, the coastal district which lies between Carthage and Egypt, and that a naval force had been sent there also.

Belisarius decided that no further time must be lost. We sailed out from Catania and touched at the small islands of Gozo and Malta – it was at Malta that the Apostle Paul was once shipwrecked. Then up sprang a strong easterly wind; and by the next morning we had sighted the nearest point of the African coast, a desert promontory called Capoudia, which lies 150 miles to the east of Carthage. As soon as we were in shallow water we furled sail and anchored. Belisarius summoned a general conference of officers on the flag-ship: the question propounded being whether we should disembark here and march along the coast, protected by the fleet, or continue the voyage and make the landing at some point closer to Carthage.

The Egyptian Admiral spoke first, because he had a long experience of the coast-line. He pointed out that Carthage was nine days' march away along a harbourless coast. If the fleet kept pace with the army, standing close inshore, what would happen if a sudden storm sprang up? Two alternatives, equally dangerous, would have to be faced: of being driven ashore and wrecked or of being blown out of touch with the army. The coast was practically waterless, the sun grilling, and troops – in full equipment and carrying rations – would be exhausted by the march. He therefore proposed that we should sail up the coast to a point just short of Carthage, where there was a large lake, the Lake of Tunis, which would afford perfect anchorage.

Rufinus, speaking in support of the Admiral, reminded Belisarius that the Vandals could easily assemble an army five times our size; and that we should not have the protection of any walled towns on our nightly halts, because they had long ago dismantled the fortifications of every town in the Diocese but Carthage and Hippo Regius.

The general opinion of the conference was that the Admiral's plan was a sound one, and that to march slowly along the coast would be to risk losing the advantage of surprise. Belisarius withheld his opinion as yet. He asked the officers, each in turn, whether it was true that their troops had positively refused to fight a sea-battle if the Vandals came out against them.

They admitted that there had been talk of this sort, because the Syracusan sailors in the food-ships had told frightening and incredible yarns about the Vandal fleet – how it consisted chiefly of fast vessels of 1,500 tons burden and five banks of oars that could carve their way through our fleet as a knife through cream cheese. But they swore that they themselves were not afraid, and undertook to induce their men to fight as bravely on sea as on land.

Belisarius then spoke: 'Comrades, I trust that you will not regard what I have to say as the words of a master, or fancy that I have delayed them to the last in order to close the discussion and compel your acquiescence. We are now aware of all the chief factors in the problem and, if you permit me, I shall sum up like a judge and deliver my verdict. But it will not necessarily be a final verdict. If any flaw in my reasoning is pointed out, I shall be most willing to consider an amendment.

'In the first place: it seems that the troops have given fair warning of their refusal to fight the Vandal fleet if it comes out against us, but declare themselves perfectly ready for any battles that may be fought on dry land, whatever the odds. You know as well as I do that one cannot compel men to fight against their will; and if they will fight bravely on land at least, that is as much as it is fair to ask of landsmen. Next: I do not agree that we need forfeit the element of surprise by disembarking our army here. If we send a few fast galleys well ahead, disguised as Egyptian pirates, to seize any vessels that they encounter, we can protect our main fleet from observation. Similarly on land, our cavalry scouts can ride well ahead and prevent any information of our approach from reaching Carthage by road. The argument that a storm might scatter or wreck the ships has to be considered; but surely if a storm came it would be safer to have the troops and horses safely ashore? Worse than a storm, from a military point of view, would be a calm, which would give the Vandals time to prepare. The map shows me, moreover, that to reach the Lake of Tunis we would have to round Cape Bon, at the end of a long promontory with precipitous cliffs, and suddenly alter our course from north-east to south-west. If we had Odysseus's famous bag of winds with us, so that we could release first one and then the other, or if all our vessels were galleys, it might be a different matter; but I think that we cannot risk being delayed by a calm or a contrary wind at the turning point.

'My advice therefore is that we disembark; that the fleet accompanies us slowly as far as the neck of the promontory, from which it is only fifty miles to Carthage by land, but 150 by sea; that we then make straight for Carthage across the hills and around the Lake, and capture it; and that the fleet round the promontory as quickly as possible and join us there as soon as we signal that we need it. As for walled cities: the infantry has been trained by me in the art of digging entrenched camps, which are better than walled towns in a way, because they contain no troublesome civilian problems. Lastly, our men and horses must regain their shore-legs before they fight: a nine days' march is just what they need. Every plan has its drawbacks and dangers, but the great numerical superiority of the Vandals suggests the advantage of a plan as unsuspected as the one I have proposed. Remember, too, that the Roman Africans are Orthodox and that Geilimer's Vandals are regarded as Arian oppressors. If we behave boldly and sensibly we shall have the entire civilian population on our side and not want either for water or for provisions.'

These arguments were unanswerable. We all disembarked, but for a guard of five archers left behind in each ship, and the crews. My mistress Antonina could not be persuaded to remain in the flag-ship, being a woman of outstanding courage.

CHAPTER II

DEFEAT OF THE VANDALS

IN most histories that are published nowadays, one battle reads very much like any other. It will be a test of my historical skill henceforth if I can tell you enough about those battles fought by Belisarius to indicate their difference in character one from another, without wearying you with too much heroic military detail: as a host may give a guest famous old wines to taste without attempting to induce intoxication in him. I must show, for example, that the Battle of the Tenth Milestone differed from the two Persian battles of Daras and the Euphrates Bank in its extreme disorderliness and geographical complexity.

Shortly after landing at Capoudia on the day of St John the Baptist, which is also Midsummer Day, after this three months' voyage, we were greeted by an excellent omen: in digging camp-entrenchments for the night some soldiers unexpectedly released an abundant spring of fresh water. By canalizing this into troughs we were able to water all the horses without the trouble of disembarking water-casks. Belisarius sent a troop of his Household Regiment ahead to Sullecthum, the nearest town. They reached a ravine near the gates at dusk and hid there all night. At early dawn a long train of vegetable-carts and farmers on horses came along the road from the interior; for it was a market-day at Sullecthum. In twos and threes our cuirassiers quietly joined this stream of traffic and occupied the town, which was unwalled, without meeting any opposition. When the townspeople, Roman Africans, awoke, they were instructed to rejoice, because Belisarius was coming to free them from their Vandal oppressors. The priest and mayor and other notables announced themselves as indeed very willing to surrender the keys of the town and put post-horses and other conveniences at our disposal. On the next day we were billeted in Sullecthum, which consists of square white-washed stone houses with flat roofs, each in its well-kept garden; and since Belisarius had impressed on the troops the importance of behaving in a friendly and honest way to the natives – by flogging some men who stole fruit from an orchard – we were treated with extreme hospitality.

A royal courier of the Vandals was detained, and Belisarius, who always gave his enemies the chance to submit before attacking them, sent him to Carthage with a message to the Vandal magistrates there. He assured them that he had not come to make war upon them, but only to dethrone the usurper Geilimer and restore their rightful king, Hilderich; and he called on their assistance in Justinian's name. The sending of this letter may be regarded as an imprudent step, and in contradiction of his avowed intention to take the city by surprise: because the courier, if he rode fast, would arrive six days ahead of us and give the alarm. But Belisarius's moral scruples about fighting unnecessary battles were not easily smothered. Besides, such an open announcement of his intentions suggested that he had brought extremely strong forces with him to carry them into practice, and the Vandals might well be frightened into compliance.

King Geilimer, however, was not at Carthage, but at Bulla with most of his fighting men, some days' journey away inland. His brother Ammatas, to whom the courier delivered the message, immediately forwarded it to him. The post-system in the Vandal kingdom being very well organized, Geilimer was able to reply on the following day. His message was that Hilderich was to be put to death at once, and that Ammatas was to prepare to hold the road by which we were approaching, at the tenth milestone from Carthage, where there is a narrow defile between hills. Ammatas's forces must be in position by the third day of July. He would himself hurry up with cavalry reinforcements and take us in the rear on that day, unless the situation had meanwhile altered. Of this exchange of letters Belisarius knew nothing as yet.

We continued our march by way of Leptiminus and the great corn-port of Hadrumetum, covering twelve miles a day. Meanwhile we were well supplied with fruit and fresh bread by the country people, who greeted us with the utmost enthusiasm, poor souls. Every night we entrenched. To build the necessary stockade, each soldier carried a long, pointed stake, which was planted in the rampart. The fleet kept pace with us on our right, and the wind remained favourable. Armenian John, with 300 of the Household Regiment, formed the vanguard, and the Massagetic Huns protected our left flank. Belisarius commanded the rearguard. At last we reached the neck of the promontory and must part company with the fleet; but our regret was soothed by the beauty of the place that we came upon at this point, the Paradise of Grasse. This is a royal palace which Geiserich built and surrounded with a noble park. There are great groves of trees here, of every variety suitable to the climate, and fish-pools and fountains and lawns and shady walls and arbours and beds of flowers; and an immense orchard consisting of trees arranged in quincunx, that is, in groups of five, each quincunx consisting of trees of five different varieties. The African climate is hotter than ours, so that at midsummer there was ripe fruit, which we had not expected to find until early August – second-figs and peaches and grapes and the like. The troops camped under these trees and were permitted to eat what they could, but not to carry any fruit away. We all gorged ourselves on bullaces and damsons and figs and mulberries, yet when we marched on again the trees still seemed as heavily laden as ever.

This was the day on which we heard of the execution of Hilderich, and on which King Geilimer's scouts first made contact with our rear-guard. But Belisarius continued forward without lagging or hurrying. By the sixth day, the fourth day of July, we had crossed the peninsula and, skirting the Lake of Tunis, drawn near to the Tenth Milestone. Here there was a small village and a posting-station; we halted five miles away from it. Belisarius chose a defensible site for the usual fortified camp, where we dug ourselves to safety as usual, each man fixing his stake in the stockade.

Meanwhile the Vandal forces were closing in on us. Ammatas led out the garrison from Carthage; Geilimer's nephew, the son of Zazo, advanced against our flank; and Geilimer himself threatened our rear. Now, the Vandals, like the Goths, were fine horsemen and clever with lance and broadsword, but only their infantry carried bows. They had no recent experience of horse-archers like ours, for their only enemies in this country, the wild Moorish horsemen of the desert, used javelins. This was greatly to our advantage. As for their fighting qualities: these fair-skinned, fair-haired Northerners had now, by the third generation, become acclimatized to Africa. They had intermarried with the natives, changed their diet and yielded to the African sun (which makes for ill-temper rather than endurance) – and to such luxuries as silk clothes, frequent bathing, spiced foods, orchestral music, and massage instead of exercise. This enervating life had brought out strongly a trait common to all Germanic tribes, namely an insecure hold on the emotions. However, their fighting forces had increased in numbers since Geiserich's time from 50,000 to 80,000, apart from their numerous Moorish allies.

Armenian John with the vanguard pushed on ahead, and on the third day of July, about midday, turning a corner in the road close to the Tenth Milestone, he came upon a force of 100 well-mounted Vandal horsemen halted negligently outside the posting-station. John's men, who were riding in column, could not deploy, because of the narrowness of the defile through which the road passed at this point. There was no opportunity for using their bows, so they immediately charged with the lance, just as they were. The Vandals formed up hurriedly and stood their ground. In the ensuing skirmish twelve of our men went down; but then Armenian John pulled a weighted throwing-dart from his shield and with it struck their leader, a handsome youth in gilded armour, full in the forehead at short range. He toppled from his horse, dead, and the Vandals then broke away, with cries of dismay, pursued by our men. More Vandals, leisurely trotting up the road in troops of twenty or thirty, became involved in the rout; and as a snowball rolled down a hill picks up new snow and grows to monstrous proportions, so with the Vandals in flight. With lance and throwing-dart and arrow the cuirassiers pursued, killing methodically, not allowing the enemy the opportunity to reform, driving them headlong out of the defile.

It was possible to deploy in the plain beyond, and the slaughter was even greater there. Armenian John pushed the Vandals back to the very walls of Carthage, and by a view of the corpses dotted here and there over the plain in those ten miles one could have imagined that an army of 20,000 men, not a mere half-squadron, had been at work.

Meanwhile King Geilimer's forces and those of his nephew converged on the Tenth Milestone. In a plain which had once been a salt marsh the nephew had the ill-luck to come suddenly upon the Massagetic Huns. He outnumbered them by 3,000 to 600, but the outlandish look of these hollow-eyed, long-haired fellows (who lived, remember, a year's journey away from Carthage and had never before been seen on African soil) scared the superstitious Vandals, and the unexpected, stinging showers of arrows were terrible. They fled unanimously without coming to blows at all, and were massacred almost to a man. As for Geilimer, he was unaware of his nephew's fate and had lost touch with Belisarius's rearguard, because of the hilly nature of the ground. Belisarius knew by now that Armenian John had cleared the defile of the enemy; but had received no further reports from him, and feared that he might have been ambushed and stand in need of assistance. Leaving the infantry behind in the stockade, he ordered the Herulians under his blood-brother Pharas, and a squadron of Thracian Goths, to gallop ahead and investigate; he followed at a more leisurely pace with the main body of cavalry.

King Geilimer was close to the Tenth Milestone now, with 30,000 cavalry. At the stockade my mistress had taken command and organized the defence in a very capable way; for she had studied these matters with Belisarius, and her courage and humorous manner of address inspired great confidence in all. However, her military capacities were not put to any severe test: Geilimer passed by our stockade without seeing it, for a hill lay between. He missed Belisarius too, who was advancing by a different road.

When Pharas and the Thracian Goths reached the posting-house where the skirmish had taken place, they found the people there in a state of the greatest excitement; because the dead Vandal in the gilded armour was none other than Ammatas himself, Geilimer's brother.

Pharas and his Herulians pushed on in search of Armenian John. Hardly had they gone when a cloud of dust was seen to the southward, and a look-out signalled enormous forces of Vandal cavalry – King Geilimer's men. The Thracian Goths immediately rushed to seize the hill commanding the entrance to the defile, but the Vandals soon thrust them off it by sheer weight of numbers, and they retreated at a gallop on the main body. Thus King Geilimer, with an army five times the size of ours, was left in possession of the highly defensible defile. Armenian John and Pharas were on one side, and Belisarius on the other, our fleet was far away – the battle was as good as lost to us.

Now, in Constantinople there is a square called 'The Square of Brotherly Love' with a fine group of statuary in it, on a tall pedestal, commemorating the fraternal devotion of the sons of the Emperor Constantine – who subsequently destroyed one another without mercy. And among the Greeks and other inhabitants of the Mediterranean lands true fraternal devotion, because of the laws of inheritance, is so rare that its genuine occurrence, even in less exalted persons than young men born in the purple, would indeed be worthy of sculptural commemoration. Why, the oldest poem in the Greek language, the *Works and Days* of Hesiod, grew out of an instance of fraternal squabbling. But with the Germanic tribes brotherly devotion is the rule rather than a rarity, and the luxurious life that they lived in Africa had by no means weakened this trait in the Vandals. When, therefore, King Geilimer reached the posting-house by the Milestone in the middle of the afternoon, and the news was broken to him that his brother Ammatas had been killed, this was a terrible thing for him. He gave himself up to barbarian grief and was incapable of taking stock of the tactical position: he could think only in terms of sepulchres and funeral elegies.

Belisarius had rallied the Thracian-Gothic fugitives and pressed on with them to the Milestone, where the Vandal forces were now crowded together in complete disorder. The cavalry had descended from the commanding hill in order to observe what was happening, and remained to join in the general lamentations over Ammatas's death. Geilimer, who now heard also of the defeat and death of his nephew at the hands of the Massagetic Huns, was blubbering disconsolately, and no military thought or action could be expected of him.

Belisarius, surprised but gratified by what he saw, at once divided his squadrons into two compact masses and sent them up the hills on either side of the defile; and, when they were in position, signalled a simultaneous attack on the mass below and between. Volleys of arrows lent sting to that impetuous charge, the slope of the hill lent it irresistible momentum. Hundreds of the enemy went down at the first onset. Then our squadrons disengaged and, after withdrawing a little way up the slope and letting loose another volley of arrows, charged once more. They repeated this manoeuvre again and again. Within half an hour all the surviving Vandals but two or three squadrons, who were cut off in the defile, were away in full flight towards the salt-marsh, where a great number of them were headed off and killed by the Massagetic Huns. As for Armenian John in the plain outside Carthage, his men had become so scattered from plundering the dead that he could not easily rally them. Pharas's arrival did not help matters, for there was loot for his Herulians too, and it was some time before the combined force of 700 returned to Belisarius's assistance, arriving just before the close and completing the victory with a charge up the defile.

It was a battle of which Belisarius said: 'I am grateful but ashamed: as a hard-pressed chess-player might be when a temperamental opponent has thrown away the game by sacrificing his best pieces. Perhaps, after all, I should have taken the Admiral's advice, and made straight for Carthage by sea; for the Milestone defile was an impassable barrier, had it been resolutely held.'

On the following morning my mistress came up with the infantry' and we all went forward together to Carthage. We arrived late in the afternoon, and found the gates thrown open to us. But Belisarius forbade any of us to enter the city, not so much because he feared a possible ambush as because he could not trust the troops to refrain from plundering. Carthage was a Roman city redeemed, not a Vandal city captured, and must be offered no violence. The jubilant citizens had lighted candles and lamps in almost every window, so that the city was illuminated as if for a festival; and very beautiful it looked from where we were, being built on gradually rising ground. Excited citizens came running out to visit our camp, with wreaths and presents for the soldiers. What a pity, they cried, that we were not allowed to participate in such marvellous scenes of unrestrained jubilation. All the vile Vandals who had not been able to escape had sought sanctuary in the churches; and there were tremendous processions in the streets, led by the bishops, of singing and cheering Orthodox Christians!

That evening the fleet arrived, for the wind had turned just as they were rounding Cape Bon; and anchored in the Lake of Tunis – all but a small division of warships that went off on an unauthorized expedition to the outer port of Carthage, the crews plundering the warehouses. When Belisarius knew that the fleet had arrived he said: 'Yet if, risking unfavourable winds and a sea-battle, I had taken the Admiral's advice, I see now that I should have chosen wrong. For a sea-attack upon Carthage would have been madness. The defences of the harbour could not have been pierced, the sea-walls being lofty and well-manned. And if it had not been for the panic raised by the news of King Geilimer's defeat, which caused the Vandal garrison to remove the huge booms from the entrances to the Lake of Tunis and the outer harbour, so as to escape themselves in all the available ships, our fleet would not have been able to enter. It was a problem that had no solution. We should never have attempted the expedition with such small forces. Yet with greater forces would we have been so successful?'

The next morning, when it was fully day, he disembarked the marines. After giving strict orders as to the importance of keeping on good terms with the natives, he marched the whole army into Carthage. Then, billeting arrangements having been made on the previous night, each detachment moved off to the street assigned to it in as orderly a manner as if this had been Adrianople or Antioch or

Constantinople itself. My mistress Antonina went with Belisarius to the Royal Palace, which they made their home; we all sat down in the banquet hall at dinner-time to eat the very banquet that Ammatas had ordered for King Geilimer, the royal servants waiting upon us. Afterwards Belisarius sat on Geilimer's throne and dispensed justice in the name of the Emperor. The occupation of the city had been so quietly undertaken that business was not in the least disturbed. Apart from the matter of the warehouse robberies, into which he made a stern inquiry, there was no crime that called for punishment and very few complaints.

This day was celebrated the feast of St Cyprian, the patron of Carthage, though it wanted two months of the correct date; because St Cyprian's storm, a violent north-east wind which is expected in mid-September, had also anticipated its date and blown the fleet safely into harbour. The Cathedral of St Cyprian, which had been seized as an Arian place of worship some years before, was in the hands of the Orthodox again, so that the feast was celebrated with ecclesiastical triumph and hosannas.

The city is a grand one, full of shops and statues, and colonnades of the local yellow marble, and baths and street-markets and a huge Hippodrome on a hill – of everything in fact that a city should be, though the squares are not so large as those of Constantinople and the streets much narrower. A radiance of liberty continued to shine for weeks in the faces of the inhabitants, and every day seemed a festival. The extraordinary ease with which the Vandals had been defeated was almost the only topic of conversation, and, to account for it, everyone began recalling his or her prophetic dreams or domestic omens.

A prophetic quality was even found in a schoolchildren's rhyme, long current in the streets:

Gamma shall chase Beta out;
Again, contrariwise,
Beta shall Gamma put to rout
And sling out both his eyes.

This rhyme was based on a horn-book used in the local monastic schools for the learning of the Greek alphabet: the first letter '*alpha*' was to be memorized as being the initial letter of '*anthos*', a flower; and '*beta*' as standing for '*Balearicos*', a Balearic slinger; and '*gamma*' for '*Gallos*', a Gallic spearman. These figures were drawn by the monks in the horn-book to fix the letters in the minds of the children. But the children had a notion that the Balearic and the Gaul, on opposite pages of the parchment pamphlet, were enemies. So, in their game of 'Gaul and Balearic', one child was the Gaul and pursued another, the Balearic, with a stick; but as soon as he caught him the Gaul ran away again, and the Balearic, in pursuit, attacked him with pebbles. The rhyme referred to this game. But the popular interpretation of it as a prophecy was that King Geiserich had chased out Count Boniface, the Roman General who had invited him there from Andalusia, and now Belisarius had put King Geilimer to rout and killed his brother and nephew. For the initial letters corresponded exactly.

Belisarius himself had no time to spend on self-congratulation or the analysis of prophecies. He at once set to work a number of Vandal prisoners, and all the available masons and unskilled labourers of the city, and a great number of sailors, and whatever infantry he could spare from garrison-duty, at repairing the city-walls to landward which had fallen into a ruinous condition, and at digging a deep, stockaded trench about them. This was a great undertaking. Though the city on its swelling promontory is protected by water on three sides, its fortifications are of enormous extent: a triple line seven miles long, across the neck of the promontory, of walls forty feet high with strong towers at intervals; and a fifteen-mile inner wall, also very strong, where the land begins to rise; and coastal defences. There are two fortified harbours – the outer for merchant vessels, and the inner for warships, of which more than two hundred can be accommodated at a time. The inner harbour was empty when we arrived, the greater part of the Vandal Navy being away with Zazo at Sardinia, and other ships having been sent to Tripoli, and the garrison having escaped in the remainder.

A day or two later a Vandal warship was signalled and allowed to enter the harbour unmolested, because it was clear that the crew had no notion that their city was in our hands. The captain was arrested as soon as he disembarked, and was thunderstruck at the sudden change of sovereignty. He bore a letter for King Geilimer from his brother Zazo announcing a complete victory in Sardinia, and trusting that the Imperial fleet that had been reported on its way to Carthage had met with deserved destruction. King Geilimer was now reorganizing his forces at Bulla – an inland town four days' march away to the eastward, and the ancient capital of the Numidian kings. He had already sent a letter to Zazo, by one of his galleys stationed farther down the coast, imploring him to return.

A fortnight later Zazo was back in Africa with his entire force – Sardinia lies only 150 miles to the northward – and was embracing his brother Geilimer on the plain at Bulla. As they stood there, weeping silently together, locked in each other's arms, they formed a statue of brotherly love that would have made the fortune of any sculptor who could have reproduced it. And wordlessly, following the royal example, each one of Zazo's men singled out a man of Geilimer's for a similar embrace, and then all began weeping and wringing their hands. A most fantastic sight it must have been!

Then the combined Vandal armies moved against Carthage. Geilimer was astonished to find the outer defences protected by a newly dug, stockaded trench, and most of the weak places in the outermost of the three walls repaired. They did not dare to attack the wall, which was held by sharp-shooting infantry, and contented themselves with making a breach in the fifty-mile long aqueduct which supplies the city with water. But Belisarius had already taken the precaution of temporarily diverting the water from the baths and ornamental pools into the deep, underground, drinking-water reservoirs. The Vandals also cut off the supply of fruit and vegetables from the interior; but this made no impression on the city, which could supply itself from the sea and from its own gardens. To be a Vandal in Africa had meant to live tax-free and enjoy feudal privileges, so that the Vandal suburb of Carthage, to the right of the old city as one sails in from the sea, was composed of magnificent residences, each standing in a park with extensive orchards and kitchen-gardens. These estates Belisarius appropriated for the billeting of the troops; and as it was the fruitful autumn season we were all extremely well off for supplies. The city granaries were well stocked, too.

Then King Geilimer tried secretly to persuade some of our troops to mutiny: the Thracian Goths, who were their Arian co-religionists, and the Massagetic Huns, who had a grievance – when peace had been signed with Persia they had not been sent home to their native steppes at the other side of the Persian Empire, as had been promised, but shipped to Africa. The Goths merely laughed at the disloyal suggestion and reported it at once; but it was some time before Belisarius, by treating the Huns with particular honour and inviting them to a number of banquets, won their full confidence and made them confess that they had seriously considered the Vandal proposal – as he already knew from his lieutenant Aigan. They explained that they did not wish to be detained in Africa as garrison troops, to live and die so far from their homes. Such attractions as silk garments, and crystal drinking-vessels for their *kavasse*, and full bellies, and plump, loving women, could not outweigh their homesickness for the wide, wind-swept steppe and the wagons of their own folk. Then Belisarius swore an oath, by his own honour, that they would be allowed to go home as soon as the Vandals were conclusively defeated; and in return they swore renewed loyalty to him.

When, in early December, the wall was repaired and once more defensible throughout its seven-mile length even without the trench, Belisarius decided to lead his army out against the Vandals. If he were defeated now, he at least had a secure place for retreat. He commanded the infantry, which formed the main body, in person. The advance guard, consisting of all his cavalry except for 500 of his Household cuirassiers, whom he had kept behind with him, found the enemy at Tricamaron, twenty miles away, and attacked at once, as they had been ordered to do. The character of this battle was unusual. The Vandals, although again enormously superior in numbers, stood dully on the defensive, as if they were a poor sort of infantry recruits. Armenian John, at the head of the remaining 1,000 Household cuirassiers, tried to tempt them out against him by skirmishing attacks. At last, finding them immovable and realizing that they had lost all courage, he charged in earnest, unfurling the Imperial standard. Geilimer had, for some superstitious reason, ordered his men to discard lance and spear and fight only with their swords: which put them at a great disadvantage.

Soon Uliaris had the good fortune to kill Zazo with a lance-thrust; when his death was known the Vandal centre broke and fled back to their camp. The wings followed, as soon as the attack became general, without striking a blow. For a battle that was to settle the fate of a huge kingdom it was remarkably bloodless and one-sided, and lasted scarcely a full hour from start to finish. We lost fifty men, and they 800. Our infantry had again not come into action at all, for they were half a day's march behind. They arrived late that afternoon and prepared to attack the Vandal camp, which was a vast ring of covered country-wagons protected by a flimsy palisade.

When King Geilimer saw our main body approaching, he caught

up his favourite little nephew, Ammatas's six-year-old son, set him on the crupper of his saddle, told him to hold tight, and galloped away with him, followed by a retinue of brothers-in-law and cousins and such-like; without so much as a word of explanation or apology to his generals. Being given so commanding an example of cowardice by their sovereign, these generals did not think to organize the defence of the camp. Squadron by squadron, the army scattered in all directions: a shameful prelude to a shameful scene.

Without a blow we captured the camp and everything that it contained; the men broke ranks and the game of grab-all began at once. Never was such plunder offered to a deserving soldiery. Not only was there plunder of gold and jewels, both ecclesiastical and personal, and carved ivories and silks from chests on the wagons, but also human plunder – the Vandal women and children, whom their menfolk had basely left to their fate. Now, Belisarius had made it clear enough that, although old military custom gave the victors of a battle a right to despoil the enemy's camp, he would hang or impale any man found guilty of rape, which was an offence against the laws of God. Belisarius, as you know, was in the habit of enforcing orders of this sort, and needed only to make a law once – unlike Justinian, his master, who often issued the same edict again and again, because, lacking the resolution to enforce it, he could thus at least keep the penalties fresh in the memory of his subjects.

So no rape took place, in the sense of women being forced against their will. But there was a great deal of earnest love-making on the part of the women themselves, many of whom were extremely good-looking and nearly all delicately nurtured. For they had no reason to remain faithful to husbands who deserted them in this cowardly fashion. Moreover, they took the practical view that, faced with slavery, they had no chance now of ever resuming their comfortable life at Carthage, which had been interrupted by this disagreeable campaign, except as the wives of our men – the better men. Many of them had their children to consider, too. They assumed, as most of our men did themselves, that when the fighting was done the army of invasion would become the military aristocracy of Africa, dispossessing the Vandals, man for man, of all their personal properties. Our men had been encouraged in this view by a sermon preached at the Cathedral by the Bishop of Carthage, on the text from the Evangelist Luke: 'When a strong man, armed, keepeth his palace, his goods are at peace. But when a stronger shall come upon him, he taketh from him all his armour wherein he trusted and divideth his spoils.' This prospect of becoming noblemen in so prosperous and pleasant a land delighted them all, except only the Massagetes.

But it was hard for me to decide whether it was a comic or a tragic sight to see these women hurriedly selecting suitable husbands and offering themselves to them with promises of land and cattle and fine furnished houses in Carthage as dowries. The men, except the Thracian Goths, did not understand a word of the Vandal language. Unless a woman was particularly attractive or offered herself to a man with a store of jewels and gold in the bosom of her robe he shook her off and went in search of better bargains. In point of numbers, there was at least one Vandal woman for every man of our army. Several of the more modest women crowded around me because I was a eunuch, hoping by marriage with me to preserve their chastity as well as their freedom. My mistress, too, had innumerable offers of ladies' maids. She had been among the first to enter the camp; and it was a fine haul of treasure that she made from the wagons, with the help of her domestics.

What with plundering, and the gross enjoyment of sexual pleasure freely offered, the army became utterly disorganized. If a single troop of Vandals had attempted to recapture that camp two hours later they would have won an easy triumph. Our soldiers had been filling their helmets from the barrels of sweet wine on the wagons, and now wandered about, quarrelling, plundering, singing discordantly; selling one another unwieldy or unwanted objects for small quantities of ready cash; accepting the caresses of the women; and finally roaming outside the camp in search of more plunder that had perhaps been concealed by fugitives in neighbouring caves or under stones. This wild sort of business continued all night. Belisarius went about from one point to another with six faithful men and put down violence, wherever he came across it, with a heavy hand. The troops were so drenched by their sudden good fortune, having become quite rich men, most of them, at a single stroke, that they were all convinced that they could now retire on their earnings without any further military obligation. When early dawn came, Belisarius climbed up on a mound in the centre of the camp, with my mistress at his side, appealing loudly for discipline, and enlarging on the dangers of a counter-attack. At first he received no answer at all. Then with his own lips he blew 'Assemble the Whites!' on a trumpet, and his Household cuirassiers gradually remembered that the penalty for absence off parade was a severe flogging. So one by one they unwillingly came together, lugging their plunder along with the help of their newly acquired families. At my mistress's suggestion Belisarius sent a convoy of plunder back to Carthage, the goods tied in bundles and piled in the captured wagons: a wagon for each half-section, and the captives of that half-section walking beside it, with a responsible senior soldier in charge.

Then he sent Armenian John with 200 men in pursuit of King Geilimer, with orders to bring him back, alive or dead, wherever he might be; and Uliaris, who was justly proud of his success in killing Zazo, volunteered to go too. Belisarius now ordered a general parade and threatened to charge the drunken mob of soldiers with the lance unless they returned to duty; which they soon did. He sent the cavalry to scour the neighbouring country for Vandals; of whom thousands were found to have taken sanctuary in village churches. Their lives were spared, and they were marched back, disarmed, under infantry guard to Carthage.

Armenian John and Uliaris pursued Geilimer for five days and nights towards Hippo Regius, a prosperous port about 200 miles to the west of Carthage, and would have overtaken him on the next day but for a most unhappy accident. At dawn Uliaris, feeling cold, drank a great deal of wine to warm himself. His stomach being empty, he became intoxicated and began to talk and joke in a foolish, genial manner. An old sergeant reproved him and said: 'If your master Belisarius were to see you now, Noble Uliaris, you would be in danger of impalement.'

'Pish!' replied Uliaris. 'No man is drunk who can shoot straight.' So saying, he took aim at the first target that presented itself – a hoopoe bird, with speckled plumage and yellow crest, sitting in a thorn-tree on a mound near by. Off whizzed the arrow, and Uliaris cried out: 'Is this the shooting of a drunken man? As I told our master myself, at Abydos, no drunken man should ever handle a weapon.'

All laughed, for he shot very wide. But their laughter was soon cut short, for a cry went up from the other side of the mound that a man was wounded. It proved to be Armenian John himself, and the arrow had sunk in at his neck, beyond the barbs.

Thus the pursuit of King Geilimer ended for a while. Armenian John died a few minutes later in Uliaris's arms, and Uliaris, overcome with shame and horror, fled for sanctuary to a village shrine close by; so that the soldiers were left leaderless. John's death was the first great grief that Belisarius experienced, but he bore it without any loud outcry in the Vandal style. When the soldiers reported Uliaris's remorse and Armenian John's dying words – 'By your love for me, dearest master, I implore you not to take vengeance on our old comrade' – he forgave Uliaris. Armenian John was buried in that place, and Belisarius endowed the tomb with a perpetual income. Uliaris never again touched wine for the rest of his life, except at the Eucharist ceremony. Years later, when his campaigning days were over, he became a monk, and served God in the monastery of St Bartimaeus at Blachernae by the Golden Horn.

Belisarius himself resumed the pursuit of King Geilimer, who had almost escaped from Africa in a boat filled with treasure. He was trying to sail to his ally, the King of the Visigoths, in Spain. But a contrary wind blew him back to Hippo Regius, and he took refuge with a tribe of friendly Moors on a precipitous mountain named Pappua, not far from Hippo and overlooking the sea. The treasure ship fell into the hands of Belisarius, who could not, however, afford to wait in the neighbourhood until the spoils were completed with the crown and person of Geilimer. He was needed elsewhere. So, after receiving the submission of the local authorities at Hippo, he cast about for a responsible soldier to undertake the siege of Pappua; and hit upon his blood-brother Pharas, who undertook the charge. While Pharas and his Herulians camped at the foot of the mountain and prevented Geilimer from escaping, Belisarius continued his task of capturing and disarming fugitive Vandals throughout the Diocese. He assembled his prisoners at Carthage and used them as labourers on the fortifications.

He also sent out expeditions to the various detached parts of the Vandal Empire, to win these back to their former allegiance, increasing his army by levies of Roman Africans. He sent one expedition to Corsica and Sardinia, armed with the head of Zazo as a proof that he was not lying when he claimed to have conquered Carthage; and another to Morocco with the head of Ammatas, who had formerly governed that country; and another to Tripoli; and still another to the fertile Balearic Islands, rich in olive-oil and almonds and figs. All these islands or regions submitted at once to his authority.

The only failure that he experienced was in Sicily, where, in Justinian's name, he claimed the promontory of Lilybaeum as part of the

Vandal Empire: on the ground that it had passed to the Gothic Crown in the dowry that King Theoderich gave King Hilderich with his sister. The Goths of Sicily refused to surrender this place, though it was rocky and desolate enough, and assisted the small Vandal garrison there to drive Belisarius's men away. Then Belisarius wrote a stern letter to the Governor of Sicily, reasserting Justinian's inalienable claim to the place, and threatening war if they refused; for he was aware that a foothold in Sicily would be a security against a possible Gothic invasion of Africa. I mention this matter of Lilybaeum because it later assumed great political importance.

Now let me close this chapter with the conclusion of the story of King Geilimer. There he was with his nephews and cousins and brothers-in-law on Mount Pappua, living with the wild Moorish tribesmen, in despair of rescue – what more miserable man in all Africa? For if the Vandals could have been described as the most luxurious nation in the world, their neighbours the Moors were among the most poverty-stricken, living all the year round in underground huts which were stifling or dank according to the season. They slept on the floor, each with only a single sheepskin under him, and wore the same rough shirt and hooded burnous, winter and summer; and had no armour worth the name and few possessions. Bread, wine and oil were absent from their diet, which consisted of water and herbs and unleavened barley-cake made not of milled flour but of grains bruised in a rough mortar and baked in the embers.

The sufferings of Geilimer and his family cannot easily be understated. They were forced to be grateful to their Moorish friends for the miserable hospitality which these offered; and since Pharas was keeping strict guard, no fresh supplies could enter. Soon the barley began to give out. They had no amusements, no baths, no horses, no charming women, no music; and far in the distance below them they could see the white walls and towers of Hippo Regius, and the oval of the Hippodrome, and vessels sailing in and out of the harbour; and among the dark masses of green, which were orchards, shone little silver patches, which were cool fish-pools.

Pharas, growing weary of the siege, attempted an assault on the mountain cliff; but his Herulians were repulsed with heavy loss by the Moorish garrison, who toppled boulders down upon them. He decided to starve Geilimer out. One day he wrote him a letter which ran as follows:

Dear Sir and King, I greet you.

I am a mere barbarian and totally uneducated. But I am speaking this to a scribe who will record what I have to tell you faithfully, I trust. (If not, I will whip him well.) What in the world, my dear Geilimer, has come upon you that you and your kinsmen stay perched up on that desolate crag with a pack of naked, verminous Moors? Is it perhaps that you wish to avoid becoming a slave? What is slavery? A foolish word. What living man is not a slave? None. My men are slaves to me in all but name; and I to my *anda*, Belisarius; and he to the Emperor Justinian; and Justinian, they say, to his wife, the beautiful Theodora; and she to someone else, I know not whom, but perhaps it is her God or some bishop or other. Come down, monarch of Mount Pappua, and become a fellow-slave with the great Belisarius, my master and *anda*, to the Emperor Justinian, the slave of a slave. Belisarius is willing, I know, to spare your life and send you to Kesarorda [Constantinople] where you shall be made a patrician and given rich estates and pass the rest of your life in every comfort, among horses and fruit-trees and full-bosomed women with charmingly small noses. He will pledge you his word, I am confident, and once you have that assurance, you have everything.

Signed:

× the mark of Pharas, the Herulian

your well-wisher.

Geilimer sobbed when he had read this letter. Using the ink and parchment which Pharas had thoughtfully sent with his messenger, he answered briefly that honour forbade him to yield; for the war was an unjust one. He prayed that God would punish Belisarius one day for the misery that he had inflicted on the innocent Vandals. He ended: 'As for me, I cannot write more; for misfortune has robbed me of my wits. Farewell, then, good-hearted Pharas, and of your charity send me a harp and a sponge, and a single loaf of white bread.'

Pharas read the last sentence over and over, but could make no sense of it. The messenger then interpreted it: Geilimer wished to experience again the smell and taste of good bread, which he had not eaten for so long a time; and the sponge was to treat an inflamed eye – for the Moors suffer from ophthalmia, which is infectious; and the harp was to provide musical accompaniment to an elegy that he had composed upon his misfortunes. Then Pharas, being a man of generous feelings, sent the gifts, but did not relax his watch.

One day, when the siege had lasted three months, King Geilimer was sitting in a hut watching a Moorish woman, his hostess, making a very small barley-cake. When she had pounded the barley and made a paste of it with water and kneaded it a little, she put it to bake in the embers of her thorn fire. Two children, his little nephew and the son of his hostess, were crouched beside the hearth, both very hungry. They waited impatiently for the cake to be baked. The young Vandal was suffering severely from intestinal worms, caught from the Moorish children, which rob the stomach of its sustenance and so increase the natural appetite. The cake was only half-baked, but he could wait no longer, and snatched it from the ashes and, without dusting it or waiting for it to cool, thrust it into his mouth and began eating it. The young Moor seized him by the hair of his head, struck him on the temple with his fist, and thumped him between the shoulders, so that the cake flew out of his mouth; and then ate it himself.

This was too much for the sensitive soul of Geilimer. He immediately took a pointed stick and a torn piece of sheepskin, and ink of powdered charcoal and goat's milk, and wrote to Pharas again. He said that he surrendered on the terms that had been proposed; but he must first be given Belisarius's pledge in writing.

Thus the siege ended, for Belisarius gave the pledge required and sent an escort to bring Geilimer to him. Geilimer descended from the mountain with all his family; and a few days later, at Carthage, he met Belisarius for the first time, who came to greet him in the suburbs.

I was present at that meeting, in attendance on my mistress, and I was a witness of King Geilimer's pitiful and strange behaviour. For, as he came towards Belisarius, he smiled, and the smile changed to hysterical laughter, and the laughter to weeping. There were tears in Belisarius's eyes, too, as he took the former monarch by the hand and led him into a neighbouring house for a drink of water. He laid him down on a bed and comforted him as a woman comforts a sick child.

CHAPTER 12

BELISARIUS'S CONSULSHIP

THOUGH the Vandals were crushed beyond question, the wild Moors of the interior still constituted a threat to our men and to the 8,000,000 unwarlike Roman Africans of the Diocese. The Moors, who numbered perhaps 2,000,000, had been at constant war with the Vandals and, as the latter degenerated, had gradually encroached on their territories. When Belisarius first landed, all but a few, such as the tribe on Mount Pappua, allied themselves with him, promising to help him against his enemies and sending their children to him as hostages. These Moors live principally in Morocco, which lies opposite to Spain, but they are also settled in the interior of the whole coast from Tripoli to the Atlantic Ocean. They claim to be descendants of those Canaanites whom Joshua the son of Nun drove out of Palestine. Ever since the time when the Emperor Claudius, shortly after the time of the Crucifixion, conquered and annexed Morocco, their paramount chiefs have not been acknowledged by their vassals as worthy of obedience unless presented with insignia of office by the Emperor himself. The insignia consist of a silver staff, fluted with gold; and a crown-shaped cap of silver tissue, banded with silver; and a white Thessalian cape with a golden brooch on the right shoulder containing a medallion of the Emperor; and a gold-embroidered tunic; and a pair of gilded top-boots. During the last hundred years the chiefs had grudgingly accepted these objects from the Vandal kings, to whom the sovereignty of Africa had lapsed; but their vassals had often made it an excuse for disobedience that they were not the authentic insignia, especially the brooches. Belisarius therefore won the favour of these chiefs by presenting them with staffs, caps, capes, brooches, tunics, and top-boots, all straight from Constantinople; and, though they did not fight with him in the two battles which destroyed the Vandals' power, neither did they fight against him.

If Belisarius had been left to govern Africa peaceably in Justinian's name he would certainly have done wonders and made of it a permanent stronghold and store-house for the Empire. He would have retained the friendship of the Moors and improved their manner of living. He intended to recruit from them a permanent cavalry defence-force to be trained in modern fighting methods and attached in loyalty to him by grants of land and money. The Roman Africans would have supplied him with garrison infantry, and he was already training levies of these. But all such projects came to nothing, because Belisarius, by the jealousy of his subordinates and the suspicion of Justinian, was prevented from consolidating his task. Two of his officers, secret agents of Cappadocian John's, had sent a confidential report to Justinian: that Belisarius was openly seating himself upon the throne of Geilimer, and seemed to have every intention of holding it for himself and his heirs; that after the capture of the Vandal camp he had publicly reviled his officers and men in a most brutal and tyrannical manner; that he was in secret treaty with the savage Moors, whom he had persuaded to maintain him in his tyranny; and that he was behaving with suspicious leniency towards the Vandal captives. These officers expected the credulous Justinian to send an order for the arrest and execution of Belisarius. They hoped to be suitably rewarded for their zeal – perhaps with the governorships of Carthage and Hippo. Their names were John, the nephew of Vitalian, commonly known as 'Bloody John', and Constantine. In case the report should go astray, they had sent Justinian two copies of the same letter by different packets, one of which reached its destination. But the other my mistress, who had a suspicion of these officers, managed to intercept shortly before the packet sailed.

The letter disturbed Belisarius greatly. He could not deny that he was in treaty with the Moors for supplying him with cavalry, or that he had set many of the elder Vandals at liberty, or that he had been dispensing justice from King Geilimer's throne, or that he had reviled his officers and men, in the interests of discipline, standing on the mound that early morning in the camp at Tricamaron. It was only the conclusion as to his loyalty that was falsely drawn. He decided to take no action against Bloody John or Constantine or even to let them know that he had seen the letter. A few months later a flattering message came from Justinian, not mentioning the slander and telling him to do just as he wished – either to return to Constantinople with the spoils and Vandal prisoners or to send them back under a subordinate and remain in Africa. Then my mistress Antonina insisted that he should return promptly in order to clear himself of suspicion. She was particularly anxious lest her friend Theodora should think her disloyal or ungrateful. With this message from Justinian came cavalry reinforcements, to the number of 4,000, under good officers, including one Hildiger, who was already betrothed to my mistress's daughter, Martha; so that Belisarius now felt at liberty to withdraw most of his own Household cuirassiers, and the Massagetic Huns, to escort the Vandal prisoners.

He chose as Governor in his place the eunuch Solomon, in whom he had the greatest confidence, and by the spring, after handing over to Solomon the detailed instructions for the proper government of Africa that had come from Justinian, he could sail away, my mistress Antonina with him.

We who were returning to Constantinople did not envy Solomon his task at Carthage, for Justinian's instructions made it clear that the Governor of the newly won kingdom must not depend on Constantinople for further forces, but must raise local levies, and economize in garrison troops by repairing defence works and building blockhouses along the frontiers. Eighty thousand Vandal cavalrymen had failed to check the Moorish raids – yet their task must be successfully taken over by a tenth of that number of our men, and the lands stolen by the Moors won back. Africa must be also reassessed for taxation, and the Arian heresy and the Donatist schism sternly put down. The reason why not all Belisarius's cuirassiers had come with us was that at the last moment a report arrived at Carthage of a slight Moorish rebellion in the interior. Belisarius, at Solomon's request, left behind Rufinus and Aigan with 500 chosen men to act as a punitive force. That number seemed sufficient.

We sailed home by way of Tripoli and Crete – an uneventful voyage – and in midsummer of the year of our Lord 534 we entered the Bosphorus again. We were given a tumultuous welcome at the docks, and a royal welcome at the Palace. My mistress Antonina and the Empress Theodora embraced with tears; and Justinian was so elated by the extraordinary value of the treasure unloaded from our ships and so impressed by the sight of our 15,000 stalwart prisoners that, forgetting his suspicions of Belisarius, he called him 'our faithful benefactor' and took him by the hand. As Commander-in-Chief of the armies, however, he assumed all the official credit for the defeat of the Vandals; and in the preamble to his new Digest of Laws (published on the day of the Tricamaron battle) he had already styled himself 'Conqueror of the Vandals and Africans' – Pious, Victorious,

Happy, and Glorious – and, without mentioning that anybody else had shared in the victory, referred to 'the sweats of war and the night-watches and fasts' on his own part that had secured it. The triumph to be celebrated was his own, not Belisarius's: for no private citizen has been awarded a full triumph since the Empire was founded, lest he should be puffed up by victory and become a rival to the throne. As I say, the Emperor, even if his warlike exertions are confined to sending off an expedition from the docks with his blessing and congratulating it on its safe return a year or more later, is always the victorious Commander-in-Chief.

None the less, Theodora insisted that he play the same sedentary part in this triumph as he had played in the victory and leave the procession to the conduct of Belisarius. He agreed. On the anniversary day of the capture of Carthage, Belisarius came out from his private residence close to the Golden Gate in the Wall of Theodosius, and passed in procession down the whole two-mile length of the High Street. He went on foot, preceded by priests and bishops singing a solemn Te Deum and swinging censers; not, as the ancient custom was, riding in a chariot preceded by trumpeters. The street was decorated with flowers and coloured silk hangings and wreaths and congratulatory greetings, and thronged with wildly cheering crowds. At each of the great squares through which we passed – the Square of Arcadius, the Ox Market, the Amastrian Square, the Square of Brotherly Love, the Bull Square (where the University professors and students were assembled), and finally the Square of Constantine (where the City militia were drawn up on parade) – the City ward-masters came with gifts and words of welcome and a fanfare of trumpets was sounded. Behind Belisarius, who was accompanied by Cappadocian John and other distinguished generals, rode his cuirassiers and the marines and the Massagetic Huns (who were to return home by way of the Black Sea on the following day), and behind these the Vandal prisoners, in chains, headed by Geilimer in a purple cloak, with his cousins and brothers-in-law and nephews. Then followed all the spoils of Africa heaped on wagons.

These were extraordinary spoils, the richest ever carried in any triumph in the world before; for though the soldiers at Tricamaron had plundered the camp, that treasure was only a tithe of what was collected at Carthage and Hippo and Bulla and Grasse and elsewhere from the city treasuries and royal palaces and seats of the nobility. It consisted of the Vandals' accumulated trading profits from overseas and their revenues from Africa – the surplus of a hundred years – and the spoils of Geiserich's extensive piracy. The Vandals had been a small and oppressive aristocracy in a fertile, teeming land, and what they were too lazy to spend on public works they had hoarded. So, heaped on these carts were millions of pounds of bar-silver, and sacks of silver and gold coin, and quantities of bar-gold, and golden cups and dishes and salt-cellars encrusted with gems, and golden thrones and golden carriages of state and statues of gold, and copies of the Gospel bound in gold and studded with pearls, and heaps of golden collars and girdles, and gold-inlaid armour – in short, every luxurious and beautiful object that can be imagined, including priceless antiquities from King Geiserich's sack of the Imperial Palace at Rome and of the Temple of Jove on the Capitoline Hill. There were also a great number of sacred relics: bones of martyrs, miraculous images, authentic garments of Apostles, the nails from St Peter's cross on which he was crucified upside down.

But the most wonderful and venerable spoils of all were none other than the sacred instruments of Jewish religious worship that were made by Moses in the Wilderness at God's express command and later installed at the Temple in Jerusalem. They are described in the twenty-fifth chapter of the Book of Exodus: the sacred shew-bread table of shittim wood overlaid with pure gold, and its accompanying golden spoons and bowls and dishes; and the seven-branched candlestick of beaten gold with its tongs and snuff-dishes; and the golden Mercy Seat, and its two attendant gold cherubim with outspread wings. These things Geiserich had stolen from Rome, where they had been brought by the Emperor Titus after his capture of Jerusalem. The Ark of the Covenant itself had disappeared. Some say that it is in France somewhere, with certain other Temple spoils, in the hands of the Frankish King, and others that it is at Axum in Ethiopia, and others that it is sunk at the bottom of the River Tiber at Rome, and others that it was long ago caught up to Heaven out of the reach of sacrilegious hands.

The Senate met the procession and joined it at the Amastrian Square, and so did droves of monks, and other clergy. The monks behaved in the rowdiest way, gloating over the spoils, especially the sacred relics which Justinian had promised them for their churches.

In the days of the Roman Republic the victorious general rode with his captives through the streets of the City, and for that one day was supreme in power. The enemy king or chieftain, if he had been captured, was offered as a human sacrifice at the close of the ceremonies. How customs have changed since those heroic times! Observe Geilimer free of chains: as the procession finally reaches the Hippodrome, where Justinian is awaiting it, seated in the Royal Box, he enters with the rest. He removes his purple cloak and, mounting up to the throne, makes obeisance to Justinian; and is then graciously raised up and pardoned. He is given a royal warrant which confers on him vast estates in Galatia for himself and his family; and, in addition, the title of Illustrious Patrician if he consents to renounce his Arian heresy. Observe also Belisarius, the victor, who approaches the throne, removes his purple cloak and makes obeisance at the Emperor's feet; and is given no estate, no words of gratitude, but informed merely that he has obeyed orders well.

You may ask how Geilimer comported himself on this trying occasion. He neither laughed nor wept, but shook his head sadly and wonderingly and continued to repeat over and over again, as a sort of charm, the words of the Prophet Ecclesiastes: 'Vanity of vanities, all is vanity.' Shortly afterwards he retired with his family to Galatia, and there lived to a comfortable old age, remaining true to the Arian faith. As for the other Vandal prisoners: the most warlike of them were formed into cavalry squadrons and sent to the defence of the Persian frontier, but first Belisarius had his pick of them for his Household Regiment. The remainder were used as labourers for the building of churches or as oarsmen in the Imperial galleys.

Afterwards Justinian was told by Theodora that if he wished to win the title 'The Great' he must be magnanimous and show Belisarius some worthy mark of favour. He therefore appointed him Consul for the year following, and even struck a medal: his own head on the obverse, and Belisarius riding in full armour on the reverse, with the inscription 'The Glory of the Romans' – a unique honour in our City. Belisarius's induction as Consul took place on New Year's Day. Seated in his ivory chair of office, which was supported by Vandal captives, and with an ivory wand in his hand, he made another short progress through the City from his quarters in the Palace to the Senate House. As he went he distributed largesse to the crowd from his own private spoils of war – gold and silver coin, cups, girdles, brooches – to the value of 100,000 gold pieces. But my mistress Antonina, whose prudence in the matter of the water-bottles will be recalled, took care that he should not beggar himself. When the mob clamoured for more, she told them herself that they were shameless creatures and would strip Belisarius not only of all he had won in Africa but of what he had inherited from his parents or saved of the gifts awarded him by the Emperor. To show the foresight of my mistress in matters of economy, I must tell you that she had, while still at Carthage and without Belisarius's knowledge, removed a very large quantity of coin from Geilimer's treasure, choosing all the more recently minted Imperial money that she could find, so that its origin should not be suspected, and hidden it away against a rainy day. For Belisarius's household expenses were enormous, and there never was a more generous man to the needy and unfortunate.

The sacred relics were distributed among the churches, appropriately to the dedication of each, and every church of importance received something. But one small, anonymous community of very poor monks, who lived by begging and occupied a ruinous house in the suburb of Blachernae, did not share in all this bounty. Their abbot came to Belisarius presently and asked him, in Christ's name, whether he had perhaps some trifle of his own that he could give them; for while he was in Africa they had prayed for his success night and day.

He replied: 'Venerable Father, yours is a fraternity of poor begging brothers who have small regard for silver or gold, and I shall therefore give your house no object that may distract their minds from religious thoughts. But I shall lend you a famous relic, the begging bowl of St Bartimaeus, which the Emperor himself gave me after the fight at Daras, and you shall display it in your house and keep it as a reminder of your vows of poverty, patience and virtue. Remember, it is a loan only, since I cannot seem ungrateful to His Sacred Majesty. One day I may have need for it again.'

Thenceforth this house was never without food and drink, for it became a centre of pilgrimage, and was thereafter known as the monastery of St Bartimaeus.

As for the golden Mercy Seat and the golden seven-branched candlestick and the shew-table and the other Jewish treasures, Justinian was persuaded by the Bishop of Jerusalem to return them to that city. The Bishop argued that they had brought no luck to the men of Rome, whose dominion had passed to the barbarians, nor to the Vandals, whom Justinian himself had defeated. They plainly carried a curse with them. Justinian sent them back to Jerusalem, to the very building where they had once been stored for a thousand years – the Temple of Solomon, which was now a Christian church. What a grand source of profit for the clergy there! The Jews lamented that they were still deprived of their holy instruments of worship, and prophesied that the Christians would before long be cast out of Jerusalem; but this has not come to pass in my time.

When the news of Belisarius's conquest of Africa reached the Persian Court, King Khosrou was surprised and vexed. He sent a congratulatory embassy to Justinian asking, half in earnest, half in joke, for his share of the spoils of Carthage. But for the Persian peace, he said, Justinian would never have been able to spare troops for Carthage. Justinian pretended to take the joke in good part, and sent Khosrou a valuable gold dinner service. So the Eternal Peace still remained in force.

There is no need to give a detailed account of my mistress's life in Constantinople during the days that followed our return from Carthage. She was again in attendance on Theodora, and spent her leisure time in parties and pleasure excursions and visits to the theatre. Theodosius was constantly with her, and a good deal of loose talk about their friendship was current at Court; but Belisarius, since Theodosius was his godson, disdained to take any notice of it, treating the young man with every mark of confidence.

News had by this time come to Belisarius which grieved him greatly: that Rufinus and Aigan and the 500 cuirassiers that he had left behind with Solomon had been destroyed by the Moors. Solomon had sent them to the interior, to a town called the Royal Springs in the centre of the corn country, 100 miles inland from Hadrumetum; they were to rescue a large number of Roman African peasants who had been carried off in a Moorish raid. The cuirassiers succeeded in this task and were slowly escorting the peasants home when they were trapped in a narrow mountain-pass by a force of several thousand Moors, who cut them to pieces in a desperate fight. The Moors were now also raiding in the western parts of the Diocese, and Solomon's forces were altogether inadequate to protect the Roman Africans. Solomon wrote to the Moorish chieftains, protesting against these outrages: he reminded them that they were now Justinian's allies, that they had sent their children to Carthage as hostages of good behaviour, and that they should be warned by the fate of the Vandals. The Moors merely laughed at this letter. They pointed out in their reply that their alliance with Justinian had not improved their condition in the least. Being polygamous, they did not set much store by children, who were easily replaceable, nor did they indulge those soft sentiments of family affection which had lost Geilimer two battles and his kingdom. The defeat of the Vandals was a sadder augury for the Roman Africans than for themselves, they said. Their raids continued.

Solomon took the field against them with all his available forces. The Moors now made the mistake of concentrating in a great army, rather than breaking up into raiding parties and devastating the Diocese piecemeal. Troops as undisciplined as these Moors, who possess no body-armour and carry flimsy shields and only a couple of javelins apiece and an occasional sword, lose fighting value proportionately to their increased concentration in mass. They adopted a strange defensive formation that had once baffled the Vandals in Tripoli. They built a circular palisade at the foot of a hill; having put their women and other non-combatants behind it, they surrounded it with twelve lines of camels, tied head to tail, sideways to the enemy. When Solomon's force appeared, some of them stood on the backs of the camels, prepared to hurl javelins down, while some crouched under the beasts' bellies, prepared to rush out and stab. Their cavalry also formed up on the hill, having undertaken to charge down as soon as the camp should be attacked; these also were armed with javelins and swords.

Solomon launched his attack. But the Roman cavalry horses, being unaccustomed to the smell of camels, reared up and could not be persuaded to charge; and the Moors did a deal of damage with their javelins. Then Solomon dismounted the squadron of Thracian Goths – big, strong men in shirts of mail – and himself led them with raised shields and drawn swords against the ring of camels. They butchered 200 camels in no time, and broke the ring. The Moorish infantry fled in disorder; their cavalry did not come into action. Solomon captured all the women and all the camels; and 10,000 Moors were killed in the pursuit.

The Moors recovered from their defeat a few weeks later and invaded the corn-growing country again with the biggest army that they had ever gathered together – so big that it was not only useless but self-destructive. Solomon surprised it at dawn one day, encamped on a mountain, and stampeded it into a ravine. In the confusion of flight these savages trampled one another down, and not a man of them thought of defending himself. Incredible though this may seem, 50,000 of them perished before the sun was high, and not a single Roman soldier received so much as a scratch. So great was the number of captive women and children that a healthy Moorish boy, whose price in the Constantinople market would not be less than ten gold pieces, could be bought here for two pieces of silver, the price of a fat sheep. Thus Rufinus and Aigan were avenged.

The survivors of the Moors took refuge with their kinsmen on Mount Aures, a huge mountain thirteen days' journey inland from Carthage on the border of Morocco. This mountain, which is sixty miles in circumference, is very easy to defend, and most fertile on its upper slopes, with plentiful springs of water. Thirty thousand fighting men now made it their headquarters for raids.

As for the rest of Roman Africa: the inhabitants were now heartily wishing the Vandals back again – not only because of the Moorish raids, but because of Justinian's tax-gatherers, who settled like hungry leeches on the land. The Vandals had also been leeches, but gorged leeches: they only taxed the farmers one-tenth of their produce, and were negligent in their collection of it. Justinian, on the other hand, required one-third, and made sure that he was paid promptly. Then, again, there was discontent in the Army because of the soldiers' Vandal wives. It seemed no more than justice that the victorious soldiers should be awarded the fertile lands and well-built houses of those whom they had dispossessed. But by Justinian's orders these properties were sequestrated and sold on behalf of the Imperial Treasury. The troops were given nothing of what they expected, but sent away to build and guard remote block-houses and expected to cultivate poor and waterless lands in the neighbourhood. The Vandal women made the loudest outcry against the injustice of this arrangement, goading their new husbands to insist upon proper redress. But Solomon had no authority to satisfy their demands.

There was still another cause for complaint in the Army, and a fair one in my opinion, caused by Justinian's foolish zeal for the Orthodox faith. Solomon's forces included, as you know, a squadron of 500 Thracian Goths and Pharas's 300 Herulians, and about 200 other barbarians from beyond the Danube: these were all Arian heretics. But Justinian had sent an order for the extirpation of the Arian heresy and the persecution of Arian priests; he forbade any Arian to receive any of the Sacraments unless he recanted, or to have his children baptized.

This rule applied not only to the surviving Vandals – old men and women, and the wives and stepchildren of the soldiers – and to Roman African converts to the heresy, but also to these brave soldiers, who never before had been thus affronted.

Solomon's reports of the situation in Africa were so disquieting that Belisarius pleaded with Justinian that the Arian soldiers should be allowed to receive the Sacraments from their own priests, as was customary. But Justinian protested that to do this would be an impious act and would imperil his own chances of salvation. Belisarius could not press the matter. He next asked Justinian to find reinforcements for Solomon (who had also been obliged to send an expedition against bandits in Sardinia) to be used as block-house troops, while the original troops should be garrisoned in Carthage and given, not palaces and parks perhaps, but decent houses and lands to content them. Justinian seemed to agree, and gathered a force of 20,000 men from Thrace and the Persian frontier, replacing them with the new Vandal squadrons. Then he told Belisarius in a public audience that he must soon return to Carthage with them and take over the governorship from Solomon. However, this was all a deception. Justinian had another war in mind. The troops were not intended for Africa, but for the conquest of Sicily.

I have mentioned the claim made by Belisarius, on Justinian's behalf, to the promontory of Lilybaeum. It was referred by the Gothic Governor of Sicily to Queen Amalasontha, Regent of Italy and Sicily and Dalmatia and South-eastern France for her young son Athalrich, with whom Justinian had made the treaty which enabled Belisarius to revictual at Syracuse on his way to the capture of Carthage. Queen Amalasontha officially took the view that on the extinction of the Vandal monarchy Lilybaeum had reverted to her own patrimony. But privately she did not wish to quarrel with Justinian, since it was a most precarious position to be queen over the Goths, who had always thought it below their dignity to be ruled by a woman.

Her father, the great King Theoderich, had been a miracle among barbarians. He was of that Ostrogothic nation which won the great victory at Adrianople, as related in a former chapter, and subsequently became allied to the Emperor of the East and protected his frontiers for him. Not many years later, at the suggestion of the Emperor of the East, nearly the whole nation, led by Theoderich from Thrace, migrated in wagons to Italy, to make war against a barbarian general who had deposed the Emperor of the West. Only a few thousands remained behind. King Theoderich conquered and killed the usurper, and seized Italy for himself and his people. Ruling justly, wisely, and long, he restored prosperity to the whole of Italy; and, while nominally the vassal of the Emperor at Constantinople, retained complete independence of action. Though no scholar himself, Theoderich was a friend to learning. The Goths – who, like all Germans, prefer barbaric to civilized virtues – could not accuse him of softness; for he was the best horseman and the best archer in his dominions, and avoided luxury like the plague. His noblest quality was his religious tolerance: though an Arian heretic, he permitted complete religious liberty to Orthodox Christians, and to heretics of any reputable sort, throughout his dominions.

Amalasontha inherited her father's courage and ability, and was, besides, very beautiful. But she had few friends among the Gothic nobility; when at Theoderich's death the crown passed to her ten-year-old son, Athalrich, with herself as regent, they interfered in all her arrangements, even in Athalrich's education. Theoderich had wished him to become a cultivated man, capable of conversing on equal terms with Emperor or Pope or Roman senator, and had put him under grave tutors; but this barbarian gentry insisted that the youth be allowed to run wild with companions of his own age and learn to drink and drab and ride cock-horse and swagger about with his sword loose in his scabbard, just as they themselves had done when young.

The result was that Athalrich grew to be a young ruffian. He came to despise his mother and, egged on by his companions, openly threatened to seize the management of the country from her. She treated him with gentle scorn, but secretly prepared to leave Italy with a shipful of treasure – a quarter of a million in gold coin – and take refuge with Justinian at Constantinople. She even sent a letter informing him of her intentions, and he replied with a warm welcome. However, she succeeded in assassinating the three young nobles who were causing her the most trouble; and thus found it unnecessary to sail. But it is a long way from Ravenna, where Amalasontha's Court was, to Constantinople. Justinian became impatient for further news. He sent an envoy to Amalasontha, ostensibly to take up the matter of Lilybaeum with her, but in reality to find out why she did not come; and he also sent two bishops, ostensibly to confer with the Pope on a knotty point of doctrine, but in reality for secret talks with a certain

Theudahad, Theoderich's nephew, who had inherited great estates in Tuscany – the district lying on the coast northward from Rome. Now, Amalasontha had recently summoned Theudahad to Ravenna and reproached him for his unjust seizure of the lands of Roman citizens, his neighbours, as also of lands belonging to the Crown; and had obliged him to make restoration and apology.

The envoy and the bishops returned, with the welcome news that Theudahad, in return for a settled income and an estate at Constantinople, was willing, for hatred of Amalasontha, to betray Tuscany to Justinian's soldiers whenever he cared to send an army of occupation; and that Amalasontha was secretly willing to transfer her regency of Italy to Justinian on the same terms – since she could not long continue to control her son. But her official reply in the matter of Lilybaeum was a denial that Justinian had any right to it.

Then a sudden event changed the whole complexion of events. Young Athalrich, his health undermined by drink and debauchery, fell into a decline and died. Amalasontha, who only ruled by virtue of being his mother, was thus, according to Gothic law, relegated to private citizenship. She decided to choose at once a noble Goth, by marriage to whom she could still remain queen. There was, she thought, no more suitable person to become her husband than this same Theudahad, her cousin (of whose intrigues with Justinian she was unaware, as he of hers): an elderly, unsoldierly man, unlike any other of the Goths in having taken to the study of philosophy and to the writing of Latin hexameter verse. He would no doubt feel honoured by a union with herself, and would allow her to rule in his name without interference. She therefore proposed marriage to him, emphasizing the advantage of thus protecting himself against the hostility both of the Gothic nobility, who despised him for his learning, and of the Italians, who hated him for his rapacity. Nobody had a better claim to the throne than he, she said, but without her he could not hope either to seize or hold it. He consented, with every appearance of pleasure, and was duly crowned king, and acclaimed as such by the Goths; for no other claimant of royal blood appeared. But Amalasontha had over-reached herself. What should Theudahad do, as soon as he had the crown on his head, but violate his sacred oath to her that he would not meddle in public business. He actually excluded her from his council room and carried her off to a small island of his in a Tuscan lake, keeping her a close prisoner there.

When Justinian heard of Theudahad's action, he was more pleased than he pretended to be. He sent another envoy to Italy, to inform Amalasontha that she would be given all the support against her enemies that she needed; and the envoy had instructions not to conceal this message from Theudahad or from any of his nobles. He hoped thus to throw the whole kingdom into confusion. But by the time that the envoy arrived in Italy, Amalasontha was dead: the relatives of the three young men whom she had killed had persuaded Theudahad to avenge their death. She was surprised one summer afternoon as she was bathing with her women in the lake, and her head forced under the water until she drowned.

Now, though Justinian continued to protest his great love for Theodora, she also was relieved at this queen's death, whom she regarded as a rival. It was true that Amalasontha, whom Justinian had known when she was a child, was of better birth than Theodora and a little younger and far more beautiful. Cappadocian John put it about that Theodora had arranged the assassination herself.

Here then was Justinian's pretext for a war – the murder of an innocent woman, his ally. He found an augury of success in the unpopularity and inefficacy of King Theudahad, whose verses did not even scan, it was said, and whose philosophical capacity was nothing. But Theudahad heard and believed a rumour, arising out of Theodora's jealousy of Amalasontha, that the perfidious Justinian had indeed intended to invade Italy with his army and marry Amalasontha, having first divorced Theodora; further, that he had planned to persecute the Goths as heretics. He offered this story to his Court as an excuse for the murder of his wife. They approved of his actions; for it was now clear at least that Amalasontha had been carrying on a treasonable correspondence with Justinian. But Theudahad officially assured Justinian's envoy that the murder had been committed without his knowledge and against his wishes.

I have now made it clear why Belisarius was ordered to take an army to the invasion of Sicily, which lay at the extremity of King Theudahad's dominions, and the population of which, moreover, was highly discontented. Sicily, the granary of Rome, had for some time been suffering from poor harvests due to bad weather and an exhaustion of the soil, so that the farmers did not find it easy to pay the tithe-tax that the Goths levied on them. In the autumn of the year of his Consulship, Belisarius set sail for this island. Antonina came with him (and I with her), and her boy Photius, and Theodosius too. But the forces under his command amounted only to 12,000, not 20,000. At the last moment Justinian detached 8,000 and sent them to Mundus (the Commander of the armies in Illyria who had assisted Belisarius in quelling the Victory Riots) with orders that he should lead them against the Goths in Dalmatia, as a diversion. Dalmatia, with the whole of the north-eastern coast of the Adriatic sea, was under Gothic rule at this time. Justinian also planned to injure the Goths in yet another quarter. He wrote to the Franks, who since the baptism of King Clovis had been Orthodox Christians, that they would now have a chance to invade the Gothic territories between the Alps and the Rhône; and that this would be a holy war against Arian heretics, blessed by their spiritual father, the Pope.

The weather was favourable and the voyage pleasant. We landed at Catania early in the month of December. The people there, remembering how honestly we had treated them on our former visit, gave us a welcome. They complained greatly of the Goths, and asked us whether we could not stay a little longer with them this time; for nobody but Belisarius knew that we were not continuing our voyage to Carthage, as had been announced. At last Belisarius openly declared his intentions, announcing himself as their protector and sending messengers to all the principal cities with invitations to submission. Within a few days the whole of Sicily had surrendered to him without a blow, with the single exception of Palermo. Here the Gothic forces of the island concentrated, taking refuge behind the fine fortifications. But even Palermo yielded with unexpected suddenness. Belisarius sailed into the harbour, which was not protected by a boom, and found that the masts of most of his vessels were considerably higher than the adjacent fortifications. What was easier than to hoist up boats by a pulley between mainmast and foremast and fill them with trained archers? (Yet so simple a plan would not perhaps have occurred to an ordinary general.) These archers could shoot straight along the streets of the city and prevent anyone from showing his head out of a doorway, unless in a side-street. Belisarius threatened, unless Palermo yielded speedily, to shoot fire-arrows and burn the houses down. So the townsfolk compelled the Goths to surrender.

You may doubt whether so short a paragraph as the last can decently cover the story of how a fertile island, full of splendid cities and no less than 70,000 square miles in extent, was recaptured from the barbarians by our Imperial troops. Yet I cannot recall any relevant circumstance that I have omitted which would swell the single paragraph to two. It was the name of Belisarius that captured Sicily rather than his army – assisted by the short-sighted zeal of the Orthodox Christians, who expected to receive better treatment at the hands of Justinian, their co-religionist, than from the Arian king. On the last day of the year, then, when Belisarius's term of office as Consul expired, he marched unopposed into the capital city of Syracuse, and there laid down his rods and axe, as the expression was. As he entered, he distributed largesse of gold and silver to the citizens from the personal treasure captured from the Goths who had opposed him at Palermo; and was hailed as their deliverer.

Justinian's envoy remained in Italy and observed the disturbing effect on King Theudahad of the news of Belisarius's landing at Catania, and of the news that simultaneously came from Dalmatia to the effect that Mundus had stormed Spalato. Theudahad saw himself threatened with the fate of King Geilimer the Vandal, his kinsman – for Geilimer and he had an aunt in common. Without consulting with his Council, he made a secret offer to the envoy to cede Sicily to Justinian and send him beside a yearly tribute of a crown of gold weighing 300 pounds; and a permanent detachment of 3,000 Gothic cavalrymen and their horses to serve either in North Africa or on the Persian frontier, as Justinian pleased, and to be kept up to strength with yearly drafts of men and remounts. He also renounced his right to sentence Italian priests and patricians to death, or to confer patrician rank on any person without the consent of Justinian or his successors. He even agreed that the responses of the factions in the Hippodrome at Rome, whenever he took his place as President, should couple in loyal salutation Justinian's name with his own, and that a statue of Justinian should flank every statue raised to himself, standing on the right side, which is the more honourable one. This was to acknowledge the suzerainty of the East over the West. Theudahad put these undertakings in writing. He was in great terror, and wished to lay up a treasure of gratitude for himself in Constantinople, if ever it should be necessary for him to escape there from Italy.

But when further news came of the fall of Palermo and of the bloodless occupation of Sicily, Theudahad's heart failed him. He wondered whether the terms he had offered Justinian to prevent him from pressing the invasion of Italy were not perhaps insufficient; to promise Sicily to Justinian when he had already taken it might be regarded as an impudence – and of what worth was an offer of 3,000 soldiers and a yearly tribute amounting to a mere 20,000 in gold, and an abandonment of the right to create or punish patricians? He recalled the envoy, who was already on his way back, and took him into his intimate confidence, first binding him with the most dreadful oaths to keep the secret. The secret was that if Justinian rejected these terms Theudahad was prepared to better them. He would resign his title of kingship and hand over to Justinian the whole government of Italy. All that he asked in return was a comfortable private life, preferably near some centre of learning in Asia Minor, on a freehold estate with a secure annual rent-roll of at least 80,000 gold pieces a year. A messenger of his own accompanied the envoy with this offer in writing, but it was only to be produced if Justinian did not accept the other one.

Ambassadors are chosen for their loyalty and self-sacrifice to the cause of their royal master; thus Justinian's envoy did not hesitate to risk spiritual disaster by breaking his oath to Theudahad. He advised Justinian to refuse the first offer, for Theudahad's messenger had a better one in readiness for him. This offer was then produced, and Justinian accepted it with alacrity. None the less, he was for haggling about the rent-roll of the estate, until Theodora laughed at his notion of business – to risk losing all Italy for the sake of a few sacks of coin.

So far, everything was going so well for Justinian that he can hardly have been blamed for believing that God regarded him with especial favour – a belief of which the servility of his courtiers did nothing to disabuse him. But, before the envoy had time to return to Italy and ratify the treaty with Theudahad, the whole political situation suddenly changed again. Two pieces of news persuaded Theudahad that he had been a fool after all and had over-estimated Justinian's power to hurt him.

The first piece of news concerned Mundus. After his capture of Spalato, he had come in contact with a large Gothic army and, after a stubborn battle in which both sides lost heavily, defeated it – but had himself been killed in pursuing the beaten enemy. It was reported that the Imperial forces were so reduced in numbers and spirit by this unlucky victory that they had returned to Illyria without even leaving a garrison behind at Spalato. The other piece of news was that a serious mutiny had broken out in North Africa, and that Belisarius was about to withdraw his forces from Sicily in order to restore order there. How true this African news was I shall presently tell. But its effect on Theudahad was so great that he spoke most insultingly to Justinian's envoy when he arrived, and even threatened to kill him on a baseless charge of adultery with a lady of the Court; he greatly repented of having written as he had to Justinian, and now declared that the envoy lied and that the two offers signed by himself were forgeries.

The Gothic noblemen of the Council believed Theudahad. They could not think that their elected king had been so cowardly and treacherous as appeared from Justinian's message, which agreed to take Italy under his sovereignty and give Theudahad the estate that he demanded. They decided that the embassy was merely a clever manoeuvre on Justinian's part to set them at odds with their king. So the envoy and his suite were kept close prisoners, and Theudahad sent a message of defiance to Justinian by a common trader, accusing him of double-dealing and treachery – Theudahad knew that the Goths would kill him if he did not immediately vindicate his honour by some vigorous action. He also sent an army to re-occupy Spalato, since the Romans had retired from it again; and began to behave oppressively to Orthodox priests throughout Italy, and threatened the Pope with death or dismissal if he was caught in any further secret dealings with Constantinople.

The Goths had little confidence in Theudahad, nevertheless, because he wrote verses in Latin and argued with Greek rhetoricians and prided himself upon his far-fetched learning. For them a few wild German ballads of battle, together with the Paternoster and the Arian Creed in the same tongue, were sufficient culture. They had not degenerated, as the Vandals had, under the luxurious spell of civilization; but neither had they profited by their sixty years' residence in Italy to improve their good sense by literary education. That they had little respect for Theudahad was due not so much to the sterile character of his learning as to the very fact of his having learning. Thus they neglected to reinforce their barbarian fighting qualities with such military knowledge as can be derived from books. In especial, they had not studied the arts of fortification or siege-craft.

CHAPTER 13

TROUBLE IN AFRICA AND IN SICILY

CONSIDER the matter from the Gothic point of view. What danger could they reasonably fear from a mere 12,000 men, a large part of whom were infantry? Italy was theirs, and they had been living on the friendliest terms with the native population for two generations. They had plentiful supplies of food, and a fleet and money and military stores; they could easily put 100,000 horsemen into the field and 100,000 foot-archers; they possessed a number of very strong walled cities. Add to this that the Imperial troops who had landed in Sicily, though professedly champions of the Orthodox faith, were for the most part Christians only by courtesy, and could not even make themselves understood by the native Italians, who spoke Latin, not Greek; and you will understand that when the Goths heard of the African mutiny and of the death of Mundus they no longer considered the name of Belisarius to be a serious factor in the situation.

To tell of the mutiny. It broke out at Easter of the following year, the year of our Lord 536. A few days later Solomon landed at Syracuse from an open boat with a few exhausted companions, and stumbled up from the quay to Belisarius's headquarters in the Governor's Palace. It so happened, that afternoon, that I was in a small room with my mistress and Belisarius and Theodosius, where we had retired after luncheon, and something not unlike an argument was in progress. Theodosius had made a rather too pointed joke at the expense of some tenet of the Orthodox faith, to the amusement of my mistress Antonina.

Belisarius did not smile, but asked Theodosius in a puzzled way whether he had relapsed to Eunomianism.

'No,' replied Theodosius. 'Indeed, I never held that opinion seriously.'

'Well. But since you have become converted to true doctrine I do not understand why you should joke as you do.'

Antonina defended Theodosius: she said that to laugh at the things that one held dear was not inconsistent with loyalty to them. When Belisarius disagreed, she changed from defence to attack, and asked him why, if Orthodoxy meant so much to him, he allowed heretics of every variety to enlist in his Household Regiment.

Belisarius answered: 'That is another matter altogether. Every man has a right to what religious beliefs he pleases, and a duty to himself not to be persuaded from them by force; but he has no right to injure his neighbour's sensibilities by asserting such beliefs offensively. I was born in the Orthodox faith, and early pledged myself to it. It offends me to hear its doctrines idly abused, as I would not myself idly abuse the faith of any honest man.'

'And if you had been born an Arian?'

'Doubtless I should have remained an Arian.'

'Then all religious views are true doctrine if sincerely held?' my mistress pressed him.

'I do not accept that. But I say that it is good to keep faith and good to respect the feelings of others.'

Theodosius made no apology for the joke that had offended his godfather. All that he would say was: 'I hold no brief for any heresy. I grant you that Orthodox doctrine can be logically defended against all heresies – especially given certain mystical premisses, such as that the Pope at Rome holds the keys of Heaven in succession to St Peter.'

Belisarius replied, stiffly: 'I do not see that logic has any part in true religion.'

Theodosius laughed. 'A sceptical comment indeed, Godfather.'

Belisarius explained, his temper still unruffled: 'Religion is faith, not philosophy. The Ionian Greeks invented philosophy to take the place of religion; and it made a cowardly and deceitful race of them.'

Then my mistress Antonina asked: 'But is not philosophy needed to steel one against possible injuries? Is it good to keep faith with those who may injure one?'

'It is good to keep faith and to forgive injuries. To break one's faith is to injure oneself.'

Theodosius remarked: 'But the weaker a man's faith, the less he will injure himself by breaking it.'

Belisarius replied gently: 'Do not let that concern us, Godson. We are all people of honour here.'

Here I intercepted a swift glance that passed between my mistress and Theodosius, as if to say: 'Ah, dear Belisarius, you flatter us. Perhaps our sense of honour is not so fanatical as yours.'

I have never forgotten that conversation, and that glance, in the light of my mistress's subsequent relations with Theodosius. This at least is sure: that Theodosius had allowed himself to be baptized only as an aid to personal advancement, and was no more a Christian than I or my mistress. He once confessed to her: 'The only writer on Christianity that I have ever read with satisfaction was Celsus.' This Celsus is anathema. He lived in pagan times, and wrote about the early Christians with witty severity. He even went to Palestine to investigate the parentage of Jesus, and claimed to have found Him recorded in the military records as the son of one Pantherus, a Greek soldier of Samaria. 'And it is noteworthy,' Theodosius said, 'that, according to the Evangelist John, Jesus did not deny His Samaritan origin when the priests charged him with it.'

Everyone is entitled to his own faith or opinions, as Belisarius maintained. But Theodosius concealed his thoughts from everyone but my mistress Antonina – if indeed he revealed them to her. Although I did not believe the stupid servants' gossip about my mistress and Theodosius – such as that they had once been observed kissing behind a screen and, on another occasion, emerging together from a dark cellar – I nevertheless felt a strong presentiment that one day passion would seize hold of my mistress and the young man and bring ill luck both on Belisarius and on themselves. For being an atheist, or at least a sceptic, what moral scruples had Theodosius? As for my mistress, she had lived a very loose life in the old days, and had not by any means been faithful to her husband the merchant, looking upon her body as her own possession to dispose of as it best pleased her. Her love for Belisarius was undeniable; but whether it would restrain her from indulging any passion that she might feel for Theodosius I could not foresee.

When Belisarius said: 'We are all people of honour here,' I was sad. I loved him as a noble hero, and my loyalty to him was only second to the loyalty that I felt for my mistress, in gratitude for the great consideration with which she had always treated me.

It was at this moment that Solomon was announced. He came panting into the room, hardly able to speak. My mistress sent me for a cup of wine to revive him, which he presently drank. My discretion being beyond question, I was permitted to remain and hear the story that he told us.

The Vandal women were at the bottom of the trouble, Solomon said. They had persuaded their new husbands that the Emperor had defrauded them of their marriage-dowries – of the houses and lands that belonged to them in their own right. These same women had also stirred up indignation against Justinian's oppressive religious edicts: all Arians being strictly debarred from the Sacraments and even forbidden a little holy water with which to sprinkle their children for baptismal purposes. There was now a whole crop of newly born Arian children who, if they happened to die without baptism, would be damned everlastingly; and this caused their fathers, Thracian Goths and Herulian Huns, great concern. The mutiny had been agreed upon for Easter Sunday, which fell that year on the twenty-third day of March. The conspirators decided to assassinate Solomon as he was attending a ceremony in honour of the Resurrection of Christ, in the Cathedral of St Cyprian. Solomon did not have the least suspicion of his danger, because the secret had been extraordinarily well kept. Yet half the soldiers of his own bodyguard were in the plot, being married to Vandal wives and wishing to share in the distribution of land and houses.

The moment chosen for the assassination was that of the solemn elevation of the Host before the high altar (an action which is held to endow it with miraculous properties); for the whole congregation would then be prostrated in reverence, and a sudden, murderous blow could easily be struck. But when the Arian soldiers entered with their hands on the hilts of their daggers, encouraging one another with nods and nudges, they were overcome by a sudden sense of awe. The vastness and richness of the Cathedral, the soft, solemn chanting of the choir, the candles and the incense, the banners and the garlands of spring flowers, the venerable priests in their embroidered robes, the unarmed congregation at prayer in festival dress – all this created a profound impression on the Arians. They could commit murder but not sacrilege. As they halted, irresolute, the silent-footed sacristans and dog-beadles came gliding up to them, plucking at their sleeves imperiously, motioning for them to prostrate themselves with the rest. One by one they obeyed, and took part in the remaining ceremonies just as if they had been of the Orthodox faith. But when they were outside again, each of them accused his neighbour of cowardice and softness and swore that he himself would have dared the deed if only a single other man had stood by him.

They made these quarrelsome declarations in the public market-place, and Solomon soon came to hear of the matter; but when he ordered their arrest the men of his bodyguard showed no readiness to obey him. Then the conspirators, joined by a number of other dissatisfied soldiers, left Carthage and began plundering in the suburbs.

Solomon found himself powerless against these malcontents: his own troops refused to march against them. On the fifth day he called a general assembly in the Hippodrome, where he addressed the assembled soldiers and sailors and police-officers, attempting to win a renewed oath of loyalty from them. But they howled him down and threw stones, and presently began beating and killing their own officers. They cut the throat of Solomon's Chief of Staff; and then Pharas the Herulian, who resolutely proclaimed himself loyal to his blood-brother Belisarius, was mortally wounded by the arrows of his own men. These Herulians had been brewing *kavasse* again, for the bee had been restored to them.

Soon the mutiny became general, the whole army began to plunder the shopping district in the centre of Carthage and the warehouses by the harbour. Then, but for their not burning any houses down or wearing Green or Blue favours, it might have been Constantinople in the Victory Riots – with no Belisarius at hand to restore order. For the time being Solomon took sanctuary in the Lady Chapel of Geilimer's Palace, but escaped as soon as he was able and made for the docks. There he commandeered a boat and, after ten days' rowing, here at last he was.

When Belisarius had asked Solomon a few questions he announced to Antonina: 'I am going to Carthage immediately. It is what the Emperor would expect of me. Do you stay here and act as my Deputy.'

'What troops will you take with you?'

'A hundred cuirassiers.'

'You will be killed, madman.'

'I shall be safely back here before the month is out.'

'I must come with you, Belisarius.'

'I can trust only you with my affairs here.'

'I cannot trust myself. Let me come with you. I will not be denied.'

'Antonina, in this you must obey me. I order you in the Emperor's name.'

Thus it was that my mistress, though against her will, remained behind at Syracuse with Theodosius; and she did not expect to see Belisarius again. If it is true that she ever broke her marriage-vows sworn to Belisarius, this was the occasion. But she always denied that she had done so, and none could contradict her, for she had always been a very discreet woman. It is my task as a historian to tell the truth, but it is also my duty as a faithful domestic not to traduce my mistress. Fortunately this task and that duty do not conflict. I know nothing for certain: so much I can swear.

In Carthage the mutineers, having plundered the city to their hearts' content and taken formal possession of what houses and lands they fancied, marched out to join forces with another group of mutineers of the column to which Solomon had entrusted the wearisome siege of Mount Aures. Their combined squadrons soon amounted to 7,000 men, and in addition there were a thousand Vandals. Four hundred of these were escaped captives. They had lately been on their way to the Persian frontier from Constantinople; but off the Island of Lesbos they had overpowered the crews of their transports and sailed not to Antioch but back to North Africa, where they disembarked in a lonely spot near Mount Pappua and marched to Mount Aures. They had intended to ally themselves with the rebel Moors, but instead joined the Imperial mutineers, who welcomed them warmly. The remaining Vandals were refugees who had been hiding in obscure places ever since the capture of Carthage and now dared to come into the open at last. Horses were found for them at the posting-houses.

The mutineers chose as their commander a private soldier, an energetic and capable Thracian named Stotzas, and then marched back to Carthage, proclaiming the whole Diocese a Soldiers' Republic. No opposition at all was expected from the citizens. They arrived outside the walls at dusk on the seventh day of April and bivouacked there, planning to march in on the following morning. But that very evening Belisarius arrived by sea with his 100 chosen cuirassiers and immediately began to search through plundered Carthage for a few loyal troops; and before morning had gathered together 2,000. Of these, 600 were Roman African recruits of the cavalry police-force, and 500 were Vandals, men beyond middle age, whom Belisarius had allowed to live unmolested in their homes, and who in gratitude now volunteered to help him. There was also a number of friendly Moors. Of soldiers who had not mutinied there were no more than 500. But it was a saying that Belisarius's name was worth 50,000 men. When the mutineers heard of his sudden arrival, they considered themselves outnumbered by 52,000 to 8,000, and immediately broke camp and fled back to the interior. They were heading for Mount Aures, where they intended to make common cause with the Moors. Belisarius pursued and overtook them fifty miles out of the city, at Membresa, an unwalled town by the River Bagrades. Here was a new sort of battle for him to fight: against his own soldiers.

The honour of the victory is now popularly given to St Cyprian – whom legend also credits with having made a personal appearance in his cathedral on that Easter morning (disguised as a dog-beadle, but his halo plainly showing) to disarm the assassins and force them upon their faces. For at Membresa St Cyprian's wind sprang up suddenly, out of season again, and blew hard in the faces of the mutineers just as the two armies were about to engage. Stotzas realized that the arrows of his men would lose velocity because of the wind, and therefore ordered one-half of his cavalry to wheel over to a sheltered position on the right flank and use their bows from there. The manoeuvre was executed slowly and with some disorder. Belisarius, at the head of his cavalry, immediately charged against the point of greatest confusion, which was the Vandal squadron. For the Vandals, not being archers, were uncertain whether they were intended to move or stay. The sudden charge broke them, and the mutineers' army was cut into two parts; both of which gave way when Belisarius's column divided and swung round at full gallop against the rear of each.

Thus it happened that many of the Vandal women changed husbands a second time. They were left behind in the camp when the mutineers scattered into the desert, every man for himself; and were captured by Belisarius's men with the rest of the plunder. Most of the dead were Vandals; because as soon as victory seemed certain, Belisarius had ordered his men to refrain from attacking the mutineers, who might presently return to their allegiance; and indeed a thousand of the fugitives surrendered gladly and were granted a free pardon.

Belisarius would have continued the pursuit and summoned the still loyal garrison of Hippo, and the troops stationed in Morocco, to help him in stamping out the mutiny. But having only a single body, and that not divine, he could not be both in Sicily and Africa at the same time; and a messenger had just arrived from my mistress Antonina, reporting the outbreak of another mutiny at Syracuse. There was nothing for it but to leave Hildiger, his future son-in-law, in temporary command of the army in Africa. He returned with his 100 men to Carthage, and so by sea to Syracuse.

Nevertheless, there was no soldiers' mutiny in Sicily, as it proved, but only a refusal of an infantry general named Constantine to take orders from my mistress Antonina as Belisarius's lieutenant. He declared that it was no part of his duty to obey any woman, unless it were the Empress in certain civil matters of which the Emperor had delegated the control to her: according to immemorial Roman custom women could not be appointed military commanders. My mistress had placed Constantine under close arrest; and his fellow-generals, sympathizing with him, ceased to send in their daily reports to my mistress, referring everything instead to the senior officer among them, who was Bloody John. On his return Belisarius released Constantine from arrest, but spoke very severely to him and to the other generals, and told them that he regarded their action as both ignorant and insulting to himself. It had long ago been proved that a woman of sense and courage could not only command troops with resolution (as his wife the Illustrious Lady Antonina had done during the march to Carthage) but lead them to victory. Had not Zenobia of Palmyra, riding mail-clad at the head of her troops, preserved the Eastern Empire from the invasion of Persian Sapor? The Lady Antonina was, moreover, his declared representative and held his seal. By this untimely insubordination they had forced his recall from Africa, and prevented him from completing his action against the mutineers. The soldier Stotzas was still at large and likely to cause more trouble.

They said little in answer, but Constantine hinted obscurely that Belisarius did not know both sides of the story. He had had no intention of insulting Belisarius, but rather of honouring him in giving no obedience to a wife who did not consult his true interests. Constantine would say no more, and left Belisarius puzzled.

But on that same evening one of my fellow-domestics, a girl named Macedonia, came privately to Belisarius and warned him that my mistress Antonina and Theodosius were lovers, and that this had become a common scandal. She said that it was no doubt because of this that Constantine and the generals had been so unwilling to obey our mistress. Macedonia made the disclosure out of revenge, for my mistress had tied her to a bed-post two days before and whipped her for misbehaviour. The misbehaviour was an ignoble love-affair with the seventeen-year-old Photius, who had come with us to Sicily. Macedonia thought it unjust that our mistress, who was a married woman, should commit adultery and yet unmercifully whip her for mere fornication. But she had no proof of our mistress's guilt and was therefore obliged to invent evidence. She persuaded two little pages, Moorish royal hostages, to support her story. They wanted revenge on our mistress because as hostages they had expected to be treated as princes; but when their parents revolted our mistress gave them menial work to do and also whipped them when they pilfered or behaved in an unseemly way. They were such accomplished liars, or Macedonia had schooled them so well, that Belisarius could not but believe their story, which was most circumstantial; and it was to him as if he were on a vessel whose anchor-cable had snapped in a sudden storm. But Macedonia had bound him by an oath not to reveal to his wife from whom the accusation had come, or to call herself and the pages in witness to any charge of adultery. Belisarius's hands were thus tied. I had no notion myself of what was on foot, but I could see that he was suddenly most miserable and also angry beyond measure. However, he contrived to hide his feelings from his wife, pleading a sick stomach and anxieties about affairs at Carthage and about the insubordination of his generals.

What thoughts were passing through his mind I cannot tell, but I can make a fair guess. In the first place, I think, he wished to kill Theodosius for his ingratitude and treachery, and a natural jealousy was not absent from his heart either. Next, he wished to kill my mistress Antonina for her faithlessness to him, especially as he had trusted her absolutely and lived a chaste life. Next, he wished to kill himself, for very shame: Theodosius was his adopted son, and the crime was therefore incest. On the other hand, it was his duty as a Christian to forgive his enemies. My mistress had hitherto been the best of wives to him, and he still loved her passionately; and he remembered that lately she had pleaded to be allowed to accompany him to Carthage, though it might be to her death. She had, moreover, told him plainly that she did not trust herself alone in Syracuse; so it seemed to Belisarius that Theodosius had seduced her by some evil art or other, against her inclinations.

I shall not wrong Belisarius by suggesting that there was another consideration that weighed with him, though it would have been foremost in the mind of any other man in his position: that my mistress would be supported by Theodora, who would not hesitate to punish him 'for putting on airs' if he took any revenge for her adultery. To be tossed in a blanket was the least punishment that he could expect in such a case. Fear of Theodora would not have swerved him from any course that he regarded as the honest one; but it is possible that even in his anguish of mind he remembered his loyalty to Justinian, who had ordered him to prosecute this war against the Goths. Any hasty or violent action that he might take in the matter would provoke the enmity of Theodora; and, if he were recalled, North Africa and Sicily would soon be lost again to the Empire. As he was aware, none of his subordinates, though many of them were brave men, had any grasp of the strategical situation, or any capacity for leadership.

He sent for me that same evening and spoke to me alone and said: 'Eugenius, you have been more than a servant, you have been a good friend to your mistress and myself. Can I trust you with a secret mission? Unless it is swiftly accomplished by some discreet person I think that I shall go mad.'

I said: 'Yes, my lord. If it concerns either your welfare or that of my mistress.'

He charged me with fearful threats not to reveal the mission to a soul; and presently told me what I was to do. I was to go to Theodosius and tell him: 'Here is a monk's robe, and here are scissors with which to clip your hair in monkish fashion, and here is a purse of money and at the docks there is a vessel sailing for Ephesus tomorrow at dawn. The master's name is So-and-So. If you do not go aboard her at once, you will be a dead man. At Ephesus you must enter a monastery and take vows of perpetual chastity.' But I was not to mention the name of Belisarius on any account.

I grew afraid. I had never seen the equable Belisarius so excited in all my experience of him, not even on that early morning in the captured camp at Tricamaron. Yet I also feared my mistress. If Theodosius were to tell her from whom this warning message came, she would suspect me of plotting against her, and perhaps kill me. It was dangerous to give Theodosius such a message without reporting it first to her, yet I could not refuse the mission; and, besides, I considered it to my mistress's advantage that Theodosius should be removed from the scene without further scandal. I went trembling to Theodosius and gave him the message, telling him how unwilling a messenger I was. Knowing my character, he believed me and recognized that the warning was a serious one.

He guessed from whom it had come, and said: 'Tell my godfather that truly I do not know why he is angry with me, unless I have been unjustly slandered. I have a clean conscience but many enemies.'

When I begged him not to tell my mistress Antonina that the message had come through me, he swore that he would not. He kept the oath honourably, I must allow. He took the robe and the scissors and the money and went straight to the docks, without sending any message to Antonina. Then I went back and reported Theodosius's words to Belisarius.

You may imagine how frantic with alarm my mistress was when her dear Theodosius disappeared without a word: she naturally feared that he had been murdered, perhaps by Constantine, and was inconsolable. Not suspecting Belisarius, she called on him to institute an immediate search for Theodosius, which he consented to do. I myself was commissioned to find out when and where he was last seen. It was not difficult for me to set my mistress's mind at rest, knowing where to look. I soon found a couple of soldiers at the docks who could swear to having seen Theodosius; for it seems that he had not adopted the monk's habit until he was aboard. Thus she knew at least that he had gone voluntarily. But she was resolved to get to the bottom of the matter. Some new air of triumph in the demeanour of Photius, whom she knew to be jealous of Theodosius, aroused her suspicions; it was easy to deduce that Macedonia was concerned with Theodosius's disappearance. In the end she frightened a full confession out of the two pages.

Meanwhile, Photius had injudiciously confided the secret to Constantine; and Constantine, still smarting from my mistress Antonina's treatment of him, was only too pleased to have the laugh of her and Belisarius. On the morning of the second day after Theodosius's disappearance, meeting Belisarius in the principal square, he saluted him and said, grinning: 'You were right to chase away that Thracian Paris, great Menelaus; but the fault lay rather with Queen Helen.'

Belisarius did not trust himself to make any reply, and therefore turned his back on Constantine. Many soldiers saw him do so, who had not heard the original remark, and it caused a bad impression.

My mistress Antonina now spoke openly to Belisarius. What passed between them I do not know. But she convinced him that Macedonia had been lying, and it was clear that he felt both exceedingly relieved and exceedingly ashamed of himself. He sent a fast vessel to recall Theodosius; and Macedonia was whipped, branded, and confined to a nunnery for the rest of her life. The page-boys were also whipped and branded, and sent to work in the silver-mines. That my mistress with my help pulled out Macedonia's tongue, cut her in pieces, and threw the pieces into the sea is a lie told many years later by the secretary Procopius to discredit her. I do not say that Macedonia was undeserving of this punishment, or that my mistress did not threaten it in her anger.

Soon all was well again between my mistress and her husband. But Theodosius had not yet returned to us, the ship that was sent after him having failed to overtake him. However, Belisarius wrote to him at Ephesus, urging him to return, and also made a public confession of his own mistake, on the day of Macedonia's trial. All talkative tongues were silenced for fear.

Belisarius now awaited Justinian's order for the invasion of Italy; but it was long in coming, because Justinian had been disconcerted by the news of Mundus's death. He was instructed to do nothing as yet, but to hold himself in readiness until he should hear of the recapture of Spalato; and then march against Rome. Spalato was re-occupied in September by the reinforced Illyrian army, and in October Belisarius heard news of this and was able to begin his march. He had been greatly assisted in his plans by my mistress, who during his absence in Africa had been carrying on secret negotiations with King Theudahad's son-in-law, who commanded the Gothic forces in Southern Italy. She had persuaded this fellow, with whom she had contrived to become acquainted, to promise to desert his army on the day that our invasion of his territory began. Therefore, when Belisarius, leaving garrisons behind at Palermo and Syracuse, the defences of which he had greatly improved, crossed the Straits of Messina and marched against the town of Reggio (where the gold-mines are), this Vandal coward deserted to us with a few of his companions, and left his men leaderless. He went to Constantinople, where, renouncing his Arian faith, he was made a patrician and given great estates. King Theudahad, hearing the news, envied him.

The invasion of Southern Italy was thus not a running battle but a progress, the Goths scattering in all directions. We encountered not the least opposition as we marched up the coast accompanied by the fleet, until early in November when we came to Naples. This noble city was strongly fortified, and held by a garrison of Goths which was said nearly to equal our own army in numbers.

There are four ways of dealing with a reputedly impregnable fortress. The first is to leave it alone and attack the enemy in some weaker place. The second is to starve it out. The third is to force its capitulation by bribe, threat, or deceit. The fourth is to take it by surprise, after discovering that it has, after all, some weak spot which the enemy in his confidence has overlooked. Belisarius could not leave Naples alone; if he did, it would serve as a rallying point for all the scattered Gothic forces within a hundred miles. From the shelter of those massive walls, columns could be detached for the re-conquest of Southern Italy – the small garrisons that he had left behind in its principal cities would be overwhelmed. Nor could he starve Naples out, since it was plentifully supplied with grain, the principal granaries of the African corn-trade being situated within the walls; besides, delay at Naples would give the Goths time to assemble a huge army against him in the North. But it was not impossible that the city might be persuaded to capitulate by an impressive threat.

First he anchored his fleet in the harbour out of range of the siege-engines on the city-walls and camped in the suburbs, where in an attack at dawn he easily captured an outwork of the fortifications by escalade. Then he sent a letter to the Neapolitan City Fathers, informing them briefly that he expected them to surrender the city to him without further delay.

The Italian mayor came to him, under a flag of truce, but with two Goths as witnesses; he was not at all obliging, and as good as told Belisarius that he was trying to create a false impression of overwhelming military strength when his forces were extremely meagre. 'I regard it as a most unfriendly action,' the Mayor said, 'to put on us native Italians the burden of replying to your message. The soldiers of the garrison are Goths, and we dare not oppose them, since we are unarmed. Nor will they surrender to bribes and threats, because King Theudahad sent them here only the other day with orders to hold out to the last man – first taking their wives and children away from them as hostages, threatening to kill them if the city were lost. My suggestion is that you do not waste time here, but push on to Rome. For if you take Rome, Naples will certainly surrender also, and if you fail to take Rome, Naples will not be of much service to you.'

Belisarius answered curtly: 'I do not ask you for any lessons in strategy. But I will tell you this. I have soldiered for many years now, and I have seen many cruel sights in the sack of places which have not surrendered when called upon. I heartily wish to avoid such experiences at Naples. If you persuade the Gothic garrison to surrender, all your ancient privileges shall be confirmed and increased, and the garrison shall be at liberty either to join the Imperial forces or to march out of the city under safe conduct. But' – here he turned to the Gothic witnesses – 'I warn you Goths that, if you choose to fight, your fate will be that of King Geilimer and his Vandals.'

A Goth answered: 'Is it not true that Carthage, which lived happily under the Vandals and surrendered at discretion to your army, has recently been plundered by the Emperor's soldiers?'

Belisarius replied: 'Not by the Emperor's soldiers, but by those of the Devil.'

The Goth said: 'That is all one to us.'

Then the conference broke up; but the Mayor secretly assured Belisarius that he would do his best to persuade his fellow-citizens to open the gates in defiance of the Goths, who in reality numbered only 1,500 men. However, 300 good men would have sufficed to hold so strong a city against 30,000, and Belisarius had no more than 10,000 troops with him, having been obliged to detach 2,000 men for garrison duty in Sicily and Southern Italy.

Naples would yield neither for famine nor thirst. The Jewish merchants who controlled the corn-trade put their granaries at the public disposal, and offered the services of a number of Jewish marines and watchmen in their employment, who were trained to arms. If Belisarius cut the city aqueduct – as he was soon to do – there were sufficient wells inside the city to supply water for all household purposes. The City Fathers sent a message to Theudahad, assuring him of their loyalty but asking him to send an army to their relief.

The only hope now left of taking Naples lay in the method of surprise. But where was the vulnerable spot in the defences to be found?

CHAPTER 14
THE SIEGE OF NAPLES

BELISARIUS studied the fortifications of Naples from every angle. He could detect no weak place in the whole circuit that would repay the use of battering-ram or mine, but tried a surprise assault from the harbour by night; sending a party of Isaurian mountaineers, who are born cragsmen, to scramble up the lofty walls at a point where rotting mortar provided hand-holds and foot-holds. One man reached the battlements and quietly made a rope fast to a merlon, and then his companions swarmed up by this rope; but they were detected by a Jewish sentry, who roused his fellow-Jews in a neighbouring guard-house. Before more than four or five of the mountaineers had gained a lodgement, the rope was cut by the Jews, and they were all hurled to death over the battlements. The same ill-luck also overtook an attempt on the landward side. Here at dusk Belisarius managed to draw a long, thick rope across a projecting turret – by first shooting an arrow across it, that carried a silken thread, to which a string was then attached and pulled across, which in turn drew with it a cord, which cord served to pull across the rope. The two ends of the rope were then tied together, and men swarmed up on either side, balancing one another. But again the sentries were alert, and cut the rope, so that the men fell to their deaths. Belisarius also tried to burn a gate down by heaping barrels of oil and resin against it, but it was flanked by two strong towers, and our men were driven off with stones and javelins, and many were left dead at the gate.

After the siege had been in progress for eighteen days a former member of the Household Regiment, an Isaurian now serving as an officer in the Isaurian infantry, came to Belisarius and asked: 'Lord, what is the worth of Naples to you?'

Belisarius replied smiling: 'If it were given me now, so that I could march on to capture Rome before winter sets in, it would be worth a million in gold. If the gift were delayed until the spring I should have small use for it.'

The Isaurian said: 'One hundred gold pieces for every man in my company and five hundred each for my officers and one thousand for myself and two thousand for the private soldier who has found the weak spot that you told us to find for you!'

'I would double that,' cried Belisarius, starting up. 'But I pay only when the keys of the city are in my hand.'

'Agreed,' said the Isaurian. Then he brought forward the private soldier.

This man, a rough, unkempt fellow, told Belisarius his story. It had occurred to him to crawl along the dry conduit of the aqueduct, from the point where it had been cut, a mile or more away, to where it entered the city. He wished to see whether the end was perhaps closed by a grating or some other obstacle. It was an easy journey – he was able to walk nearly upright, and there were frequent ventilation holes above him in the brick vaulting. At last he reached a place where the tunnel narrowed to a hole in a rock, large enough to admit a boy, though impassable by a soldier in full armour. This rock was not granite, but some soft, volcanic rock which could easily be cut away with a pickaxe. He could see, a few yards away on the other side, light coming from above as if the aqueduct was unroofed at that point, and he could also make out a number of wind-fallen olives, a ragged headkerchief, and some broken crockery. He had then returned and next day walked along the road beside the aqueduct, looking for signs of an olive-tree overhanging the roof at any point, but could see none. He therefore concluded that the rock was inside the city somewhere.

Belisarius took twenty Isaurians of this man's company into the secret, but nobody else. He gave them muffled hammers and chisels and baskets and set them at enlarging the hole, which he first inspected himself. They must work as silently as possible. At midday they reported that the hole was large enough to admit the passage of a man in full armour, and that beyond it the aqueduct tunnel was three times the height of a man, and that a part of the brick roof had fallen in at this spot. The roots of an olive-tree had broken through the lower course of brick-work, deriving sustenance in normal times from the water of the aqueduct. The tree itself was outside the aqueduct, but one of its branches was spread across the hole in the roof. They brought the ragged headkerchief back with them, and some olives. Belisarius examined these things and said: 'The cotton kerchief has been newly washed and blown from where it was put to dry; and these are cultivated olives, not wild ones. Be sure that the tree is growing in some old woman's backyard.'

Then he sent another warning to the Neapolitan City Fathers: 'If you do not surrender your city tonight you will have lost it tomorrow, for I know how to take it. I swear this on my honour, which I am not accustomed to pledge idly. If you disbelieve me I shall be offended. When we storm the walls, I cannot promise that there will be no violence.'

But they did not believe him.

That night he sent 600 mail-clad men down the aqueduct, though at first they were most unwilling to go, saying that they were soldiers, not sewer-rats. My mistress's son Photius asked to have the honour of leading them, but Belisarius would not entrust so difficult an undertaking to a mere boy; though he allowed him to bring up the rear and be responsible for reporting progress. It occurred to Belisarius that 600 men in armour, stumbling however carefully down the dark aqueduct, would surely make a great noise; so he decided to drown the noise by a diversion.

He had with him an old acquaintance – Bessas, the Thracian Goth, who had been present at the banquet of Modestus. He was a veteran of fifty now, but still strong and full of fight. Belisarius desired this Bessas to go out with some of his fellow-Goths to a point near the entrance of the aqueduct and there engage the enemy sentries in talk in their own language, as if trying to bribe them to surrender the city. Bessas's men were to make as much clatter as possible, scuffling among the stones in the dark and indulging in loud horse-play as if drunken.

The ruse succeeded. Insults, shouts, cheers, jokes were exchanged, Gothic ballads were sung, Bessas loudly proclaimed his loyalty to the Emperor Justinian and the Gothic sentries theirs to King Theudahad; and the 600 men passed through the aqueduct without being overheard. They carried lanterns with them, to give them courage.

The leading man, the Isaurian who had originally discovered the way, wore no mail-coat, and was armed only with a dagger. When he reached the place where the roof was broken, he climbed up the side of the aqueduct from the shoulders of a comrade. Gaining a hand-hold on a projecting brick, he mounted higher, and after a struggle reached the top. A long strap was thrown to him; this he fastened to the branch of the olive-tree and then put a leg over the wall and looked around him. As Belisarius had foreseen, it was the courtyard of a house. Nobody was about. He beckoned with his hand, and four men in armour, including an officer, soon joined him in the court. Then he stole into the house, which was ruinous but occupied. It was now past midnight.

As he climbed in through the window his nostrils were assailed by the sour smell of poverty. He was in the kitchen; in the moonlight he saw a single cup and a single plate on a wretched table, where the owner had supped. Pausing, he heard a weak cough from the next room and a mumbling noise that could only come from an aged woman in prayer. He was upon her before she could scream, his dagger raised; but this was only for a moment. He took from his bosom the same ragged kerchief that he had shown to Belisarius, and returned it to her with a smile of friendship. He also gave her a lump of cheese, which she smelt and then ate delightedly. The officer now came in. He asked in Latin where her house was situated and who her neighbours were. She described its location and said that her neighbours were poor folk like herself, from whom there was nothing to fear. The 600 men were signalled to climb up. They stepped into the courtyard, which was a large one, one by one, massing themselves together. Photius returned to report to Belisarius that all was well so far.

Belisarius had a party with scaling-ladders ready in a lemon-grove not far from the aqueduct. As soon as he heard the two trumpet-flourishes from the city, and saw from the swinging of lanterns where exactly on the northern course of the circuit-wall the Isaurians had gained a lodgement, he brought these ladders up hurriedly and ordered an escalade. Constantine, to whom had been entrusted the task of preparing the ladders, had under-estimated the height of the wall, so that they were short by a good twenty feet; he lengthened them, however, by lashing them together, two and two, and little time was lost. The Isaurians had captured two towers and a considerable stretch of wall between them, so it was not long before 2,000 men had mounted and joined them there. Naples was as good as captured.

The only defenders who fought with true courage were the Jews. They knew that they had little hope of freedom if captured, Justinian being a persecutor of their religion; he blamed all Jews for the complicity of their ancestors in the crucifixion of Jesus Christ. But at last they, too, were overpowered. The gates being opened by some of the citizens, in swarmed the rest of the army.

Naples was given up to plunder for the rest of the night, and many acts of savagery were done which Belisarius was powerless to prevent. Especially violent were 200 Massagetic Huns, heathen, who had elected not to return to their own country, preferring to serve with Belisarius. They broke into the churches, robbed the church-treasuries, and killed the priests at the altars – a sacrilege which distressed Belisarius when it was reported to him, especially as these were churches of the Orthodox faith. In the morning he announced an amnesty and put an end to the looting. The soldiers had to be content with their plunder of money and jewels and silver plate, for he took away from them the Neapolitan women and children whom they had seized as slaves and restored them to their families. Then he held a court of justice, as he had done in Carthage at its capture. He informed the 800 Gothic prisoners that they would be sent to Constantinople and there given the choice either of becoming unpaid manual labourers or of serving as paid soldiers of the Emperor on the Persian frontier. They assured him that they would choose to remain soldiers, and he praised them.

While this court was in progress, an official messenger of the Italian Civil Service – ghastly faced, exhausted, spattered with mud – was admitted to Belisarius's presence. He carried with him a letter from King Theudahad to Honorius, the City Governor of Rome. He had not broken the seals, but believed it to be a message of the utmost importance and secrecy, for he had been roused from sleep long after midnight and kept waiting for six hours while it was being penned. Being a loyal Roman who hated the heretical Goths, he had at great danger to himself passed disguised down the Appian Way and brought this letter to the hand of conquering Belisarius, Vice-Regent to His Sacred Majesty the Emperor Justinian, who was Vice-Regent to God Himself. As he passed through the town of Terracina, at dusk, he had been questioned by a Gothic officer; to avoid capture or delay, he had stabbed the Goth in the belly and left him dying on the road.

Belisarius broke the seals of the letter and soon began to laugh so heartily that we feared for his senses. At last, recovering his gravity, he read out to the assembled company, in sonorous tones, the following document:

King Theudahad to the Illustrious Honorius, Governor of the Eternal City Rome, Greeting!

We regret to learn from your report that the brazen elephants placed in the Sacred Way (so named after the many superstitions to which it was consecrated of old) are falling into decay.

It is to be much regretted that, whereas these animals live in the flesh for more than a thousand years, their brazen effigies should be so soon crumbling to ruin. See, therefore, that their gaping limbs be strengthened by iron hooks, and that their sagging bellies be underpinned by massive masonry.

The living elephant, when it falls prostrate on the ground, as often occurs when it is helping men to fell trees, cannot rise again unaided. This is because it has no joints in its feet; and accordingly in the torrid lands frequented by these beasts you may often see numbers of them lying as if dead until men approach to help them to stand upright again. Thus this creature, so terrible by its size, is in point of fact not equally endowed by Nature with the tiny ant.

That the elephant, however, surpasses all other animals in intelligence is proved by the adoration which it renders to Him whom it understands to be the Almighty Ruler of all. Moreover, it pays to good princes a homage which it refuses to tyrants.

This beast uses its proboscis, that nosëd hand which Nature has awarded it in compensation for its very short neck, for the benefit of its master, accepting those presents which will be most profitable to him. It always walks cautiously, mindful of that fatal fall into the hunter's pit which was the prelude to its captivity. At its master's bidding it will exhale its breath – which is said to be a remedy for the human headache, especially if it sneezes.

When the elephant comes to water, it sucks up in its trunk a vast quantity, which at a word of command it will squirt forth like a shower. If anyone has treated it with contempt, it will pour forth such a stream of dirty water over him that one would believe a river had entered his house. For this beast has a wonderfully long memory, both of injury and of kindness. Its eyes are small but move solemnly. There is a sort of regal dignity in its appearance, and while it recognizes with pleasure all that is honourable, it evidently despises scurrilous jests. Its skin is furrowed by deep channels, like those of the victims of the foreign disease named after it, *elephantiasis*. It is on account of the impenetrability of its hide that the Persian Kings use the elephant in war.

It is most desirable that we should preserve the likeness of these creatures, and that our citizens should thus be familiarized with the sight of the denizens of foreign lands. Do not therefore permit them to perish, since it adds to the glory of Rome to collect all specimens of processes by which the art of workmen has imitated the productions of wealthy Nature in far parts of the world.

Farewell!

The messenger was crestfallen and angry that the letter was such a silly one; but Belisarius soothed him with compliments upon his courage and loyalty. He gave him a reward of five pounds of gold, which is 360 gold pieces, and enrolled him as a courier on his own staff. Belisarius said that the letter was of far greater value than appeared at first reading: it indicated clearly that King Theudahad was busying himself with scholarly trifles instead of attending to the defence of his kingdom. 'Now I can march against Rome without anxiety,' he told us.

Had this King continued in command of the Gothic armies, Belisarius's task would have been a light one indeed. For he had made no warlike preparations at all, assuring his nobles that all was well: a mongrel barking at a pack of wolves would very soon be eaten up. Theudahad regarded it as unnecessary to send a relief force to Naples, which could stand a siege, he said, twice the length of that to which Troy had been subjected by the Greeks of old. He would not listen to any remonstrances. 'Let Belisarius first break his teeth on Naples; afterwards we can fill his mouth with mud.'

Then when news came that Naples had fallen, the patience of his nobles was at an end. They declared that he had evidently sold the city to the Emperor; that to live in scholarly ease somewhere, anywhere, enriched through the betrayal of his subjects, was now his only object in life. They called an assembly at Lake Regillus, not far from Terracina, to which he was not invited. There they raised on their shields a brave general named Wittich, and acclaimed him king. This Wittich, who was of humble birth, had not many years previously gained a great victory for Theoderich against the savage Gepids on the banks of the Save. So little of a scholar was he that he could hardly sign his own name.

King Theudahad, who was on his way from Tivoli to Rome, to consult some works in the public library there, did not delay for a moment when he heard the news – spurring off to his palace at Ravenna. Ravenna was the securest place of refuge in Italy, being protected by marshes (over which ran two defensible causeways) and by a sea too shallow to allow ships of war to approach the fortifications. But Wittich sent a man to hunt him down, who rode harder for revenge than Theudahad rode for fear, having lately been deprived by Theudahad's order of a beautiful heiress promised to him in marriage. This man galloped day and night and finally overtook Theudahad, after a ride of 200 miles, at the very gateway to Ravenna. There he caught him by the collar, pulled him from his horse, and cut his throat as if he had been a hog or wether.

King Wittich marched to Rome, ahead of Belisarius. There he announced his election to the kingship and called a grand council of Goths. It became clear at this council that Gothic affairs were all in confusion. Not only were the forces for home defence scattered all over Italy, but the principal field army had gone north-westward across the Alps, to protect Gothic possessions this side of the Rhône against the Franks whom Justinian had bribed to attack them. Another army was in Dalmatia before Spalato. When Wittich reckoned up the forces at his immediate disposal, they amounted to no more than 20,000 trained men; and to outnumber Belisarius merely by two to one did not afford him the least confidence of victory.

He therefore decided to leave a garrison in Rome strong enough to defend it against assault, to make peace with the Franks, to marshal his forces at Ravenna, and within a few weeks to be back again in overwhelming strength to drive us into the sea. The Roman Senate assured King Wittich of their loyalty, which he strengthened by taking distinguished hostages from them; and the Pope Silverius himself, who had been under Theudahad's suspicion of secret correspondence with Constantinople, swore a solemn oath of allegiance to him. Then Wittich marched to Ravenna, and at Ravenna he married (though much against her will) Matasontha, Amalasontha's only daughter, and thus engrafted himself into the house of Theoderich. From Ravenna he sent messages of friendship to Justinian, asking him to withdraw his armies: for the death of Amalasontha, he said, had been avenged by that of Theudahad.

Justinian paid no attention, trusting that all Italy would soon be his. As for the Franks, Wittich made peace with them, paying them 150,000 in gold – the sum already promised by Theudahad – and yielding them the Gothic territories between the Alps and the Rhône on condition that they should send troops to help him against Belisarius. But the Franks, wishing to seem on good terms with us still, would promise none of their own troops; armies of their subject allies would be sent in due time, they said.

Then we marched on Rome, by the Latin Way, which runs through Capua, parallel with the coast about thirty miles inland; for the shorter Appian Way was readily defensible at Terracina and several other points, and Belisarius could not afford delay or further loss of men. Everywhere we were greeted with joy by the natives, and especially by the priests. The soldiers had strict orders to pay for all provisions that they might need and to act with politeness. To us domestics the sights of Italy, ancient and modern, were of great interest; but our mistress had no eyes for them and involved us in her own gloomy feelings. A letter had at last come from Theodosius, who had become a monk at Ephesus, just as Belisarius had advised him to do. In it he protested his love and gratitude to Belisarius, but excused himself from returning to us at present. 'I cannot come, my dearest Godparents, while your son Photius is with you: for you tell me that Macedonia has been punished, and I fear her lover's revenge. I do not charge him with having incited her to slander me, but you must know that he hated me even before this. For you gave me many gifts, dear Godmother Antonina; and these he regarded as stolen from his own inheritance.'

Belisarius wished to revive my mistress from her melancholy and at the same time to make generous amends to Theodosius for his former suspicions of him. He therefore sent Photius back to Constantinople; who took with him, for Justinian, the keys of Naples, the Gothic prisoners, and a letter requesting immediate reinforcements. Then Belisarius wrote to tell Theodosius that he could now return without fear. But my mistress thought it a weary time to wait.

The Gothic garrison at Rome was surprised by our arrival: their advance-guard, posted on the Appian Way, had believed us still to be at Naples. Once more the name of Belisarius proved its value. The people of Rome were convinced that the City must fall to him, and were anxious to avoid the fate of the Neapolitans. The Pope Silverius then violated his oath to Wittich, with the excuse that it was sworn under duress and to a heretic. He sent Belisarius a letter inviting him to enter without fear, since he would soon persuade the Gothic garrison to march out. As we descended the long ridge of Albano and entered the city by the Asinarian Gate, the Gothic garrison marched out of the Flaminian, to the northward. Only their commander refused to desert his post. Belisarius took him alive and sent him to Constantinople with the keys of the city.

I confess that the sight of Rome disappointed me. It is venerable and vast indeed, and contains most remarkable buildings, the greatest of them overshadowing anything that we can show in Constantinople. But in three things it is inferior in my mind even to Carthage: it is a city that has greatly declined in riches and population, it does not lie upon the sea, the climate is unhealthy.

The Roman Senators and clergy greeted us warmly and urged us to push on to Ravenna and destroy the usurper Wittich before he had time to assemble his forces. But they were distressed when Belisarius replied that he preferred to remain awhile in the city and enjoy its hospitality, and especially when he began to repair the city defences, which were in a ruinous condition. The Pope Silverius himself came to my mistress secretly, and said to her – I was present – 'Most Virtuous and Illustrious daughter, perhaps you will be able to persuade the victorious Belisarius, your husband, to give over his unwise intentions. It seems that he is intending to stand a siege in our Holy Rome, which (though abundantly blessed by God) is the least defensible city in the world, and in twelve hundred years of its history has never successfully stood a long siege. Its circuit walls, as you can see, are twelve miles in length and rise from a level plain; it is without sufficient food for its many hundred thousands of souls, and cannot easily be provisioned from the sea – as Naples, for instance, could be. Since your forces are insufficient, why not return to Naples and leave us Romans in peace?'

My mistress Antonina replied: 'Beloved of Christ, Most Holy and Eminent Silverius, fix your thoughts rather on the Heavenly City, and my husband and I will concern ourselves with this earthly one. Permit me to warn Your Holiness that it is to your advantage not to meddle in our affairs.'

Pope Silverius went away offended, not offering my mistress his customary blessing – which, as you may imagine, did not greatly distress her. Enmity sprang up between them, and he repented of having welcomed our small army. He was convinced that we would be overwhelmed, and that Wittich would depose him for his breach of faith.

Belisarius, having sent out Constantine and Bessas with a small force to win Tuscany over to our arms, set his remaining troops to work at strengthening the ancient city ramparts, clearing and deepening the choked fosse, and patching up the gates. Since early in Theoderich's reign no one had troubled about the repair of the ramparts. They consisted of the customary broad terrace of earth enclosed between two battlemented walls, with guard-towers at intervals. Belisarius now improved on the battlements by adding a defensive wing to each of them, on the left; so that to birds or angels looking down from the sky they would appear thus: ΓΓΓΓΓ, like the letter *Gamma* written many times over. He employed all the available masons and labourers in the city on this work, as he had done at Carthage. He also filled the Roman granaries with corn that he had brought from Sicily and requisitioned all stocks of grain within 100 miles of the city; paying for them at a fair price.

We had entered Rome on the tenth day of December; three months were gone before King Wittich came against us with his army. But by then it was a very strong army, drawn from every part of Italy and from across the Alps – consisting for the most part of heavy cavalry. Tuscany had yielded to our arms, but Belisarius now recalled from there all but the garrisons which he had put into Perugia and Narni and Spoleto, a mere thousand men. With the marines whom he took from the fleet, he had 10,000 men of all arms to oppose to 150,000 Goths. Thus the siege of Rome began.

Wittich rode southward at the head of his army, which strung out behind him on the Flaminian Way for a hundred miles and with only a little interval between division and division. Not far from Rome, he met a priest being carried out from the city in a sedan-chair on his way to take up a bishopric in the North. Wittich asked this priest: 'What news, Holy Father? Is Belisarius still at Rome? Do you think that we shall catch him before he falls back on Naples?'

The priest, who was a man of penetration, replied: 'There is no need to hurry, King Wittich. The Lady Antonina, wife of this Belisarius, is reglazing the windows of a palace which they are to occupy, and putting new hinges on the doors and buying furniture and pictures, and re-planting the garden with rose-trees and building a new north porch. Belisarius himself is doing the same sort of thing for the city defences – when you reach the Tiber you will find a new sort of north porch that he has built at the Mulvian Bridge.'

There are many bridges over the Tiber. The Mulvian is the only one near Rome that is not part of the city fortifications, lying two miles to the northward. Belisarius had built two strong stone towers here and garrisoned them with a detachment of 150 cavalrymen, whom he provided with catapults and scorpions to sink any boat in which the Goths might attempt to cross the river and take them in the rear. He intended the fortification of this bridge to delay Wittich's advance, obliging him either to make a long detour or to send his men across the river by tens or twenties in a few small ferry-boats – he had removed all larger boats and barges himself. Whichever choice Wittich made, his army was so huge that Belisarius would gain something like twenty days for completing his work on the city fortifications; and in those twenty days the reinforcements that he was expecting from Constantinople might well arrive. Perhaps he would also be able to delay the enemy's crossing at another point.

The Mulvian Bridge garrison proved cowardly. When they saw the Gothic knights approaching in their hundreds and thousands and tens of thousands, mounted on fine horses, the spring sunshine twinkling on helmets and armour and lance-points and frontlets and poitrails, they said to one another: 'Why should we stay here and be killed to please Belisarius? Not even he would care to face the odds of a thousand to one.' Some of them were Thracian Goths, who suddenly realized that this impressive army consisted of their kinsmen and co-religionists. What quarrel had they with them? At dusk the garrison fled: the Thracian Goths as deserters to Wittich, the remainder in the direction of Campania, being ashamed or afraid to return to Rome.

On the following morning Belisarius rode out towards the Mulvian Bridge with a thousand men of the Household Regiment, to hear what news there might be of the Goths; the usual dawn report from the officer commanding the Bridge garrison had not reached him. He was mounted on Balan, the white-faced bay charger that Theodora had given him after Daras, and was only a mile away from the Bridge when, emerging from a wood with his staff, he suddenly came upon an unexpected and unwelcome sight: four or five Gothic squadrons, already across the river, trotting in mass towards him over a large grassy meadow. Not hesitating for a moment, he charged straight at them, yelling to his leading troop to follow. When they came pouring up behind, shooting from the saddle as they rode, they found him and his staff doing the bloody work of common troopers; nor would he then draw out, but forced his way deeper into the fight.

Among the enemy were the deserters of the Thracian Goths, who recognized Belisarius and cried out to their companions: 'Aim at the bay and end the war at one stroke!' And 'Aim at the bay!' was the cry that every Goth took up.

Then began a fiercer encounter even than the conflict with the Persians on the Euphrates bank. Not only was Belisarius's squadron fighting against enormous odds, but every man of the Goths was eager to win imperishable renown by killing 'the Greek on the white-faced bay', as they called him. Never, I think, was such a bitter struggle seen since the world began. Belisarius's staff fought desperately at his side, warding off javelin-casts and spear-thrusts; Belisarius himself, cutting and thrusting and parrying with his sword, pressed forward into the very heart of the enemy. His horse Balan fought with him, having been trained to rear up and strike with his fore-hooves and savage an enemy. Still the cry continued in the Gothic tongue, 'Aim at the bay!' 'Kill the Greek on the white-faced bay!' Belisarius shouted for a new sword, for his own was blunted with use. A dying groom, one Maxentius, gave him his. Belisarius soon broke off this gift-sword close to the hilt, and a third one was found for him, taken from a dead Gothic nobleman, which lasted him through that battle and many another. After three hours or more of this fighting the Goths had their bellyful and turned in flight, leaving a full thousand dead behind them on the meadow. (Four times that number had been engaged.) They say that Belisarius had accounted for sixty or more with his own right arm. He was bespattered with the blood that had spurted on him from lopped limbs and severed necks, but by some miracle had not been so much as scratched by any Gothic weapon. When Belisarius fought he did not smile and joke as most of his men did; he considered it a very serious matter to kill a man, especially a fellow-Christian. Nor did he ever boast of his battle exploits.

The wounded men rode back to Rome in small parties. The last of them to arrive brought the news that Belisarius was killed; because when Maxentius died the groom was confused with the master. Then all of us in the city gave ourselves up for lost, except my mistress Antonina, who would not believe the news, and behaved with the greatest fortitude. After a tour of the sentries on the walls and an inspection of the garrisons at the gates, to encourage the men and forestall treachery, she took up her station at the Flaminian Gate. My mistress was popular with the men – courage is a commodity that is always prized. Also, she was not above exchanging bawdy jokes with them, and was free with her money, and could sit a horse well and even handle a bow.

Meanwhile Belisarius pursued the fleeing enemy towards the bridge, hoping to drive them back across the river and thus to relieve the detachment which, for all he knew, was still desperately holding out in the flanking towers at the bridge. But by this time a strong force of Gothic infantry had also crossed the river. They opened their ranks for a moment to receive the cavalry fugitives, then closed them again and held their ground, greeting our men with a shower of arrows. Belisarius wheeled round his squadron, now greatly reduced in numbers, and seized a hill near by from which he could see clearly whether the Imperial banner still flew from the towers. It had gone. Then 10,000 Gothic cavalry thundered against him and he was forced from his position. His men still had their quivers full of arrows, for the fighting had been hand to hand. They were now able, by picking off the leading horsemen of the enemy, to fight a profitable rearguard action all the way back to Rome.

Belisarius arrived at the Salarian Gate at dusk with large forces of the enemy pursuing him, just out of bowshot.

As I have said, my mistress Antonina was at the Flaminian Gate, a whole mile to the west of the Salarian, where there was a guard of marines. The marines had heard the news of Belisarius's death, and could not believe that it was indeed he who was clamouring for admission. They suspected a trick. Belisarius crossed the bridge over the fosse and came close to the Gate shouting: 'Do you not know Belisarius? Open at once, Sailors, or I will come round by the Flaminian Gate and flog every second man of you.'

His face was unrecognizable for blood and dust; but some of the men knew his voice and were for admitting him. Others were afraid, lest they should admit the Goths too. The gates remained shut, Belisarius and his bodyguard crowding up against them between the two flanking towers. The Goths halted in disorder on the other side of the bridge and began encouraging one another to charge across. Then Belisarius, who was never at a loss, dug his heels into Balan, uttered his war-cry, and charged fiercely back with his exhausted men across the bridge. In the growing darkness the Goths supposed that a new force of the enemy had sallied from the Gate. They fled in all directions.

At this, the marines at last opened to Belisarius. They humbly begged his pardon, which he granted; and soon he was embracing his Antonina and asking her for the news of the day. She told him of the measures that she had taken on her own initiative for the defence of the city. When the rumour came of his death she had strengthened the guards on the wall: she had dealt out picks to the common Roman labourers, and detailed them for duty, a few to each guard-tower. She had told them: 'It is a simple task. Keep your eyes open. If you see a Goth climbing up the wall, shout "Turn out, the guard!" loudly and, at the same moment, strike him with your pick!' She had also enlisted, from the unemployed artisans: masons and smiths with their sledge-hammers, timber-men and butchers with their axes, and watermen with their boat-hooks. She had said: 'I do not need to teach you how to handle your arms.' But she had given them helmets to remind them that they were soldiers. Belisarius greatly approved of her work.

Then, wearied as he was, and having eaten nothing since the morning, he yet made a tour of the fortifications to see that everything was in order and every man at his post. There are fourteen main gates to Rome and several more postern gates; it was midnight before he had completed his rounds. He went round right-handed, that is to say the way of the sun; but when he reached the Tiburtine Gate to the east of the city a messenger from Bessas overtook him, having run from the Praenestine Gate which Belisarius had just quitted. He brought alarming news. Bessas had heard that the Goths had broken in on the other side of the city, by the Janiculan Hill, and were already close to the Capitol.

The news caused a panic among the Isaurians who were guarding the Tiburtine Gate; but Belisarius, questioning the messenger, soon began to doubt the story, especially as Bessas's sole informant had been a priest of St Peter's Cathedral. He sent scouts at once to investigate; and presently they returned, reporting that no Goths had been seen anywhere. So he circulated an order to all officers that they were to believe no rumours put about by enemies inside the walls to frighten them from their posts. If danger came he undertook to inform them of it himself; but they must stand fast, each trusting that his brave comrades at other parts of the walls were doing the same. He ordered fires to be lighted along the whole circuit of the walls, so that the Goths might see that Rome was well guarded and the citizens might sleep more securely.

When he came round to the Salarian Gate again he found a crowd of soldiers and Roman citizens listening to the speech of a Gothic nobleman. The Goth addressed himself to the citizens in good Latin (which the marines did not understand), reproaching them for their faithlessness in admitting a pack of Greeks from Constantinople into their city. 'Greeks!' he cried, contemptuously. 'What salvation do you expect from a pack of Greeks? Surely you know what Greeks are from those whom you have seen – those companies of strutting Greek actors and those lewd pantomime dancers and those thieving, cowardly sailors?'

Belisarius turned to the marines and said to them smiling: 'I wish that you understood Latin.'

They asked: 'What does he say?'

'He is particularly abusing you sailors, and some of the things that he says are true.'

My mistress persuaded him to eat a little bread and meat and drink a cup of wine. As he was eating, five of the leading Senators came to him trembling, and asked: 'Tomorrow, General, you will yield?'

He laughed: 'Treat the Goths with contempt, my illustrious friends, for they are beaten already.'

They looked away from him and exchanged glances of wonder. He told them: 'I am not either joking or bragging, for today I learned that the victory is ours if we behave with ordinary prudence.'

'But, Illustrious Belisarius, the arrows of their infantry headed you away from the Mulvian Bridge, and their cavalry in enormous strength chased you all the way back to Rome.'

Belisarius wiped his lips with a napkin and said: 'Excellent fellow-patricians, you have described exactly what happened, and this is the reason why I say that the Goths are already beaten.'

They muttered indignantly to themselves that he must be mad. But anyone with the least common sense would have seen at once what he meant. Their infantry had shown only defensive powers against him, and their cavalry also had been unable to ride him down, even with enormous superiority in numbers, and fresh horses. For, not being archers, they were obliged to keep their distance. We recalled another remark of Belisarius's, made at Daras: rare as was a general who could handle 40,000 men, he was rarer still who could handle 80,000. What of Wittich, who had brought nearly twice that number against us?

The first night of the Defence of Rome passed, and no attack was made at dawn.

CHAPTER 15
THE DEFENCE OF ROME

THE first action that the Goths took against the city was to build six fortified camps, complete with ditch, rampart, and palisade. These were sited at intervals around the whole northern circuit, at distances from the walls varying between three hundred paces and one mile. Their next action was to cut every one of the fourteen aqueducts that had for centuries past supplied the city with abundant pure water fetched from a great distance. However, there were rain-water wells, and the western wall enclosed a stretch of the River Tiber, so we were by no means waterless; but the richer citizens took it very ill that they were obliged to drink rain-water and, if they wished to keep clean, to bathe in the river, being deprived of their own commodious baths. Belisarius was careful to stop up the aqueduct conduits with masonry at convenient points. He also built semicircular screens enclosing several of the city gates from inside, with only a small, well-guarded door in each of them, to prevent the citizens from making a sudden treacherous rush and admitting the enemy. The Flaminian Gate was so closely threatened by a Gothic camp that he blocked it altogether. He inspected the whole course of the defences very carefully, both from inside and outside, in search of a weak spot, inquiring especially about the exits of the city sewers; but he found that these emptied into the Tiber, under the water, so that nobody could enter by them.

The greatest inconvenience that we suffered at first was from the stoppage of the public corn-mills on the Janiculan Hill, which were worked by water from Trajan's aqueduct. Since we had no horses or oxen in the city to spare for turning the cranks, for the time being we were compelled to use slaves. But Belisarius soon had the mills working again by water-power. Just below the Aurelian Bridge he tied two stout ropes across the river, tightened them with a winch, and used them to hold two large barges in position, head-on to the current and only two feet apart. He put a corn-mill in each barge, geared to a mill-wheel suspended between them, which the rush of water from under the arch of the bridge turned round at a good speed. When he saw that the method was successful he strengthened the ropes; and forty more barges, in couples with mill-wheels between them, were tied on to the original pair in a long line downstream. Thenceforward we had no difficulty in grinding our corn; except when a few days later the Goths, having heard of the mills from deserters, sent trunks of trees floating down the river, some of which were carried against the mill-wheels and broke them. Belisarius then tied an iron chain-work across the bridge, constructed like a shallow fishing-seine. The floating tree-trunks were caught in this, and boatmen pulled them ashore to cut up as fuel for the public bakeries.

The citizens of Rome had hitherto been entirely unacquainted with the trials and perils of war, but Belisarius soon let them know that they must not expect to be inactive spectators, like the audience at a play: what privations the soldiers suffered, they must suffer too. In order to spare a reserve force of fighting men who could be hurried to any part of the walls threatened by attack, he enrolled still more unemployed labourers as sentries. He gave some of them daily archery practice in the Fields of Mars, and others he trained as spearmen. But they were sulky soldiers and remained a rabble, however hard the officers and sergeants worked at them.

Wherever Belisarius went in the city, Romans of both sexes and every social class had only black looks for him. They were angry that he had dared to take the field against the Goths before he had received sufficient troops from the Emperor, and thus involved them in a siege that threatened to end in starvation and massacre. King Wittich was told by deserters that the Senate was especially indignant against Belisarius; and therefore sent envoys to the city to take advantage of the disharmony.

These Goths, brought blindfolded into the Senate House, were permitted to address the Senators in the presence of Belisarius and his staff. They forgot the courtesies of the occasion and spoke roughly to the luxurious patricians, accusing them of having broken faith with the Gothic Army of National Defence and admitted a mixed force of 'Greek interlopers' to man the fortifications of the city. On Wittich's behalf they offered a general amnesty conditional upon Belisarius's quitting the city at once; they would even undertake to give him ten days' grace before starting in pursuit, which was most generous, they said, considering that the forces at his disposal were wholly inadequate to the defence of so enormous a stretch of walls.

Belisarius replied briefly that the Roman patricians had not been treacherous: they had merely admitted fellow-patricians into the city, together with the Imperial Forces that these noblemen lawfully commanded. 'My Gothic lords, I am empowered to answer with the voice of this loyal Senate, being of high rank among them, as well as with that of my Serene Master. I reply, then, that it was not Goths or any other Germans who originally built this city or these walls – why, you have not even kept them in good repair! Thus it is you who are the interlopers and without any title to possession. Wittich, your king, is not even recognized by my Serene Master as his vassal. So away now, I advise you, excellent Goths, and use your eloquence to persuade your compatriots of their folly; or the time will come, I warn you, when you and they will be glad to hide your heads in bramble-bushes and thistle-patches to avoid our lances. Meanwhile, understand well that Rome is only to be won from us by siege-craft and hard fighting. Siege-craft is an art in which no Goth, fortunately for ourselves, was ever adept; therefore our forces, though small at present, are more than adequate to defend the walls which our ancestors built and which you Goths have abandoned without a struggle.'

King Wittich was anxious to hear from the returning envoys what sort of a man this Belisarius was. They told him: 'He is a bearded lion of a man, has no fear, uses few unnecessary words; in feature and colour and bodily build resembles ourselves (but that his hair is dark and his eyes, which are blue like our own, are set deep in his head). His swift look and gracious bearing impose respect on all about him. We also saw Antonina, his wife, a lioness of the same breed, red-haired. King Wittich, you must be prepared to fight energetically.'

It was a fortnight before Wittich could complete his preparations for the assault. When, one morning at dawn, Belisarius saw from the rampart what these preparations were, he began to laugh; which caused a scandal among the citizens. They asked one another indignantly: 'Does he laugh that we are to be eaten up by these Arian beasts?'

I must confesss that I, too, did not see where the joke lay, for as I looked I could make out, a quarter of a mile away, a number of formidable framework structures on wheels, being drawn towards us by teams of oxen and escorted by swarms of Gothic lancers. They were like towers, each with an inside stairway mounting to a platform at the top, and seemed to be of an equal height with our wall. There were also a great number of long scaling-ladders being carried forward by their infantry, and wagons piled high with what appeared to be bundles of faggots, and more wagons loaded with planks. It was plain that their intention was to fill up a part of our moat with the faggots, then wheel the towers across a plank road resting on the faggots and take the walls by escalade. There were also four smaller wheeled structures encased in horse-hide, each with an iron-tipped beam protruding. These I recognized as battering-rams; the beam is swung on ropes within the structure and by repeated pounding will eventually knock a hole in even the stoutest wall.

They chose the Salarian Gate as the main point of their attack, and Belisarius immediately concentrated on the neighbouring towers all the defensive artillery within reach. This consisted of scorpions, which are small stone-throwing machines worked by the tight twisting and sudden release of a hemp rope; and wild asses, a larger sort of scorpion; and catapults, which are mechanical bows, worked on the same principle as these other machines, from the grooves of which thick bolts with wooden feathers are shot with force sufficient to outrange any ordinary bow. We had a few wolves also, which are machines for hooking the head of a battering-ram as it strikes and hauling it sideways, with a pulley, so that the tower overturns.

Belisarius called calmly to his armour-bearer, Chorsomantis, a Massagetic Hun, and said: 'Fetch me my hunting-bow and two deer-arrows, Chorsomantis.' These were his weapons of precision. A Gothic nobleman, a cousin as it proved to King Wittich, was superintending the advance of the enemy siege-engines. He was armed in gilded armour and wore a tall purple plume. But while he was still out of bow-shot, as he thought, death overtook him: Belisarius, with careful aim, struck him in the throat with a deer-arrow, so that he toppled dead from his horse. The range was not less than 200 paces. Unaware that this was Belisarius's customary accuracy of aim, the Goths were appalled by so evil an omen. A taunting cheer went up from the walls, and the Goths paused for a while while the dead man was carried away. Another nobleman, his brother, then took command; but as he signalled for the cavalcade to advance, Belisarius aimed again and proved, to anyone who might doubt it, that the first shot had not been a matter of mere luck. This time the arrow struck the Goth in the mouth, as he was shouting something, and the barbed head stood out through the back of his neck; he, too, fell dead. I began dancing for joy and cried: 'Oh, well done, my lord! Give us leave to shoot now!' For I had a bow in my hand, as had all my fellow-domestics.

He said: 'Wait until the trumpet blows the signal. Then let everyone about me aim at the oxen.'

The trumpet sounded, we all bent our bows and let fly. More than a thousand Goths fell, and all the oxen, poor beasts. A fearful cry went up. Then, I remember, I aimed at a tall infantryman as he ran forward with a bundle of faggots; but I missed my mark, and the arrow struck a horse in the rump, which reared up and threw his rider. I aimed at the horseman as he lay senseless; after three shots my arrow kissed his shoulder and glanced off. Since he continued to lie there as if dead, I looked for other targets, but saw none; for the Goths had retreated in consternation and taken up positions out of arrow range.

A large Gothic force of all arms then moved off out of sight. Though we did not know it, they were ordered to attack the Wild Beast Pen near the Praenestine Gate, two miles away to the right of us. But since 40,000 men remained as a threat to the Salarian Gate, Belisarius could not spare any troops from here as reinforcements elsewhere.

In the meanwhile there was great danger at the Aelian Gate across the river, where Constantine was in command. Only a stone's throw from the walls, just across the Aelian Bridge which leads to St Peter's Cathedral, stands the marble mausoleum of the Emperor Hadrian. This is a square building surmounted by a cylindrical drum around which runs a covered colonnade; the drum is capped by a rounded dome. In the construction of this wonderful edifice, no mortar at all was used, but only white marble stones, jointed together. Along the colonnade at intervals stand equestrian statues, also in white marble; they represent, I believe, the generals who served under Hadrian in his wars. The mausoleum was used as an outwork of the fortifications, the bridge being an extension of the City wall. It was here that Constantine's 300 men stood on guard, with catapults and sharp-shooting archers and a small detachment of army-farriers provided with heavy hammers.

The Gothic commander of the force ordered to assault this place was a man of discretion. Realizing that the part of the main wall which was protected by the river on either side of the Aelian Bridge would be weakly held, he kept a number of boats ready for an attack at a favourable point half a mile away upstream. This was a mud-flat under the walls sufficiently firm and wide to plant scaling-ladders upon. Here it was his plan to send an escalade party across in the boats, as soon as the attack against the mausoleum itself had been launched.

He handled the mausoleum attack ably enough. His men – heavy-armed infantry, with scaling-ladders – moved under his direction down the covered cloisters which run from St Peter's Cathedral to within a very short distance of the mausoleum. Constantine's men in the colonnade of statues, though on the alert, could do nothing until the Goths emerged from the cloisters. They then defended themselves vigorously, but only with arrows and darts: the catapults could not be depressed to fire at such a steep angle. Next, large bodies of Gothic archers, covering all four corners of the mausoleum and protected by huge shields, opened a most harassing cross-fire upon the colonnade, causing the defenders heavy losses. The situation grew dangerous. Constantine, warned of the impending attack from the mud-flat, had to leave hastily with twenty men to repel it. There was no capable officer to take over the command from him.

Soon scaling-ladders were planted against the mausoleum walls, and up clambered the Goths in complete mail-armour. The defenders' arrows and darts made little impression upon them. Then Rome would have been lost but for the sudden thought of a brave sergeant of farriers. He struck with his hammer at one of the statues and broke off a leg. His neighbour seized this huge lump of marble and hurled it down the ladder. The leading Goth fell stunned, involving in his crashing fall a whole row of climbing men behind him. The same farrier-sergeant broke off another leg, and down came the statue; this he frantically beat into convenient pieces which his neighbour distributed to all who needed them. Then the Goths were pelted from all their ladders with the mutilated limbs and trunks of these antique heroes and their steeds. They ran bawling away into the open, pursued by arrows; where they soon came within catapult-range. The whir of the great bolts, that would drive right through a man or a tree, made them run all the faster. Constantine easily checked the attack from the mud-flat, so that here on the western side the Goths failed in their hopes, as they failed also eastward at the Tiburtine Gate and northward at the Flaminian, where in each case the walls rise from a steep slope, disadvantageous for assault.

At the Salarian Gate the main Gothic force still threatened, but by now they kept well out of range, warned by the fate of one of their chiefs; he had been standing perched on the branch of a pine-tree, close to the trunk, shooting at us on the battlements. My mistress Antonina was managing a catapult, for she had learned how to lay a sight with these machines. Two men would wind the crank until the manager signed 'enough'; while he was studying his target, his mate would put a bolt in the horn groove and release the catch when the signal came. I was acting as mate to my mistress, and two Roman artisans were at the crank. She laid carefully on this sharp-shooting Goth, and presently signalled 'Release'. I pressed the lever, and the bolt whizzed out. Then a fearful sight was seen. The bolt, striking the Goth fair and square in the middle of his corselet, drove through and sunk for half its length into the tree; he was pinned there like a crow nailed to a barn-door as a warning to other crows.

My mistress was commanding here as lieutenant for Belisarius, who had now hurried away to help Bessas and his men at the Wild Beast Pen – a place close to the Praenestine Gate – where a strong attack had been launched. It was triangular in shape, formed by two weak outer walls at right-angles to each other built up against the main wall; and had formerly been used as a pen for lions destined for sport in the Colosseum. The outer walls could not be held by us, being low and of insufficient thickness to allow a breastwork to be built upon them. Wittich was aware, moreover, that the main wall which they enclosed was ruinous, and that it would soon yield to the pounding of a battering-ram. Gothic infantry clambered across the fosse with picks to undermine one of the outer walls, which would meanwhile screen them somewhat against arrow-attack from the battlements. Once the Pen was captured he could have hopes of victory. Faggots and planks were ready, and scaling-towers and ladders, just as at the Salarian Gate. A large force of Gothic lancers stood by.

The Goths across the fosse swung their picks industriously; and after a time a portion of the wall fell outward with a crash and they swarmed into the Pen. Belisarius at once sent two strong parties of Isaurians down over the main wall, by ladders, upon the outer walls. From here they leaped among the crowded Goths and closed the entrance of the Pen; then butchered them at their leisure. For whereas the Isaurians carried short cutlasses, which are excellent for fighting in cramped quarters, the Goths had two-handed broadswords, which need plenty of space for effective use. More Gothic infantry ran forward to assist their comrades, but suddenly the Praenestine Gate near by swung open: out poured a column of cuirassiers of Belisarius's Household, together with a few Thracian Goths. They charged the barbarian lancers, who were standing about in no regular order, and drove them in rout with heavy loss back to their camp, half a mile away. Then the cuirassiers turned and set fire to the scaling-towers and rams and ladders, which made a huge blaze; and so rode back in safety. A sudden sally was also made at the Salarian Gate, at my mistress's order, with the same success: here also the Goths fled and the engines were burned. Then our men hurried out and stripped the dead. With my mistress's permission, I went out with them and found the man whom I had killed: I saw that his neck had been broken. I took away his golden torque and the golden-hilted dagger from his belt – a eunuch house-slave playing the hero!

By the late afternoon the attack had everywhere failed. In shooting against so dense a mass as the Goths presented, the worst archers in the world could hardly have failed to cause great destruction; and we had a number of quick-firing marksmen with us and a plentiful supply of arrows. We reckoned the enemy losses that day as upward of 20,000 killed or disabled. The Goths withdrew sullenly to their camps, and all that night we could hear psalm-singing and lamentations as they buried their dead. On the following morning we were ready for them again; but no new attack was made at any point, nor for many days afterwards.

Belisarius had written to Justinian once more, explaining his need of 30,000 reinforcements and urging that at least 10,000 be sent without an hour's delay. Before the letter could reach Constantinople news came that reinforcements were already on their way. But it seemed that they numbered a mere 2,000 and had been forced by bad weather to winter in Greece, unable to cross the Adriatic Sea. There was no indication that they were the advance-guard of an army of reputable size. Belisarius knew now that he would be confined within the walls of Rome for three or four months longer at least. Provisions were still being brought into the city at night, by the gates on the southern side, but not in sufficient quantities to feed 600,000 persons for any length of time. He therefore ordered the speedy evacuation to Naples of all women, children, and aged people, and of all other civilians, except priests and senators and such, who were incapable of bearing arms.

Between dusk and dawn the Goths now kept close inside their palisaded camps; this was the fighting hour of the Moors, who were excused ordinary duty, but spent their nights outside the city walls. They would ride out in parties of three or four, wearing clothes of the colour of mud; and, tethering their horses in some clump of trees, hide in ditches by the wayside, or behind bushes. They would then spring upon single soldiers, cut their throats, rob them, and gallop away. Sometimes, combining their parties, they would destroy quite large companies of Goths. They used especially to lie in wait near the Gothic camp latrines, which were in each case dug outside the ditch, in order to catch men who were taken short in the night. They also haunted the horse-lines and the grazing paddocks. It was from fear of these Moors, as I say, that the Goths learned to keep close to their camps all night. So the long processions of evacuated civilians went out unmolested, night after night; and no Gothic camp covered the road that they took.

The first party was sent to the Port of Rome, where our fleet was; from there they took ship to Naples. But the rest were forced to go on foot all the way, carrying bundles or pushing handcarts heaped with household treasures. Processions of 50,000 and upwards went out nightly, straggling down the Appian Way. It was a lamentable sight to see them go, and many were the tears shed by these poor folk at the Appian Gate, and by the men whom they left behind. But at least they had a good road to travel by. The Appian Way is built of hard lava, as firm and unbroken as when it was first paved, hundreds of years ago under the Republic. Furthermore, Belisarius provided each party in turn with a cavalry escort for the first stage of the journey, and gave them sufficient food to last until they came to Naples.

On the day after the departure of the first party from the Port of Rome, which lies eighteen miles from the city, King Wittich seized the fortifications at this place; we had been unable to spare troops to guard them, and sailors are not fighters. Hitherto convoys of stores had reached us in barges from the Port, hauled up the river by oxen. We were now cut off from the sea, and our fleet retired to Naples. This occurred in April. In May we were put on half-rations of corn. In June the reinforcements arrived from Greece, under a general named Martin: 1,600 heathen Slavs and Bulgarian Huns.

These Slavs, who have curiously European features for so wild a race, had recently appeared in great force on the banks of the Danube, dispossessing the Gepids. They are horse-archers and excellent fighters if well fed, well paid and well led; and are also men of their word, but very dirty in their habits. Justinian had provided them with body-armour and helmets – usually they wear only leather jerkins and trews. He had also paid a great sum of money on their account to the priests of their tribe: for the Slavs have all things in common, and the priests, by whose ministrations they worship the Lightning God, act as their treasurers. When these Slavs learned that Belisarius was of their race and even knew a little of their language, they became well disposed to him; and so did the Huns (whom I have already described) on finding a few fellow-tribesmen of theirs in his Household Regiment held in great honour.

Belisarius now proposed to take the offensive against the Goths, though 1,600 men are not 10,000. He did not wish the new arrivals to feel that they were cooped up like prisoners in the city; as soon as they had been posted to their stations and given instruction in their guard-duties he staged a demonstration for their benefit. In broad daylight he sent out from the Salarian Gate 200 of his Household cuirassiers, under an Illyrian named Trajan, a troop commander and a wonderfully cool fellow. Following the orders that they had received, these men galloped to a little hill within sight of the walls and there formed up in a ring. Out rushed the indignant Goths from the nearest camp, snatching up their weapons and mounting their horses in great eagerness to attack them. By the time that it takes a Christian to say a Paternoster slowly, Trajan's men had shot 4,000 arrows into their disorderly column and killed or wounded 800 horsemen; but as soon as the Gothic infantry began to arrive Trajan's men galloped off, shooting from the saddle. They accounted for 200 more Goths before they returned, without a single casualty, to the shelter of the gate, where they entered under covering fire from a massed battery of catapults. Observe: the Gothic horsemen were armed only with lance and sword, and those of their infantry who were archers wore no body-armour and would go nowhere without the escort of mail-clad spearmen, who were very slow of foot. It was not to be wondered at that Trajan's men had it all their own way. A few days later a second force of 200 cuirassiers went out, but with a hundred Slavs attached to them for instructional purposes. They, too, seized a small hill, shot down Goths by the hundred, retired. A few days later still another force, Household cuirassiers and Bulgars, did the same thing. In these skirmishes the Goths lost 4,000 men; yet Wittich did not draw the obvious moral as to the inferiority of his armament, believing that the success of our men had been due merely to their daring. He ordered 500 of his own Royal Lancers to make a similar demonstration on a hill near the Asinarian Gate. Belisarius sent out a thousand Thracian cavalry under Bessas; the Goths were shot to pieces, hardly a hundred escaping back to their camp. The next day Wittich, who had reviled the survivors for cowards, sent out another lancer squadron of similar size. Belisarius let the Slavs and Bulgars loose on them, and every Goth was killed or taken prisoner.

The summer advanced slowly. One night a convoy came up from Terracina with sacks of coin for the payment of the troops, and with another sort of treasure for my mistress's household, namely the person of Theodosius. I must record that, although she greeted him very kindly, my mistress was so busy with her management of military affairs that the young man no longer seemed half her life; she had little time now for his sly witticisms and graces. She was prouder than ever before of being Belisarius's wife: there were continual praises of him in every common soldier's mouth and in almost every officer's, and her name was respectfully coupled with his. Theodosius, on the other hand, was a person of little importance, after all. He was not even a good marksman with a bow, and only a fair horseman – my mistress judged people mainly by these standards now, taking her duties very seriously. But she found a use for him as legal secretary to her husband. Soon it came to my ears that Constantine was reviving the old scandal among his brother-officers; and that the Catholic clergy were privately using the scandal to discredit our household among the civil population. But I said nothing, since we had troubles enough.

The same convoy also brought in a number of wagons of corn. They were the last that reached us, for the Goths now began to blockade the roads closely. Seven miles south-westward from the city two great aqueducts intersected, enclosing a considerable space with their enormous brick arches; by filling up the open intervals with clay and stones the Goths made a strong fortress, to which they built outworks. Here they placed a garrison of 7,000 men and were thus in command of both the Latin Way and the Appian Way. Even before the winter closed down on us there was great distress in Rome for lack of food. The remaining citizens, though impressed by Belisarius's frequent successes, refused to volunteer for active service; they grew more disaffected than ever, especially after a partial reverse that we suffered, which I shall soon describe.

It was by my mistress Antonina's vigilance that the treachery of the Pope Silverius was revealed. Belisarius had deputed to her the task of granting civilians permission to leave the city on business. She was very sharp in detecting any fraud – before she undertook this task a great number of Romans needed for defence work had managed to escape on various pretexts. One day a smooth-spoken priest came before her and asked permission to be absent for two or three nights: he had left a book in the sacristy-cupboard of his parish church near the Mulvian Bridge, and now wished to consult it. My mistress asked: 'What book?' He answered that it was the letters of St Jerome. She knew that no priest in his senses would risk passing through the Gothic lines merely to fetch these out-of-date, ill-tempered letters – of which, moreover, copies were surely to be had in any church library in Rome. But she concealed her suspicions and granted him a pass. The priest was arrested that night as he was passing out of the Pincian postern-gate. Sewn in his skirt was found a letter to King Wittich, signed by all the leading senators and by the Pope himself, offering to open the Asinarian Gate to admit the Gothic army on such a night as Wittich might appoint.

I should explain that Belisarius, in order to be as free as possible from judicial work that might interfere with his military duties, had also deputed to Antonina the settling of all civilian disputes and the punishment of all civilian offenders, though disputes and crimes of the military still came up before him. My mistress held a daily court in her quarters at the Pincian Palace. When she told him the names of the traitors and showed him the letter, he was angry but not astonished: he was aware that Wittich had threatened to kill the Roman hostages that he had at Ravenna if Italy continued to hold out against him. Belisarius did not think it just, however, that merely because the traitors were persons of such distinction they should be tried by himself rather than by her. Indeed, he was glad that the case lay in Antonina's jurisdiction: he would have been ashamed, as a devout Christian, to sit in judgement on the spiritual head of his Church. My mistress certainly had no such scruples, being still a pagan at heart. She said: 'A traitor in a mitre, or a traitor in a helmet – where is the difference?' Nevertheless, Belisarius was present at the trial, not wishing to seem a shirker of responsibility. My mistress, being unwell that day, reclined on a couch; he sat at her feet as her coädjutor.

The Pope Silverius, summoned before the court, appeared in full regalia of gold and purple and white silk, as if to overawe my mistress. He had his Fisherman's ring on his finger, his pastoral staff in his hand, the great jewelled tiara on his head. Behind him followed a retinue of bishops and deacons, splendidly gowned. But these were instructed by my mistress Antonina to wait in the first and second ante-chambers, according to their rank.

The Pope Silverius rapped with his staff on the floor and asked my mistress: 'Why, Illustrious Antonina, Sister in Christ, have you brought us here, rudely interrupting our devotions with your impetuous summons? What ails you that you could not instead come to our Palace, as courtesy demanded?'

She bent her brows in the style of Theodora and, disdaining any reply to his question, asked him directly: 'Pope Silverius, what have we done to you that you should betray us to the Goths?'

He feigned indignation: 'Would you accuse the anointed successor of the Holy Apostle Peter of a miserable felony?'

But she: 'Do you think that because tradition entrusts you with the Keys of Heaven you have power also over the keys of the Asinarian Gate?'

'Who accuses us of this treachery?'

'Your own signature and seal.' She showed him the intercepted letter.

'Adulteress, it is a forgery,' he bellowed at her.

'Be respectful to the court, cleric, or you shall be scourged,' she threatened. Then she confronted him with the parish priest, who had made a full confession without any necessity of torture.

The Pope Silverius trembled for shame, yet continued to deny his guilt. The nine senators who had also signed the letter were now produced in witness against him. They had already thrown themselves on the mercy of my mistress, and tearfully blamed the Pope to his face for seducing them from their loyalty.

My mistress delivered her verdict, after a short conference with Belisarius: 'Whereas the sentence that the Law requires to be inflicted on traitors, during the defence of a city, is mutilation of the features, and to be paraded for public insult through the streets, and then to be put to a disgraceful death at the stake, we yet have more regard for the good name of the Church than to keep strictly to the letter of the law. None the less, a shepherd who sells his flock to the Arian wolf cannot be allowed to retain his crook. Eugenius, disrobe this priest and give him the monk's robe hanging on the peg yonder. Silverius, you are deposed from your bishopric, and leave the city tonight.'

Although the clerics of the Papal retinue were appalled at the sacrilege when the sentence was announced to them, they could not dispute the human justice of it. I approached the Pope and took away his pastoral staff, his ring, and his tiara, laying them upon a table. Then I conducted him to a room where the regional sub-deacon was waiting. He removed all Silverius's priestly garments, until he stood before us only in his shirt – and not a hair-shirt, either, but a fine silk one embroidered with flowers like a woman's chemise. Then we gave him the monk's robe and put it over his head, and tied the cord for him, all without a word.

When we brought him back into the court my mistress addressed him, saying: 'Spend the rest of your days in repentance, Brother Silverius, as did your illustrious predecessor, the first Bishop of Rome, after similarly breaking faith with his Master. He finally made amends by martyrdom in the Hippodrome of Caligula, close to the city – but so much sanctity we do not expect of you.'

Belisarius said nothing all this time, and appeared very ill at ease.

Silverius was escorted out of the Palace by two Massagetic Huns, who placed him in the guard-room at the Pincian Gate; that night he left the city for Naples, and the East.

His subordinates met to elect a new Pope. The deacon Vigilius was the successful candidate – having gone to the trouble of bribing the electors with a matter of 15,000 gold pieces. Gold was more highly prized by these greedy clerics than ever before. The civil population was allowed only a very small corn-ration, which it would eke out with cabbage and such green herbs as nettle and dandelion and hare's ear; but good food in plenty only gold could purchase. During that summer soldiers took to making nightly raids on the harvest-fields behind the Gothic lines, cutting the heads of corn off by the handful with sickles and thrusting them into sacks slung over the backs of their horses. A sack of corn fetched a hundred times its peace-time price.

As winter drew on, these supplies ceased: sausages made from mule-flesh were the only palatable supplement to the meagre corn-ration that even the wealthiest purse could buy. Cats, rats, and axle-grease were eaten. Of wine alone there was no great shortage, since Belisarius had requisitioned all stocks from private cellars for public distribution. The city was very close to famine; yet, strangely enough, I never saw a single under-nourished priest. 'Ah,' said my mistress drily, when I remarked on this to her, 'the ravens feed them, as they miraculously fed the Prophet Elijah.'

As for the nine senators who had attached their names to the intercepted letter, Antonina could not in justice punish them more severely than the Pope. She banished them, confiscated their goods, and sent them out of the city in Brother Silverius's company. Belisarius was still uneasy: other Romans as well might be implicated in the plot. He therefore employed locksmiths to change or interchange the locks of all the gates twice a month, so that it would be more difficult for traitors to obtain a key to fit them. He also appointed officers for guard duty at these gates according to an irregular roster, to make it impossible for any of them to be bribed in advance to open any particular gate on any agreed night. To make the watches less tedious my mistress had formed bands of musicians from the theatre to give frequent concerts at every gate; but for greater vigilance on these occasions Belisarius set outposts beyond the fosse, chiefly Moors, and every outpost had a watchdog trained to growl at the least sound of approaching feet.

I must pause here just long enough to relate how cleverly my mistress Antonina managed these musicians. If any musician played ill my mistress would seize his instrument from him and show him: 'The tune goes so.' And she would taunt them, 'O you miserable Romans, you cannot fight and you cannot fiddle. Of what use are you?' To this an aggrieved daring musician once replied, attempting to abash her with obscenity: 'We are great adepts at procreation.' She replied coldly: 'In this at least you surpass your fathers.' The joke was repeated from mouth to mouth, and has become one of the most famous of her many sayings.

The reverse of which I promised to tell was due to the elation of our troops at the success of the cavalry skirmishes. They were impatient of Belisarius's policy of gradually wearing down the enemy's forces and courage, and clamoured for a general engagement. It was his policy never to discourage a warlike spirit in his men, but he did not think that the time was yet ripe for a pitched battle. The enormous difference in size between the armies still remained, and the Goths, though discouraged, were still fighting courageously. He tried to keep his men busy with more frequent sorties. But on two or three occasions he found that the Goths were ready for him, having been warned of his intentions by deserters. The Roman population now began to clamour for a battle too – or at least for a speedy end to the siege, one way or the other. He could no longer refuse the plea: he must not lose the respect of his men, or allow the civil population to become unmanageable.

The largest Gothic camp lay a mile beyond the mausoleum of Hadrian in what is called the Plain of Nero. Belisarius was anxious that his main attack against the camps outside the Pincian and Salarian Gates should not be hindered by enemy reinforcements hurried up from that quarter. He therefore ordered the Moorish cavalry to make a feint against the Goths there as soon as he was engaged; they were to ride out from the Aelian Gate under an officer named Valentine. After them would follow a force of city infantry, drawing up in defensive formation a short distance outside the gate. He told these Romans to look as much like soldiers as possible, but did not expect any serious fighting from them. His main attack he would make with cavalry alone. He had increased his cavalry forces by 1,000: in the recent fighting a great number of riderless horses had been captured, and part of the Isaurian infantry had converted itself – very successfully – into cavalry. The remaining Isaurians pleaded to be allowed also to take part in the battle. He could not refuse them, but stipulated that a few of them must remain on the walls and at the gates, to stiffen the city levies and to manage the catapults and scorpions and wild asses.

Early one autumn morning Belisarius led out his cavalry through the Pincian and Salarian Gates; the Isaurian infantry followed behind. Wittich was waiting for them, warned as usual. He had mustered every available man from his four northern camps, drawing up his infantry in the centre of his line and his cavalry on the wings; he stood at a distance of half a mile from the city, to allow more room for pursuit when he had overwhelmed us.

At nine o'clock the battle began, and Belisarius did just as he pleased at first, because the Goths stood on the defensive. He had divided his cavalry into two columns, one to each flank, which poured thousands of arrows into their dense mass. But to keep their infantry amused, a few small bodies of our Isaurian spearmen came up between, very close to their centre, and challenged equal bodies of Goths to combat; they were victorious in every such encounter. After a while the enemy cavalry began to retreat, their infantry keeping pace with them. By midday our men had pressed them back against their most distant camps. But here their archers came into action at last and, protected by huge shields, began shooting at our horses from the top of the ramparts. Before long so many of our cavalry were either wounded or unhorsed that no more than four full squadrons survived to resist fifty of theirs. To have broken off the engagement at this point, however, would have meant abandoning our infantry to its fate. At last the Gothic right wing took courage and charged. Bessas, who was commanding the cavalry on our left, fell back on the infantry; the infantry did not hold, and the whole line began to retire. It was easy enough for our cavalry to fight a rearguard action, but the slower-moving infantry suffered heavily. In all we lost a thousand men, whom we could ill spare, before covering fire from the siege-engines on the walls halted the rush of the enemy. Some of the Roman soldiers shut the Pincian Gate against the returning men, but my mistress and I were there with a few trusty spearmen. We resisted, killing several, and opened the gate again.

In the Plain of Nero meanwhile the two other armies had stood facing each other for a long time – the city levies drawn up in a formidable line, several thousand strong, with a screen of Moorish cavalry in front. The Goths had acquired a superstitious fear of the black-faced Moors by now; the Moors knew this, and kept harrying them with sudden charges, hurling their javelins and retiring with whoops of laughter. At midday the Moors made an unexpected charge in mass. The Goths, who outnumbered them by thirty to one, turned and fled to the Vatican Hill, leaving their camp unguarded. Valentine marched the whole army forward across the plain, intending to seize the Gothic camp and leave the Roman infantry to guard it while he and the Moors made a raid northward to destroy the Mulvian Bridge. Had this plan succeeded, Wittich would have been compelled to abandon his northern camps, since all food supplies for them came down the Flaminian Way and across this bridge. But when the rabble of Roman infantry began to plunder the Gothic camp, the Moors were loath to be deprived of their share of the plunder and joined in the merry work. Presently a few enemy scouts ventured down from the Vatican Hill and observed what was happening. They prevailed on the others to make an effort to recapture the camp. Soon the Goths came charging back in their thousands, and Valentine could not restore order in time: he was driven from the camp and forced back to the walls again, with heavy losses.

This was the last pitched battle which Belisarius consented to fight during the long defence of Rome.

Still no reinforcements arrived from Constantinople. Though we did not know it at the time, it was Cappadocian John who prevented their dispatch: apparently he insisted to Justinian that not another man could be spared. My mistress was for writing to Theodora, but Belisarius did not think it appropriate that his wife should appeal to the Empress in a military matter which directly concerned neither of them. Nevertheless, she did write, secretly, at the end of November, on the day that Silverius was deposed, making her plea a postscript to her lively account of the trial. Theodora would, my mistress knew, be delighted to hear of Silverius's humiliation, for he had angered her recently by refusing a request of hers – not backed by Justinian's authority – to reinstate a Patriarch who, though a most energetic and worthy man, had been removed from his see for Monophysite leanings. 'The new Pope promises to be more obliging', my mistress Antonina wrote to Theodora.

It was now very difficult for Belisarius to keep the civil population in good heart, for they were subsisting on a diet consisting almost wholly of herbs. Pestilence broke out and carried off 12,000 of them; but the soldiers still had their daily corn-ration and their wine and a little salted meat, so not many of them died. Sorties were made every two or three days, when it was found that the Goths were by no means so eager as before to come to grips with our horse-archers. Nobody enjoys being shot at and being unable to reply; but Wittich had not thought to form a corps of horse-archers of his own.

Of the smaller incidents of the siege I could write endlessly. There are a few stories concerned with wounds that must not be left untold. On the day that Theodosius entered Rome with the convoy Belisarius had engaged the attention of the enemy with brisk skirmishes at the other gates. The Household Regiment was heavily engaged, and on their return that evening two of the cuirassiers presented an extraordinary sight. One of them, Arzes, a Persian formerly belonging to the Immortals, came riding back with an arrow sunk in his face close to his nose; and another, a Thracian called Cutilas, came back with a javelin sticking in his head and waving about like a plume. Neither of them had paid the least attention to these wounds, but had continued fighting indefatigably, to the horror and alarm of the Goths, who cried: 'These are not men but demons.'

The javelin was afterwards drawn from Cutilas's head by a surgeon; but the wound grew inflamed, and he was dead in two days. Arzes, however, was examined by the same surgeon, who pressed the back of his neck and asked: 'Does this pressure hurt?' 'Yes,' replied Arzes. Then the surgeon opened the skin at the back of Arzes' neck. He found the point of the arrow, caught hold of it with a pair of forceps and, having first cut off the shaft close to the nose, tugged the arrow through, barb and all. Arzes fainted with the pain, but his blood was healthy: the wound healed up without any suppuration. He led the next sally, and survived the war.

On another occasion, Trajan, the troop-commander whose exploits I have already mentioned, was pierced close above the right eye and near the nose by the long, barbed head of an arrow. The shaft had been insecurely fastened to it, and fell off at the moment of impact. Trajan continued fighting. For days and months after his comrades expected him to drop dead at any moment; but he lived on and suffered no pain or inconvenience, though the barbed head remained imbedded in his flesh. Five years later it began slowly to emerge again. Twelve years more, and he was able to pluck it out like a thorn.

But as strange a story as any concerns the wound of Chorsomantis, Belisarius's armour-bearer. This was not a deep or a very remarkable wound, being a mere spear-prick in his shin, but it kept him in his quarters for several days, with poultices of wound-wort wrapped around it. In consequence he was absent from the pitched battle, in which a number of his comrades distinguished themselves. When he was well again he swore to be avenged on the Goths for this 'insult to his shin', as he called it. His white mare having recently foaled, he now had the necessary milk from her for brewing *kavasse*; and *kavasse* he brewed. One day after his midday meal, having drunk a good deal of this liquor, Chorsomantis armed himself, mounted his mare, and rode to the Pincian postern-gate. He told the sentry on duty there that the Illustrious Lord Belisarius had entrusted him with a mission to the enemy's camp. As Chorsomantis was known to enjoy Belisarius's fullest confidence, the sentry did not doubt his word; the gate was unlocked for him.

The sentry watched Chorsomantis ride easily over the plain until an outpost of the Goths, a party of twenty men, sighted him. Taking him for a deserter, they came spurring eagerly forward, each hoping to win the mare for his own booty. Chorsomantis drew his bow.

Twang! twang! twang! – down went three Goths, and the others turned hurriedly about. He shot three more of them as they fled, then returned towards the city at a slow walk, holding in his mettlesome mare. A troop of sixty Goths now came charging down on him, but he turned and galloped about them in a half-circle. He killed two more men, wounded two, and completed the circle with the slaughter of four more. I happened to be watching from the rampart, ran hurriedly and called to my mistress, who was in conference with the officers of a guard-house near by, begging her not to miss this extraordinary spectacle. 'Here's a man has gone mad,' I cried.

She recognized the mare: 'No, not mad, my good Eugenius. That is only our Chorsomantis avenging the insult to his shin.'

Then Chorsomantis was caught between two enemy troops; but he charged clean through the nearer one, using his lance and sword this time. We cheered loudly, for we saw that he was safe at last, if he wished. My mistress ordered a strong covering fire from the catapults to assist his return, but our cheer determined him to continue the fight. He turned yet again and disappeared from our view, driving some of the enemy before him, but pursued by others. We heard distant shouts and cries for a good while longer as the fight continued towards their camp.

In the end a Gothic cheer from close to their palisade informed us that Chorsomantis was no more. While many Christians made the sign of the Cross upon their breasts and offered a prayer for his soul my mistress cried out with a loud pagan oath: 'By the body of Bacchus and the club of Hercules, that was an angry man!'

CHAPTER 16

RETIREMENT OF THE GOTHS

THE news that had come from Africa in the spring of this year was gloomy indeed. Solomon had recently sent a column of Imperial troops against Stotzas from Numidia, but Stotzas had persuaded them to join in the mutiny, in spite of the prestige that he had lost through his defeat by Belisarius. Except for the towns of Carthage and Hippo Regius and Hadrumetum, the whole Diocese was lost to Justinian again. However, it was one thing to be the ring-leader of a successful mutiny and another to govern a Diocese: Stotzas found that he had little authority over his men, who complained that he did not provide them with regular rations or pay or attend to their comforts, and that they were little better off now than before. Later in the year we heard that Justinian had sent his nephew Germanus to proclaim an amnesty in his name to all deserters; and that the mutineers considered the offer a very handsome one, since it included back pay for all the months of the mutiny. Stotzas's forces were now gradually melting away. At last we heard that Germanus had defeated Stotzas and his Moorish allies in the field, and that Stotzas had fled to the interior of Morocco in the company of a few Vandals; and that all was quiet again, though the whole Diocese was greatly impoverished. Belisarius wrote to Germanus, suggesting that he send him as reinforcements the Herulians and Thracian Goths who had been among the mutineers; in Italy there were no laws forbidding the Sacraments to Arians, and he could make good use of these brave men.

At Rome there was plain famine now. The distressed citizens came again to plead with Belisarius to fight another pitched battle, and so end the siege, one way or the other, at a single stroke. They even told him: 'Our misery has become so profound that it has actually inspired us with a sort of courage, and we are ready, if you insist, to take up arms and march with you against the Goths. Rather die under the merciful sword-stroke or lance-thrust than from the slow and tearing pangs of hunger.'

Belisarius was ashamed to hear so degrading an avowal from the mouths of men who still bore the proud name of Romans. In dismissing them he said that if they had volunteered twelve months previously to learn the business of fighting, by now he might have good use for them: as it was, they were useless to him. Belisarius was aware that the Goths were in a very difficult position themselves – the pestilence had spread to their camps, which were insanitary, and destroyed many thousands of them. There had also been a breakdown in their food-supply from the north, owing to floods and mismanagement. But his own position was worse; and if the relieving force that was rumoured to be on its way did not soon arrive he was lost.

He now took the bold step of secretly sending out two columns, of 500 good troops and 1,000 Roman levies each, to surprise and occupy the fortified towns of Tivoli and Terracina. If both actions were successful he would not only have decreased his ration-strength but turned from besieged to besieger: Tivoli and Terracina commanded the roads by which food-convoys were now reaching the Goths. He urged my mistress Antonina to leave Rome with the force sent against Terracina, and from there continue to Naples and hurry the reinforcements forward to him as soon as they arrived. In reality he was anxious for her health, because her great exertions and the badness of the food had weakened her greatly; and she had frequent fainting fits. Besides, to be the only woman in a besieged city is no happy fate. After some hesitation she agreed to go, resolved by whatever means to revitual the city before another month had passed.

On the last night of November we slipped out of the city, 1,500 of us, by the Appian Gate. I, for one, was so happy to be away that I began to sing a Hippodrome song, 'The Chariots Fly', forgetting the order of silence; an officer struck me roughly over the shoulder with the flat of his sword, and I ceased singing in the middle of my verse. We passed the aqueduct fortress in safety, the Goths having abandoned it because of the pestilence; and a few days later we occupied Terracina without incident, for the small Gothic garrison fled at sight of our banner. We filled our bellies in this place, eating cheese and butter and fresh sea-fish for the first time for many months.

My mistress and I and Procopius the secretary, who came with us, set out from Terracina with an escort of twenty soldiers; yet we reached Naples with more than 500! Our way had taken us past the encampment of those cavalrymen who had deserted at the Mulvian Bridge long before. A number of other deserters had since joined them there. When my mistress offered them all a free pardon, they fell in behind her. And at Baiae we found a number of our wounded, who had been sent to take the waters there, now sufficiently recovered to be able to fight again. But Naples – where the volcano Vesuvius was rumbling ominously, and scattering the ashes that induce such fertility in the vineyards that they fall upon – Naples had happy news for us. A fleet had just arrived from the East with 3,000 Isaurian infantry on board, and was anchored in the bay; and, besides this, 2,000 cavalry under Bloody John had landed at Otranto and were moving up towards us by rapid marches.

Soon our army of 5,500 men was ready to march to the relief of Rome. We had collected great quantities of grain and oil and sausages and wine to take with us. Bloody John had assembled a large number of farm-wagons, requisitioned with their teams in his passage through Calabria; we loaded the grain on these. John undertook to escort the convoy into Rome along the Appian Way – if the Goths attacked, the wagons would provide him with a useful barricade in the barbarian style. My mistress took command of the Isaurian fleet itself, storing all the other provisions in it. The weather being fine, we sailed to Ostia at once, agreeing to meet John there four days before Christmas Day.

At the mouth of the River Tiber is an island two miles long and two miles broad. On the northern side is the strongly fortified Port of Rome, connected with the city by a good road along which, in times of peace, barges are drawn up the current by teams of oxen. On the southern side is Ostia, which was once of greater importance than the Port of Rome, but has long lost its trade and declined to a mere open village. This is because the road from here to Rome is unsuitable as a towpath: it was found cheaper to tow goods up the river in barges than to haul them along the road in wagons. Besides, the harbour of Ostia had grown too shallow for convenient use, a great quantity of silt having been carried down the river and retained by the artificial island built at the harbour mouth. However, the Goths now held the Port of Rome, and Ostia was the only other port in the neighbourhood; so to Ostia we went, and found it undefended.

Meanwhile Belisarius, informed of the approach of the convoy, decided to deal the Goths a heavy blow to the northward, in order to distract their attention from what was happening on the river. One early morning, therefore, he ordered a thousand light cavalry under Trajan to ride out from the Pincian Gate against the nearest Gothic camp and shoot arrows over the palisade, inviting a skirmish. The Gothic cavalry soon gathered from the other camps. Trajan retired, according to orders, as soon as they charged, and was pursued back to the city walls. This was only the beginning of the battle. The Goths did not know that our men had been busy in the night removing the buttressed wall with which the Flaminian Gate had long been blocked from inside. From this unexpected quarter burst Belisarius himself at the head of his Household Regiment and, forcing his way through an intervening outpost, charged their confused column in the flank. Then Trajan's men turned about, and the Goths were caught between the two forces. Very few escaped.

King Wittich was greatly disheartened by this battle and by the messages that now reached him from some of his spies in the city. For my mistress had caught a ring of them just before she left, and Theodosius, who took over this work in her absence, forced them by threats of torture to send out letters containing misleading news. According to these letters, the vanguard of an enormous army – at least 60,000 men – was advancing from Naples. Wittich's own forces had been reduced by battle and sickness to 50,000 men; two large convoys of grain that he needed urgently had been captured by the Tivoli garrison; desertions became frequent. He decided to sue for peace.

Accordingly, he sent three envoys to Rome. Belisarius admitted them as before, blindfolded, and had them speak their messages in the Senate House before him. Their spokesman, a Roman friendly to the Goths, stated King Wittich's case ably and at some length. The whole question at issue, he said, was whether the Goths had a right in Italy or not. If they had a right, as he could prove, then Justinian was acting unjustly in sending an army against them, not having himself been injured by them in any way. The facts were as follows. Theoderich, their former king, who had patrician rank at Constantinople, had been commissioned by the then Emperor of the East to invade Italy and seize the government from the hands of certain barbarian generals who had deposed his colleague, the Emperor of the West. This commission Theoderich had successfully undertaken; and in all the long years of his reign had preserved the Italian Constitution in its entirety. He had made no new laws nor repealed any old ones, leaving the civil government entirely in the hands of Italians, and acting merely as commander-in-chief of the forces which protected the country against Franks, Gepids, Burgundians, and similar barbarians. Moreover, though Arians, Theoderich and his successors had behaved with noble tolerance towards the Orthodox Christians and shown veneration for their shrines; and it would therefore be ridiculous to pretend that the present inexcusable invasion was a war of religious liberation.

Belisarius replied: 'Theoderich was sent to Italy to win back the country for the Emperor of the East, surely, not to seize it for himself? It would have been no advantage to the then Emperor that Italy should be governed by this barbarian usurper as opposed to that.'

The envoy said: 'Let that pass. Sensible men do not argue about dim historical incidents. But I have come to tell you this: that if you consent to withdraw your army from Italy, my royal master will freely cede to your Emperor the whole fruitful island of three-cornered Sicily.'

Belisarius laughed and replied scornfully: 'Fair is fair. And we will freely cede to you the whole fruitful island of three-cornered Britain, which is much larger than Sicily and used to be a source of great riches to us – before we lost it.'

'Suppose that my Master agrees to let you keep Naples and the whole of Campania?'

'My orders are to reconquer Italy for its rightful owner, and I propose to carry them out. I am not empowered to make any arrangements that would prejudice the Emperor's claim to the entire peninsula and all its dependencies.'

'Will you agree to a three months' armistice while King Wittich sends proposals for peace to Constantinople?'

'I shall never stand in the way of an enemy who genuinely desires to make peace with his Serene Highness, my Master.'

An armistice was agreed upon, therefore, and an exchange of hostages. But before it was ratified Belisarius heard of our arrival at Ostia by land and sea. He could not restrain himself, but rode out one night at dusk with a hundred men to welcome his Antonina. He passed safely through the Gothic lines and dined with us that night in our entrenched and barricaded camp. He promised that as we came up the road the next day with our wagons, he would, if necessary, sally out to our assistance. At midnight he rode back again, eluding the enemy outposts as before.

In our pleasure at seeing him and hearing his account of the fight outside the Flaminian Gate, we had omitted to tell him of our transport difficulties. I was present with my mistress at a council of war the next morning when these difficulties were discussed. The Ostia road was a neglected, muddy track, and the wagon oxen were so worn out by their long forced march from Calabria that they were still lying half-dead where they had halted the night before, unable even to eat the cut grass that their drivers had spread before them. Neither whip nor goad would persuade them to haul wagons that day.

It was my mistress Antonina who made the suggestion that we should load the corn on our smaller rowing-galleys, board them in against enemy arrow or javelin attack, and fit them with very wide sails. The wind was steady from the West and, with the help of oars at the bends of the river, it should not be impossible to make progress against the current as far as the city. The cavalry could follow along the bank and occasionally haul on ropes where sail and oars both failed to carry a boat upstream.

The plan was successful: after an all-day voyage the boats reached Rome safely at dusk. The Goths had offered no hindrance, not wishing to prejudice the signing of the armistice. The wind remained steady, and the boats returned to Ostia on the next day for a further cargo. Within a few days the whole of the stores had been conveyed into Rome, the famine was at an end, the fleet had returned to winter at Naples, and the armistice, which bound both sides to refrain from 'all acts or threats of force whatsoever', was signed and sealed. Wittich's ambassadors then set out for Constantinople; but Belisarius sent a letter to Justinian urging him to pay no attention to their proposed terms unless these amounted to a capitulation.

Hildiger, my mistress's son-in-law, arrived from Carthage on New Year's Day with what was left of the Herulians and Thracian Goths – 600 vigorous, shame-faced men. Belisarius welcomed them without any taunting reference to their part in the mutiny. On the same day the Gothic garrison abandoned the Port of Rome, Wittich being unable to keep this place provisioned; the Isaurian force which we had posted at Ostia occupied it. The Tuscan city of Civita Vecchia was abandoned by its garrison for the same reason, and likewise occupied by us. Wittich protested that this was a violation of the armistice, but Belisarius ignored the protest; for neither arms nor threats had been used on his side. He now sent a large cavalry column under the command of Bloody John to winter near the Fucine Lake, about seventy miles eastward from Rome; John was to remain there quietly until further orders, exercising the troops in archery and rapid manoeuvre.

If the Goths broke the armistice he would be in a position to do them a great deal of harm.

Wittich, whose army continued to occupy its original camps, treacherously made three attempts at capturing the city by surprise. The first method he tried was the one by which Belisarius had captured Naples: entry by an aqueduct. A party of Goths stole along the dry conduit of the Virgin Water until they came to the masonry block far inside the city, near the Baths of Agrippa, and began to chip it away. But this aqueduct passes over the Pincian Hill at ground level, and a sentry on duty at the Palace happened to see the light of their torches shining through two holes in the brick-work. Trajan, going the rounds of the sentries, asked him: 'Have you anything unusual to report?' The sentry replied: 'Yes, sir, I saw a wolf's eyes flashing red in the dark yonder.'

Trajan could not understand how a wolf could have entered Rome through the closely guarded gates. It occurred to him, too, that a wolf's eyes only appear to flash red in the dark when a light catches them, whereas the sentry was standing in a particularly dark spot. But the man was positive that he had seen a something flashing from beside the aqueduct, and what could it be but a wolf's eyes? Trajan happened to mention this trivial incident when he breakfasted with us at headquarters the next morning. My mistress Antonina, who was present, said to Belisarius: 'If it had been a wolf, the wolf-hounds would have given tongue from the kennels. They can scent a wolf from a mile away. Trajan, see that the mystery is cleared up!' Trajan made the sentry point out exactly where the wolf had been seen. There he discovered the two holes, where a long staple had once been hammered into the brickwork. A breach was at once made in the aqueduct and the droppings of Gothic torches were found, with signs of demolition work at the masonry block. The breach was sealed up again, but when the Goths came next night to resume work they were confronted by a placard reading: 'Road closed. By Order of Belisarius.' They hurried back, fearing an ambush.

Wittich's next attempt was a surprise cavalry raid against the Pincian Gate one day at noon. His men had scaling-ladders with them, and also numerous flasks containing a combustible mixture for use against the gate, which was made of wood. However, our look-out on the tower signalled an unusual activity in the enemy's camp. Hildiger, who was on his way to luncheon with us at the Palace, happened to see the signal. He immediately alarmed a squadron of the Household Regiment, rode out with them against the Goths, and stifled the assault before it was well launched.

Wittich's third and last attempt was against the part of the walls which is washed by the Tiber and has no protecting towers – the very spot where Constantine had repelled an attack during the fight at the mausoleum. It was to be a night attack in force. Wittich had bribed two Roman sacristans from the Cathedral of St Peter to prepare the way for him. They were to cultivate the friendship of the guards on this lonely stretch of wall; then, on the appointed night, visit them with a skin of wine, make them drunk, and doctor their wine-cups with an opiate which he provided. When the sacristans signalled with a torch that the coast was clear, the Goths would cross the river in skiffs, plant their ladders on the mud-flat and seize the city. It was a plan that might well have succeeded, had not one of the sacristans betrayed the other, who confessed as soon as the phial of opiate was discovered in his house. Belisarius punished the traitor in the traditional way, by cutting off his nose and ears and mounting him backwards on an ass. But instead of being exposed to the insults of the mob in the streets – the usual sequel – he was sent along the road into Wittich's camp.

After these flagrant breaches of the armistice had been committed, Belisarius wrote to Bloody John: 'Overrun the Gothic lands in Picenum; carry off all the valuables that you find; capture the Gothic women and children, but do no violence to them. This booty is to be shared among the whole army; keep it intact. On no account forfeit the goodwill of the native Italians. Seize what fortresses you can, and either garrison them or dismantle their fortifications, but leave none still held by the enemy behind you as you advance.'

Bloody John found his task an easy one, since almost every Goth capable of bearing arms was away at the siege of Rome, and there were only small garrisons left in the fortified towns. His booty was enormous. Not content with raiding Picenum, he pushed up the eastern coast for 200 miles. He thereby disregarded Belisarius's orders; for he left in his rear the fortified towns of Urbino and Osimo. But a subordinate has a right to disobey orders if he thoroughly understands them and becomes aware of circumstances that make them out of date; and here was a case in point. For when the Gothic garrison of Rimini heard of John's approach they had fled to Ravenna, which is only a day's march away, and the City Fathers of Rimini had invited John to enter. Bloody John judged that as soon as Wittich heard that the Romans held Rimini he would raise the siege of Rome and march back, for fear of losing Ravenna too; and he was correct in this forecast. Also, Wittich's wife Matasontha, who was at Ravenna and had never ceased to resent the marriage to which she had been forced, had opened a secret correspondence with Bloody John, offering him every assistance that would contribute to her husband's defeat and death. So he did right in pushing on to Rimini. Once Wittich acknowledged failure by a retreat from Rome, the end of his reign was near.

Now, Constantine was angry that Bloody John had been preferred to him in the command of this raiding expedition. Constantine had fought bravely and energetically enough throughout the siege, but nourished an ever-growing jealousy of Belisarius, whose victories he ascribed entirely to luck. Three years before, it will be recalled, he had been one of the signatories to the secret letter in which Belisarius was absurdly accused to Justinian of aiming at the sovereignty of North Africa. Belisarius had never told Constantine that the letter had been intercepted, but my mistress Antonina had recently hinted that she knew that a copy of it had reached the Emperor. Constantine was persuaded that, in revenge for the letter, Belisarius had, ever since the landing in Sicily, given him the most difficult, most inglorious, and most unprofitable tasks to perform. He therefore wrote to Justinian again, accusing Belisarius of having forged the evidence by means of which the Pope had been deposed, and – more absurd still – of having taken bribes from King Wittich to sign an armistice on better terms than the Goths had any right to expect.

He applied for leave to go hunting near the Port of Rome – not to return to his post at the Aelian Gate until the following morning. At the Port of Rome he gave the letter to the commander of a packet-ship that was to sail for Constantinople that day, telling him that it was a private letter for the Emperor from Belisarius. But the next day as soon as he returned he was handed a subpoena to attend Belisarius's military court at the Pincian Palace. Constantine naturally concluded that some spy had followed him and that the letter was now in Belisarius's hands; but he swaggered off defiantly to the Palace, ready to justify his action, if necessary. For he had a secret commission, signed by Justinian himself, to report at once upon any action on Belisarius's part that showed the least taint of disloyalty. This commission had been sent to him at Carthage two years previously, in answer to his original report. It was still valid.

As it happened, the case which he had been summoned to attend merely concerned two daggers with amethyst-mounted hilts and a golden double-scabbard belonging to an Italian resident of Ravenna named Praesidius. Praesidius, who had fled to Rome at the outbreak of hostilities, prized these daggers as heirlooms, but had been robbed of them by one of Constantine's personal attendants; Constantine himself now wore them openly. During the siege Praesidius had made several appeals for their return, but was given only insults in reply. He had not brought a civil charge against Constantine, hardly expecting that in such times a mere civilian refugee would be given any satisfaction against a distinguished cavalry commander. But when the armistice was signed Praesidius at last made an application at the Palace for permission to swear a warrant against Constantine for theft. Theodosius, who as Belisarius's legal secretary was charged to settle as many cases as possible out of court, dissuaded him from proceeding. Constantine was nevertheless sent a note by Theodosius in Belisarius's name, asking him to restore the daggers – if they were indeed stolen property. Constantine disregarded this note, confident that the charge would not be pressed. In reply to a second note, signed by my mistress and written in a more peremptory style, he wrote a smooth denial of all knowledge of the matter. Praesidius, upon being shown this letter by Theodosius, grew very angry. It was St Anthony's Day (the same day that Constantine went hunting at the Port of Rome) and he waited in the Market Place until Belisarius came riding through on the way to attend divine service in St Anthony's Church. Then, darting forward from among the crowd, Praesidius caught hold of Balan's bridle and called out in a loud voice: 'Do the laws of his Sacred Majesty Justinian permit an Italian refugee to be robbed of his family heirlooms by Greek soldiers?'

Belisarius's attendants threatened Praesidius and told him to be off; but he shouted and screamed, and would not release his hold on the bridle until Belisarius had undertaken to inquire personally into the matter on the very next day. Constantine, knowing nothing of all this, arrived at the Palace wearing in his belt the very daggers that were in dispute and of which he had disclaimed knowledge.

The charge was read out. Belisarius first examined the documents in the case, including Constantine's letter of denial. Then he heard Praesidius's own evidence, and then the evidence of his friends. It appeared that the daggers had been forcibly taken from Praesidius's person by Constantine's servant Maxentiolus; that Constantine then wore them himself and persistently refused to return them, alleging that he had bought them from Maxentiolus, who had found them on a Gothic corpse.

'Is it true that you made this statement, noble Constantine?'

'Yes, my lord Belisarius, and I hold to it. This impudent fellow Praesidius is quite mistaken in thinking them his.'

'Praesidius, do you see anyone in this court now wearing your daggers?'

Praesidius replied: 'Those are they, Illustrious Belisarius, that the general is as usual wearing.'

'Can you prove that they are yours?'

'I can. My father's name, Marcus Praesidius, is damascened in gold on the blade of each.'

'Noble Constantine, do any such names appear on the daggers you are wearing?' Belisarius asked.

Constantine flew into a rage. 'What if they do? The daggers are mine by purchase. I would rather throw them into the Tiber than give them to a man who has publicly insulted me as a thief.'

'I desire you to hand me the daggers for examination, my Lord.'

'I refuse.'

Belisarius clapped his hands. In marched ten troopers of the bodyguard, lining up beside the door. Out of respect for Constantine's rank nobody had hitherto been admitted to the court-room (besides the two witnesses) but Hildiger, Bessas, and three other generals of equal rank with him.

Constantine cried: 'You intend to murder me, do you?' His conscience was troubling him in the matter of the letter to Justinian.

'By no means. But I intend to see that your man Maxentiolus returns to this Italian gentleman the daggers that he stole from him – if those are they.'

Constantine seized one of the daggers and with a great roar rushed at Belisarius, who was wearing no armour. He would have slit his belly open, but Belisarius side-stepped like a boxer and dodged behind Bessas, who was wearing a coat of mail. Constantine pushed Bessas aside furiously and made a second rush at Belisarius. Then Hildiger and Valerian, another general, caught Constantine from behind and disarmed him. He was led off to confinement.

Later, this same Maxentiolus, examined by my mistress Antonina, told her that on the previous day he had seen Constantine hand a letter to the master of the packet, and heard him say that it came from Belisarius. Since the weather was unfavourable for sailing, the packet was still at its moorings; and the letter was soon in her hands. She read it, and made up her mind that Constantine was too dangerous an enemy to be allowed to live. Without a word to Belisarius, she sent one of my fellow-domestics to kill Constantine in his prison-chamber, of which she had the key. She was then for giving out that it had been a suicide; but Belisarius, who was both vexed and relieved at Constantine's death, would not tell lies of that sort. He preferred to take full responsibility for Constantine's execution and to justify it, in his report to Justinian, as a military necessity. Bessas, Hildiger, and Valerian countersigned this report, testifying to Constantine's mutinous words and murderous attack. Then Hildiger, at my mistress's suggestion, added (truly enough) that Constantine had lately been airing views on the nature of the Son which were not only highly heretical but attributable to the teachings of no reputable sect – too illogical, indeed, to be anything but the product of his own wild brain, notoriously unhinged since his sunstroke in Africa. So Justinian approved the sentence. But it was a great shame to Belisarius to learn, from the secret commission that was found on Constantine's dead body, that Justinian doubted his faith and employed agents to spy on him. He agreed with Antonina that, brave fighter though he had proved, Constantine's death was a public benefit.

On the twenty-first of March the armistice came to an end. At dawn of the same day King Wittich – having received by way of reply from Justinian no more than a curt: 'I have received your letter and am considering what action to adopt' – raised the siege and marched back across the Mulvian Bridge with the remains of his army. He had given Belisarius warning of his intention by setting fire to all the huts, siege-engines, palisades, and other wooden material in his camps. It was Belisarius's principle not to press a retreating enemy with too great rigour, but these bonfires were lighted in defiance, and the Gothic divisions still preserved good military discipline. It would not be right to let them escape without one last blow. But Belisarius's forces had lately become so reduced by the detachment of garrisons and raiding parties to various parts of Italy that he dared not risk a battle on equal terms. What he did was to call all his best remaining troops and hold them in readiness at the Pincian Gate until the look-outs on the walls reported that nearly half the Gothic army had now crossed the bridge. Then he led them out quickly and made a strong attack on the Goths drawn up near the bridge, waiting their turn to cross. Many men fell on both sides, for the fighting was hand to hand, until a charge of the Household Regiment broke the Gothic line. At this the whole disheartened mass streamed towards the bridge, with no thought in any man's mind but to get across it somehow. The confusion and slaughter in their ranks cannot easily be described, so fearful it was. Their cavalry rode down their infantry, and any man who slipped and fell was likely to be trampled to death. Moreover, our archers' fire was now concentrated upon the bridge, which was soon heaped high with corpses, and a great number of mail-clad men fell or were pushed over the arches into the water, where they were drowned by the weight of their armour. Ten thousand Goths died that morning at the Mulvian Bridge.

So ended the defence of Rome which Belisarius had first begun, contrary to all advice, in the December of the year before the last. I do not think that all history can show so large a city held for so long a time by a garrison so grossly outnumbered.

King Wittich retreated sullenly towards Ravenna, detaching large garrisons as he went for the defence of Osimo, Urbino, and other smaller fortresses. Belisarius felt the need of Bloody John and his 2,000 cavalry, and sent Hildiger hurrying to Rimini by another route to order his withdrawal. Rimini could more profitably be held by a detachment of infantry which had just landed from Dalmatia at Ancona, a port not far off. (Dalmatia was now ours again, Wittich having withdrawn to Italy the forces that were besieging Spalato; and troops could therefore be spared.) But Bloody John refused to withdraw.

This time he was not justified in disobeying orders. The fact was, he had a great deal of Gothic treasure collected in the city which he wished to retain for his own use instead of sharing it with the rest of the army. Hildiger therefore left at Rimini the infantry that he had brought from Ancona; but persuaded the 800 men of the Household Regiment, whom Belisarius had lent to Bloody John, to withdraw with him. King Wittich, determined to win here the success that had eluded him at Rome, settled down to besiege the city; and soon

Bloody John began to repent of having disobeyed orders, for there was great scarcity of provisions in Rimini, and Wittich was attacking with great resolution.

Now, it is not my purpose to write a history of the wars, but to tell the story of Belisarius. I forbear therefore to give a detailed account of this siege, yet I will say that Wittich attacked with scaling-towers propelled by hand from inside, not drawn by oxen; that Bloody John prevented their advance by hurried trenching; and that Wittich then decided to starve him out.

The situation at Rimini was soon more desperate than Belisarius realized. Nor was he in any position to march to the relief of his disobedient lieutenant, having sent a considerable part of his forces to Northern Italy, with the fleet, to capture Pavia and Milan; besides, the fortified towns of Todi and Chiusi, which lay between him and Rimini, must first be reduced. Nevertheless, the news that Wittich was besieging Rimini caused him such anxiety that, leaving only the Roman levies to garrison the city, he marched northward to its relief; and presently Todi and Chiusi surrendered to the terror of his name. He sent the Gothic garrison under escort to Naples and Sicily and continued forward. But our total forces did not now amount to 3,000 men, whereas King Wittich had increased his strength to 100,000 with new forces from Dalmatia.

Fortunately the letter addressed by my mistress to Theodora had taken effect at last. We had the welcome news that 7,000 further reinforcements had landed at Fermo in Picenum, on the eastern coast. Who should be in command of this army but the eunuch Chamberlain Narses! 'Ah,' said my mistress Antonina to Belisarius, laughing, 'I am glad that I sympathized with his military ambitions on our journey together to Daras. And he will prove a capable officer in spite of his age, I believe, if he can learn a little humility. But at the Court he has been accustomed to take orders from the Emperor and Empress only; you and I must handle him tactfully.'

Hildiger rejoined us at Chiusi, and we marched across Italy until we came in sight of the Adriatic Sea. At Fermo (which is a day's march away from Osimo) we joined forces with Narses, whom Belisarius and my mistress greeted in the friendliest possible way. But there was much merriment among the household at Narses' appearance. That he was dwarfish and big-buttocked and had a squint and a twisted lip had not seemed very ridiculous when he was gliding along the Palace corridors with his usual great roll of documents in his hand, wearing his scarlet-and-white silk uniform and a golden chain of honour. But to see Narses, who had already long passed the grand climacteric of his years, strutting about in the latest fashion of plate-armour (inlaid with fishes and crosses and other Christian symbols) and high ostrich-plumed helmet and brocaded purple cloak, trailing a full-sized sword which was continually catching between his legs and tripping him up – that I assure you was a sight to raise a smile on the face of a man dying of the cholera. My mistress, though hardly able to keep a sober face herself, warned us privately not in any way to offend Narses' sensibilities; since he was in the Emperor's confidence, and could either greatly help or greatly injure Belisarius's cause, as he pleased – and Belisarius's cause was ours. With Narses came Justin the son of Germanus, grand-nephew to the Emperor.

King Wittich had sent 25,000 men to increase the garrison of Osimo, and this army barred the way to Rimini. An immediate council of war was held, at which Belisarius invited the general officers present to give their views in rising order of seniority. Valerian and Hildiger spoke first, expressing that, since Bloody John had twice disobeyed orders, first in advancing beyond Osimo without reducing it and then in not withdrawing from Rimini when desired to do so, he should be left to extricate himself from the difficulty as best he could. To march to his relief, skirting Osimo, was to endanger the whole army for the sake of 2,000 men. Between the Goths at Osimo and Wittich's field army encamped outside Rimini we would be caught as between hammer and anvil. Bessas agreed and added piously that Bloody John's avariciousness deserved whatever punishment God might think fit to impose. But Narses intervened; he pointed out, as though Belisarius had already agreed to follow their advice, that Bloody John's disobedience of orders was no reason for sentencing the brave soldiers under his command to massacre or slavery. 'To do so, indeed, is to injure your own cause, and that of the Emperor. You may laugh at me as a mere theorist of warfare, but I shall not consent to any plan of action that sacrifices Rimini to private revenge.'

Belisarius raised his brows at this outburst. He replied: 'Distinguished Chamberlain, is it not more charitable to withold condemnation of an offence until that offence is committed?' He was about to give his own opinion on the proper course to pursue, when the meeting was interrupted by a message from Bloody John, smuggled through the Gothic lines by a daring Isaurian soldier. The message was that Rimini could not hold out more than seven days longer at most, after which it would surrender from starvation.

Belisarius then delivered his opinion: which was that Osimo must be masked by a small force – no more than a thousand men could be spared – encamped twenty miles away; the remainder of the army must hurry forward to the relief of Bloody John and his men. The only hope of forcing Wittich to abandon the siege was to deceive him as to our numbers, and for this reason we must divide into three armies and converge on Rimini with all speed. One army must march up the coast under Martin, a recently arrived general, and the fleet under Hildiger must keep pace with it. Narses and himself, with the best of the cavalry, must take the Apennine ridge-track, far inland. To this plan everyone agreed; and the start was made that very morning. My mistress went with Belisarius and Narses, and I with her, riding on a mule behind her palfrey. And a rough ride it was indeed, and an extremely hot one – for this was July, with not a breath of wind stirring among the rocks and pines. The mountain villages through which we passed were inhabited by miserable half-starved savages, who not only were not Christians but had never been converted to a belief in the Olympian Gods and still worshipped obscure aboriginal deities. But there was plenty of game in the valleys, and our scouts had fine sport. One of them even shot a bear, an animal which we had thought was extinct in Italy since the time of the Emperor Augustus. On the fifth day, after travelling some 200 miles and on a diet mainly of army biscuit and salt pork, we reached Sarsina, which is only one day's journey inland from Osimo. There our scouts came suddenly on a Gothic foraging party and drove them off with loss. Belisarius, in the vanguard, could easily have captured them all, but preferred to let them escape and spread the alarming news of our approach.

King Wittich, to whom the fugitives had given a very exaggerated account of our strength, expected us to march down the valley of the Rubicon and attack him from the north-west. But on the following evening he saw the distant glare of our camp-fires to the westward, and very numerous these were: every soldier had been instructed to light one and keep it heaped with fuel all night. To the south-eastward he saw the camp-fires of what seemed to be another huge army, which was Martin's brigade. And when day broke the sea was covered with ships, and armed galleys came steering menacingly towards the harbour. The Gothic army abandoned its camp in a panic. Nobody obeyed orders or had any thought at all but to be the first man off up the Aemilian Way and into Ravenna. If Bloody John had been able to make a sortie at that moment the result might well have been decisive; but his men were so weak from starvation that they could hardly mount their horses, which themselves were mere bags of bones, since there was practically no grazing in Rimini.

Hildiger landed with a battalion of marines and captured the enemy camp, which contained a good deal of treasure and 500 badly wounded Goths. Belisarius did not arrive until midday. The boisterous and indiscreet Uliaris, who had accompanied Hildiger, told Bloody John that Belisarius, enraged with him for disobeying orders, had reproved Narses in a very rude manner for urging the immediate relief of Rimini. This was Uliaris's notion of a joke; Bloody John took it seriously as coming from one of Belisarius's oldest friends and was extremely angry.

Belisarius greeted him in a somewhat reserved way, but seeing how pale and emaciated the man looked said no more in the way of rebuke than: 'You owe a great debt of gratitude to Hildiger, Distinguished John!'

Bloody John replied sourly: 'No, but rather to Narses.' Saluting, he turned on his heel without another word.

As for the treasure that Bloody John had collected for himself and stored at Rimini, Belisarius distributed it equally among all the troops who had served with him before the arrival of Narses. This angered Bloody John still more. He went to Narses, whom he had known for some years, having been in command of a company of Palace Ushers, and complained that Belisarius had treated him very shabbily. Narses sympathized, and the two of them became fast friends, forming a coalition against Belisarius. Narses believed that it was disgraceful for an old, experienced statesman like himself, who shared the secrets of the Emperor, to take orders from a man half his age, a mere general; and also that he should be recompensed for having given up his secure and comfortable post at the Palace by being allowed to share the glories of the campaign with Belisarius. He meant by this, to share the command with him. Bloody John pointed out that nearly all Belisarius's own troops were now garrisoning various towns in Italy and Sicily – 200 men here, 500 there, 1,000 in another place – and that his marching army was thus reduced to 2,000 swords; whereas Narses and John himself commanded five times that amount.

Now that Rimini had been relieved, Belisarius felt free to attack Osimo; but Narses began to oppose this and every other project that he put forward, trying to force him either to share or to resign his command. Valuable time was thus wasted, though the news that arrived from other parts of Italy was most disquieting and called for instant action. At last on my mistress's suggestion Belisarius called a council of generals and spoke frankly to them.

He said: 'I am sorry to find, my lords and gentlemen, that you and I are in disagreement as to the proper conduct of this war. Most of you, I mean, are under the impression that the Goths are already completely conquered. This is far from being the case. King Wittich is at Ravenna with 60,000 Goths; there are nearly 30,000 more behind the walls of Osimo; between here and Rome there are several other fortified towns strongly held. Wittich has now sent an army under his nephew Uriah against our small garrison at Milan, and Liguria is his again. Worse: a large army of Franks, or at least of Burgundians, who are allies of the Franks, have recently crossed the Ligurian Alps and are reported to be joining forces with this Uriah. I have repeatedly urged upon you my considered opinion: that we should march against Osimo without further delay, meanwhile masking Ravenna with a small force, and also send a large relief force to Milan. You have sullenly opposed these plans. I shall now assert my authority, by converting them into definite orders.'

Nobody replied for some time. Then Narses spoke. 'It is not practicable to divide our forces in this way, my lord. The soundest strategy would be to march northward past Ravenna and seize the whole Venetian coast, thus drawing Uriah away from Milan; and at the same time to blockade Ravenna by sea and land. To attack Osimo would be a waste of energy, since Osimo will fall when Ravenna does. But do you take your own few forces to Milan or Osimo or the Moon or wherever else you wish. I intend to do as I have said with the men whom I have brought with me.'

Belisarius asked: 'And our garrison at Milan, Distinguished Chamberlain? What of them?'

Narses replied: 'They must extricate themselves as best they can – just as Bloody John would have been forced to do at Rimini but for my insistence.'

Belisarius controlled his rising indignation. 'My Lord Narses,' he said gently, 'you forget yourself – and the truth.' Then he called to his secretary Procopius: 'Where is the document that recently came for me from the Emperor?'

Procopius found the document. It was one that Justinian had signed without Narses' knowledge, being forced to do so by Theodora. Belisarius read out in his low, even voice:

'We have today sent our Lord Chamberlain, the Distinguished Narses, to Picenum with certain of our regiments. But he shall have authority over our armies in Italy only as specifically appointed to a command by the Illustrious Belisarius, who has held and must continue to hold the supreme authority under us. It is the duty of all Imperial officers serving in the Western Empire to obey the said Belisarius implicitly, for the public good of our Empire.'

Narses' ugly face turned still uglier as he listened. When Belisarius had finished, he snatched the letter from his hands and read it over to himself, hoping to twist some meaning from it that was not there. He had a mind well-sharpened by years of petty intrigue, and it was therefore not difficult for him to find a flaw in the wording. 'There!' he cried in triumph, pointing to the last words. 'We are to obey you implicitly, but only for the public good of His Serene Majesty's Empire. Illustrious Belisarius, your military plans are thoroughly unsound, and in no way conduce to the public good. I, for one, do not feel bound by this document to obey you. And you, Distinguished John?'

Bloody John answered: 'I, too, think that to send another expedition to Milan and attack Osimo with reduced forces is a most dangerous plan, especially with Wittich stationed at Ravenna.'

Hildiger exclaimed indignantly: 'While we command the sea King Wittich can be held a close prisoner at Ravenna. The only approach is by the causeways across the marshes. A thousand men could block these effectively. I stand by my Lord Belisarius.'

But Narses' party prevailed.

Then my mistress Antonina spoke angrily to Narses and said: 'Her Resplendency the Empress Theodora will give you a whipping for this day's work when you return, eunuch – if you are lucky enough to return.'

CHAPTER 17
A DIADEM REFUSED

BELISARIUS wrote to the Emperor, acquainting him drily with Narses' 'loyal scruples' against deferring to his military judgement; he asked for a new warrant confirming his authority as supreme commander of the Armies in Italy. My mistress Antonina wrote to Theodora at the same time, using a less diplomatic term for Narses' disgraceful behaviour. Justinian's answer was long in coming.

Meanwhile Belisarius kept his patience and even managed to persuade Narses to join him in the siege of Urbino. This city is built on a steep hill, and has only one approach on level ground, namely from the north, where the walls are raised higher in compensation. The Gothic garrison, confident in the strength of their walls and their well-stocked granaries, refused an invitation to surrender; Belisarius would have to take the city by assault or stratagem. There was no aqueduct entrance to explore, the inhabitants being supplied with water by a perpetual spring within the city; he must therefore attempt to breach the walls. With this end in view he had a cloister built, superintending the work himself. A cloister is a connected series of pent-houses on wheels, each pent-house consisting of a stout timber frame roofed with osier hurdles of the sort that shepherds use to form their sheep-cotes, the hurdles being covered with raw hides. This cloister was to be advanced against the northern stretch of the fortifications, and under its protection a large number of soldiers with picks and shovels would begin undermining the wall. Usually the posts of a cloister are eight feet high, but Belisarius added another yard to them in order to leave space for a subsidiary roof, for greater protection. The roof of a cloister is built at a steep angle so that stones bounce off harmlessly; the hides are kept constantly damp to prevent them from being set on fire. Belisarius incorporated half a dozen battering-rams in the cloister.

The walls of Urbino were very solid and the ground very rocky: which accounted for there being no fosse. Narses and Bloody John had already lost patience, Bloody John swearing that the place was impregnable – had he not made an unsuccessful attempt upon it himself on his way to Rimini when it was held only by a few men? So on the tenth night of the siege they marched their divisions away, without informing Belisarius where they were going. Narses went to hold Rimini, Bloody John to raid along the coast beyond Ravenna as a means of enriching himself: for in all that north-eastern territory of Aemilia and Venetia there were no strong fortresses to which the Goths could retreat in safety with their treasures.

Belisarius was left to press the siege of Urbino with 1,800 men. The 2,000 Goths of the garrison, aware of what had happened, laughed and jeered at him. But the cloister was soon in position, while his best archers, perched on a scaffolding behind and protected by a screen, picked off the sentries on the battlements.

Though the miners worked vigorously, by the third day they had not yet dug down to the foundations of the wall, and the rams, swung in unison, still made no noticeable impression on it. Then the Goths succeeded in pushing down a whole merlon upon the roof of the cloister. It broke through, but killed nobody, for the archers on the scaffolding gave warning in time. Belisarius reckoned that it would be two months at least before the wall collapsed, and made no secret of this to his remaining officers. Judge then of his surprise, and ours, when on the fourth day, having been strangely quiet for the two preceding days, the Goths of the garrison appeared between the embrasures of the battlements with their hands raised in token of surrender. By midday the terms had been agreed upon between Belisarius and their commander, and Urbino was ours.

What had occurred must be ascribed to plain good luck, but plain good luck was no more than Belisarius deserved at this juncture. Narses would not have agreed about this. Indeed, when the news reached him at Rimini he was so overcome with jealousy that for days he would not eat at the common mess-table, for fear that he might betray his real feelings and so seem disloyal to the Emperor. Narses, by the way, carried about with him, in a gilt shrine, a little glass image of the Virgin Mother of Jesus, which he would consult before undertaking any important step. He used to tell his officers: 'Our Lady has warned me not to listen to the plan you suggest.' Or: 'Our Lady agrees with me that the project I have formed is a sound one.' On this occasion the Virgin had said nothing. She might well have notified him that the perpetual water supply at Urbino would suddenly fail and the garrison surrender from thirst – for then he would not have put himself in so foolish a position.

Now, in digging the usual fosse for his camp, Narses had accidentally struck a spring of water and, on Bloody John's advice, diverted it into troughs in his horse-lines for the more convenient watering of his horses – just as Belisarius had once done at Capoudia. This diversion of the spring had an unsuspected connexion with the failure of the city's water supply. The irony of it was that Narses was really responsible for the fall of Urbino – and, moreover, never knew! By restoring the water to its former channel we were able to quench Urbino's thirst again. Nobody was admitted to the secret but myself and two of my fellow-domestics, masons by trade, who came with me to the abandoned camp and did the necessary work under my direction. We had orders to hide the spring again under a pile of rocks, for Belisarius might find it necessary to hold Urbino against enemy attack one day.

The motto 'Patience in Poverty', on the bowl of St Bartimaeus, which Justinian had given to Belisarius and Belisarius had lent to the monks, recurred to my mind. Our forces were still further reduced by the necessity of sending Martin with a thousand men to the relief of Milan. Belisarius (my mistress Antonina always at his side) undertook the siege of Orvieto with the mere 800 trained men left him, and some Italian recruits: the town lay too close to Rome to be allowed to remain in Gothic hands.

Martin was no hero. When he reached the right bank of the River Po he was afraid to cross with so small a force against Uriah's army of Burgundians and Goths – which consisted of not less than 70,000 men. Uliaris, who was with Martin, in command of a half-squadron of the Household Regiment, agreed with him that the odds were too great to face. The Governor of Milan sent a messenger to Martin – the messenger passed in disguise through the Gothic lines and swam across the river – imploring that an army be sent at once to his relief. Milan, which is a city of 300,000 inhabitants and next to Rome the most beautiful and prosperous in all Italy, was facing starvation. 'We are reduced to eating dogs and rats and mice and dormice; and several cases of cannibalism have already been reported.'

Martin made excuses: he had no boats in which to transport his stores across the river. But he undertook that the siege would be raised within three weeks if they could hold out so long. He sent a messenger to Belisarius at Orvieto, with orders to ride night and day: Belisarius was begged to send Bloody John inland up the valley of the

Po from Aemilia. 'With John's help', Martin wrote, 'we can perhaps save Milan.'

Belisarius then sent a fast messenger to Bloody John, acquainting him with the straits in which the Milanese were, and ordering him to join forces with Martin and relieve the city.

Bloody John wrote back in downright refusal – he would take orders from Narses alone. He added unfeelingly: 'So the Milanese are eating dormice? I have read in the *Natural History* of the celebrated Pliny that these little creatures were forbidden to the Romans of old by Cato the Censor as being too luxurious a delicacy for the table.'

Thereupon Belisarius wrote to Narses at Rimini, reminding him that the divisions of an army are like the limbs of a human being, and must be controlled and directed by a single authority, the head. 'I would abandon the siege of Orvieto and hurry to Milan with my 800 cuirassiers, but that I must remain in the neighbourhood of Rome – I cannot leave the defence of the city wholly to the Roman levies. Also, a forced march of 300 miles through Tuscany in the present bad weather would be the ruin of my horses. I implore you in the name of God, send your friend John, and Justin the grand-nephew of our master the Emperor, with all available forces to assist Martin. Or go yourself, and derive whatever glory from the campaign you may desire.'

Thus pleadingly addressed, Narses gave Bloody John the required permission; but it was too late. Consider. Martin's messenger had 300 miles to cover from the Po to Orvieto; and Belisarius's messenger 300 miles to cover before he reached Bloody John, who was at Padua; and Bloody John's messenger to Belisarius 300 miles likewise, not hurrying either; and then Belisarius's messenger to Narses at Rimini nearly 200 miles more. There was a further delay caused by Bloody John's having an unseasonable bout of malarial fever. By the time that he had recovered and was ready to set out for Milan with 4,000 cavalry, and boats on ox-wagons for the passage of the Po, the city had fallen. This was already the beginning of the year 539, the year of the tailed comet.

The lives of the thousand men of Belisarius's garrison at Milan were spared by the Goths and Burgundians on their entry; but by order of Uriah all males of the civil population except mere children were butchered, to the number of 100,000, and at the very altars of the churches where they took sanctuary. The soldiers made free with the women, of whom as many as were of any use were taken away as slaves; the Burgundians being allowed first choice in recognition of their services. The old and ugly and infirm were left behind to starve. All the children were taken off by the Goths. The fortifications of Milan were dismantled and the churches levelled to the ground: the Catholic churches by the Arian Goths, but the Arian ones by the Catholic Burgundians. Great fires started and spread unchecked, and one-half of the city was demolished.

Martin and Uliaris returned to Orvieto. When Belisarius heard of the fate of Milan he was so shocked that he would not admit them to his presence, and throughout that campaign he did not speak another word to Uliaris except to give him necessary orders. Uliaris, he said, could have done some small thing for the honour of the Household Regiment – could at least have raided the Gothic communications.

At last a message came from the Emperor Justinian, recalling Narses on the ground that he could no longer be spared from his office as Court Chamberlain, and confirming Belisarius's appointment as supreme commander, under himself, of the Armies in Italy. Justinian did not reprove Narses, even when he learned of the massacre at Milan, which Narses might have prevented, but continued to behave with great friendliness towards him. Narses took away from Italy a thousand of the men whom he had enlisted for service there. Also, his departure was the excuse for a revolt of the 2,000 Herulian cavalry who were under his direct command. They refused to accept orders from Belisarius and marched into Liguria, pillaging the open country as they went; there they concluded a peace treaty with Uriah, selling him all their slaves and spare possessions and being granted fertile lands to colonize in the neighbourhood of Como. But by a sudden change of heart, to which these barbarous people are no less liable than a city mob, they repented and marched all the way back to Constantinople by way of Macedonia, hoping to be pardoned by the Emperor through the intercession of Narses. (Narses did not fail them.)

Thus Belisarius was left in supreme command indeed, but with a field army, you would say, of no more than 6,000 trained men. However, he had now recalled the garrisons left behind in Sicily and the South of Italy and replaced them with Roman levies, and he had also made soldiers of a sort out of the Italian peasantry, so that 25,000 men were available for campaigning purposes. Five thousand he sent under Justin to besiege Fiesole. Three thousand under Bloody John, together with 3,000 more under another John, who was surnamed The Epicure, he sent up the Po valley to resist any attempt on Uriah's part to join forces with Wittich at Ravenna. Belisarius himself with 11,000 men settled down to the siege of Osimo, the capital city of Picenum.

At this point the bounds of my story widen again. To the westward they cross the River Rhône in France, to the eastward they cross the Euphrates, to the northward the Danube, to the southward the deserts of Africa. King Wittich was still at Ravenna. The garrison of Osimo now appealed for assistance, but he replied only with empty assurances that God was on the side of the Goths. He did not dare to lead his troops out of the city, since our infantry outposts guarded the causeways over the marshes, being posted behind strong barricades. Rimini, too, was in our hands; cavalry could be summoned from there by bonfire signal at short notice should Wittich's Goths attempt to force the barricades. Uriah's return from Milan was blocked by the forces under Bloody John and John the Epicure, and his Burgundian allies had returned to their own country. Wittich felt like a creature trapped.

Then an old merchant of the large Syrian colony resident at Ravenna came to him and said: 'How is it that the Emperor Justinian has been able to spare forces for the conquest of Africa and of so much of your own dominions? It is surely because he first bought peace with the Persians, and thus could spare Belisarius, the commander of his Eastern armies, for service here in the West. If you were to persuade the Great King to cross the Euphrates in force, then Belisarius would soon be recalled to the East to deal with the new threat. For the Emperor has only this one general of genius, and must pass him up and down across his dominions like the shuttle across the web of a loom. King Wittich, send an embassy to the Great King and, at the same time, another embassy to Theudebert, King of the Franks. Let these embassies inform each monarch that the other has promised to make a flank attack in force against the Roman Empire.'

Wittich asked: 'But how can any of us Goths go safely on embassies across the entire Eastern Empire? The Emperor's men would surely arrest my envoys. Moreover, none of us can speak the Persian tongue.'

The Syrian replied: 'Send priests. They will not be suspected. Let them travel in the company of Syrians, who go everywhere, know every language, have friends in every land.'

Wittich embraced the idea. Willing priests were found, and Syrian guides, the priest destined for Persia assuming the temporary rank of bishop for greater security. The two embassies went out by sea together, in two small boats, taking advantage of the tide on the next moonless night, and eluded our flotilla. At Ravenna there are tides, a common phenomenon on the shores of the Ocean but not seen elsewhere in the Mediterranean. (It has recently been observed that tides are regulated by the moon.) Only at certain hours can ships navigate the channel across the extensive shallows and enter the port; which is what protects Ravenna so securely against attack from the sea.

A month later, considering the matter again, King Wittich sent two more embassies, similarly composed, to the Moors in Africa, and to the Lombards, a Germanic race recently arrived on the farther bank of the Upper Danube, suggesting that they, too, should strike in concert with the Persians and Franks. The four embassies all succeeded in reaching their destinations. In every case but that of the Lombards the answer was: 'Yes, we will strike, and soon.' The Lombards replied cautiously: 'We will do nothing until we have news that the armies of the other nations are in motion; for we are at present the trusted allies of the Emperor.'

None of us would have suspected King Wittich of understanding world politics sufficiently to foment trouble on distant frontiers of our Empire; for no German had ever considered doing such a thing before. But he was hard pressed, and ready to accept the advice even of Syrians, whom usually he despised as lying Oriental heretics.

The year drew on; it was now the fifth since we had first landed in Sicily. Fiesole and Osimo both refused to capitulate. The Gothic garrisons being large and the defences strong, our only hope was to reduce these fortresses by famine. Belisarius did not allow his army to deteriorate and diminish during the siege, as Wittich had done with his before Rome. On the contrary, he employed these months in the training of his Italian levies, exercising them in continual manoeuvres; he made their rates of pay correspond with the skill that they had attained in the handling of arms and other military arts. He also raised several fresh battalions, providing officers from the ranks of the Household Regiment – among his 'biscuit-eaters' there were numerous Thracians and Illyrians whose native dialect was a sort of Latin. But the new levies were no great improvement upon the Roman city troops. The Italian soil, once so prolific of heroes, has become exhausted in the course of centuries: the Italian has no stomach for a fight, for all his bluster and boasting. Belisarius regretted that he could not use the Gothic prisoners that he captured, for they were strong, bold men, easily trained. Instead, they were being sent to the East and to Africa to fight for the Emperor there.

Of the siege of Osimo I can recall few incidents worth relating. Old soldiers have told me that their experience confirms mine: the incidents at the beginning of a campaign recur sharply to the memory, but as the years of war drag on a man notices less and less and becomes sluggish, so that his attention is not stirred except by some extraordinary sight.

There were frequent skirmishes that summer on the slope of the hill between the city walls of Osimo and our camp. The Goths would creep out at dusk to cut fodder for their horses, and our patrols would engage them; on moonlight nights there would be very sharp fighting. It was down that hill one morning, against a battalion of our infantry advancing in line, that the Goths suddenly rolled a huge number of wagon-wheels with long knives and sickles lashed to the hubs. By good luck not a man of ours was hurt; the Goths had miscalculated the direction of the slope, and the wheels swerved harmlessly away into a wood, from which we recovered them. It was on that slope too that, riding out one morning with my mistress, I was witness to an unforgettable sight. A number of Goths under an officer were out on the hill-side cutting fodder by daylight; and a company of Moors, dismounted, went out to stalk them, creeping up a grassy ravine. But the fodder-cutting party was a bait concealing an ambush: as the Moors emerged from the ravine with a loud yell, up sprang another party of Goths to meet them and there was a hand-to-hand tussle, many men falling on both sides. The officer in command of the fodder-cutting party, who was wearing gilded plate-armour but no helmet, was killed by an upward stab of a Moorish javelin in the groin – plate-armour, intended for mounted use, has a weakness at this spot. The Moor who had struck the blow uttered a cry of triumph and, seizing the corpse by its yellow hair, began dragging it off. Then a Gothic spear flew and neatly transfixed the Moor's two calves a few inches above each heel, as one skewers a hare's hind-legs with a twig for greater ease in carrying it home. But the Moor did not release his hold. He crawled slowly downhill like a caterpillar, arching and flattening out, dragging the corpse behind him. All this my mistress and I saw with our own eyes from the shelter of a holly tree. One of our trumpeters now blew the Alarm, and a troop of Bulgarian Huns galloped past us up the hill to the rescue. The leading Hun picked up the Moor, javelin and all, and threw him across the back of his horse. The Moor would still not let go his corpse, which bumped and clattered along the ground as they rode back to safety.

Another memorable occasion was the fight at the cistern. This cistern was built on the steep ground to the northward of Osimo, close to the walls. It provided the garrison's chief, but not only, water-supply; it was fed by a small trickle of pure water and protected by a vault to keep the water cool. The Goths used to fill their pitchers at it by night, with a strong covering party posted all around. Five Isaurians now volunteered to destroy it, if they were provided with the necessary cold chisels, hammers, and crowbars, and protected while they worked. Early the next day Belisarius brought up his whole army and posted them in a circle at intervals around the wall. Long ladders were held in readiness, as if for an escalade. When the Advance was sounded and the attention of the Goths engaged, the five Isaurians would slip unobtrusively inside the cistern and begin their work of demolition.

The enemy waited quietly for the expected attack and held their fire until our men should be within easy range. The trumpets blew, there was shouting and shooting from our men, but the ladders were advanced only at a single point, 300 paces from the cistern; here the Goths came crowding up to repel the attack. In spite of this diversion the Isaurians did not escape notice as they scrambled up the rock and stole inside the cistern. The Goths realized that they were the victims of a ruse and made a furious sortie from the postern-gate close by, intending to capture the five men. Belisarius led an immediate counter-attack and held them off. It was bitter work, for the Goths were more numerous and had the advantage of the steep hill; but Belisarius's companions were sure-footed Isaurians and Armenian mountaineers, who loved this sort of fighting. Like them, Belisarius fought on foot, wearing only a buff-coat and armed with two javelins and a cutlass. He kept urging them to renewed efforts, though their losses were heavy. The longer the five Isaurians could work undisturbed in the cistern, he reckoned, the shorter would the siege be.

The Goths retreated about midday. As Belisarius rushed forward in pursuit a sentry on the neighbouring tower took a steady aim at him with a javelin; he cast, and the javelin came darting surely down. Belisarius did not see it, for the sun was shining in his eyes from the south, immediately over the edge of the battlements. It was the spearman Unigatus, at Belisarius's side, who saved his life. Being a much shorter man than his master, he was already under the shadow of the wall and could see the javelin coming. He leaped forward and sideways, catching at it. The long head pierced his palm and cut all the sinews of the fingers, so that he was crippled in that hand for the rest of his life. But he said: 'To save my lord Belisarius, I would gladly have interposed my breast.'

Belisarius went down into the cistern himself. Though the Isaurians had been hammering and heaving away with all their might at the big stone blocks, they had not succeeded in shifting so much as a pebble. It was the habit of the men of old to build not for a year, or even for a lifetime, but for ever. The stones were jointed so closely together and the interstices filled with so iron-hard a cement that it seemed a place hollowed out of the living rock. There was nothing else for it but to do what Belisarius had a natural repugnance against doing: he fouled the good water by throwing into the cistern the corpses of horses and quicklime and poisonous shrubs. The Goths, who were already reduced to eating grass, must now rely on a single well inside the fortifications and on rain-water from the house-roofs caught in tubs. But this was a year of drought, and no rain fell.

Fiesole yielded from famine in the month of August, and Belisarius displayed the captive leaders to the garrison at Osimo, hoping to persuade them to yield. Yield at last they did, for Belisarius offered them generous terms. He would not make slaves of them, but they must renounce their allegiance to King Wittich and swear loyalty to the Emperor Justinian, and also give up half their wealth to our men in lieu of plunder. By now they were angry with Wittich for abandoning them to their fate when his armies were still much more numerous than those of Belisarius – who was a soldier after their own hearts. They all volunteered to serve in the Household Regiment. They were picked men, and Belisarius enrolled them gladly. Thus the last of the fortresses southward from Ravenna had fallen to our arms.

Meanwhile King Wittich's nephew Uriah had been encamped at Pavia on the upper Po, prevented by the two Johns from marching to help his uncle at Ravenna. One day in June he heard good news – the embassy to King Theudebert had taken effect and 100,000 Franks had crossed the Alps and were marching to his aid through Liguria. These

Franks are Catholics in name only, and still retain many of their bloodthirsty old German customs; they have, moreover, a greater reputation for perfidy than any race in Europe. They are not horsemen, like the Goths and Vandals, their distant kinsmen, except that a few lancers accompany each of their princes and that every gau-leader is mounted as a mark of dignity. They are infantry, very brave and very undisciplined; and are armed with broadswords, shields, and their dreaded *franciscas*. These franciscas are short-handled, double-headed axes which, as they charge, they throw in a concerted volley; the blow from such an axe will shatter any ordinary shield and kill the man behind it.

Soon King Theudebert's forces reached the bridge-head over the Po at Pavia, which Uriah held; and the Goths welcomed them heartily. But the moment that the first battalions of the Franks had crossed unmolested, a dreadful surprise awaited Uriah. The Franks broke ranks and ran here and there, chasing Gothic women and children; and sacrificed those they captured, as the first fruits of war, by hurling them headlong into the river! This was an old custom of their pre-Christian days, but they justified it on Orthodox grounds: as the fitting treatment for Arian heretics who denied that Jesus Christ was the equal of His Almighty Father! Uriah's Goths were so taken aback by the horror of this sight that they fled away in a mad rush to their camp. Pursued with volleys of hurtling axes, they did not stop to defend the camp – there was a general stampede down the road towards Ravenna. They burst through Bloody John's outposts in their tens of thousands; and hundreds were shot down as they streamed past his camp.

Then Bloody John gathered his bodyguard together and galloped towards the Gothic camp, believing that Belisarius had made a surprise move through Tuscany, and that it was he who had routed the Goths. By the time that he had learned his mistake the Franks were swarming down the road; he fought a sharp engagement and was worsted. Abandoning his camp, with all his pillage of two years in it, he retreated to Tuscany. King Theudebert had won the whole western part of Liguria at a single stroke.

It had been a year of drought; and, because of the dangers of the time, farming activities had been interrupted throughout the north of Italy. The little corn that had been planted withered before it came to an ear, and the stocks in the granaries and barns had long ago been commandeered by King Wittich for his armies, or by the Milanese who had revolted against him, or by the Herulians in their raids. Consequently, when the Franks had consumed the provisions which they found in the two captured camps, they were forced to subsist on the flesh of oxen cooked in the waters of the Po, which was running very low that year and was tainted with corpses. An army composed entirely of infantry has a narrower range of foraging than a cavalry army, and the Franks are heavy eaters. Thus they suffered great distress. When August came they were attacked by dysentery, and no less than 35,000 of them died.

Belisarius wrote King Theudebert a letter reproaching him for the breach of faith with his ally the Emperor Justinian; he suggested that the pestilence was a divine retribution for this and for the cruel murder of the Gothic women and children. Theudebert did not contradict him, and presently marched home. But Western Liguria was left a desert, and it is computed that 50,000 Italian peasants died of starvation that summer.

The Moors in Africa were also defeated in this year by Solomon; and the Lombards therefore thought it convenient to remain where they were, unless perhaps the Persians should strike their promised blow and Justinian be forced to draw away all his western armies to save Syria and Asia Minor from invasion. Then, unsolicited, a powerful nation drove at the Empire from another quarter – the Bulgarian Huns, united under a powerful Cham for the first time for thirty years. They were easily able to force the passage of the Lower Danube. Justinian had, for years past, been gradually denuding his northern frontier fortresses of men to supply his armies in the West, and this without raising a single new battalion or squadron; and had allowed the fortresses themselves to fall into disrepair, considering the building of new churches to be a more glorious practice than the patching of old ramparts. I must here interrupt my account of the great Hunnish raid with a description of a Paradise which Justinian, at enormous expense, had constructed for Theodora and himself on the Asiatic coast of the Sea of Marmora, not far from the city, and on the site of a temple of Hera. The Summer Palace of this Paradise, surrounded by trees and vines and flowers, was at once acknowledged the most beautiful private building in the world, just as St Sophia was the most beautiful sacred one. Marble and the precious metals were lavished upon it, and the baths and colonnades outshone in luxury any that Corinth itself had boasted before the earthquake. Because of the difficulties of the currents in the Straits, Justinian built out two long jetties here – sinking countless chests full of cement in the deep water, to form a private harbour. This great undertaking is worthy of mention here not only because it represented an additional drain on the Treasury, but also because it was the southern tide-mark of the Hunnish raid.

The Bulgars, then, overran the whole of the Balkans as far southward as the Isthmus of Corinth, capturing no less than thirty-two fortresses as they went; and the whole diocese of Thrace as far as Constantinople itself, where they broke through the long walls of Anastasius and were only restrained by the inner wall that the Emperor Theodosius had built, stoutly defended by Narses. Some of them crossed the Hellespont from Sestos to Abydos and raided in Asia Minor, being with difficulty driven off from the gates of Justinian's new Paradise. Two hundred thousand prisoners, 500,000 dead, vast quantities of treasure, the destruction of fifty prosperous towns: such was the price that the Bulgars exacted of Justinian for his false economy in the matter of troops and fortifications. They returned home unmolested.

Belisarius was gathering all his forces to press the siege of Ravenna; and another small Imperial army sailed over to assist him from Dalmatia. But Ravenna is the most difficult city in the world to capture, because of its geographical position. The great Theoderich besieged it unsuccessfully for three years; on the landward side the marshes kept him out, and on the seaward side the shallows and fortifications – that he won it at last was a diplomatic not a military victory. It seemed likely that Belisarius, too, must be content to wait for three years. King Wittich had huge stocks of corn and oil and wine in the city, and at his request an additional supply was being sent by Uriah down the River Po from Mantua.

But a few weeks later, in spite of all this, Wittich was in a most difficult position with regard to food supplies. First, the drought had so shrunken the stream that Uriah's corn barges grounded in the shallows at the mouth of the river and were unable to proceed southward through the connected series of lagoons which form the waterway to Ravenna; the entire convoy was captured by Hildiger, whose patrols were very active and alert in this quarter. Then a second blow was struck against Wittich in Ravenna itself by his own wife, Matasontha. She contrived, during a thunderstorm, to set fire secretly to the two largest granaries in the city. The damage was ascribed to lightning. Wittich conceived the idea that God hated him and was grinding his face in the dust.

King Theudebert of the Franks now sent envoys to Wittich at Ravenna. Because the Franks were still supposedly his allies, Belisarius permitted them to pass through his lines, but only on condition that his own envoys should be permitted to accompany them and hear what they had to say to Wittich, and plead the cause of the Empire. Theodosius was chosen as Belisarius's representative and acquitted himself well enough.

The Frankish envoys proposed an offensive and defensive alliance with the Goths, boasting that they could send half a million men across the Alps and bury 'the Greeks' under a mound of axes. They said that they would be content to take no more than one-half of Italy in payment for their aid.

Theodosius then pointed out that the Franks were wholly untrustworthy as allies, having accepted subsidies from both sides and made war on both; that mobs of infantry would stand no chance of victory against disciplined bodies of cavalry; and that to offer a Frank half a loaf of bread was to give away the whole loaf, together with bread-knife and platter. If King Wittich made his peace with the Emperor he would at least save something from the wreck of his hopes. The Gothic ambassadors sent to Constantinople during the armistice at the close of the siege of Rome had asked for terms which neither justice nor the military situation warranted; Wittich would be well advised now to throw himself upon the clemency of the Emperor, whose generosity to a fallen foe had been proved in the case of King Geilimer and of many a lesser chief.

King Wittich listened attentively to Theodosius, dismissed the Franks, and sent fresh ambassadors to Constantinople. While he waited for their return, the Gothic Alpine garrisons made their submission to Belisarius; and Uriah's army, moving down from Mantua, was so reduced by desertions that he could do nothing more to assist his uncle, but must turn back again as far as Como.

We camped outside Ravenna, and the winter drew on. There was no fighting, but the vigilance of our guards and patrols was not relaxed. Not a single sack of corn was allowed to enter Ravenna, nor a single ship to run the blockade. It was during this period that my mistress renewed her former intimacy with Theodosius, to relieve the tedium of her life. He had a good singing voice and revealed a talent for musical composition; they would sing duets together, very prettily, and accompany themselves on a lyre and a fiddle. One of Theodosius's songs was an outline of why the Italians should love the Greeks: this war of liberation had given them a merry time indeed – massacre, rape, arson, enslavement, famine, plague, cannibalism. The verses were so graceful that nobody could think the sentiments they expressed disloyal. Throughout this period Theodosius and my mistress behaved towards each other with exemplary discretion.

It was in this summer that Theodora's brother-in-law Sittas, who was commanding in the East as Belisarius's successor, was killed in a casual border skirmish in Armenia. He was the only general of reputation in these parts, and his death caused the Persians great joy. King Khosrou decided to break the Eternal Peace in the following spring. Wittich's priestly ambassadors had assured him, through their Syrian interpreter, that the Franks and Moors would assist the Goths by campaigns in the West. Khosrou's first answer had been: 'If we strike from the East, our royal cousin Justinian will abandon his conquests in the West and bring Belisarius against us with all his forces. For Rome is far away from his capital, but Antioch is near. This will benefit your Goths, but not us.'

The priests could not find a convincing answer. But the interpreter was equal to the occasion. I must now disclose a circumstance of which I became aware only after this Syrian plot had matured, but which I shall not withhold from you here – since it will perhaps add to your interest in what I am about to relate: the interpreter was none other than my former master Barak! In a private audience with the Great King, Barak protested that there was nothing to fear from Belisarius. It was an open secret, he said, that Belisarius intended to remain in Italy. In the new year he would throw off his allegiance to Justinian, proclaim himself Emperor of the Western World, and make common cause with the Goths and the Franks; North Africa would be included in his dominions.

'When we have news that Belisarius has so proclaimed himself, we shall invade Syria at once,' said Khosrou, well pleased.

But Barak said: 'King of Kings, it surely would be more consonant with your dignity if you struck without waiting for Belisarius to act? Then his assumption of the Diadem might seem to be encouraged by your invasion of Syria, rather than contrariwise.'

Khosrou seemed impressed by this argument and, recalling Wittich's envoys, gave them the promise to do what they asked of him.

Returning to Italy, these priests re-entered Ravenna, pretending that they had merely been on a pilgrimage to the Holy Places, and gave Wittich their hopeful news. But Barak went to Pavia and there told Uriah, as a joke, of the ingenious lie that he had invented for Khosrou's benefit.

Justinian had spies everywhere, even in the Persian Court, and he heard the story long before Uriah did. Believing that Belisarius was indeed about to betray him, he grew very troubled. He immediately called Narses and Cappadocian John and Theodora to a consultation.

Theodora said: 'That is a mere Syrian tale and without foundation. Because you choose to surround yourself with liars, rogues, and cheats at Court, do you refuse to recognize that such a thing as honour can exist among the officers of your armies?'

But Narses said: 'I suspected this very thing, Majesty. That is why I withheld my obedience from Belisarius.'

And Cappadocian John: 'He has been planning this for many years. Why else did he put the responsibility on Your Clemency for refusing Wittich's peace-terms during the siege of Rome? It was partly to draw more reinforcements to his standards and partly to discredit Your Clemency; so that when he at last proclaims himself Emperor his mildness will be contrasted with your severity.'

Narses said: 'The Italian levies he is raising are another proof of his intentions.'

And Cappadocian John: 'He was planning this revolt six years ago when he was at Carthage, as Constantine and his brother-officers wrote to warn your Clemency. He delayed it then for strategical reasons, considering that while Sicily and Italy were in Gothic hands Africa could not be safely held. But now that the Goths are so near defeat he aims higher.'

Justinian asked: 'What shall we do, friends? Advise us. We are in great fear.'

Narses answered: 'Without delay, offer King Wittich such easy terms as he will be glad to accept. Then Belisarius will not dare to proclaim himself Emperor, being unable to out-bid your Clemency in generosity to the Goths. As for our own officers in Italy, they are weary of war. It is all one to them what treaty you sign with King Wittich.'

Cappadocian John agreed. 'Allow King Wittich to keep one-half of his treasure and all his Italian dominions that lie to the north of the Po.'

But Theodora said: 'Truly it surprises me that with so many false friends and open enemies in the East, Belisarius does not in fact do what he is unjustly accused of planning to do. Count Boniface long ago was forced to treachery in Africa by similar libels against him at the Emperor's Court. So Africa was lost to us.'

Justinian replied softly: 'My dearest, do not meddle in this matter, we beg. Our mind is made up.'

Thus it was that ambassadors arrived from Constantinople with such terms as Wittich was overjoyed to accept. Belisarius, leading them to the gates of Ravenna, inquired of them what precisely the terms were; but they said that they were forbidden to tell him as yet. When they came out again and showed him the treaty signed by Wittich and merely needing Belisarius's own signature for ratification, he was aghast. He could only think that the Emperor had been misinformed as to the hopeless military situation of the Goths. He refused to sign until a confirmation in writing, duly sealed, should arrive from Constantinople.

Then Bloody John and Martin and John the Epicure and Valerian and even Bessas began criticizing him behind his back for prolonging the war unnecessarily. Belisarius, hearing of this, called them all to a conference and asked them to speak frankly: did they really consider that the terms were appropriate ones?

They all said: 'Yes, we think so. We cannot capture Ravenna, and it is too much to ask our men to stay encamped on the fringe of these marshes for who knows how many years. In any case, the Emperor has evidently decided to end the war as soon as possible.'

'Then I do not wish to implicate you in the apparently disloyal action that I am taking in withholding my signature from this treaty. As you are aware, the Code makes the infringement of orders by an officer in war-time a capital offence, and His Serenity the Emperor is my supreme commander. I shall ask you to put in writing the view that you have just expressed.' But he meant equally that, if he could force Wittich to sign a treaty more favourable to ourselves, this document with their signatures would be evidence to Justinian of the difficulties that he had to contend with among his own staff. For he still held the view that Justinian trusted him to act according to his discretion.

They consented to sign.

A most strange thing now happened. Uriah, thinking over the ingenious lie which Barak had told King Khosrou, decided that it would be an extremely happy solution if Belisarius did indeed proclaim himself Emperor! No nobler or more capable man existed, and it would be fatal for Italy to be ruled not from Rome or Ravenna but from distant Constantinople: Africa had already felt the cruel disadvantages of a lost independence of government. With Belisarius as Emperor, the Goths would naturally remain the dominant military power, the Italians being unfit for any but civil duties, and would have the benefit of Belisarius's instruction in the art of winning battles. Uriah smuggled a message into Ravenna to his Aunt Matasontha, whom he knew to be disaffected to his Uncle Wittich, telling her that if the Gothic nobles inside the city invited Belisarius to become their sovereign, he could answer for those outside. She called a secret Council, at which Uriah's suggestion was voted upon and carried by a large majority. The nobles despised Wittich and held Belisarius in admiration; besides, Ravenna could not have resisted long in any case, because of the destruction of the granaries.

Thus Belisarius received a secret invitation from the Gothic Council to become Emperor of the West. Their messenger was soon followed by another from Wittich, who had heard of the Council vote. Wittich declared that he was perfectly willing either to resign his monarchy or pay homage to Belisarius as Emperor.

Belisarius informed nobody of this offer except my mistress Antonina. He cried indignantly: 'How can they mistake me for a traitor to my Emperor? What have I ever done to earn such an insult?'

Antonina laughed and said: 'But the Emperor himself is of their opinion.'

'How do you mean?'

'Read this!'

The letter she gave him to read was one that she had just received from Theodora. It gave a sour account of the meeting between Justinian, Narses, Cappadocian John, and herself. Theodora was greatly angered at Justinian's ill-mannered rebuke to her in the presence of the two councillors, and had evidently written the letter as a sort of revenge. The letter closed in something of this style: 'My dearest friend Antonina, if it is true after all, which I greatly doubt, that you husband contemplates this bold step, do not in loyalty to me dissuade him from it. If he has never contemplated it, persuade him to it. For he is the only man alive who is capable of restoring law, order, and prosperity to Italy and Africa, and thus defending our western flank. Only let him send back to us his Eastern troops when he can spare them, and remain at peace with us. Do you be my royal cousin at Rome, and think tenderly of me, and send me frequent news of yourself, and for the sake of old times favour the Blue faction in your Hippodrome. Then I shall continue to love you as always. To explain shortly: my Sacred Husband is jealous of your Illustrious husband's victories. I cannot promise that he will not do him some great injury one day. If Belisarius were to break his allegiance now it would be a wise and justifiable act, and of great benefit to the world.'

Belisarius's eyes flashed as he thrust Theodora's letter into the live coals of a charcoal brazier; he did not speak until the parchment was wholly consumed. Then he said: 'The faith of Belisarius is worth more to him than fifty Italies and a hundred Africas.'

Then he called his officers together. 'Tomorrow,' he announced, 'we enter Ravenna in peace. Warn your men.'

They all stared at him. Justinian's ambassadors were present too.

'Does this not please you?'

'Oh, my lord! But the Goths? Do they surrender?'

'How else should we enter?'

Belisarius secretly assured the Gothic envoys that none of the citizens of Ravenna should be either robbed or enslaved, and swore an oath to that effect on a copy of the Gospels. But he said: 'As to the title of Emperor, give me leave not to assume it by proclamation until I am inside your city. When King Wittich does homage to me, that will be the sign for the trumpets to sound the Imperial salute.'

The next day we marched along the causeway into the city and took possession of it. As our men passed through the streets in close order the Gothic women, watching in their doorways, spat in their husbands' faces, saying: 'So few, and such miserable little men! Yet you always allowed them to defeat you.'

The husbands answered: 'No, it was not they! It was that handsome tall general who rode by at their head on the white-faced bay. He did everything. He is to be our new ruler. He is the wisest, noblest, boldest man who ever lived. He is Belisarius.'

Belisarius accepted the submission, not the homage, of Wittich; and, though the Goths expected him at any moment to proclaim himself Emperor, he gave no sign. But they were satisfied to wait, because he kept his oath about not enslaving or plundering the people of Ravenna, seizing only the royal treasures in the Emperor's name, and because he brought in a few ship-loads of provisions. Further, he allowed all the Goths who owned lands to the south of the Po to leave the city and return to cultivate them. This was a safe step, for all the fortified towns in the South were now garrisoned by his troops.

For the first few days Belisarius was certainly allowing the Goths to believe that he would, before long, accept the Diadem. My mistress Antonina, growing hopeful, asked him: 'Have you then taken the wise decision?' To which he replied: 'Yes, that of continuing loyal to my oath as a general. It would have been wrong to let slip any opportunity for occupying the enemy's capital without loss of life.'

My mistress Antonina was so angry with him for respecting an oath sworn long ago to a scoundrel that she would hardly speak to him. Theodosius seemed angry too, perhaps because he had been promised by her the governorship of Rome when Belisarius became Emperor. He told Antonina in private: 'In order that Belisarius may keep his faith virginal, Italy must be destroyed.'

She asked: 'How destroyed?'

Theodosius answered: 'Belisarius will be recalled, and the destruction will come about through greedy tax-gatherers, unjust laws, stupid generals, wilful subalterns, mutiny, revolt, invasion. You will see.'

CHAPTER 18

A COLD WELCOME HOME

RAVENNA is a city of paradoxes. It is built on piles in a lagoon. 'The frogs in Ravenna greatly outnumber the citizens,' they say, 'and its mosquitoes outnumber even the angels of Heaven.' The sea, however, is gradually receding from the coast, so that the harbour which the Emperor Augustus built is now orchard land. 'Apples grow on the masts in Ravenna harbour,' they say. A yard or two below the surface of the soil water is always struck, which is inconvenient for the building of walls and the burial of corpses; but the water is brackish, and the inhabitants rely on rain-catchment for drinking and cooking. They say: 'Here the dead swim and the living go thirsty. Here waters stand and walls fall.' A colony of retired Syrian traders is settled at Ravenna, all very pious; whereas the local priests are mercenary and inclined to disregard Canon law. 'Here Syrians pray, but priests practise usury,' they say. There is no hunting to be had in the neighbourhood, and no sport but hand-ball at the baths; nevertheless, because of the damp a man must take vigorous exercise to keep in health. As a result, many wealthy civilians belong to a militia and practise military exercises on the parade-ground and in the tilt-yard; but the garrison-officers, from sheer boredom, join literary clubs in order to improve their education. 'Here men of letters play at being soldiers, and soldiers at being men of letters,' they say. To these many paradoxes was now added a man who could have been a sovereign but would not, and a man who would have liked to remain a sovereign but could not.

Paradoxical, too, was the discovery that my former master Barak, so knowledgeable in relics, had been piously adoring in a local church a relic of St Vitalis which, as any historical expert would tell you, cannot possibly have been his: I found a votive offering hanging in the church to commemorate Barak's miraculous cure from gall-stones by means of this relic. And for Barak a whole series of paradoxes was in store. He came to Ravenna to claim a great reward from Belisarius for having suggested to the Goths that he should be invited to become Emperor of the West. But Belisarius, so far from rewarding him, arrested him at my instance on that thirty-three-year-old charge of forgery, and sent him under guard to Constantinople to stand his trial. However, in his report on the case Belisarius did not mention Barak's part in the plot to make him Emperor: he regarded the whole transaction with such distaste that he preferred to suppress all reference to it. At Constantinople Barak secured an honourable release by bribery, and though by now seventy years of age, resumed his long-interrupted task as overseer of monuments in the Holy Places. It was his pleasure to refresh the blood-marks on the pillar of scourging; and to renew the hyssop-sponge at Golgotha, which the piety of pilgrims had worn almost to nothing; and to discover at Joppa, buried in an old chest during the persecutions of the Emperor Nero, a startling number of early Christian relics of the first importance and in an agreeably sound state of preservation.

Fortunately we left Ravenna before the mosquito season began. Bloody John had written a warning letter to Justinian as soon as he became aware that the Goths had offered the Diadem to Belisarius. Justinian immediately recalled Belisarius, commending him warmly for his magnificent services and hinting that he would soon be employed in a yet wider field. Belisarius would have wished first to settle accounts with Uriah's army, now reduced to a mere thousand men, but he would not risk Justinian's displeasure by any further act of apparent disobedience. He therefore ordered his household to begin packing up, preparatory to moving. When Uriah at Pavia heard of this he was surprised and greatly disappointed; for he had believed that Belisarius still intended to proclaim himself Emperor. He concluded that Belisarius, weighing the strength of the Imperial troops hostile to him against that of the Gothic armies, considered that the step was too risky. He therefore persuaded his fellow-nobles to elect as Gothic king a certain Hildibald, who was a nephew of the Visigothic King of Spain; the prospect of a military alliance between the Goths of Italy and the Goths of Spain would perhaps tip the balance of Belisarius's judgement in favour of accepting the Diadem. Hildibald undertook to go to Ravenna and there do homage to Belisarius at once.

But Belisarius scornfully refused this renewed offer, and in the spring of the year of our Lord 540 we set sail for Constantinople again, leaving Pavia still untaken. Justinian meanwhile appointed eleven generals of equal rank – including Bloody John – to command the armies in Italy; these were united only in their jealousy of Belisarius and in their greed of money and power. At Belisarius's departure they proved incapable of concerted action, and did not even make any serious attempt to capture Pavia. However, Bloody John arranged for Uriah's murder by the new king, Hildibald; and then Uriah's death was avenged on Hildibald himself; and then one Erarich was elected but soon assassinated. Finally, the dangerous crown passed to Hildibald's young nephew Teudel. Thus in seven years seven monarchs had reigned over the Goths.

The civil governor appointed to rule Italy for Justinian was Alexander, surnamed 'The Scissors'; formerly a money-changer, he had first come to the attention of the authorities at Constantinople as an adept clipper of the gold coinage. From every fifty coins that passed through his hands he would clip the equivalent of five, and this without making the coins seem any smaller. Cappadocian John, so far from punishing him for this fraud, had employed him in increasing the face-value of the gold in the Military Treasury by the same methods, and in other dishonest transactions. The Scissors soon showed such ingenuity in finding new ways of raising taxes that he was adjudged worthy of the highest offices. He had recently acted as chief tax-gatherer under Solomon in Africa. The problem of procuring money for Justinian's enormous expenditure was more pressing than ever now, because of the Bulgarian raids which had impoverished so wide an extent of country. The Scissors practised his usual extortions on Italy; and whatever treasure the war had spared he contrived to seize for his royal Master, who allowed him to retain five per cent of his takings as commission. Moreover, nobody could accuse The Scissors of partiality: he snipped away not only the fortunes of the Goths and Italians but the pay and rations of the Imperial troops as well. Theodosius's gloomy forecast of the future of Italy was proving correct in every article. But of this more will be told later.

Just before we had sailed King Khosrou of Persia had begun his threatened invasion of Syria. It was not an altogether unjustified one, because Justinian had been in secret treaty with the White Huns who live beyond the Caspian Sea, trying to bribe them to invade Persia from the North; and with the old King of the Saracens, trying to detach him from his allegiance. Being dissatisfied with the terms he offered, they had put Khosrou in possession of both sets of correspondence. Khosrou tried the southern route once more, marching along the right bank of the Euphrates from the plains of Babylon, and crossed the frontier unopposed. Having only cavalry with him, he reached

Sura after six days' march; and captured it by a trick during a truce arranged for the discussion of capitulation terms. After a conference with the Imperial representative, the bishop of the town, he had escorted him back with honour to the principal gate – then sent a party of men rushing forward with a baulk of timber to block the gateway. Before the people of Sura could remove the baulk a squadron of Persian cavalry had swept in and down the main street. Sura was sacked and burned to the ground; its inhabitants enslaved and taken away to Persia.

Our commander in Syria was the same Boutzes who had fought on the left wing at Daras. His headquarters were at Hierapolis, another six days' march up the river. On hearing of Khosrou's approach, Boutzes exhorted the citizens and soldiers to a resolute defence of the city – then, collecting his light cavalry, took to flight with the utmost speed. Khosrou marched against Hierapolis. Finding that the fortifications were strong, he agreed not to press the siege if he were given a ransom of 100,000 pieces of gold. The citizens, alarmed by the fate of Sura, paid the money. After this, Khosrou turned westward and came to Beroea, where he found the fortifications more vulnerable than those of Hierapolis and therefore fixed the ransom-money at 200,000 pieces of gold. Here, too, the citizens consented, but when they came to collect the money they found that they could only raise one-half of it; the Imperial tax-gatherers – especially my mistress's son Photius, who had become one of Justinian's most heartlessly efficient agents – had been busy in this country of late. Fearful of Khosrou's anger, therefore, the principal citizens and the soldiers of the garrison deserted the walls of Beroea and fled for safety to the citadel. Khosrou stormed the deserted walls and, furious at being trifled with, as he put it, burned half the city down. However, upon finding that the money had not been paid simply because there was none, he forgave the debt and continued his march towards Antioch.

Justinian, when the news of the invasion reached him, had immediately sent his nephew Germanus – the one who had helped to put down the mutiny in Africa – to inspect the defences of Antioch. These were in good enough repair, but had one vulnerable point: a large broad rock, Orocasias, which stood close up against the walls at the highest point of the circuit. Just as Hadrian's mausoleum had been a standing threat to the walls of Rome until it had been incorporated in them as an outwork, so with this rock Orocasias. Germanus decided that it must be fortified at once. The only alternative was to cut a broad, deep fosse to separate the wall from the rock (which stood only fifteen feet below the level of the battlements), and to raise the height of the wall. But the civic authorities of Antioch refused to do anything in the matter. They said that there was no time to complete any building or trenching before Khosrou arrived, and that to be interrupted in the work would be to reveal gratuitously the one weak part of the defences. If they found themselves unable to defend the city, they would try to buy Khosrou off; in fact, the Patriarch Ephraim wrote secretly to Khosrou, offering to collect any reasonable sum in ransom – he suggested 100,000 in gold. But Justinian now sent a circular letter to all governors of cities, forbidding them to pay ransom money under penalty of death. The Patriarch, afraid to face Khosrou empty-handed, fled northward into Cilicia, as a number of other rich citizens prudently did. Six thousand cavalry now arrived from the Lebanon to reinforce the garrison; their commanders closed the gates, so that flight became impossible.

King Khosrou's advance-guard soon appeared within sight of Antioch. His ambassador came under the walls and declared the Persian demands – they exactly corresponded with the Patriarch's offer. For 100,000 he would spare the city and pass on with his army.

The inhabitants of Antioch are a very disorderly, unserious sort of people. They treated the ambassador with no sort of respect – pelting him with filth and shooting arrows all about him. If Belisarius with only 5,000 trained men, they argued, could hold a much bigger city for a whole year against 150,000 Goths, why should not they with 9,000 hold Antioch against Khosrou's army of 50,000 Persians? Moreover, Belisarius had been given little help by the unwarlike Roman civilians, whereas in Antioch the Blues and Greens had formed a sort of local militia; their faction-fights, which were conducted in a more open and courageous fashion than at Constantinople, had given them soldierly enthusiasm. So it happened, after all, that 10,000 volunteers swelled the regular forces, and one-half of these at least wore chain-armour and carried weapons. Unfortunately, the rock Orocasias itself was not defended. It is my opinion that if 300 good men had climbed outside the fortifications and stationed themselves on its steep crest they could have warded off any attack. But a different plan was adopted: long wooden stages were slung from ropes between the towers at this point, so that the defenders could fight from two tiers –

with arrows and javelins from the staging above, with swords and spears from the battlements below.

On the morning following the refusal of his peace-terms King Khosrou sent part of his army down into the valley of the Orontes, to make assaults at various points of the city wall there while he went up the hill with a picked force against Orocasias. Those wooden stages were the undoing of Antioch. As the archers and javelin-men stationed on them were working hard to make the Persians keep their distance, with reinforcements continually rushing down from the towers to them, suddenly the ropes gave way – and planks and soldiers fell with a tremendous crash on top of the crowded parapet beneath. Hundreds were either killed or gravely injured; and horrible cries went up, which the Persians answered with yells of triumph.

The men in the adjoining towers, not knowing what had happened, imagined that the wall itself had collapsed and that the Persians were forcing an entrance. They deserted their posts and rushed downhill into the city; arrived at the gate which leads to the suburb of Daphne, they shouted that they had seen Boutzes in the distance coming to their relief with an army and must hurry out to join forces with him. Nobody believed this story, but there was an immediate rush of civilians to quit Antioch while a chance still offered, the Daphne gate being the only one against which the Persians were making no attack. Then the whole cavalry force withdrew from the fortifications and converged at a gallop on this single gate, riding down the civilians and clambering out over a barrier of dead and dying. Soon Antioch was deserted of all troops except a few regular infantry and the city militia. The militia-men who had survived the collapse of the staging abandoned the Orocasias wall as soon as they realized that their flanks were no longer protected by the regulars. They drew up at the bottom of the hill, resolved to defend the streets. The Persians scaled the walls with ladders and entered without difficulty.

The militia-men then gave a brisk display of street-fighting in the approved Hippodrome tradition, with cobblestones and rapiers and bludgeons. The Blues attacked with their war-cry 'Down with the Greens!' and the Greens with their war-cry 'Down with the Blues!', and the Persians were forced to give ground against them. But King Khosrou, posted in a captured tower, observed that this was only a rabble army, and sent a squadron of his Immortals charging up the street. The militia broke, and a massacre began in which immense numbers of people of both sexes perished. Antioch was sacked, and in the Cathedral Khosrou found extraordinary stores of gold and silver, enough to pay for the whole campaign twice over. As a punishment for the street-fighting, he ordered the whole city to be burned down, with the exception of the Cathedral – for he said that he had no quarrel with the Patriarch. Even the suburbs were destroyed, more thoroughly even than by the earthquake of thirteen years previously. Half a million people were left homeless and starving. He assembled 100,000 of the younger and more active sort and comforted them thus: 'I shall bring you back safely with me to my own country and build you a new city on the banks of the Euphrates, which is a finer river by far than your Orontes. You shall have baths and market-places and a public library and a hippodrome – everything that you could possibly desire!'

Then he marched to Seleucia, the port of Antioch, and bathed in the sea, in fulfilment of a vow that he had made to the Sun God; and then up the Orontes to Apamea, where he again enriched himself with church treasures. There the people opened their gates to him, so he did not burn the city, and even allowed them to keep their most priceless possession – a half-yard of wood sawn from the base of the True Cross. Age and rottenness had made this relic phosphorescent, so that it shone in the dark, which was held miraculous. The priests kept it in a golden chest studded with jewels. But Khosrou took the chest.

It was at Apamea that he ordered a chariot-race in his own honour. 'Mark you,' he said, 'the Green Colour must be given the precedence, since the Emperor Justinian and his Empress have, my ministers inform me, too long shown an unjust bias in favour of the Blue.' In Persia chariots are used only in parades and ceremonial processions; Khosrou therefore did not realize that the sport was competitive. The four chariots were released from the 'prisons', the charioteers strove with cry and blow for the lead, and the First Blue soon gained the inner berth: he shot fifty paces ahead of the Second Blue, with the two Greens a long way behind. Khosrou grew very angry and, seeing in the Blue chariots an emblem of the Emperor, he cried out: 'Stop the race, stop that Caesar! He has impertinently stolen the lead from my two chariots.' Persian soldiers rushed out into the arena and formed a barrier with lances. The Blue charioteers pulled up, for fear of impaling their horses, and the Green chariots were allowed to take the lead and win. This was the foullest race ever seen in a hippodrome (and I could tell you of some pretty foul ones). The audience laughed uproariously, and Khosrou beamed at them, not realizing that the joke was against himself. 'Stop that Caesar' became a catchword in racing circles all over the world. Khosrou was of a naturally irritable and sarcastic temper. For example, he would ridicule the misfortunes of the people whose cities he destroyed by pretending to weep and saying: 'Alas, poor Christians, it was your misguided loyalty to our foolish, greedy cousin of Constantinople that brought you to this!' He was not altogether a bad man, however.

From Apamea he returned home, not by the way that he had come but by Edessa and Carrhae and Constantina and Daras. He accepted a mere 5,000 in gold as ransom-money from Edessa, though at first he had intended to storm it, because the Mages with him advised him against any such attempt. For his vanguard twice missed their road on their way there, and when at last they found it he suddenly began to suffer great pain from an abscess under a tooth in his lower jaw. The people of Edessa were not surprised to escape so slightly. They claim that Jesus Christ Himself once sent a letter to a citizen of Edessa who had invited Him to leave the foolish Galileans to their fate and come as an honoured guest to teach in Edessa. Jesus is supposed to have written: 'I cannot come, because of the prophecies in the Scriptures, but all good fortune shall attend you as long as you live, and I shall protect your city from attack by the Persians for ever.' This does not read to me as a likely reply in the circumstances: there was no threat from Persia in Jesus's day. Nevertheless, the men of Edessa have inscribed it in gold letters on the city gate; and as a protective charm it has only once failed to work.

While King Khosrou was still close to Edessa an embassy arrived from Justinian, agreeing to the terms suggested as a price for the restoration of the Eternal Peace – namely, an annual payment of 400,000 in gold, besides what had already been taken in the course of the campaign. As an act of grace Khosrou now offered to sell all the captives that he was bringing back from Antioch at a bargain price to the people of Edessa – who are notoriously kind-hearted. They collected, in addition to the ransom money of 5,000 pieces, the equivalent of fully 50,000. This sum was made up in silver and small money, and even in cattle and sheep, the voluntary contributions of farmers. The very prostitutes held a meeting, at which it was decided that all jewels whatsoever belonging to members of their guild should be added to the ransom money. Unfortunately, Boutzes arrived at this point, and announced that Edessa had disobeyed the Emperor in paying Khosrou the 5,000. He forbade any more to be paid, and informed Khosrou that the people of Edessa had reconsidered the matter and would not conclude the bargain. He was angry with Khosrou that the ransom-price for his own brother Coutzes, captured thirteen years previously, had been fixed at an impossible sum, so that Coutzes had died in prison. As an act of private justice, Boutzes kept all the money from Edessa for himself; and Khosrou carried the captives off with him.

This was early in July. The news now reached King Khosrou that Belisarius had returned to Constantinople. He hurried home, contenting himself with extorting small sums of protection money from Constantina and the other cities through which he passed. He refused money from Carrhae, on the ground that it was not a Christian city but continued true to the Old Gods. At Daras he made a demonstration; then, levying a further 5,000 pieces there, passed back across the Persian frontier, well pleased with himself. As for the captives, he built them their new Antioch by the Euphrates, and they were by no means disappointed with it: a great many of them renounced Christianity and returned to the worship of the Old Gods in the temples that he built for them. Symmachus, the Athenian philosopher, came here too and opened an academy for the study of the doctrine called neo-Platonism – a sort of Christianity not complicated by the story of Jesus Christ or by arguments as to His nature. At the Hippodrome of New Antioch the Green Colour was under King Khosrou's particular protection, and was given all the best horses.

But as soon as Justinian heard that Khosrou was back in Persia he tore up the new treaty.

This, then, was the shameful story that greeted us in July on our arrival at Constantinople from Ravenna: in the three months Khosrou had cost Justinian a sum that ran into I cannot say how many millions, and exposed both the weakness of his defences and the cowardice of his troops. Few officers of distinction had accompanied Belisarius and my mistress home, and no troops except the Household Regiment, which by enlistment of Goths, Moors, and Vandals had now swelled to 7,000 men. These were all bold, sturdy fellows; for if ever any outstanding courage was shown by any fighter, whether he belonged to enemy or allied forces, Belisarius was always quick to engage him and turn him into a first-class soldier. At the defence of Rome the Household Regiment had so often borne the brunt of the Gothic attack that the Romans used to exclaim in wonder: 'The Empire of Theoderich undermined by the household of a single man!'

With us came a large train of captives, headed by King Wittich and Queen Matasontha and the children of King Hildibald. We also brought all the public treasures of Ravenna. These consisted of some ten millions in gold and silver bars and coin; the ancient regalia of the Empire of the West; great quantities of miscellaneous gold and silver plate, including the treasures captured by Theoderich in his wars in France and the treasures of the Arian Church (which Justinian had ordered to be dissolved); and the Roman standards captured long ago at the Battle of Adrianople, together with the very diadem that the Emperor Valens had worn on that disastrous day.

Of the standards and the crown Belisarius said, as we were nearing home: 'The defeat at Adrianople is avenged at last. Ah, if my Uncle Modestus had only lived to see me bring these back, what a classical banquet he would have spread for us!'

My mistress agreed: 'Yes, and what a more than classical speech he would have delivered!'

Belisarius was, I think, contrasting in his mind the sort of welcome that his uncle would have given him with what might, in the worst case, be expected from Justinian because of this atmosphere of slander and suspicion at Court. It was not that Belisarius was ambitious of honours and titles: he was satisfied merely with the sense of a task well done. But being naturally warm-hearted he was easily chilled by ungenerosity in others. He was hoping, no doubt, for Justinian's sake as much as for his own, that all suspicions would vanish upon his return and the slanderers be confounded.

If I am right in so interpreting his thoughts, a great disappointment was in store for him. Never before in the world, I think, has a loyal and victorious general received so cold a welcome home from his Emperor. The city mob went perfectly wild in its expressions of admiration for Belisarius, acclaiming him as their only sure defender against the Persians. But Justinian was so jealous that he withheld the deserved triumph; nor did he even make a public exhibition of the Gothic spoils. These were landed privately at the Imperial port and stored in the Porphyry Palace, where none but members of the Senate were permitted to view them. Justinian was for not giving any of the money to Belisarius; for fear, I suppose, that he would scatter it to the crowd as largesse and so increase his popularity. But Theodora insisted that he should have at least half a million for the expenses of his household, because the men drew no pay or rations from public funds unless on active service. During all his wars, Belisarius not only gave his Household Troops extra pay and rations out of his own pocket, but made good their losses in arms and equipment – which was not at all a usual practice: he also awarded them rings and chains of honour for any signal military exploit and pensioned off the sick and wounded who were incapacitated for further fighting. More than this, if any old soldier came to him and said, as it might be, 'I lost an arm in your first Persian campaign and have come to beggary at last,' he would give him money, though the man had not been under his direct command at all. Such generosity, of course, increased the suspicion of Justinian whose standard of what was due to distressed veterans was a niggardly one.

The citizens used to say of Belisarius: 'He is a sort of monster. No man ever saw him drunk; he dresses as simply as his station allows; so far from being lecherous, he has not so much as cast a longing eye on a single one of his captured women though greater beauties than the Vandal and Gothic ladies do not exist in the world; he is not even a religious enthusiast.' Accompanied by my mistress and a large retinue of cuirassiers, he would leave his house in the High Street on foot every day and walk all the way to the Square of Augustus to attend to his business at the War Office, and later to pay his duty to his Sovereigns. The crowd never tired of staring at his tall figure and frank, grave face, and at the soldiers marching with even tread behind him. These were dark-skinned, delicate-featured Persians, and blond, yellow-haired Vandals, and big-limbed, auburn-haired Goths, and bow-legged, slant-eyed Huns, and Moors with crinkly black hair and hooked noses and thick lips. People used to stare at my mistress and whisper: 'She is a sort of monster, too. She destroyed many Goths herself, aiming with a catapult, and it was she who relieved Rome.' I once overheard a priest say of her: 'Well did Solomon prophesy of this harlot in the Books of Proverbs: "She hath cast down many wounded; yea, many strong men have been slain by her. Her house is the way to Hell, going down to the chambers of death."'

Then, although only a distorted imagination could have read Belisarius's genuine modesty as affectation, Narses and Cappadocian John told Justinian: 'He is contemplating a rebellion. Look how he courts the favour of the mob, so that his least movement through the streets becomes a sort of festival procession. The radiance of Your Own Glorious Majesty is by contrast dimmed for the vulgar eye. He believes now that the two Empires are his for the taking: he has come here to Constantinople to make a parade of his captives, and will in due time attempt to snatch the Diadem from Your Serenity's sacred brow. Be the first to act.'

Justinian, being cowardly, put them off, saying: 'I have no evidence as yet.' He was afraid of Theodora, to whom my mistress Antonina was so dear a friend; besides, if Khosrou made another invasion in the following year, Belisarius alone would be capable of stemming the attack.

As for King Wittich, he paid homage to Justinian and even renounced his Arian errors; so that he was raised to patrician rank and given great estates in Galatia – which marched with those that had been awarded to Geilimer. But the marriage between him and Matasontha was dissolved at their joint request. As a reward for her services in the matter of the burned granaries, Matasontha was permitted to marry Justinian's own nephew Germanus, the one who had helped to put down the mutiny of Stotzas. The other Gothic captives were formed into cavalry units and sent to guard the Danube frontier. So much, then, for the Goths.

At Constantinople we saw for the first time the completed church of St Sophia. The architect was Anthemius of Tralles. Justinian had told him: 'Spare no expense to make this the most beautiful and lasting building in the world, that God's name and mine may be glorified.' Anthemius was equal to the task. It is his name that deserves the principal glory; for Justinian merely approved his designs. If any other names are to be honoured, let them be those of Isidore of Miletus, Anthemius's assistant, and of Belisarius, whose Vandalic victory provided both the treasure which paid for the construction of the Cathedral and the necessary slave-labour.

The Cathedral overtops all the neighbouring buildings, lofty though they are. To compare greater with less, it is like some huge merchant ship anchored among ferry-boats in the Horn. Its proportions are so nicely calculated, however, that there is nothing brutal or forbidding in its size. It has, on the contrary, a graceful but serious nobility which I can only express by saying: 'Had Belisarius been as fine an architect as he was a soldier, that is the sort of church which he would have built.'

St Sophia's is more than 200 feet broad, and 300 feet long and 150 feet high. A huge cupola crowns it; and, as one gazes up from within at the ceiling, which is inlaid throughout with pure gold, it seems as though the whole structure must collapse at any moment, for there are no cross-beams or central piers to support it, but each part springs inward and upward to the central point of the cupola. The citizens tell country visitors: 'A demon, at the Emperor's command, suspended the cupola from the sky by a golden chain until the other parts were raised to meet it.' Many visitors take this pleasantry for truth.

There are two porticoes, each with a domed roof inlaid with gold, one for male and one for female worshippers. Who could worthily describe the beauty of the carved columns and the mosaics with which the building is adorned? The place resembles nothing so much as a spring meadow under a broad golden sun, with the great freestone pillars of the transept rising from it like trees; many different colours of marble have been worked into the walls and floor – red and green and speckled purple and straw-colour and butter-yellow and pure white, with here and there the blue sheen of lapis-lazuli. Exquisite carving and chasing and moulding make every detail delightful, and the numerous windows in the walls and cupola flood the transept with light. To appreciate this building and to worship in it the Wisdom to which it is dedicated one does not need to be an Orthodox Christian; and it is open at all times even to poor worshippers, so long as they have not offended against the laws and behave in a seemly manner. A beggar can enter and imagine himself an emperor, standing in the midst of such lavish splendour; only a few parts of the building are barred to him – such as the sanctuary, which is plated with 40,000 pounds' weight of glittering silver, and certain private chapels. As for relics of the saints and martyrs, they are stored here in profusion, and some of the inner doors are made of wood that (they say) once formed part of Noah's ark.

It was during a visit to St Sophia's, I believe, that the conviction came upon Theodosius that he was living a very aimless life, and that he would be at ease again only if he returned to his monastery. It was not that he was more truly a Christian now than before, but that at Ephesus his life had been regulated according to a strict rule and he had not needed ever to think what to do next. Theodosius was no vicious man; indeed, in accepting the monastic restraint upon the passions, he was enduring what most men would have found unbearable. He was aware, too, that he was the subject of continual gossip in connexion with my mistress Antonina, being called her pleasure-boy; and my mistress, in order to stifle this gossip, always addressed him with humiliating harshness in public, though very affectionately in private. Theodosius was also very weary of war and could not face the prospect of still another campaign – especially in the East, where Belisarius was likely soon to be sent: great heat always made him sick and empty-headed. He therefore secretly packed up a few possessions one night, took a passage on a fast merchant vessel, and went off to Ephesus; leaving behind him a short note of apology and farewell.

My mistress was so grieved at his disappearance that she could not touch food or conduct her daily business, and presently took to her bed. She was forty years old now, and the anxieties of the Italian campaign had given her an anxious, haggard look, of which no cosmetics or massage could rid her. Also, the change of her blood had recently begun, so that she was in a nervous and irritable state; she fell into a melancholy from which Belisarius, for all his love and patience, could not rouse her. It seems that she took Theodosius's departure as a sign that her great beauty (which he used to celebrate, courtier-fashion, in songs of his own making) had left her, together with all her widely acknowledged wit and charm. I consider that Belisarius showed true magnanimity on this occasion. When she confessed that only the presence of Theodosius could revive her, he went directly to Justinian and made a humble petition that Theodosius be recalled.

Justinian consented to write to the Abbot of Ephesus, desiring him to release Theodosius from his vows and send him back; but Theodosius claimed the right to become a monk as one that no human authority, not even the Emperor's, could deny him.

When, in the spring, King Khosrou resumed his military operations and Belisarius was sent hurriedly to the frontier to oppose him, my mistress remained behind in the city, saying that in such low spirits she would be only a hindrance to him.

CHAPTER 19
VICTORY AT CARCHEMISH

Now my story enters on a phase in which I have no pleasure, since it was one of great unhappiness for my mistress Antonina and greater unhappiness, even, for Belisarius, her husband; and this despite a remarkable victory that he won over the Persians. But the evil must be told with the good.

My mistress, as I have said, remained in Constantinople while Belisarius was sent against King Khosrou in the late spring of the year of our Lord 541. He had spent as much of his time as his Court duties permitted in training the Gothic recruits of the Household Regiment in the use of the bow and his own well-tried system of cavalry tactics. But there was a very different sort of fighting material waiting for him in the East. On his arrival at Daras – a place, he wrote, sweetened for him by the memory of her visit to him there – he found the Imperial Forces sunk into a sadly low state of discipline and training; and, as for courage, they trembled at the very name of Persia. His own 7,000 men were all that he could count upon for serious fighting. Many regular regiments, of full strength according to the Army List and drawing full pay and rations, were short of several hundred men, and of the so-called trained men one-half were unarmed labourers employed on improving the fortifications of Daras and other places – according to the plan which Belisarius had himself drawn up twelve years before, and of which the necessity had only lately been discovered.

King Khosrou differed from most Eastern monarchs with military ambitions, whose practice is to undertake easy objectives in person while consigning the hazardous ones to their lieutenants: contrariwise, he always chose the post of greatest difficulty. On the invitation of the native Colchians, who were being shamefully squeezed by Justinian's tax-gatherers (though their land was only a Roman protectorate, not a possession), he invaded Colchis by a route through the foot-hills of the Caucasus which no Persian army had ever taken before and which had always been considered impossible. He had sent a large force of pioneers ahead of him to hack a road, through virgin forest and across the face of precipices, sufficiently broad and firm even for the transport of elephants. His design was not suspected, because he had given out that the expedition was against a tribe of Huns that had been raiding into Persian Iberia. To be short: he penetrated to the coast of Colchis, captured the principal Roman fortress of Petra, killed the Roman Governor, was acclaimed by the Colchians as a deliverer, took possession of the country.

Belisarius heard of the expedition from his spies across the Mesopotamian border, though no news of its outcome was obtainable as yet. He decided that the only hope for Colchis lay in his drawing Khosrou back in a hurry by some counter-stroke. He summoned all available forces from the various garrison cities and spoke very bluntly to his generals, reproaching them for having neglected the forces under their command. He threatened that, unless these were properly armed, equipped, and brought up to strength within two months' time he would see to it that they were all degraded in rank. He also insisted that as generalissimo he expected unhesitating obedience. 'Nevertheless,' he said, 'I have been ten years in the Western Empire, and cannot be expected to appreciate the present strategic position in every detail. I should be glad to have a frank opinion from every one of you as to the practicability of an immediate cavalry-raid across the frontier. The Great King is far away. Though he has no doubt left his frontier fortresses well guarded, this is perhaps an excellent opportunity for avenging his sack of Antioch and for restoring the offensive capacities of our men. The Emperor has sent me here for the express purpose of upholding the honour of the Roman Army.'

Boutzes, anxious to regain Belisarius's good opinion of him, agreed that a raid would be an excellent thing; and so did Peter, the Governor of Daras, for the same reason. But the joint-commanders of the Thracian troops from the Lebanon – the same two who had betrayed Antioch by escaping with all their men from the Daphne gate – made difficulties. If they came with Belisarius, they said, there was nothing to prevent the King of the Saracens from raiding Syria and Palestine in their absence.

Belisarius answered: 'I have been away from the East, as I say, for ten years, but have not forgotten so much as you may suppose. These Saracens are about to begin their Ramadan fast, when out of respect for their Sun God they fast all the daylight hours and abstain from any fighting for two whole months.' This silenced them.

A few days later Belisarius led his field army of 15,000 men across the Persian frontier and encamped about eight miles from Nisibis. With him, too, came 5,000 Arabs under the same King Harith ibn Gabala of Bostra, who had deserted him ten years before during the Unnecessary Battle, but who had been freely forgiven by Justinian for his perfidy. The Persians had learned such contempt for our armies that it was likely that they would leave the protection of their strong fortifications and come out against Belisarius. He hoped thus to defeat them and, heading off their main retreat and allowing only a squadron or so to escape to Nisibis, to capture the city, by sending a party of men, dressed in Persian armour, to mingle with these fugitives and keep the gates open for him. However, this plan was opposed by Peter, who thought that the Persians should be intimidated by a nearer approach. He insisted on encamping only a mile and a half away from the city.

Belisarius sent a message to Peter, saying that his courage was commendable but that if he fought and defeated the Persians where he was encamped they would have to retreat only a short distance to reach safety; and that he was acting directly against orders in taking up that position.

Peter replied: 'I served with you some years ago on the Euphrates, where, though the Persians were then hundreds of miles away from a fortress, you hesitated to attack them. I pride myself that I am not afraid of the Persians. As for obedience, I am informed that recently at Ravenna you overrode the orders of the Emperor himself. Yet no harm came of it for you.'

Belisarius wrote again: 'Circumstances alter cases. However, I do not propose to argue with you. If, against my orders, you maintain your bravado, do at least, I beg of you, be careful of a surprise attack, especially at the dinner-hour.'

The weather being extremely hot at midday, Peter's men took off their armour and stacked their arms, and a number of them went out in twos and threes to steal melons from the kitchen-gardens a few hundred yards from the walls of Nisibis. The Persian cavalry made a sudden sally from three gates and chased the melon-stealers back to their palisaded camp. The camp guards snatched up their arms in a hurry and ran to the help of their comrades, but were driven back in confusion. Peter was soon forced to abandon his camp with the loss not only of fifty men but of his regimental standard.

Fortunately Belisarius's look-out men had seen a cloud of dust from the direction of Nisibis, and reported this at once. It was a standing order in Belisarius's camp that dinner should be served in relays, only one-third of the men being off duty at a time; so within one minute of the trumpeter's blowing the Alarm the Household cuirassiers were pelting down the Nisibis road to Peter's rescue. Belisarius was at their head, with his Gothic recruits mounted on heavy horses, and found the Persians busy reforming their ranks after a hurried plunder of the camp. Separating into two columns for a double flank attack, they converged on the enemy at a gallop, shooting from the saddle and charging home with their long lances. The enemy arrows did not stop them, since, as I have already explained, Persian bows are too light for effective use against heavily armoured cavalry. The Goths had the satisfaction of breaking the Persian line at the first onset and driving them back in confusion on Nisibis. Peter's regiment was saved – but at the expense of Belisarius's plans; for the Persians, of whom 150 men fell in the skirmish, realized that Belisarius was back again on the frontier and had lost none of his former vigour. They did not venture to go out against him from the city; but displayed Peter's regimental standard from one of their towers, wreathing it in black sausages for derision.

Now that Belisarius had no hope of taking Nisibis by surprise, he decided to push on beyond it, knowing that no ordinary siege-craft could reduce it in less than twelve months or a year. The next fortress to the east was Sisauranum, some thirty-five miles distant; the garrison there, including the local militia, consisted of 4,000 men. Belisarius could afford to leave Nisibis with its garrison of 6,000 in his rear, but not both Sisauranum and Nisibis. He decided therefore to lay siege to Sisaruranum with his main forces, leaving a small containing force behind at Nisibis, and to send King Harith with his Arabs raiding across the River Tigris into the province of Assyria.

This part of Assyria had been free from Roman raids for centuries. The inhabitants lived in perfect security and were extremely rich. With King Khosrou absent in Colchis and the Persian frontier forces pinned in Nisibis and Sisauranum, King Harith's men found such easy plundering as they had never enjoyed before in all their lives. King Harith considered that it would be a great pity to share all this wealth with the Roman armies in his rear, as the agreement was, and therefore decided to return to his Court at Bostra by another way. With him had come a squadron of the Household Regiment under Trajan, and another of Thracians under John the Epicure, to stiffen the Arab forces in case any serious resistance was encountered. But Harith deceived Trajan and John by instructing his scouts to report that a large army of Persians had cut in from the North behind the expedition and were lying in wait for their return at the Tigris bridge by which they had crossed. He announced that he was going home at once. John the Epicure, encumbered with booty, baulked at dealing with a whole army by himself and decided to follow Harith's example. Trajan, being his junior in rank, was forced to keep him company. The whole expedition therefore marched southward along the River Tigris until they came to the bridge at Nineveh, where they crossed over; John the Epicure and Trajan then returned to Roman territory across the desert by way of Singara and the lower reaches of the Aborrhas. King Harith reached Bostra in safety, with his booty, after a still longer march. (Justinian once more forgave this perfidious Arab, and some years afterwards, when he destroyed an army of the King of the Saracens, raised him to patrician rank, and received him with honour at Constantinople.)

Meanwhile Belisarius was expecting word from King Harith – or, failing him, from Trajan – as to what progress had been made and what Persian forces were stationed in Assyria. Receiving no message at all, he began to grow anxious. But he succeeded in capturing Sisauranum: being crowded with peasant refugees, it surrendered from famine after a six weeks' siege. Unlike the frontier cities of Daras and Nisibis, this city kept no permanent store of food as a safeguard against siege, and the suddenness of Belisarius's appearance had not permitted the collection of stocks of corn from the surrounding country. Belisarius's terms were generous: a free pardon for all the citizens – who were Christians of Roman descent, this being one of the cities handed over to Persia a century and a half before by the disgraceful treaty of Jovian – and for the 800 Persian horsemen of the garrison a choice between common slavery and enlistment in the Emperor Justinian's army. They chose to serve under Justinian and were later transferred to Italy to fight against the Goths – as the Goths enlisted in the Household Regiment had been transferred to Mesopotamia to fight against the Persians. The fortifications of Sisauranum were razed to the ground.

Still no news came from King Harith, and Belisarius feared that the whole expeditionary force had been ambushed and destroyed. He now called a council of war and pressed for an advance across the Tigris – perhaps Harith was still holding out in some captured city or other, waiting for relief. But not one of the generals would support him in this project. Those from the Lebanon insisted on returning with their troops, now that the Saracens' Ramadan was over; while the others pointed out that their troops were suffering so severely from the heat that fully one-third of them were incapacitated for fighting. They began a disorderly clamour, the refrain of which was: 'Take us back again. We will not cross the Tigris. We refuse to go farther. Take us back again.'

Thus by the bravado of Peter, the treachery of King Harith, the credulousness of John the Epicure, the cowardice of these other generals, Belisarius was robbed of what might have been the greatest of his victories. For when King Khosrou in Colchis heard of the Arab raid in Assyria and of Belisarius's capture of Sisauranum, he came hurrying back by the road which passes to the westward of Lake Van and along the eastern bank of the Tigris. He had already lost nearly one-half of his army by a cholera epidemic. He now lost one-half of what remained to him by a breakdown of his food supply – the frightening news of the cholera turned his commissariat-trains back to Iberia. He was delayed further by a landslide which carried away his new road at the most difficult point of the journey, so that he had to cut it afresh in order to pass. If Belisarius had now been able to cross the Tigris he would have intercepted Khosrou and, the Persians being in a pitiful state of starvation and disorder, would doubtless have added a third captured king to the gifts he had made to Justinian.

But it was not to be: Belisarius could not persuade his generals to march. He laid his sick in carts and retired past Nisibis to Daras.

In Constantinople strange things had been happening. To begin with, there appeared in the city an illegitimate son of Theodora's, born to her in Egypt during that one unlucky year when she went off to Pentapolis from the club-house. The father was a person of no importance – an Arabian merchant, recently dead; he had taken the boy (whom he christened John) off her hands. Theodora had told Justinian that she had never had a child; and when he conferred patrician rank on her she signed a document solemnly affirming this. Cappadocian John's hold on Theodora was his knowledge that this child existed:

his agents in Egypt had brought the story to him, but without any details to confirm it. Theodora could not be sure whether or not he was in possession of any evidence that would carry weight with Justinian; she herself had never been able to discover where her son was. At last the young man, John the Bastard, was told the secret of his birth by his dying father and came to Constantinople from Aden on the Red Sea, where they lived. He approached Theodora through my mistress Antonina, whose first husband, he knew, had been a business associate of his father's. If he expected to be greeted with maternal tears and kisses and given a prominent position at Court he was much mistaken. Theodora wasted no time, but declared him a lunatic and shut him up in a Bedlam, where he soon died. She had not loved the father, why should she love the son? Besides, he was a greedy, vain, illiterate fellow.

Theodora, with sighs of relief, told my mistress: 'Now at last, my dearest, we can settle our account with Cappadocian John: I no longer have anything to fear from him.'

But Theodora knew that until Theodosius was brought back from Ephesus my mistress would be in no state of mind to assist in any plot of revenge. So, though my mistress was convinced that Theodosius would never be tempted to leave his retreat, Theodora let the Bishop of Ephesus, one of her Monophysite nominees, know that he must contrive to send the monk Theodosius back to Constantinople at once. The Bishop ordered the Abbot of the monastery, which had a very easy rule, to impose such heavy penances and restrictions on Theodosius that he would voluntarily demand absolution from his vows.

My mistress's hopes began to revive a little at this news, and she began thinking of ways to entrap and ruin Cappadocian John. Her first step was to cultivate the acquaintance of John's only daughter, Euphemia, a clever girl to whom he was devoted. Theodora had chosen a husband for her whom she did not in the least wish to marry. My mistress, playing upon Euphemia's bitterness against Theodora, gradually won her sympathies. Euphemia asked her one evening: 'Illustrious Lady Antonina, dearest friend, why is it that you look so sad these days and scarcely smile at all? Is it anxiety for your brave husband at the wars?'

My mistress, who certainly had no intention of confiding to Euphemia how much she missed Theodosius, answered shortly: 'I have little anxiety for my husband's safety in the field.' Then, by a sudden inspiration she continued: 'What distresses me is that the Emperor is so unreasonably suspicious of my husband's loyalty. I fear far more for his safety when he is here at Constantinople.'

Euphemia exclaimed: 'Suspicious of Belisarius's loyalty! Why, nobody in the Empire is so devoted to the Emperor as he, surely?'

My mistress rose, carefully shut all the doors, and then whispered: 'I have long been wishing to confide in someone, dearest child, for my heart is full to bursting with indignation at the ungrateful treatment that my noble Belisarius has received. He has enlarged the Emperor's dominions by tens of thousands of square miles and his treasure by tens of millions in gold, and brought him home captive two powerful kings – not to mention his quelling of the Victory riots, when the Emperor nearly lost his throne. But this miserable Justinian is jealous and treats him like a dog or criminal. Belisarius told me before he left: "Better any other Emperor than this! I feel absolved from my vows of loyalty to him, because of my prolonged ill-treatment at his hands." '

Euphemia replied: 'You and Belisarius have only yourselves to blame, dearest friend; for though you have the power, you hesitate to use it.'

My mistress replied without hesitation: 'But child, we cannot undertake a military revolution unless we have the assistance of powerful ministers at Court. Your illustrious father, for instance, does not see eye to eye with us at all. If we had *him* on our side . . . By the way, he is the very man for Emperor in Justinian's place. My husband himself has no ambitions in that way, as you know: he is interested only in soldiering.'

Euphemia's anxiety to escape from her unwelcome marriage made her particularly eloquent in presenting the case to her father. But her task was an easy one, because Cappadocian John cherished a secret belief that he would eventually wear the Diadem. An old astrologer at the Hippodrome, perhaps the same who had prophesied so truly for Theodora and my mistress, had many years before told him: 'My son, the robe of Augustus will one day be put upon you by the Palace soldiers, and that will be a day of great rejoicing at Court.' John was therefore pleased beyond measure at Euphemia's account of the conversation. He told Euphemia to assure my mistress Antonina that she could count on him absolutely in all things that would contribute to Justinian's downfall. My mistress embraced Euphemia and swore by the Holy Ghost that her father could depend on Belisarius and herself for the same vigour of purpose that he himself displayed.

Before the plot developed any further, Theodosius, to my mistress Antonina's inexpressible joy, returned to us from Ephesus, weary of the penitential rigours that the Abbot had imposed upon him. He was a monk no longer and soon resumed his old ways – rich robes, perfumes, singing and guitar-playing, fashionable sneers, lively frolics about nothing. How to explain this change of mood – as unaccountable as his sudden plunge into the religious life? Well, there are characters of his sort, especially among the Thracians, whose contradictoriness we could waste a long time in discussing – their love of being discussed being perhaps the clue to the mystery. So let us say no more about Theodosius's motives, contenting ourselves with an account of his words and deeds.

My mistress's son Photius happened to be out of the city at the time, though he had been staying with us ever since Belisarius's departure. He had incurred enormous debts by commercial speculation at Antioch before the city was destroyed, and from betting at the races and the bear-fighting. If he could not soon meet his obligations he would be degraded, as a bankrupt, from the Patrician Order; but he felt sure that his mother would come to the rescue to avoid a family scandal. Perhaps she would have done so, had Theodosius not told her a story that angered her exceedingly. He said that he had run away to Ephesus because Photius had threatened to kill both her and him unless he left the city at once: this was why he had been so reluctant to return.

A great to-do followed. My mistress, of course, refused to pay Photius's debts; and because, on hearing the story, she had asked for police protection for Theodosius and herself and the whole matter had therefore become public, she sent Belisarius a full report. She also threatened Photius with severe punishment at Theodora's hands.

Photius hurriedly crossed the Bosphorus and took a post-chaise to the Persian frontier, to throw himself on Belisarius's protection. Exactly what he told Belisarius I do not know, but the gist of it was that when Theodosius went to Ephesus the second time it was with the intention of returning to my mistress at Constantinople as soon as Belisarius was out of the way; that he had so returned, and that the two of them were now living in open sin together. He further complained that my mistress had stolen a large sum of his money from him and conferred it on her paramour; and that in addition to having brought him to the verge of bankruptcy, she was persecuting him in every possible way because he knew too much about her.

Belisarius heard this horrible tale from Photius on the very day that he was holding his council of war at Sisauranum. To think that it influenced him in his decision to retire from Persian territory might be natural, were it not so manifest that he put his duty as a soldier before all personal considerations. At least his military associates should have been aware of this trait in him. Nevertheless, the suggestion went the rounds, given circulation by the very generals who had been most timorous about crossing the Tigris.

After the council of war, Belisarius had further talk with Photius, who swore by the Holy Ghost – the most terrible oath that a Christian can swear, and one which if broken consigns the soul, they say, to everlasting torment in Hell – that he spoke the truth. To support his testimony he had brought two of my fellow-domestics as witnesses, and a Senator who happened to be one of his principal creditors and was nearly bankrupt himself. These, with Photius, succeeded in convincing Belisarius. Perhaps his disappointment with the campaign and the shaky state of his health after a month of dysentery played a part in confusing his usually clear powers of judgement. Furthermore, it should be said in his defence that my mistress's relations with Theodosius certainly did give a very mysterious impression. Even I, as I have already confessed earlier in this work, could never make up my mind as to their true character. At all events, Belisarius succumbed to an attack of jealous rage; all his officers were aghast at the change in him. For once in his life he forgot to be patient or gentle with his men, acting just like any other general, except that in his furies he refrained from blasphemy. Nor was his condition improved by a letter from my mistress, in which she wrote that Photius had escaped from Constantinople with his mouth full of slander and that she was following in haste to fill it with mud. She informed him that Theodosius, for fear of assassination by Photius's friends, was temporarily returning to Ephesus in her absence.

However, the affair of Cappadocian John had to be settled before she set out; otherwise the plot might turn against her. So she sent me to Cappadocian John to say that she was setting out for Daras at once, for the purpose of persuading Belisarius that a move for Justinian's overthrow and supersession could now be safely made. I arranged that

Cappadocian John should meet my mistress secretly on the following midnight in an orchard of Belisarius's estate at Rufinianae, a suburb of Constantinople across the Bosphorus: this would be her first stopping-place after leaving the city. She had no doubt but that he would fall into her trap – for had she not used the name of the Holy Ghost to Euphemia in asseverating the earnestness of Belisarius's intentions and her own?

My mistress reported my success to Theodora, who took into her confidence Narses (now on bad terms with Cappadocian John) and Marcellus, the Commander of the Imperial Guards. Narses and Marcellus went to Rufinianae in disguise, with a party of soldiers; and by the agreed hour were at their posts in the orchard – some of them concealed behind a cistern and others among the boughs of the apple-trees. They say that Justinian had got wind that something was astir, but that it was reported to him as a genuine plot against the Throne; and that he sent this message to Cappadocian John: 'We know all. Desist, or you die. Your confederate Antonina is under our displeasure.' But if it is true that Cappadocian John received this message, he must have considered it more dangerous to reply to it than to continue with the plot, and taken the reference to my mistress as a clear proof of her sincerity. However it was, when Cappadocian John slipped out of the city with a party of armed attendants to keep his appointment that night, he had made up his mind to accompany her to Daras.

It was pitch dark in the orchard, and my teeth were chattering with apprehension as I stood waiting beside my mistress Antonina, thinking how much was at stake. Like her, I was wearing a mail shirt under my cloak. At midnight a glove came flying over the garden-gate; I threw it back – the agreed signal. John was admitted with his twelve Cappadocian guards.

He and my mistress clasped hands like true conspirators, and at once he began cursing Justinian for a monster and a tyrant and a coward; it was not necessary for her to commit herself at all. And it is a curious thing that, as he raved on, it suddenly came to my mistress that the mysterious superintendent of police who had spoken to her in the church that day long ago, as she was on her way to Blachernae from the Palace, had been John himself in disguise; for he now happened to mispronounce an uncommon Greek word in just the same way that the other man had.

She could not help laughing at this. Cappadocian John paused, suspicious at once, and began to look about him. Then Narses and Marcellus sprang from their ambuscade with a shout, and a fierce fight began. My mistress, to keep up the farce, cried out: 'Oh, Oh, we are betrayed,' and pretended to struggle with Narses. I ran off. Marcellus was struck down and seriously wounded in the neck before the twelve Cappadocians were overpowered. In the confusion their master climbed over a wall and escaped.

If the foolish man had ridden straight back to the Palace and reported to Justinian that he had gone to Rufinianae on Justinian's own behalf, intending to trick Antonina into a public confession of her treachery, he might have been able to turn the tables on her. Instead, he grew panic-stricken and took sanctuary in St Irene's Church, so that when at dawn Theodora and Narses denounced him to Justinian there was no possible conclusion but that he was guilty.

This church of St Irene's, burned down during the Victory Riots, had been magnificently rebuilt by Justinian, and it was a sanctuary that he would never have ventured to violate. So Cappadocian John suffered no more severe punishment than the confiscation of all his estates and – strange proceeding – a condemnation to take holy orders!

Cappadocian John became a priest much against his will, for he was thus debarred by law from ever again holding secular office. But the old prophecy was fulfilled. The Palace Guards put on him the robe of Augustus – that is to say the priestly robe of an archdeacon who had just died, whose name happened to be Augustus; and there was great rejoicing in the Palace, where he was much hated. He was sent from St Irene's to a church at Cyzicus, a trading city on the Asiatic shore of the Sea of Marmora. Justinian was vexed, not so much that Cappadocian John had attempted to betray him as that Theodora was thus so triumphantly justified: he had always refused to believe her when she denounced John as a traitor. To spite her, he subsequently restored most of John's fortune to him, in the name of Christian charity; John lived in peace and security at Cyzicus for two or three years more. But Justinian could not thwart Theodora's resolve to harry her enemy. The Bishop of Cyzicus, under whose authority Cappadocian John had come, was informed by her that the new priest must not be allowed to live an easy life. John was therefore kept to a scrupulously exact routine; which irked him greatly.

We continued our journey to Daras by land. When we reached the fortress my mistress was met by Trajan, who had returned safely with his force and his plunder from Assyria. He led her to the room where Belisarius awaited her. There Belisarius, ignoring her affectionate greeting, confronted her at once with Photius's sworn testimony as to her adultery, and the depositions of the Senator and the two domestics. He shouted angrily at her: 'This is the end, Antonina. Your conduct as my wife should have been such as to make it impossible for me ever to reproach you with your past. That reproach you now hear from me: I am reminded of what your condition was when I first became acquainted with you.'

She met his severity with a severity of her own. Taking the parchment from his hand, she read it coldly, ripped it across, and let the pieces fall to the ground. She said that she would not demean herself by denying these charges, but in answer to his gross reproach of her she would say this: she could not feel any of the pain and misery that he clearly intended her to feel, but must think of him henceforward as a buffoon unworthy to be the husband of a woman like herself.

My mistress's demeanour was not a guilty one and, indeed, she fully expected to convince Belisarius that he was once more mistaken. But though Belisarius, in spite of his glowing rage, still loved her exceedingly, he could not return to his simple faith in her as readily as he had once done at Syracuse. He pressed her: 'Do you mean to tell me, wife, that your son Photius would swear by the Holy Ghost unless he was certain, beyond all argument, that he was speaking the truth?'

She replied scornfully: 'Do you think that everyone takes an oath as seriously as yourself – especially one to so obscure a concept as the Holy Ghost? Did not our master Justinian once swear this oath to Vitalian on the Bread and Wine, and then break it cheerfully for urgent reasons of state, on the sophistical ground that Vitalian was a heretic? Why, the day before I left Constantinople I myself swore by the Holy Ghost, for what might also be called urgent reasons of state – and I cannot regard myself as a particularly dishonest woman.'

Then she told him the whole story of the plot against Cappadocian John. When Belisarius heard that she, his trusted wife Antonina, had solemnly pledged his honour for the sake of a freakish plot of revenge, he felt dizzy and was obliged to sit down on a stool. When his head cleared he asked her: 'Tell me, Antonina, have I served my Emperor so frivolously that anyone can be made to believe me capable of playing the traitor? What amorous or magical arts did you use with Cappadocian John to persuade him of this impossible thing? What rights over me do you think that you hold, that you dare to bandy my name among scoundrels? And what did you think to gain by this wickedness? Was it perhaps the Empress's protection for an incestuous union with our godson?'

Instead of defending herself, she attacked him in what she knew to be his most sensitive feelings: his religion and his manhood. 'It seems that all but myself are to benefit by your famous Christian forbearance. But who could say whether it was piety or cowardice that has resigned you to Justinian's contemptuous treatment of you! He has whipped you and kicked you like a dog, and like a dog you come crawling and fawning to his feet. In crediting you even in jest with a desire to regain your lost self-respect by rebellion I did you an honour that you did not deserve.'

Belisarius could stand no more. He called Trajan from the anteroom. 'Convey the Lady Antonina to her quarters and post a guard at the door. She is to remain under close arrest until further notice.'

Trajan was dumbfounded.

My mistress felt that here indeed was a Belisarius that she had never encountered before. She was frightened at the sudden chasm that gaped between them and at the dreadful things that she had said to him. But she was also indignant that her liberty to behave how she pleased had been challenged, and this affected her far more strongly than his doubts of her chastity. She followed Trajan with a set face.

I shared in her confinement. For a long time all that she would say to me was the often-repeated: 'When the Empress releases me it will be a bad day for my Lord Belisarius.'

I contrived to get word to the Empress of what had happened. Within a month, namely at the end of September, Belisarius was ordered to set my mistress Antonina free and return to Constantinople immediately. Our confinement had not been over-tedious, and my mistress had not been subjected to any indignities, Belisarius not being of a revengeful nature.

Photius had meanwhile gone to Ephesus to seize Theodosius and bring him back to Daras for punishment, though Belisarius had given him no such commission, and was indeed unaware of his intentions. Photius managed, by tricking the Bishop of Ephesus into believing that he was Theodora's agent, to remove Theodosius from the church of St John the Evangelist; he had fled here for sanctuary. Photius carried him away to the mountain resort in Cilicia where the sick men of the Household Regiment had been sent to recuperate; and there confined him in a hut, as if on Belisarius's own orders. He had already robbed Theodosius of a large sack of gold which he had brought with him to the church of St John. It was money that my mistress Antonina had asked him to bank at Ephesus – she made a practice of depositing money in different Asiatic cities, as a security against evil times.

When we arrived at Constantinople, Belisarius boldly came before the Empress and asked her for justice against my mistress Antonina, telling her all that had passed. But the Empress raged against him like a tigress and ordered him to be immediately reconciled with his wife.

He replied: 'So long as my godson Theodosius is alive no reconciliation is possible; for the Lady Antonina is bewitched by him, and has behaved towards me in a criminal manner.'

Theodora tried to break down his assurance: 'And I suppose that you have never once been unfaithful to Antonina in all your life.'

'She would not accuse me of that, surely?'

Theodora was a just woman in her way, and took no direct action against Belisarius. But she could not refrain from injuring him through his intimate friends, charging them with real but forgotten offences that had been noted in the books for an emergency of this sort. Some were banished, others imprisoned. For Photius, worse was in store. Theodora sent after him to Cilicia and had him arrested for fraud, perjury, and theft; and, though of Consular rank, he was stripped and lashed and tortured before her until he confessed that he had lied to Belisarius, and until he revealed where Theodosius was being detained.

As for Photius's associate, the Senator: Theodora deprived him of all his property and had him immured in a dark underground stable, where a curiously loathsome treatment was meted out to him. He was tied to a manger with a short halter, his hands shackled behind him. There the poor wretch stood like an ass, unable to move or lie down, but ate and slept and fulfilled all the other needs of nature on his feet. This extreme torture was not only on my mistress Antonina's account: Theodora had a long-standing grudge against the man, who had once insulted her in our club-house days and called her a two-legged ass. He went mad after a few months of stable-life and began braying aloud; she then released him, but he died almost at once. Photius was confined in a corner of the same stable, though spared the manger and halter. I may as well tell the rest of his story here. Twice, with secret aid from Justinian, who had always found him a useful agent, Photius managed to escape from his prison and reach a city sanctuary: each time Theodora violated the sanctuary and returned him to his stable. On the third occasion he got clear away to Jerusalem, where he took monastic vows and remained safe from further vengeance.

Theodosius was brought back from Cilicia by Theodora's agents about the end of November. Theodora did not immediately report his arrival to my mistress, but told her gaily at the conclusion of the next audience: 'My dearest Lady Antonina, a most remarkable pearl has just come into my hands, and I should like your opinion of it. Will you come with me and judge of it?'

In the room to which Theodora led her, Theodosius was discovered, looking none the worse for his adventures and playing on a couch with one of the Palace cats. My poor mistress was speechless. She had refused to believe that he was safe in Cilicia, as Photius had said. Theodora left them alone together, after promising that in compensation for his sufferings and the calumnies sworn against him, Theodosius would be advanced to general's rank, and inviting him to live in her wing of the Palace, for safety's sake.

Thus this evil year came to an end, Belisarius and my mistress continuing estranged.

Early in the spring of the following year, the year of our Lord 542, King Khosrou once more crossed our frontier; this time with the largest army that he had yet brought together, little short of 200,000 men. His forces included several divisions of the White Huns whom Justinian had unsuccessfully tried to bribe to war against him. Hearing of the success of the Syrian raid of the previous year, they volunteered to join Khosrou, in hopes of spoil. Khosrou again took the southern route along the right bank of the Euphrates. But, aware that he had already sucked Syria almost dry of its silver and gold, he decided to waste no time here, but to march forward into Palestine. Now that Antioch had been destroyed, Jerusalem was easily the richest city of the East. The Holy Places there glittered with treasure, and the pilgrim trade had enriched the inhabitants, both Jews and Christians, to a fabulous degree.

After Belisarius's recall the command in the East had been entrusted to Boutzes. But Boutzes shut himself up in the fortress of Hierapolis with his small army, and was afraid even to send out scouts for news of Khosrou's progress. He wrote to Justinian asking for at least 50,000 reinforcements, though well aware that to raise such an army Justinian must denude the home provinces of their entire garrisons – a large expedition had recently been sent to Italy, consisting of all available reserves of regular troops.

Justinian called Belisarius to him and said: 'Most loyal and excellent general, we forgive you all the evil you have done us in the past and remember only your services. Take what men you have with you and go immediately to Syria to protect our holy city of Jerusalem from this heathen King, who, we are informed by our General Boutzes, has boasted that it will be his before the Easter festival. If you do this we will love you for ever more.'

Belisarius was too respectful a subject to argue with his Emperor that he had never done him any evil; and swallowed the reproach. It was his view that so long as a man acted uprightly and according to his own conscience such insults could not harm him. There is a Christian saying, that to forgive your enemy and to return good for evil is like heaping coals of fire upon his head. Justinian's hair was constantly being singed by the warmth of Belisarius's unexampled services. A paradox: if from some small touch of rebelliousness, some pettiness of injured pride, some slight defeat, Belisarius had ranged himself with Justinian's other generals and become a candidate for forgiveness, all would have been well. But nothing is so galling to a man of Justinian's character as to be dependent for his fame and the secure tenure of his throne on a man not only immeasurably more kingly than himself in every respect, but one who never seemed to make a mistake. Time after time, Belisarius accomplished the seemingly impossible, and Justinian felt more and more humiliated to stand so heavily in his debt. I shall have more to write upon this head before I have done.

Belisarius set out for Hierapolis with twenty men, using relays of post-horses and travelling eighty miles a day. He ordered the remainder of the Household Regiment to follow as soon as possible, and during his passage through Cilicia collected his now recovered sick from Daras, 1,500 in number. A messenger, instructed to ride ahead and take the fastest horse from each post-house, arrived at Hierapolis three days before him and announced his approach. As Belisarius was crossing the Cilician border into Syria this messenger met him with a letter from Boutzes urging him to take refuge in Hierapolis and assist in its defence. 'For it is essential that you should seek safety and not expose yourself to capture by the Persians, who would regard this as a greater victory than the capture of a whole province.'

Belisarius returned a characteristic reply: 'Are you unaware that King Khosrou is threatening the capture of Jerusalem? Be sure, I never fight a battle if I can possibly avoid doing so; but to seek safety in Hierapolis while the Persians were marching on Jerusalem, through territory almost destitute of troops, I would consider the act of a traitor. Come to me at Carchemish with all your men. It is better to face King Khosrou in the open. Five hundred men will suffice for the defence of Hierapolis.'

Belisarius encamped at Carchemish. He had already been informed by smoke-signal from down the river that King Khosrou's army included several divisions of infantry. He argued from this that Khosrou did not intend this time to raid across the desert to Chalcis, but to follow up the river until he reached Zeugma, with its hospitable and unfortressed road to Antioch. But before coming to Zeugma Khosrou would have to pass by Hierapolis and Carchemish (Carchemish is one day's march down the river from Zeugma, but Hierapolis three days' march, a little to the westward). He would be surprised to find an army opposing him at Carchemish, an open town, instead of being locked up safely in Hierapolis. To Carchemish presently came the remaining 5,000 men of the Household Regiment, and Boutzes from Hierapolis with 5,000, and 2,000 more from Carrhae and Zeugma. This made 13,000 men in all.

King Khosrou, travelling slowly with his 200,000, had now reached Barbalissus, where the Euphrates makes its right-angled turn. He did not know what was best for him to do. He had expected that the mere threat of his approach would clear the way for him, but his scouts reported a large Roman army at Carchemish, commanded by Belisarius. He could not now raid into Palestine with his cavalry alone, because that would mean leaving his infantry behind: unsupported by cavalry and unprotected by walls, it would be an easy prey to the enemy. He could proceed up the river and fight with this army at Carchemish; but, in order to do so, would it not be wise first to capture Hierapolis, which threatened his flank? And when had Belisarius ever lost a battle fought on the defensive? If he only knew what forces Belisarius commanded he could decide whether or not to risk a battle. He therefore sent an ambassador to Belisarius, ostensibly to discuss peace terms, but actually to look about him and report on the condition of the Imperial Army.

Belisarius, being warned that the Ambassador was on his way, guessed his intentions. He went out a few miles beyond Carchemish with the Household Regiment and encamped on a hill; and there made careful preparations for the Ambassador's reception. By his orders, none of the men wore mail-shirts or helmets or carried shields; each was armed with some slight weapon only – a bow, an axe, or a lance, according to his race – and clothed in clean white-linen tunic and trousers.

As the Ambassador, a Mage, came riding that afternoon along the river-road, a hare darted by, pursued by a number of dark men with hooked noses, mounted on racing horses; and as the hare doubled the leader killed it with a javelin cast. They paid no attention to the Ambassador until he greeted them, in Persian. They answered in Camp Latin, which the Mage understood; and he learned that they were Moors – not Assyrians as he had supposed – from beyond the Pillars of Hercules.

'How do you happen to be here so far away from your homes?' asked the surprised Ambassador.

'Oh,' they replied, 'Belisarius forced our kings to submit to him, and we gladly enlisted in his service, because he is the greatest general that the world has ever known and has made us rich and famous. But who are you?'

'I am the Ambassador of the Great King of Persia.'

'Oh, yes,' they replied politely. 'The same whose armies our Lord Belisarius defeated at Daras and at Sisauranum. Do you perhaps wish to see our master? He is most hospitable. Let us escort you to his tent.'

They led the way forward, and presently they passed two parties of horsemen on a level plain tilting together with blunt lances. The men of one party had fair hair and ruddy faces; those of the other, for the most part, auburn hair and delicate skins; both were large, strong men on large, strong horses. The Ambassador asked: 'What men are those?'

'Oh, those are Ostrogoths and Vandals. The Vandals come from the coast of North Africa about Carthage, which my Lord Belisarius won back for the Empire; but the Goths from Italy, another of his conquests. Would you care to observe these men closely? They are new-comers to your part of the world.'

The Moors whistled on their fingers, and a mixed party of Goths and Vandals rode up.

The Ambassador spoke to them. 'So you are captives, eh, forced to serve the Emperor of the Romans?'

A Goth replied: 'We serve no man unwillingly. It is our pleasure to serve the Lord Belisarius because he is making us perfect in the arts of war. When we return to our own lands we shall be men of credit.'

Next, a troop of slant-eyed, short-legged Huns dashed past the Ambassador with a wild shout; he learned that they were Herulians from beyond the Black Sea. They also spoke in reverent praise of Belisarius. All around him in the plain the Mage could see groups of the Household Regiment at their field-sports – tilting, shooting at a mark, spearing tent-pegs, wrestling from horseback, driving a leather ball about with crooked sticks.

Then suddenly the trumpet blew the Alert. In a moment all games ceased; every troop formed up speedily under its pennant and trotted to join its own squadron. At another trumpet call, with promptness and precision, the squadrons formed up in two long double lines, making an avenue of welcome. The Ambassador passed through, feeling rather uncomfortable, I imagine. There were 6,000 of them, and never was a finer choice of men ever brought together. They appeared far less interested in him than he in them, and eager to return to their sports. At the top of the hill was pitched Belisarius's tent of plain canvas. Belisarius sat before it on a tree-stump, without even his general's cloak, wearing white linen like his men, and looking as if he had never a care in the world. After exchanging salutations with the Ambassador he ordered the trumpeter to blow the Dismiss. The 6,000 men returned with a cheer to the plain.

The Ambassador asked: 'Are you indeed Belisarius? I expected to find a man in gilded armour, with servitors in crimson-silk uniform ranged about him.'

Belisarius replied: 'Had your royal Master warned us of your approach, we should have received you with greater formality, not in this undress. However, we are soldiers, not courtiers, and wear no scarlet or gold.'

The Ambassador delivered his message. He said that the Great King was at hand, his armies being like locusts in numbers, and wished to discuss peace terms.

Belisarius laughed softly. 'I have fought in many lands and observed many strange customs, but never before have I met a case like this – a king who is at pains to bring 200,000 soldiers with him in order to discuss peace terms. Tell your royal Master that our country, though hospitable, cannot act as host for so lavish a retinue as this. When he has dismissed them I shall be prepared to discuss peace terms in an amicable fashion. I will grant him an armistice of five days in which to send them back home across the Euphrates. I thank your Excellency for visiting us.'

The Ambassador returned and reported to Khosrou: 'My advice, Great King, is to return home at once. If their main body resemble their advance guard in the least respect, then you are utterly lost. For discipline, manliness, and skill in arms I have never seen their like. Moreover, it is clear that they are very numerous; they would not otherwise dare to base themselves on an unwalled town like Carchemish or behave with such confidence when on outpost duty. As for their general, Belisarius: in my quality of Mage I am accustomed to read the souls of men, and I see joined in him all the military and moral virtues which our primitive ancestors esteemed. You cannot risk a battle with such a man. If you make the smallest mistake, not one of your men will ever see Babylon again.'

Khosrou believed the Ambassador because he spoke without flattery. He decided to return, though even this seemed a dangerous course to take, with Belisarius's army threatening his rear. The nearest way home was over the Euphrates and back by way of Mesopotamia, but on the farther bank of the river he had seen ten or twenty troops of Roman cavalry, who appeared, by the continual smoke-signals that they sent back across the plain towards Edessa, to be the vanguard of another army. He was afraid to attempt a crossing, for fear of being attacked in the midst of operations; though this 'other army' had no real existence – what Khosrou had seen was only 1,000 of Belisarius's troops from Carrhae, making the most of themselves. But the Mage pointed out that Belisarius had never yet broken his word and that if King Khosrou crossed the river within the five days allowed, he would be safe enough.

Khosrou crossed in a hurry, unmolested. Persian armies always carry bridging material with them (short timbers which hook together), and therefore the widest and swiftest streams present no obstacle to them. As soon as he was safe on the farther bank he sent a message to Belisarius, asking for an ambassador to discuss peace terms as he had promised.

Belisarius himself then crossed the Euphrates at Zeugma with all his forces. He sent an ambassador to tell King Khosrou that, if the Persian Army returned through Roman territory without doing any damage, Justinian would arrange with him that the terms agreed upon in the previous year were put into effect.

Khosrou consented to this, and the next day began his homeward march. But he was afraid to pass through Mesopotamia because of the imaginary army; so returned along the left bank of the Euphrates, putting his men on short rations. Belisarius began following him, always one day's journey behind, as he had done many years before with the Persian general Azareth. However, when he reached a point just opposite Barbalissus he was obliged to desist: he himself and nearly all his generals were recalled to Constantinople by a peremptory summons from the Emperor.

The pursuit could not be safely trusted to any officer that remained. King Khosrou, aware that he was no longer being followed, continued to the city of Callinicum and captured it without difficulty. As it unluckily happened, Justinian had ordered the defences to be repaired, and the masons had just torn down the half of one wall in order to build it more securely; so the garrison, unable to close the breach, had fled. Khosrou, determined to have something to show for his invasion, disregarded his promise, and carried the entire population of Callinicum into captivity, having levelled the city with the ground. Thus the White Huns gained their expected plunder.

Palestine, however, was saved. Belisarius admitted afterwards that only 40,000 men could have engaged the Persian armies at Carchemish with any confidence of success; and he had had no more than 12,000. Carchemish, he said, was the sweetest of all his victories. He had routed 200,000 Persians with his unarmed Household alone, and not lost a single man. He said too: 'The Persians were like locusts, but we frightened them from our fields with the clash of steel and the sound of trumpets.'

CHAPTER 20
DISGRACE

Let no one think that Belisarius was summoned from the East to receive some great reward from his Emperor for this bloodless and glorious victory at Carchemish. The circumstances that led to his recall were far from pleasant ones. I shall relate them without delay.

Now, this was the year of the plague, which was of the sort called bubonic. It had not caused such extensive havoc since a thousand years before, when the historian Thucydides described its occurrence at Athens. Between war and disease there is a close connexion. In my opinion it is not merely that the pollution caused by fighting – corpses unburied, aqueducts broken, public sanitation neglected – breeds disease, but that the emotions which war excites weaken the mind and make bodies susceptible to every evil physical influence. The plague is a disease which baffles doctors, strikes and spares indiscriminately, is horrible in its symptoms.

The infection had originally been carried from China towards the end of the previous year in a bale of carpets consigned to a merchant of Pelusium in Egypt. He sickened; but the nature of the disease was not recognized, for the first symptoms are always slight and accompanied by no fever. He had infected his fellow-merchants and his family before the characteristic tumours appeared which give their name to the disease. Soon there were a thousand cases in Pelusium; from where it spread westward to Alexandria and beyond, and northward to Palestine. In the spring the grain-ships carried the plague to Constantinople, where my mistress was, and I with her. For grain-ships are always full of rats, and rats are subject to the infection and carry the seeds of it about in their furs. These grain-ship rats communicated the plague to the dock-rats of the Golden Horn, a very numerous colony, and they to the sewer-rats, and thus the infection spread throughout the city. At first there were no more than ten cases a day, but soon there were a hundred and then a thousand, and then, in the height of the summer, ten and twenty thousand a day.

The tumours formed usually on the groin, but also under the armpits, and in some cases behind the ears. In the later stages of the disease there was a great variation of symptoms. Some sufferers fell into a deep coma. They would consent to eat and drink and perform other habitual actions indicated for them to do – if they had friends or slaves faithful enough to nurse them – but behaved like sleep-walkers, not recognizing anyone, not noticing anything, remaining passive and perfectly unaware of the passage of time. Others, however, were seized with a violent delirium; these had to be strapped to their beds, or they would run off down the streets bawling or shrieking that the Devil was in their house, or the Bulgarian Huns perhaps – and many who had nobody to restrain them rushed to the harbour or the straits and plunged in and were drowned. In some cases, again, there was neither coma nor delirium: the sufferers remained clear-minded until the tumour mortified, and they died screaming for pain. In still other cases no pain was felt at all, and death came as peacefully as in old age. Often the whole body broke out in black pustules of the size of a pea, or there was a vomiting of blood; when either of these things happened death always ensued.

Many were utterly immune from the disease, even physicians and undertakers who handled the sick or dead by the thousand; while others who had fled away to the hills of Thrace at the first alarm, and lived there in the pure air remote from all contact with their fellow men, died nevertheless. Neither degree of susceptibility nor peculiarity of symptoms could be foretold according to sex, age, class, profession, faith, or race.

Before the plague reached its full vehemence the dead were buried with the customary rites, each household disposing of its own corpses. But it fast became impossible to display such piety: old tombs were broken into by night for new tenants to be thrust into them. Finally in thousands of houses, even those of very rich citizens, every person was either dead or fled, and the corpses lay rotting unburied. Justinian ordered his Registrar-General to take the matter in hand. The neglected corpses were buried in trenches; but soon the supply of labourers was insufficient to the task. Then the towers of the fortifications at Sycae on the other side of the Horn were used as charnel-houses, the dead being flung in through holes in the roof until there was room for no more. Though the roofs were sealed again a ghastly stench pervaded the city – especially when the wind blew from the north.

At the height of the pestilence more than 20,000 a day were dying. All trade and industry in the city came to an end, and of course social gatherings were out of the question. But there were services in the churches, which were thronged with terrified believers and became notorious centres of infection. The municipal food-supply failed, because no grain-ship captains dared to anchor in the harbour and the plague had spread to the farming districts too. Thousands who escaped the plague died of starvation. It was a time of signs and visions: ghosts paraded the daylight streets, and, greatest marvel of all, for once there was even peace between the Blue and Green factions. More nobility and virtue and loving-kindness were now shown by penitent evil-doers than ever before or since. Theodosius said to my mistress in this context: 'Our Lady Plague has a more persuasive voice by far, Godmother, than our Saviour, the Lord Jesus.' He always used a contemptuous tone in discussing the horrors around us, and made his own continued health seem to be a matter of good taste rather than good fortune. My mistress and I were also blessed with immunity. Whether or not this was due to frequent fumigation of the house with sulphur I do not know, but very few of my fellow-domestics sickened. Other houses, equally fortunate, ascribed their immunity to some Christian relic or heathen charm, or to some specific in which they had faith, such as curds or lemon-water or plum-pickle.

At about the time that the mortality began to decrease slightly, a whisper went through the Palace: 'His Sacred Majesty, the Emperor himself, is sick. It was thought to be a mere cold, but today a tumour has appeared on the groin. He is in a deep coma, and cannot even be persuaded to eat. It is impossible that he will live, the doctors agree.'

Then came the headless rumour spreading swiftly throughout the Empire: 'He is dead.' Even in that horrible time – for by now every diocese almost was afflicted – the people found heart to thank God that the evil were slain as well as the good. And they prayed that the next Emperor might be kinder to his subjects and more true to his word. When the rumour reached Belisarius he was at Carchemish – it was just before the five days' armistice. His officers came in a body and asked him: 'From whom do you take orders now, Illustrious Belisarius?'

He answered at once, not wishing to seem evasive or equivocal: 'The choice remains with the Senate. But my vote will go to Justin, the late Emperor's nephew and nearest of kin, who is highest in rank of all the Imperial Family.' (This was not Justin, the son of Germanus, but another, the son of Justinian's sister Vigilantia.)

They said: 'But, my lord, the oath of allegiance which all officers have been required to swear is jointly to Justinian as Emperor and Theodora as his wife.'

He replied: 'That may be. It happens that I swore my oath, under the old form, to Justinian alone. It is unconstitutional for a woman to be Empress in her own right. Though I regard Her Resplendency as a most capable and energetic administrator, I do not approve that a thousand-year-old rule should be broken in her favour. For this reason alone: the Goths and Armenians and Moors and many another race in the Empire would never consent to be ruled by a woman, and would remain in a constant state of rebellion so long as she lived.'

Boutzes agreed, adding: 'For my part, even if this were not the case, I should refuse to obey Theodora, who (I may now speak without disloyalty, the Emperor being dead) is no less of a monster than he was, but fiercer and more cunning even.'

The others all thought the same thing, but did not express themselves with such freedom.

Then came the news that Justinian was, after all, not dead. Though now in his sixtieth year (held to be the most dangerous time of life), he had recovered sufficiently from his coma to recognize Theodora and Narses. Moreover, the tumour on his groin, having swollen to a great size, had begun to suppurate slightly – a sign that he was on his way to recovery. The tumour broke; presently he was on his feet again and well enough, except that his speech was affected by a partial paralysis of the tongue.

During the coma, his living phantasm, which emitted a greenish-violet light, had been seen gliding about the Palace corridors and passing with ease through doors and walls, and sometimes floating feet foremost in and out of windows in a most gruesome manner, frightening the guards and servants out of their wits. On two or three occasions the phantasm was heard to speak. In each case the words were reported as follows: 'O sweet Beelzebub, saviour of monarchs! Take me not yet, Beelzebub – the Angel would soar.' Some put one interpretation on this, and some another; but a few of us understood the Angel as Belisarius, whose wings Justinian kept so jealously clipped.

Belisarius, however, had now not merely one Imperial enemy but two. For a distorted version of what he had said to his generals at Carchemish was at once sent back to Theodora by John the Epicure and

Peter, his secret enemies, to cancel any report that might have reached her of their own lack of warmth in her cause. This, then, was the reason why all these generals were summoned back from Barbalissus to Constantinople.

At Constantinople the plague had now abated somewhat, and city life was resuming its former factious gaiety; a lively interest was taken in the coming judicial inquiry. As soon as Belisarius and the other generals arrived, they were informed that they were under arrest. The charge was high treason. Belisarius was temporarily relieved of his command in the East, which was handed over to Martin.

Belisarius was astonished. He declared himself ready to face his accusers with a cheerful conscience; for he had said nothing either untrue or disloyal. To the officers and men of his Household Regiment who had come with him he sent this message: 'It seems that I have been unjustly slandered to His Clemency the Emperor, but I have every confidence that I shall be a free man before long. I charge you, by your love of me, to abstain from any rebellious or criminal act which would prejudice my acquittal. Obey the Emperor's officers in everything. Be patient.'

The trial was held at the Palace behind closed doors; and no report of the judicial findings – Theodora herself was the judge – was published. Belisarius conducted his own defence, and by cross-examining John the Epicure and Peter separately drove them to contradict each other. He tried to convince the Court, too, that they had been inefficient, quarrelsome, rapacious, disobedient officers, and ungrateful ones besides. He admitted that he had advised against Theodora's election as sole monarch; but was able to produce the minutes of the meeting, which his secretary had taken down, in proof of the innocence of his remarks: he had, he protested, merely upheld the Roman Constitution. Theodora could not convict him for treason. Yet she was resolved to harm him as much as she possibly could, for not having recommended her to his subordinates as Justinian's natural successor.

John the Epicure and Peter were complimented for their loyalty to the Throne and given presents of money and new titles.

The sentence on two or three of the offending generals, including Boutzes, was close confinement during their Majesties' pleasure. Boutzes was lowered into an unlighted dungeon, where he had nobody to share his misery and not even a word from the gaolers; scraps of meat and bread were thrown to him once a day, as to a wild beast in a pen. It was only after two years and four months that he was released. By then he was broken by ill-health and had taken to crawling on his hands and knees, which were covered with callouses, and he had lost all his hair and most of his teeth. Moreover, the sudden return to the light of day was too much for his eyes – he was thereafter never able to read or distinguish objects clearly. Thus were avenged the inhabitants of Antioch, whose ransom-money Boutzes had stolen from the kind-hearted people of Edessa.

Belisarius, though proved not guilty of treason, was found guilty of 'giving credence and currency to damaging rumours' (of Justinian's death), of failing to punish Boutzes for his disloyal words – and of permitting the capture of Callinicum! His removal from his command was confirmed, and all his property whatsoever in land, goods, or money was forfeited to the Crown.

Belisarius heard the sentence with dignity, and made no appeal against it. His only comment was that without funds he could not continue to equip, pay, and feed the Household Regiment, which had served the Emperor faithfully in many wars.

Theodora replied: 'They rank as slaves of your household, and you need not, therefore, have any concern for their fate. They are forfeited too.'

At this he remained silent, but it was observed that he clenched his fists until the knuckles whitened. He loved the men of his Household Regiment, and could hardly bear that they should be taken from him to be mishandled by the generals of the common sort.

Theodora called to Narses and said: 'The slaves of the former Commander of Armies in the East, this Belisarius, are to be divided up among the Palace generals and colonels, yourself to have the first choice. If any are left whom no Palace officer can afford to maintain, let the Secretaries of State draw lots for them.' Thus Belisarius had the pain of seeing many of the hardy men whom he had perfected in the arts of war become the door-keepers and attendants of perfumed eunuchs.

Belisarius lost not only the half-squadron of men who had come to Constantinople with him, but the remainder of his Household, now also recalled. He sent word around to them again, secretly: 'Patience, comrades, I implore you! All will be well before long. Enjoy your holiday in the city, keep yourselves in training as I have taught you to do, express no pity for me, swallow all insults. Patience!' They obeyed him, though unwillingly.

The city mob, who are notoriously as incapable of sound judgement as they are unstable of purpose, had heard the sentence on Belisarius with secret glee. They reasoned in the wine-shops: 'Be sure, the Emperor and Empress have now at last ruined themselves by their ingratitude. Our Belisarius will not submit to such injustice. He is too bold and proud a man. Only wait: soon there will be news of a sudden rising by the Household Regiment and of bloody murder in the Sacred Apartments of the Palace.'

They waited with growing impatience. Nothing at all happened. They muttered in disgust among themselves that their former idol, their glorious hero Belisarius, was submitting to the spite and ingratitude of his sovereigns with a patience as abject as that in use among the penitential monks. (These squat like toads in their cells while the flagellant of the week, coming around with his wire scourge, flogs their backs until the old scars open again.) When at first the citizens had crowded about him in the street with shouts of indignant pity he repulsed them angrily, crying: 'Gentlemen, be silent, this affair is between the Emperor and myself. Leave me, I beg you, and go about your businesses.'

He had a meagre attendance of four or five young officers, who clung to him from loyalty, though warned by Narses that they would thereby come under the Imperial suspicion and lose all chance of promotion. All his other associates were careful not to greet him – although, had he raised the standard of revolt, most of them would have rallied to it at once. He took mean lodgings near the Bull Square in a house attached to the Entertainment Halls. This is a group of halls, built around a central fountain, which families who have houses of only modest size can hire for wedding and funeral feasts and suchlike. Here he was dependent on these same young officers even for the necessities of life. But for them he must have applied for a wooden ticket and drawn the common dole. Theodora had not only stripped him of all his wealth in the city: she had also sent to Edessa, where he had banked a large sum of money for war-expenses, and made that hers too.

Every day he went to pay his respects at the Palace, as he would ordinarily have done. Justinian tried to goad him to rebellion by sneers and gibes; for the man's patience exasperated him. One morning he refused to see Belisarius, alleging a press of business, and ordered him to wait outside the Palace Gates until the evening. Belisarius obeyed, standing all day outside the Gates without food, exposed to public curiosity. Then the mob, disgusted by what they regarded as miserable slavishness, pelted him with rotten fruit and filth, so that his patrician's gown was disgracefully stained. He uttered not a single word, and did not even stoop to avoid the missiles. But he dealt sternly with an impudent youth who came sneaking up along the wall and attempted to pull his beard. He seized the fellow by the breeches and tossed him a great distance; it is said that this youth suffered injuries which kept him an invalid for many years.

At dusk he was at last admitted to the Palace, and there begged leave to present an appeal to the Emperor. Justinian consented to consider the appeal, hoping that he had at last moved Belisarius to open resentment. He was disappointed: all that Belisarius asked was a new gown, so that he could present himself decently at the next audience.

Justinian replied tartly: 'We have no money to clothe you, my Lord Belisarius. If you cannot afford to keep yourself in gowns, we had better strike your name from the roll of patricians: thus you will be released from all ceremonial obligations.'

Belisarius bowed low and replied: 'In whatever rank or capacity I am permitted to serve your Majesty, I can be counted upon to do my duty faithfully.'

His name was removed from the roll, and he did not return to the Palace for many months.

All this time, of course, my mistress continued to enjoy Theodora's friendship and, so far from being deprived of any of her possessions, was made richer by the grant of much of Belisarius's property, including his large estate at Rufinianae. She pretended to be much more indifferent to her husband's misfortunes than, I know, she actually was. For my part I never mentioned Belisarius's affairs to her if I could avoid doing so; and whenever she alluded to them herself I was careful not to commit myself to any attitude. But it made my blood boil to see Theodosius pride it at Belisarius's expense. He was a great man at the Palace in those days, and went about attended by a train of 400 Thracians of the Household Regiment, whom Theodora had presented to him. He was constantly closeted with Theodora, having been appointed Master of Palace Entertainments.

Of the inner history of what occurred next many versions are current – some plausible, some ridiculous, none authentic. At all events, the essential happening was that Theodosius died of a dysentery on St Stephen's Day, which is the day following Christmas Day; and whether this was a sheer accident or whether he was poisoned at the Christmas feast, and if so by whom, was never brought to the light of history. The few who examined his corpse inclined to the view that he was poisoned.

This much can be confidently said: his death is not to be laid at Belisarius's door, nor was any friend of Photius's responsible for it. It is not outside the limits of credibility that some officious domestic of my mistress Antonina thought thus to anticipate her wishes. I cannot discuss this. Needless to say, suspicion never fell upon Eugenius.

My mistress's feelings on Theodosius's death were confused. She had recently changed towards him, and with strange suddenness. She had come to believe, rightly or wrongly, that her favourite, by using the same courtier's arts that he had used with her, had now made himself a lover of Theodora's. He certainly was then treating my mistress with an indifference which she must have felt very galling, though she did her best to conceal the smart from everyone.

Theodora took the death lightly; she did not even interest herself in its cause. Yet she showed my mistress unaffected sympathy in her loss, and seemed to have no notion whatsoever that she had been nourishing such bitter jealousy. Some said that this lightness of heart was assumed by Theodora in order to deprive Justinian of satisfaction in her grief; for they said that it was the Emperor himself who had arranged Theodosius's murder, in jealousy of his wife's pleasure in him, and that in truth she felt his loss very keenly. But that was nonsense.

My mistress now fell into a deep melancholy; sleeplessness and lack of appetite wore her so thin that she looked ten years more than her age, which was now two-and-forty.

One day when I went into her boudoir she looked up, with eyes red from weeping. Though I had often seen her sullen, fretful, angry, despairing, I had not seen her weep since her girlhood.

I said to her gently: 'Mistress, I was your first slave, and I have been faithful to you all my life. I am devoted to you, above everything in the world, and would die for your sake, as you know. Let me share in your misery, learning the cause of it. O Lady Antonina, my heart sinks when I see you weeping.'

The tears burst out afresh; but she did not reply.

Then I asked: 'Mistress, dearest mistress, is it that you mourn for Theodosius?'

She cried out: 'No, Eugenius, my faithful friend, no! By Hera and Aphrodite, no! It is not of Theodosius that I am thinking – but of my husband Belisarius. I must confide in you again, as I did long ago in my club-house days, lest my silence consume me. O dear Eugenius, I would give all I possess never to have cast eyes on false Theodosius. Belisarius has always been my real love – and, like a fool, I have utterly ruined him. Nor is there any undoing of my folly.'

I wept with her. 'A reconciliation must be brought about at once,' I cried impulsively. But she answered that neither Belisarius's pride nor hers permitted a reconciliation. Moreover, Theodora had by no means forgiven Belisarius, and the Emperor hated him above all human beings.

After a little thought, I said: 'I believe that I understand the whole case and can find a way out.'

'There is no way out, Eugenius.'

Nevertheless, I went on boldly: 'Mistress, it appears to me that if I were to go to Belisarius and tell him, what I believe has never been revealed to him, that Photius confessed under torture to having slandered you; and if I were to swear to him that you and Theodosius were never lovers; and if I were to tell him further that your oaths to Cappadocian John were sworn – were they not? – at the order of the Empress and that you have asked pardon of God for this offence and for your other blasphemies – would you not do that immediately, dearest mistress, to placate Belisarius? – and that you have far more cause to be offended by him than he by you . . .'

'O wise Eugenius, go with my blessing. Yes, I will ask pardon of God – I would certainly not let that trifle stand in my way. Tell him all that you have just said; and then, if he forgets his pride and anger, you may assure him that I never did love anyone else but himself, and that I will not rest until he is restored to freedom and honour – then he and I will never again be parted.'

'You will appeal to the Empress?'

'I will. I will remind her of the services that I rendered her lately in the matter of Cappadocian John, and of our old friendship, and of the friendship existing between her father, the Bear Master, and mine, the charioteer. . . .'

But I said: 'Dearest mistress, I have a further suggestion to make. I believe that I am in a position to accomplish the final ruin of Cappadocian John myself. If this is done and if you take the credit for it, surely the Empress will give you everything you ask?'

'How?' she asked, eagerly. 'How can you bring this about?'

I replied: 'This afternoon, in a wine-shop, I fell in conversation with a poor young man of Cyzicus, who is dying of a wasting disease and has not long to live. He and his whole family, old grandparents and wife and three young children, have been driven from their home by order of the Bishop of Cyzicus. He came alone on foot to Constantinople, and today applied for justice and relief at the Palace; but the officials drove him away, because the Bishop is in good standing at Court. I sympathized with him, and gave him a piece of silver, telling him to meet me under the statue of the Elephant of Severus tomorrow at noon. I did not disclose my name or that of my employer, and I am not known in that wine-shop.'

'Well?'

'Give me five hundred pieces in gold, mistress, and that will be sufficient to destroy Cappadocian John.'

'I do not understand.'

'Give me the money and trust me to undertake the matter.'

'If you succeed, Eugenius, I will give you fifty thousand and your freedom.'

'What is money but bodily comforts, which I already possess? What is "freedom" but to be well considered, as I already am? No, Mistress, my sufficient reward will be that you and my Lord Belisarius and the Empress are relieved of an old enemy, and that the death of your father Damocles, my former master, is avenged, and that I shall have been the means of reconciling the Empress to my Lord Belisarius.'

That evening I sought out Belisarius at his mean lodgings. Though weak from a return of his malarial fever, he rose from his couch to welcome me. With a smile that concealed the depth of his feeling, he asked: 'And are you not afraid to visit me, Eugenius, old friend?'

I answered: 'No, Illustrious Lord. With the message that I bring I would have risked passing through fire or a camp of Bulgarian Huns.'

He grew a little impatient: 'Do not address me by titles of which I have been deprived. What is the message?'

I related, as from myself, all that I had agreed with my mistress to say. He listened most eagerly, crying 'Ah!' when I told him that his wife had asked pardon of God. Then I showed him the State papers in which Photius's confession was recorded – having bribed the copying clerk to the Assistant-Registrar for a day's loan of them. Belisarius read them hastily, and then again with great care, and at last he beat his breast and said: 'For my jealous rage and my credulity I deserve all that I have suffered. But alas, Eugenius, it is too late now. Your mistress will never forgive me for what I did to her at Daras, even if I make her a full apology.'

I urged him to be of good courage: all would yet be well. Then I repeated my mistress's message, which at first he would not believe to be authentic. He said: 'If your mistress Antonina will indeed still listen to any words of mine, tell her that the fault was wholly on my side – but that it was only an excess of love for her that made me guilty of such madness.'

That night Belisarius and my mistress met secretly at his lodgings. Nobody but myself knew of it. Both embraced me, kissing me on the cheeks, and said that they owed their lives to me.

On the next day I met the young man from Cyzicus under the statue of the Elephant. I drew him aside to a private place and said to him: 'Here in this bag are five hundred pieces of gold. They will keep your family in decent plenty for the rest of their lives. But in order to earn them you must do a desperate thing.'

He asked: 'What can that be, benefactor?'

'You must kill the Bishop of Cyzicus. He is an enemy of my master's, whose gold this is.'

'Your words frighten me,' he cried.

'How, when you have so few months to live in any case, and when by this deed you will, at a stroke, secure both revenge for your injuries and provision for your destitute family?'

He asked: 'Who is your master?'

I answered: 'I do not hesitate to tell you that. He is Cappadocian John, now a priest of the Cathedral at Cyzicus.'

I made him believe that I was in earnest about the gold; when I gave him ten gold pieces on account he undertook to commit the murder and went cheerfully away.

Soon the expected news came from Cyzicus. The young man had fulfilled his obligation. He had waited outside the Cathedral porch after Mass and, as the Bishop emerged, sunk a long dagger into him.

He was arrested and threatened with the rack unless he revealed the motives of this sacrilegious deed. As I had expected, he avoided mention of his own wrongs, telling the officers merely that he had been bribed to the deed by a gift of ten pieces of gold from Cappadocian John. Cappadocian John's enmity towards the Bishop was well known. He was arrested and tried before the judges of that place, found guilty as accessory to the murder, and sentenced to death. By my mistress's intercession with Theodora the young man's life was spared, and later I sent the remainder of the 500 gold pieces to him. How long he lived afterwards, I do not know.

Cappadocian John's life, too, was spared by Justinian, with the excuse that his guilt was insufficiently proved. Nevertheless, he was stripped of his robe and thrashed and made to confess to his past sins; though he would not own to murder, the rest of the tale was disgraceful enough to have hanged him a dozen times over. All his goods were forfeited to the Crown, and he was set naked on a trading-ship bound for Egypt (but for charity someone lent him a rough blanket); whereever the ship touched he was made to go ashore and beg for bread and coppers on the quay. Thus vengeance was at last fully accomplished; for it was to John's nakedness and beggary that Theodora and my mistress had pledged themselves, not to his death by violence. The soul of the charioteer Damocles, my former master, had peace by the banks of Styx.

My mistress could now go before Theodora and beg her to receive Belisarius back into favour; saying that she herself proposed to forgive and live with him again. Her devotion to Theodora's cause was once more proved, and Belisarius would do nothing further to earn the displeasure of his Empress – of that she could be assured.

Theodora did not reject the plea. She sent an Imperial messenger to Belisarius with a letter which ran as follows: 'You are yourself well aware, best of men, how you have wronged your Sovereigns. But since I am greatly indebted to your wife for her services to me, I have, at her request, expunged from the records all charges against you, and given you my gracious pardon. For the future, then, you need not fear as to your safety or your prosperity; but we shall judge your behaviour not only by your actions in regard to ourselves, but by your attitude to her.'

Thus Belisarius was restored to favour again, for even Justinian considered that his pride had now been sufficiently humbled; and one-half of his treasure was given back to him, and all the land and houses. Justinian held back the remainder of the treasure, which amounted to one-quarter of a million gold pieces, saying that the possession of so much money did not become a subject when there was such urgent need of funds in the Imperial Treasury.

As a tribute to the close friendship existing between my mistress Antonina's family and her own, Theodora now decided that Joannina, my mistress's child by Belisarius, should be betrothed to her own nearest relative, Anastasius 'Longlegs', son of Sittas the general and her sister Anastasia. It was to this youth that she intended the Diadem to pass, after Justinian's death and her own: the marriage would greatly strengthen his position in the city. So this was done.

It may seem strange that I have made no reference to Joannina since her birth just before Belisarius's expedition to Carthage. The fact is that she had enjoyed no intimate life with either of her parents. My mistress Antonina had not taken the child with her to the wars, but placed her under the tutelage of Theodora, who came to regard her as her own daughter. Joannina remained with Theodora in the Sacred Apartments of the Palace even when her parents happened to be back in the city. My mistress was content that this should be so: her chief maternal feelings were for Martha, Hildiger's wife – who unfortunately fell a victim to the plague. But it saddened Belisarius that he should be estranged from his only child. He sent her frequent letters and presents from overseas, fondly reminding her that she had a father. But whenever they met, during his occasional respites from war, it was always in the shadow of the Throne; and Joannina treated his affectionate advances with embarrassment. With Antonina the child was more at ease, as with a good-natured, fashionable aunt.

The news of Joannina's engagement set a public seal on the reconciliation of Theodora and my mistress with Belisarius. Theodora even persuaded the Emperor to witness the ceremonial exchange of gifts at Belisarius's house; and his presence there seemed a good omen for the renewed prosperity of Belisarius's domestic affairs. Belisarius and my mistress were escorted by a remnant of his Household Regiment – 400 Thracians who had passed to my mistress at Theodosius's death, and were now restored to their former master. But their 6,500 comrades-in-arms were still withheld from him.

Belisarius's recall from the East had brought disaster there. Justinian ordered an invasion of Persian Armenia, and reinforced the frontier armies until they amounted to nearly 30,000 men; but divided the command between no less than fifteen generals. Each general favoured and pursued a plan of campaign of his own; at Dubis, on the River Araxes, their disunited forces were routed by an army of only 4,000 Persians and fled wildly home, abandoning their plunder, their standards, and their arms. Several of these generals continued in their flight until their horses foundered, though there was now no enemy within thirty miles of them. Then Our Lady Plague proved an unexpected ally, spreading suddenly into Persian territory, which she had hitherto spared, and killing one man in every three throughout the Great King's dominions: else it would have gone ill with the Roman Empire. For, of 30,000 men, 10,000 men were killed at Dubis and 10,000 captured, together with all the transport of the army, heaped with baggage and plunder.

When Belisarius volunteered to go again to the East and rally the survivors, Justinian haughtily refused this plea. He withheld the true explanation, which was that he did not wish Belisarius to succeed once more where others had failed, and thus seem indispensable; but said, in his odious smiling way, that the Lady Antonina must henceforth accompany her husband on his campaigns as a surety for his loyal behaviour, and that the Lady Antonina would 'no doubt dislike a visit to the Persian frontier in view of her unfortunate experiences on a previous visit.'

Then he went on to say that if Belisarius greatly hungered for the battlefield he might return to Italy, to complete the task which he had neglected to finish. 'It was most unwise and not altogether loyal, my Lord Belisarius, to return to us at Constantinople before you had properly stamped out the last sparks of Gothic rebellion, which have smouldered ever since and at last burst into a menacing blaze.'

Belisarius answered him, as patiently as ever: 'Give me back the remainder of my Household Regiment, Your Majesty, and I will do my best in the matter.'

Justinian sneered: 'For some new treachery, I suppose? No, no, General, I am too old and experienced a hare to be lured by such a lettuce-leaf. Besides, your former troops, all but a very few, have lately been taken from my Palace officers and drafted, as you know, to the Persian frontier – from where we cannot spare them. But why do you argue with us, you who were so recently a beggar? We will give you permission to recruit new troops wherever you please in our dominions; but since the recrudescence of war in Italy is clearly due to your former negligence, we shall require you to finance the expedition yourself. We have no money, but you are still possessed of an ample fortune. If you accept this charge we will bestow on you a great honour: we will create you Count of the Royal Stables. Let us know your mind tomorrow.'

Then he dismissed him.

Belisarius accepted the terms – for he disdained to bargain. Presently he sailed for Italy with my mistress Antonina, whom I accompanied, and his 400 Thracians. His new title gave my mistress much amusement. She would say such things as this: 'My poor husband, you are created Count of the Augean Stables, but forbidden to cleanse them!' (The hero Hercules was commanded, as his fifth Labour, to cleanse the stables of Augeas in one day; accomplishing this by leading the Rivers Alpheus and Peneus through them.)

It was about this time that Solomon was killed in Africa, in battle with a raiding army of Moors. He had been a most capable Governor, though greatly hampered by an insufficiency of troops. The Roman Africans had long regretted those happy days of Vandal rule when the Moors were restrained in their hill-fortresses and the tax-gatherers from Constantinople had not yet begun to eat up the land. After Solomon's death the Moors massacred, burned, and destroyed without pity or fear of reprisal. The poorer the Diocese grew, the more heavily did the taxes fall on what wealth survived; for the assessment made in the year of Belisarius's Consulship had never been modified. Then came the plague. In those years of general disaster five millions of the population perished; then, so many fields being left untilled and unwatered, the desert broke in upon them. I think this fertile land will never recover from its misfortunes – or at least not so long as it remains within the Empire.

CHAPTER 21

EXILE IN ITALY

WHAT now follows is an account of five years of the most thankless campaigning, surely, that any general of repute ever undertook. Disappointment wearies, not only in the experience but in the telling of it. I shall therefore be brief and write down only enough of this, Belisarius's last campaign in the West, to prove that his courage and resource and vigour remained unaffected by thirty years of almost continuous campaigning, and that he did all that could possibly have been expected of him, and more.

It will be remembered that the Gothic crown had passed to a young prince named Teudel who could command at first no more than a thousand lances and had only one fortified city of any strength in his possession – Pavia. But he was the first capable sovereign to rule over the Goths since the death of Theoderich. By the quarrelsomeness and inactivity of the eleven Imperial generals that opposed him, he was able to increase his forces to 5,000 men and organize them into a well-equipped army. In the same year that Belisarius quarrelled with my mistress at Daras, Bloody John, Bessas, and the rest had received instructions from Justinian to 'crush the last remnants of the Goths'; but he was unwilling to entrust the supreme command to any one of them. They took the field with 12,000 men, including the garrison of Sisauranum that Belisarius had captured and that had just arrived from the East. Chiefly because of their disagreement as to the equitable distribution of the booty that they expected to take, they were ingloriously defeated by Teudel, at Faenza: many thousands of their men were killed or captured and – unique disgrace – every single regimental standard was abandoned, though every single general escaped. Only the Persian squadron fought with courage, and for this reason lost more heavily than any other. Then each of the eleven generals led what remained of his own command into the shelter of a different fortress, so that the whole of Italy now lay open to Teudel's army.

Bloody John took the field again with reinforcements from Ravenna. Though still outnumbered, Teudel scattered Bloody John's army at a battle near Florence, and not only caused him heavy losses in killed and wounded but persuaded a great many of his men to desert to the Gothic army. Alexander ('The Scissors') had reduced the armies in Italy to a most despondent condition by stealing their pay and rations. No soldiers will fight for long without pay or proper food, except in the defence of their own homes and under a courageous leader. Besides, if there is discord among the officers, as here, the ranks soon come to know of it, and confidence is destroyed. Those who deserted to Teudel were putting themselves under the protection of a king who was a man of his word – a bold, active, generous leader who did not share his command with rivals.

In the next spring, the same spring in which Belisarius was sent against King Khosrou in Syria, Teudel, leaving the Imperial generals to skulk in their fortresses of the North-East of Italy, marched down to the almost unprotected South. He overran it with ease, capturing the fortresses of Benevento, where he destroyed the fortifications, and Cumae, where he found great quantities of treasure, and soon he was besieging Naples.

From Ravenna Bloody John, in the name of all the generals, wrote to Justinian for reinforcements. With unexpected promptness, Justinian sent a senator, Maximinus, with a huge fleet and all the troops that could be gathered together from the training depots and garrison towns of the East. Maximinus was given authority as Commander of the Armies in Italy. He was a coward, and totally without experience of war. A great deal of his time was spent in prayer and fasting. Justinian hated to entrust large armies to experienced generals, lest they should prove rebellious. He seemed to be under the impression that victories are won on one's knees, not in the saddle.

The expedition ended disastrously, as might have been expected. First, Maximinus delayed for months in Greece, sending one of his generals ahead with a number of supply ships but inadequate forces to the relief of Naples. Teudel's cavalry surprised this small fleet as the crews disembarked carelessly at Salerno, to take in water and stretch their legs, and captured nearly the whole of it. Then Maximinus himself sailed to Syracuse in Sicily, from where he now sent the rest of his army in the rest of his ships, to the further relief of Naples. This was already November, too late in the year for safe voyages. A violent north-westerly wind overtook the expedition when close to Naples, driving the ships ashore – and where else but on the very beach where King Teudel was encamped with his Goths? Of the soldiers who managed to escape from the fury of the waves many hundreds were hurled back into the sea by the pitiless Goths, who did not wish to be encumbered with prisoners. The Roman general in command of the expedition was, however, spared. They made him go with a halter around his neck to advise the Neapolitans to capitulate, since they could expect no succour now and were hard-pressed by famine. Teudel undertook to spare their lives.

Thereupon Naples surrendered. When Teudel saw how utterly emaciated the citizens were, he acted with a humanity and understanding remarkable in a barbarian. He made it his care that they should not fill their empty bellies suddenly and so destroy themselves – building up their strength with a gradual increase of rations. He took no vengeance on them, either, even allowing the garrison to march out with the honours of war and providing them with pack animals to take them to Rome. Moreover, as an example to his own men and an encouragement to the native population, he executed a Gothic soldier for the rape of an Italian girl and awarded her as a dowry all the soldier's possessions. But he razed the fortifications of Naples to the ground so that, though recaptured, the city could never again be used against the Goths as a base of operations.

King Teudel would have next marched on to the capture of Rome, where Bloody John was commanding the garrison; for the citizens were well-disposed to the Gothic cause and prepared to welcome him. But the plague had now reached Italy, and the streets of Rome were full of unburied corpses. Teudel hurried away from the infection. Part of his army he sent to besiege Otranto, while with the remainder he besieged Osimo and Tivoli. Tivoli fell to him by an act of treachery; and the communications between Rome and Tuscany, on which the citizens of Rome relied for provisions, were thereby cut. The Imperial Forces degenerated more and more as Teudel's force improved. Their pay, which depended on the Italian revenues, could no longer be found, because the Goths now held nearly the whole of the countryside; and their fighting capacities depended largely on their pay.

Such was the state of affairs in Italy when Belisarius brought us there from Constantinople. He had first made a recruiting march through Thrace with his 400 cuirassiers. This was the first time for a great many years that he had visited Tchermen, his birthplace, or Adrianople, where he had begun his military career. He received a great welcome from his fellow-countrymen. At every town to which he came a civic reception was waiting for him: the march became almost a royal progress. The 400 men, all Thracians and heroes of the Gothic, Vandal, and Persian campaigns, were so fine and martial-looking in their mail-shirts and white-plumed helmets, sat their chestnut horses so well, and spoke with such admiration and love of Belisarius that no less than 4,000 recruits enlisted under his standard – of whom 1,500 were from Adrianople alone. They called him 'Lucky Belisarius' in Thrace, because not only had he himself never been wounded, but of his Household Regiment that had fought in so many glorious battles very few men had fallen – at least while serving under his direct command – and very many had made their fortunes. He had hoped to procure arms and armour here for his recruits, there being a supply of such things at the Imperial arms factory at Adrianople; but they were refused him, even for ready gold. The Bulgarian Huns had also made a clean sweep of the horses of Thrace in their recent raid, except for the Imperial herds, which had been got away in time behind the walls of Salonica; so that he was also unable to mount his recruits. No arms, armour, horses – and to forge a raw recruit into an efficient cuirassier, even if he is already accustomed to horses, is a work of two years or more.

From Thrace we sailed around the coast of Greece to Spalato, where we revictualled; there arms, but not armour, were found for the recruits. From Spalato Belisarius sent to the relief of Otranto that Valentine who had commanded the Roman militia in the Plain of Nero during the defence of Rome: with 2,000 men, untrained for the most part, and a year's supply of corn. Valentine accomplished the relief of Otranto just in time: the garrison had decided to capitulate to the Goths four days later, on account of famine. Belisarius could not attempt a landing in the neighbourhood of Rome, for the enemy, with the captured warships, controlled the whole western coast. He brought us to Ravenna by way of Pola.

At Ravenna he exhorted the resident Goths to persuade those of their kinsmen who were fighting with King Teudel to resume their allegiance to the Emperor. But not even the name of Belisarius could draw away a single man. He sent up into Aemilia, to secure that district at least, a hundred of the trained men of his Household and 200 of the most promising recruits, for whom he had found horses and armour in Ravenna; and 2,000 Illyrian infantry. Bologna, the capital, surrendered. but provisions were scanty. Besides, the Illyrians had received no pay for eighteen months and were disgusted that during their absence in Italy the Bulgarian Huns had been allowed to raid Illyria and carry their wives and children into captivity. They suddenly announced that they were going home; which they did, leaving the 400 men of the Household to their own devices. (Justinian was angry with these Illyrians at first, but afterwards forgave them.) So all Aemilia was yielded to the enemy except the fortress of Piacenza. The only lucky circumstance of the expedition was that the men of the Household, commanded by Thurimuth, a Thracian, contrived to cut their way through to Ravenna and to bring back 200 horses and 300 suits of armour belonging to Goths whom they had killed in ambuscades.

Belisarius then sent Thurimuth to Osimo, which King Teudel was besieging, with a thousand men, all that he could spare. Thurimuth managed to slip through the Gothic lines into the city, without loss; but he soon realized, after making a bold sortie, that his thousand men were no match for the 30,000 to which the Gothic Army had now swelled by desertions from the Imperial Army. Nor could he rely on the remainder of the garrison for any military assistance. He consulted with the commander, who agreed with him that the continued presence of the relieving force would be a hindrance rather than a help, meaning merely more mouths to feed; so he removed by night. The Goths were warned of his plans by a deserter, and ambushed him four miles outside the city. He lost 200 men and all his pack animals; with the rest he escaped clear away to Rimini.

Teudel had destroyed the ramparts of all the cities that had yielded to him. Belisarius, who needed a more convenient base than Ravenna, determined to refortify Pesaro, an Umbrian port between Rimini and Osimo, where there was good grazing for horses in the river valley. The walls of Pesaro had been torn down to half their height, and the gates removed; but with his usual resource he sent agents to measure the gateways, and at Ravenna new oaken gates were made, bound with wrought iron, of the required height and breadth. Thurimuth took these in boats to Pesaro, and fitted them in place; and set the townspeople hastily to work at rebuilding the walls. He had 3,000 men with him, nearly all Thracian recruits. By the time that Teudel had arrived with his army from before Osimo, the walls were high enough to defend. Belisarius had been busily training these recruits in archery, so that they gave a good account of themselves. Teudel withdrew, baffled.

Belisarius wrote to Justinian in the following terms:

Most Mighty Emperor,

I have arrived in Italy without horses or armour – for these were unobtainable in Thrace – and with no money but what I have in my private purse for the payment of my recently-raised Thracian recruits. These are few, untrained as yet, ill-armed, and without horses. Your Majesty's regular troops and militia, which we found here, are no match either in number or courage for the enemy. King Teudel holds the whole of Italy – except for a few cities, which with the forces at my disposal I am unable to relieve – and in consequence the Imperial revenues cannot be collected. The fact is that even the troops at Ravenna are owed such long arrears of pay by Your Majesty that I am quite unable to persuade them to fight. More than one-half of them have already deserted to the enemy.

If my mere presence in Italy were sufficient to bring the war to a victorious conclusion, all would be well: for I have advertised my arrival by every means at my disposal. But let Your Majesty consider that a general without troops is like a head shorn at the neck. I respectfully suggest that the men of my Household Regiment, whom you have sent to the Persian frontier, be recalled and dispatched to me here at once; and with them a large force of Herulian or other Huns, if Your Majesty will be at the expense of engaging their services with a substantial sum of money. If my request cannot be granted, little or nothing can be accomplished by Your Majesty's most loyal and obedient servant

Belisarius, Count of the Royal Stables,
At present commanding the Imperial Armies in Italy.

Bloody John, handing over his command at Rome to Bessas, undertook to deliver this letter to Justinian at Constantinople and to urge him to remedy the desperate condition in which we found ourselves. John set out at the close of this year, the year of our Lord 545. Belisarius meanwhile remained at Ravenna, training his recruits, using the few horses at his disposal in rotation for their cavalry exercises. The men learned handiness with their bows, lances, darts, swords, either on foot or mounted – he made them ride wooden horses, like children.

Osimo surrendered to Teudel on account of famine, and next Fermo and Ascoli, which are also in Picenum. Then Spoleto and Assisi in Tuscany. Only Perugia held out, though Teudel contrived the assassination of Cyprian, the general who commanded the garrison.

Bloody John did not deliver the letter to the Emperor, speaking to him of the matter in vague terms only. He was weary of the Italian war, and did not wish to be sent back at once from the comforts of Constantinople, where he was well received, to the discomforts and anxieties of campaigning. He devoted himself to the task of achieving a distinguished marriage, and presently became the husband of Germanus's daughter, young Justin's sister and grand-niece to the Emperor. (By so doing he made himself an enemy of the Empress Theodora, who regarded this as an act of great presumption, almost as a declaration that he was a candidate for the Throne at Justinian's death.)

Receiving no reply, Belisarius wrote again, in exact repetition of his former letter, except that he gave news of Teudel's latest successes. He now reported that Rome, which Bessas held with 3,000 men, was threatened with famine – Teudel's fleet based on the Lipari Islands was intercepting the corn-ships from Sicily – and could not hold out many months longer. Piacenza, the last fortress in the North to remain loyal to the Romans, had already surrendered from famine. He added (prompted by my mistress) that, since His Gracious Majesty appeared to be not alarmed by the condition of affairs in Italy as reported to him in the letter entrusted to John, or at any rate unable to remedy them, he would consider himself at liberty to retire with his wife and bodyguard to Durazzo on the farther side of the Adriatic Sea. There the climate was less relaxing than that of Ravenna, and communication with Constantinople – should the Emperor deign to send him any further instructions – more convenient. The Emperor's grand-nephew Justin would remain in command at Ravenna.

The letter was perfectly respectful and proper in its form, but Justinian felt that it contained a concealed reproach; which decided him to do nothing about the matter, especially as Bloody John denied having been entrusted with any previous letter. However, my mistress had sent a letter to Theodora along with this second letter of Belisarius's, in which she said that Justinian must make up his mind whether to retain possession of Italy by paying the armies there and by sending reinforcements, or whether he wished to resign his claim to it. Theodora at last prevailed on Justinian to withdraw some troops from the Persian frontier, where the danger of invasion seemed to have passed with the plague, and to send Narses to the Crimea to hire a strong force of Herulian Huns to accompany the expedition to Italy. But it was late autumn before these reinforcements, with Bloody

John at their head, arrived at Durazzo; and meanwhile conditions at Rome were growing worse and worse. The most that Belisarius had been able to do was to send a thousand men, half of whom were members of the Household Regiment, across Italy to assist the weak garrison at the Port of Rome – the continued possession of which was essential if Rome was to be relieved by the Imperial Fleet. Valentine, who commanded these troops, had instructions to avoid any battle that might involve him in serious loss. He eluded the Goths and reached his destination in safety.

The Pope Vigilius, the same who had succeeded to the deposed Silverius, had lately been ordered to go from Rome to Sicily, there to await a summons to Constantinople. Justinian (who wished to be remembered as Great for his theological talents as well as for his other qualities and feats) was working on a treatise, for which he wanted the Pope Vigilius's approval. A nice point had arisen in the doctrine of the relations between the First and Second Persons of the Trinity, and it seemed advisable to discuss it with the Pope before venturing farther. The object of the treatise was to suggest a compromise between those who believed in the Son's single nature and those who believed that He had two natures. A great number of heretics might thus be restored to the Orthodox communion. I spare you the details of this argument. Pope Vigilius could not take a serious view of the Emperor's theology, which was muddled and contradictory; yet neither could he afford to give offence. What concerned him far more nearly was an alarming report that reached him of the state of affairs at Rome: that a bushel of grain was selling for five gold pieces there, and an ox for fifty, while the poor were already eating nettles and grass, as during the previous siege. Being a man of generosity and, despite having bribed himself into office, an honest Christian, he remembered Jesus's three times repeated injunction to the Apostle Peter, 'Feed My Sheep': he engaged at his own expense a small fleet of cornships to sail to the Port of Rome with provisions for the city population.

The Pope sent this fleet under the guidance of a bishop who, avoiding the Gothic blockading squadron at the Lipari Islands by a wide detour, brought the ships safely to port; and was relieved on his arrival to see the Imperial standard still flying from the tower and the garrison waving their cloaks wildly from the battlements. Unfortunately, he misread the signal, which was one not of encouragement but of warning. No sooner were his ships tied up securely to the quay, with the help of the dock-men, when there was a sudden barbaric yell, and two squadrons of Teudel's Goths burst from their ambush behind a warehouse. They seized the ships and murdered every man on board, with the sole exception of the bishop, whom they carried away captive to Teudel. The fact was that Valentine, disobeying Belisarius's instructions, had a day or two before led his thousand men in a sally against the Goths, but had been cut off: he was killed, with almost every man in his command. The besiegers had then sighted the bishop's fleet from a hill, and what was left of the garrison was too weak to prevent them from laying this successful ambush in the harbour. The captured bishop (his name happened also to be Valentine) was closely questioned by King Teudel, who hoped to obtain valuable military information from him. But the bishop evaded Teudel's questions, like a good Roman, even when threatened with torture. Teudel lost patience with him and ordered both his hands to be hacked off. We greatly pitied this good man.

In Rome there were many suicides from famine. The veteran Bessas, whom resentment against Justinian's neglect of the Italian situation had soured, was concerned chiefly with enriching himself at the expense of the citizens. By his orders, no commoner was allowed to leave the city unless he paid 5,000 gold pieces for the privilege; a patrician was asked to pay 100,000. Most patricians considered the price exorbitant and preferred to stay, at whatever inconvenience to themselves. The only grain remaining was in the military granaries. Bessas sold a little of this at a time at increasingly high prices, more and more adulterated with bran – which was to rob his horses, too. When gold currency failed he accepted in payment ancient silver dishes and flagons, family heirlooms – but only for their weight in silver, not for their value as antique pieces. It was his intention, I believe, to capitulate before long, on condition that he and his soldiers – who had also grown rich by selling part of their rations – should be allowed to march out with the honours of war and keep their private fortunes.

One morning the city mob came howling to the gates of the Pincian Palace, Bessas's headquarters. And a dreadful sight they must have presented, with their gaunt, discoloured faces and wind-swollen stomachs; for dogs, mules, asses, cats, rats, mice being all consumed, nothing but nettles now remained to eat that could be eaten – unless they secretly ate horse dung or the flesh of murdered children. The guards tried to drive these poor creatures away, but they fell when struck, and could not rise up again for weakness, lying wriggling like wasps or flies with singed wings. Their petition was: 'For God's sake do one of three things – either feed us, or let us quit the city without payment, or put us out of our misery by killing us.' Bessas replied: 'I cannot feed you, having no corn except just sufficient for my men; nor kill you, for that would be murder; nor let you quit the city, for fear that the Goths should take advantage of the opening of the gates to force their way inside. Courage! Belisarius will soon be here with enough food for everyone.'

Nevertheless, he gradually lowered the leaving-fee for all but the patricians – until it lay within reach of the most modest purses. Soon the city was almost empty. Most of the fugitives died by the way, from utter exhaustion; many were killed by the Goths, whose forces had now increased to some 60,000 men; a few escaped to the South. But Rome still held out, as did also the garrison of the Port of Rome; and Belisarius was coming to their relief from Durazzo in Dalmatia, the reinforcements having just arrived.

Bloody John wished the whole army, which now numbered 20,000 men, to cross the narrow sea to Brindisi and march in a body across Italy to Rome. But Belisarius pointed out that, even if they met with no serious opposition, the march to Rome would occupy forty days, whereas to go by sea in the galleys would occupy only five days, if the winds were favourable. With famine threatening Rome, every day was precious. His new Household Troops were by no means uselesss soldiers; and he succeeded in buying armour and horses for one half of them at Durazzo. He embarked them in the swiftest of the galleys and ordered Bloody John to follow as soon as possible.

My mistress behaved with the greatest tenderness and consideration towards Belisarius throughout all this time, and their confidence in each other sustained them through many evil days; nor was there ever again the least word of scandal spoken against my mistress's private life. To me they were most attentive and entrusted me with many important secrets.

Belisarius and my mistress, whom I accompanied, sailed in the flagship; we looked forward to this new campaign with some misgiving, but once embarked were eager to be in Italy again. A violent southeasterly wind forced us to run for safety to the harbour of Otranto. The Gothic soldiers who were still besieging this town, not realizing that our presence was accidental, retired in fear to Brindisi, two days' journey to the northward. The wind changed on the next day and we sailed southward again and through the Straits of Messina; the Goths congratulated themselves that the danger was past.

We arrived six days later at the Port of Rome, which was still holding out; but nothing could be done until Bloody John arrived, our forces being so small. We waited for several days and, receiving no news, concluded that his fleet had been sunk or scattered by the storm that we had ourselves encountered. At last a dispatch came from John, by a trading-vessel, announcing that he was adhering to his original plan of marching across Italy. He had already met with some success: he had ferried his troops across to Otranto unperceived by the Goths and, first capturing a large herd of remounts, had surprised the enemy at Brindisi, overwhelmed their camp, and killed a great number of them. He was now advancing north-westward in the direction of Rome.

Belisarius cried: 'Will no general of mine ever obey me? I fear that by the time this John arrives, Rome will have fallen.' But he smuggled a message into the city to Bessas, begging him to hold out a little longer.

King Teudel did not underestimate Belisarius's courage or resource. He knew that he would do his best to bring provisions up the Tiber in boats, and therefore decided to block the way against him. At a point where the river narrows, about three miles downstream from Rome, he built two strong wooden towers, one on either bank, connected them with a boom of heavy timbers, and manned them with the best men in his army. Wittich would never have had the wit to think of so ingenious a scheme as that.

Belisarius was not dismayed by Teudel's boom and towers. He sent two of his most reliable guardsmen to the spot; they were to pretend to be deserters, and to measure the towers with their eye. These guardsmen parleyed with the sentries at the tower on the right bank; and, affecting to be dissatisfied with the Gothic offers, presently came away again. Now that Belisarius had the measure, he constructed a tower, twenty feet higher than Teudel's, upon two cement-barges lashed together. At the top, from a pair of projecting davits, he slung a long-boat. He also had 200 galleys boarded in with fences six feet high and embrasures cut in the fences sufficient for archers to shoot through. These galleys he manned with his best troops, and loaded them with grain, sausages, dried meat, oil, cheese, figs, and other foods.

Another message came from Bloody John by a priest disguised as a peasant. John was at pains to say, first, that the native population had welcomed him with enthusiasm throughout his progress from Brindisi; but unfortunately Teudel had garrisoned Capua and so barred his road to Rome. Capua was impregnable, and one should never advance past a strongly held fortress – as Belisarius himself had often pointed out. He had therefore turned back, and was now hunting down the scattered Gothic war-bands in Lucania.

Belisarius learned from the priest that this Capua garrison consisted of a mere half-squadron of lancers. He realized that Bloody John, caring nothing for the fate of Rome – and perhaps wishing to be revenged on Bessas, who had shown no sympathy for him when he was besieged in Rimini some years before – preferred the easy task of plundering unoccupied country. If Rome was to be relieved this must be done by Belisarius's own unaided resources, whatever the odds.

He gave the command of the Port of Rome to an Armenian named Isaac; my mistress would also be there to advise and assist. A half-squadron of cavalry was stationed on either side of the river, with supporting infantry, and ordered to hold out to the last man if the Port should be attacked. Belisarius took personal command of the fleet of boarded-in galleys. He sent a message to Bessas: 'Expect my arrival by way of the river in the early afternoon of tomorrow. I have means to break the boom. I count upon you to make a sudden raid against the Gothic camp shortly after noon, as a diversion. I have plentiful provisions for you in my boats.'

The next day, the sixth of December, was the feast of Bishop Nicholas, the patron saint of children. St Nicholas was much cultivated by Justinian, who built a church in his honour at Constantinople. About him more absurd miracles are related, I verily believe, than about any other saint in the Calendar: no sooner was he born than he stood up and lisped thanks to Almighty God for the gift of existence, and as an infant he rigidly observed the canonical fasts of Wednesdays and Fridays, by abstaining on those days from sucking the breasts of his mother Joanna – to her great discomfort but greater wonder. For some unexplained reason, St Nicholas has become the heir of the Sea-God Poseidon, whose temples have nearly all been rededicated to him; as the heiress to the Goddess Venus is the Virgin Mary, and the heir to the Dog Cerberus is the Apostle Peter (Jesus Himself being heir to Orpheus, who tamed savage things with his charming melodies). Every saint acknowledged by the Church has his peculiar character and virtue, Nicholas has come to be an emblem of child-like simplicity. On this occasion the Thracian soldiers, being of the Orthodox faith, regarded the day as of particularly good omen, since it was recorded of Nicholas that at the famous Council of Nicaea he was carried away by his hot religious feelings and dealt his fellow-cleric Arius, the founder of the Arian heresy (which the Goths profess), a tremendous box on the ear.

Early in the morning of St Nicholas's Day, then, Belisarius was ready to begin his voyage up the river with oars and sails. Two thousand of his Household Troops, those for whom he had no horses, kept pace on either side of the stream, and his remaining squadron of cavalry acted as a screen. My mistress embraced him and wished him godspeed and victory, and he departed. We who remained waited anxiously on the battlements.

About noon a mounted messenger came back with glorious news. Belisarius's fleet had first encountered a chain net fixed across the river a little distance below the boom – the very same chain that he had himself used for protecting the water-mills during his defence of the city – but the infantry, with a volley of arrows and a charge, had scattered the guards posted at either end; they unhooked the obstruction and proceeded. The tall, floating tower, with the long-boat suspended from the top of it, had been pulled up the tow-path by a number of pack animals. Then, while the archers in the galleys and the infantry on the banks hotly engaged the Goths in the twin land-towers, this floating tower was warped up into position against the land-tower on the tow-path. Now Belisarius's intentions were disclosed. The long-boat was lowered from the davits with a rush: as it fell among the crowded Goths in the tower, a dozen flaming torches were thrown into it. The boat had been filled with pitch and oil and resin and other combustible materials, so that in less than a minute the whole Gothic tower was ablaze. A squadron of Goths came charging down the tow-path, but hesitated at the sight of the burning tower and at the sound of men screaming from the fiery mass. Our infantry drove them back in disorder. Belisarius began destroying the boom, and was ready to continue his advance as soon as Bessas should make his sortie. Two hundred Goths had been burned alive in the tower. The garrison of the other tower had fled.

When Isaac the Armenian heard this news he shouted for joy, as we all did at the Port. He decided to win his share of glory by an attack on a stockaded Gothic camp which lay at half a mile's distance, guarding Ostia. Gathering a hundred horsemen together, he spurred out from the fortress into the delta of the river and cried to my mistress Antonina as he went: 'The fortress is safe under your guardianship, gracious lady; soon I shall return with gifts.'

Isaac never returned. He carried the camp at his first charge, scattered the garrison, and mortally wounded their commander. But the Goths realized that this was not the vanguard of a large army, it was merely a madman with a hundred adventurers behind him. They came rushing back to find Isaac's men busily engaged in plundering the huts. Isaac was struck down, and not ten of his hundred men won safely back to the fortifications. One man, finding his return barred, escaped by galloping away up to the head of the delta. He shouted across the stream to an outpost which Belisarius had left there: 'O comrades, Isaac is killed, and I alone of his men am left; and I am wounded in the side. Fetch me across the river, I beg.' With that he fainted.

While they ferried him and his horse across the river on a raft, one of them galloped up the tow-path to take the bad news to Belisarius at the boom. What he said was: 'Alas, General, all is lost at the Port of Rome. Isaac and the entire garrison have been killed by the Goths – all but one man, your guardsman Sisifried, who has escaped and been fetched wounded across the river at the delta head.'

Belisarius knew Sisifried as a bold, loyal, resourceful soldier, and the messenger also as a very trusty man, so he could not but believe the news. The first question he asked, with a sort of gasp, was: 'And my wife, the Lady Antonina?'

The messenger answered: 'I do not know. Sisifried's words were: "I alone am left of Isaac's men."'

At this Belisarius swayed upon his feet. Tears burst from his eyes, and for a while he stood speechless. He crossed himself, muttering a broken prayer. But in a little while he regained control of his feelings: perhaps he recalled how Geilimer, the Vandal King, had lost a battle by untimely grief for a dear one. It was now three o'clock, and Bessas had not made the expected sortie, though aware of the burning of the tower and the destruction of the boom. Must he engage the whole Gothic Army by himself? That would be foolhardy to the point of madness. Nevertheless, he would have done so, in the hope of aid from Bessas as soon as the galleys drew near to the city; but that, with the Port taken, he was cut off from the sea – for Ostian was also held by the enemy, and defeat now would be disaster. His only hope lay in immediate return and the recapture of the Port. He ordered the helms of his galleys to be turned hard about, and, taking the infantry aboard, recalled his cavalry by trumpet-blast and hurried downstream. Perhaps it was still not too late to wrest the fortress from the enemy and avenge his dead.

When we at the Port saw his boats returning we were filled with amazement, but not so great an amazement as he himself felt on observing our sentries still at the gates of the fortress. Then relief and disgust struggled for mastery in his mind – relief that the report was an error, disgust at having, from foolish credulity, abandoned an attempt so well begun. He said bitterly: 'This is the day of St Nicholas, when children find sweetmeats hidden in their shoes, and when old soldiers turn simpletons.'

That night his malarial fever came back upon him. The restless and unhappy condition of his mind aggravated the attack; he grew very sick indeed, and was soon raving in delirium. He kept calling for my mistress, not recognizing her at his bedside. Her heart was pierced when in the wanderings of his mind he relived the anguish that he had suffered in the belief that she was killed. 'What remains for me now?' he continually cried. 'Antonina is dead.'

At the height of his fever, we who attended him were obliged to call the assistance of eight of his strongest guardsmen to restrain him from doing some wild deed. Now he imagined that he was fighting the Goths outside the walls of Rome, and now that it was the Persians at Daras. Once he uttered his war-cry in a terrible voice and caught two men in his arms, nearly crushing them to death; but suddenly fell gasping.

CHAPTER 22

RECALL AND FORGIVENESS

Belisarius was confined to his chamber for ten days. On the eleventh day King Teudel took Rome, being admitted one night with all his army by four treacherous Isaurian soldiers at the Asinarian Gate. Bessas had not constantly changed the duty roster for his guards, as Belisarius had done, or changed the locks on the gates; thus the soldiers had been able to agree with Teudel for an exact hour some days in advance. The cause of their treachery was a grievance against the captain of their company for holding back part of their corn ration in order to sell it to patricians.

King Teudel's Goths immediately set about plundering the great houses of the patricians, allowing Bessas and his garrison to escape without hindrance. Teudel contented himself with what he found in the Pincian Palace – Bessas's evilly won store, which had the appearance of a royal treasury or the hoard of a successful admiral of pirates. In all Rome, a city that had recently housed half a million souls, the Goths found no more than 500 commoners and 400 persons of patrician blood – nearly all women and children, these, since most of the patricians themselves had escaped with the garrison. Teudel began pulling down the fortifications; and swore that, for its ungrateful hostility to the benignant Gothic rule of Theoderich and his descendants, the city had earned no better fate than to be burned down and reduced to the level of a sheep-walk.

Belisarius learned of this threat and wrote to him from the Port of Rome: 'King Teudel, if you do as you have threatened with Rome, the birthplace of Empire, will your name not stink in the nostrils of posterity? Be sure that it will be told and written of you: "What fifty generations of Romans toiled to build, bringing together the noblest materials and the finest architects and craftsmen procurable in the entire world, a German princeling, insulting the great dead, burned down one day as an act of spite, and at a time when it stood empty because of plague and famine." '

Teudel reflected, and refrained. Belisarius had been right in supposing that, with a Gothic King, the hypothetical verdict of posterity would weigh more than his own natural inclinations or the most practical advice of his wisest counsellors. Nevertheless, Teudel dismantled three miles of the fortifications, and removed all the gates, making an open city of it. Then, leaving strong forces behind him in the neighbourhood to pin down our forces at the Port of Rome, he set out against Bloody John, who was now at Taranto.

Bloody John did not dare to face Teudel, and so retreated hurriedly to Otranto; by which action Southern Italy, that had seemed securely his, was handed back to its Gothic rulers. Teudel, considering that the capture of Otranto was a matter of little importance, so long as Bloody John could be immobilized there, decided to march up the Adriatic coast to Ravenna, the inhabitants of which were clearly disaffected to the Imperial cause and likely to open the gates to him. With Ravenna in his hands he would be the undoubted master of Italy.

King Teudel had already begun his march up the coast when he was recalled by news which filled him with astonishment and indignation. Belisarius, true to his reputation for attempting the seemingly impossible, was once more holding Rome and ready to dispute its possession against all the Goths in Italy!

'But how,' you may well ask, 'could even Belisarius dare with his miserably inadequate forces to hold an open city against an army which could now muster 80,000 men?'

Belisarius's own answer to this question would have been: 'We must dare to make amends for our former failures.'

As soon as he was sufficiently well to sit his horse, Belisarius had reconnoitred the city with a thousand horsemen, riding out by night from the Port. He had found it wholly deserted (for the first time in its history, I suppose) and even encountered a small pack of wolves roaming in the Field of Mars – which the soldiers refrained from shooting. These wolves were regarded as a good omen, because they were animals once held sacred by the ancient Romans, Romulus the founder of Rome having been suckled by a she-wolf. Belisarius made a careful tour of the walls and finally pronounced: 'All is well, friends.'

They thought that his wits were still deranged by the fever, but he explained: 'King Teudel, being a barbarian, has scamped his task of destruction, as I expected. He has been content merely to dislodge the upper courses of stone from the rampart and push the rubble forward into the fosse. Working with vigour, we can repair the damage in a short time.'

The Gothic retaining army, informed that Belisarius was returning to the Port from his reconnaissance, ambushed him at four several points. In each case he divided his forces into three parts: one half-squadron held its ground while the other two pressed forward on either flank and enveloped the enemy, distressing them with arrows until they abandoned their position. On this homeward ride Belisarius killed or captured more than the number of his own forces, losing some thirty men, because the Gothic squadrons consisted of lancers only and were given no opportunity to come to close quarters, but overwhelmed by arrows. Though numbering fully 15,000, this Gothic army did not again venture from its camp; and Belisarius, leaving only 500 men to guard the Port, could throw all his forces into Rome. He had with him his own 4,000 Thracians, diminished by 300, and 2,000 of Bessas's men who had fled to him when Rome was taken, and 500 regular troops, former deserters to Teudel at Spoleto, who had been persuaded to return to their allegiance. There were also a few hundred sturdy labourers gathered from the villages in the neighbourhood, mostly refugees from the city, who gladly offered to work for him if they were paid with corn and meat and a little wine.

Count Belisarius entered Rome on the Feast of the Three Kings; King Teudel did not return until the first day of February (of this new year of our Lord 547). In those twenty-five days a miracle had been accomplished. The whole fosse had been cleared of earth and rubble and planted with pointed stakes cut from the rafters of ruined houses; and the dressed stones of the rampart had been collected and laid back in place, though without mortar. The walls presented a bold face again to the enemy, and only fell short by a few feet, in the rebuilt places, of their original height. Only there were no gates, and for lack of skilled smiths and carpenters none could be improvised in that short time. Belisarius was therefore obliged to resort to the tactics of the ancient Spartans: he closed the gateways with human gates, which were his best spearmen drawn up in phalanx. We had all worked in the eight-hour shifts: soldiers, domestics, civilians, including women and children – not one of us was allowed to avoid the *corvée*. I, a pampered eunuch, broke my well-trimmed nails on the rough stones and wearied my plump shoulders carrying baskets of earth. Belisarius was everywhere at once, like lightning in a storm.

I had been sent by Belisarius to the municipal lime kilns on the first days to see whether any lime was available for making mortar, so that at least the angles of the walls might be strengthened; but I found only a few bags. Nailed to the wall in the President's office was a parchment document which, since it was no longer valid, I took down and kept as a memento of the siege. I copy it out here as a curiosity. It was the President's official appointment by Theoderich some years previously.

King Theoderich to the Distinguished Faustulus, President of the Lime Kilns, greeting!

It is a glorious labour indeed to serve the City of Rome! Who can doubt that lime, which is snow-white in hue and imponderable as an African sponge, is of mighty service in the construction of the most magnificent edifices? In proportion as it is itself debilitated and broken down by the fierce breath of fire, so does it lend force to massive masonry. It is a dissolvable stone, a petrifying downiness, a sandy pebble which (O wonder) burns the best when abundantly watered, without which stones do not stay nor grains of gravel commodiously cohere.

Therefore we set you, our industrious lord Faustulus, over the burning of lime and its decent distribution; that there may be plenty of this substance available both for public and private works, and that thereby people may be persuaded and encouraged confidently to build and rebuild our beloved City. Perform this well, and you shall be promoted to yet more honourable offices!

When I first read these elegant words I did not know whether to laugh or weep, they seemed so incongruous to the present desolation of the city and the barbarous Camp Latin of the soldiers who now formed its principal population. A philosophical train of thought was started in my mind, about the essentially evil nature of war, however just the cause; which I instantly smothered as monkish Christian and no more congruous to the situation than the document itself. But enough of this.

When King Teudel came within sight of the city he made an immediate attack upon us from the north-east, sending his men in mass against the Nomentan, Tiburtine, and Praenestine Gates. I think that he expected the rebuilt walls to fall at the mere noise of his war-horns, as the walls of Jericho are said to have fallen to the war-horns of Jewish Joshua. I witnessed the cavalry-charge at the Tiburtine Gate, where I was once more at the same task that had me occupied ten years previously – serving a catapult with bolts while my mistress laid the sights. There were 10,000 Gothic lancers drawn up just out of range, and squadron by squadron they charged in column with levelled lances at the bridge that guarded the gate. It was like pouring wine into a bottle with an obstruction in the neck.

Few indeed of the Goths reached the gate, over a mound of dead and dying, to spit themselves there upon the spears of the phalanx as an Indian bear upon the quills of a porcupine. Their fearful losses were due not merely to our heavy and accurate fire from the walls, with bows, catapults, scorpions, wild asses, but to the iron caltrops which guarded the approach – a device never before used against the Goths. I have remarked that the necessary artisans for the making of new city gates were not available; but the farrier-sergeants of the army had been working night and day, employing all skilled and half-skilled men in the manufacture of these iron caltrops. A caltrop consists of four stout spikes, each a foot in length, fitted to an iron ball at such an angle that all their points are equidistant from one another. Thus, however thrown upon the ground, the caltrop always rests upon a firm triangle of spikes, with one spike sticking threateningly upward. Some call it the 'Devil's tripod'. The caltrop was the family badge of Belisarius, and was embroidered in gold by my mistress's women upon the white Household standard. The motto read: '*Quocunque jeceris, stabit*' – 'wheresoever you cast it, it will find its feet'. Cavalry cannot pass a position heavily strewn with caltrops unless they first dismount and carry them away one by one; otherwise the horses catch their feet in the spikes and stumble and fall impaled.

Five squadrons in succession charged this fearful barrier. The mound of dead rose higher and higher until every upward spike had spitted a man or a horse. Thus – as the rhetoricians would put it – the bridge became passable at last by reason of its very impassability. There was heavy fighting at the gate, the Gothic infantry being now engaged, and from the flanking-towers stones, boiling water, and beams came showering down upon them. Our spearmen, Isaurians, fought in relays; but since there were only fifty men in each team and the Goths came pressing forward in their hundreds and hundreds, they grew very weary. It was only my mistress's heartening presence and her promise of great rewards to every man who survived the day that kept them at their post. By midday our catapults had exhausted their supply of bolts and the wild-asses had kicked themselves to pieces. I seized a bow and found that I had not altogether forgotten my former archery practice, though my arms were feeble.

There was no pause for dinner, but we snatched mouthfuls of bread and cheese as we fought, and slaves carried around pitchers of sour wine. In the afternoon it rained heavily, the rain turned to sleet, and our bow-strings became useless. Even soldiers who usually took an honest pleasure in fighting began groaning and cursing in their distress. But the Goths suffered more than we. The approach to the gate became very slippery; our spearmen, to whom my mistress gave rough cloths to tie about their feet, had a great advantage over the enemy, who staggered and slid here and there on their wet leather soles.

The battle ended at nightfall, the Goths being held at every gate. They retired for the night, and we sent out the labourers in gangs with torches to recover bolts and arrows, for which we paid them by the bundle of fifty; while we ourselves cleared the bridges, freeing the bloody caltrops of their dead and taking plunder of golden torques and rings and shirts of mail.

King Teudel attacked again shortly after dawn, and again there was the same dreadful drama of slaughter, and again every bridge was held. I killed a Goth with my second arrow, striking him in the face at short range. They withdrew at noon, pursued by two squadrons of Household cuirassiers from the Praenestine Gate; but rallied a mile away. Our whole cavalry was sent out to support these squadrons. In the battle which followed, bow and arrow once more prevailed over the lance. During these two days 15,000 Goths had been killed and many more carried away seriously wounded. Twenty thousand dead horses also strewed the battlefield. Our total losses were 450, 200 of whom were killed in the cavalry engagements.

A few days later the Goths returned to attack for the third time, but with such evident reluctance that Belisarius – who knew better than any general who ever lived, I suppose, exactly when to turn from the defensive to the offensive – went out himself against them with all the cavalry. They say that from a quarter of a mile's distance, with his strongest bow, Belisarius aimed at the Gothic standard-bearer riding ahead of the line. There was a following wind, or the shot would have been impossible: the arrow, falling from a great height, struck the standard-bearer in the groin, and pinned him to the saddle, so that the horse, pricked by the arrow, reared up and threw him. Others, jealous perhaps of Belisarius's feats, claim that the arrow was not fired by Belisarius, but by Sisifried, the guardsman who had survived Isaac's defeat; but if so, Sisifried did something extraordinary and far beyond his usual powers. The more natural account is that the arrow was Belisarius's, though perhaps Sisifried also aimed one at the standard-bearer.

King Teudel's standard tumbled to the ground; which was the worst of omens. At once our leading squadron charged to seize it, shooting from the saddle as they went, and there was bitter fighting for its possession. Two Gothic lancers were tugging at one end and two Household cuirassiers at the other. A Gothic officer hacked the staff through with a blow of his sword, and our men had to be content with the butt. This same officer chopped off the left forearm of the standard-bearer, because around the wrist was buckled a golden bracelet set with rubies and emeralds which he wished to deny to us. Then the Goths retreated, and in the pursuit lost 3,000 men more. When Belisarius returned that night he had horses to mount the remainder of his Thracians, and every man of them could at last be dressed in a mail shirt. He had lost nine men only.

Teudel broke the siege on the next day, and retired to Tivoli, first destroying all the bridges over the Tiber, upstream from Rome, with the single exception of the Mulvian, which Belisarius had already seized. Teudel was forced to bear the angry reproaches of his surviving noblemen that he had been hoodwinked by Belisarius's letter into sparing Rome from complete destruction. If he had kept to his original threat and levelled the whole city to a sheep-walk, they said, the war would not have taken this evil turn for the Goths. But when he came to Tivoli, he asked them: 'And suppose all Tivoli had been levelled with the ground? Come now, my lords, the fault at Rome – if fault it was – lies with you; for I entrusted each of you with the pulling down of a part of the Roman ramparts, but you were lazy and left too much standing. Fortunately, you have done the same thing here: so that the credit of quickly rebuilding the walls of Tivoli will be yours, as well as the fault at Rome. To work, to work, and let posterity praise you!'

Belisarius now found the necessary artisans for making new city gates. Soon the task was done and the gates in position. Before the end of February he could send a set of keys to Justinian at Constantinople; asking, in return, for reinforcements to enable him to complete the reconquest of Italy, and money to pay the troops under his command. 'He gives twice, who gives quickly,' Belisarius wrote, 'and I trust to make speedy repayment with the person and treasures of another captive king.'

He wrote not once but three times, and my mistress wrote also to Theodora. No reply and no reinforcements came. When he had put the necessary garrisons into Ostia and Civita Vecchia, he stood in greater need of a field army than ever before, and he was now paying the regular troops as well as those of his Household with treasure from his own purse. Nor was it possible, though he tried this, to lay even the smallest taxes upon the impoverished Italians. They possessed neither money nor anything that could be exchanged for money.

Justinian at length replied that he had already sent a large army to Italy under Valerian. He commanded Belisarius and Bloody John (who had not met for three years now) to be reconciled to each other. They were to join forces at Taranto, where this army should by now have arrived.

But Valerian remained for months on the farther shore of the Adriatic, detaching only 300 men for service in Italy. It was no fault of his: Illyria was being raided again – not by Bulgars this time, but by Slavs, in enormous undisciplined numbers – and Valerian had orders not to leave Durazzo until the danger had passed. The general commanding the Imperial Forces in Illyria dared not risk an engagement with the horde of Slavs, but followed ineffectively in their rear from district to district. His caution was due to the mutinous mood of the troops, who had not been paid for several months, and, in lieu of pay, now plundered the already plundered countryside. The whole Diocese had reached the condition described by the Jewish prophet Joel: 'That which the palmer-worm hath left, hath the locust eaten; and that which the locust hath left, hath the canker-worm eaten; and that which the canker-worm hath left, hath the caterpillar eaten.'

We did not know of this Slav invasion, or of Valerian's delay, and sailed for Taranto cheerfully. With us were all the troops that could be spared from garrison service – a mere 700 horsemen and 200 infantry. I, for one, was not sorry to say good-bye to Rome. As we left the Port of Rome early in June and were carried by a favourable breeze towards the Straits of Messina, we all had hopes of a speedy and victorious return to Constantinople. After passing through the Straits our sailing ships, now towed by the galleys, struggled against the wind along the 'sole of the buskin', as that part of Southern Italy is called because of its shape on the map. We were headed for Taranto, which lies in the angle of the buskin's high heel. But, to continue this geographical figure, we had not yet passed the ball of the foot when a tremendous north-easterly gale struck us and we were driven to take refuge at Cotrone, where was the only safe anchorage within a great many miles. At first it seemed a dangerous position: few troops, an unwalled town, the Gothic army not far away, grain scarce, the wind continuing to blow strongly from the north-east. Belisarius persuaded all the able-bodied inhabitants of the town, men and women, to assist his infantry in fortifying the city with a stockaded rampart and a fosse; and sent the 700 cavalry ahead to hold two narrow defiles in the range of mountains, at the instep of the buskin, which enclose and protect this district of Cotrone. But the longer he viewed the situation, the better he liked it. The district was rich in grazing grounds and well stocked with cattle. He pointed out to his officers that the mountains made it a natural fortress, far more convenient for organizing his forces than Taranto. 'It was a lucky wind blew us here,' he said. 'This will be the assembly-place of the armies.'

Then, while he supervised the facing of the rampart with stones and the construction of towers, still waiting for the wind to change, disaster came upon him. His 700 horsemen had hardly reached the mountain passes which he had directed them to occupy when they sighted a large force of King Teudel's lancers. These Goths were on the way to besiege Rossano, a neighbouring city on the coast between Cotrone and Taranto. It was in Rossano that Bloody John had stored all his plunder of the last three years, and many Italian noblemen had also taken refuge there. The 700 laid an ambush and routed the lancers, killing 200 of them. But victory gave them a false sense of security, so that with no Belisarius to watch them they neglected their duties, posted no sentries in the passes, despised the enemy. They spent their time foraging in small parties, or playing games, or hunting. King Teudel suddenly came against them in person one day at dawn at the head of 3,000 life-guards and caught them entirely unprepared. They fought bravely, but to no purpose. Teudel's Goths rode down all but fifty of them, who reached Cotrone with the news only a few minutes before the arrival of Teudel. The fortifications of the town were not yet completed, for they were planned on a large scale, and Belisarius had no choice but to re-embark instantly with the 200 infantry and the fifty survivors of his cavalry. Cotrone was left in Teudel's hands. The gale which had delayed our voyage to Taranto was still blowing, and carried us in a single day the whole distance to Messina in Sicily, which is 100 miles.

There is not much more to relate of Belisarius's last campaign in Italy. He drew 2,000 men from the garrisons of Sicily, and embarked them in ships for Otranto, which we reached without further accident. The 'large army' promised by Justinian presently arrived there from Spalato under Valerian, and another 'large army', direct from Constantinople, which was intended, I suppose, to clinch matters. The combined forces amounted to barely 3,000 men, most of them being untrained recruits!

Belisarius said to my mistress: 'My dearest, this army is like three drops of water on the tongue of a man dying from thirst. I confess to you that my resources are at an end. I have now spent all my personal treasure in the expenses of this war, except for a few thousand gold pieces; I have mortgaged half my property in Constantinople and sold outright my estates at Tchermen and Adrianople. Much money is owed me that I cannot collect. There is, for example, the matter that I have concealed from you, for shame – my dealings with Herodian, the general who commanded at Spoleto two years ago. He had borrowed fifty thousand gold pieces from me for three months, without interest; telling me, truly enough, that he had been left a large legacy by an uncle, and that he needed money for paying and feeding his troops. When, after six months, I asked him for repayment, knowing that the legacy money had arrived for him at Ravenna, he insolently threatened to sell Spoleto to the Goths if I pressed him so barbarously, and to pay me with the proceeds. When I reproached him for this answer he did indeed sell Spoleto, and became one of Teudel's boon companions. He now has my money, his legacy, and the reward for betraying Spoleto; I have nothing. The Emperor himself owes me an enormous sum for what I have advanced to the regular troops on his behalf. Of that I make no complaint; I dedicate my life to the Emperor's service, and am honoured to be his debtor. But without men and money no war can be fought.'

My mistress replied: 'Let me go in person to Constantinople, my dearest husband. I undertake that the Empress will persuade the Emperor that either a great army and plenty of treasure must be sent for the reconquest of Italy or that Italy must be abandoned to the Goths. You may be sure, my love, that I shall not delay over the business.'

So she sailed away, and I with her; and it was now mid-July. The journey was tedious because of contrary winds. We were coasting around Greece, having just passed the island of Salamis, when a ship from Salonica came bowling down the breeze on our starboard. I was standing on the forecastle, and shouted out in Latin: 'What good news have you, sailors?' For it is unlucky at sea to ask for any but good news.

The mate of the vessel shouted back: 'Good news indeed. The Beast is dead.'

I cried: 'What Beast, excellent man?'

There was a confused shout in answer. The ship was almost out of hail as I shrilly repeated, 'What Beast?'

A sailor, making a trumpet of his hands, bawled back into the wind: '*Perierunt ambo*', meaning 'Both are dead.'

Then we heard a great shout of laughter, but nothing more.

We guessed the name of one of the two Beasts correctly – the whale Porphyry; but there was much speculation in our vessel as to the identity of the other. So Porphyry had met his death at last! The account we heard at our next port of call was somewhat absurd. We were well aware that Porphyry, because of the construction of his throat, only ate small fry; but he was now credited with having pursued a flock of dolphins into shallow water close to the mouth of the river Sangarius (which flows into the Black Sea about a hundred miles to the eastward of the Bosphorus) and engulfed a dozen of them, and to have been busy chewing their bones when found stranded on a mud-bank close to the shore. What really happened, I believe, was that Porphyry and the dolphins were both in pursuit of a very large shoal of little fish, and that Porphyry was enticed into shallow water by the dolphins. In any case, the fishermen of the neighbourhood came up in boats and attacked Porphyry with axes and boat-hooks. He was so fast in the mud that he could not hoist up his tail to destroy them. However, he seemed proof against all their weapons, so they passed a number of heavy ropes around him and, by means of a pulley attached to a great tree by the river-bank, hauled him ashore. Then they fetched soldiers from a neighbouring post, who dispatched him with long spears. Porphyry measured forty-five feet in length and fifteen feet at his broadest part. He provided the district with food for many months; since what meat they could not eat fresh they smoked or pickled. In the flesh of his head – or her head, for Porphyry proved to be a cow whale – they found embedded a long arrow with white feathers, doubtless the same that Belisarius had once fired, but in the throat no blue-painted catapult-spear.

The other Beast to which the sailor had referred was no Beast at all, to my mistress's way of thinking. Indeed, so far from being good news, it was the worst news that we could possibly have received from the city: Theodora was dead. A sudden cancer beginning in her breast had spread rapidly through the whole of her body, and she had died, not without courage, after a few weeks' sickness and much pain.

Our grief was mixed with wonder. It was recollected now that the whale's first appearance in the Straits had coincided to a day with Theodora's first arrival in the city with Acacius her father – as its death had coincided with hers to the hour; and further that on the day that Belisarius and the Blue militia went out against Porphyry and wounded the beast, Theodora had been struck with a fearful aching of the head which had plagued her intermittently ever since. Was Porphyry, then, her familiar spirit?

My mistress Antonina immediately went into mourning for Theodora, and later sacrificed a black ram with pagan prayers for her ghost. She said: 'The Christian God has been placated by many masses. But Theodora secretly reverenced the Old Gods also.'

We nevertheless continued our voyage, since my mistress felt that, having come so far, she should at least attempt to make Justinian see reason about the Italian campaign.

My mistress found the Emperor by no means grieving for Theodora's death, but very jolly, like a little boy whose nurse or mother has suddenly fallen sick and left him at liberty to do all the naughty things he pleases. He had been removing from their sees or cures all the clergy with Monophysite leanings whom Theodora had protected. Also, though he was sixty-five years of age, he had begun a career of promiscuous passion, to make up for all the years of restraint under Theodora. His virility lasted him, indeed, for another fifteen years. His agents constantly searched the slave-markets for good-looking girls; and besides this he debauched the daughters of many of Theodora's ladies. To the Lady Chrysomallo's grand-daughter, who shrunk from his embraces, he said affably: 'Your grandmother was just the same, my dear. But she did what I required of her, because that was her obligation.'

He made himself Theodora's sole heir, cancelling all her legacies – including a very large one indeed to my mistress, and 5,000 in gold for myself, who was mentioned very graciously in the will.

At the audience which he granted my mistress immediately upon her arrival, she told him very plainly and precisely how matters stood in Italy. He listened with apparent concern. But, at the news that Belisarius had only 150 men of his bodyguard with him at Otranto – 100 were defending Rossano, and the rest were either killed or had been left behind in the neighbourhood of Rome – and that he was a poor man again, this evil Emperor could not conceal his satisfaction.

He said to my mistress: 'So the victorious Belisarius has acknowledged failure at last, eh? But, no, no, we cannot repay the money that he has foolishly spent in his ridiculous campaigning. Why, what a cowardly way to manage a war – to sail from this port to that, to shelter behind fortresses, to avoid battle! Eh, Narses? He should have taken a lesson from our brave John, who fears nothing. Certainly we cannot send him either more men or more money. This Count Belisarius cries in the voice of the horse-leech's daughters mentioned by King Solomon: "Give! Give!" Solomon, you will recall, held that four things are never satisfied – the grave, the lechery of a barren woman, sandy soil, fire. Had wise Solomon been living now, he would doubtless have added the name of Count Belisarius as fifth insatiate.'

When he had finished, my mistress asked quietly: 'But Italy, Your Clemency? Are you prepared to lose your dominion over Italy?'

He replied: 'No, indeed, Illustrious Lady Antonina, and for that reason we shall now recall your husband from that land and appoint a more capable commander in his stead. But we do not wish to humiliate the good fellow: we shall be careful to state in the letter that his services are needed once more against the Persians, who still dispute the possession of Colchis with us.'

She made an obeisance. 'As Your Serenity pleases. Let the order of recall be made at once. No doubt your Grand Chamberlain, the brave Narses, will be equal to the task in which my Belisarius has failed.'

Justinian replied, disregarding the irony: 'We shall give your suggestion the fullest consideration.'

He called for parchment and ink and seemed about to sign the recall there and then, but suddenly laid down the purple-stained goose-quill which had been placed in his hand. He said: 'Softly, softly! We require an undertaking from you first, best of women.'

My mistress answered: 'If it lies in my power, I will give it.'

He informed her with a crafty smile: 'We require that you sign a document breaking off the marriage-engagement between your daughter Joannina and Anastasius, my late Empress's nephew.'

My mistress Antonina thought quickly. There seemed to be no reason for refusing his demand, since at Theodora's death Anastasius had ceased to be a person of any importance. It might be that Justinian intended the girl as a bride for one of his nephews or grand-nephews – perhaps Germanus's son Justin – believing that she would bring a handsome dowry with her.

My mistress replied: 'It is my pleasure and my husband's to obey Your Serenity in all things.'

When she had signed the document that was thereupon made out for her, someone – I think young Justin – sniggered. The snigger spread among those standing near him. Justinian looked about him encouragingly and began to chuckle and roll about on his throne; unrestrained laughter soon possessed the whole audience-chamber. My mistress was embarrassed, angry, and puzzled. She made another obeisance and retired.

The fact was that my mistress had been cruelly tricked. She was wholly unaware of what had been happening all this time to her gay daughter Joannina. Joannina, now in her fifteenth year, had long anticipated her marriage-day, which had been postponed until her parents could be present at it; for with Theodora's consent she had until recently occupied a suite of the Palace with this Anastasius 'Long-Legs', with whom she was much in love, just as if she were his wife. Upon Theodora's death the usual Christian conventions had been restored at Court; Joannina was desired to return to her own suite. But although Justinian would have discountenanced the marriage of a patrician with a woman who was undeniably not a virgin, Anastasius meant to keep to the contract, being in love with the poor girl. Now my mistress had broken the contract irrevocably, had unwittingly signed away Joannina's chance of ever marrying a man of her own rank. This was a bitter shame to my mistress, and to Belisarius when he heard of it. Joannina pleaded that Theodora had forced this sin upon her, but he saw that this was clearly not the case. Justinian openly exulted in his unkingly triumph. Joannina, remaining unmarried, took the penitent's veil, for the shame that she had brought upon herself and her parents.

Meanwhile Belisarius had organized his small army, to which Bloody John joined his own – now reduced to a thousand light cavalry. They sailed from Otranto to the relief of Rossano, but a hurricane scattered the fleet, sinking some vessels. The remainder re-assembled at Cotrone, some days later, and once more steered for Rossano, past which they had been blown. But by this time King Teudel was there, ready to oppose the landing. On the narrow beach his life-guards were lined up in close and embattled order, with archers well posted: it would have been suicidal to attempt a disembarkation. Nor were there any other landing-places on that dangerous coast. With grief in his heart Belisarius drew away again to Cotrone and left the garrison to choose between death and surrender. A hundred of his brave Thracians were among them.

At a council of war it was decided that Bloody John and Valerian should use their cavalry to raid Teudel's lines of communications, while Belisarius returned to Rome to strengthen the fortifications and encourage the garrison there. The war was not yet lost.

But then the summons came from Constantinople. As soon as the news that Belisarius was being recalled reached Rossano, the town surrendered. The surrender of Perugia followed. Ill consequences also attended the arrival of the news at Rome. Already there had been mutiny in the city: the soldiers had killed their new governor for selling military stores at high prices to civilians, but returned to discipline under the leadership of Diogenes, one of Belisarius's few surviving veteran officers. Diogenes prepared for the expected siege by sowing every available garden, park, and waste patch in the city with corn; and, though King Teudel, returning from Rossano, captured the Port of Rome and thus cut off communications with the sea, all his attempts on the city walls were frustrated. Diogenes had now been besieged in Rome three times and well understood the task of defence. Yet there could only be one ending to the business, because the soldiers of the garrison had lost all hope of relief when they learned that Belisarius was gone.

Even the men of the Household Regiment became disaffected, complaining that they had volunteered to serve with glory under Belisarius, not to rot unpaid, ill-fed, and leaderless, in ruinous Rome. It was a party of Isaurians, however, not they, who sold the city again to Teudel; and Rome changed masters for the fourth time in a few years. The escaping garrison was ambushed, and only about a hundred men reached safety at Civita Vecchia, the last Imperial stronghold in the West; where Diogenes, wounded, took command. Nevertheless, a few veterans of the Household Regiment still continued to hold the mausoleum of Hadrian against all attacks – until, after many days, they, too, capitulated from a horror of eating horse-flesh; but demanded and were granted the honours of war.

King Teudel next invaded Sicily. Our troops there shut themselves up in the sea-ports and allowed him to ravage the entire island. Italy was abandoned to the Goths, except for a small fortress here and there, and Ravenna.

When Belisarius returned to Constantinople Justinian first reproached him in a blackguardly style and then – an insult scarcely to be borne – bestowed his forgiveness upon him. Belisarius, conscious that he had done far more than could be expected of a subject by the greediest and most capricious monarch, made no reply but that he remained always at the Emperor's service. His loyalty and pride forbade him to answer otherwise.

Nor had his return been altogether without danger. There was a Palace conspiracy on foot, led by a bold and revengeful Armenian general named Artaban, to assassinate the Emperor and place on the throne his nephew Germanus, whom he had treated very badly. The attempt was delayed for a few days until Belisarius should arrive in the city. It was not that Artaban and his fellow-conspirators (who included Marcellus, the Commander of the Guards) believed that Belisarius might assist them; but that, knowing of his inflexible loyalty to the Throne, they considered it safer to murder him too. He was to be struck down as he passed through the suburbs to pay his respects at the Palace. Germanus, however, when the plot was disclosed to him, pretended compliance, but hastened to inform Justinian, being in reality horrified by the infamous proposal. The conspirators were arrested on the very day that Belisarius landed, and he reached the Palace unharmed.

In the end Justinian pardoned the conspirators.

Count Belisarius was a poor man now, and could not afford to engage any more soldiers for his bodyguard. He was dependent on my mistress Antonina for everything, including his daily expenses. Yet no false shame prevented him from being her pensioner in this way. He said: 'We are not merely husband and wife, but old comrades of war whose purses are at each other's disposal, freely.' She drew upon her hidden reserves of money, and redeemed his mortgaged property. They lived quietly in a house close to the arch of Honorius on the western side of the Bull Square. (It is on this Arch that certain brass replicas of noxious insects are fixed: Apollonius of Tyana, the celebrated magician, is said to have put them there as a charm against various diseases.)

Justinian did not send Belisarius to the war in Colchis, preferring to keep him unemployed in the city. He bestowed on him his old title, 'Commander of the Armies in the East', and presently also that of 'Commander of the Imperial Guards', but allowed him to play no part whatsoever in military affairs; nor did he once call on him for advice.

Justinian's theological pamphlets had brought him little glory; and the Council that he now summoned of all the bishops in Christendom (180 or more) brought little glory on the Church. Though he forced the Council with threats to anathematize certain works repugnant to the Monophysites, whose favour he was now courting, these heretics did not in gratitude return to the Orthodox communion, but stayed obstinately outside. Moreover, the Pope Vigilius had disagreed totally with his fellow-prelates and with the Emperor as to the propriety of the anathema, and done all that he could to avoid committing himself. At last, in fear of his life, he had taken sanctuary in the Church of the Apostle Peter at Constantinople; and only after much temporizing and tergiversation consented – not being of the stuff of martyrs – to approve the findings of the Council. On his return to Italy he found himself faced with a schism; for the clergy of nearly the whole Western Church regarded the anathematized works as sound doctrine. All those bishops, however, whose sees could be controlled by the military forces of Constantinople – chiefly those in Africa and Illyria – were disciplined into conformity or else deposed and imprisoned. Those whose sees were in Italy, Sicily, France, or Spain continued obdurate.

The bishops of the West, though they had hated Theodora as a Monophysite, greatly regretted her death. They said: 'Had she been alive, she would have laughed the Emperor out of his theological pretensions, and the Council would never have been called.'

CHAPTER 23

THREE HUNDRED VETERANS

I INTEND now to close a number of lesser histories; and then to tell of Count Belisarius's last battle, which is a tale of tales, 'the crowning jewel in his diadem of victories', as the panegyric writers said. But after that there will still remain one more chapter, which disquiets me and makes me tremble when I consider that I must write it.

To begin, then, with the East. King Khosroü is still alive in this year of our Lord 571, when I write this book. He has abstained from any further invasions of Roman Mesopotamia or Syria, ever since Belisarius turned him back at Carchemish; though the Saracens, his allies, are harassing our frontiers again. But he let the war in Colchis drag on, with alternate victory and defeat, until ten years ago: when another Eternal Peace was signed, under which he withdrew his claim to the sovereignty of Colchis and Justinian agreed to pay him a small annual tribute. (As I write, this Peace, too, has been broken – by the Romans this time. There has also been a successful revolt of the native Christians in Persian Armenia, which has placed itself under Roman protection.) Khosrou, like each of his ancestors in turn, has experienced greatest hostility from those most nearly related to him by blood; since Persian women are held in no honour and have no power to restrain their men-folk from mutual murder. His favourite son, born of a Christian woman, embraced Christianity when he came of age, and not long since rebelled, with a large part of the army; Khosrou crushed him in battle and he died.

Khosrou, though at first suspicious of Greek philosophy, has in his mature years studied it eagerly, engrafting it upon the Magian faith. Thus the torch of the Old Religion, quenched at Athens by Justinian, has been relighted not only in New Antioch, on the Euphrates, but in Persia itself at Khosrou's great university of Gondi Sapor, near Susa. There the best of the Greek Classics have been translated into Persian, together with works from the Latin and Sanskrit languages. But Khosrou abhors and persecutes Christianity, as a religion that 'leads men to neglect their duty in this life for hope of salvation in the next, and that tends to dishonour the Royal House of Persia by awarding

Divinity to a Jew of obscure parentage and rebellious spirit.' He also persecutes a doctrine called Communism; this was first preached by one Mazdak, who derived it from early Christian practice, but who wished the community of possession to include not only goods and money but also women. Khosrou enjoys good health, and rules vigorously. I do not know whether it was the Mages or the Greek philosophers who persuaded him that the admiration of posterity for a sovereign is secured less by aggressive war against neighbours than by a record of generosity, justice, culture, the resolute defence of his country, and the energetic pursuance of his subjects' welfare at home and abroad. This, at least, is King Khosrou's present view. Ever since the ravages of the plague, which he regarded as a warning sign from Heaven, he has been most attentive to his people, in a despotic way, and has rebuilt, repopulated, and restocked all those districts which suffered from Roman, Arab, or Hun invasion. Already his grace-name is *Nushirvan* ('The Generous Mind'), and it will be long celebrated in Persian history. They will say of him: 'He protected trade, agriculture, and learning – those were the good days.' For Persia is now strong, prosperous, contented. If only the same could be truly said of our own Empire after the long reign of his ambitious contemporary Justinian!

Now, of King Teudel in the West. Four years after having tacitly agreed, by the recall of Belisarius, to yield all Italy to the Goths – except the city of Ravenna – Justinian found it necessary to renew the war: it was inconvenient for his religious policy that the bishops of North Italy should have broken communion with the Pope Vigilius, and that Arianism should not yet be crushed. He consented to renew the war, but could not bring himself either to provide sufficient forces or to choose a general to command them. On one point only he was resolved: that he would not give Belisarius any further opportunity to distinguish himself. Here was a continual comedy for my mistress and myself to watch, now that we were safe in Constantinople: Justinian playing the capricious tricks that had been so inconvenient to us in Italy. Belisarius made no comment on these matters to us; and I verily believe that he refrained from all hostile criticisms of Imperial policy even in his private mind.

First, Justinian sent Germanus with 5,000 men to Sicily. Then he began to consider that Germanus had been the person recently selected for Emperor by the Armenian assassin, Artaban, and that he was far too closely related to the Goths – he had married Matasontha, formerly King Wittich's wife, and his young son by her was the only surviving male descendant of the great Theoderich. Recalling Germanus suddenly, Justinian gave the command to one Liberius, an old, harmless patrician with no fighting experience at all.

Then someone suggested that Liberius's views on the Incarnation were not quite sound; so he recalled Liberius and (of all people in the world) appointed Artaban, whom he had now forgiven for the attempt on his life and elevated in rank!

But, on second or third thoughts, Artaban might, after all, be ambitious and seek to make himself Emperor of the West. Justinian therefore appointed Germanus again, remembering that it was through his carelessness about the fortification of the rock Orocasias that Antioch had fallen – a man with so black a mark on his record could not be regarded as a rival to himself!

Germanus died, suddenly, on his way to Italy; poisoned, some say, by Matasontha. His command devolved jointly on his lieutenants – Bloody John and Germanus's elder son, Justinian's namesake. Justinian did not wish to give the sole command to Bloody John and thus dishonour his grand-nephew and namesake; nor did he wish any other person with the name of Justinian to win glory. He recalled both officers.

'What next?' my mistress and I asked each other. 'What is the fifth episode of this play, "The Suspicious Glutton"?' Then one day a confidential servant of Narses' came to me and said: 'Friend Eugenius, if I may speak to you unofficially as one domestic to another: is it possible that your mistress, the Illustrious Antonina, would be willing to speak a few words in private to my master, if he suggested it?'

I replied: 'If your master, the Distinguished Narses, has pleasant news for my mistress, she will, of course, be disposed to hear it: at least she will not treat your master with the disrespect that he once showed her and her husband, the Count Belisarius, in Italy. Moreover, my mistress and your master have found themselves working together in harmony on one occasion at least since then – when the trap was laid at Rufinianae for Cappadocian John. The meeting can surely be arranged.'

That preliminary settled, an interview was officially requested and granted. Here was old Narses asking pardon of my mistress for the wrong that he had done her and Belisarius twelve years before! He wished to know whether Belisarius would forgive him sufficiently to offer him advice on a matter of State importance.

My mistress Antonina, who did not underrate Narses' powers and was softened by his apology, offered to act as mediator between Belisarius and himself. Thus a second interview was arranged. Here again all was friendliness. Narses reiterated his regret for having formerly opposed Belisarius's orders and entertained suspicions of his loyalty. Belisarius replied generously, taking Narses' right hand in his own and embracing him.

Narses' question was briefly this: 'Dear friend, do you advise me to accept the honour that the Emperor presses upon me – to command the expedition against the Goths? And if so, upon what terms should I accept it? For I cannot estimate the military situation in Italy, and yours is the only view that would weigh with me.'

The nobility of Belisarius was never shown more clearly than in his answer: 'Dear friend, accept the honour. I know of nobody who has greater capacity than yourself for the task, which is one that must be accomplished for the credit of the Empire; and action must be taken before the Goths recover their former strength. You are asking me, I think, to estimate the number and composition of the forces without which it would be unwise for any general, however energetic, to attempt the reconquest of Italy. My answer is: he would need 30,000 men, and at least 20,000 of these should be cavalry, well mounted, and should include the flower of the Roman army – the scattered squadrons of my Household Regiment which I have trained and tested against the Goths. Also, he would need abundance of money, not only to pay his army well but to win back the allegiance of the soldiers in Italy who for want of money have deserted to the Goths.'

Narses was a shrewd judge of men. He recognized Belisarius as a man incapable of guile and of perfect devotion to the Emperor. He paused awhile and then said: 'I thank you, Belisarius, not merely for your advice but for sparing to remind me of my obstinacy. If it had not been for that, Milan need never have been destroyed.'

Belisarius replied: 'Narses, I honour you for your generosity, and my prayers will go with you.'

Narses accepted the commission from Justinian, but insisted on the terms – not mentioning that Belisarius had framed them. The men and money were found immediately! Narses came again to Belisarius, and with decent humility begged him, in the name of their new friendship, for advice as to the best military means of defeating the Goths.

Belisarius said: 'Offer King Teudel a pitched battle as soon as you have landed, before he has time to collect his troops from the fortresses; no Gothic King can resist a pitched battle, even when his forces are greatly inferior in numbers to the enemy. Stand on the defensive as we did at Daras, posting your foot-archers well forward on either flank, facing inwards. Bait the trap with mail-clad spearmen: King Teudel has had reason to despise the Imperial infantry, who seldom face a cavalry charge.'

Narses objected: 'But if I do as you advise, will not King Teudel, swallowing the bait, carry the trap away with him?'

Belisarius replied: 'There is that danger, and I was therefore about to suggest that your spearmen should be dismounted cavalry, whose courage would be of a higher order.'

'Good. And I must place my light cavalry forward on the flanks, I suppose?'

'Yes. Keep them thrust well out, not near enough to invite attack, but near enough to act as a menace. Hold my Household Regiment, with your other heavy cavalry, in reserve.'

Narses asked: 'But if Teudel attacks the foot-archers first?'

'It would be against the Gothic code of kingly honour to do so. Mailed horseman disdains to attack leather-coated archer.'

Thus the famous Battle of Taginae was won already at the Brazen House at Constantinople, and by Belisarius, though Narses never acknowledged his indebtedness to him, nor did Belisarius ever seek to diminish from Narses' glory by recalling it. The battle, which King Teudel eagerly accepted, began with his lancers charging into the re-entrant that Narses offered them and being raked with distant flanking fire from 8,000 long bows. The confusion caused by the uncontrollable kicking and plunging of a huge number of wounded horses and by the death or unhorsing of most of the chieftains, conspicuous by their armour and trappings, slackened the charge from a gallop to a trot, from a trot to a walk. When momentum is lost, charging cavalry are no match for courageous mail-clad spearmen, and their horses offer a most vulnerable target. Teudel's leading squadron could not break the line of spears; the squadrons behind could do nothing to assist them, and lost heavily from continuous arrow-fire. At last Teudel himself was wounded. The Goths wavered. The Roman spearmen then opened their ranks and the Household Regiment swept through the gap; and it was to the war-cry 'Belisarius' that the Gothic lancers were thrown back upon their own infantry, who became involved in the rout and scattered in all directions.

King Teudel was overtaken and killed a few miles from the battle-field. His blood-stained garments and his jewelled hat were dispatched as trophies of victory to the Emperor at Constantinople.

The dismantling of the fortifications of so many cities by the Goths proved their undoing: there was nothing to oppose Narses' progress. Rome was captured at the first assault by one of his generals. Then the Gothic fleet came over to him. Within two months, after a last engagement on the banks of the Sarno, in the neighbourhood of Mount Vesuvius, the war was won. The surviving Goths were broken in spirit; they agreed either to quit Italy or to submit to Justinian.

Shortly before this agreement was made a venerable institution came to a sudden end. For of the Roman Senators and their families, 300 persons whom Teudel had kept as hostages beyond the Po were butchered in revenge for his death; and the rest, hurrying from Sicily to Rome on news of its capture, were intercepted by the Goths near Vesuvius and likewise destroyed without mercy. The Order had not been revived, and never, I think, will be. Its only excuse for continuance during the last few hundred years had been its riches and its ancient traditions of culture. Justinian inherited the riches; the traditions could not be either recovered or established afresh. So much then for the Senatorial Order of the West, and for King Teudel, and for the Goths – whose name is now extinct in Italy, though there are still Visigothic Kings ruling in Spain.

The end of Bessas: he redeemed his loss of Rome by his success in Colchis, where he recaptured Petra, the capital, from the Persians; and died in honour at Constantinople, not long afterwards. But Petra was once more taken by the Persians. Then a strange coincidence – Dagistheus, the Roman commander at Petra, redeemed his loss of that city by his success in Italy; for it was he who recaptured Rome, lost by Bessas, for Narses.

Narses, who remained in Italy as Governor, won a second great battle on his own account, so that this time the credit goes to his own studies of the art of war. A huge army of Franks had marched down into Southern Italy. Narses surprised their main body at Casilinum in Campania when (as before in Belisarius's time) they had lost half their numbers from dysentery. The Frankish army consisted wholly of infantry armed with sword, spear, and throwing-axe. Narses offered to oppose them with his own infantry; but, as the Franks charged in column, he enveloped their flanks with his squadrons and shot them to pieces at a hundred paces' distance, which was out of the range of their axes. The Franks dared not move forward for fear of being charged on either flank, nor did they dare to break column and attack the cavalry – their art of war demands that they keep close order on all occasions. They died together in a heap, and only five men of 30,000 succeeded in escaping. Narses, perhaps to avoid Justinian's jealousy, ascribed the credit for this victory entirely to the miraculous image of the Virgin that he carried with him, who warned him of all important events.

When Justinian heard of Taginae and Casilinum he praised God and was exceedingly happy. 'Ah,' he is reported to have said, 'why did we not think to send our valiant Narses to Italy long ago? Why did we recall him from the previous campaign, upon a jealous complaint of Count Belisarius? Many lives would have been saved and much treasure spared if we had only trusted to our Narses. We blame ourselves for displaying too great consideration for the feelings of Belisarius, a cowardly and stupid officer; but perhaps such excess of generosity is pardonable in a sovereign.'

Then he returned to his theological studies and, convinced that Italy was safe, that King Khosrou meditated no further mischief on the Eastern frontier, and that the barbarians to the North could be bribed or tricked into fighting one another, he neglected his armies and fortifications more than ever before.

Belisarius, as Commander of the Armies in the East and of the Imperial Guards, three times approached him, begging him to consider the danger to the Empire. After the third attempt an Imperial order came: 'His Serenity forbids this subject to be raised again. God will defend His people who trust in Him, with a strong right hand.'

*

One day, in the autumn of the year of our Lord 558 – which was the year of Bloody John's death, in a hunting accident, after having obediently served with Narses in his Italian campaign, and the tenth year of our renewed residence in Constantinople – Belisarius was handed a message by the master of a Black Sea trading vessel. It was written in the shaking hand of an old man, on a dirty strip of parchment.

'Most Illustrious Belisarius, who rescued my life from Cappadocian John fifty years and more ago, in an inn near Adrianople in Thrace, when you were only a little lad: the time has come to show that Simeon the burgess does not forget this debt of gratitude. The Bulgarian Huns carried me off as a slave long ago in a raid upon Thrace, but have treated me with indulgence because of my skill as a saddler. I have learned their barbarous language and am admitted to their councils, and I confess that I am now better situated in many ways than when I was the slave of rapacious tax-collectors. Only, I miss the good wine of Thrace and the warmth of my well-built house. Know, then, that this winter, if the Danube freezes again, as the weather prophets foretell, a Bulgarian horde will overrun Thrace. They boast that they will attack Constantinople itself and take such plunder as was never taken before since the world began. Zabergan leads them, a capable Cham. Twenty thousand men ride with him. Warn the Emperor. Farewell.'

Belisarius brought the letter to the Emperor's attention. Justinian asked: 'Why this torn strip of parchment, reeking of the docks? Is this a proper document to show an Emperor?'

'A dirty beggar, Your Majesty, who sees smoke curling from the upper windows of a great house, is privileged to come rushing into the hall with a warning cry of "Fire!" The inmates thank him for his timely warning and excuse his rags and rude address.'

Justinian said: 'This, Illustrious Belisarius, is surely one of those military ruses for which you are justly famous? You wish to frighten us by a forgery into increasing our armies and rebuilding the fortifications of the city, knowing well that we have forbidden you to mention the matter directly. We are not deceived, but forgive you for your errors. See to it, my lord, that all disloyalty be banished from your heart. For in times of old there have been generals in this Court who urged upon their Emperors the raising of new armies, pretending an emergency, but planning to use them against the State. Search your heart, my lord, and if you find sin there, pluck it out with Christ's help, for He will grant you strength.'

Now, in the Square of Augustus, opposite the Senate House, Justinian had placed a colossal equestrian statue of himself; it stands upon a very lofty pedestal plated with the finest pale brass. He is shown there in armour of antique pattern and wearing a helmet with an immensely long plume. In his left hand is an orb surmounted by a cross. His right hand is raised in a gesture which is intended to mean: 'Begone, enemies!' But he carries no arms, not even a dagger, as if the gesture and the frown on his face were sufficient discouragement. And indeed in the latter part of his reign he treated his armies as if he had no further use for them. The fact was that Justinian, ambitious of greatness, had acted like the nameless rich man, mentioned in an anecdote by Jesus Christ, who began building a house for himself without first counting the cost, and so fell into debt and ridicule. Justinian's eye, it was said in the city, was the bully of his stomach: he wasted his substance on vain religious luxuries, neglecting his practical military needs.

All agreed that he should never, in the first place, have attempted the conquest and occupation of Africa and Italy with the meagre forces at his disposal. Despite the almost miraculous successes of Belisarius, the double task had proved too heavy for the Imperial armies to perform. True, they still held Carthage and Ravenna, but protracted campaigns had brought these prosperous and well-governed lands to almost complete ruin. Meanwhile, the Northern and Eastern frontiers were weakened by the absence of their garrisons and reserves, and many times breached by invasion, so that a general catastrophe had been only narrowly avoided. The price for the reconquest of the Western Empire was, in a word, its devastation, and the devastation also of Syria, Colchis, Roman Mesopotamia, Illyria, and Thrace: the revenues of which diminished pitiably. Justinian was now obliged to institute a policy of retrenchment; and characteristically began to apply it in the department of Imperial Defence, rather than in that of Ecclesiastical Endowment; hoping, by the foundation or embellishment of still more monasteries, nunneries, churches, to bribe the angelic hosts to assist him, as at other times he had bribed Franks, Slavs, and Huns with gifts of gold or military equipment. He publicly justified his superstitious confidence by the words spoken by Jesus to the Apostle Peter when he resisted the guards of the Jewish High Priest and cut off the ear of one of them: 'Put up again thy sword into its place. For all they that take the sword shall perish with the sword.' He was the more wedded to his pacifism in that he had no fears for his own safety: the soothsayers whom he secretly consulted had all assured him that he would meet a natural death at last in his own bed in the Sacred Apartments of the Palace.

On Christmas Day the Huns crossed the frozen Danube. When the news reached the Court the Emperor ordered masses to be said in all the principal sanctuaries, and spent his whole night in vigil at St Irene's Church; but took no other action. The Huns divided into two bodies, the one to ravage Greece, the other under their Cham Zabergan himself to capture the city. They swept across Thrace unopposed. Being heathen, they felt no respect for churches or convents: they robbed and raped indiscriminately, sending back wagon-loads of treasure and droves of captives along the winter roads and across the Danube. The escorts of these convoys, savage horsemen, forced the pace with whips or the prick of swords; and any captive who fell and did not instantly rise was killed without mercy – even women overtaken with labour pains. The Huns, though in general well-behaved among themselves, count the whole world of Christians as their natural prey, and would think no more of spitting a baptized infant on a lance than they would of transfixing a fawn in the chase.

Zabergan pressed on. The long walls of Anastasius, built across the peninsula at thirty-two miles' distance from the city, were no obstacle to his horsemen: being ruinous in very many places, with no soldiers available to man the breaches, no catapults or other engines ready for use in the towers. On the Feast of the Three Kings, Zabergan camped by the banks of the river Athyras, twenty miles from the city, and panic suddenly overcame the Constantinopolitans. For the public squares were full of unhappy refugees from the villages, with grey faces and small bundles, shouting: 'They come, the Huns come – like a furious herd of wild bulls destroying as they go! O God have mercy upon us!'

This cry spread through the streets: 'God have mercy upon us!' Then every citizen asked his neighbour: 'Where are the men of the Imperial Guard? Where are the city militia? Will no one restrain these Bulgarian devils from storming the inner walls and burning the city down, and destroying every one of us?'

Great crowds of them hired boats and fled across the Bosphorus into Asia Minor, 50,000 persons crossing in a single day.

The Emperor Justinian spent the greater part of these days kneeling in his private chapel. He repeated again and again: 'The Lord is strong. He will deliver us.' The only step of a practical nature that he took was to order that all churches in the suburbs, and all his villas too, should be immediately stripped of their treasures, and these conveyed to the Imperial private port, to be loaded on barges.

At last he sent for Belisarius, and asked: 'How is it, Illustrious Belisarius, Count of our Stables and Commander of our Guards, that you have sent no soldiers to repel these heathen savages?'

Belisarius replied: 'Your Sacred Majesty gave me titles of honour but not the authority that customarily goes with them; and forbade me to mention the unprepared and undisciplined condition of your forces. Three times, on my return from Italy, I presented the same report to you: pointing out that your ministers sold commissions in the Guards to untrained civilians, that no military drill was practised by the soldiers nor any weapons provided, that your stables were empty of cavalry-horses. You ordered me to have no fear for the safety of this city.'

'You lie, you lie,' yelled Justinian. 'If ever by the grace of God we survive this trial of our faith, you shall be made to suffer dreadful things for your neglect of our armies and fortifications, and not all your boasted victories will save you from the rope.'

Belisarius asked: 'But my order meanwhile, Your Majesty?'

'Go and die like a brave man, though you have lived a coward. Gather together what forces you can and meet the Bulgars in the field, thus imitating my gallant Narses – not skulking behind walls as your custom is. Only in this way can you atone for your follies.'

Belisarius made his obeisance, and left the Sacred Presence. But Justinian called his admiral and asked him secretly: 'Is my fleet well provisioned? What weather can we expect in the Mediterranean if we are obliged to sail?'

Belisarius sent a crier through the streets to shout as follows: 'Count Belisarius, by order of his Sacred Majesty the Emperor, will lead an army against the Hunnish invaders. The city militia will take their stations upon the wall of Theodosius according to their Colours, and will provide themselves with what arms they can find. The Imperial Guards will parade under their officers, whose duty it is to see that they are horsed and fully armed, and march down to the Golden Gate, there to await further orders. All veteran soldiers present in this city who have ever served as cuirassiers with the said Count Belisarius in the wars are desired to gather forthwith on the Parade Ground; he will put himself at their head and provide them with arms and horses.'

Belisarius went to the Dancing Masters of the Green and Blue factions. 'In the Emperor's name, I commandeer all the shirts of mail and spears and shields that are worn in the Hippodrome spectacles and in the stage-plays.' He also went to the Race Masters of the Green and Blue factions. 'In the Emperor's name, I commandeer all the horses in the Hippodrome stables.' Of bows and arrows he found sufficient at the Palace and a number of carriage-horses in the Imperial stables, and a few chargers. Thus he found equipment for his veterans.

The Parade Ground is famous in history as the place where Alexander the Great reviewed his troops before setting out for the conquest of the East. Here Belisarius's veterans came crowding from every part of the city – men on whom the years had bestowed most dissimilar fortunes. Some were well-clothed and stout, some in rags and pale, some limped, some strutted. But the light of valour shone in every face, and they cried one to another: 'Greetings, comrade! It is good when old soldiers meet together.'

There were many reunions between former comrades-in-arms who had not met for a number of years, the city being so large. It was: 'You still alive, old Sisifried? I had thought you died with Diogenes on the retreat from Rome', and 'Why, comrade Unigatus, I saw you last at the siege of Osimo, when the javelin pierced your hand', and 'Hey, comrade, do you not know me? We bivouacked together in the Paradise of Grasse under a quincunx of fruit-trees, four and twenty years ago, a few days before the Battle of the Tenth Milestone.' I was there with my mistress Antonina, and had many affectionate greetings from old associates, which warmed my heart.

But there were some who had even longer campaigning memories than myself. There were two men who had raided with Belisarius against the Gepids and these same Bulgarians when he was a beardless young officer.

From a wrestling-school in the suburbs came white-haired Andreas, Belisarius's former satchel-slave and bath-attendant, who had retired from the wars after his two great feats of single combat before Daras. He said: 'In my wrestling-school I have kept supple and strong, my Lord Belisarius, though I am sixty-five years of age. See, I wear the white-plumed helmet that you gave me as a reward at Daras. I have kept it well scoured with sand. Let me be your standard-bearer!'

When they were all assembled, a few more than 300 men, there came sliding up a tall figure, lean with fasting and clad in a monk's robe. He caught at Belisarius's bridle and said: 'O my brother Belisarius, for this one day I put off my robe and lay down my scourge and resume chain-armour. For though I trust that I have made my peace with Heaven for my sins and follies, and especially for the killing of our dear comrade, Armenian John, I cannot die content until I have regained your trust and affection, which I forfeited by my negligence before Milan.'

Belisarius dismounted from his horse and embraced the monk, replying: 'Uliaris, you shall command a hundred men of this force. I have heard of your holiness and good works among the begging brothers of St Bartimaeus, and I accept you as a loan from God.'

Trajan (recently rid of the arrow-head which had been lodged so long in the flesh of his face) commanded another hundred men. He had gained great glory with Narses in Italy. He now kept a tavern at the docks. Thurimuth, the same who had fought so well in Belisarius's second Italian campaign, commanded the remaining troop. He had fallen on evil days and had not long been released from prison; but I do not recall whether it was for felony or heresy that he had been imprisoned. Belisarius allotted each man to a troop, and it was seen that he remembered the name of every one of them who had ever been among his biscuit-eaters, and his record. Next he mounted them, and gave them arms and armour. They were all greatly exhilarated by now. 'Belisarius for ever!' they cried, and 'Lead us at once against the enemy!'

Belisarius was moved. But he replied: 'Comrades, in remembering the glorious battles of long ago do not forget how they were won. They were won not only by courage and skill with arms but by prudence.'

They rode in column, clattering down the High Street. The people cheered and cried: 'Evidently God is with us still – for here comes Belisarius!'

My mistress rode beside him on a palfrey, carrying her head like a young bride; and I followed close behind her on a jennet. She wore a fine red wig, her face was brave with rouge and white lead, and her shrunken bosom well padded. It was only standing close that one could read her age in the wrinkled hands and yellowed eyes, the drawn cheeks and flabby neck.

We came through the suburb of Deuteron to the Golden Gate, where all was confusion – everyone shouting orders, nobody obeying. Not more than fifty of the 2,000 men of the Guards who had answered the summons were provided with horses; nor, apart from two or three officers, did I see a single man wearing a mail-shirt or properly armed; one could be sure that not as many as would make a full company had ever attended a military parade. Even the city militia were a better force of men; for a few score of both the Blue and Green contingents had practised archery at the city butts (shooting on feast-days for the prize of a goose or a sucking-pig or a flagon of wine); and many more had fought by night with swords in faction-feuds.

Belisarius would have added these archers to his small army, but they refused, saying that their obligation was to defend the walls only, and that it was against the laws to lead them out of the city.

From a tower beside the gate we heard the Demarch of the Blues (for the Greens held the other half of the wall) shouting: 'Is there never a man among you all who understands the management of a catapult? There are catapults in every tower and a good store of bolts.'

My mistress Antonina cried out gaily in answer: 'No, never a man, but an old woman in a red wig, a veteran of two defences of Rome! To me she said: 'Come, Eugenius, old soldier, let us teach these recruits their trade.'

So we two dismounted and went up into the tower, where we renewed the ropes of the catapults, which were rotten, and oiled the winches. Then we went from tower to tower, instructing the men at the catapults and scorpions how to repair and handle their machines, and how to lay a sight. If any man did not pay proper attention, or seemed clumsy, my mistress would call him 'bastard of a Green heretic' and switch him over the shoulders with her riding-whip, shaming him before his mates.

Meanwhile Belisarius gathered the weaponless Guards together and added a thousand able-bodied Thracian peasants to them, taken from among the refugees. He told the officers: 'Yonder is a pleasure park of the Emperor's, surrounded by a palisade of stakes. Lead your men there and let them bring back two stakes each from the palisade. These must serve instead of swords and spears. For shield, collect metal salvers and dishes from private houses.'

Then this unwarlike rabble marched out through the gates, Belisarius riding at the head with his 300 veterans. My mistress and I watched him go, with pride and foreboding. She said softly, disregarding the regiment of civilians who followed unhappily behind, like a train of captives: 'Three hundred was the number of the Greeks at Thermopylae, according to the old song. Not a man of them returned, but their name will live for ever.'

I replied, with a smile, to cheer her: 'Unlucky souls, who had no Belisarius to command them!'

But she: 'Against ten or twenty thousand Huns what are these few worn-out men riding out to meet them in battle, by the orders of the Emperor? You expect a miracle, Eugenius?'

I replied: 'I do, having seen many.'

At the village of Chettos, two miles from Melantias, where the Cham Zabergan was encamped, Belisarius set his men to dig a ditch and pile a rampart; and every man planted one of his two stakes on the rampart to form the stockade, keeping the other to carry as a spear. Belisarius sent his veterans forward to dispose themselves as if they were cavalry pickets of a large, widely extended army. Behind them, on a front of five miles, the infantry burned numerous sentry-fires at night; and by day (for the weather had been rainless) dragged bushes along the roads and raised huge clouds of dust.

On the second night an important message came, carried by a peasant boy. It was from old Simeon again, whom the Huns had brought with them as a guide and interpreter. He reported that Zabergan's forces numbered not much more than 7,000 picked cavalry, the remainder of his force having taken the road to Greece; and that they would attack the camp in three days' time, because this was a lucky day in their Calendar.

'And in mine,' cried Belisarius, 'for it is the birthday of my wife Antonina.'

The camp at Chettos was further strengthened with a barrier of thorn-bushes; ploughshares and harrows were scattered in front of the gates to do the work of caltrops. The veterans joked together, calling this 'The Pincian Gate', and that 'The Flaminian', and a little hill to the south was 'The Mausoleum of Hadrian'.

Zabergan learned at last that he had no army against him worth the name, but only the aged Belisarius and a few reckless men. He therefore thought it sufficient to send 2,000 Huns, under his brother, to overwhelm the Imperial camp. Their way led through a wide, thick forest, in which there was a narrow defile; this was a notorious haunt of bandits, whose habit it was to lie in wait for prey among the thick bushes that fringed the track. Here Belisarius prepared an ambush. On one side of the track he hid Trajan's troop, on the other Thurimuth's; and behind them, lining the steep sides of the defile, his army of 'spectators', as he called his stake-armed infantry.

Let me not lengthen the tale unnecessarily. The Huns rode into the ambush without a thought of danger. At the trumpet signal Belisarius and Uliaris charged them suddenly with the remaining troop – Andreas, well ahead of the rest, carried the standard. After the lance, the sword: Belisarius fought in the front rank, cutting and thrusting with all his old precision. For a moment the standard was in jeopardy; but Andreas killed a Hun who tried to snatch it from him, plunging a dagger in his belly. Then Trajan and Thurimuth charged from the rear with their troops, while every man of the spectators yelled as fiercely as if this had been a chariot-race, clashing stakes against mock-shields as though impatient for the order to charge. The Bulgars were terrified. They could not use their bows in that narrow place, nor display their skill in cavalry manoeuvre. They were wearing only buff-coats; which made them the less able to resist the furious onslaught of the mail-clad veterans. They gave way suddenly and streamed back in headlong rout.

Belisarius pressed the pursuit, not heeding the arrows that the Huns fired as they fled; his horses could not easily be wounded, because of the metal poitrails he had improvised for them. His own arrows stung more than the Huns'. Four hundred of the enemy were killed, including the brother of Zabergan, whom Uliaris had transfixed with his lance in the first charge. The remainder fled back to Melantias, crying: 'Home, brothers, home! The spirits of the dead are upon us – aged men with fiery eyes and white hair streaming!' They gashed their cheeks with their nails in sign of lamentation.

The Cham Zabergan broke camp and retreated with his whole army. Belisarius followed him, stage by stage. He had entered that battle with 300 armed men only and finished it with 500. The newcomers were Thracian peasants, chosen from among the recruits as men accustomed to horses and to the use of a light bow for hunting; they had been given the horses and arms of the dead Bulgars. Belisarius's dead numbered three only, though many were wounded; Unigatus, who had fought bravely with his one good arm, died of his wounds a few days later.

Belisarius sent a dispatch to the Emperor: 'Obeying your Sacred orders, we have conquered the enemy and are pursuing him.'

In the streets, jubilation and ceaseless praise for Belisarius – 'This victory of his outshines every former one'; in the Palace, mortification and muttering.

Justinian told his admiral: 'Discharge the cargoes of the vessels. We shall not sail.' His Chamberlain (another than Narses, who was still in Italy) cried in pretended indignation: 'Are the citizens mad that they give thanks for their deliverance not to Your Glorious Serenity who ordained the battle, but to Belisarius – by whose neglect Thrace had been wasted and the city all but lost?'

Justinian sent this message to Belisarius: 'Enough now. Let the Huns go in peace, not wasting lives in vain battles. We may have need for their services in wars against our other enemies. If you pursue them farther you will fall under our displeasure.'

Belisarius obeyed. Then Justinian's messengers rode forward to Zabergan's camp. 'The Emperor's message. Following the example of the Glorious Christ who once, in flesh, ordered His servant Peter to put up his sword after he had valiantly struck at a Jewish officer and wounded him, we have likewise called off our armies. But we conjure you in Christ's name to be gone in peace.'

The Cham Zabergan was puzzled by this message, but understood at least that Belisarius had been recalled. Regaining courage, he continued in Thrace all the summer long, burning and pillaging. In the autumn Justinian offered him money to be gone, and Zabergan, afraid lest his retreat might be cut by a flotilla of armed vessels sent up the Danube from the Black Sea, signed a treaty and withdrew.

Justinian now set himself feverishly to the task of rebuilding the long wall of Anastasius – though he took no steps for the training of a proper defence force. The courtiers cried: 'See how the Father of his people puts his negligent officers to shame!'

When Belisarius and his 300 returned by the Fountain Gate, the Guards and peasants behind them singing the paean of victory, they were greeted with garlands and palms and kisses from the enthusiastic citizenry. From the Palace came only a single, curt message: 'Count Belisarius has overstepped his authority in dismantling the palings of our park at the Golden Gate without a signed authority from the Keeper of the Parks. Let these stakes be restored forthwith.' The last phrase became a byword in the wine-shops: if a man who had done his neighbour a signal service was afterwards taken up sharply by him for some slight fault, the outraged benefactor would exclaim: 'Ay, ay, dear sir, and let the stakes be restored forthwith.'

This Battle of Chettos was the last battle that Count Belisarius fought; and let none doubt that my account is true, since these things were not done far away on a distant frontier, but here close by, not a day's journey from a city of a million inhabitants. One may ride out for an afternoon's pleasure to view the defile, and the two camps, the Cham Zabergan's at Melantias and Count Belisarius's at Chettos, and return to the city again before evening falls.

CHAPTER 24

THE LAST INGRATITUDE

How can I bear to tell of the final cruelty, not possessing his patience or great heart who suffered it? My story has reached the year of our Lord 564, when Justinian had completed the eightieth year of his life and the thirty-seventh of his reign. The Empire was at peace at last, but it was such peace as a sick man attains after the crisis of a violent fever; and none can say, will he recover or will he die.

The Emperor had grown slovenly in appearance and slovenly in speech; and – this stout champion of Orthodoxy, this harsh persecutor of heretics – had now himself lapsed into a scandalous heresy concerning the nature of the Son.

It had been Theodora's view that the body of Jesus Christ had been insensible to fleshly passions and weaknesses, and was in fact incorruptible flesh, and therefore not human flesh; for the character of all ordinary flesh is to corrupt, she said, unless it be converted into a mummy, in the Egyptian fashion, or frozen by accident in a solid block of ice. But the Orthodox view was that Jesus, until the Resurrection, subsisted in corruptible human flesh, and that to deny this was Monophysitism, and detracting from the greatness of the sacrifice that Jesus had made for mankind.

Justinian brought forward Theodora's view (which in her lifetime he had always opposed) as a new discovery of his own; having her arguments fresh in his memory. In an edict he stigmatized those who held the opposite view as 'worshippers of the corruptible'. He required all patriarchs and bishops to assent to this novel article of faith. In trepidation they begged leave to consider the matter for a while. But the Patriarch of Constantinople, who was a careful scholar and a very upright man, tore his clothing and put dust on his head, exclaiming in such terms as these: 'This is worse even than the heresy of the Monophysites – it verges upon the blasphemy of the filthy Manichees, who declare that the two natures of the Son are contradictory. For, my dear brothers, if Jesus Christ, when living here upon earth, was in truth insensible to passions and weaknesses (as His Clemency would have us believe) what shall we say of the famous weeping for Lazarus, and of those protests on the Cross – the plea that the cup of suffering be put from Him? Such acts, testified to by the Holy Evangelists, would be either madness or false feigning if the body of Jesus had, forsooth, been the invulnerable body of a deity.'

The Cathedral clerics informed against the Patriarch, and he was deposed.

Belisarius expressed no opinion on these matters. When Sergius, a leading Senator, questioned him about them, he replied: 'It is difficult enough to live according to the commands of Christ, without perplexing oneself with philosophical inquiries as to His nature. I would as soon busy myself with a critical study of the personal character of the Emperor.'

Sergius looked closely at him to see whether there was sharp satire hidden in his words, but answered: 'Best of men, would not such a study be most illuminating?'

Every day Belisarius attended the Emperor at the Palace; unless the Court was in recess, when he would visit his estates and go hunting there. He remained frugal in habits, generous to the poor, beloved by his friends, and between him and my dear mistress Antonina no words ever passed but words of love and understanding. My mistress conformed to the Christian code of manners, and had by this time abandoned all her pagan ways – except that she still used certain innocent charms for the cure of toothaches and headaches and for immunity from witchcraft. So calm and orderly was the tenor of their lives that it seemed as if they were taking a slow walk together towards the grave, hand in hand, and that no further obstacle would be set in their path, or disaster overtake them.

But Justinian hated Belisarius with an unconquerable hate, and loathed the prospect of dying, to leave his enemy in the enjoyment of unchecked fame and prosperity. 'He has stolen our glory,' was Justinian's cry. 'Our ungrateful subjects have a greater regard for him than for the Sacred Person of their Emperor.'

The infamous Procopius, who had been military secretary to Belisarius in all his wars, had spent some years in writing a long history of them. Being a downright, cantankerous man, not given to flattery, he had told the bitter truth, concealing little or nothing about the treachery of this general and the incompetence of that, and had given due credit to Belisarius for his many victories gained against such enormous odds. He had not directly blamed Justinian for his caprice, incompetence, cruelty, procrastination, meanness, ingratitude, yet had told the historical facts in so straightforward a way that no person with sense, reading them, could fail to form a most unfavourable opinion of the monarch or to conceive the greatest admiration for the general. This history was at last sent to the copying schools at Alexandria, where it was published. It had circulated widely before Justinian became aware of its existence, some five years before the Battle of Chettos.

When Procopius heard that the Emperor was angry and realized that he was in danger of death, he wrote an abject apology. He begged his Master to believe that, if he had written ill, Belisarius was to blame for having given him false information; and he undertook not only to withdraw all copies of the book, but also to write a historical work in eulogy of Justinian's own mighty deeds. Justinian pardoned him, gave him a pension, and raised him to patrician rank. Procopius took good care to speak only slightingly of his former patron, whom he no longer saluted in the streets, in order to retain the Emperor's favour. But Justinian was greatly dissatisfied when the work of eulogy was at last delivered to him. It proved to be only an account of his abstemiousness, his learning and piety, of churches built and fortifications raised. He had expected the former history to be rewritten in another style, so that he and not his subject Belisarius would be given credit for the conquest of Africa and Italy. He stopped Procopius's pension.

Then Procopius in the bitterness of his heart wrote a book of libels not only upon Belisarius and my mistress Antonina but upon the Emperor himself and dead Theodora. Sometimes he told the truth, sometimes he distorted the facts, sometimes he lied – according to his vindictive purposes. (Even I, Eugenius, was introduced into this farrago: for example, I was supposed to have assisted my mistress in the murder of the maid Macedonia: whose tongue, he said, was cut in little pieces and cast into the sea.) Procopius boasted to his friends: 'I have written a book that will put mildew and blight upon the names of certain great ones who have wronged me.' But he kept the book from all eyes, intending it for posterity.

In the autumn after the Battle of Chettos, a fresh conspiracy to assassinate the Emperor was formed by a group of senators, headed by Sergius and Marcellus (the same who had been forgiven by the Emperor for his part in the former plot of Artaban the Armenian). The conspiracy was accidentally discovered and the leaders forced to betray the names of their accomplices. Among these leaders was Herodian, the general who had once surrendered Spoleto to King Teudel as an act of spite against Belisarius and then deserted to the Goths; after Teudel's death he had surrendered Cumae to Narses, and been pardoned by Justinian. On Herodian's return to Constantinople, Belisarius had taken action against him in the courts and recovered the debt of 50,000 pieces of gold which had figured in the story of the surrender of Spoleto. Herodian now, to escape the certain punishment of death, ransomed himself by a false confession that Belisarius was the originator of the plot against Justinian's life. At his suggestion Apion the Public Prosecutor sent his agents to break into Procopius's house in search of documents incriminating Belisarius. Here, locked in a chest, they found the revengeful book of anecdotes. Apion read it, and thereupon threatened that Procopius would be strangled for his insults to the Emperor's Majesty – unless he consented to give such evidence as would secure Belisarius's conviction as a traitor. Procopius consented, and the book was returned to him. Now it will be understood why I name him the infamous Procopius.

Apion came to Belisarius's house early one morning, accompanied by two shorthand writers to the Crown and a party of soldiers. They found him playing at hand-ball before his plunge in the swimming-pool. I was among the players, keeping the goal. Belisarius greeted Apion cheerfully and said: 'Are you not the newly appointed Public Prosecutor? This is indeed an early call. Will you join us at breakfast after I have had my plunge?'

Apion answered very gravely: 'His Sacred Majesty's business cannot wait either for your breakfast or mine, nor for any cold plunge. Put on your garments immediately, Count Belisarius. I have a warrant for your arrest on a charge of high treason. Soldiers, seize these domestics; their evidence will be needed.'

Belisarius said to me: 'Eugenius, note down the score of goals; we will conclude this game at some other time. Then beg your mistress, the Lady Antonina, to descend as soon as she conveniently can.'

But they prevented me from fetching my mistress. Apion said: 'The domestics of the Illustrious Antonina are also to be detained.'

Belisarius dressed himself and invited Apion and the soldiers to come into the tepid room, the day being cold. There Apion read out his warrant, in some such words as these:

To the Illustrious Patrician Belisarius, Count of the Imperial Stables, Commander of the Imperial Bodyguard and of the Armies in the East, Greeting!

Know, Belisarius, by these presents that we Justinian, your Emperor, are displeased with you and require you to submit peacefully to our officer, the Distinguished Public Prosecutor Apion, when he comes with soldiers to apprehend you.

You have repeatedly, over a course of many years, proved yourself a disloyal and mischievous subject, caring more for your own safety, wealth, and glory than for the Sacred Interests of your Master; as the following record will make clear.

First, in the fifth year of our reign, you did permit half of our City of Constantinople to be plundered and burned by the factious mob, before taking action against the ring-leaders, the traitors Hypatius and Pompey.

Item, when we sent you against the Vandals in Africa in the sixth year of our reign you did propose and intend to usurp our sovereignty in that Diocese; but certain loyal generals warned us of your guilt and we recalled you before you could do us that mischief.

Item, when we sent you against the Goths in Italy, in the eighth year of our reign, you did wilfully disregard our written instructions and conclude a peace with the enemy other than that we had authorized. You furthermore did enter into secret correspondence with the Goths and offer yourself to them as a candidate for the Empire of the West, again intending and proposing to usurp our sovereignty; but once more we prevented you. You returned home to this City leaving the Goths unconquered, which was a great hindrance to us.

Item, when we sent you against the Persians, in the thirteenth year of our reign, you avoided battle with them and allowed them to return home unmolested and to destroy our great city of Callinicum.

Item, in the fourteenth year of our reign, when we sent you once more against the Persians, you failed to take advantage of the King's absence, he being then at the task of devastating our territory of Colchis: you did not cross over into Assyria and lay waste the land and rescue the captives taken at Antioch, though that would have been an easy matter; nor did you cut off the King's retreat from the said territory of Colchis.

Item, in the same year you also uttered treasonable words against our beloved Empress, Theodora, now with God.

Item, in the seventeenth year of our reign, when we sent you once more against the Goths in Italy, you accomplished nothing of note, wasted our treasure and forces and returned home after five years, leaving the Goths to be defeated at last by our faithful Chamberlain Narses. From Italy you wrote contumacious and threatening letters to us, and on your return were a party to a conspiracy against our life made by Artaban the Armenian.

Item, in the thirty-second year of our reign, after you had neglected our fortifications and the troops under your command, thus encouraging a barbarian inroad, you arrogated for yourself the glory of the repulse of these Huns, which belonged first to God Almighty and next to ourselves; just as in former times you had attempted to usurp the glory which we won against the Persians, Vandals, Moors, Goths, Franks, and other nations, making a show of yourself to the City mob and courting their favour with largesse.

What patience and long-suffering we have displayed, how many times we have pardoned you for your impudent acts and words!

Now, in this thirty-seventh year of our reign, it has come to our notice that you are implicated in another plot against our life. Our generals Herodian and John (vulgarly surnamed 'The Epicure') confess that you attempted to seduce them from their loyalty to us, and the Distinguished Patrician, Lord Procopius, who was formerly your military secretary, has denounced you to us for the same heinous crime. These confess that you agreed with them for a set day when a murderous attack should be made upon us with swords in our very Council Chamber, while we sat upon our Throne, and wore the Sacred vestments of Royalty. They feigned to consent, but were full of fear and repeated your words to our officers.

Know then, Traitor, that our royal pardon, so often freely granted, must be withheld at last; for a criminal who sinned constantly when his locks were black, and sins still while his locks are white, is not redeemable to virtue. It would be weakness in us to forgive beyond the scriptural limit of seventy times seven.

Obey!

Belisarius asked Apion when he had finished: 'Who prepared this warrant for His Clemency's signature?'

Apion answered: 'I myself.'

'You seem by your speech to be a Thracian from the district of Adrianople. Do I recognize you after the lapse of so many years? Were we not schoolmates together under the learned Malthus?'

Apion's face grew red, for he could not forget what a mean figure he had cut in the eyes of his schoolfellows. He answered: 'That is neither here nor there.'

We domestics were led away to the prison and put to the torture, one by one – both slaves and freedmen, from the youngest foot-page to Andreas and myself, who were both close upon seventy years of age. We were racked and scourged; and twisted cords were bound tightly around our foreheads, and our feet were burned in a charcoal brazier. For some the torture was made more severe than for others. I was chained in a cell with Andreas before we were taken out to the torture. He had witnessed the arrest of Belisarius, and was hot with fury against Apion. 'The Public Prosecutor has followed a most glorious career while his schoolfellow was commanding the armies of the Emperor – quills, ink, parchment, humility, bribery! After twenty years as spare clerk, he attains the dignity of shorthand writer to the Crown; twenty years more and he is Assistant Registrar-General. Five more and he is Public Prosecutor, waited upon subserviently by the whole tribe – copy-clerks, messengers, process-servers, gaolers, policemen. A little copy-clerk boasts to his comrades: "The Distinguished Apion honoured me with a smile today, and remembered my name." Now bribes are taken, not offered; humility is laid aside. He is the fearful Torture-Master – lord of chains, scourges, racks, branding-irons, the taste of which now awaits us.' Andreas also said: 'That snivelling little Apion! I can still see him crouched in a corner of the schoolroom, glowering at us because he was given no spiced bun – having shirked the snow-battle with the oblates. O bun of discord! I think we must persuade the President of the Streets to remove the Elephant from his pedestal and set up a statue of the distinguished Apion in his place.'

Andreas died under the torture, but in order to vex Apion he did not utter a single cry. I yelled and screamed without ceasing. I knew that to do so would either satisfy the officer of the torture chamber or else disconcert him, so that he would say to the slave: 'Enough for the moment, fellow: relax the cords, unscrew!' All my cries were: 'Long life to his Gracious Majesty!' and 'I know nothing, nothing.' So I escaped. Of the bodily injuries that I received that day I shall not trouble you. I am a person of no importance.

The inquisitors asked me again and again: 'Did you not hear the traitor Belisarius in conversation with Marcellus the Patrician – did he not utter treasonable phrases? See, here are written the words which your fellow-domestics heard him speak one evening at dinner with your mistress. Are you sure that you did not hear the same words yourself? They all swear that you were present.'

I denied everything and maintained that Belisarius was the best and kindest and most loyal of men. However, others confessed to all that was necessary, because of the torture.

I was not present at the trial, which took place in the month of January behind closed doors. They say that Belisarius made no reply to any of the charges except to deny them. There were wilder ones than those of treason. For he was accused of committing sodomy upon his adopted son Theodosius and filthiness upon his stepdaughter Martha. He asked leave to cross-examine the witnesses for the prosecution – Herodian, John the Epicure, and Procopius; but this was refused by Justinian, who judged the case in person. They say also that when Justinian taunted him with the mockery of a fair trial, by asking: 'Are there any reputable witnesses whom you would wish to call, my lord, to testify that you are no traitor?' he replied: 'There are four.'

'And who are they? Are they present in the city?'

'No, Clemency.'

'Name them, nevertheless.'

'Geilimer, formerly King of the Vandals; Wittich, formerly King of the Goths; Khosrou, the Great King of Persia; Zabergan, Grand Cham of the Bulgarian Huns. These know to their cost that I am no traitor.'

*

My mistress Antonina was charged as an accomplice. They say that when she was brought into Court she spoke in a rambling way, as if already in her dotage, bringing up foul memories of Justinian's life before he became Emperor. Her talk, they say, was very fanciful and sarcastic. She said: 'My friend Theodora of the Blue club-house had a little lap-dog, most gluttonous and lecherous. She used to talk theological nonsense to him all night and feed him with lumps of raw meat; and he was a fawning, inquisitive little dog and would lick every foot in the city and sniff at every street corner. We called him Caesar, but he had a barbarous Gothic name before that.'

She also said: 'Your worship, I knew a little, smiling, rosy-cheeked man once who committed fornication with three generations of women.' (She meant the Lady Chrysomallo, her daughter, and granddaughter.) 'He offered prayers to Beelzebub and never learned to speak good Greek. But in pity I was courteous to such a little, smiling, rosy-cheeked man.'

Justinian was agitated. He closed her case in haste: 'This noble lady has lost her wits. She must be put in charge of doctors. She is not fit to plead.'

Yet my mistress continued: 'The pretty girls of the Blue club-house all made the same complaints about Phagon the Glutton. They said that his demands on them were unnatural; that he was stingy with love-gifts; that he confused spiritual ecstasy with that of flesh – worshipping the corruptible; and that he smelt of goat.'

'Remove her, remove her!' Justinian cried in a shrill voice.

'Of goat and incense mixed. He was a bed-wetter, also, and had warts upon his thighs.'

The sentences were promulgated. The penalties were various. To some death by the axe, to some death by the rope, to others lifelong imprisonment. To Herodian and John the Epicure, pardon.

My mistress was confined in the Castle of Repentance which Theodora had built at Hieron, and her property given into the keeping of the Church. Belisarius's life was spared. But he was deprived of all his honours and all his possessions in land and treasure, and disqualified even from drawing the common dole. But still another fearful vengeance was taken upon him. Alas, now! Let me write it quickly: the light of both his eyes was quenched in the Brazen House that same evening with red-hot needles.

*

My mistress, prostrate on her pallet in the sick ward of the Castle, called for me at midnight and said: 'Eugenius, do you fear the Emperor more than you love me and my dear husband?'

'What do you ask of me, mistress? I am yours to command.'

'Eugenius, take a boat across the Bosphorus and stand near the Brazen House, but out of sight; and be ready to act as a guide to my Belisarius when he is set free tomorrow. They will release him very early before the streets are full of people.'

I waited in the Square of Augustus, near the Brazen House, for many hours. At dawn I saw him rudely thrust out of the gate by two drunken soldiers. One cried: 'Go and seek your fortune now, old man. You are free as air.'

'Ay,' cried the other. 'No money, no home, no eyes, no fame!'

But a young corporal came out and reproved them: 'You are two ill-conditioned beasts, who have never raised your heads above your trough of swill. Go now at once, I order you, and lie upon your backs on the pavement of the Brazen House. Gaze up at the mosaics on the ceiling and observe the pictured battles there. You will see the great victories of the Tenth Milestone and Tricameron, and the capture of Naples, and the defence of Rome, and the victory at the Mulvian Bridge. From whom does the Emperor in those pictures receive the spoils of victory – kings and kingdoms and all that is most valued by monarchs? Why, from this Belisarius, whom you now insult in his blindness, denying that any fame remains to him!'

Belisarius, turning his sightless face towards the Corporal, said: 'Softly, best of men! Whom the Emperor hates, shall his soldiers praise?'

The Corporal replied: 'My father fought in Persia and in Africa with your Household Squadron, and fell at Rome defending Hadrian's mausoleum. If these ruffians take fame from you, they dishonour my father's memory. Accept this broken spear-staff, brave one, to steady your faltering steps. I do not care who hears me say: "Fame cannot be quenched with a needle."'

The streets were empty of all but scavengers and homeless beggars. Belisarius, staff in hand, walked with many pauses down the High Street, across the coloured marble flags of the pavement; I followed him at a little distance. When he reached the statue of the Elephant he stopped to finger the rugged legs of the beast. I heard him mutter idly to himself: 'Behold now Behemoth whom I made with thee; he eateth grass like an ox. His bones are as strong pieces of brass, his bones are like bars of iron. He is the chief of the ways of God.'

Presently he spoke again more to the purpose, quoting from the same book: 'Behold I cry out of wrong but I am not heard, I cry aloud but there is not judgement. He hath fenced up my way that I cannot pass, and he hath set darkness in my paths. He hath stripped me of my glory.'

Then I spoke softly from behind him and said: 'My lord, this is I, Eugenius the eunuch. My dear mistress Antonina sent me here to be your guide.'

He turned and reached out his hand for mine, drew me to him, and embraced me. Then he asked anxiously after my mistress, and I gave him her sorrowful messages of love. As we walked on, he ate the white bread and fruit that I had brought from her for his breakfast.

Belisarius asked me to guide him to the suburb of Blachernae; he went with such great strides through the empty squares and streets that it seemed rather that he was guiding me than I him. Nobody heeded us. An easterly wind brought the smell of new bread from the municipal bakeries, which he remarked upon; and as we passed through the docks in the district of Zeugma he snuffed with his nose and said: 'I smell cinnamon and sandalwood and sailors. This blindness will make a very dog of me.'

At last we came to the monastery of St Bartimaeus at Blachernae. There Belisarius rapped with his staff on the postern gate, and a lay-brother opened.

Belisarius demanded to see the Abbot, but the lay-brother replied: 'He is at his accounts; I cannot disturb him for such as you.'

Belisarius said: 'Tell him, I beg, that my name is Belisarius.'

The lay-brother laughed at what he judged to be a pleasantry. For Belisarius was dressed in a commoner's tunic, soiled by prison wear, and had a dirty clout fastened over his eyes.

The lay-brother joked: 'And my name is the Apostle Peter.'

Through the door I perceived the monk Uliaris passing along a passage on some errand. I cried out to him: 'Brother Uliaris, to the rescue!'

Uliaris hurried to the door. When he perceived Belisarius's fate, he wept bitterly and cried out: 'O dear friend, O dear friend!' – not finding other words.

Belisarius said: 'Uliaris, beloved comrade, go, I beg you, to your reverend Abbot and obtain from him a certain possession of mine, which I once lent to his predecessor until I should have need of it. It is the wooden begging bowl of St Bartimaeus, your patron: the hour of my need is now.'

Uliaris went to the Abbot, who at first would not yield up the bowl. He protested that it was a sacred relic, not to be handled by profane hands, and, moreover, a great source of revenue to the monastery; and that the Emperor would be angry if charity were shown to Belisarius.

Uliaris told the Abbot: 'God will assuredly curse our house if we withhold this bowl from the rightful owner, by whose generosity we have benefited these thirty years.'

Then the Abbot consented, though unwillingly, and gave Uliaris the key to the jewelled chest in which the bowl was kept. Uliaris came out again to us and delivered up the bowl.

Belisarius traced the carved inscription with his finger, repeating aloud the words 'Poverty and Patience'. Uliaris was still so oppressed by grief and astonishment that he found no words of farewell. He embraced Belisarius and went inside again.

Belisarius and I now made our way to the suburb of Deuteron by the Golden Gate. We stopped at the portico of a church of the Virgin. Here Belisarius sat down to beg on the steps; but the beadle, not knowing him, drove him away roughly. He suffered the same treatment at the Churches of St Anne, St George, St Paul, and the Martyr Zoe. For these beadles reserve the church steps for certain professional beggars who pay them a proportion of their alms in return for the privilege. At last he asked me to guide him to the monastery of Job the Prophet, not far off, where at last he met with kindness. For a beggar already posted there recognized him and rushed to weep upon his neck; it was Thurimuth, the guardsman, again fallen on evil times.

Belisarius sat down against a buttress of the cloister, crossing his legs. By this time the streets had begun to fill. With the bowl upon his lap he called in a clear, proud voice: 'Alms, alms! Spare a copper for Belisarius! Spare a copper for Belisarius who once scattered gold in these streets! Spare a copper for Belisarius, good people of Constantinople! Alms, alms!'

At this strange cry, which seemed a command rather than a plea, a great crowd began to gather; and a common wonder gave place to common indignation when they recognized their former hero and saviour – a blind beggar at the roadside. Soon money rained into the bowl, silver and gold pieces mixing with the copper. Though some shrouded their faces with their cloaks as they gave, there were many men of rank and substance who did not so conceal themselves, and also many women.

Now certain of his veterans gathered at the news. They formed as it were a bodyguard to prevent the people from pressing too closely upon him, so that each passed by singly, paying his debt of gratitude to Belisarius for the city's deliverance from the Huns. Thurimuth had fetched a sack: as often as the bowl was filled he emptied the coins into the sack and gave the bowl to Belisarius again. Before evening fell forty thousand people had passed, and there were many sacks full of money. But still Belisarius chanted: 'Spare a copper for Belisarius, good people of Constantinople! Alms, alms!' All gave according to their quality – poor old women gave farthings, and children halfpence. Even the prostitutes contributed silver from their night earnings. One man brought a broad gold piece, quoting: 'Whose is the image and superscription?' It was an example of the medal struck after the conquest of Africa, proclaiming Belisarius 'The Glory of the Romans'.

When Justinian heard what was happening he was both angry and alarmed. The temper of the people was rising, and there were disloyal shouts in the streets and demonstrations before the Palace. On the walls of the public buildings were scrawled in chalk such phrases as these: in Latin, '*Justinianus ab injustitiis*' (Justinian, so called for his injustices) and, in Greek, 'Samson in his blindness destroyed a King and his Court.'

Justinian sent hurriedly for his Chamberlain, and ordered that a pardon be drafted; which he signed, restoring to Belisarius all his titles and property. Presently the blind man was escorted in honour back to his own house by his faithful veterans. He divided among them the money which he had collected – it amounted to 200 gold pieces for each man. But the bowl he returned to the Abbot.

My mistress Antonina was now released from the Castle of Repentance. For the few weeks that remained to Belisarius of life, he enjoyed perfect serenity. My mistress Antonina was constantly by his side; and every day three or four of his veterans called upon him for a gossip about old times, arranging the turns among themselves. He was forbidden to leave the grounds of his house, for Justinian was afraid of the people; but such regard was shown for him, and so many people were anxious to call upon him, that it seemed rather that he held a Court here than lived under a sentence of detention.

Belisarius died in his sleep on the thirteenth day of March in the year of our Lord 565. It was thought a remarkable thing, when his body was laid out for burial, that he had no scars at all to show for so many bloody battles fought all the world over. My mistress Antonina, who took his death calmly, as he would have wished, said: 'Ay, the only injuries that he ever suffered were at the hands of his own Emperor.'

Before the year was out, on the thirteenth day of November, Justinian, too, was dead, of a gangrene. Where the souls of each went, let the Christians dispute. But they say that Justinian's end was both noisome and weird; and that as he finally gave up the ghost, squeaking with terror, the voice of the Father of Lies rang through the Palace rooms, in sinister parody of the Scriptures: 'This is my beloved Son, in whom I am well pleased.'

Justinian had his desire in outliving his enemy Belisarius. But, of the four persons so closely linked together in this story – Justinian, Theodora, Belisarius, Antonina – the longest-lived was my dear mistress. After Belisarius's death she became very quiet, and soon I was the only person for whom she had a word. Finally, she asked me to take her to the convent where her daughter Joannina was now Abbess; and there, not long after making her peace with Joannina, she died. She bequeathed all her money to the same convent, except for an annuity sufficient for my needs.

I outlive even Narses. Let me tell of his end and then be done. At Justinian's death, Justin succeeded to the Empire – not his grand-nephew Justin, Germanus's son, but an elderly cousin, the son of Justinian's sister Vigilantia. Then Narses, still the Governor of Italy, was informed against by a deputation of Italians who came to Justin at Constantinople. Narses had ruled well and firmly, but the poverty of the country was such that his collection of the revenues could not but seem oppressive. Justin consented to dismiss Narses, writing to Italy that he was excused from further command because of his great age. Narses, yielding his authority and title to a certain Longinus, left his Palace at Ravenna, and retired to a villa at Naples. There he received an offensive private letter from Sophia, grand-daughter of Theodora's sister Anastasia, now Justin's Empress: in it Sophia cruelly observed that he did well to leave the profession of arms to men, and enjoined him to resume his former occupation of wool-spinning among the Palace maidens. The reason for this expression of ill-will was an unforgiven slight that Narses had once put upon her while he was Chamberlain.

When Narses read her letter, he cried aloud: 'I will spin Her Resplendency such a thread as she shall not unravel all her life.' Thereupon he proceeded to spin a thread of intrigue with the enemy across the Northern frontier. (Though you may disbelieve it, Narses was ninety-four years of age, but as active in mind and body as many a man of fifty. At the age of ninety-one he had gained a great victory in the North against one Count Vidinus, a rebel, and against the Franks and Alemans who supported him.)

Justin had been aware that the savage Lombards were meditating an invasion of Italy, and was anxious that his friend Longinus, the new Governor of Italy, should gain the glory of repelling them. But Narses, having determined to be revenged on the Empress Sophia, sent a messenger to King Alboin of the Lombards, saying: 'The Emperor has removed me from my command and thrown open the fertile fields of Italy to your resolute warriors.'

These Germans thereupon invaded Northern Italy by way of the

Brenner Pass. Narses wrote to Justin, volunteering to repel Alboin if immediately restored to his command. But Justin paid no attention to him. Then the Lombards, whom Longinus lacked the resolution to oppose, seized all Italy to the north of the Po, and occupy it securely to this day.

Narses died of remorse.

*

Now what must be said of Belisarius's patient submission to the cruelty and caprice of Justinian, his Emperor? Some have held, because of this, that his character stands far higher than an ordinary man's; others that it falls far below, being equal to that of a poltroon. The matter could be disputed endlessly. What holds more weight with me than any idle philosophical argument is my knowledge of Belisarius's own views. For, just as he did not hold with the Donatists of Africa, who refused to accept the Sacraments from the hands of an evil-living priest but only from one of unblemished reputation; so he did not hold with political Donatists, who constituted themselves critics of those set in authority over them, and ruined all by their disobedience and ignorance. For my part, being a domestic, I find the surest index to a man's character in his treatment of domestics: it mirrors the dignity with which he comports himself towards those set in authority over him. Belisarius was the sweetest master, I believe, that ever servant had.

There is this to be noted: though Justinian treated Belisarius execrably, he never once ordered him to perform any act that was plainly against the laws of God; for Belisarius would not have obeyed, be sure, holding the laws of God as superior to any commands of man.

And there is this too: Justinian, for all his supposed dealings with Beelzebub, was very zealous for the Christian faith. He kept vigils, fasted, built and enriched monasteries and churches, discouraged infidelity, enlarged the temporal powers of the bishops – and obeyed in all seriousness the ironic injunction of Jesus to turn the other cheek to those who smote it. Thus: he paid money to the Cham Zabergan who had devastated Thrace, he conferred patrician rank on Artaban the assassin, he honoured such proved traitors as Herodian and John the Epicure. After Theodora's death he even recalled the beggared Cappadocian John to the city from Alexandria and cosseted him again. Yes, to evil-doers the Emperor was extravagantly forgiving. But with honest men he was at a loss, since Christian doctrine chiefly instructs how to treat with sinners, oppressors, slanderers, and traitors, but gives little indication for the reward of natural virtue. (It is more blessed to give than to receive; to forgive than to be forgiven.) Thus Justinian rewarded Hypatius with death for his uprightness of conduct during the Victory Riots; and treated the noble Germanus with suspicion and disdain; and with Belisarius played the very fiend. My meaning is: I think that Belisarius pitied Justinian for wishing to be a Christian and yet wanting the knowledge of how to set about it.

According to the Evangelists, Jesus Christ spoke a parable once about a strayed sheep rescued at last by the shepherd; and drew the moral that there is more joy in Heaven over one sinner who repents than over ninety-nine just men who have no need for repentance. Here, no doubt, Jesus spoke ironically again, meaning by 'just men' the mean and self-righteous. But Justinian, in his old age, absurdly improving on the parable, seemed to have decided that the shepherd must insult and torture the single sheep who remained dutifully in the sheep-fold rather than stray out with his ninety-nine depraved fellows; and to have drawn the moral that there is indignation in Heaven when any person (other than the Son of God Himself) behaves with inflexible probity. This view is not uncommon among eminent theologians, luxuriously aware of their own sinful impulses.

'Under the Old Gods', my former master Damocles used to say, somewhat exaggerating the case, 'virtue was always honoured, ignominy frowned upon; the felon's cross was not gilded and jewelled; man did not revel in self-abasement.' But let anyone believe what he pleases. And if he happens to be a simple devotee of virtue, not a logic-chopping, hypocritical theologian or perverted ascetic, this story will not offend him, but contrariwise confirm him in his principles. For Count Belisarius had such a simple devotion to virtue, from which he never declined. Those of you for whom the Gospel story carries historical weight may perhaps say that Belisarius behaved at his trial before Justinian very much as his Master had done before Pontius Pilate, the Governor of Judaea – when unjustly accused of the very same crime, namely treason against the Empire; and that he suffered no less patiently.

So much, then, for these things.

THE END

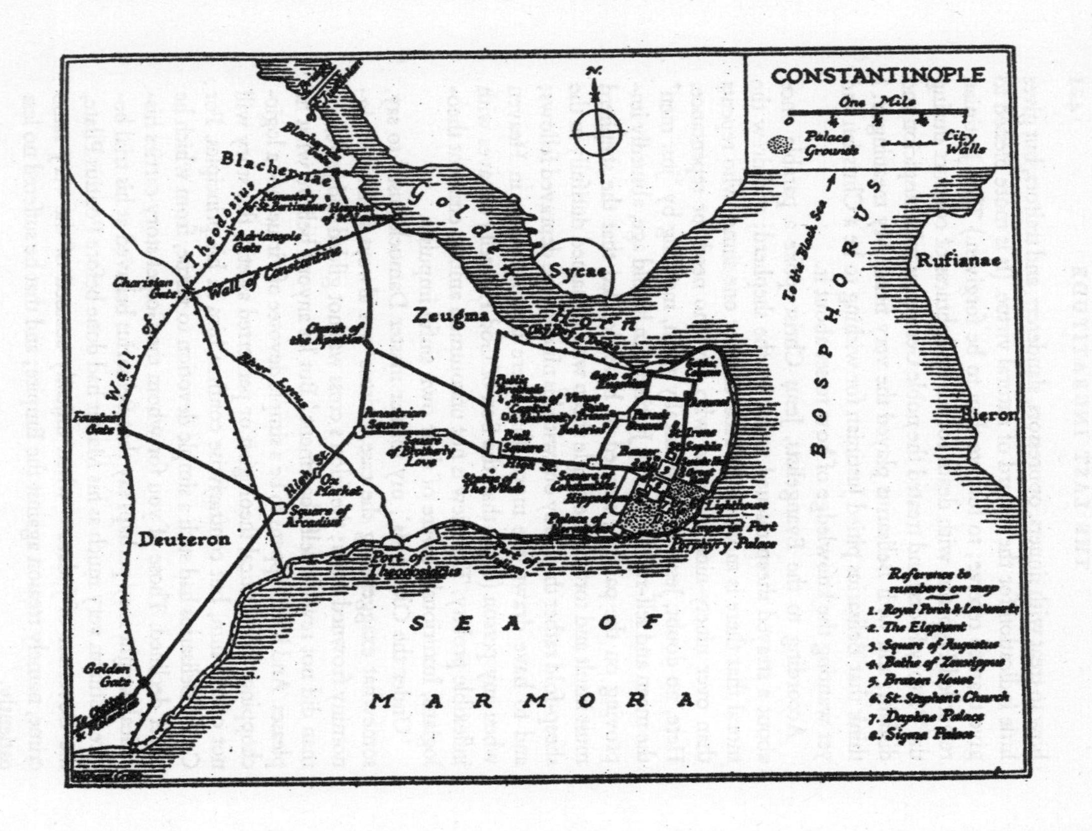
CONSTANTINOPLE
One Mile
0
1
Palace Grounds
City Walls
N.
To the Black Sea
BOSPHORUS
Rufianae
Hieron
Golden Horn
Sycae
Zeugma
Blachernae
Wall of Theodosius
Adrianople Gate
Wall of Constantine
Charisian Gate
Church of the Apostles
River Lycus
Fountain Gate
Amastrian Square
Square of Brotherly Love
Bull Square
High St.
Ox Market
Square of Arcadius
Statue of The Winds
Square of Constantine
Hippodrome
Deuteron
Port of Theodosius
Lighthouse
Imperial Port
Porphyry Palace
Arsenal
St. Irene
St. Sophia
Golden Gate
SEA OF MARMORA
Reference to numbers on map
1. Royal Porch & Lavatory
2. The Elephant
3. Square of Augustus
4. Baths of Zeuxippus
5. Brazen House
6. St. Stephen's Church
7. Daphne Palace
8. Sigma Palace

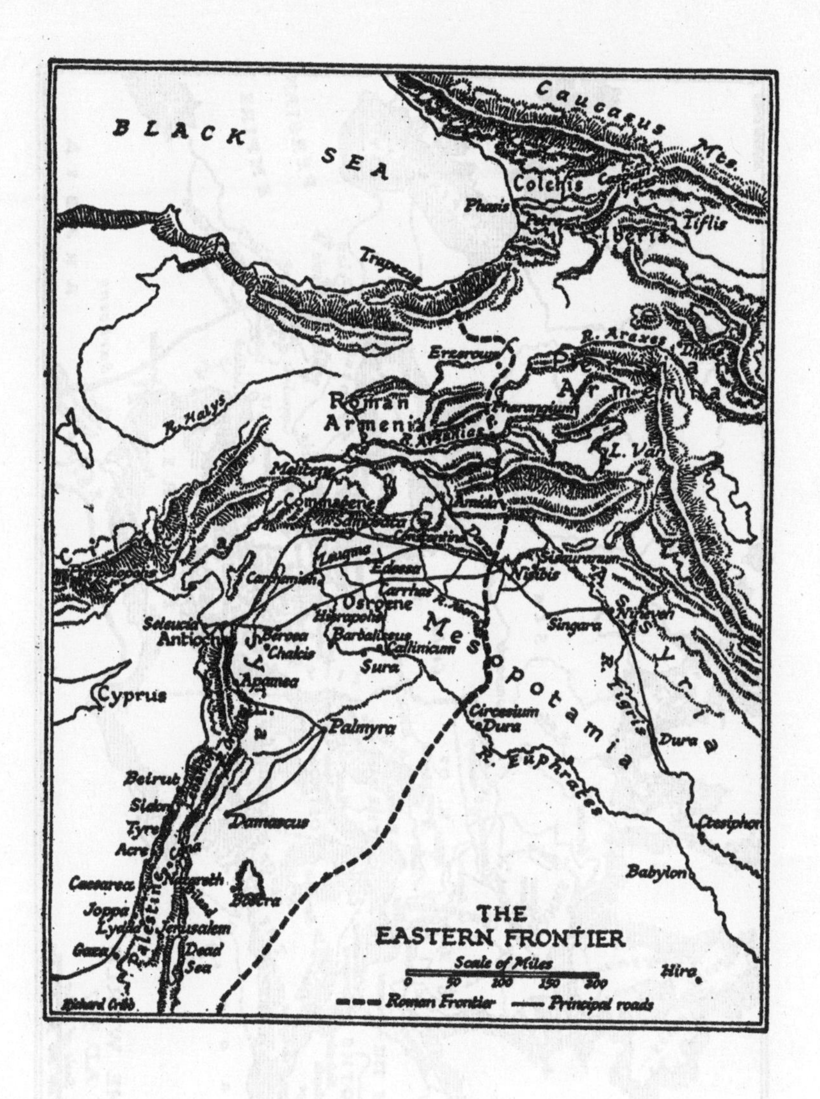
BLACK SEA
Caucasus Mts.
Colchis
Phasis
Tiflis
Iberia
Trapezus
R. Araxes
Erzeroum
Persarmenia
Roman Armenia
R. Halys
L. Van
Melitene
Commagene
Amida
Edessa
Nisibis
Carrhae
Osrhoene
Mesopotamia
Assyria
Nineveh
Singara
Seleucia
Antioch
Beroea
Chalcis
Barbalissus
Callinicum
Sura
Apamea
Cyprus
Circesium
Dura
Palmyra
R. Tigris
R. Euphrates
Beirut
Sidon
Tyre
Acre
Damascus
Caesarea
Nazareth
Bostra
Joppa
Lydda
Jerusalem
Gaza
Palestine
Dead Sea
Ctesiphon
Babylon
Hira
THE EASTERN FRONTIER
Scale of Miles
0 50 100 150 200
Roman Frontier
Principal roads
Richard Cribb

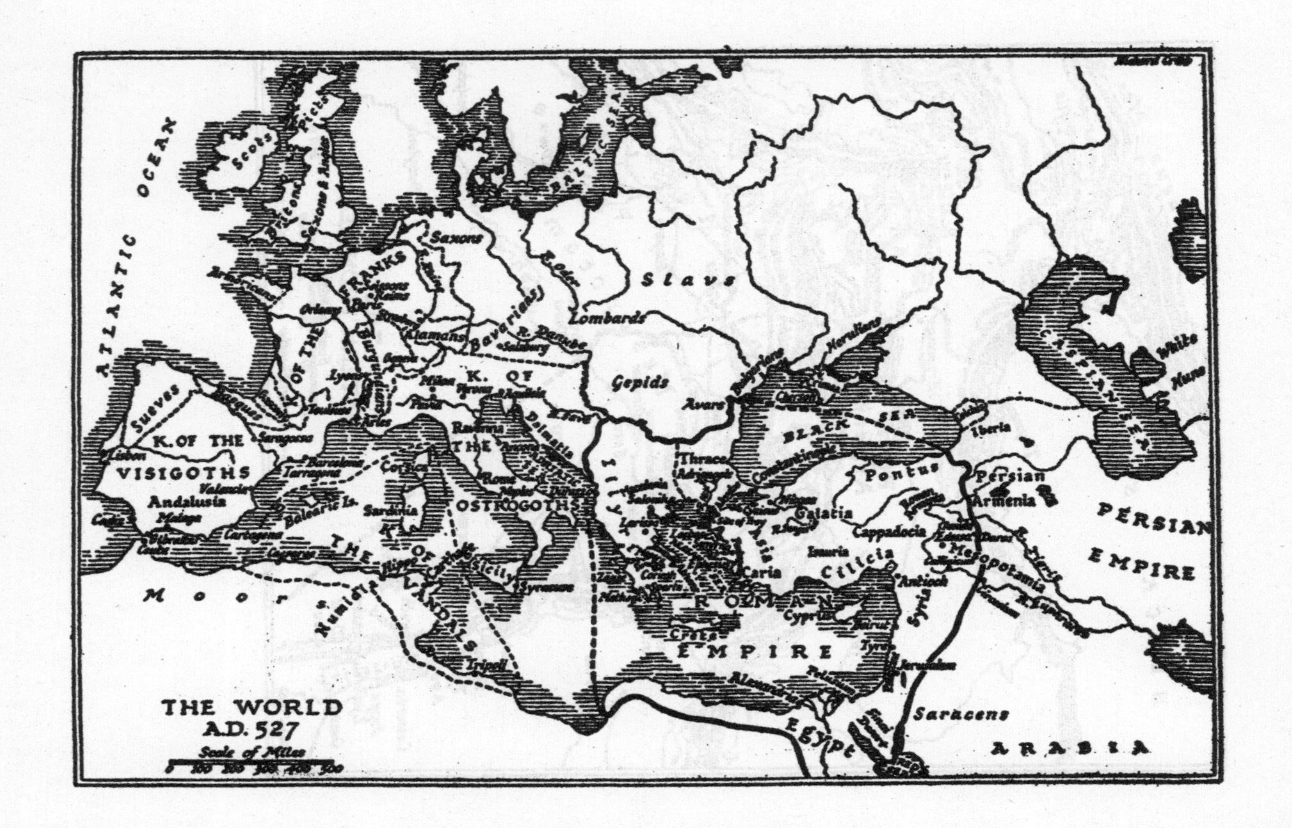

ATLANTIC OCEAN
Scots
Picts
Britons
Saxons & Angles
Armoricans
FRANKS
Saxons
Paris
Orleans
K. OF THE Burgundians
Lyons
Toulouse
Arles
Alamans
Bavarians
R. Danube
Salzburg
BALTIC SEA
R. Oder
Slavs
Lombards
Gepids
Avars
Herulians
K. OF THE OSTROGOTHS
Milan
Verona
Pavia
Ravenna
Rome
Naples
Dalmatia
R. Save
Corsica
Sardinia
Sicily
Syracuse
Suevès
Basques
K. OF THE VISIGOTHS
Lisbon
Saragossa
Barcelona
Tarragona
Valencia
Andalusia
Malaga
Cadiz
Gibraltar
Ceuta
Cartagena
Balearic Is.
Caesarea
K. OF THE VANDALS
Hippo
Carthage
Tripoli
Numidia
Moors
Illyria
Thrace
Adrianople
Constantinople
BLACK SEA
Chersonesus
Iberia
CASPIAN SEA
White Huns
Pontus
Galatia
Cappadocia
Isauria
Cilicia
Asia
Caria
Corinth
Sparta
Crete
Cyprus
ROMAN EMPIRE
Antioch
Syria
Beirut
Tyre
Jerusalem
Alexandria
Egypt
Saracens
ARABIA
Persian Armenia
Mesopotamia
R. Tigris
R. Euphrates
PERSIAN EMPIRE
THE WORLD
A.D. 527
Scale of Miles
0 100 200 300 400 500

ITALY AND AFRICA
Scale of Miles
Milan
Ravenna
Florence
Chiusi
Orvieto
Perugia
Assisi
Spoleto
Ancona
Ascoli
Tivoli
Fucine Lake
Rome
Port of Ostia
Benevento
LIGURIA
TUSCANY
PICENUM
APULIA
CALABRIA
LUCANIA
CAMPANIA
ADRIATIC SEA
SARDINIA
TYRRHENIAN
SEA
Lipari Is
Palermo
Lilybaeum
SICILY
Catania
Syracuse
Reggio
Cotrone
Appian Way
Hippo Regius
Tricamaron
Royal Springs
Hadrumetum
Cape Bona
AFRICA

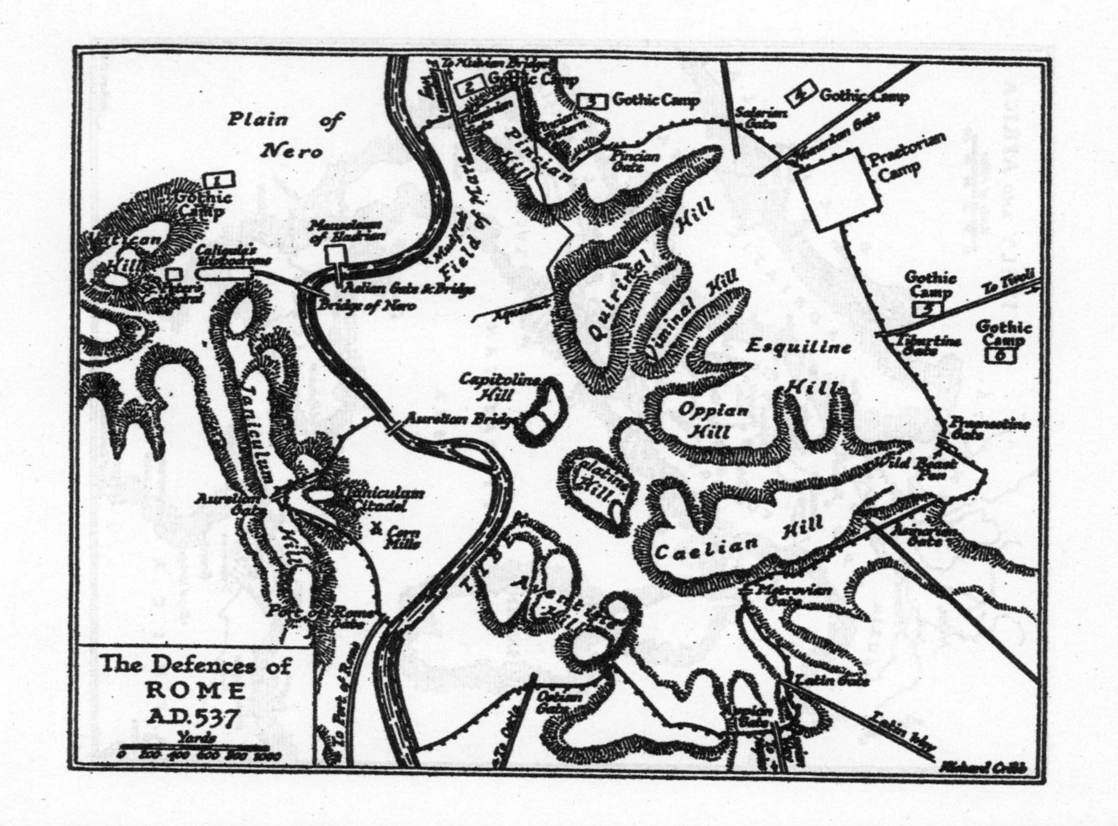
The Defences of
ROME
A.D. 537
Yards
0 200 400 600 800 1000
Plain of
Nero
Gothic Camp
Mausoleum of Hadrian
Caligula's Hippodrome
Aelian Gate & Bridge
Bridge of Nero
Field of Mars
To Milvian Bridge
Gothic Camp
Gothic Camp
Pincian Hill
Pincian Gate
Salarian Gate
Gothic Camp
Praetorian Camp
Quirinal Hill
Viminal Hill
Esquiline
Hill
Gothic Camp
To Tivoli
Gothic Camp
Tiburtine Gate
Praenestine Gate
Capitoline Hill
Aurelian Bridge
Oppian Hill
Wild Beast Pen
Janiculum
Hill
Aurelian Gate
Janiculum Citadel
Corn Mills
Port of Rome Gate
To Port of Rome
Caelian Hill
Asinarian Gate
Metrovian Gate
Latin Gate
Latin Way
Appian Gate
Ostian Gate
Richard Cribb

PENGUIN MODERN CLASSICS

THE COMPLETE POEMS
ROBERT GRAVES

'A monumental basis for looking at the poems afresh ... No one else offers his precise combination of criticism, nightmare and epigram' Sean O'Brien, *Guardian*

One of the most remarkable writers of the twentieth century, Robert Graves published more than a thousand poems over some seventy years. Primarily known for his love poetry, Graves combined irony with passion, the intensely personal with the universal, inspired by his Muses – the White and Black Goddesses. But there are also works of harsh realism, written after his traumatic experience in the First World War and the aftermath of shell shock and religious crisis. Melancholy and fear run through many poems, but balanced by humour and moments of pure lyrical beauty. Bringing together those that appeared in his lifetime, along with posthumously published poems, this volume represents the most comprehensive collection ever of Graves's poetic work.

'A Renaissance figure, among the most generous, self-willed, unseemly and brilliant writers of our century' D. M. Thomas, *The New York Times*

Edited by Beryl Graves and Dunstan Ward

Penguin Modern Classics

GOODBYE TO ALL THAT
ROBERT GRAVES

'His wonderful autobiography' Jeremy Paxman, *Daily Mail*

In 1929 Robert Graves went to live abroad permanently, vowing 'never to make England my home again'. This is his superb account of his life up until that 'bitter leave-taking': from his childhood and desperately unhappy school days at Charterhouse, to his time serving as a young officer in the First World War that was to haunt him throughout his life. It also contains memorable encounters with fellow writers and poets, including Siegfried Sassoon and Thomas Hardy, and covers his increasingly unhappy marriage to Nancy Nicholson. *Goodbye to All That*, with its vivid, harrowing descriptions of the Western Front, is a classic war document, and also has immense value as one of the most candid self-portraits of an artist ever written.

PENGUIN MODERN CLASSICS

CLAUDIUS THE GOD

ROBERT GRAVES

'*I, Claudius* and *Claudius the God* are an imaginative and hugely readable account of the early decades of the Roman Empire … racy, inventive, often comic' *Daily Telegraph*

Claudius has survived the murderous intrigues of his predecessors to become, reluctantly, Emperor of Rome. Here he recounts his surprisingly successful reign: how he cultivates the loyalty of the army and the common people to repair the damage caused by Caligula; his relations with the Jewish King Herod Agrippa; and his invasion of Britain. But the growing paranoia of absolute power and the infidelity of his promiscuous young wife Messalina mean that his good fortune will not last forever. In this second part of Robert Graves's fictionalized autobiography, Claudius – wry, rueful, always inquisitive – brings to life some of the most scandalous and violent times in history.

With a new Introduction by Barry Unsworth

PENGUIN MODERN CLASSICS

GIOVANNI'S ROOM
JAMES BALDWIN

'Exquisite … a feat of fire-breathing, imaginative daring' *Guardian*

David, a young American in 1950s Paris, is waiting for his fiancée to return from vacation in Spain. But when he meets Giovanni, a handsome Italian barman, the two men are drawn into an intense affair. After three months David's fiancée returns, and, denying his true nature, David rejects Giovanni for a 'safe' future as a married man. His decision eventually brings tragedy.

Full of passion, regret and longing, this story of a fated love triangle has become a landmark in gay writing, but its appeal is broader. James Baldwin caused outrage as a black author writing about white homosexuals, yet for him the issues of race, sexuality and personal freedom were eternally intertwined.

'Audacious … remarkable … elegant and courageous' Caryl Phillips

With a new Introduction by Caryl Phillips

PENGUIN MODERN CLASSICS

UNDERTONES OF WAR
EDMUND BLUNDEN

'An established classic ... accurate and detailed in observation of the war scene and its human figures' D. J. Enright

In one of the finest autobiographies to come out of the First World War, the poet Edmund Blunden records his devastating experiences in France and Flanders. Enlisting at the age of twenty, he took part in the disastrous battles of the Somme, Ypres and Passchendaele, describing the latter as 'murder, not only to the troops but to their singing faiths and hopes'. In his compassionate yet unsentimental prose, he tells of the endurance, heroism – and despair – among the men of his battalion.

This volume, which contains a selection of Blunden's war poems, also reveals his close affinity with the natural world: the 'shepherd in a soldier's coat' whose love of the rural landscape gave him some refuge from the terrible betrayal enacted in Flanders fields.

read more 

PENGUIN MODERN CLASSICS

UNDER FIRE
HENRI BARBUSSE

'One of the most influential of all war novels' *History Today*

Under Fire follows the fortunes of the French Sixth Battalion during the First World War. For this group of ordinary men, thrown together from all over France and longing for home, war is simply a matter of survival, and the arrival of their rations, a glimpse of a pretty girl or a brief reprieve in hospital is all they can hope for.

Written during the War and based on his own experiences, Henri Barbusse's novel is a powerful account of one of the greatest horrors mankind has inflicted upon itself and a critique of the inequality between ranks and of the incomprehension of those who have managed to avoid active service. It vividly evokes life in the trenches – the mud, stench and monotony of waiting, while under fire in an eternal battlefield.

Translated by Robin Buss With an Introduction by Jay Winter

read more 

Penguin Modern Classics

CHRIST STOPPED AT EBOLI
CARLO LEVI

'No message, human or divine, has reached this stubborn poverty … to this shadowy land … Christ did not come. Christ stopped at Eboli.'

Carlo Levi, one of the twentieth-century's most incisive commentators, was exiled to a remote and barren corner of southern Italy for his opposition to Mussolini. He entered a world cut off from history and the state, hedged in by custom and sorrow, without comfort or solace, where, eternally patient, the peasants lived in an age-old stillness and in the presence of death – for Christ did stop at Eboli.

'One of the most poetic and penetrating first-hand accounts of the confrontation between cultures' *The Times Literary Supplement*

Translated by Frances Frenaye

PENGUIN MODERN CLASSICS

THE LEVANT TRILOGY
OLIVIA MANNING

THE DANGER TREE/ THE BATTLE LOST AND WON/ THE SUM OF THINGS

'The finest fictional record of the war produced by a British writer'
Anthony Burgess

Leaving behind Hitler's Europe, Guy and Harriet Pringle find refuge in Cairo, a city tense with fear and expectation. Also newly arrived is Simon Boulderstone, an inexperienced young officer who falls in love with Harriet's fun-loving friend Edwina. While the Pringles struggle for survival in the city Simon becomes involved in the bitter fighting in the desert.

For each of them there is disillusionment and isolation as they battle with their own unresolved problems heightened by the uncertainties of war. Olivia Manning's evocative work brilliantly captures the mood of the Near and Middle East in wartime and the sense of irrevocable change.

read more 

PENGUIN MODERN CLASSICS

HOMAGE TO CATALONIA
GEORGE ORWELL

'An unrivalled picture of the rumours, suspicions and treachery of civil war' Anthony Beevor

'Every line of serious work that I have written since 1936 has been written, directly or indirectly, against totalitarianism and for democratic socialism as I understand it.' Thus wrote Orwell following his experiences as a militiaman in the Spanish Civil War, chronicled in *Homage to Catalonia*. Here he brings to bear all the force of his humanity, passion and clarity, describing with bitter intensity the bright hopes and cynical betrayals of that chaotic episode.

'A war story that is both brutally honest and lyrically beautiful' Michael Shelden, *Daily Telegraph*, Books of the Century

With an Introduction by Julian Symons

THE AUTHORITATIVE TEXT

read more 

PENGUIN MODERN CLASSICS

ONE DAY IN THE LIFE OF IVAN DENISOVICH
ALEKSANDR SOLZHENITSYN

'It is a blow struck for human freedom all over the world ... and it is gloriously readable' *Sunday Times*

This brutal, shattering glimpse of the fate of millions of Russians under Stalin shook Russia and shocked the world when it first appeared.

Discover the importance of a piece of bread or an extra bowl of soup, the incredible luxury of a book, the ingenious possibilities of a nail, a piece of string or a single match in a world where survival is all. Here safety, warmth and food are the first objectives. Reading this book, you enter a world of incarceration, brutality, hard manual labour and freezing cold – and participate in the struggle of men to survive both the terrible rigours of nature and the inhumanity of the system that defines their conditions of life.

Translated by Ralph Parker

WINNER OF THE NOBEL PRIZE FOR LITERATURE

PENGUIN MODERN CLASSICS

MOMENTS OF REPRIEVE
PRIMO LEVI

'One of the most important and gifted writers of our time' Italo Calvino

Primo Levi was one of the most astonishing voices to emerge from the twentieth century: a man who survived one of the ugliest times in history, yet who was able to describe his own Auschwitz experience with an unaffected tenderness.

Levi was a master storyteller but he did not write fairytales. These stories are an elegy to the human figures who stood out against the tragic background of Auschwitz, 'the ones in whom I had recognised the will and capacity to react, and hence a rudiment of virtue'. Each centres on an individual who – whether it be through a juggling trick, a slice of apple or a letter – discovers one of the 'bizarre, marginal moments of reprieve'.

Translated by Ruth Feldman

With an Introduction by Michael Ignatieff